THE MODERN LIBRARY
of the World's Best Books

>>>

SELECTED WRITINGS OF
HERMAN MELVILLE

SELECTED WRITINGS OF

HERMAN

MELVILLE

>>

COMPLETE SHORT STORIES

TYPEE

BILLY BUDD, FORETOPMAN

>>

THE MODERN LIBRARY · NEW YORK

THE MODERN LIBRARY

IS PUBLISHED BY

RANDOM HOUSE, INC.

BENNETT A. CERF · DONALD S. KLOPFER · ROBERT K. HAAS

Manufactured in the United States of America
By H. Wolff

Contents

Note

THREE different periods of Melville's literary production are represented in this selection. *Typee* was his first novel, and *Billy Budd, Foretopman,* finished some forty-six years later, was his tenth and last. The stories, chronologically, came near the beginning of his literary life, since they were all completed within the decade following the publication year of *Typee.* But if they are considered in relation to the bulk of Melville's fiction, they stand as late works, since seven of his novels had already been published before he began writing stories.

Except for *Billy Budd,* all of Melville's known prose fiction was written in the amazingly brief span of years from 1845, when *Typee* was finished, to 1857, when his ninth novel, *The Confidence-Man,* was published. From 1857 until the end of 1888, when he began *Billy Budd,* he apparently wrote no fiction at all, but devoted his limited writing time exclusively to poetry.

Typee was first published in London (February-March, 1846) and a month later in New York. A second "revised" American edition appeared in the same year, slightly expurgated and without the "Appendix" of the first printing, but with the addition of "The Story of Toby." The complete, original text used here was set up from a copy of the first English edition, to which has been added "The Story of Toby" from the second American edition. *Typee* was a great critical success on both sides of the Atlantic, and it has always been one of the most widely popular of Melville's books.

The fifteen stories printed here represent all of Melville's finished work in the short-story form. All were written in the four-year period (1853-1856) shortly after the publication of *Moby Dick* (1851) and *Pierre* (1852), and all but two appeared in magazines during that time: "The Two Temples," which survives in manuscript, was never printed during his lifetime, and "The Piazza" was apparently written as a title-piece to the volume called *The Piazza Tales* (1856), which contained also "Bartleby," "The Encantadas," "The Lightning-Rod Man," "Benito Cereno," and "The Bell Tower." The stories were never collected in a single volume until 1949, when Random House published *The Complete Stories of Herman Melville,* with an introduction and notes by Jay Leyda, who devoted much time and care to the preparation of an authentic text, removing the various printing and editorial errors that had accumulated in previously published versions. The plates of that volume are used in this Modern Library edition.

This text of *Billy Budd* is based on existing editions, with corrections made by a comparison with the manuscript at the Houghton Library of Harvard University. According to Melville's notes, *Billy Budd* was begun on November 16, 1888, and finished on April 19, 1891, five months before his death. Along with other papers, the manuscript was preserved by Melville's wife, but its existence was not known until 1921, when his granddaughter, Mrs. Eleanor Melville Metcalf, allowed Raymond Weaver to see the contents of the small box in which the papers were kept. *Billy Budd* was first published in London in 1924, but not in New York until 1928—eighty-two years after the publication of *Typee*.

The Editors of the Modern Library

SELECTED WRITINGS OF

HERMAN MELVILLE

Bartleby

I AM a rather elderly man. The nature of my avocations, for the last thirty years, has brought me into more than ordinary contact with what would seem an interesting and somewhat singular set of men, of whom, as yet, nothing, that I know of, has ever been written—I mean, the law-copyists, or scriveners. I have known very many of them, professionally and privately, and, if I pleased, could relate divers histories, at which good-natured gentlemen might smile, and sentimental souls might weep. But I waive the biographies of all other scriveners, for a few passages in the life of Bartleby, who was a scrivener, the strangest I ever saw, or heard of. While, of other law-copyists, I might write the complete life, of Bartleby nothing of that sort can be done. I believe that no materials exist, for a full and satisfactory biography of this man. It is an irreparable loss to literature. Bartleby was one of those beings of whom nothing is ascertainable, except from the original sources, and, in his case, those are very small. What my own astonished eyes saw of Bartleby, *that* is all I know of him, except, indeed, one vague report, which will appear in the sequel.

Ere introducing the scrivener, as he first appeared to me, it is fit I make some mention of myself, my *employés*, my business, my chambers, and general surroundings; because some such description is indispensable to an adequate understanding of the chief character about to be presented. Imprimis: I am a man who, from his youth upwards, has been filled with a profound conviction that the easiest way of life is the best. Hence, though I belong to a profession proverbially energetic and nervous, even to turbulence, at times, yet nothing of that sort have I ever suffered to invade my peace. I am one of those unambitious lawyers who never address a jury, or in any way draw down public applause; but, in the cool tranquillity of a snug retreat, do a snug business among rich men's bonds, and mortgages, and title-deeds. All who know me, consider me an eminently *safe* man. The late John Jacob Astor, a personage little given to poetic enthusiasm, had no hesitation in pronouncing my first grand point to be prudence; my next, method. I do not speak it in vanity, but simply record the fact, that I was not unemployed in my profession by the late John Jacob Astor; a name which, I admit, I love to repeat; for it hath a rounded and orbicular sound to it, and rings like unto bullion. I will freely add, that I was not insensible to the late John Jacob Astor's good opinion.

Some time prior to the period at which this little history begins, my avocations had been largely increased. The good old office, now extinct in the State of New York, of a Master in Chancery, had been conferred upon me. It was not a very arduous office, but very pleasantly remunerative. I seldom lose my temper; much more seldom indulge in dangerous indignation at wrongs and outrages; but I must be permitted to be rash here and declare, that I consider the sudden and violent abrogation of the office of Master in Chancery, by the new Constitution, as a —— premature act; inasmuch as I had counted upon a life-lease of the profits, whereas I only received those of a few short years. But this is by the way.

My chambers were up stairs, at No. —— Wall Street. At one end, they looked upon the white wall of the interior of a spacious sky-light shaft, penetrating the building from top to bottom.

This view might have been considered rather tame than otherwise, deficient in what landscape painters call "life." But, if so, the view from the other end of my chambers offered, at least, a contrast, if nothing more. In that direction, my windows commanded an unobstructed view of a lofty brick wall, black by age and everlasting shade; which wall required no spy-glass to bring out its lurking beauties, but, for the benefit of all near-sighted spectators, was pushed up to within ten feet of my window-panes. Owing to the great height of the surrounding buildings, and my chambers being on the second floor, the interval between this wall and mine not a little resembled a huge square cistern.

At the period just preceding the advent of Bartleby, I had two persons as copyists in my employment, and a promising lad as an office-boy. First, Turkey; second, Nippers; third, Ginger Nut. These may seem names, the like of which are not usually found in the Directory. In truth, they were nicknames, mutually conferred upon each other by my three clerks, and were deemed expressive of their respective persons or characters. Turkey was a short, pursy Englishman, of about my own age—that is, somewhere not far from sixty. In the morning, one might say, his face was of a fine florid hue, but after twelve o'clock, meridian—his dinner hour—it blazed like a grate full of Christmas coals; and continued blazing—but, as it were, with a gradual wane—till six o'clock, P.M., or thereabouts; after which, I saw no more of the proprietor of the face, which, gaining its meridian with the sun, seemed to set with it, to rise, culminate, and decline the following day, with the like regularity and undiminished glory. There are many singular coincidences I have known in the course of my life, not the least among which was the fact, that, exactly when Turkey displayed his fullest beams from his red and radiant countenance, just then, too, at that critical moment, began the daily period when I considered his business capacities as seriously disturbed for the remainder of the twenty-four hours. Not that he was absolutely idle, or averse to business then; far from it. The difficulty was, he was apt to be altogether too energetic. There was a strange, inflamed, flurried, flighty recklessness of activity about him. He would be incautious in dipping his pen into his inkstand. All his blots upon my documents were dropped there after twelve o'clock, meridian. Indeed, not only would he be reckless, and sadly given to making blots in the afternoon, but, some days, he went further, and was rather noisy. At such times, too, his face flamed with augmented blazonry, as if cannel coal had been heaped on anthracite. He made an unpleasant racket with his chair; spilled his sand-box; in mending his pens, impatiently split them all to pieces, and threw them on the floor in a sudden passion; stood up, and leaned over his table, boxing his papers about in a most indecorous manner, very sad to behold in an elderly man like him. Nevertheless, as he was in many ways a most valuable person to me, and all the time before twelve o'clock, meridian, was the quickest, steadiest creature, too, accomplishing a great deal of work in a style not easily to be matched—for these reasons, I was willing to overlook his eccentricities, though, indeed, occasionally, I remonstrated with him. I did this very gently, however, because, though the civilest, nay, the blandest and most reverential of men in the morning, yet, in the afternoon, he was disposed, upon provocation, to be slightly rash with his tongue—in fact, insolent. Now, valuing his morning services as I did, and resolved not to lose them—yet, at the same time, made uncomfortable by his inflamed ways after twelve o'clock—and being a man of peace, unwilling by my admonitions to call forth unseemly retorts from him, I took upon me, one Saturday noon (he was always worse on Saturdays) to hint to him, very kindly, that, perhaps, now that he was growing old, it might be well to abridge his labors; in short, he need not come to my chambers after twelve o'clock, but, dinner over, had best go home to his lodgings, and rest himself till tea-time. But no; he insisted upon his afternoon devotions. His countenance became intolerably fervid, as he oratorically assured me—gesticulating with a long ruler at the other end of the room—that if his services in the morning were useful, how indispensable, then, in the afternoon?

"With submission, sir," said Turkey, on this occasion, "I consider myself your right-hand man. In the morning I but marshal and deploy my columns; but in the afternoon I put myself at their head, and gallantly charge the foe, thus"—and he made a violent thrust with the ruler.

"But the blots, Turkey," intimated I.

"True; but, with submission, sir, behold these hairs! I am getting old. Surely, sir, a blot or two of a warm afternoon is not to be severely urged against gray hairs. Old age —even if it blot the page—is honorable. With submission, sir, we *both* are getting old."

This appeal to my fellow-feeling was hardly to be resisted. At all events, I saw that go he would not. So, I made up my mind to let him stay, resolving, nevertheless, to see to it that, during the afternoon, he had to do with my less important papers.

Nippers, the second on my list, was a whiskered, sallow, and, upon the whole, rather piratical-looking young man, of about five-and-twenty. I always deemed him the victim of two evil powers—ambition and indigestion. The ambition was evinced by a certain impatience of the duties of a mere copyist, an unwarrantable usurpation of strictly professional affairs, such as the original drawing up of legal documents. The indigestion seemed betokened in an occasional nervous testiness and grinning irritability, causing the teeth to audibly grind together over mistakes committed

in copying; unnecessary maledictions, hissed, rather than
spoken, in the heat of business; and especially by a continual discontent with the height of the table where he
worked. Though of a very ingenious mechanical turn,
Nippers could never get this table to suit him. He put chips
under it, blocks of various sorts, bits of pasteboard, and at
last went so far as to attempt an exquisite adjustment, by
final pieces of folded blotting-paper. But no invention
would answer. If, for the sake of easing his back, he
brought the table-lid at a sharp angle well up towards his
chin, and wrote there like a man using the steep roof of a
Dutch house for his desk, then he declared that it stopped
the circulation in his arms. If now he lowered the table to
his waistbands, and stooped over it in writing, then there
was a sore aching in his back. In short, the truth of the
matter was, Nippers knew not what he wanted. Or, if he
wanted anything, it was to be rid of a scrivener's table altogether. Among the manifestations of his diseased ambition
was a fondness he had for receiving visits from certain
ambiguous-looking fellows in seedy coats, whom he called
his clients. Indeed, I was aware that not only was he, at
times, considerable of a ward-politician, but he occasionally
did a little business at the Justices' courts, and was not unknown on the steps of the Tombs. I have good reason to
believe, however, that one individual who called upon him
at my chambers, and who, with a grand air, he insisted was
his client, was no other than a dun, and the alleged title-
deed, a bill. But, with all his failings, and the annoyances
he caused me, Nippers, like his compatriot Turkey, was a
very useful man to me; wrote a neat, swift hand; and, when
he chose, was not deficient in a gentlemanly sort of deportment. Added to this, he always dressed in a gentlemanly
sort of way; and so, incidentally, reflected credit upon my
chambers. Whereas, with respect to Turkey, I had much
ado to keep him from being a reproach to me. His clothes

were apt to look oily, and smell of eating-houses. He wore his pantaloons very loose and baggy in summer. His coats were execrable; his hat not to be handled. But while the hat was a thing of indifference to me, inasmuch as his natural civility and deference, as a dependent Englishman, always led him to doff it the moment he entered the room, yet his coat was another matter. Concerning his coats, I reasoned with him; but with no effect. The truth was, I suppose, that a man with so small an income could not afford to sport such a lustrous face and a lustrous coat at one and the same time. As Nippers once observed, Turkey's money went chiefly for red ink. One winter day, I presented Turkey with a highly respectable-looking coat of my own—a padded gray coat, of a most comfortable warmth, and which buttoned straight up from the knee to the neck. I thought Turkey would appreciate the favor, and abate his rashness and obstreperousness of afternoons. But no; I verily believe that buttoning himself up in so downy and blanket-like a coat had a pernicious effect upon him—upon the same principle that too much oats are bad for horses. In fact, precisely as a rash, restive horse is said to feel his oats, so Turkey felt his coat. It made him insolent. He was a man whom prosperity harmed.

Though, concerning the self-indulgent habits of Turkey, I had my own private surmises, yet, touching Nippers, I was well persuaded that, whatever might be his faults in other respects, he was, at least, a temperate young man. But, indeed, nature herself seemed to have been his vintner, and, at his birth, charged him so thoroughly with an irritable, brandy-like disposition, that all subsequent potations were needless. When I consider how, amid the stillness of my chambers, Nippers would sometimes impatiently rise from his seat, and stooping over his table, spread his arms wide apart, seize the whole desk, and move it, and jerk it, with a grim, grinding motion on the floor, as if the table were a perverse voluntary agent, intent on thwarting and vexing him, I plainly perceive that, for Nippers, brandy-and-water were altogether superfluous.

It was fortunate for me that, owing to its peculiar cause —indigestion—the irritability and consequent nervousness of Nippers were mainly observable in the morning, while in the afternoon he was comparatively mild. So that, Turkey's paroxysms only coming on about twelve o'clock, I never had to do with their eccentricities at one time. Their fits relieved each other, like guards. When Nippers's was on, Turkey's was off; and *vice versa*. This was a good natural arrangement, under the circumstances.

Ginger Nut, the third on my list, was a lad, some twelve years old. His father was a carman, ambitious of seeing his son on the bench instead of a cart, before he died. So he sent him to my office, as student at law, errand-boy, cleaner and sweeper, at the rate of one dollar a week. He had a little desk to himself, but he did not use it much. Upon inspection, the drawer exhibited a great array of the shells of various sorts of nuts. Indeed, to this quick-witted youth, the whole noble science of the law was contained in a nutshell. Not the least among the employments of Ginger Nut, as well as one which he discharged with the most alacrity, was his duty as cake and apple purveyor for Turkey and Nippers. Copying law-papers being proverbially a dry, husky sort of business, my two scriveners were fain to moisten their mouths very often with Spitzenbergs, to be had at the numerous stalls nigh the Custom House and Post Office. Also, they sent Ginger Nut very frequently for that peculiar cake—small, flat, round, and very spicy—after which he had been named by them. Of a cold morning, when business was but dull, Turkey would gobble up scores of these cakes, as if they were mere wafers—indeed, they sell them at the rate of six or eight for a penny—the scrape of his pen blending with the crunching of the crisp particles in his mouth. Of all the fiery afternoon blunders and flurried rashnesses of Turkey, was his once moistening a ginger-cake between his lips, and clapping it on to a mortgage, for a seal. I came within an ace of dismissing him then. But he mollified me by making an oriental bow, and saying—

"With submission, sir, it was generous of me to find you in stationery on my own account."

Now my original business—that of a conveyancer and title hunter, and drawer-up of recondite documents of all sorts—was considerably increased by receiving the Master's office. There was now great work for scriveners. Not only must I push the clerks already with me, but I must have additional help.

In answer to my advertisement, a motionless young man one morning stood upon my office threshold, the door being open, for it was summer. I can see that figure now—pallidly neat, pitiably respectable, incurably forlorn! It was Bartleby.

After a few words touching his qualifications, I engaged him, glad to have among my corps of copyists a man of so singularly sedate an aspect, which I thought might operate beneficially upon the flighty temper of Turkey, and the fiery one of Nippers.

I should have stated before that ground-glass folding-doors divided my premises into two parts, one of which was occupied by my scriveners, the other by myself. According to my humor, I threw open these doors, or closed them. I resolved to assign Bartleby a corner by the folding-doors, but on my side of them, so as to have this quiet man within easy call, in case any trifling thing was to be done. I placed his desk close up to a small side-window in that part of the room, a window which originally had afforded a lateral view of certain grimy backyards and bricks, but which, owing to subsequent erections, commanded at present no view at all, though it gave some light. Within three feet of the panes was a wall, and the light came down from far above, between two lofty buildings, as from a very small opening in a dome. Still further to a satisfactory arrangement, I procured a high green folding screen, which might entirely isolate Bartleby from my sight, though not remove him from my voice. And thus, in a manner, privacy and society were conjoined.

At first, Bartleby did an extraordinary quantity of writing. As if long famishing for something to copy, he seemed to gorge himself on my documents. There was no pause for digestion. He ran a day and night line, copying by sunlight and by candle-light. I should have been quite delighted with his application, had he been cheerfully industrious. But he wrote on silently, palely, mechanically.

It is, of course, an indispensable part of a scrivener's business to verify the accuracy of his copy, word by word. Where there are two or more scriveners in an office, they assist each other in this examination, one reading from the copy, the other holding the original. It is a very dull, wearisome, and lethargic affair. I can readily imagine that, to some sanguine temperaments, it would be altogether intolerable. For example, I cannot credit that the mettlesome poet, Byron, would have contentedly sat down with Bartleby to examine a law document of, say five hundred pages, closely written in a crimpy hand.

Now and then, in the haste of business, it had been my habit to assist in comparing some brief document myself, calling Turkey or Nippers for this purpose. One object I had, in placing Bartleby so handy to me behind the screen, was, to avail myself of his services on such trivial occasions. It was on the third day, I think, of his being with me, and before any necessity had arisen for having his own writing examined, that, being much hurried to complete a small affair I had in hand, I abruptly called to Bartleby. In my haste and natural expectancy of instant compliance, I sat with my head bent over the original on my desk, and my right hand sideways, and somewhat nervously extended with the copy, so that, immediately upon emerging from his retreat, Bartleby might snatch it and proceed to business without the least delay.

In this very attitude did I sit when I called to him, rapidly stating what it was I wanted him to do—namely, to examine a small paper with me. Imagine my surprise, nay, my consternation, when, without moving from his privacy, Bartleby, in a singularly mild, firm voice, replied, "I would prefer not to."

I sat awhile in perfect silence, rallying my stunned faculties. Immediately it occurred to me that my ears had deceived me, or Bartleby had entirely misunderstood my meaning. I repeated my request in the clearest tone I could assume; but in quite as clear a one came the previous reply, "I would prefer not to."

"Prefer not to," echoed I, rising in high excitement, and crossing the room with a stride. "What do you mean? Are you moon-struck? I want you to help me compare this sheet here—take it," and I thrust it towards him.

"I would prefer not to," said he.

I looked at him steadfastly. His face was leanly composed; his gray eye dimly calm. Not a wrinkle of agitation rippled him. Had there been the least uneasiness, anger, impatience or impertinence in his manner; in other words, had there been anything ordinarily human about him, doubtless I should have violently dismissed him from the premises. But as it was, I should have as soon thought of turning my pale plaster-of-paris bust of Cicero out of doors. I stood gazing at him awhile, as he went on with his own writing, and then reseated myself at my desk. This is very strange, thought I. What had one best do? But my business hurried me. I concluded to forget the matter for the present, reserving it for my future leisure. So, calling Nippers from the other room, the paper was speedily examined.

A few days after this, Bartleby concluded four lengthy documents, being quadruplicates of a week's testimony taken before me in my High Court of Chancery. It became necessary to examine them. It was an important suit, and great accuracy was imperative. Having all things arranged, I called Turkey, Nippers and Ginger Nut, from the next room, meaning to place the four copies in the hands of my four clerks, while I should read from the original. Accordingly, Turkey, Nippers, and Ginger Nut had taken their seats in a row, each with his document in his hand, when I called to Bartleby to join this interesting group.

"Bartleby! quick, I am waiting."

I heard a slow scrape of his chair legs on the uncarpeted floor, and soon he appeared standing at the entrance of his hermitage.

"What is wanted?" said he, mildly.

"The copies, the copies," said I, hurriedly. "We are going to examine them. There"—and I held towards him the fourth quadruplicate.

"I would prefer not to," he said, and gently disappeared behind the screen.

For a few moments I was turned into a pillar of salt, standing at the head of my seated column of clerks. Recovering myself, I advanced towards the screen, and demanded the reason for such extraordinary conduct.

"*Why* do you refuse?"

"I would prefer not to."

With any other man I should have flown outright into a dreadful passion, scorned all further words, and thrust him ignominiously from my presence. But there was something about Bartleby that not only strangely disarmed me, but, in a wonderful manner, touched and disconcerted me. I began to reason with him.

"These are your own copies we are about to examine. It is labor saving to you, because one examination will answer for your four papers. It is common usage. Every copyist is bound to help examine his copy. Is it not so? Will you not speak? Answer!"

"I prefer not to," he replied in a flute-like tone. It seemed to me that, while I had been addressing him, he carefully revolved every statement that I made; fully comprehended the meaning; could not gainsay the irresistible conclusion; but, at the same time, some paramount consideration prevailed with him to reply as he did.

"You are decided, then, not to comply with my request—a request made according to common usage and common sense?"

He briefly gave me to understand, that on that point my judgment was sound. Yes: his decision was irreversible.

It is not seldom the case that, when a man is browbeaten in some unprecedented and violently unreasonable way, he begins to stagger in his own plainest faith. He begins, as it were, vaguely to surmise that, wonderful as it may be, all the justice and all the reason is on the other side. Accordingly, if any disinterested persons are present, he turns to them for some reinforcement for his own faltering mind.

"Turkey," said I, "what do you think of this? Am I not right?"

"With submission, sir," said Turkey, in his blandest tone, "I think that you are."

"Nippers," said I, "what do *you* think of it?"

"I think I should kick him out of the office."

(The reader of nice perceptions will here perceive that, it being morning, Turkey's answer is couched in polite and tranquil terms, but Nippers replies in ill-tempered ones. Or, to repeat a previous sentence, Nippers's ugly mood was on duty, and Turkey's off.)

"Ginger Nut," said I, willing to enlist the smallest suffrage in my behalf, "what do *you* think of it?"

"I think, sir, he's a little *luny*," replied Ginger Nut, with a grin.

"You hear what they say," said I, turning towards the screen, "come forth and do your duty."

But he vouchsafed no reply. I pondered a moment in sore perplexity. But once more business hurried me. I determined again to postpone the consideration of this dilemma to my future leisure. With a little trouble we made out to examine the papers without Bartleby, though at every page or two Turkey deferentially dropped his opinion, that this proceeding was quite out of the common; while Nippers, twitching in his chair with a dyspeptic nervousness, ground out, between his set teeth, occasional hissing maledictions against the stubborn oaf behind the screen. And for his (Nippers's) part, this was the first and the last time he would do another man's business without pay.

Meanwhile Bartleby sat in his hermitage, oblivious to everything but his own peculiar business there.

Some days passed, the scrivener being employed upon another lengthy work. His late remarkable conduct led me to regard his ways narrowly. I observed that he never went to dinner; indeed, that he never went anywhere. As yet I had never, of my personal knowledge, known him to be outside of my office. He was a perpetual sentry in the corner. At about eleven o'clock though, in the morning, I noticed that Ginger Nut would advance toward the opening in Bartleby's screen, as if silently beckoned thither by a gesture invisible to me where I sat. The boy would then leave the office, jingling a few pence, and reappear with a handful of ginger-nuts, which he delivered in the hermitage, receiving two of the cakes for his trouble.

He lives, then, on ginger-nuts, thought I; never eats a dinner, properly speaking; he must be a vegetarian, then, but no; he never eats even vegetables, he eats nothing but ginger-nuts. My mind then ran on in reveries concerning the probable effects upon the human constitution of living entirely on ginger-nuts. Ginger-nuts are so called, because they contain ginger as one of their peculiar constituents, and the final flavoring one. Now, what was ginger? A hot, spicy thing. Was Bartleby hot and spicy? Not at all. Ginger, then, had no effect upon Bartleby. Probably he preferred it should have none.

Nothing so aggravates an earnest person as a passive resistance. If the individual so resisted be of a not inhumane temper, and the resisting one perfectly harmless in his passivity, then, in the better moods of the former, he will endeavor charitably to construe to his imagination what proves impossible to be solved by his judgment. Even so, for the most part, I regarded Bartleby and his ways. Poor fellow! thought I, he means no mischief; it is plain he intends no insolence; his aspect sufficiently evinces that his eccentricities are involuntary. He is useful to me. I can get along with him. If I turn him away, the chances are he will fall in with some less indulgent employer, and then he will be rudely treated, and perhaps driven forth miserably to starve. Yes. Here I can cheaply purchase a delicious self-approval. To befriend Bartleby; to humor him in his strange wilfulness, will cost me little or nothing, while I lay up in my soul what will eventually prove a sweet morsel for my conscience. But this mood was not invariable with me. The passiveness of Bartleby sometimes irritated me. I felt strangely goaded on to encounter him in new opposition— to elicit some angry spark from him answerable to my own. But, indeed, I might as well have essayed to strike fire with my knuckles against a bit of Windsor soap. But one afternoon the evil impulse in me mastered me, and the following little scene ensued:

"Bartleby," said I, "when those papers are all copied, I will compare them with you."

"I would prefer not to."

"How? Surely you do not mean to persist in that mulish vagary?"

No answer.

I threw open the folding-doors near by, and, turning upon Turkey and Nippers, exclaimed:

"Bartleby a second time says, he won't examine his papers. What do you think of it, Turkey?"

It was afternoon, be it remembered. Turkey sat glowing like a brass boiler; his bald head steaming; his hands reeling among his blotted papers.

"Think of it?" roared Turkey. "I think I'll just step behind his screen, and black his eyes for him!"

So saying, Turkey rose to his feet and threw his arms into a pugilistic position. He was hurrying away to make good his promise, when I detained him, alarmed at the effect of incautiously rousing Turkey's combativeness after dinner.

"Sit down, Turkey," said I, "and hear what Nippers has to say. What do you think of it, Nippers? Would I not be justified in immediately dismissing Bartleby?"

"Excuse me, that is for you to decide, sir. I think his conduct quite unusual, and, indeed, unjust, as regards Turkey and myself. But it may only be a passing whim."

"Ah," exclaimed I, "you have strangely changed your mind, then—you speak very gently of him now."

"All beer," cried Turkey; "gentleness is effects of beer—Nippers and I dined together to-day. You see how gentle I am, sir. Shall I go and black his eyes?"

"You refer to Bartleby, I suppose. No, not to-day, Turkey," I replied; "pray, put up your fists."

I closed the doors, and again advanced towards Bartleby. I felt additional incentives tempting me to my fate. I burned to be rebelled against again. I remembered that Bartleby never left the office.

"Bartleby," said I, "Ginger Nut is away; just step around to the Post Office, won't you?" (it was but a three minutes' walk) "and see if there is anything for me."

"I would prefer not to."

"You *will* not?"

"I *prefer* not."

I staggered to my desk, and sat there in a deep study. My blind inveteracy returned. Was there any other thing in which I could procure myself to be ignominiously repulsed by this lean, penniless wight?—my hired clerk? What added thing is there, perfectly reasonable, that he will be sure to refuse to do?

"Bartleby!"

No answer.

"Bartleby," in a louder tone.

No answer.

"Bartleby," I roared.

Like a very ghost, agreeably to the laws of magical invocation, at the third summons, he appeared at the entrance of his hermitage.

"Go to the next room, and tell Nippers to come to me."

"I prefer not to," he respectfully and slowly said, and mildly disappeared.

"Very good, Bartleby," said I, in a quiet sort of serenely-severe self-possessed tone, intimating the unalterable purpose of some terrible retribution very close at hand. At the moment I half intended something of the kind. But upon the whole, as it was drawing towards my dinner-hour, I thought it best to put on my hat and walk home for the day, suffering much from perplexity and distress of mind.

Shall I acknowledge it? The conclusion of this whole business was, that it soon became a fixed fact of my chambers, that a pale young scrivener, by the name of Bartleby, had a desk there; that he copied for me at the usual rate of four cents a folio (one hundred words); but he was permanently exempt from examining the work done by him, that duty being transferred to Turkey and Nippers, out of compliment, doubtless, to their superior acuteness; moreover, said Bartleby was never, on any account, to be dispatched on the most trivial errand of any sort; and that even if entreated to take upon him such a matter, it was generally understood that he would "prefer not to"—in other words, that he would refuse point-blank.

As days passed on, I became considerably reconciled to Bartleby. His steadiness, his freedom from all dissipation, his incessant industry (except when he chose to throw himself into a standing revery behind his screen), his great stillness, his unalterableness of demeanor under all circumstances, made him a valuable acquisition. One prime thing was this—*he was always there*—first in the morning, continually through the day, and the last at night. I had a singular confidence in his honesty. I felt my most precious papers perfectly safe in his hands. Sometimes, to be sure, I could not, for the very soul of me, avoid falling into sudden spasmodic passions with him. For it was exceeding difficult to bear in mind all the time those strange peculiarities, privileges, and unheard-of exemptions, forming the tacit stipulations on Bartleby's part under which he remained in my office. Now and then, in the eagerness of dispatching pressing business, I would inadvertently summon Bartleby, in a short, rapid tone, to put his finger, say, on the incipient tie of a bit of red tape with which I was about compressing some papers. Of course, from behind the screen the usual answer, "I prefer not to," was sure to come; and then, how could a human creature, with the common infirmities of our nature, refrain from bitterly exclaiming upon such perverseness—such unreasonableness? However, every added repulse of this sort which I received only tended to lessen the probability of my repeating the inadvertence.

Here it must be said, that, according to the custom of most legal gentlemen occupying chambers in densely-populated law buildings, there were several keys to my door. One was kept by a woman residing in the attic, which person weekly scrubbed and daily swept and dusted my apartments. Another was kept by Turkey for convenience sake. The third I sometimes carried in my own pocket. The fourth I knew not who had.

Now, one Sunday morning I happened to go to Trinity Church, to hear a celebrated preacher, and finding myself rather early on the ground I thought I would walk round to my chambers for a while. Luckily I had my key with me; but upon applying it to the lock, I found it resisted by something inserted from the inside. Quite surprised, I called out; when to my consternation a key was turned from within; and thrusting his lean visage at me, and holding the door ajar, the apparition of Bartleby appeared, in his shirt-sleeves, and otherwise in a strangely tattered deshabille, saying quietly that he was sorry, but he was deeply engaged just then, and—preferred not admitting me at present. In a brief word or two, he moreover added, that perhaps I had better walk round the block two or three times, and by that time he would probably have concluded his affairs.

Now, the utterly unsurmised appearance of Bartleby, tenanting my law-chambers of a Sunday morning, with his cadaverously gentlemanly *nonchalance*, yet withal firm and self-possessed, had such a strange effect upon me, that incontinently I slunk away from my own door, and did as desired. But not without sundry twinges of impotent rebellion against the mild effrontery of this unaccountable scrivener. Indeed, it was his wonderful mildness chiefly, which not only disarmed me, but unmanned me, as it were. For I consider that one, for the time, is a sort of unmanned when he tranquilly permits his hired clerk to dictate to him, and order him away from his own premises. Furthermore, I was full of uneasiness as to what Bartleby could possibly be doing in my office in his shirt-sleeves, and in an otherwise dismantled condition of a Sunday morning. Was anything amiss going on? Nay, that was out of the question. It was not to be thought of for a moment that Bartleby was an immoral person. But what could he be doing there?—copying? Nay again, whatever might be his eccentricities, Bartleby was an eminently decorous person. He would be the last man to sit down to his desk in any state approaching to nudity. Besides, it was Sunday; and there was something about Bartleby that forbade the supposition that he would by any secular occupation violate the proprieties of the day.

Nevertheless, my mind was not pacified; and full of a restless curiosity, at last I returned to the door. Without hindrance I inserted my key, opened it, and entered. Bartleby was not to be seen. I looked round anxiously, peeped behind his screen; but it was very plain that he was gone. Upon more closely examining the place, I surmised that for an indefinite period Bartleby must have ate, dressed, and slept in my office, and that too without plate, mirror, or bed. The cushioned seat of a rickety old sofa in one corner bore the faint impress of a lean, reclining form. Rolled away under his desk, I found a blanket; under the empty grate, a blacking box and brush; on a chair, a tin basin, with soap and a ragged towel; in a newspaper a few crumbs of ginger-nuts and a morsel of cheese. Yes, thought I, it is evident enough that Bartleby has been making his home here, keeping bachelor's hall all by himself. Immediately then the thought came sweeping across me, what miserable friendlessness and loneliness are here revealed! His poverty is great; but his solitude, how horrible! Think of it. Of a Sunday, Wall Street is deserted as Petra; and every night of every day it is an emptiness. This building, too, which of week-days hums with industry and life, at nightfall echoes with sheer vacancy, and all through Sunday is forlorn. And here Bartleby makes his home; sole spectator of a solitude which he has seen all populous—a sort of innocent and transformed Marius brooding among the ruins of Carthage!

For the first time in my life a feeling of overpowering stinging melancholy seized me. Before, I had never experienced aught but a not unpleasing sadness. The bond of a common humanity now drew me irresistibly to gloom. A fraternal melancholy! For both I and Bartleby were sons of Adam. I remembered the bright silks and sparkling faces I had seen that day, in gala trim, swan-like sailing down the Mississippi of Broadway; and I contrasted them with the pallid copyist, and thought to myself, Ah, happiness courts the light, so we deem the world is gay; but misery hides aloof, so we deem that misery there is none. These sad fancyings—chimeras, doubtless, of a sick and silly brain— led on to other and more special thoughts, concerning the eccentricities of Bartleby. Presentiments of strange discoveries hovered round me. The scrivener's pale form appeared to me laid out, among uncaring strangers, in its shivering winding-sheet.

Suddenly I was attracted by Bartleby's closed desk, the key in open sight left in the lock.

I mean no mischief, seek the gratification of no heartless curiosity, thought I; besides, the desk is mine, and its contents, too, so I will make bold to look within. Everything was methodically arranged, the papers smoothly placed. The pigeon-holes were deep, and removing the files of documents, I groped into their recesses. Presently I felt something there, and dragged it out. It was an old bandanna handkerchief, heavy and knotted. I opened it, and saw it was a saving's bank.

I now recalled all the quiet mysteries which I had noted

in the man. I remembered that he never spoke but to answer; that, though at intervals he had considerable time to himself, yet I had never seen him reading—no, not even a newspaper; that for long periods he would stand looking out, at his pale window behind the screen, upon the dead brick wall; I was quite sure he never visited any refectory or eating-house; while his pale face clearly indicated that he never drank beer like Turkey, or tea and coffee even, like other men; that he never went anywhere in particular that I could learn; never went out for a walk, unless, indeed, that was the case at present; that he had declined telling who he was, or whence he came, or whether he had any relatives in the world; that though so thin and pale, he never complained of ill-health. And more than all, I remembered a certain unconscious air of pallid— how shall I call it?—of pallid haughtiness, say, or rather an austere reserve about him, which had positively awed me into my tame compliance with his eccentricities, when I had feared to ask him to do the slightest incidental thing for me, even though I might know, from his long-continued motion-lessness, that behind his screen he must be standing in one of those dead-wall reveries of his.

Revolving all these things, and coupling them with the recently discovered fact, that he made my office his constant abiding place and home, and not forgetful of his morbid moodiness; revolving all these things, a prudential feeling began to steal over me. My first emotions had been those of pure melancholy and sincerest pity; but just in proportion as the forlornness of Bartleby grew and grew to my imagination, did that same melancholy merge into fear, that pity into repulsion. So true it is, and so terrible, too, that up to a certain point the thought or sight of misery enlists our best affections; but, in certain special cases, beyond that point it does not. They err who would assert that invariably this is owing to the inherent selfishness of the human heart.

It rather proceeds from a certain hopelessness of remedying excessive and organic ill. To a sensitive being, pity is not seldom pain. And when at last it is perceived that such pity cannot lead to effectual succor, common sense bids the soul be rid of it. What I saw that morning persuaded me that the scrivener was the victim of innate and incurable disorder. I might give alms to his body; but his body did not pain him; it was his soul that suffered, and his soul I could not reach.

I did not accomplish the purpose of going to Trinity Church that morning. Somehow, the things I had seen disqualified me for the time from church-going. I walked homeward, thinking what I would do with Bartleby. Finally, I resolved upon this—I would put certain calm questions to him the next morning, touching his history, etc., and if he declined to answer them openly and unreservedly (and I supposed he would prefer not), then to give him a twenty dollar bill over and above whatever I might owe him, and tell him his services were no longer required; but that if in any other way I could assist him, I would be happy to do so, especially if he desired to return to his native place, wherever that might be, I would willingly help to defray the expenses. Morever, if, after reaching home, he found himself at any time in want of aid, a letter from him would be sure of a reply.

The next morning came.

"Bartleby," said I, gently calling to him behind his screen.

No reply.

"Bartleby," said I, in a still gentler tone, "come here; I am not going to ask you to do anything you would prefer not to do—I simply wish to speak to you."

Upon this he noiselessly slid into view.

"Will you tell me, Bartleby, where you were born?"

"I would prefer not to."

"Will you tell me *anything* about yourself?"

"I would prefer not to."

"But what reasonable objection can you have to speak to me? I feel friendly towards you."

He did not look at me while I spoke, but kept his glance fixed upon my bust of Cicero, which, as I then sat, was directly behind me, some six inches above my head.

"What is your answer, Bartleby?" said I, after waiting a considerable time for a reply, during which his countenance remained immovable, only there was the faintest conceivable tremor of the white attenuated mouth.

"At present I prefer to give no answer," he said, and retired into his hermitage.

It was rather weak in me I confess, but his manner, on this occasion, nettled me. Not only did there seem to lurk in it a certain calm disdain, but his perverseness seemed ungrateful, considering the undeniable good usage and indulgence he had received from me.

Again I sat ruminating what I should do. Mortified as I was at his behavior, and resolved as I had been to dismiss him when I entered my office, nevertheless I strangely felt something superstitious knocking at my heart, and forbidding me to carry out my purpose, and denouncing me for a villain if I dared to breathe one bitter word against this forlornest of mankind. At last, familiarly drawing my chair behind his screen, I sat down and said: "Bartleby, never mind, then, about revealing your history; but let me entreat you, as a friend, to comply as far as may be with the usages of this office. Say now, you will help to examine papers to-morrow or next day: in short, say now, that in a day or two you will begin to be a little reasonable: —say so, Bartleby."

"At present I would prefer not to be a little reasonable," was his mildly cadaverous reply.

Just then the folding-doors opened, and Nippers

approached. He seemed suffering from an unusually bad night's rest, induced by severer indigestion than common. He overheard those final words of Bartleby.

"*Prefer not, eh?*" gritted Nippers—"I'd *prefer* him, if I were you, sir," addressing me—"I'd *prefer* him; I'd give him preferences, the stubborn mule! What is it, sir, pray, that he *prefers* not to do now?"

Bartleby moved not a limb.

"Mr. Nippers," said I, "I'd prefer that you would with-draw for the present."

Somehow, of late, I had got into the way of involuntarily using this word "prefer" upon all sorts of not exactly suitable occasions. And I trembled to think that my contact with the scrivener had already and seriously affected me in a mental way. And what further and deeper aberration might it not yet produce? This apprehension had not been without efficacy in determining me to summary measures.

As Nippers, looking very sour and sulky, was departing, Turkey blandly and deferentially approached.

"With submission, sir," said he, "yesterday I was thinking about Bartleby here, and I think that if he would but prefer to take a quart of good ale every day, it would do much towards mending him, and enabling him to assist in examining his papers."

"So you have got the word, too," said I, slightly excited.

"With submission, what word, sir?" asked Turkey, respectfully crowding himself into the contracted space behind the screen, and by so doing, making me jostle the scrivener. "What word, sir?"

"I would prefer to be left alone here," said Bartleby, as if offended at being mobbed in his privacy.

"*That's* the word, Turkey," said I—"*that's* it."

"Oh, *prefer?* oh yes—queer word. I never use it myself. But, sir, as I was saying, if he would but prefer—"

"Turkey," interrupted I, "you will please withdraw."

"Oh certainly, sir, if you prefer that I should."

As he opened the folding-door to retire, Nippers at his desk caught a glimpse of me, and asked whether I would prefer to have a certain paper copied on blue paper or white. He did not in the least roguishly accent the word "prefer." It was plain that it involuntarily rolled from his tongue. I thought to myself, surely I must get rid of a demented man, who already has in some degree turned the tongues, if not the heads of myself and clerks. But I thought it prudent not to break the dismission at once.

The next day I noticed that Bartleby did nothing but stand at his window in his dead-wall revery. Upon asking him why he did not write, he said that he had decided upon doing no more writing.

"Why, how now? what next?" exclaimed I, "do no more writing?"

"No more."

"And what is the reason?"

"Do you not see the reason for yourself?" he indifferently replied.

I looked steadfastly at him, and perceived that his eyes looked dull and glazed. Instantly it occurred to me, that his unexampled diligence in copying by his dim window for the first few weeks of his stay with me might have temporarily impaired his vision.

I was touched. I said something in condolence with him. I hinted that of course he did wisely in abstaining from writing for a while; and urged him to embrace that opportunity of taking wholesome exercise in the open air. This, however, he did not do. A few days after this, my other clerks being absent, and being in a great hurry to dispatch certain letters by the mail, I thought that, having nothing else earthly to do, Bartleby would surely be less inflexible than usual, and carry these letters to the post office. But he blankly declined. So, much to my inconvenience, I went myself.

Still added days went by. Whether Bartleby's eyes improved or not, I could not say. To all appearance, I thought they did. But when I asked him if they did, he vouchsafed no answer. At all events, he would do no copying. At last, in reply to my urgings, he informed me that he had permanently given up copying.

"What!" exclaimed I; "suppose your eyes should get entirely well—better than ever before—would you not copy then?"

"I have given up copying," he answered, and slid aside.

He remained as ever, a fixture in my chamber. Nay—if that were possible—he became still more of a fixture than before. What was to be done? He would do nothing in the office; why should he stay there? In plain fact, he had now become a millstone to me, not only useless as a necklace, but afflictive to bear. Yet I was sorry for him. I speak less than truth when I say that, on his own account, he occasioned me uneasiness. If he would but have named a single relative or friend, I would instantly have written, and urged their taking the poor fellow away to some convenient retreat. But he seemed alone, absolutely alone in the universe. A bit of wreck in the mid-Atlantic. At length, necessities connected with my business tyrannized over all other considerations. Decently as I could, I told Bartleby that in six days' time he must unconditionally leave the office. I warned him to take measures, in the interval, for procuring some other abode. I offered to assist him in this endeavor, if he himself would but take the first step towards a removal. "And when you finally quit me, Bartleby," added I, "I shall see that you go not away entirely unprovided. Six days from this hour, remember."

At the expiration of that period, I peeped behind the screen, and lo! Bartleby was there.

I buttoned up my coat, balanced myself; advanced slowly towards him, touched his shoulder, and said, "The time has come; you must quit this place; I am sorry for you; here is money; but you must go."

"I would prefer not," he replied, with his back still towards me.

"You *must*."

He remained silent.

Now I had an unbounded confidence in this man's common honesty. He had frequently restored to me sixpences and shillings carelessly dropped upon the floor, for I am apt to be very reckless in such shirt-button affairs. The proceeding, then, which followed will not be deemed extraordinary.

"Bartleby," said I, "I owe you twelve dollars on account; here are thirty-two; the odd twenty are yours—Will you take it?" and I handed the bills towards him.

But he made no motion.

"I will leave them here, then," putting them under a weight on the table. Then taking my hat and cane and going to the door, I tranquilly turned and added—"After you have removed your things from these offices, Bartleby, you will of course lock the door—since every one is now gone for the day but you—and if you please, slip your key underneath the mat, so that I may have it in the morning. I shall not see you again; so good-bye to you. If, hereafter, in your new place of abode, I can be of any service to you, do not fail to advise me by letter. Good-bye, Bartleby, and fare you well."

But he answered not a word; like the last column of some ruined temple, he remained standing mute and solitary in the middle of the otherwise deserted room.

As I walked home in a pensive mood, my vanity got the better of my pity. I could not but highly plume myself on my masterly management in getting rid of Bartleby. Mas-

terly I call it, and such it must appear to any dispassionate
thinker. The beauty of my procedure seemed to consist in
its perfect quietness. There was no vulgar bullying, no
bravado of any sort, no choleric hectoring, and striding to
and fro across the apartment, jerking out vehement commands for Bartleby to bundle himself off with his beggarly
traps. Nothing of the kind. Without loudly bidding Bartleby depart—as an inferior genius might have done—I
assumed the ground that depart he must; and upon that
assumption built all I had to say. The more I thought over
my procedure, the more I was charmed with it. Nevertheless, next morning, upon awakening, I had my doubts—I
had somehow slept off the fumes of vanity. One of the coolest and wisest hours a man has, is just after he awakes in the
morning. My procedure seemed as sagacious as ever—but
only in theory. How it would prove in practice—there was
the rub. It was truly a beautiful thought to have assumed
Bartleby's departure; but, after all, that assumption was
simply my own, and none of Bartleby's. The great point
was, not whether I had assumed that he would quit me,
but whether he would prefer so to do. He was more a man
of preferences than assumptions.

After breakfast, I walked down town, arguing the proba-
bilities *pro* and *con*. One moment I thought it would prove
a miserable failure, and Bartleby would be found all alive at
my office as usual; the next moment it seemed certain that
I should find his chair empty. And so I kept veering about.
At the corner of Broadway and Canal Street, I saw quite
an excited group of people standing in earnest conversation.

"I'll take odds he doesn't," said a voice as I passed.

"Doesn't go?—done!" said I, "put up your money."

I was instinctively putting my hand in my pocket to
produce my own, when I remembered that this was an
election day. The words I had overheard bore no reference
to Bartleby, but to the success or non-success of some candi-

date for the mayoralty. In my intent frame of mind, I had,
as it were, imagined that all Broadway shared in my excitement, and were debating the same question with me. I
passed on, very thankful that the uproar of the street
screened my momentary absent-mindedness.

As I had intended, I was earlier than usual at my office
door. I stood listening for a moment. All was still. He must
be gone. I tried the knob. The door was locked. Yes, my
procedure had worked to a charm; he indeed must be vanished. Yet a certain melancholy mixed with this: I was
almost sorry for my brilliant success. I was fumbling under
the door mat for the key, which Bartleby was to have left
there for me, when accidentally my knee knocked against a
panel, producing a summoning sound, and in response a
voice came to me from within—"Not yet; I am occupied."

It was Bartleby.

I was thunderstruck. For an instant I stood like the man
who, pipe in mouth, was killed one cloudless afternoon long
ago in Virginia, by summer lightning; at his own warm open
window he was killed, and remained leaning out there
upon the dreamy afternoon, till some one touched him,
when he fell.

"Not gone!" I murmured at last. But again obeying that
wondrous ascendancy which the inscrutable scrivener had
over me, and from which ascendancy, for all my chafing, I
could not completely escape, I slowly went down stairs and
out into the street, and while walking round the block,
considered what I should next do in this unheard-of perplexity. Turn the man out by an actual thrusting I could
not; to drive him away by calling him hard names would
not do; calling in the police was an unpleasant idea; and
yet, permit him to enjoy his cadaverous triumph over me—
this, too, I could not think of. What was to be done? or, if
nothing could be done, was there anything further that I
could *assume* in the matter? Yes, as before I had prospec

tively assumed that Bartleby would depart, so now I might retrospectively assume that departed he was. In the legitimate carrying out of this assumption, I might enter my office in a great hurry, and pretending not to see Bartleby at all, walk straight against him as if he were air. Such a proceeding would in a singular degree have the appearance of a home-thrust. It was hardly possible that Bartleby could withstand such an application of the doctrine of assumptions. But upon second thoughts the success of the plan seemed rather dubious. I resolved to argue the matter over with him again.

"Bartleby," said I, entering the office, with a quietly severe expression, "I am seriously displeased. I am pained, Bartleby. I had thought better of you. I had imagined you of such a gentlemanly organization, that in any delicate dilemma a slight hint would suffice—in short, an assumption. But it appears I am deceived. Why," I added, unaffectedly starting, "you have not even touched that money yet," pointing to it, just where I had left it the evening previous.

He answered nothing.

"Will you, or will you not, quit me?" I now demanded in a sudden passion, advancing close to him.

"I would prefer *not* to quit you," he replied, gently emphasizing the *not*.

"What earthly right have you to stay here? Do you pay any rent? Do you pay my taxes? Or is this property yours?"

He answered nothing.

"Are you ready to go on and write now? Are your eyes recovered? Could you copy a small paper for me this morning? or help examine a few lines? or step round to the post-office? In a word, will you do anything at all, to give a coloring to your refusal to depart the premises?"

He silently retired into his hermitage.

I was now in such a state of nervous resentment that I

thought it but prudent to check myself at present from further demonstrations. Bartleby and I were alone. I remembered the tragedy of the unfortunate Adams and the still more unfortunate Colt in the solitary office of the latter; and how poor Colt, being dreadfully incensed by Adams, and imprudently permitting himself to get wildly excited, was at unawares hurried into his fatal act—an act which certainly no man could possibly deplore more than the actor himself. Often it had occurred to me in my ponderings upon the subject that had that altercation taken place in the public street, or at a private residence, it would not have terminated as it did. It was the circumstance of being alone in a solitary office, up stairs, of a building entirely unhallowed by humanizing domestic associations —an uncarpeted office, doubtless, of a dusty, haggard sort of appearance—this it must have been, which greatly helped to enhance the irritable desperation of the hapless Colt.

But when this old Adam of resentment rose in me and tempted me concerning Bartleby, I grappled him and threw him. How? Why, simply by recalling the divine injunction: "A new commandment give I unto you, that ye love one another." Yes, this it was that saved me. Aside from higher considerations, charity often operates as a vastly wise and prudent principle—a great safeguard to its possessor. Men have committed murder for jealousy's sake, and anger's sake, and hatred's sake, and selfishness' sake, and spiritual pride's sake; but no man, that ever I heard of, ever committed a diabolical murder for sweet charity's sake. Mere self-interest, then, if no better motive can be enlisted, should, especially with high-tempered men, prompt all beings to charity and philanthropy. At any rate, upon the occasion in question, I strove to drown my exasperated feelings towards the scrivener by benevolently construing his conduct. Poor fellow, poor fellow! thought

I, he don't mean anything; and besides, he has seen hard times, and ought to be indulged.

I endeavored, also, immediately to occupy myself, and at the same time to comfort my despondency. I tried to fancy, that in the course of the morning, at such time as might prove agreeable to him, Bartleby, of his own free accord, would emerge from his hermitage and take up some decided line of march in the direction of the door. But no. Half-past twelve o'clock came; Turkey began to glow in the face, overturn his inkstand, and become generally obstreperous; Nippers abated down into quietude and courtesy; Ginger Nut munched his noon apple; and Bartleby remained standing at his window in one of his profoundest dead-wall reveries. Will it be credited? Ought I to acknowledge it? That afternoon I left the office without saying one further word to him.

Some days now passed, during which, at leisure intervals I looked a little into "Edwards on the Will," and "Priestley on Necessity." Under the circumstances, those books induced a salutary feeling. Gradually I slid into the persuasion that these troubles of mine, touching the scrivener, had been all predestinated from eternity, and Bartleby was billeted upon me for some mysterious purpose of an allwise Providence, which it was not for a mere mortal like me to fathom. Yes, Bartleby, stay there behind your screen, thought I; I shall persecute you no more; you are harmless and noiseless as any of these old chairs; in short, I never feel so private as when I know you are here. At last I see it, I feel it; I penetrate to the predestinated purpose of my life. I am content. Others may have loftier parts to enact; but my mission in this world, Bartleby, is to furnish you with office-room for such period as you may see fit to remain.

I believe that this wise and blessed frame of mind would have continued with me, had it not been for the unsolicited and uncharitable remarks obtruded upon me by my professional friends who visited the rooms. But thus it often is, that the constant friction of illiberal minds wears out at last the best resolves of the more generous. Though to be sure, when I reflected upon it, it was not strange that people entering my office should be struck by the peculiar aspect of the unaccountable Bartleby, and so be tempted to throw out some sinister observations concerning him. Sometimes an attorney, having business with me, and calling at my office, and finding no one but the scrivener there, would undertake to obtain some sort of precise information from him touching my whereabouts; but without heeding his idle talk, Bartleby would remain standing immovable in the middle of the room. So after contemplating him in that position for a time, the attorney would depart, no wiser than he came.

Also, when a reference was going on, and the room full of lawyers and witnesses, and business driving fast, some deeply-occupied legal gentleman present, seeing Bartleby wholly unemployed, would request him to run round to his (the legal gentleman's) office and fetch some papers for him. Thereupon, Bartleby would tranquilly decline, and yet remain idle as before. Then the lawyer would give a great stare, and turn to me. And what could I say? At last I was made aware that all through the circle of my professional acquaintance, a whisper of wonder was running round, having reference to the strange creature I kept at my office. This worried me very much. And as the idea came upon me of his possibly turning out a long-lived man, and keep occupying my chambers, and denying my authority; and perplexing my visitors; and scandalizing my professional reputation; and casting a general gloom over the premises; keeping soul and body together to the last upon his savings (for doubtless he spent but half a dime a day), and in the end perhaps outlive me, and claim possession of my office by right of his perpetual occupancy: as all these dark anticipations crowded upon me more and more, and my friends continually intruded their relentless remarks upon the apparition in my room; a great change was wrought in me. I resolved to gather all my faculties together, and forever rid me of this intolerable incubus.

Ere revolving any complicated project, however, adapted to this end, I first simply suggested to Bartleby the propriety of his permanent departure. In a calm and serious tone, I commended the idea to his careful and mature consideration. But, having taken three days to meditate upon it, he apprised me, that his original determination remained the same; in short, that he still preferred to abide with me.

What shall I do? I now said to myself, buttoning up my coat to the last button. What shall I do? what ought I to do? what does conscience say I *should* do with this man, or, rather, ghost. Rid myself of him, I must; go, he shall. But how? You will not thrust him, the poor, pale, passive mortal —you will not thrust such a helpless creature out of your door? you will not dishonor yourself by such cruelty? No, I will not, I cannot do that. Rather would I let him live and die here, and then mason up his remains in the wall. What, then, will you do? For all your coaxing, he will not budge. Bribes he leaves under your own paper-weight on your table; in short, it is quite plain that he prefers to cling to you.

Then something severe, something unusual must be done. What! surely you will not have him collared by a constable, and commit his innocent pallor to the common jail? And upon what ground could you procure such a thing to be done?—a vagrant, is he? What! he a vagrant, a wanderer, who refuses to budge? It is because he will *not* be a vagrant, then, that you seek to count him *as* a vagrant. That is too absurd. No visible means of support: there I have him. Wrong again: for indubitably he *does* support himself, and that is the only unanswerable proof that any man can show of his possessing the means so to do. No more, then. Since he will not quit me, I must quit him. I will change my offices; I will move elsewhere, and give him fair notice, that if I find him on my new premises I will then proceed against him as a common trespasser.

Acting accordingly, next day I thus addressed him: "I find these chambers too far from the City Hall; the air is unwholesome. In a word, I propose to remove my offices next week, and shall no longer require your services. I tell you this now, in order that you may seek another place."

He made no reply, and nothing more was said.

On the appointed day I engaged carts and men, proceeded to my chambers, and, having but little furniture, everything was removed in a few hours. Throughout, the scrivener remained standing behind the screen, which I directed to be removed the last thing. It was withdrawn; and, being folded up like a huge folio, left him the motionless occupant of a naked room. I stood in the entry watching him a moment, while something from within me upbraided me.

I re-entered, with my hand in my pocket—and—and my heart in my mouth.

"Good-bye, Bartleby; I am going—good-bye, and God some way bless you; and take that," slipping something in his hand. But it dropped upon the floor, and then—strange to say—I tore myself from him whom I had so longed to be rid of.

Established in my new quarters, for a day or two I kept the door locked, and started at every footfall in the passages. When I returned to my rooms, after any little absence, I would pause at the threshold for an instant, and attentively listen, ere applying my key. But these fears were needless. Bartleby never came nigh me.

I thought all was going well, when a perturbed-looking stranger visited me, inquiring whether I was the person who had recently occupied rooms at No. — Wall Street.

Full of forebodings, I replied that I was.

"Then, sir," said the stranger, who proved a lawyer, "you are responsible for the man you left there. He refuses to do any copying; he refuses to do anything; he says he prefers not to; and he refuses to quit the premises."

"I am very sorry, sir," said I, with assumed tranquillity, but an inward tremor, "but, really, the man you allude to is nothing to me—he is no relation or apprentice of mine, that you should hold me responsible for him."

"In mercy's name, who is he?"

"I certainly cannot inform you. I know nothing about him. Formerly I employed him as a copyist; but he has done nothing for me now for some time past."

"I shall settle him, then—good morning, sir."

Several days passed, and I heard nothing more; and, though I often felt a charitable prompting to call at the place and see poor Bartleby, yet a certain squeamishness, of I know not what, withheld me.

All is over with him, by this time, thought I, at last, when, through another week, no further intelligence reached me. But, coming to my room the day after, I found several persons waiting at my door in a high state of nervous excitement.

"That's the man—here he comes," cried the foremost one, whom I recognized as the lawyer who had previously called upon me alone.

"You must take him away, sir, at once," cried a portly person among them, advancing upon me, and whom I knew to be the landlord of No. — Wall Street. "These gentlemen, my tenants, cannot stand it any longer; Mr. B——," pointing to the lawyer, "has turned him out of his room, and he now persists in haunting the building generally, sitting upon the banisters of the stairs by day, and sleeping in the entry by night. Everybody is concerned;

clients are leaving the offices; some fears are entertained of a mob; something you must do, and that without delay."

Aghast at this torrent, I fell back before it, and would fain have locked myself in my new quarters. In vain I persisted that Bartleby was nothing to me—no more than to any one else. In vain—I was the last person known to have anything to do with him, and they held me to the terrible account. Fearful, then, of being exposed in the papers (as one person present obscurely threatened), I considered the matter, and, at length, said, that if the lawyer would give me a confidential interview with the scrivener, in his (the lawyer's) own room, I would, that afternoon, strive my best to rid them of the nuisance they complained of.

Going up stairs to my old haunt, there was Bartleby silently sitting upon the banister at the landing.

"What are you doing here, Bartleby?" said I.

"Sitting upon the banister," he mildly replied.

I motioned him into the lawyer's room, who then left us.

"Bartleby," said I, "are you aware that you are the cause of great tribulation to me, by persisting in occupying the entry after being dismissed from the office?"

No answer.

"Now one of two things must take place. Either you must do something, or something must be done to you. Now what sort of business would you like to engage in? Would you like to re-engage in copying for some one?"

"No; I would prefer not to make any change."

"Would you like a clerkship in a dry-goods store?"

"There is too much confinement about that. No, I would not like a clerkship; but I am not particular."

"Too much confinement," I cried, "why, you keep yourself confined all the time!"

"I would prefer not to take a clerkship," he rejoined, as if to settle that little item at once.

"How would a bar-tender's business suit you? There is no trying of the eye-sight in that."

"I would not like it at all; though, as I said before, I am not particular."

His unwonted wordiness inspirited me. I returned to the charge.

"Well, then, would you like to travel through the country collecting bills for the merchants? That would improve your health."

"No, I would prefer to be doing something else."

"How, then, would going as a companion to Europe, to entertain some young gentleman with your conversation—how would that suit you?"

"Not at all. It does not strike me that there is anything definite about that. I like to be stationary. But I am not particular."

"Stationary you shall be, then," I cried, now losing all patience, and, for the first time in all my exasperating connection with him, fairly flying into a passion. "If you do not go away from these premises before night, I shall feel bound—indeed, I *am* bound—to—to—to quit the premises myself!" I rather absurdly concluded, knowing not with what possible threat to try to frighten his immobility into compliance. Despairing of all further efforts, I was precipitately leaving him, when a final thought occurred to me —one which had not been wholly unindulged before.

"Bartleby," said I, in the kindest tone I could assume under such exciting circumstances, "will you go home with me now—not to my office, but my dwelling—and remain there till we can conclude upon some convenient arrangement for you at our leisure? Come, let us start now, right away."

"No: at present I would prefer not to make any change at all."

I answered nothing; but, effectually dodging every one

by the suddenness and rapidity of my flight, rushed from the building, ran up Wall Street towards Broadway, and, jumping into the first omnibus, was soon removed from pursuit. As soon as tranquillity returned, I distinctly perceived that I had now done all that I possibly could, both in respect to the demands of the landlord and his tenants, and with regard to my own desire and sense of duty, to benefit Bartleby, and shield him from rude persecution. I now strove to be entirely care-free and quiescent; and my conscience justified me in the attempt; though, indeed, it was not so successful as I could have wished. So fearful was I of being again hunted out by the incensed landlord and his exasperated tenants, that, surrendering my business to Nippers, for a few days, I drove about the upper part of the town and through the suburbs, in my rockaway; crossed over to Jersey City and Hoboken, and paid fugitive visits to Manhattanville and Astoria. In fact, I almost lived in my rockaway for the time.

When again I entered my office, lo, a note from the landlord lay upon the desk. I opened it with trembling hands. It informed me that the writer had sent to the police, and had Bartleby removed to the Tombs as a vagrant. Moreover, since I knew more about him than any one else, he wished me to appear at that place, and make a suitable statement of the facts. These tidings had a conflicting effect upon me. At first I was indignant; but, at last, almost approved. The landlord's energetic, summary disposition, had led him to adopt a procedure which I do not think I would have decided upon myself; and yet, as a last resort, under such peculiar circumstances, it seemed the only plan.

As I afterwards learned, the poor scrivener, when told that he must be conducted to the Tombs, offered not the slightest obstacle, but, in his pale, unmoving way, silently acquiesced.

Some of the compassionate and curious by-standers joined

the party; and headed by one of the constables arm-in-arm with Bartleby, the silent procession filed its way through all the noise, and heat, and joy of the roaring thoroughfares at noon.

The same day I received the note, I went to the Tombs, or, to speak more properly, the Halls of Justice. Seeking the right officer, I stated the purpose of my call, and was informed that the individual I described was, indeed, within. I then assured the functionary that Bartleby was a perfectly honest man, and greatly to be compassionated, however unaccountably eccentric. I narrated all I knew, and closed by suggesting the idea of letting him remain in as indulgent confinement as possible, till something less harsh might be done—though, indeed, I hardly knew what. At all events, if nothing else could be decided upon, the alms-house must receive him. I then begged to have an interview.

Being under no disgraceful charge, and quite serene and harmless in all his ways, they had permitted him freely to wander about the prison, and, especially, in the inclosed grass-platted yards thereof. And so I found him there, standing all alone in the quietest of the yards, his face towards a high wall, while all around, from the narrow slits of the jail windows, I thought I saw peering out upon him the eyes of murderers and thieves.

"Bartleby!"

"I know you," he said, without looking round—"and I want nothing to say to you."

"It was not I that brought you here, Bartleby," said I, keenly pained at his implied suspicion. "And to you, this should not be so vile a place. Nothing reproachful attaches to you by being here. And see, it is not so sad a place as one might think. Look, there is the sky, and here is the grass."

"I know where I am," he replied, but would say nothing more, and so I left him.

As I entered the corridor again, a broad meat-like man, in

an apron, accosted me, and, jerking his thumb over his shoulder, said—"Is that your friend?"

"Yes."

"Does he want to starve? If he does, let him live on the prison fare, that's all."

"Who are you?" asked I, not knowing what to make of such an unofficially speaking person in such a place.

"I am the grub-man. Such gentlemen as have friends here, hire me to provide them with something good to eat."

"Is this so?" said I, turning to the turnkey.

He said it was.

"Well, then," said I, slipping some silver into the grub-man's hands (for so they called him), "I want you to give particular attention to my friend there; let him have the best dinner you can get. And you must be as polite to him as possible."

"Introduce me, will you?" said the grub-man, looking at me with an expression which seemed to say he was all impatience for an opportunity to give a specimen of his breeding.

Thinking it would prove of benefit to the scrivener, I acquiesced; and, asking the grub-man his name, went up with him to Bartleby.

"Bartleby, this is a friend; you will find him very useful to you."

"Your sarvant, sir, your sarvant," said the grub-man, making a low salutation behind his apron. "Hope you find it pleasant here, sir; nice grounds—cool apartments—hope you'll stay with us some time—try to make it agreeable. What will you have for dinner to-day?"

"I prefer not to dine to-day," said Bartleby, turning away. "It would disagree with me; I am unused to dinners." So saying, he slowly moved to the other side of the inclosure, and took up a position fronting the dead-wall.

"How's this?" said the grub-man, addressing me with a stare of astonishment. "He's odd, ain't he?"

"I think he is a little deranged," said I, sadly.

"Deranged? deranged is it? Well, now, upon my word, I thought that friend of yourn was a gentleman forger; they are always pale and genteel-like, them forgers. I can't help pity 'em—can't help it, sir. Did you know Monroe Edwards?" he added, touchingly, and paused. Then, laying his hand piteously on my shoulder, sighed, "he died of consumption at Sing-Sing. So you weren't acquainted with Monroe?"

"No, I was never socially acquainted with any forgers. But I cannot stop longer. Look to my friend yonder. You will not lose by it. I will see you again."

Some few days after this, I again obtained admission to the Tombs, and went through the corridors in quest of Bartleby; but without finding him.

"I saw him coming from his cell not long ago," said a turnkey, "may be he's gone to loiter in the yards."

So I went in that direction.

"Are you looking for the silent man?" said another turnkey, passing me. "Yonder he lies—sleeping in the yard there. 'Tis not twenty minutes since I saw him lie down."

The yard was entirely quiet. It was not accessible to the common prisoners. The surrounding walls, of amazing thickness, kept off all sounds behind them. The Egyptian character of the masonry weighed upon me with its gloom. But a soft imprisoned turf grew under foot. The heart of the eternal pyramids, it seemed, wherein, by some strange magic, through the clefts, grass-seed, dropped by birds, had sprung.

Strangely huddled at the base of the wall, his knees drawn up, and lying on his side, his head touching the cold stones, I saw the wasted Bartleby. But nothing stirred. I paused; then went close up to him; stooped over, and saw that his dim eyes were open; otherwise he seemed profoundly sleeping. Something prompted me to touch him. I felt his hand, when a tingling shiver ran up my arm and down my spine to my feet.

The round face of the grub-man peered upon me now. "His dinner is ready. Won't he dine to-day, either? Or does he live without dining?"

"Lives without dining," said I, and closed the eyes.

"Eh!—He's asleep, ain't he?"

"With kings and counselors," murmured I.

* * *

There would seem little need for proceeding further in this history. Imagination will readily supply the meagre recital of poor Bartleby's interment. But, ere parting with the reader, let me say, that if this little narrative has sufficently interested him, to awaken curiosity as to who Bartleby was, and what manner of life he led prior to the present narrator's making his acquaintance, I can only reply, that in such curiosity I fully share, but am wholly unable to gratify it. Yet here I hardly know whether I should divulge one little item of rumor, which came to my ear a few months after the scrivener's decease. Upon what basis it rested, I could never ascertain; and hence, how true it is I cannot now tell. But, inasmuch as this vague report has not been without a certain suggestive interest to me, however sad, it may prove the same with some others; and so I will briefly mention it. The report was this: that Bartleby had been a subordinate clerk in the Dead Letter Office at Washington, from which he had been suddenly removed by a change in the administration. When I think over this rumor, hardly can I express the emotions which seize me. Dead letters! does it not sound like dead men? Conceive a man by nature and misfortune prone to a pallid hopelessness, can any business seem more fitted to heighten it than that of continually handling these dead letters, and assorting them for the flames? For by the cart-load they are annually burned. Sometimes from out the folded paper the pale clerk takes a ring—the finger it was meant for, perhaps, moulders in the grave; a bank-note sent in swiftest charity —he whom it would relieve, nor eats nor hungers any more; pardon for those who died despairing; hope for those who died unhoping; good tidings for those who died stifled by unrelieved calamities. On errands of life, these letters speed to death.

Ah, Bartleby! Ah, humanity!

The Encantadas OR *Enchanted Isles*

The Isles at Large

That may not be, said then the Ferryman,
Least we unweeting hap to be fordonne:
For those same Islands, seeming now and than,
Are not firme land, nor any certein wonne,
But stragling plots, which to and fro do ronne
In the wide waters; therefore are they hight
The Wandring Islands: Therefore doe them shonne;
For they have oft drawne many a wandring wight
Into most deadly daunger and distressed plight;
For whosoever once hath fastened
His foot thereon, may never it recure,
But wandreth evermore uncertein and unsure.

Darke, dolefull, dreary, like a greedy grave,
That still for carrion carcases doth crave:
On top whereof ay dwelt the ghastly owle,
Shrieking his balefull note, which ever drave
Far from that haunt all other chearefull fowle;
And all about it wandring ghostes did wayle and howle.

TAKE five-and-twenty heaps of cinders dumped here and there in an outside city lot; imagine some of them magnified into mountains, and the vacant lot the sea; and you will have a fit idea of the general aspect of the Encantadas, or Enchanted Isles. A group rather of extinct volcanoes than of isles; looking much as the world at large might, after a penal conflagration.

It is to be doubted whether any spot of earth can, in desolateness, furnish a parallel to this group. Abandoned cemeteries of long ago, old cities by piecemeal tumbling to their ruin, these are melancholy enough; but, like all else which has but once been associated with humanity, they still awaken in us some thoughts of sympathy, however sad. Hence, even the Dead Sea, along with whatever other emotions it may at times inspire, does not fail to touch in the pilgrim some of his less unpleasurable feelings.

And as for solitariness; the great forests of the north, the expanses of unnavigated waters, the Greenland ice-fields, are the profoundest of solitudes to a human observer; still the magic of their changeable tides and seasons mitigates their terror; because, though unvisited by men, those forests are visited by the May; the remotest seas reflect familiar stars even as Lake Erie does; and in the clear air of a fine Polar day, the irradiated, azure ice shows beautifully as malachite.

But the special curse, as one may call it, of the Encantadas, that which exalts them in desolation above Idumea and the Pole, is, that to them change never comes; neither the change of seasons nor of sorrows. Cut by the Equator, they know not autumn, and they know not spring; while already reduced to the lees of fire, ruin itself can work little more upon them. The showers refresh the deserts; but in these isles, rain never falls. Like split Syrian gourds left withering in the sun, they are cracked by an everlasting drought beneath a torrid sky. "Have mercy on me," the wailing spirit of the Encantadas seems to cry, "and send Lazarus that he may dip the tip of his finger in water and cool my tongue, for I am tormented in this flame."

Another feature in these isles is their emphatic uninhabitableness. It is deemed a fit type of all-forsaken overthrow, that the jackal should den in the wastes of weedy Babylon; but the Encantadas refuse to harbor even the outcasts of the beasts. Man and wolf alike disown them. Little but reptile life is here found: tortoises, lizards, immense spiders, snakes, and that strangest anomaly of outlandish nature, the *iguana*. No voice, no low, no howl is heard; the chief sound of life here is a hiss.

On most of the isles where vegetation is found at all, it is more ungrateful than the blankness of Atacama. Tangled thickets of wiry bushes, without fruit and without a name, springing up among deep fissures of calcined rock, and treacherously masking them; or a parched growth of distorted cactus trees.

In many places the coast is rock-bound, or, more properly, clinker-bound; tumbled masses of blackish or greenish stuff like the dross of an iron-furnace, forming dark clefts and caves here and there, into which a ceaseless sea pours a fury of foam; overhanging them with a swirl of gray, haggard mist, amidst which sail screaming flights of unearthly birds heightening the dismal din. However calm the sea without, there is no rest for these swells and those rocks; they lash and are lashed, even when the outer ocean is most at peace with itself. On the oppressive, clouded days, such as are peculiar to this part of the watery Equator, the dark, vitrified masses, many of which raise themselves among white whirlpools and breakers in detached and perilous places off the shore, present a most Plutonian sight. In no world but a fallen one could such lands exist.

Those parts of the strand free from the marks of fire, stretch away in wide level beaches of multitudinous dead shells, with here and there decayed bits of sugar-cane, bamboos, and cocoanuts, washed upon this other and darker world from the charming palm isles to the westward and southward; all the way from Paradise to Tartarus; while mixed with the relics of distant beauty you will sometimes see fragments of charred wood and mouldering ribs of wrecks. Neither will any one be surprised at meeting these last, after observing the conflicting currents which eddy throughout nearly all the wide channels of the entire group.

The capriciousness of the tides of air sympathizes with those of the sea. Nowhere is the wind so light, baffling, and every way unreliable, and so given to perplexing calms, as at the Encantadas. Nigh a month has been spent by a ship going from one isle to another, though but ninety miles between; for owing to the force of the current, the boats employed to tow barely suffice to keep the craft from sweeping upon the cliffs, but do nothing towards accelerating her voyage. Sometimes it is impossible for a vessel from afar to fetch up with the group itself, unless large allowances for prospective lee-way have been made ere its coming in sight. And yet, at other times, there is a mysterious indraft, which irresistibly draws a passing vessel among the isles, though not bound to them.

True, at one period, as to some extent at the present day, large fleets of whalemen cruised for spermaceti upon what some seamen call the Enchanted Ground. But this, as in due place will be described, was off the great outer isle of Albemarle, away from the intricacies of the smaller isles, where there is plenty of sea-room; and hence, to that vicinity, the above remarks do not altogether apply; though even there the current runs at times with singular force, shifting, too, with as singular a caprice.

Indeed, there are seasons when currents quite unaccountable prevail for a great distance round about the total group, and are so strong and irregular as to change a vessel's course against the helm, though sailing at the rate of four or five miles the hour. The difference in the reckonings of navigators, produced by these causes, along with the light and variable winds, long nourished a persuasion, that there existed two distinct clusters of isles in the parallel of the Encantadas, about a hundred leagues apart. Such was the idea of their earlier visitors, the Buccaneers; and as late as 1750, the charts of that part of the Pacific accorded with the strange delusion. And this apparent fleetingness and unreality of the locality of the isles was most probably one reason for the Spaniards calling them the Encantada, or Enchanted Group.

But not uninfluenced by their character, as they now confessedly exist, the modern voyager will be inclined to fancy that the bestowal of this name might have in part originated in that air of spell-bound desertness which so significantly invests the isles. Nothing can better suggest the aspect of once living things malignly crumbled from ruddiness into ashes. Apples of Sodom, after touching, seem these isles.

However wavering their place may seem by reason of the currents, they themselves, at least to one upon the shore, appear invariably the same: fixed, cast, glued into the very body of cadaverous death.

Nor would the appellation, enchanted, seem misapplied in still another sense. For concerning the peculiar reptile inhabitant of these wilds—whose presence gives the group its second Spanish name, Galapagos—concerning the tortoises found here, most mariners have long cherished a superstition, not more frightful than grotesque. They earnestly believe that all wicked sea-officers, more especially commodores and captains, are at death (and, in some cases, before death) transformed into tortoises; thenceforth dwelling upon these hot aridities, sole solitary lords of Asphaltum.

Doubtless, so quaintly dolorous a thought was originally inspired by the woe-begone landscape itself; but more particularly, perhaps, by the tortoises. For, apart from their strictly physical features, there is something strangely self-condemned in the appearance of these creatures. Lasting sorrow and penal hopelessness are in no animal form so suppliantly expressed as in theirs; while the thought of their wonderful longevity does not fail to enhance the impression.

Nor even at the risk of meriting the charge of absurdly

believing in enchantments, can I restrain the admission that sometimes, even now, when leaving the crowded city to wander out July and August among the Adirondack Mountains, far from the influences of towns and proportionally nigh to the mysterious ones of nature; when at such times I sit me down in the mossy head of some deep-wooded gorge, surrounded by prostrate trunks of blasted pines, and recall, as in a dream, my other and far-distant rovings in the baked heart of the charmed isles; and remember the sudden glimpses of dusky shells, and long languid necks protruded from the leafless thickets; and again have beheld the vitreous inland rocks worn down and grooved into deep ruts by ages and ages of the slow draggings of tortoises in quest of pools of scanty water; I can hardly resist the feeling that in my time I have indeed slept upon evilly enchanted ground.

Nay, such is the vividness of my memory, or the magic of my fancy, that I know not whether I am not the occasional victim of optical delusion concerning the Galapagos. For, often in scenes of social merriment, and especially at revels held by candle-light in old-fashioned mansions, so that shadows are thrown into the further recesses of an angular and spacious room, making them put on a look of haunted undergrowth of lonely woods, I have drawn the attention of my comrades by my fixed gaze and sudden change of air, as I have seemed to see, slowly emerging from those imagined solitudes, and heavily crawling along the floor, the ghost of a gigantic tortoise, with "Memento * * * * *" burning in live letters upon his back.

Two Sides to a Tortoise

Most ugly shapes and horrible aspects,
Such as Dame Nature selfe mote feare to see,
Or shame, that ever should so fowle defects
From her most cunning hand escaped bee;
All dreadfull pourtraicts of deformitee:
Ne wonder, if these do a man appall;
For all that here at home we dreadfull hold,
Be but as bugs to fearen babes withall,
Compared to the creatures in these isles' entrall.

"Feare nought," then saide the Palmer well aviz'd,
"For these same monsters are not these in deed,
But are into these fearfull shapes disguiz'd."
And lifting up his vertuous staffe on hye,
Then all that dreadfull armie fast can flye
Into great Tethys bosome, where they hidden lye.

IN VIEW of the description given, may one be gay upon the Encantadas? Yes: that is, find one the gaiety, and he will be gay. And, indeed, sackcloth and ashes as they are, the isles are not perhaps unmitigated gloom. For while no spectator can deny their claims to a most solemn and superstitious consideration, no more than my firmest resolutions can decline to behold the spectre-tortoise when emerging from its shadowy recess; yet even the tortoise, dark and melancholy as it is upon the back, still possesses a bright side; its calipee or breast-plate being sometimes of a faint yellowish or golden tinge. Moreover, every one knows that tortoises as well as turtles are of such a make, that if you but put them on their backs you thereby expose their bright sides without the possibility of their recovering

55

themselves, and turning into view the other. But after you have done this, and because you have done this, you should not swear that the tortoise has no dark side. Enjoy the bright, keep it turned up perpetually if you can, but be honest, and don't deny the black. Neither should he, who cannot turn the tortoise from its natural position so as to hide the darker and expose his livelier aspect, like a great October pumpkin in the sun, for that cause declare the creature to be one total inky blot. The tortoise is both black and bright. But let us to particulars.

Some months before my first stepping ashore upon the group, my ship was cruising in its close vicinity. One noon we found ourselves off the South Head of Albemarle, and not very far from the land. Partly by way of freak, and partly by way of spying out so strange a country, a boat's crew was sent ashore, with orders to see all they could, and besides, bring back whatever tortoises they could conveniently transport.

It was after sunset, when the adventurers returned. I looked down over the ship's high side as if looking down over the curb of a well, and dimly saw the damp boat deep in the sea with some unwonted weight. Ropes were dropt over, and presently three huge antediluvian-looking tortoises, after much straining, were landed on deck. They seemed hardly of the seed of earth. We had been abroad upon the waters for five long months, a period amply sufficient to make all things of the land wear a fabulous hue to the dreamy mind. Had three Spanish custom-house officers boarded us then, it is not unlikely that I should have curiously stared at them, felt of them, and stroked them much as savages serve civilized guests. But instead of three custom-house officers, behold these really wondrous tortoises—none of your schoolboy mud-turtles—but black as widower's weeds, heavy as chests of plate, with vast shells medallioned and orbed like shields, and dented and blistered like shields that have breasted a battle, shaggy, too, here and there, with dark green moss, and slimy with the spray of the sea. These mystic creatures, suddenly translated by night from unutterable solitudes to our peopled deck, affected me in a manner not easy to unfold. They seemed newly crawled forth from beneath the foundations of the world. Yea, they seemed the identical tortoises whereon the Hindoo plants this total sphere. With a lantern I inspected them more closely. Such worshipful venerableness of aspect! Such furry greenness mantling the rude peelings and healing the fissures of their shattered shells. I no more saw three tortoises. They expanded—became transfigured. I seemed to see three Roman Coliseums in magnificent decay.

Ye oldest inhabitants of this, or any other isle, said I, pray, give me the freedom of your three walled towns.

The great feeling inspired by these creatures was that of age:—dateless, indefinite endurance. And, in fact, that any other creature can live and breathe as long as the tortoise of the Encantadas, I will not readily believe. Not to hint of their known capacity of sustaining life, while going without food for an entire year, consider that impregnable armor of their living mail. What other bodily being possesses such a citadel wherein to resist the assaults of Time?

As, lantern in hand, I scraped among the moss and beheld the ancient scars of bruises received in many a sullen fall among the marly mountains of the isle—scars strangely widened, swollen, half obliterate, and yet distorted like those sometimes found in the bark of very hoary trees, I seemed an antiquary of a geologist, studying the bird-tracks and ciphers upon the exhumed slates trod by incredible creatures whose very ghosts are now defunct.

As I lay in my hammock that night, overhead I heard the slow weary draggings of the three ponderous strangers

along the encumbered deck. Their stupidity or their resolution was so great, that they never went aside for any
impediment. One ceased his movements altogether just
before the mid-watch. At sunrise I found him butted like
a battering-ram against the immovable foot of the foremast,
and still striving, tooth and nail, to force the impossible
passage. That these tortoises are the victims of a penal, or
malignant, or perhaps a downright diabolical enchanter,
seems in nothing more likely than in that strange infatuation of hopeless toil which so often possesses them. I have
known them in their journeyings ram themselves heroically
against rocks, and long abide there, nudging, wriggling,
wedging, in order to displace them, and so hold on their
inflexible path. Their crowning curse is their drudging
impulse to straightforwardness in a belittered world.

Meeting with no such hinderance as their companion
did, the other tortoises merely fell foul of small stumbling-
blocks—buckets, blocks, and coils of rigging—and at times
in the act of crawling over them would slip with an
astounding rattle to the deck. Listening to these draggings
and concussions, I thought me of the haunt from which
they came; an isle full of metallic ravines and gulches, sunk
bottomlessly into the hearts of splintered mountains, and
covered for many miles with inextricable thickets. I then
pictured these three straightforward monsters, century after
century, writhing through the shades, grim as blacksmiths;
crawling so slowly and ponderously, that not only did toadstools and all fungous things grow beneath their feet, but a
sooty moss sprouted upon their backs. With them I lost
myself in volcanic mazes; brushed away endless boughs of
rotting thickets; till finally in a dream I found myself sitting
cross-legged upon the foremost, a Brahmin similarly
mounted upon either side, forming a tripod of foreheads
which upheld the universal cope.

Such was the wild nightmare begot by my first impression of the Encantadas tortoise. But next evening, strange to say, I sat down with my shipmates, and made a merry repast from tortoise steaks and tortoise stews; and supper over, out knife, and helped convert the three mighty concave shells into three fanciful soup-tureens, and polished the three flat yellowish calipees into three gorgeous salvers.

Rock Rodondo

For thy this hight the Rock of vile Reproch,
A daungerous and dreadfull place,
To which nor fish nor fowle did once approch,
But yelling meawes, with seagulles hoars and bace,
And cormoyrants, with birds of ravenous race,
Which still sit waiting on that dreadfull clift.

With that the rolling sea resounding soft,
In his big base them fitly answered;
And on the Rock the waves breaking aloft
A solemne meane unto them measured;
Then he the Boteman bad row easily,
And let him heare some part of that rare melody.

Suddeinly an innumerable flight
Of harmefull fowles about them fluttering cride,
And with their wicked wings them oft did smight,
And sore annoyed, groping in that griesly night.
Even all the nation of unfortunate
And fatall birds about them flocked were.

To go up into a high stone tower is not only a very fine thing in itself, but the very best mode of gaining a comprehensive view of the region round about. It is all the better if this tower stand solitary and alone, like that mysterious Newport one, or else be sole survivor of some perished castle.

Now, with reference to the Enchanted Isles, we are fortunately supplied with just such a noble point of observation in a remarkable rock, from its peculiar figure called of old by the Spaniards, Rock Rodondo, or Round Rock. Some two hundred and fifty feet high, rising straight from the sea ten miles from land, with the whole mountainous group to the south and east, Rock Rodondo occupies, on a large scale, very much the position which the famous Campanile or detached Bell-Tower of St. Mark does with respect to the tangled group of hoary edifices around it.

Ere ascending, however, to gaze abroad upon the Encantadas, this sea-tower itself claims attention. It is visible at the distance of thirty miles; and, fully participating in that enchantment which pervades the group, when first seen afar invariably is mistaken for a sail. Four leagues away, of a golden, hazy noon, it seems some Spanish Admiral's ship, stacked up with glittering canvas. *Sail ho! Sail ho! Sail ho!* from all three masts. But coming nigh, the enchanted frigate is transformed apace into a craggy keep.

My first visit to the spot was made in the gray of the morning. With a view of fishing, we had lowered three boats, and pulling some two miles from our vessel, found ourselves just before dawn of day close under the moon-shadow of Rodondo. Its aspect was heightened, and yet softened, by the strange double twilight of the hour. The great full moon burnt in the low west like a half-spent beacon, casting a soft mellow tinge upon the sea like that cast by a waning fire of embers upon a midnight hearth; while along the entire east the invisible sun sent pallid intimations of his coming. The wind was light; the waves languid; the stars twinkled with a faint effulgence; all nature seemed supine with the long night watch, and half-suspended in jaded expectation of the sun. This was the critical hour to catch Rodondo in his perfect mood. The twilight was just enough to reveal every striking point, without tearing away the dim investiture of wonder.

From a broken stair-like base, washed, as the steps of a water-palace, by the waves, the tower rose in entablatures of strata to a shaven summit. These uniform layers, which compose the mass, form its most peculiar feature. For at their lines of junction they project flatly into encircling shelves, from top to bottom, rising one above another in graduated series. And as the eaves of any old barn or abbey are alive with swallows, so were all these rocky ledges with unnumbered sea-fowl. Eaves upon eaves, and nests upon nests. Here and there were long birdlime streaks of a ghostly white staining the tower from sea to air, readily accounting for its sail-like look afar. All would have been bewitchingly quiescent, were it not for the demoniac din created by the birds. Not only were the eaves rustling with them, but they flew densely overhead, spreading themselves into a winged and continually shifting canopy. The tower is the resort of aquatic birds for hundreds of leagues around. To the north, to the east, to the west, stretches nothing but eternal ocean; so that the man-of-war hawk coming from the coasts of North America, Polynesia, or Peru, makes his first land at Rodondo. And yet though Rodondo be terra firma, no land-bird ever lighted on it. Fancy a red-robin or a canary there! What a falling into the hands of the Philistines, when the poor warbler should be surrounded by such locust-flights of strong bandit birds, with long bills cruel as daggers.

I know not where one can better study the Natural History of strange sea-fowl than at Rodondo. It is the aviary of Ocean. Birds light here which never touched mast or tree; hermit-birds, which ever fly alone; cloud-birds, familiar with unpierced zones of air.

Let us first glance low down to the lowermost shelf of all, which is the widest, too, and but a little space from high-water mark. What outlandish beings are these? Erect as men, but hardly as symmetrical, they stand all round the rock like sculptured caryatides, supporting the next range of eaves above. Their bodies are grotesquely misshapen; their bills short; their feet seemingly legless; while the members at their sides are neither fin, wing, nor arm. And truly neither fish, flesh, nor fowl is the penguin; as an edible, pertaining neither to Carnival nor Lent; without exception the most ambiguous and least lovely creature yet discovered by man. Though dabbling in all three elements, and indeed possessing some rudimental claims to all, the penguin is at home in none. On land it stumps; afloat it sculls; in the air it flops. As if ashamed of her failure, Nature keeps this ungainly child hidden away at the ends of the earth, in the Straits of Magellan, and on the abased sea-story of Rodondo.

But look, what are yon woe-begone regiments drawn up on the next shelf above? what rank and file of large strange fowl? what sea Friars of Orders Gray? Pelicans. Their elongated bills, and heavy leathern pouches suspended thereto, give them the most lugubrious expression. A pensive race, they stand for hours together without motion. Their dull, ashy plumage imparts an aspect as if they had been powdered over with cinders. A penitential bird, indeed, fitly haunting the shores of the clinkered Encantadas, whereon tormented Job himself might have well sat down and scraped himself with potsherds.

Higher up now we mark the gony, or gray albatross, anomalously so called, an unsightly, unpoetic bird, unlike its storied kinsman, which is the snow-white ghost of the haunted Capes of Hope and Horn.

As we still ascend from shelf to shelf, we find the tenants of the tower serially disposed in order of their magnitude:—gannets, black and speckled haglets, jays, sea-hens, sperm-whale-birds, gulls of all varieties:—thrones, princedoms, powers, dominating one above another in senatorial array; while, sprinkled over all, like an ever-repeated fly in a great piece of broidery, the stormy petrel or Mother Cary's chicken sounds his continual challenge and alarm. That this mysterious humming-bird of ocean— which, had it but brilliancy of hue, might, from its evanescent liveliness, be almost called its butterfly, yet whose chirrup under the stern is ominous to mariners as to the peasant the death-tick sounding from behind the chimney jamb—should have its special haunt at the Encantadas, contributes, in the seaman's mind, not a little to their dreary spell.

As day advances the dissonant din augments. With ear-splitting cries the wild birds celebrate their matins. Each moment, flights push from the tower, and join the aerial choir hovering overhead, while their places below are supplied by darting myriads. But down through all this discord of commotion, I hear clear, silver, bugle-like notes unbrokenly falling, like oblique lines of swift-slanting rain in a cascading shower. I gaze far up, and behold a snow-white angelic thing, with one long, lance-like feather thrust out behind. It is the bright, inspiriting chanticleer of ocean, the beauteous bird, from its bestirring whistle of musical invocation, fitly styled the "Boatswain's Mate."

The winged life clouding Rodondo had its full counter-part in the finny hosts which peopled the waters at its base. Below the waterline, the rock seemed one honey-comb of grottoes, affording labyrinthine lurking-places for swarms of fairy fish. All were strange; many exceedingly beautiful; and would have well graced the costliest glass globes in which gold-fish are kept for a show. Nothing was more strik-ing than the complete novelty of many individuals of this multitude. Here hues were seen as yet unpainted, and fig-ures which are unengraved.

To show the multitude, avidity, and nameless fearless-ness and tameness of these fish, let me say, that often, mark-ing through clear spaces of water—temporarily made so by the concentric dartings of the fish above the surface—cer-tain larger and less unwary wights, which swam slow and deep, our anglers would cautiously essay to drop their lines down to these last. But in vain; there was no passing the uppermost zone. No sooner did the hook touch the sea, than a hundred infatuates contended for the honor of capture. Poor fish of Rodondo! in your victimized confidence, you are of the number of those who inconsiderately trust, while they do not understand, human nature.

But the dawn is now fairly day. Band after band, the sea-fowl sail away to forage the deep for their food. The tower is left solitary, save the fish-caves at its base. Its birdlime gleams in the golden rays like the whitewash of a tall lighthouse, or the lofty sails of a cruiser. This moment, doubtless, while we know it to be a dead desert rock, other voyagers are taking oaths it is a glad populous ship.

But ropes now, and let us ascend. Yet soft, this is not so easy.

A Pisgah View from the Rock

That done, he leads him to the highest Mount,
From whence, far off he unto him did shew . . .

IF YOU seek to ascend Rock Rodondo, take the following
prescription. Go three voyages round the world as a
main-royal-man of the tallest frigate that floats; then
serve a year or two apprenticeship to the guides who conduct strangers up the Peak of Teneriffe; and as many more
respectively to a rope-dancer, an Indian juggler, and a
chamois. This done, come and be rewarded by the view
from our tower. How we get there, we alone know. If we
sought to tell others, what the wiser were they? Suffice it,
that here at the summit you and I stand. Does any balloon-
ist, does the outlooking man in the moon, take a broader
view of space? Much thus, one fancies, looks the universe
from Milton's celestial battlements. A boundless watery
Kentucky. Here Daniel Boone would have dwelt content.

Never heed for the present yonder Burnt District of the
Enchanted Isles. Look edgeways, as it were, past them, to
the south. You see nothing; but permit me to point out the
direction, if not the place, of certain interesting objects in
the vast sea, which, kissing this tower's base, we behold
unscrolling itself towards the Antarctic Pole.

We stand now ten miles from the Equator. Yonder, to
the east, some six hundred miles, lies the continent; this
Rock being just about on the parallel of Quito.

Observe another thing here. We are at one of three
uninhabited clusters, which, at pretty nearly uniform distances from the main, sentinel, at long intervals from each

66

other, the entire coast of South America. In a peculiar manner, also, they terminate the South American character of country. Of the unnumbered Polynesian chains to the westward, not one partakes of the qualities of the Encantadas or Galapagos, the isles of San Felix and San Ambrosio, the isles Juan Fernandez and Mas-a-Fuera. Of the first, it needs not here to speak. The second lie a little above the Southern Tropic; lofty, inhospitable, and uninhabitable rocks, one of which, presenting two round hummocks connected by a low reef, exactly resembles a huge double-headed shot. The last lie in the latitude of 33°; high, wild and cloven. Juan Fernandez is sufficiently famous without further description. Mas-a-Fuera is a Spanish name, expressive of the fact, that the isle so called lies *more without,* that is, further off the main than its neighbor Juan. This isle Mas-a-Fuera has a very imposing aspect at a distance of eight or ten miles. Approached in one direction, in cloudy weather, its great overhanging height and rugged contour, and more especially a peculiar slope of its broad summits, give it much the air of a vast iceberg drifting in tremendous poise. Its sides are split with dark cavernous recesses, as an old cathedral with its gloomy lateral chapels. Drawing nigh one of these gorges from sea, after a long voyage, and beholding some tatterdemalion outlaw, staff in hand, descending its steep rocks toward you, conveys a very queer emotion to a lover of the picturesque.

On fishing parties from ships, at various times, I have chanced to visit each of these groups. The impression they give to the stranger pulling close up in his boat under their grim cliffs is, that surely he must be their first discoverer, such, for the most part, is the unimpaired . . . . . . silence and solitude. And here, by the way, the mode in which these isles were really first lighted upon by Europeans is not unworthy of mention, especially as what is about to be said, likewise applies to the original discovery of our Encantadas.

Prior to the year 1563, the voyages made by Spanish ships from Peru to Chile, were full of difficulty. Along this coast, the winds from the South most generally prevail; and it had been an invariable custom to keep close in with the land, from a superstitious conceit on the part of the Spaniards, that were they to lose sight of it, the eternal trade-wind would waft them into unending waters, from whence would be no return. Here, involved among tortuous capes and headlands, shoals and reefs, beating, too, against a continual head wind, often light, and sometimes for days and weeks sunk into utter calm, the provincial vessels, in many cases, suffered the extremest hardships, in passages, which at the present day seem to have been incredibly protracted. There is on record in some collections of nautical disasters, an account of one of these ships, which, starting on a voyage whose duration was estimated at ten days, spent four months at sea, and indeed never again entered harbor, for in the end she was cast away. Singular to tell, this craft never encountered a gale, but was the vexed sport of malicious calms and currents. Thrice, out of provisions, she put back to an intermediate port, and started afresh, but only yet again to return. Frequent fogs enveloped her; so that no observation could be had of her place, and once, when all hands were joyously anticipating sight of their destination, lo! the vapors lifted and disclosed the mountains from which they had taken their first departure. In the like deceptive vapors she at last struck upon a reef, whence ensued a long series of calamities too sad to detail.

It was the famous pilot, Juan Fernandez, immortalized by the island named after him, who put an end to these coasting tribulations, by boldly venturing the experiment— as De Gama did before him with respect to Europe—of standing broad out from land. Here he found the winds favorable for getting to the South, and by running westward till beyond the influences of the trades, he regained the coast without difficulty; making the passage which, though in a high degree circuitous, proved far more expeditious than the nominally direct one. Now it was upon these new tracks, and about the year 1670, or thereabouts, that the Enchanted Isles, and the rest of the sentinel groups, as they may be called, were discovered. Though I know of no account as to whether any of them were found inhabited or no, it may be reasonably concluded that they have been immemorial solitudes. But let us return to Rodondo.

Southwest from our tower lies all Polynesia, hundreds of leagues away; but straight west, on the precise line of his parallel, no land rises till your keel is beached upon the Kingsmills, a nice little sail of, say 5000 miles.

Having thus by such distant references—with Rodondo the only possible ones—settled our relative place on the sea, let us consider objects not quite so remote. Behold the grim and charred Enchanted Isles. This nearest crater-shaped headland is part of Albemarle, the largest of the group, being some sixty miles or more long, and fifteen broad. Did you ever lay eye on the real genuine Equator? Have you ever, in the largest sense, toed the Line? Well, that identical crater-shaped headland there, all yellow lava, is cut by the Equator exactly as a knife cuts straight through the centre of a pumpkin pie. If you could only see so far, just to one side of that same headland, across yon low dikey ground, you would catch sight of the isle of Narborough, the loftiest land of the cluster; no soil whatever; one seamed clinker from top to bottom; abounding in black caves like smithies; its metallic shore ringing under foot like plates of iron; its central volcanoes standing grouped like a gigantic chimney-stack.

Narborough and Albemarle are neighbors after a quite

curious fashion. A familiar diagram will illustrate this strange neighborhood:

Ħ

Cut a channel at the above letter joint, and the middle transverse limb is Narborough, and all the rest is Albemarle. Volcanic Narborough lies in the black jaws of Albemarle like a wolf's red tongue in his open mouth.

If now you desire the population of Albemarle, I will give you, in round numbers, the statistics, according to the most reliable estimates made upon the spot:

Men,	none
Ant-eaters,	unknown
Man-haters,	unknown
Lizards,	500,000
Snakes,	500,000
Spiders,	10,000,000
Salamanders,	unknown
Devils,	do.

Making a clean total of ......11,000,000 exclusive of an incomputable host of fiends, ant-eaters, man-haters, and salamanders.

Albemarle opens his mouth towards the setting sun. His distended jaws form a great bay, which Narborough, his tongue, divides into halves, one whereof is called Weather Bay, the other Lee Bay; while the volcanic promontories, terminating his coasts, are styled South Head and North Head. I note this, because these bays are famous in the annals of the Sperm Whale Fishery. The whales come here at certain seasons to calve. When ships first cruised hereabouts, I am told, they used to blockade the entrance of Lee Bay, when their boats going round by Weather Bay, passed through Narborough channel, and so had the Leviathans very neatly in a pen.

The day after we took fish at the base of this Round
Tower, we had a fine wind, and shooting round the north
headland, suddenly descried a fleet of full thirty sail, all
beating to windward like a squadron in line. A brave sight
as ever man saw. A most harmonious concord of rushing
keels. Their thirty kelsons hummed like thirty harp-strings,
and looked as straight whilst they left their parallel traces
on the sea. But there proved too many hunters for the
game. The fleet broke up, and went their separate ways out
of sight, leaving my own ship and two trim gentlemen of
London. These last, finding no luck either, likewise vanished; and Lee Bay, with all its appurtenances, and without
a rival, devolved to us.

The way of cruising here is this. You keep hovering
about the entrance of the bay, in one beat and out the
next. But at times—not always, as in other parts of the
group—a race-horse of a current sweeps right across its
mouth. So, with all sails set, you carefully ply your tacks.
How often, standing at the foremast head at sunrise, with
our patient prow pointed in between these isles, did I gaze
upon that land, not of cakes, but of clinkers, not of streams
of sparkling water, but arrested torrents of tormented lava.

As the ship runs in from the open sea, Narborough
presents its side in one dark craggy mass, soaring up some
five or six thousand feet, at which point it hoods itself in
heavy clouds, whose lowest level fold is as clearly defined
against the rocks as the snow-line against the Andes. There
is dire mischief going on in that upper dark. There toil
the demons of fire, who, at intervals, irradiate the nights
with a strange spectral illumination for miles and miles
around, but unaccompanied by any further demonstration;
or else, suddenly announce themselves by terrific concussions, and the full drama of a volcanic eruption. The blacker
that cloud by day, the more may you look for light by
night. Often whalemen have found themselves cruising

nigh that burning mountain when all aglow with a ball-room blaze. Or, rather, glass-works, you may call this same vitreous isle of Narborough, with its tall chimney-stacks.

Where we still stand, here on Rodondo, we cannot see all the other isles, but it is a good place from which to point out where they lie. Yonder, though, to the E.N.E., I mark a distant dusky ridge. It is Abington Isle, one of the most northerly of the group; so solitary, remote, and blank, it looks like No-Man's Land seen off our northern shore. I doubt whether two human beings ever touched upon that spot. So far as yon Abington Isle is concerned, Adam and his billions of posterity remain uncreated.

Ranging south of Abington, and quite out of sight behind the long spine of Albemarle, lies James's Isle, so called by the early Buccaneers after the luckless Stuart, Duke of York. Observe here, by the way, that, excepting the isles particularized in comparatively recent times, and which mostly received the names of famous Admirals, the En-cantadas were first christened by the Spaniards; but these Spanish names were generally effaced on English charts by the subsequent christenings of the Buccaneers, who, in the middle of the seventeenth century, called them after Eng-lish noblemen and kings. Of these loyal freebooters and the things which associate their name with the Encantadas, we shall hear anon. Nay, for one little item, immediately; for between James's Isle and Albemarle, lies a fantastic islet, strangely known as "Cowley's Enchanted Isle." But, as all the group is deemed enchanted, the reason must be given for the spell within a spell involved by this particular designation. The name was bestowed by that excellent Buccaneer himself, on his first visit here. Speaking in his published voyages of this spot, he says—"My fancy led me to call it Cowley's Enchanted Isle, for, we having had a Sight of it upon several Points of the Compass, it appear'd always in as many different Forms; sometimes like a ruined Fortification, upon another Point, like a great City, &c." No wonder though, that among the Encantadas all sorts of ocular deceptions and mirages should be met.

That Cowley linked his name with this self-transforming and bemocking isle, suggests the possibility that it conveyed to him some meditative image of himself. At least, as is not impossible, if he were any relative of the mildly-thoughtful and self-upbraiding poet Cowley, who lived about his time, the conceit might seem not unwarranted; for that sort of thing evinced in the naming of this isle runs in the blood, and may be seen in pirates as in poets.

Still south of James's Isle lie Jervis Isle, Duncan Isle, Crossman's Isle, Brattle Isle, Wood's Isle, Chatham Isle, and various lesser isles, for the most part an archipelago of aridities, without inhabitant, history, or hope of either in all time to come. But not far from these are rather notable isles—Barrington, Charles's, Norfolk, and Hood's. Succeeding chapters will reveal some ground for their notability.

The Frigate, and Ship Flyaway

Looking far foorth into the ocean wide,
A goodly ship with banners bravely dight,
And flag in her top-gallant I espide
Through the maine sea making her merry flight.

ERE quitting Rodondo, it must not be omitted that here, in 1813, the U. S. frigate *Essex*, Captain David Porter, came near leaving her bones. Lying becalmed one morning with a strong current setting her rapidly towards the rock, a strange sail was descried, which —not out of keeping with alleged enchantments of the neighborhood—seemed to be staggering under a violent wind, while the frigate lay lifeless as if spell-bound. But a light air springing up, all sail was made by the frigate in chase of the enemy, as supposed—he being deemed an English whale-ship—but the rapidity of the current was so great, that soon all sight was lost of him; and, at meridian, the *Essex*, spite of her drags, was driven so close under the foam-lashed cliffs of Rodondo that, for a time, all hands gave her up. A smart breeze, however, at last helped her off, though the escape was so critical as to seem almost miraculous.

Thus saved from destruction herself, she now made use of that salvation to destroy the other vessel, if possible. Renewing the chase in the direction in which the stranger had disappeared, sight was caught of him the following morning. Upon being descried he hoisted American colors and stood away from the *Essex*. A calm ensued; when, still confident that the stranger was an Englishman, Porter dispatched a cutter, not to board the enemy, but drive back his boats engaged in towing him. The cutter succeeded. Cutters were subsequently sent to capture him; the stranger now showing English colors in place of American. But, when the frigate's boats were within a short distance of their hoped-for prize, another sudden breeze sprang up; the stranger, under all sail, bore off to the westward, and, ere night, was hull down ahead of the *Essex*, which, all this time, lay perfectly becalmed.

This enigmatic craft—American in the morning, and English in the evening—her sails full of wind in a calm— was never again beheld. An enchanted ship no doubt. So, at least, the sailors swore.

This cruise of the *Essex* in the Pacific during the war of 1812, is, perhaps, the strangest and most stirring to be found in the history of the American navy. She captured the furthest wandering vessels; visited the remotest seas and isles; long hovered in the charmed vicinity of the enchanted group; and, finally, valiantly gave up the ghost fighting two English frigates in the harbor of Valparaiso. Mention is made of her here for the same reason that the Buccaneers will likewise receive record; because, like them, by long cruising among the isles, tortoise-hunting upon their shores, and generally exploring them; for these and other reasons, the *Essex* is peculiarly associated with the Encantadas.

Here be it said that you have but three eye-witness authorities worth mentioning touching the Enchanted Isles:—Cowley, the Buccaneer (1684); Colnett, the whaling-ground explorer (1793); Porter, the post captair. (1813). Other than these you have but barren, bootless allusions from some few passing voyagers or compilers.

Barrington Isle and the Buccaneers

Let us all servile base subjection scorne;
And, as we bee sonnes of the earth so wide,
Let us our fathers heritage divide,
And chalenge to our selves our portions dew
Of all the patrimonie, which a few
Now hold in hugger-mugger in their hand . . .
Lords of the world, and so will wander free,
Where so us listeth, uncontrol'd of anie.

How bravely now we live, how jocund, how
near the first inheritance, without fear, how
free from little troubles!

NEAR two centuries ago Barrington Isle was the resort of that famous wing of the West Indian Buccaneers, which, upon their repulse from the Cuban waters, crossing the Isthmus of Darien, ravaged the Pacific side of the Spanish colonies, and, with the regularity and timing of a modern mail, waylaid the royal treasure-ships plying between Manila and Acapulco. After the toils of piratic war, here they came to say their prayers, enjoy their free-and-easies, count their crackers from the cask, their doubloons from the keg, and measure their silks of Asia with long Toledos for their yard-sticks.

As a secure retreat, an undiscoverable hiding-place, no spot in those days could have been better fitted. In the centre of a vast and silent sea, but very little traversed—surrounded by islands, whose inhospitable aspect might well drive away the chance navigator—and yet within a few days' sail of the opulent countries which they made their prey—the unmolested Buccaneers found here that tran-

quillity which they fiercely denied to every civilized harbor
in that part of the world. Here, after stress of weather, or
a temporary drubbing at the hands of their vindictive foes,
or in swift flight with golden booty, those old marauders
came, and lay snugly out of all harm's reach. But not only
was the place a harbor of safety, and a bower of ease, but
for utility in other things it was most admirable.

Barrington Isle is, in many respects, singularly adapted
to careening, refitting, refreshing, and other seamen's purposes. Not only has it good water, and good anchorage, well
sheltered from all winds by the high land of Albemarle,
but it is the least unproductive isle of the group. Tortoises
good for food, trees good for fuel, and long grass good for
bedding, abound here, and there are pretty natural walks,
and several landscapes to be seen. Indeed, though in its
locality belonging to the Enchanted group, Barrington Isle
is so unlike most of its neighbors, that it would hardly seem
of kin to them.

"I once landed on its western side," says a sentimental
voyager long ago, "where it faces the black buttress of Albemarle. I walked beneath groves of trees—not very lofty,
and not palm trees, or orange trees, or peach trees, to be
sure—but, for all that, after a long sea-faring, very beautiful to walk under, even though they supplied no fruit.
And here, in calm spaces at the heads of glades, and on the
shaded tops of slopes commanding the most quiet scenery—
what do you think I saw? Seats which might have served
Brahmins and presidents of peace societies. Fine old ruins
of what had once been symmetric lounges of stone and turf,
they bore every mark both of artificialness and age, and
were, undoubtedly, made by the Buccaneers. One had been
a long sofa, with back and arms, just such a sofa as the poet
Gray might have loved to throw himself upon, his Cré-
billon in hand.

"Though they sometimes tarried here for months at a

time, and used the spot for a storing-place for spare spars, sails, and casks; yet it is highly improbable that the Buccaneers ever erected dwelling-houses upon the isle. They never were here except their ships remained, and they would most likely have slept on board. I mention this, because I cannot avoid the thought, that it is hard to impute the construction of these romantic seats to any other motive than one of pure peacefulness and kindly fellowship with nature. That the Buccaneers perpetrated the greatest outrages is very true—that some of them were mere cut-throats is not to be denied; but we know that here and there among their host was a Dampier, a Wafer, and a Cowley, and likewise other men, whose worst reproach was their desperate fortunes—whom persecution, or adversity, or secret and unavengeable wrongs, had driven from Christian society to seek the melancholy solitude or the guilty adventures of the sea. At any rate, long as those ruins of seats on Barrington remain, the most singular monuments are furnished to the fact, that all of the Buccaneers were not unmitigated monsters.

"But during my ramble on the isle I was not long in discovering other tokens, of things quite in accordance with those wild traits, popularly, and no doubt truly enough, imputed to the freebooters at large. Had I picked up old sails and rusty hoops I would only have thought of the ship's carpenter and cooper. But I found old cutlasses and daggers reduced to mere threads of rust, which, doubtless, had stuck between Spanish ribs ere now. These were signs of the murderer and robber; the reveler likewise had left his trace. Mixed with shells, fragments of broken jars were lying here and there, high up upon the beach. They were precisely like the jars now used upon the Spanish coast for the wine and Pisco spirits of that country.

"With a rusty dagger-fragment in one hand, and a bit of a wine-jar in another, I sat me down on the ruinous green sofa I have spoken of, and bethought me long and deeply of these same Buccaneers. Could it be possible, that they robbed and murdered one day, reveled the next, and rested themselves by turning meditative philosophers, rural poets, and seat-builders on the third? Not very improbable, after all. For consider the vacillations of a man. Still, strange as it may seem, I must also abide by the more charitable thought; namely, that among these adventurers were some gentlemanly, companionable souls, capable of genuine tranquillity and virtue."

Charles's Isle and the Dog-King

Loe with outragious cry
A thousand villeins round about him swarmd
Out of the rockes and caves adjoyning nye;
Vile caitive wretches, ragged, rude, deformd,
All threatning death, all in straunge manner armd;
Some with unweldy clubs, some with long speares,
Some rusty knives, some staves in fier warmd.

We will not be of anie occupation,
Let such vile vassalls borne to base vocation
Drudge in the world, and for their living droyle,
Which have no wit to live withouten toyle.

SOUTHWEST of Barrington lies Charles's Isle. And hereby hangs a history which I gathered long ago from a shipmate learned in all the lore of outlandish life.

During the successful revolt of the Spanish provinces from Old Spain, there fought on behalf of Peru a certain Creole adventurer from Cuba, who, by his bravery and good fortune, at length advanced himself to high rank in the patriot army. The war being ended, Peru found itself like many valorous gentlemen, free and independent enough, but with few shot in the locker. In other words, Peru had not wherewithal to pay off its troops. But the Creole—I forget his name—volunteered to take his pay in lands. So they told him he might have his pick of the Enchanted Isles, which were then, as they still remain, the nominal appanage of Peru. The soldier straightway embarks thither, explores the group, returns to Callao, and says he will take a deed of Charles's Isle. Moreover, this deed must stipulate that thenceforth Charles's Isle is not only the sole property of the Creole, but is forever free of Peru, even as Peru of Spain. To be short, this adventurer procures himself to be made in effect Supreme Lord of the Island, one of the princes of the powers of the earth.*

He now sends forth a proclamation inviting subjects to his as yet unpopulated kingdom. Some eighty souls, men and women, respond; and being provided by their leader with necessaries, and tools of various sorts, together with a few cattle and goats, take ship for the promised land; the last arrival on board, prior to sailing, being the Creole himself, accompanied, strange to say, by a disciplined cavalry company of large grim dogs. These, it was observed on the passage, refusing to consort with the emigrants, remained aristocratically grouped around their master on the elevated quarter-deck, casting disdainful glances forward upon the inferior rabble there; much as, from the ramparts, the soldiers of a garrison, thrown into a conquered town, eye the inglorious citizen-mob over which they are set to watch.

Now Charles's Isle not only resembles Barrington Isle in being much more inhabitable than other parts of the group, but it is double the size of Barrington, say forty or fifty miles in circuit.

Safely debarked at last, the company, under direction of their lord and patron, forthwith proceeded to build their capital city. They make considerable advance in the way of walls of clinkers, and lava floors, nicely sanded with cinders. On the least barren hills they pasture their cattle,

* The American Spaniards have long been in the habit of making presents of islands to deserving individuals. The pilot Juan Fernandez procured a deed of the isle named after him, and for some years resided there before Selkirk came. It is supposed, however, that he eventually contracted the blues upon his princely property, for after a time he returned to the main, and as report goes, became a very garrulous barber in the city of Lima.

while the goats, adventurers by nature, explore the far inland solitudes for a scanty livelihood of lofty herbage. Meantime, abundance of fish and tortoises supply their other wants.

The disorders incident to settling all primitive regions, in the present case were heightened by the peculiarly untoward character of many of the pilgrims. His Majesty was forced at last to proclaim martial law, and actually hunted and shot with his own hand several of his rebellious subjects, who, with most questionable intentions, had clandestinely encamped in the interior, whence they stole by night, to prowl barefooted on tiptoe round the precincts of the lava-palace. It is to be remarked, however, that prior to such stern proceedings, the more reliable men had been judiciously picked out for an infantry body-guard, subordinate to the cavalry body-guard of dogs. But the state of politics in this unhappy nation may be somewhat imagined, from the circumstance that all who were not of the body-guard were downright plotters and malignant traitors. At length the death penalty was tacitly abolished, owing to the timely thought, that were strict sportsman's justice to be dispensed among such subjects, ere long the Nimrod King would have little or no remaining game to shoot. The human part of the life-guard was now disbanded, and set to work cultivating the soil, and raising potatoes; the regular army now solely consisting of the dog-regiment. These, as I have heard, were of a singularly ferocious character, though by severe training rendered docile to their master. Armed to the teeth, the Creole now goes in state, surrounded by his canine janizaries, whose terrific bayings prove quite as serviceable as bayonets in keeping down the surgings of revolt.

But the census of the isle, sadly lessened by the dispensation of justice, and not materially recruited by matrimony, began to fill his mind with sad mistrust. Some way the population must be increased. Now, from its possessing a little water, and its comparative pleasantness of aspect, Charles's Isle at this period was occasionally visited by foreign whalers. These His Majesty had always levied upon for port charges, thereby contributing to his revenue. But now he had additional designs. By insidious arts he, from time to time, cajoles certain sailors to desert their ships, and enlist beneath his banner. Soon as missed, their captains crave permission to go and hunt them up. Whereupon His Majesty first hides them very carefully away, and then freely permits the search. In consequence, the delinquents are never found, and the ships retire without them.

Thus, by a two-edged policy of this crafty monarch, foreign nations were crippled in the number of their subjects, and his own were greatly multiplied. He particularly petted these renegado strangers. But alas for the deep-laid schemes of ambitious princes, and alas for the vanity of glory. As the foreign-born Prætorians, unwisely introduced into the Roman state, and still more unwisely made favorites of the Emperors, at last insulted and overturned the throne, even so these lawless mariners, with all the rest of the body-guard and all the populace, broke out into a terrible mutiny, and defied their master. He marched against them with all his dogs. A deadly battle ensued upon the beach. It raged for three hours, the dogs fighting with determined valor, and the sailors reckless of everything but victory. Three men and thirteen dogs were left dead upon the field, many on both sides were wounded, and the king was forced to fly with the remainder of his canine regiment. The enemy pursued, stoning the dogs with their master into the wilderness of the interior. Discontinuing the pursuit, the victors returned to the village on the shore, stove the spirit casks, and proclaimed a Republic. The dead men were interred with the honors of war, and the dead dogs ignominiously thrown into the sea. At last, forced by stress of suffering, the fugitive Creole came down from the hills and offered to treat for peace. But the rebels refused it on any other terms than his unconditional banishment. Accordingly, the next ship that arrived carried away the ex-king to Peru.

The history of the king of Charles's Island furnishes another illustration of the difficulty of colonizing barren islands with unprincipled pilgrims.

Doubtless for a long time the exiled monarch, pensively ruralizing in Peru, which afforded him a safe asylum in his calamity, watched every arrival from the Encantadas, to hear news of the failure of the Republic, the consequent penitence of the rebels, and his own recall to royalty. Doubtless he deemed the Republic but a miserable experiment which would soon explode. But no, the insurgents had confederated themselves into a democracy neither Grecian, Roman, nor American. Nay, it was no democracy at all, but a permanent *Riotocracy*, which gloried in having no law but lawlessness. Great inducements being offered to deserters, their ranks were swelled by accessions of scamps from every ship which touched their shores. Charles's Island was proclaimed the asylum of the oppressed of all navies. Each runaway tar was hailed as a martyr in the cause of freedom, and became immediately installed a ragged citizen of this universal nation. In vain the captains of absconding seamen strove to regain them. Their new compatriots were ready to give any number of ornamental eyes in their behalf. They had few cannon, but their fists were not to be trifled with. So at last it came to pass that no vessels acquainted with the character of that country durst touch there, however sorely in want of refreshment. It became Anathema—a sea Alsatia—the unassailed lurking-place of all sorts of desperadoes, who in the name of liberty did just what they pleased. They continually fluctuated in their numbers. Sailors, deserting ships at other islands, or in boats at sea anywhere in that vicinity, steered for Charles's Isle, as to their sure home of refuge; while, sated with the life of the isle, numbers from time to time crossed the water to the neighboring ones, and there presenting themselves to strange captains as shipwrecked seamen, often succeeded in getting on board vessels bound to the Spanish coast, and having a compassionate purse made up for them on landing there.

One warm night during my first visit to the group, our ship was floating along in languid stillness, when some one on the forecastle shouted "Light ho!" We looked and saw a beacon burning on some obscure land off the beam. Our third mate was not intimate with this part of the world. Going to the captain he said, "Sir, shall I put off in a boat? These must be shipwrecked men."

The captain laughed rather grimly, as, shaking his fist towards the beacon, he rapped out an oath, and said—"No, no, you precious rascals, you don't juggle one of my boats ashore this blessed night. You do well, you thieves—you do benevolently to hoist a light yonder as on a dangerous shoal. It tempts no wise man to pull off and see what's the matter, but bids him steer small and keep off shore—that is Charles's Island; brace up, Mr. Mate, and keep the light astern."

Norfolk Isle and the Chola Widow

At last they in an Island did espy
A seemely woman, sitting by the shore,
That with great sorrow and sad agony
Seemed some great misfortune to deplore,
And lowd to them for succour called evermore.

Blacke hys eye as the midnyghte sky,
Whyte hys neck as the driven snowe,
Redde hys cheek as the mornynge lyghte,
Cold he lys ynne the ground belowe;
Mie love ys dedde,
Gon to hys deathe-bedde,
All under the cactus tree.

Each lonely scene shall thee restore,
For thee the tear be duly shed;
Belov'd till life can charm no more,
And mourn'd till Pity's self be dead.

FAR to the northeast of Charles's Isle, sequestered from the rest, lies Norfolk Isle; and, however insignificant to most voyagers, to me, through sympathy, that lone island has become a spot made sacred by the strangest trials of humanity.

It was my first visit to the Encantadas. Two days had been spent ashore in hunting tortoises. There was not time to capture many; so on the third afternoon we loosed our sails. We were just in the act of getting under way, the uprooted anchor yet suspended and invisibly swaying beneath the wave, as the good ship gradually turned her heel to leave the isle behind, when the seaman who heaved with me at the windlass paused suddenly, and directed my attention to something moving on the land, not along the beach, but somewhat back, fluttering from a height.

In view of the sequel of this little story, be it here narrated how it came to pass, that an object which partly from its being so small was quite lost to every other man on board, still caught the eye of my handspike companion. The rest of the crew, myself included, merely stood up to our spikes in heaving, whereas, unwontedly exhilarated, at every turn of the ponderous windlass, my belted comrade leaped atop of it, with might and main giving a downward, thewy, perpendicular heave, his raised eye bent in cheery animation upon the slowly receding shore. Being high lifted above all others was the reason he perceived the object, otherwise unperceivable; and this elevation of his eye was owing to the elevation of his spirits; and this again—for truth must out—to a dram of Peruvian pisco, in guerdon for some kindness done, secretly administered to him that morning by our mulatto steward. Now, certainly, pisco does a deal of mischief in the world; yet seeing that, in the present case, it was the means, though indirect, of rescuing a human being from the most dreadful fate, must we not also needs admit that sometimes pisco does a deal of good?

Glancing across the water in the direction pointed out, I saw some white thing hanging from an inland rock, perhaps half a mile from the sea.

"It is a bird; a white-winged bird; perhaps a——no; it is——it is a handkerchief!"

"Aye, a handkerchief!" echoed my comrade, and with a louder shout apprised the captain.

Quickly now—like the running out and training of a great gun—the long cabin spy-glass was thrust through the mizzen-rigging from the high platform of the poop; whereupon a human figure was plainly seen upon the inland rock, eagerly waving towards us what seemed to be the handkerchief.

Our captain was a prompt, good fellow. Dropping the glass, he lustily ran forward, ordering the anchor to be dropped again; hands to stand by a boat, and lower away.

In a half-hour's time the swift boat returned. It went with six and came with seven; and the seventh was a woman.

It is not artistic heartlessness, but I wish I could but draw in crayons; for this woman was a most touching sight; and crayons, tracing softly melancholy lines, would best depict the mournful image of the dark-damasked Chola widow.

Her story was soon told, and though given in her own strange language was as quickly understood; for our captain, from long trading on the Chilean coast, was well versed in the Spanish. A Cholo, or half-breed Indian woman of Payta in Peru, three years gone by, with her young new-wedded husband Felipe, of pure Castilian blood, and her one only Indian brother, Truxill, Hunilla had taken passage on the main in a French whaler, commanded by a joyous man; which vessel, bound to the cruising grounds beyond the Enchanted Isles, proposed passing close by their vicinity. The object of the little party was to procure tortoise oil, a fluid which for its great purity and delicacy is held in high estimation wherever known; and it is well known all along this part of the Pacific coast. With a chest of clothes, tools, cooking utensils, a rude apparatus for trying out the oil, some casks of biscuit, and other things, not omitting two favorite dogs, of which faithful animal all the Cholos are very fond, Hunilla and her companions were safely landed at their chosen place; the Frenchman, according to the contract made ere sailing, engaged to take them off upon returning from a four months' cruise in the westward seas; which

interval the three adventurers deemed quite sufficient for
their purposes.

On the isle's lone beach they paid him in silver for their
passage out, the stranger having declined to carry them at
all except upon that condition; though willing to take every
means to insure the due fulfillment of his promise. Felipe
had striven hard to have this payment put off to the period of
the ship's return. But in vain. Still they thought they had, in
another way, ample pledge of the good faith of the Frenchman. It was arranged that the expenses of the passage home
should not be payable in silver, but in tortoises; one hundred tortoises ready captured to the returning captain's
hand. These the Cholos meant to secure after their own
work was done, against the probable time of the Frenchman's coming back; and no doubt in prospect already felt,
that in those hundred tortoises—now somewhere ranging
the isle's interior—they possessed one hundred hostages.
Enough: the vessel sailed; the gazing three on shore
answered the loud glee of the singing crew; and ere evening, the French craft was hull down in the distant sea, its
masts three faintest lines which quickly faded from Hunilla's eye.

The stranger had given a blithesome promise, and
anchored it with oaths; but oaths and anchors equally will
drag; naught else abides on fickle earth but unkept promises
of joy. Contrary winds from out unstable skies, or contrary
moods of his more varying mind, or shipwreck and sudden
death in solitary waves; whatever was the cause, the blithe
stranger never was seen again.

Yet, however dire a calamity was here in store, misgivings of it ere due time never disturbed the Cholos' busy
minds, now all intent upon the toilsome matter which had
brought them hither. Nay, by swift doom coming like the
thief at night, ere seven weeks went by, two of the little

party were removed from all anxieties of land or sea. No more they sought to gaze with feverish fear, or still more feverish hope, beyond the present's horizon line; but into the furthest future their own silent spirits sailed. By persevering labor beneath that burning sun, Felipe and Truxill had brought down to their hut many scores of tortoises, and tried out the oil, when, elated with their good success, and to reward themselves for such hard work, they, too hastily, made a catamaran, or Indian raft, much used on the Spanish main, and merrily started on a fishing trip, just without a long reef with many jagged gaps, running parallel with the shore, about half a mile from it. By some bad tide or hap, or natural negligence of joyfulness (for though they could not be heard, yet by their gestures they seemed singing at the time), forced in deep water against that iron bar, the ill-made catamaran was overset, and came all to pieces; when dashed by broad-chested swells between their broken logs and the sharp teeth of the reef, both adventurers perished before Hunilla's eyes.

Before Hunilla's eyes they sank. The real woe of this event passed before her sight as some sham tragedy on the stage. She was seated in a rude bower among the withered thickets, crowning a lofty cliff, a little back from the beach. The thickets were so disposed, that in looking upon the sea at large she peered out from among the branches as from the lattice of a high balcony. But upon the day we speak of here, the better to watch the adventure of those two hearts she loved, Hunilla had withdrawn the branches to one side, and held them so. They formed an oval frame, through which the bluely boundless sea rolled like a painted one. And there, the invisible painter painted to her view the wave-tossed and disjointed raft, its once level logs slantingly upheaved, as raking masts, and the four struggling arms undistinguishable among them; and then all subsided into smooth-flowing creamy waters, slowly drifting the splintered wreck; while first and last, no sound of any sort was heard. Death in a silent picture; a dream of the eye; such vanishing shapes as the mirage shows.

So instant was the scene, so trance-like its mild pictorial effect, so distant from her blasted bower and her common sense of things, that Hunilla gazed and gazed, nor raised a finger or a wail. But as good to sit thus dumb, in stupor staring on that dumb show, for all that otherwise might be done. With half a mile of sea between, how could her two enchanted arms aid those four fated ones? The distance long, the time one sand. After the lightning is beheld, what fool shall stay the thunder-bolt? Felipe's body was washed ashore, but Truxill's never came; only his gay, braided hat of golden straw—that same sunflower thing he waved to her, pushing from the strand—and now, to the last gallant, it still saluted her. But Felipe's body floated to the marge, with one arm encirclingly outstretched. Lock-jawed in grim death, the lover-husband softly clasped his bride, true to her even in death's dream. Ah, Heaven, when man thus keeps his faith, wilt Thou be faithless who created the faithful one? But they cannot break faith who never plighted it.

It needs not to be said what nameless misery now wrapped the lonely widow. In telling her own story she passed this almost entirely over, simply recounting the event. Construe the comment of her features as you might, from her mere words little would you have weened that Hunilla was herself the heroine of her tale. But not thus did she defraud us of our tears. All hearts bled that grief could be so brave.

She but showed us her soul's lid, and the strange ciphers thereon engraved; all within, with pride's timidity, was withheld. Yet was there one exception. Holding out her small olive hand before her captain, she said in mild and slowest Spanish, "Señor, I buried him," then paused, struggled as against the writhed coilings of a snake, and cringing suddenly, leaped up, repeating in impassioned pain, "I buried him, my life, my soul!"

Doubtless, it was by half-unconscious, automatic motions of her hands, that this heavy-hearted one performed the final office for Felipe, and planted a rude cross of withered sticks —no green ones might be had—at the head of that lonely grave, where rested now in lasting uncomplaint and quiet haven he whom untranquil seas had overthrown.

But some dull sense of another body that should be interred, of another cross that should hallow another grave —unmade as yet—some dull anxiety and pain touching her undiscovered brother, now haunted the oppressed Hunilla. Her hands fresh from the burial earth, she slowly went back to the beach, with unshaped purposes wandering there, her spell-bound eye bent upon the incessant waves. But they bore nothing to her but a dirge, which maddened her to think that murderers should mourn. As time went by, and these things came less dreamingly to her mind, the strong persuasions of her Romish faith, which sets peculiar store by consecrated urns, prompted her to resume in waking earnest that pious search which had but been begun as in somnambulism. Day after day, week after week, she trod the cindery beach, till at length a double motive edged every eager glance. With equal longing she now looked for the living and the dead; the brother and the captain; alike vanished, never to return. Little accurate note of time had Hunilla taken under such emotions as were hers, and little, outside herself, served for calendar or dial. As to poor Crusoe in the self-same sea, no saint's bell pealed forth the lapse of week or month; each day went by unchallenged; no chanticleer announced those sultry dawns, no lowing herds those poisonous nights. All wonted and steadily recurring sounds, human, or humanized by sweet fellowship with man, but one stirred that torrid trance—the cry of dogs; save which naught but the rolling sea invaded it; an all-pervading monotone; and to the widow that was the least loved voice she could have heard.

No wonder, that as her thoughts now wandered to the unreturning ship, and were beaten back again, the hope against hope so struggled in her soul, that at length she desperately said, "Not yet, not yet; my foolish heart runs on too fast." So she forced patience for some further weeks. But to those whom earth's sure indraft draws, patience or impatience is still the same.

Hunilla now sought to settle precisely in her mind, to an hour, how long it was since the ship had sailed; and then, with the same precision, how long a space remained to pass. But this proved impossible. What present day or month it was she could not say. Time was her labyrinth, in which Hunilla was entirely lost.

And now follows——

Against my own purposes a pause descends upon me here. One knows not whether nature doth not impose some secrecy upon him who has been privy to certain things. At least, it is to be doubted whether it be good to blazon such. If some books are deemed most baneful and their sale forbid, how, then, with deadlier facts, not dreams of doting men? Those whom books will hurt will not be proof against events. Events, not books, should be forbid. But in all things man sows upon the wind, which bloweth just there whither it listeth; for ill or good, man cannot know. Often ill comes from the good, as good from ill.

When Hunilla——

Dire sight it is to see some silken beast long dally with a golden lizard ere she devour. More terrible, to see how feline Fate will sometimes dally with a human soul, and by a nameless magic make it repulse a sane despair with a hope which is but mad. Unwittingly I imp this cat-like thing, sporting with the heart of him who reads; for if he feel not he reads in vain.

—"The ship sails this day, to-day," at last said Hunilla to herself; "this gives me certain time to stand on; without certainty I go mad. In loose ignorance I have hoped and hoped; now in firm knowledge I will but wait. Now I live and no longer perish in bewilderings. Holy Virgin, aid me! Thou wilt waft back the ship. Oh, past length of weary weeks—all to be dragged over—to buy the certainty of to-day, I freely give ye, though I tear ye from me!"

As mariners, tost in tempest on some desolate ledge, patch them a boat out of the remnants of their vessel's wreck, and launch it in the self-same waves, see here Hunilla, this lone shipwrecked soul, out of treachery invoking trust. Humanity, thou strong thing, I worship thee, not in the laureled victor, but in this vanquished one.

Truly Hunilla leaned upon a reed, a real one; no metaphor: a real Eastern reed. A piece of hollow cane, drifted from unknown isles, and found upon the beach, its once jagged ends rubbed smoothly even as by sand-paper; its golden glazing gone. Long ground between the sea and land, upper and nether stone, the unvarnished substance was filed bare, and wore another polish now, one with itself, the polish of its agony. Circular lines at intervals cut all round this surface, divided it into six panels of unequal length. In the first were scored the days, each tenth one marked by a longer and deeper notch; the second was scored for the number of sea-fowl eggs for sustenance, picked out from the rocky nests; the third, how many fish had been caught from the shore; the fourth, how many small tortoises found inland; the fifth, how many days of sun; the sixth, of clouds; which last, of the two, was the greater one. Long night of busy numbering, misery's mathematics, to weary her too-wakeful soul to sleep; yet sleep for that was none.

The panel of the days was deeply worn—the long tenth notches half effaced, as alphabets of the blind. Ten thousand times the longing widow had traced her finger over the bamboo—dull flute, which played on, gave no sound—as if counting birds flown by in air would hasten tortoises creeping through the woods.

After the one hundred and eightieth day no further mark was seen; that last one was the faintest, as the first the deepest.

"There were more days," said our Captain; "many, many more; why did you not go on and notch them, too, Hunilla?"

"Señor, ask me not."

"And meantime, did no other vessel pass the isle?"

"Nay, Señor;—but——"

"You do not speak; but *what,* Hunilla?"

"Ask me not, Señor."

"You saw ships pass, far away; you waved to them; they passed on;—was that it, Hunilla?"

"Señor, be it as you say."

Braced against her woe, Hunilla would not, durst not trust the weakness of her tongue. Then when our Captain asked whether any whale-boats had——

But no, I will not file this thing complete for scoffing souls to quote, and call it firm proof upon their side. The half shall here remain untold. Those two unnamed events which befell Hunilla on this isle, let them abide between her and her God. In nature, as in law, it may be libelous to speak some truths.

Still, how it was that, although our vessel had lain three days anchored nigh the isle, its one human tenant should not have discovered us till just upon the point of sailing, never to revisit so lone and far a spot, this needs explaining ere the sequel come.

The place where the French captain had landed the little party was on the further and opposite end of the isle. There, too, it was that they had afterwards built their hut. Nor did the widow in her solitude desert the spot where her loved ones had dwelt with her, and where the dearest of the twain now slept his last long sleep, and all her plaints awaked him not, and he of husbands the most faithful during life.

Now, high broken land rises between the opposite extremities of the isle. A ship anchored at one side is invisible from the other. Neither is the isle so small, but a considerable company might wander for days through the wilderness of one side, and never be seen, or their halloos heard, by any stranger holding aloof on the other. Hence Hunilla, who naturally associated the possible coming of ships with her own part of the isle, might to the end have remained quite ignorant of the presence of our vessel, were it not for a mysterious presentiment, borne to her, so our mariners averred, by this isle's enchanted air. Nor did the widow's answer undo the thought.

"How did you come to cross the isle this morning, then, Hunilla?" said our Captain.

"Señor, something came flitting by me. It touched my cheek, my heart, Señor."

"What do you say, Hunilla?"

"I have said, Señor, something came through the air."

It was a narrow chance. For when in crossing the isle Hunilla gained the high land in the centre, she must then for the first have perceived our masts, and also marked that their sails were being loosed, perhaps even heard the echoing chorus of the windlass song. The strange ship was about to sail, and she behind. With all haste she now descends the height on the hither side, but soon loses sight of the ship among the sunken jungles at the mountain's base. She struggles on through the withered branches,

which seek at every step to bar her path, till she comes to
the isolated rock, still some way from the water. This she
climbs, to reassure herself. The ship is still in plainest sight.
But now, worn out with over-tension, Hunilla all but faints;
she fears to step down from her giddy perch; she is fain to
pause, there where she is, and as a last resort catches the
turban from her head, unfurls and waves it over the jungles
towards us.

During the telling of her story the mariners formed a
voiceless circle round Hunilla and the Captain; and when
at length the word was given to man the fastest boat, and
pull round to the isle's thither side, to bring away Hunilla's
chest and the tortoise oil, such alacrity of both cheery and
sad obedience seldom before was seen. Little ado was made.
Already the anchor had been recommitted to the bottom, and
the ship swung calmly to it.

But Hunilla insisted upon accompanying the boat as
indispensable pilot to her hidden hut. So being refreshed
with the best the steward could supply, she started with us.
Nor did ever any wife of the most famous admiral, in her
husband's barge, receive more silent reverence of respect
than poor Hunilla from this boat's crew.

Rounding many a vitreous cape and bluff, in two hours'
time we shot inside the fatal reef; wound into a secret cove,
looked up along a green many-gabled lava wall, and saw
the island's solitary dwelling.

It hung upon an impending cliff, sheltered on two sides
by tangled thickets, and half-screened from view in front
by juttings of the rude stairway, which climbed the preci·
pice from the sea. Built of canes, it was thatched with long,
mildewed grass. It seemed an abandoned hay-rick, whose
haymakers were now no more. The roof inclined but one
way; the eaves coming to within two feet of the ground.
And here was a simple apparatus to collect the dews, or
rather doubly-distilled and finest winnowed rains, which, in

mercy or in mockery, the night-skies sometimes drop upon
these blighted Encantadas. All along beneath the eaves, a
spotted sheet, quite weather-stained, was spread, pinned to
short, upright stakes, set in the shallow sand. A small
clinker, thrown into the cloth, weighed its middle down,
thereby straining all moisture into a calabash placed below.
This vessel supplied each drop of water ever drunk upon
the isle by the Cholos. Hunilla told us the calabash would
sometimes, but not often, be half filled overnight. It held
six quarts, perhaps. "But," said she, "we were used to thirst.
At sandy Payta, where I live, no shower from heaven
ever fell; all the water there is brought on mules from the
inland vales."

Tied among the thickets were some twenty moaning
tortoises, supplying Hunilla's lonely larder; while hundreds
of vast tableted black bucklers, like displaced, shattered
tomb-stones of dark slate, were also scattered round. These
were the skeleton backs of those great tortoises from which
Felipe and Truxill had made their precious oil. Several
large calabashes and two goodly kegs were filled with it. In
a pot near by were the caked crusts of a quantity which
had been permitted to evaporate. "They meant to have
strained it off next day," said Hunilla, as she turned aside.

I forgot to mention the most singular sight of all, though
the first that greeted us after landing.

Some ten small, soft-haired, ringleted dogs, of a beautiful breed, peculiar to Peru, set up a concert of glad wel-
comings when we gained the beach, which was responded
to by Hunilla. Some of these dogs had, since her widow-
hood, been born upon the isle, the progeny of the two
brought from Payta. Owing to the jagged steeps and pitfalls,
tortuous thickets, sunken clefts and perilous intricacies of
all sorts in the interior, Hunilla, admonished by the loss of
one favorite among them, never allowed these delicate
creatures to follow her in her occasional birds'-nests climbs

and other wanderings; so that, through long habituation, they offered not to follow, when that morning she crossed the land, and her own soul was then too full of other things to heed their lingering behind. Yet, all along she had so clung to them, that, besides what moisture they lapped up at early daybreak from the small scoop-holes among the adjacent rocks, she had shared the dew of her calabash among them; never laying by any considerable store against those prolonged and utter droughts which, in some disastrous seasons, warp these isles.

Having pointed out, at our desire, what few things she would like transported to the ship—her chest, the oil, not omitting the live tortoises which she intended for a grateful present to our Captain—we immediately set to work, carrying them to the boat down the long, sloping stair of deeply-shadowed rock. While my comrades were thus employed, I looked and Hunilla had disappeared.

It was not curiosity alone, but, it seems to me, something different mingled with it, which prompted me to drop my tortoise, and once more gaze slowly around. I remembered the husband buried by Hunilla's hands. A narrow pathway led into a dense part of the thickets. Following it through many mazes, I came out upon a small, round, open space, deeply chambered there.

The mound rose in the middle; a bare heap of finest sand, like that unverdured heap found at the bottom of an hour-glass run out. At its head stood the cross of withered sticks; the dry, peeled bark still fraying from it; its transverse limb tied up with rope, and forlornly adroop in the silent air.

Hunilla was partly prostrate upon the grave; her dark head bowed, and lost in her long, loosened Indian hair; her hands extended to the cross-foot, with a little brass crucifix clasped between; a crucifix worn featureless, like an ancient graven knocker long plied in vain. She did not see me, and I made no noise, but slid aside, and left the spot.

A few moments ere all was ready for our going, she reappeared among us. I looked into her eyes, but saw no tear. There was something which seemed strangely haughty in her air, and yet it was the air of woe. A Spanish and an Indian grief, which would not visibly lament. Pride's height in vain abased to proneness on the rack; nature's pride subduing nature's torture.

Like pages the small and silken dogs surrounded her, as she slowly descended towards the beach. She caught the two most eager creatures in her arms—*"Tita mia! Tomotita mia!"*—and fondling them, inquired how many could we take on board.

The mate commanded the boat's crew; not a hard-hearted man, but his way of life had been such that in most things, even in the smallest, simple utility was his leading motive.

"We cannot take them all, Hunilla; our supplies are short; the winds are unreliable; we may be a good many days going to Tumbez. So take those you have, Hunilla; but no more."

She was in the boat; the oarsmen, too, were seated, all save one, who stood ready to push off and then spring himself. With the sagacity of their race, the dogs now seemed aware that they were in the very instant of being deserted upon a barren strand. The gunwales of the boat were high; its prow—presented inland— was lifted; so owing to the water, which they seemed instinctively to shun, the dogs could not well leap into the little craft. But their busy paws hard scraped the prow, as it had been some farmer's door shutting them out from shelter in a winter storm. A clamorous agony of alarm. They did not howl, or whine; they all but spoke.

"Push off! Give way!" cried the mate. The boat gave one heavy drag and lurch, and next moment shot swiftly from the beach, turned on her heel, and sped. The dogs ran howling along the water's marge; now pausing to gaze at the flying boat, then motioning as if to leap in chase, but mysteriously withheld themselves; and again ran howling along the beach. Had they been human beings, hardly would they have more vividly inspired the sense of desolation. The oars were plied as confederate feathers of two wings. No one spoke. I looked back upon the beach, and then upon Hunilla, but her face was set in a stern dusky calm. The dogs crouching in her lap vainly licked her rigid hands. She never looked behind her, but sat motionless, till we turned a promontory of the coast and lost all sights and sounds astern. She seemed as one who, having experienced the sharpest of mortal pangs, was henceforth content to have all lesser heart-strings riven, one by one. To Hunilla, pain seemed so necessary, that pain in other beings, though by love and sympathy made her own, was unrepiningly to be borne. A heart of yearning in a frame of steel. A heart of earthly yearning, frozen by the frost which falleth from the sky.

The sequel is soon told. After a long passage, vexed by calms and baffling winds, we made the little port of Tumbez in Peru, there to recruit the ship. Payta was not very distant. Our captain sold the tortoise oil to a Tumbez merchant; and adding to the silver a contribution from all hands, gave it to our silent passenger, who knew not what the mariners had done.

The last seen of lone Hunilla she was passing into Payta town, riding upon a small gray ass; and before her on the ass's shoulders, she eyed the jointed workings of the beast's armorial cross.

Hood's Isle and the Hermit Oberlus

That darkesome glen they enter, where they find
That cursed man, low sitting on the ground,
Musing full sadly in his sullein mind;
His griesie lockes, long growen and unbound,
Disordred hong about his shoulders round,
And hid his face; through which his hollow eyne
Lookt deadly dull, and stared as astound;
His raw-bone cheekes, through penurie and pine,
Were shronke into his jawes, as he did never dine.
His garment nought but many ragged clouts,
With thornes together pind and patched was,
The which his naked sides he wrapt abouts.

SOUTHEAST of Crossman's Isle lies Hood's Isle, or McCain's Beclouded Isle; and upon its south side is a vitreous cove with a wide strand of dark pounded black lava, called Black Beach, or Oberlus's Landing. It might fitly have been styled Charon's.

It received its name from a wild white creature who spent many years here; in the person of a European bringing into this savage region qualities more diabolical than are to be found among any of the surrounding cannibals.

About half a century ago, Oberlus deserted at the above-named island, then, as now, a solitude. He built himself a den of lava and clinkers, about a mile from the Landing, subsequently called after him, in a vale, or expanded gulch, containing here and there among the rocks about two acres of soil capable of rude cultivation; the only place on the isle not too blasted for that purpose. Here he succeeded in raising a sort of degenerate potatoes and pumpkins, which from time to time he exchanged with needy whalemen passing, for spirits or dollars.

His appearance, from all accounts, was that of the victim of some malignant sorceress; he seemed to have drunk of Circe's cup; beast-like; rags insufficient to hide his nakedness; his befreckled skin blistered by continual exposure to the sun; nose flat; countenance contorted, heavy, earthy; hair and beard unshorn, profuse, and of fiery red. He struck strangers much as if he were a volcanic creature thrown up by the same convulsion which exploded into sight the isle. All bepatched and coiled asleep in his lonely lava den among the mountains, he looked, they say, as a heaped drift of withered leaves, torn from autumn trees, and so left in some hidden nook by the whirling halt for an instant of a fierce night-wind, which then ruthlessly sweeps on, somewhere else to repeat the capricious act. It is also reported to have been the strangest sight, this same Oberlus, of a sultry, cloudy morning, hidden under his shocking old black tarpaulin hat, hoeing potatoes among the lava. So warped and crooked was his strange nature, that the very handle of his hoe seemed gradually to have shrunk and twisted in his grasp, being a wretched bent stick, elbowed more like a savage's war-sickle than a civilized hoe-handle. It was his mysterious custom upon a first encounter with a stranger ever to present his back; possibly, because that was his better side, since it revealed the least. If the encounter chanced in his garden, as it sometimes did—the new-landed strangers going from the sea-side straight through the gorge, to hunt up the queer green-grocer reported doing business here—Oberlus for a time hoed on, unmindful of all greeting, jovial or bland; as the curious stranger would turn to face him, the recluse, hoe in hand, as diligently would avert himself; bowed over, and sullenly revolving round his murphy hill. Thus far for hoeing. When planting, his whole aspect and all his gestures were so malevolently and uselessly sinister and secret, that he seemed rather in act of dropping poison into wells than potatoes into soil. But among his lesser and more harmless marvels was an idea he ever had, that his visitors came equally as well led by longings to behold the mighty hermit Oberlus in his royal state of solitude, as simply to obtain potatoes, or find whatever company might be upon a barren isle. It seems incredible that such a being should possess such vanity; a misanthrope be conceited; but he really had his notion; and upon the strength of it, often gave himself amusing airs to captains. But after all, this is somewhat of a piece with the well-known eccentricity of some convicts, proud of that very hatefulness which makes them notorious. At other times, another unaccountable whim would seize him, and he would long dodge advancing strangers round the clinkered corners of his hut; sometimes like a stealthy bear, he would slink through the withered thickets up the mountains, and refuse to see the human face.

Except his occasional visitors from the sea, for a long period, the only companions of Oberlus were the crawling tortoises; and he seemed more than degraded to their level, having no desires for a time beyond theirs, unless it were for the stupor brought on by drunkenness. But sufficiently debased as he appeared, there yet lurked in him, only awaiting occasion for discovery, a still further proneness. Indeed, the sole superiority of Oberlus over the tortoises was his possession of a larger capacity of degradation; and along with that, something like an intelligent will to it. Moreover, what is about to be revealed, perhaps will show, that selfish ambition, or the love of rule for its own sake, far from being the peculiar infirmity of noble minds, is shared by beings which have no mind at all. No creatures are so selfishly tyrannical as some brutes; as any one who has observed the tenants of the pasture must occasionally have observed.

"This island's mine by Sycorax my mother," said Oberlus to himself, glaring round upon his haggard solitude. By some means, barter or theft—for in those days ships at intervals still kept touching at his Landing—he obtained an old musket, with a few charges of powder and ball. Possessed of arms, he was stimulated to enterprise, as a tiger that first feels the coming of its claws. The long habit of sole dominion over every object round him, his almost unbroken solitude, his never encountering humanity except on terms of misanthropic independence, or mercantile craftiness, and even such encounters being comparatively but rare; all this must have gradually nourished in him a vast idea of his own importance, together with a pure animal sort of scorn for all the rest of the universe.

The unfortunate Creole, who enjoyed his brief term of royalty at Charles's Isle was perhaps in some degree influenced by not unworthy motives; such as prompt other adventurous spirits to lead colonists into distant regions and assume political pre-eminence over them. His summary execution of many of his Peruvians is quite pardonable, considering the desperate characters he had to deal with; while his offering canine battle to the banded rebels seems under the circumstances altogether just. But for this King Oberlus and what shortly follows, no shade of palliation can be given. He acted out of mere delight in tyranny and cruelty, by virtue of a quality in him inherited from Sycorax his mother. Armed now with that shocking blunderbuss, strong in the thought of being master of that horrid isle, he panted for a chance to prove his potency upon the first specimen of humanity which should fall unbefriended into his hands.

Nor was he long without it. One day he spied a boat

upon the beach, with one man, a negro, standing by it.
Some distance off was a ship, and Oberlus immediately
knew how matters stood. The vessel had put in for wood,
and the boat's crew had gone into the thickets for it. From
a convenient spot he kept watch of the boat, till presently
a straggling company appeared loaded with billets. Throwing these on the beach, they again went into the thickets,
while the negro proceeded to load the boat.

Oberlus now makes all haste and accosts the negro, who,
aghast at seeing any living being inhabiting such a solitude,
and especially so horrific a one, immediately falls into a
panic, not at all lessened by the ursine suavity of Oberlus,
who begs the favor of assisting him in his labors. The negro
stands with several billets on his shoulder, in act of shoul-
dering others; and Oberlus, with a short cord concealed in
his bosom, kindly proceeds to lift those other billets to
their place. In so doing, he persists in keeping behind the
negro, who, rightly suspicious of this, in vain dodges about
to gain the front of Oberlus; but Oberlus dodges also; till
at last, weary of this bootless attempt at treachery, or fearful of being surprised by the remainder of the party,
Oberlus runs off a little space to a bush, and fetching his
blunderbuss, savagely commands the negro to desist work
and follow him. He refuses. Whereupon, presenting his
piece, Oberlus snaps at him. Luckily the blunderbuss misses
fire; but by this time, frightened out of his wits, the negro,
upon a second intrepid summons, drops his billets, surrenders at discretion, and follows on. By a narrow defile
familiar to him, Oberlus speedily removes out of sight of
the water.

On their way up the mountains, he exultingly informs
the negro that henceforth he is to work for him, and be
his slave, and that his treatment would entirely depend on
his future conduct. But Oberlus, deceived by the first impulsive cowardice of the black, in an evil moment slackens

his vigilance. Passing through a narrow way, and perceiving his leader quite off his guard, the negro, a powerful fellow, suddenly grasps him in his arms, throws him down, wrests his musketoon from him, ties his hands with the monster's own cord, shoulders him, and returns with him down to the boat. When the rest of the party arrive, Oberlus is carried on board the ship. This proved an Englishman, and a smuggler; a sort of craft not apt to be over-charitable. Oberlus is severely whipped, then handcuffed, taken ashore, and compelled to make known his habitation and produce his property. His potatoes, pumpkins, and tortoises, with a pile of dollars he had hoarded from his mercantile operations were secured on the spot. But while the too vindictive smugglers were busy destroying his hut and garden, Oberlus makes his escape into the mountains, and conceals himself there in impenetrable recesses, only known to himself, till the ship sails, when he ventures back, and by means of an old file which he sticks into a tree, contrives to free himself from his handcuffs.

Brooding among the ruins of his hut, and the desolate clinkers and extinct volcanoes of this outcast isle, the insulted misanthrope now meditates a signal revenge upon humanity, but conceals his purposes. Vessels still touch the Landing at times; and by and by Oberlus is enabled to supply them with some vegetables.

Warned by his former failure in kidnapping strangers, he now pursues a quite different plan. When seamen come ashore, he makes up to them like a free-and-easy comrade, invites them to his hut, and with whatever affability his red-haired grimness may assume, entreats them to drink his liquor and be merry. But his guests need little pressing; and so, soon as rendered insensible, are tied hand and foot, and pitched among the clinkers, are there concealed till the ship departs, when, finding themselves entirely dependent upon Oberlus, alarmed at his changed demeanor, his savage threats, and above all, that shocking blunderbuss, they willingly enlist under him, becoming his humble slaves, and Oberlus the most incredible of tyrants. So much so, that two or three perish beneath his initiating process. He sets the remainder—four of them—to breaking the caked soil; transporting upon their backs loads of loamy earth, scooped up in moist clefts among the mountains; keeps them on the roughest fare; presents his piece at the slightest hint of insurrection; and in all respects converts them into reptiles at his feet—plebeian garter-snakes to this Lord Anaconda.

At last, Oberlus contrives to stock his arsenal with four rusty cutlasses, and an added supply of powder and ball intended for his blunderbuss. Remitting in good part the labor of his slaves, he now approves himself a man, or rather devil, of great abilities in the way of cajoling or coercing others into acquiescence with his own ulterior designs, however at first abhorrent to them. But indeed, prepared for almost any eventual evil by their previous lawless life, as a sort of ranging Cow-Boys of the sea, which had dissolved within them the whole moral man, so that they were ready to concrete in the first offered mold of baseness now; rotted down from manhood by their hopeless misery on the isle; wonted to cringe in all things to their lord, himself the worst of slaves; these wretches were now become wholly corrupted to his hands. He used them as creatures of an inferior race; in short, he gaffles his four animals, and makes murderers of them; out of cowards fitly manufacturing bravoes.

Now, sword or dagger, human arms are but artificial claws and fangs, tied on like false spurs to the fighting cock. So, we repeat, Oberlus, czar of the isle, gaffles his four subjects; that is, with intent of glory, puts four rusty cutlasses into their hands. Like any other autocrat, he had a noble army now.

It might be thought a servile war would hereupon ensue. Arms in the hands of trodden slaves? how indiscreet of Emperor Oberlus! Nay, they had but cutlasses—sad old scythes enough—he a blunderbuss, which by its blind scatterings of all sorts of boulders, clinkers, and other scoria would annihilate all four mutineers, like four pigeons at one shot. Besides, at first he did not sleep in his accustomed hut; every lurid sunset, for a time, he might have been seen wending his way among the riven mountains, there to secrete himself till dawn in some sulphurous pitfall, undiscoverable to his gang; but finding this at last too troublesome, he now each evening tied his slaves hand and foot, hid the cutlasses, and thrusting them into his barracks, shut to the door, and lying down before it, beneath a rude shed lately added, slept out the night, blunderbuss in hand.

It is supposed that not content with daily parading over a cindery solitude at the head of his fine army, Oberlus now meditated the most active mischief; his probable object being to surprise some passing ship touching at his dominions, massacre the crew, and run away with her to parts unknown. While these plans were simmering in his head, two ships touch in company at the isle, on the opposite side to his; when his designs undergo a sudden change.

The ships are in want of vegetables, which Oberlus promises in great abundance, provided they send their boats round to his Landing, so that the crews may bring the vegetables from his garden; informing the two captains, at the same time, that his rascals—slaves and soldiers—had become so abominably lazy and good-for-nothing of late, that he could not make them work by ordinary inducements, and did not have the heart to be severe with them.

The arrangement was agreed to, and the boats were sent and hauled upon the beach. The crews went to the lava hut; but to their surprise nobody was there. After waiting till their patience was exhausted, they returned to the shore, when lo, some stranger—not the Good Samaritan either—seems to have very recently passed that way. Three of the boats were broken in a thousand pieces, and the fourth was missing. By hard toil over the mountains and through the clinkers, some of the strangers succeeded in returning to that side of the isle where the ships lay, when fresh boats are sent to the relief of the rest of the hapless party.

However amazed at the treachery of Oberlus, the two captains, afraid of new and still more mysterious atrocities —and indeed, half imputing such strange events to the enchantments associated with these isles—perceive no security but in instant flight; leaving Oberlus and his army in quiet possession of the stolen boat.

On the eve of sailing they put a letter in a keg, giving the Pacific Ocean intelligence of the affair, and moored the keg in the bay. Some time subsequent, the keg was opened by another captain chancing to anchor there, but not until after he had dispatched a boat round to Oberlus's Landing. As may be readily surmised, he felt no little inquietude till the boat's return; when another letter was handed him, giving Oberlus's version of the affair. This precious document had been found pinned half-mildewed to the clinker wall of the sulphurous and deserted hut. It ran as follows: showing that Oberlus was at least an accomplished writer, and no mere boor; and what is more, was capable of the most tristful eloquence.

"*Sir: I am the most unfortunate ill-treated gentleman that lives. I am a patriot, exiled from my country by the cruel hand of tyranny.*

"*Banished to these Enchanted Isles, I have again and again besought captains of ships to sell me a boat, but always have been refused, though I offered the handsomest prices in Mexican dollars. At length an opportunity pre-*

sented of possessing myself of one, and I did not let it slip.

"I have been long endeavoring, by hard labor and much solitary suffering, to accumulate something to make myself comfortable in a virtuous though unhappy old age; but at various times have been robbed and beaten by men professing to be Christians.

"To-day I sail from the Enchanted group in the good boat Charity bound to the Feejee Isles.

FATHERLESS OBERLUS

"P.S.—Behind the clinkers, nigh the oven, you will find the old fowl. Do not kill it; be patient; I leave it setting; if it shall have any chicks, I hereby bequeath them to you, whoever you may be. But don't count your chicks before they are hatched."

The fowl proved a starveling rooster, reduced to a sitting posture by sheer debility.

Oberlus declares that he was bound to the Feejee Isles; but this was only to throw pursuers on a false scent. For, after a long time, he arrived, alone in his open boat, at Guayaquil. As his miscreants were never again beheld on Hood's Isle, it is supposed, either that they perished for want of water on the passage to Guayaquil, or, what is quite as probable, were thrown overboard by Oberlus, when he found the water growing scarce.

From Guayaquil Oberlus proceeded to Payta; and there, with that nameless witchery peculiar to some of the ugliest animals, wound himself into the affections of a tawny damsel; prevailing upon her to accompany him back to his Enchanted Isle; which doubtless he painted as a Paradise of flowers, not a Tartarus of clinkers.

But unfortunately for the colonization of Hood's Isle with a choice variety of animated nature, the extraordinary and devilish aspect of Oberlus made him to be regarded in Payta as a highly suspicious character. So that being found concealed one night, with matches in his pocket, under the hull of a small vessel just ready to be launched, he was seized and thrown into jail.

The jails in most South American towns are generally of the least wholesome sort. Built of huge cakes of sunburnt brick, and containing but one room, without windows or yard, and but one door heavily grated with wooden bars, they present both within and without the grimmest aspect. As public edifices they conspicuously stand upon the hot and dusty Plaza, offering to view, through the gratings, their villainous and hopeless inmates, burrowing in all sorts of tragic squalor. And here, for a long time, Oberlus was seen; the central figure of a mongrel and assassin band; a creature whom it is religion to detest, since it is philanthropy to hate a misanthrope.

Note.—They who may be disposed to question the possibility of the character above depicted, are referred to the 2d vol. of Porter's *Voyage into the Pacific*, where they will recognize many sentences, for expedition's sake derived verbatim from thence, and incorporated here; the main difference—save a few passing reflections—between the two accounts being, that the present writer has added to Porter's facts accessory ones picked up in the Pacific from reliable sources; and where facts conflict, has naturally preferred his own authorities to Porter's. As, for instance, *his* authorities place Oberlus on Hood's Isle: Porter's, on Charles's Isle. The letter found in the hut is also somewhat different; for while at the Encantadas he was informed that, not only did it evince a certain clerkliness, but was full of the strangest satiric effrontery which does not adequately appear in Porter's version. I accordingly altered it to suit the general character of its author.

Runaways, Castaways, Solitaries, Grave-Stones, Etc.

And all about old stockes and stubs of trees,
Whereon nor fruit nor leafe was ever seen,
Did hang upon the ragged rocky knees;
On which had many wretches hanged beene.

SOME relics of the hut of Oberlus partially remain to this day at the head of the clinkered valley. Nor does the stranger, wandering among other of the Enchanted Isles, fail to stumble upon still other solitary abodes, long abandoned to the tortoise and the lizard. Probably few parts of earth have, in modern times, sheltered so many solitaries. The reason is, that these isles are situated in a distant sea, and the vessels which occasionally visit them are mostly all whalers, or ships bound on dreary and protracted voyages, exempting them in a good degree from both the oversight and the memory of human law. Such is the character of some commanders and some seamen, that under these untoward circumstances, it is quite impossible but that scenes of unpleasantness and discord should occur between them. A sullen hatred of the tyrannic ship will seize the sailor, and he gladly exchanges it for isles, which, though blighted as by a continual sirocco and burning breeze, still offer him, in their labyrinthine interior, a retreat beyond the possibility of capture. To flee the ship in any Peruvian or Chilean port, even the smallest and most rustical, is not unattended with great risk of apprehension, not to speak of jaguars. A reward of five pesos sends fifty dastardly Spaniards into the wood, who, with long knives, scour them day and night in eager hopes of securing their prey. Neither is it, in general, much easier to escape pursuit at the isles of Polynesia. Those of them which have felt a civilizing influence present the same difficulty to the runaway with the Peruvian ports, the advanced natives being quite as mercenary and keen of knife and scent as the retrograde Spaniards; while, owing to the bad odor in which all Europeans lie, in the minds of aboriginal savages who have chanced to hear aught of them, to desert the ship among primitive Polynesians, is, in most cases, a hope not unforlorn. Hence the Enchanted Isles become the voluntary tarrying places of all sorts of refugees; some of whom too sadly experience the fact, that flight from tyranny does not of itself insure a safe asylum, far less a happy home.

Moreover, it has not seldom happened that hermits have been made upon the isles by the accidents incident to tortoise-hunting. The interior of most of them is tangled and difficult of passage beyond description; the air is sultry and stifling; an intolerable thirst is provoked, for which no running stream offers its kind relief. In a few hours, under an equatorial sun, reduced by these causes to entire exhaustion, woe betide the straggler at the Enchanted Isles! Their extent is such as to forbid an adequate search, unless weeks are devoted to it. The impatient ship waits a day or two; when, the missing man remaining undiscovered, up goes a stake on the beach, with a letter of regret, and a keg of crackers and another of water tied to it, and away sails the craft.

Nor have there been wanting instances where the inhumanity of some captains has led them to wreak a secure revenge upon seamen who have given their caprice or pride some singular offense. Thrust ashore upon the scorching marl, such mariners are abandoned to perish outright, unless by solitary labors they succeed in discovering some precious driblets of moisture oozing from a rock or stagnant in a mountain pool.

I was well acquainted with a man, who, lost upon the Isle of Narborough, was brought to such extremes by thirst, that at last he only saved his life by taking that of another being. A large hair-seal came upon the beach. He rushed upon it, stabbed it in the neck, and then throwing himself upon the panting body quaffed at the living wound; the palpitations of the creature's dying heart injected life into the drinker.

Another seaman, thrust ashore in a boat upon an isle at which no ship ever touched, owing to its peculiar sterility and the shoals about it, and from which all other parts of the group were hidden—this man, feeling that it was sure death to remain there, and that nothing worse than death menaced him in quitting it, killed two seals, and inflating their skins, made a float, upon which he transported himself to Charles's Island, and joined the republic there.

But men, not endowed with courage equal to such desperate attempts, find their only resource in forthwith seeking some watering-place, however precarious or scanty; building a hut; catching tortoises and birds; and in all respects preparing for a hermit life, till tide of time, or a passing ship arrives to float them off.

At the foot of precipices on many of the isles, small rude basins in the rocks are found, partly filled with rotted rubbish or vegetable decay, or overgrown with thickets, and sometimes a little moist; which, upon examination, reveal plain tokens of artificial instruments employed in hollowing them out, by some poor castaway or still more miserable runaway. These basins are made in places where it was supposed some scanty drops of dew might exude into them from the upper crevices.

The relics of hermitages and stone basins are not the only signs of vanishing humanity to be found upon the isles. And, curious to say, that spot which of all others in settled communities is most animated, at the Enchanted

Isles presents the most dreary of aspects. And though it may seem very strange to talk of post-offices in this barren region, yet post-offices are occasionally to be found there. They consist of a stake and a bottle. The letters being not only sealed, but corked. They are generally deposited by captains of Nantucketers for the benefit of passing fisher-men, and contain statements as to what luck they had in whaling or tortoise-hunting. Frequently, however, long months and months, whole years glide by and no applicant appears. The stake rots and falls, presenting no very ex-hilarating object.

If now it be added that grave-stones, or rather grave-boards, are also discovered upon some of the isles, the pic-ture will be complete.

Upon the beach of James's Isle, for many years, was to be seen a rude finger-post, pointing inland. And, perhaps, taking it for some signal of possible hospitality in this other-wise desolate spot—some good hermit living there with his maple dish—the stranger would follow on in the path thus indicated, till at last he would come out in a noiseless nook, and find his only welcome, a dead man—his sole greeting the inscription over a grave. Here, in 1813, fell, in a day-break duel, a lieutenant of the U.S. frigate *Essex*, aged twenty-one: attaining his majority in death.

It is but fit that, like those old monastic institutions of Europe, whose inmates go not out of their own walls to be inurned, but are entombed there where they die, the En-cantadas, too, should bury their own dead, even as the great general monastery of earth does hers.

It is known that burial in the ocean is a pure necessity of sea-faring life, and that it is only done when land is far astern, and not clearly visible from the bow. Hence, to vessels cruising in the vicinity of the Enchanted Isles, they afford a convenient Potter's Field. The interment over, some good-natured forecastle poet and artist seizes his paint-brush, and inscribes a doggerel epitaph. When, after a long lapse of time, other good-natured seamen chance to come upon the spot, they usually make a table of the mound, and quaff a friendly can to the poor soul's repose.

As a specimen of these epitaphs, take the following, found in a bleak gorge of Chatham Isle:

> *Oh, Brother Jack, as you pass by,*
> *As you are now, so once was I.*
> *Just so game, and just so gay,*
> *But now, alack, they've stopped my pay.*
> *No more I peep out of my blinkers,*
> *Here I be—tucked in with clinkers!*

Cock-A-Doodle-Doo! OR The Crowing of the Noble Cock Beneventano

IN ALL parts of the world many high-spirited revolts from rascally despotisms had of late been knocked on the head; many dreadful casualties, by locomotive and steamer, had likewise knocked hundreds of high-spirited travelers on the head (I lost a dear friend in one of them); my own private affairs were also full of despotisms, casualties, and knockings on the head when early one morning in Spring, being too full of hypoes to sleep, I sallied out to walk on my hillside pasture.

It was a cool and misty, damp, disagreeable air. The country looked underdone, its raw juices squirting out all round. I buttoned out this squitchy air as well as I could with my lean, double-breasted dress-coat—my overcoat being so long-skirted I only used it in my wagon—and spitefully thrusting my crab-stick into the oozy sod, bent my blue form to the steep ascent of the hill. This toiling posture brought my head pretty well earthward, as if I were in the act of butting it against the world. I marked the fact, but only grinned at it with a ghastly grin.

All round me were tokens of a divided empire. The old grass and the new grass were striving together. In the low wet swales the verdure peeped out in vivid green; beyond, on the mountains, lay light patches of snow, strangely relieved against their russet sides; all the humped hills looked like brindled kine in the shivers. The woods were strewn with dry dead boughs, snapped off by the riotous winds of March, while the young trees skirting the woods were just beginning to show the first yellowish tinge of the nascent spray.

I sat down for a moment on a great rotting log nigh the top of the hill, my back to a heavy grove, my face presented toward a wide sweeping circuit of mountains enclosing a rolling, diversified country. Along the base of one long range of heights ran a lagging, fever-and-agueish river, over which was a duplicate stream of dripping mist, exactly corresponding in every meander with its parent water below. Low down, here and there, shreds of vapor listlessly wandered in the air, like abandoned or helmless nations or ships —or very soaky towels hung on criss-cross clothes-lines to dry. Afar, over a distant village lying in a bay of the plain formed by the mountains, there rested a great flat canopy of haze, like a pall. It was the condensed smoke of the chimneys, with the condensed, exhaled breath of the villagers, prevented from dispersion by the imprisoning hills. It was too heavy and lifeless to mount of itself; so there it lay, between the village and the sky, doubtless hiding many a man with the mumps, and many a queasy child.

My eye ranged over the capacious rolling country, and over the mountains, and over the village, and over a farmhouse here and there, and over woods, groves, streams, rocks, fells—and I thought to myself, what a slight mark, after all, does man make on this huge great earth. Yet the earth makes a mark on him. What a horrid accident was that on the Ohio, where my good friend and thirty other good fellows were sloped into eternity at the bidding of a thick-headed engineer, who knew not a valve from a flue. And that crash on the railroad just over yon mountains there, where two infatuate trains ran pell-mell into each other, and climbed and clawed each other's backs; and one locomotive was found fairly shelled, like a chick, inside of a passenger car in the antagonist train; and near a score of noble hearts, a bride and her groom, and an innocent little infant, were all disembarked into the grim hulk of Charon, who ferried them over, all baggageless, to some clinkered iron-foundry or other. Yet what's the use of complaining? What justice of the peace will right this matter? Yea, what's the use of bothering the very heavens about it? Don't the heavens themselves ordain these things—else they could not happen?

A miserable world! Who would take the trouble to make a fortune in it, when he knows not how long he can keep it, for the thousand villains and asses who have the management of railroads and steamboats, and innumerable other vital things in the world. If they would make me Dictator in North America a while, I'd string them up! and hang, draw, and quarter; fry, roast, and boil; stew, grill, and devil them, like so many turkey-legs—the rascally numskulls of stokers; I'd set them to stokering in Tartarus—I would.

Great improvements of the age! What! to call the facilitation of death and murder an improvement! Who wants to travel so fast? My grandfather did not, and he was no fool. Hark! here comes that old dragon again—that gigantic gad-fly of a Moloch—snort! puff! scream!—here he comes straight-bent through these vernal woods, like the Asiatic cholera cantering on a camel. Stand aside! here he comes, the chartered murderer! the death monopolizer! judge, jury, and hangman all together, whose victims die always without benefit of clergy. For two hundred and fifty miles that iron fiend goes yelling through the land, crying "More! more! more!" Would that fifty conspiring mountains would fall atop of him! And, while they were about it, would they would also fall atop of that smaller dunning fiend, my creditor, who frightens the life out of me more than any locomotive—a lantern-jawed rascal, who seems to run on a railroad track, too, and duns me even on Sunday, all the way to church and back, and comes and sits in the same pew with me, and pretending to be polite and hand me the prayer-book opened at the proper place, pokes his pesky bill under my nose in the very midst of my devotions, and so shoves himself between me and salvation; for how can one keep his temper on such occasions?

I can't pay this horrid man; and yet they say money was never so plentiful—a drug in the market; but blame me if I can get any of the drug, though there never was a sick man more in need of that particular sort of medicine. It's a lie; money ain't plentiful—feel of my pocket. Ha! here's a powder I was going to send to the sick baby in yonder hovel, where the Irish ditcher lives. That baby has the scarlet fever. They say the measles are rife in the country, too, and the varioloid, and the chicken-pox, and it's bad for teething children. And after all, I suppose many of the poor little ones, after going through all this trouble, snap off short; and so they had the measles, mumps, croup, scarlet fever, chicken-pox, cholera morbus, summer-complaint, and all else, in vain! Ah! there's that twinge of the rheumatics in my right shoulder. I got it one night on the North River, when, in a crowded boat, I gave up my berth to a sick lady, and stayed on deck till morning in drizzling weather. There's the thanks one gets for charity! Twinge! Shoot away, ye rheumatics! Ye couldn't lay on worse if I were some villain who had murdered the lady instead of befriending her. Dyspepsia too—I am troubled with that.

Hallo! here come the calves, the two-year-olds, just turned out of the barn into the pasture, after six months of cold victuals. What a miserable-looking set, to be sure! A breaking up of a hard winter, that's certain: sharp bones sticking out like elbows; all quilted with a strange stuff dried on their flanks like layers of pancakes. Hair worn quite off too, here and there; and where it ain't pancaked, or worn off, looks like the rubbed sides of mangy old hairtrunks. In fact, they are not six two-year-olds, but six abominable old hair-trunks wandering about here in this pasture.

Hark! By Jove, what's that? See! the very hair-trunks prick their ears at it, and stand and gaze away down into the rolling country yonder. Hark again! How clear! how musical! how prolonged! What a triumphant thanksgiving of a cock-crow! *"Glory be to God in the highest!"* It says those very words as plain as ever cock did in this world. Why, why, I begin to feel a little in sorts again. It ain't so very misty, after all. The sun yonder is beginning to show himself: I feel warmer.

Hark! There again! Did ever such a blessed cock-crow so ring out over the earth before! Clear, shrill, full of pluck, full of fire, full of fun, full of glee. It plainly says—*"Never say die!"* My friends, it is extraordinary, is it not?

Unwittingly, I found that I had been addressing the twoyear-olds—the calves—in my enthusiasm; which shows how one's true nature will betray itself at times in the most unconscious way. For what a very two-year-old, and calf, I had been to fall into the sulks, on a hill-top too, when a cock down in the lowlands there, without discourse of reason, and quite penniless in the world, and with death hanging over him at any moment from his hungry master, sends up a cry like a very laureate celebrating the glorious victory of New Orleans.

Hark! there it goes again! My friends, that must be a Shanghai; no domestic-born cock could crow in such prodigious exulting strains. Plainly, my friends, a Shanghai of the Emperor of China's breed.

But my friends the hair-trunks, fairly alarmed at last by such clamorously-victorious tones, were now scampering off, with their tails flirting in the air, and capering with

their legs in clumsy enough sort of style, sufficiently evincing that they had not freely flourished them for the six
months last past.

Hark! there again! Whose cock is that? Who in this
region can afford to buy such an extraordinary Shanghai?
Bless me—it makes my blood bound—I feel wild. What?
jumping on this rotten old log here, to flap my elbows and
crow too? And just now in the doleful dumps. And all this
from the simple crow of a cock. Marvelous cock! But soft
—this fellow now crows most lustily; but it's only morning;
let's see how he'll crow about noon, and toward nightfall.
Come to think of it, cocks crow mostly in the beginning of
the day. Their pluck ain't lasting, after all. Yes, yes; even
cocks have to succumb to the universal spell of tribulation:
jubilant in the beginning, but down in the mouth at the
end.

> "... Of fine mornings,
> *We fine lusty cocks begin our crows in gladness;*
> *But when eve does come we don't crow*
>   *quite so much,*
> *For then cometh despondency and madness."*

The poet had this very Shanghai in his mind when he
wrote that. But stop. There he rings out again, ten times
richer, fuller, longer, more obstreperously exulting than
before! Why, this is equal to hearing the great bell of St.
Paul's rung at a coronation! In fact, that bell ought to be
taken down, and this Shanghai put in its place. Such a
crow would jollify all London, from Mile End (which is
no end) to Primrose Hill (where there ain't any prim-
roses), and scatter the fog.

Well, I have an appetite for my breakfast this morning,
if I have not had it for a week before. I meant to have only
tea and toast; but I'll have coffee and eggs—no, brown-

stout and a beef-steak. I want something hearty. Ah, here comes the down-train: white cars, flashing through the trees like a vein of silver. How cheerfully the steam-pipe chirps! Gay are the passengers. There waves a handkerchief— going down to the city to eat oysters, and see their friends, and drop in at the circus. Look at the mist yonder; what soft curls and undulations round the hills, and the sun weaving his rays among them. See the azure smoke of the village, like the azure tester over a bridal-bed. How bright the country looks there where the river overflowed the meadows. The old grass has to knock under to the new. Well, I feel the better for this walk. Home now, and walk into that steak and crack that bottle of brown-stout; and by the time that's drank—a quart of stout—by that time, I shall feel about as stout as Samson. Come to think of it, that dun may call, though. I'll just visit the woods and cut a club. I'll club him, by Jove, if he duns me this day.

Hark! there goes Shanghai again. Shanghai says, "Bravo!" Shanghai says, "Club him!"

Oh, brave cock!

I felt in rare spirits the whole morning. The dun called about eleven. I had the boy Jake send the dun up. I was reading *Tristram Shandy,* and could not go down under the circumstances. The lean rascal (a lean farmer, too— think of that!) entered, and found me seated in an arm-chair, with my feet on the table, and the second bottle of brown-stout handy, and the book under eye.

"Sit down," said I; "I'll finish this chapter, and then attend to you. Fine morning. Ha! ha!—this is a fine joke about my Uncle Toby and the Widow Wadman! Ha! ha! ha! let me read this to you."

"I have no time; I've got my noon *chores* to do."

"To the deuce with your *chores!*" said I. "Don't drop your old tobacco about here, or I'll turn you out."

"Sir!"

"Let me read you this about the Widow Wadman. Said the Widow Wadman—"

"There's my bill, sir."

"Very good. Just twist it up, will you;—it's about my smoking time; and hand a coal, will you, from the hearth yonder!"

"My bill, sir!" said the rascal, turning pale with rage and amazement at my unwonted air (formerly I had always dodged him with a pale face), but too prudent as yet to betray the extremity of his astonishment. "My bill, sir!"— and he stiffly poked it at me.

"My friend," said I, "what a charming morning! How sweet the country looks! Pray, did you hear that extraordinary cock-crow this morning? Take a glass of my stout!"

"*Yours?* First pay your debts before you offer folks *your* stout!"

"You think, then, that, properly speaking, I have no *stout*," said I, deliberately rising. "I'll undeceive you. I'll show you stout of a superior brand to Barclay and Perkins."

Without more ado, I seized that insolent dun by the slack of his coat—(and being a lean shad-bellied wretch, there was plenty of slack to it)—I seized him that way, tied him with a sailor-knot, and, thrusting his bill between his teeth, introduced him to the open country lying round about my place of abode.

"Jake," said I, "you'll find a sack of blue-nosed potatoes lying under the shed. Drag it here, and pelt this pauper away: he's been begging pence of me, and I know he can work, but he's lazy. Pelt him away, Jake!"

Bless my stars, what a crow! Shanghai sent up such a perfect pæan and *laudamus*—such a trumpet-blast of triumph, that my soul fairly snorted in me. Duns!—I could have fought an army of them! Plainly, Shanghai was of the opinion that duns only came into the world to be kicked, banged, bruised, battered, choked, walloped, hammered, drowned, clubbed!

Returning in-doors, when the exultation of my victory over the dun had a little subsided, I fell to musing over the mysterious Shanghai. I had no idea I would hear him so nigh my house. I wondered from what rich gentleman's yard he crowed. Nor had he cut short his crows so easily as I had supposed he would. This Shanghai crowed till mid-day, at least. Would he keep a-crowing all day? I resolved to learn. Again I ascended the hill. The whole country was now bathed in a rejoicing sun-light. The warm verdure was bursting all round me. Teams were a-field. Birds, newly arrived from the South, were blithely singing in the air. Even the crows cawed with a certain unction, and seemed a shade or two less black than usual.

Hark! there goes the cock! How shall I describe the crow of the Shanghai at noon-tide? His sunrise crow was a whisper to it. It was the loudest, longest, and most strangely musical crow that ever amazed mortal man. I had heard plenty of cock-crows before, and many fine ones;—but this one! so smooth and flute-like in its very clamor—so self-possessed in its very rapture of exultation—so vast, mounting, swelling, soaring, as if spurted out from a golden throat, thrown far back. Nor did it sound like the foolish, vain-glorious crow of some young sophomorean cock, who knew not the world, and was beginning life in audacious gay spirits, because in wretched ignorance of what might be to come. It was the crow of a cock who crowed not without advice; the crow of a cock who knew a thing or two; the crow of a cock who had fought the world and got the better of it, and was now resolved to crow, though the earth should heave and the heavens should fall. It was a wise crow; an invincible crow; a philosophic crow; a crow of all crows.

I returned home once more full of reinvigorated spirits,

with a dauntless sort of feeling. I thought over my debts and other troubles, and over the unlucky risings of the poor oppressed *peoples* abroad, and over the railroad and steamboat accidents, and over even the loss of my dear friend, with a calm, good-natured rapture of defiance, which astounded myself. I felt as though I could meet Death, and invite him to dinner, and toast the Catacombs with him, in pure overflow of self-reliance and a sense of universal security.

Toward evening I went up to the hill once more to find whether, indeed, the glorious cock would prove game even from the rising of the sun unto the going down thereof. Talk of Vespers or Curfew!—the evening crow of the cock went out of his mighty throat all over the land and inhabited it, like Xerxes from the East with his double-winged host. It was miraculous. Bless me, what a crow! The cock went game to roost that night, depend upon it, victorious over the entire day, and bequeathing the echoes of his thousand crows to night.

After an unwontedly sound, refreshing sleep I rose early, feeling like a carriage-spring—light—elliptical—airy—buoyant as sturgeon-nose—and, like a football, bounded up the hill. Hark! Shanghai was up before me. The early bird that caught the worm—crowing like a bugle worked by an engine—lusty, loud, all jubilation. From the scattered farm-houses a multitude of other cocks were crowing, and replying to each other's crows. But they were as flageolets to a trombone. Shanghai would suddenly break in, and overwhelm all their crows with his one domineering blast. He seemed to have nothing to do with any other concern. He replied to no other crow, but crowed solely by himself, on his own account, in solitary scorn and independence.

Oh, brave cock!—oh, noble Shanghai!—oh, bird rightly offered up by the invincible Socrates, in testimony of his final victory over life.

As I live, thought I, this blessed day will I go and seek out the Shanghai, and buy him, if I have to clap another mortgage on my land.

I listened attentively now, striving to mark from what direction the crow came. But it so charged and replenished, and made bountiful and overflowing all the air, that it was impossible to say from what precise point the exultation came. All that I could decide upon was this: the crow came from out of the East, and not from out of the West. I then considered with myself how far a cock-crow might be heard. In this still country, shut in, too, by mountains, sounds were audible at great distances. Besides, the undulations of the land, the abuttings of the mountains into the rolling hill and valley below, produced strange echoes, and reverberations, and multiplications, and accumulations of resonance, very remarkable to hear, and very puzzling to think of. Where lurked this valiant Shanghai—this bird of cheerful Socrates—the game-fowl Greek who died unappalled? Where lurked he? Oh, noble cock, where are you? Crow once more, my Bantam! my princely, my imperial Shanghai! my bird of the Emperor of China! Brother of the Sun! Cousin of great Jove! where are you?—one crow more, and tell me your number!

Hark! like a full orchestra of the cocks of all nations, forth burst the crow. But where from? There it is; but where? There was no telling, further than it came from out the East.

After breakfast I took my stick and sallied down the road. There were many gentlemen's seats dotting the neighboring country, and I made no doubt that some of these opulent gentlemen had invested a hundred dollar bill in some royal Shanghai recently imported in the ship *Trade Wind,* or the ship *White Squall,* or the ship *Sovereign of the Seas;* for it must needs have been a brave ship with a brave name which bore the fortunes of so brave a cock. I resolved to walk the entire country, and find this noble foreigner out; but thought it would not be amiss to inquire on the way at the humblest homesteads, whether, peradventure, they had heard of a lately-imported Shanghai belonging to any of the gentlemen settlers from the city; for it was plain that no poor farmer, no poor man of any sort, could own such an Oriental trophy—such a Great Bell of St. Paul's swung in a cock's throat.

I met an old man, plowing, in a field nigh the road-side fence.

"My friend, have you heard an extraordinary cock-crow of late?"

"Well, well," he drawled, "I don't know—the Widow Crowfoot has a cock—and Squire Squaretoes has a cock—and I have a cock, and they all crow. But I don't know of any on 'em with 'strordinary crows."

"Good morning to you," said I, shortly; "it's plain that you have not heard the crow of the Emperor of China's chanticleer."

Presently I met another old man mending a tumble-down old rail-fence. The rails were rotten, and at every move of the old man's hand they crumbled into yellow ochre. He had much better let the fence alone, or else get him new rails. And here I must say, that one cause of the sad fact why idiocy more prevails among farmers than any other class of people, is owing to their undertaking the mending of rotten rail-fences in warm, relaxing spring weather. The enterprise is a hopeless one. It is a laborious one; it is a bootless one. It is an enterprise to make the heart break. Vast pains squandered upon a vanity. For how can one make rotten rail-fences stand up on their rotten pins? By what magic put pith into sticks which have lain freezing and baking through sixty consecutive winters and summers? This it is, this wretched endeavor to mend rotten rail-

fences with their own rotten rails, which drives many farmers into the asylum.

On the face of the old man in question incipient idiocy
was plainly marked. For, about sixty rods before him extended one of the most unhappy and desponding broken-
hearted Virginia rail-fences I ever saw in my life. While in
a field behind, were a set of young steers, possessed as by
devils, continually butting at this forlorn old fence, and
breaking through it here and there, causing the old man to
drop his work and chase them back within bounds. He
would chase them with a piece of rail huge as Goliath's
beam, but as light as cork. At the first flourish, it crumbled
into powder.

"My friend," said I, addressing this woeful mortal, "have
you heard an extraordinary cock-crow of late?"

I might as well have asked him if he had heard the
death-tick. He stared at me with a long, bewildered, doleful, and unutterable stare, and without reply resumed his
unhappy labors.

What a fool, thought I, to have asked such an uncheer-
ful and uncheerable creature about a cheerful cock!

I walked on. I had now descended the high land where
my house stood, and being in a low tract could not hear
the crow of the Shanghai, which, doubtless, overshot me
there. Besides, the Shanghai might be at lunch of corn
and oats, or taking a nap, and so interrupted his jubilations
for a while.

At length, I encountered, riding along the road, a portly
gentleman—nay, a *pursy* one—of great wealth, who had
recently purchased him some noble acres, and built him a
noble mansion, with a goodly fowl-house attached, the
fame whereof spread through all that country. Thought I,
Here now is the owner of the Shanghai.

"Sir," said I, "excuse me, but I am a countryman of
yours, and would ask, if so be you own any Shanghais?"

"Oh, yes; I have ten Shanghais."

"Ten!" exclaimed I, in wonder, "and do they all crow?"

"Most lustily; every soul of them; I wouldn't own a cock that wouldn't crow."

"Will you turn back, and show me those Shanghais?"

"With pleasure: I am proud of them. They cost me, in the lump, six hundred dollars."

As I walked by the side of his horse, I was thinking to myself whether possibly I had not mistaken the harmoni- ously combined crowings of ten Shanghais in a squad, for the supernatural crow of a single Shanghai by himself.

"Sir," said I, "is there one of your Shanghais which far exceeds all the others in the lustiness, musicalness, and inspiring effects of his crow?"

"They crow pretty much alike, I believe," he courteously replied. "I really don't know that I could tell their crows apart."

I began to think that, after all, my noble chanticleer might not be in the possession of this wealthy gentleman. However, we went into his fowl-yard, and I saw his Shang- hais. Let me say that hitherto I had never clapped eye on this species of imported fowl. I had heard what enormous prices were paid for them, and also that they were of an enormous size, and had somehow fancied they must be of a beauty and brilliancy proportioned both to size and price. What was my surprise, then, to see ten carrot-colored mon- sters, without the smallest pretension to effulgence of plum- age. Immediately, I determined that my royal cock was neither among these, nor could possibly be a Shanghai at all; if these gigantic gallows-bird fowl were fair speci- mens of the true Shanghai.

I walked all day, dining and resting at a farm-house, in- specting various fowl-yards, interrogating various owners of fowls, hearkening to various crows, but discovered not the mysterious chanticleer. Indeed, I had wandered so far and deviously, that I could not hear his crow. I began to suspect that this cock was a mere visitor in the country, who had taken his departure by the eleven o'clock train for the South, and was now crowing and jubilating somewhere on the verdant banks of Long Island Sound.

But next morning, again I heard the inspiring blast, again felt my blood bound in me, again felt superior to all the ills of life, again felt like turning my dun out of doors. But displeased with the reception given him at his last visit, the dun stayed away. Doubtless being in a huff; silly fellow that he was to take a harmless joke in earnest.

Several days passed, during which I made sundry excursions in the regions roundabout, but in vain sought the cock. Still, I heard him from the hill, and sometimes from the house, and sometimes in the stillness of the night. If at times I would relapse into my doleful dumps, straightway at the sound of the exultant and defiant crow, my soul, too, would turn chanticleer, and clap her wings, and throw back her throat, and breathe forth a cheerful challenge to all the world of woes.

At last, after some weeks I was necessitated to clap another mortgage on my estate, in order to pay certain debts, and among others the one I owed the dun, who of late had commenced a civil-process against me. The way the process was served was a most insulting one. In the private room I had been enjoying myself in the village tavern over a bottle of Philadelphia porter, and some Herkimer cheese, and a roll, and having apprised the landlord, who was a friend of mine, that I would settle with him when I received my next remittances, stepped to the peg where I had hung my hat in the bar-room, to get a choice cigar I had left in the hall, when lo! I found the civil-process enveloping the cigar. When I unrolled the cigar,

I unrolled the civil-process, and the constable standing by rolled out, with a thick tongue, "Take notice!" and added, in a whisper, "Put that in your pipe and smoke it!"

I turned short round upon the gentlemen then and there present in that bar-room. Said I, "Gentlemen, is this an honorable—nay, is this a lawful way of serving a civil-process? Behold!"

One and all they were of opinion, that it was a highly inelegant act in the constable to take advantage of a gentleman's lunching on cheese and porter, to be so uncivil as to slip a civil-process into his hat. It was ungenerous; it was cruel; for the sudden shock of the thing coming instanter upon the lunch, would impair the proper digestion of the cheese, which is proverbially not so easy of digestion as blancmange.

Arrived home, I read the process, and felt a twinge of melancholy. Hard world! hard world! Here I am, as good a fellow as ever lived—hospitable—open-hearted—generous to a fault: and the Fates forbid that I should possess the fortune to bless the country with my bounteousness. Nay, while many a stingy curmudgeon rolls in idle gold, I, heart of nobleness as I am, I have civil-processes served on me! I bowed my head, and felt forlorn—unjustly used—abused—unappreciated—in short, miserable.

Hark! like a clarion! yea, like a jolly bolt of thunder with bells to it—came the all-glorious and defiant crow! Ye gods, how it set me up again! Right on my pins! Yea, verily on stilts!

Oh, noble cock!

Plain as cock could speak, it said, "Let the world and all aboard of it go to pot. Do you be jolly, and never say die. What's the world compared to you? What is it, anyhow, but a lump of loam? Do you be jolly!"

Oh, noble cock!

"But, my dear and glorious cock," mused I, upon second

thought, "one can't so easily send this world to pot; one can't so easily be jolly with civil-processes in his hat or hand."

Hark! the crow again. Plain as cock could speak, it said, "Hang the process, and hang the fellow that sent it! If you have not land or cash, go and thrash the fellow, and tell him you never mean to pay him. Be jolly!"

Now this was the way—through the imperative intimations of the cock—that I came to clap the added mortgage on my estate; paid all my debts by fusing them into this one added bond and mortgage. Thus made at ease again, I renewed my search for the noble cock. But in vain, though I heard him every day. I began to think there was some sort of deception in this mysterious thing: some wonderful ventriloquist prowled around my barns, or in my cellar, or on my roof, and was minded to be gaily mischievous. But no—what ventriloquist could so crow with such an heroic and celestial crow?

At last, one morning there came to me a certain singular man, who had sawed and split my wood in March—some five-and-thirty cords of it—and now he came for his pay. He was a singular man, I say. He was tall and spare, with a long saddish face, yet somehow a latently joyous eye, which offered the strangest contrast. His air seemed staid, but undepressed. He wore a long, gray, shabby coat, and a big battered hat. This man had sawed my wood at so much a cord. He would stand and saw all day long in a driving snow-storm, and never wink at it. He never spoke unless spoken to. He only sawed. Saw, saw, saw—snow, snow, snow. The saw and the snow went together like two natural things. The first day this man came, he brought his dinner with him, and volunteered to eat it sitting on his buck in the snow-storm. From my window, where I was reading Burton's *Anatomy of Melancholy*, I saw him in the act. I burst out of doors bare-headed. "Good heavens!" cried I, "what are you doing? Come in. *This* your dinner!"

He had a hunk of stale bread and another hunk of salt beef, wrapped in a wet newspaper, and washed his morsels down by melting a handful of fresh snow in his mouth. I took this rash man in-doors, planted him by the fire, gave him a dish of hot pork and beans, and a mug of cider.

"Now," said I, "don't you bring any of your damp dinners here. You work by the job, to be sure; but I'll dine you for all that."

He expressed his acknowledgments in a calm, proud, but not ungrateful way, and dispatched his meal with satisfaction to himself, and me also. It afforded me pleasure to perceive that he quaffed down his mug of cider like a man. I honored him. When I addressed him in the way of business at his buck, I did so in a guardedly respectful and deferential manner. Interested in his singular aspect, struck by his wondrous intensity of application at his saw—a most wearisome and disgustful occupation to most people—I often sought to gather from him who he was, what sort of a life he led, where he was born, and so on. But he was mum. He came to saw my wood, and eat my dinners—if I chose to offer them—but not to gabble. At first, I somewhat resented his sullen silence under the circumstances. But better considering it, I honored him the more. I increased the respectfulness and deferentialness of my address toward him. I concluded within myself that this man had experienced hard times; that he had had many sore rubs in the world; that he was of a solemn disposition; that he was of the mind of Solomon; that he lived calmly, decorously, temperately; and though a very poor man, was, nevertheless, a highly respectable one. At times I imagined that he might even be an elder or deacon of some small country church. I thought it would not be a bad plan to run this excellent man for President of the United States. He would prove a great reformer of abuses.

His name was Merrymusk. I had often thought how jolly a name for so unjolly a wight. I inquired of people whether they knew Merrymusk. But it was some time before I learned much about him. He was by birth a Marylander, it appeared, who had long lived in the country round about; a wandering man; until within some ten years ago, a thriftless man, though perfectly innocent of crime; a man who would work hard a month with surprising soberness, and then spend all his wages in one riotous night. In youth he had been a sailor, and run away from his ship at Batavia, where he caught the fever, and came nigh dying. But he rallied, reshipped, landed home, found all his friends dead, and struck for the Northern interior, where he had since tarried. Nine years back he had married a wife, and now had four children. His wife was become a perfect invalid; one child had the white-swelling, and the rest were rickety. He and his family lived in a shanty on a lonely barren patch nigh the railroad track, where it passed close to the base of a mountain. He had bought a fine cow to have plenty of wholesome milk for his children; but the cow died during an accouchement, and he could not afford to buy another. Still, his family never suffered for lack of food. He worked hard and brought it to them.

Now, as I said before, having long previously sawed my wood, this Merrymusk came for his pay.

"My friend," said I, "do you know of any gentleman hereabouts who owns an extraordinary cock?"

The twinkle glittered quite plain in the wood-sawyer's eye.

"I know of no *gentleman*," he replied, "who has what might well be called an extraordinary cock."

Oh, thought I, this Merrymusk is not the man to enlighten me. I am afraid I shall never discover this extraordinary cock.

Not having the full change to pay Merrymusk, I gave him his due, as nigh as I could make it, and told him that in a day or two I would take a walk and visit his place, and hand him the remainder. Accordingly one fine morning I sallied forth upon the errand. I had much ado finding the best road to the shanty. No one seemed to know where it was exactly. It lay in a very lonely part of the country, a densely wooded mountain on one side (which I call October Mountain, on account of its bannered aspect in that month), and a thicketed swamp on the other, the railroad cutting the swamp. Straight as a die the railroad cut it; many times a day tantalizing the wretched shanty with the sight of all the beauty, rank, fashion, health, trunks, silver and gold, dry-goods and groceries, brides and grooms, happy wives and husbands, flying by the lonely door—no time to stop—flash! here they are—and there they go!—out of sight at both ends—as if that part of the world were only made to fly over, and not to settle upon. And this was about all the shanty saw of what people call "life."

Though puzzled somewhat, yet I knew the general direction where the shanty lay, and on I trudged. As I advanced, I was surprised to hear the mysterious cock crow with more and more distinctness. Is it possible, thought I, that any gentleman owning a Shanghai can dwell in such a lonesome, dreary region? Louder and louder, nigher and nigher, sounded the glorious and defiant clarion. Though somehow I may be out of the track to my wood-sawyer's, I said to myself, yet, thank heaven, I seem to be on the way toward that extraordinary cock. I was delighted with this auspicious accident. On I journeyed; while at intervals the crow sounded most invitingly, and jocundly, and superbly; and the last crow was ever nigher than the former one. At last, emerging from a thicket of elders, straight before me I saw the most resplendent creature that ever blessed the sight of man.

A cock, more like a golden eagle than a cock. A cock, more like a Field-Marshal than a cock. A cock, more like Lord Nelson with all his glittering arms on, standing on the *Vanguard*'s quarter-deck going into battle, than a cock. A cock, more like the Emperor Charlemagne in his robes at Aix-la-Chapelle, than a cock.

Such a cock!

He was of a haughty size, stood haughtily on his haughty legs. His colors were red, gold, and white. The red was on his crest alone, which was a mighty and symmetric crest, like unto Hector's helmet, as delineated on antique shields. His plumage was snowy, traced with gold. He walked in front of the shanty, like a peer of the realm, his crest lifted, his chest heaved out, his embroidered trappings flashing in the light. His pace was wonderful. He looked like some noble foreigner. He looked like some Oriental king in some magnificent Italian opera.

Merrymusk advanced from the door.

"Pray, is not that the Signor Beneventano?"

"Sir?"

"That's the cock," said I, a little embarrassed. The truth was, my enthusiasm had betrayed me into a rather silly inadvertence. I had made a somewhat learned sort of allusion in the presence of an unlearned man. Consequently, upon discovering it by his honest stare, I felt foolish; but carried it off by declaring that *this was the cock*.

Now, during the preceding autumn I had been to the city, and had chanced to be present at a performance of the Italian Opera. In that opera figured in some royal character a certain Signor Beneventano—a man of a tall, imposing person, clad in rich raiment, like to plumage, and with a most remarkable, majestic, scornful stride. The Signor Beneventano seemed on the point of tumbling over backward with exceeding haughtiness. And, for all the world, the proud pace of the cock seemed the very stage-pace of the Signor Beneventano.

Hark! Suddenly the cock paused, lifted his head still higher, ruffled his plumes, seemed inspired, and sent forth a lusty crow. October Mountain echoed it; other mountains sent it back; still others rebounded it; it overran the country round. Now I plainly perceived how it was I had chanced to hear the gladdening sound on my distant hill.

"Good Heavens! do you own the cock? Is that cock yours?"

"Is it my cock!" said Merrymusk, looking slyly gleeful out of the corner of his long, solemn face.

"Where did you get it?"

"It chipped the shell here. I raised it."

"You?"

Hark! Another crow. It might have raised the ghosts of all the pines and hemlocks ever cut down in that country. Marvelous cock! Having crowed, he strode on again, surrounded by a bevy of admiring hens.

"What will you take for Signor Beneventano?"

"Sir?"

"That magic cock!—what will you take for him?"

"I won't sell him."

"I will give you fifty dollars."

"Pooh!"

"One hundred!"

"Pish!"

"Five hundred!"

"Bah!"

"And you a poor man?"

"No: don't I own that cock, and haven't I refused five hundred dollars for him?"

"True," said I, in profound thought, "that's a fact. You won't sell him, then?"

"No."

"Will you give him?"

"No."

"Will you *keep* him, then!" I shouted, in a rage.

"Yes."

I stood awhile admiring the cock, and wondering at the man. At last I felt a redoubled admiration of the one, and a redoubled deference for the other.

"Won't you step in?" said Merrymusk.

"But won't the cock be prevailed upon to join us?" said I.

"Yes. Trumpet! hither, boy! hither!"

The cock turned round, and strode up to Merrymusk.

"Come!"

The cock followed us into the shanty.

"Crow!"

The roof jarred.

Oh, noble cock!

I turned in silence upon my entertainer. There he sat on an old battered chest, in his old battered gray coat, with patches at his knees and elbows, and a deplorably bunged hat. I glanced round the room. Bare rafters overhead, but solid junks of jerked beef hanging from them. Earth floor, but a heap of potatoes in one corner, and a sack of Indian meal in another. A blanket was strung across the apartment at the further end, from which came a woman's ailing voice and the voices of ailing children. But somehow in the ailing of these voices there seemed no complaint.

"Mrs. Merrymusk and children?"

"Yes."

I looked at the cock. There he stood majestically in the middle of the room. He looked like a Spanish grandee caught in a shower, and standing under some peasant's shed. There was a strange supernatural look of contrast about him. He irradiated the shanty; he glorified its meanness. He glorified the battered chest, and tattered gray coat, and the bunged hat. He glorified the very voices which came in ailing tones from behind the screen.

"Oh, father," cried a little sickly voice, "let Trumpet sound again."

"Crow," cried Merrymusk.

The cock threw himself into a posture.

The roof jarred.

"Does not this disturb Mrs. Merrymusk and the sick children?"

"Crow again, Trumpet."

The roof jarred.

"It does not disturb them, then?"

"Didn't you hear 'em *ask* for it?"

"How is it, that your sick family like this crowing?" said I. "The cock is a glorious cock, with a glorious voice, but not exactly the sort of thing for a sick chamber, one would suppose. Do they really like it?"

"Don't *you* like it? Don't it do *you* good? Ain't it inspiring? don't it impart pluck? give stuff against despair?"

"All true," said I, removing my hat with profound humility before the brave spirit disguised in the base coat.

"But then," said I, still with some misgivings, "so loud, so wonderfully clamorous a crow, methinks might be amiss to invalids, and retard their convalescence."

"Crow your best now, Trumpet!"

I leaped from my chair. The cock frightened me, like some overpowering angel in the Apocalypse. He seemed crowing over the fall of wicked Babylon, or crowing over the triumph of righteous Joshua in the vale of Ashkelon. When I regained my composure somewhat, an inquisitive thought occurred to me. I resolved to gratify it.

"Merrymusk, will you present me to your wife and children?"

"Yes. Wife, the gentleman wants to step in."

"He is very welcome," replied a weak voice.

Going behind the curtain, there lay a wasted, but strangely cheerful human face; and that was pretty much all; the body, hid by the counterpane and an old coat, seemed too shrunken to reveal itself through such impediments. At the bedside sat a pale girl, ministering. In another bed lay three children, side by side: three more pale faces.

"Oh, father, we don't mislike the gentleman, but let us see Trumpet, too."

At a word, the cock strode behind the screen, and perched himself on the children's bed. All their wasted eyes gazed at him with a wild and spiritual delight. They seemed to sun themselves in the radiant plumage of the cock.

"Better than a 'pothecary, eh?" said Merrymusk. "This is Dr. Cock himself."

We retired from the sick ones, and I reseated myself again, lost in thought, over this strange household.

"You seem a glorious independent fellow!" said I.

"And I don't think you a fool, and never did. Sir, you are a trump."

"Is there any hope of your wife's recovery?" said I, modestly seeking to turn the conversation.

"Not the least."

"The children?"

"Very little."

"It must be a doleful life, then, for all concerned. This lonely solitude—this shanty—hard work—hard times."

"Haven't I Trumpet? He's the cheerer. He crows through all; crows at the darkest; Glory to God in the highest! continually he crows it."

"Just the import I first ascribed to his crow, Merrymusk, when first I heard it from my hill. I thought some rich nabob owned some costly Shanghai; little weening any such poor man as you owned this lusty cock of a domestic breed."

"*Poor* man like *me*? Why call *me* poor? Don't the cock *I* own glorify this otherwise inglorious, lean, lantern-jawed land? Didn't *my* cock encourage *you*? And *I* give you all this glorification away gratis. I am a great philanthropist. I am a rich man—a very rich man, and a very happy one. Crow, Trumpet."

The roof jarred.

I returned home in a deep mood. I was not wholly at rest concerning the soundness of Merrymusk's views of things, though full of admiration for him. I was thinking on the matter before my door, when I heard the cock crow again. Enough. Merrymusk is right.

Oh, noble cock! oh, noble man!

I did not see Merrymusk for some weeks after this; but hearing the glorious and rejoicing crow, I supposed that all went as usual with him. My own frame of mind remained a rejoicing one. The cock still inspired me. I saw another mortgage piled on my plantation; but only bought another dozen of stout, and a dozen dozen of Philadelphia porter. Some of my relatives died; I wore no mourning, but for three days drank stout in preference to porter, stout being of the darker color. I heard the cock crow the instant I received the unwelcome tidings.

"Your health in this stout, oh noble cock!"

I thought I would call on Merrymusk again, not having seen or heard of him for some time now. Approaching the place, there were no signs of motion about the shanty. I felt a strange misgiving. But the cock crew from within doors, and the boding vanished. I knocked at the door. A feeble voice bade me enter. The curtain was no longer drawn; the whole house was a hospital now. Merrymusk lay on a heap of old clothes; wife and children were all in their beds. The cock was perched on an old hogshead hoop, swung from the ridge-pole in the middle of the shanty.

"You are sick, Merrymusk," said I, mournfully.

"No, I am well," he feebly answered. "Crow, Trumpet."

I shrunk. The strong soul in the feeble body appalled me.

But the cock crew.

The roof jarred.

"How is Mrs. Merrymusk?"

"Well."

"And the children?"

"Well. All well."

The last two words he shouted forth in a kind of wild ecstasy of triumph over ill. It was too much. His head fell back. A white napkin seemed dropped upon his face. Merrymusk was dead.

An awful fear seized me.

But the cock crew.

The cock shook his plumage as if each feather were a banner. The cock hung from the shanty roof as erewhile the trophied flags from the dome of St. Paul's. The cock terrified me with exceeding wonder.

I drew nigh the bedsides of the woman and children. They marked my look of strange affright; they knew what had happened.

"My good man is just dead," breathed the woman lowly. "Tell me true?"

"Dead," said I.

The cock crew.

She fell back, without a sigh and, through long-loving sympathy, was dead.

The cock crew.

The cock shook sparkles from his golden plumage. The cock seemed in a rapture of benevolent delight. Leaping from the hoop, he strode up majestically to the pile of old clothes, where the wood-sawyer lay, and planted himself, like an armorial supporter, at his side. Then raised one long, musical, triumphant, and final sort of crow, with throat heaved far back, as if he meant the blast to waft the wood-sawyer's soul sheer up to the seventh heavens. Then he strode, king-like, to the woman's bed. Another upturned and exultant crow, mated to the former.

The pallor of the children was changed to radiance. Their faces shone celestially through grime and dirt. They seemed children of emperors and kings, disguised. The cock sprang upon their bed, shook himself, and crowed, and crowed again, and still and still again. He seemed bent upon crowing the souls of the children out of their wasted bodies. He seemed bent upon rejoining instanter this whole family in the upper air. The children seemed to second his endeavors. Far, deep, intense longings for release transfigured them into spirits before my eyes. I saw angels where they lay.

They were dead.

The cock shook his plumage over them. The cock crew. It was now like a Bravo! like a Hurrah! like a Three-times-three! hip! hip! He strode out of the shanty. I followed. He flew upon the apex of the dwelling, spread wide his wings, sounded one supernatural note, and dropped at my feet.

The cock was dead.

If now you visit that hilly region, you will see, nigh the railroad track, just beneath October Mountain, on the other side of the swamp—there you will see a grave-stone, not with skull and cross-bones, but with a lusty cock in act of crowing, chiseled on it, with the words beneath:

O death, where is thy sting?
O grave, where is thy victory?

The wood-sawyer and his family, with the Signor Beneventano, lie in that spot; and I buried them, and planted the stone, which was a stone made to order; and never since then have I felt the doleful dumps, but under all circumstances crow late and early with a continual crow.

Cock-a-doodle-doo!—oo!—oo!—oo!—oo!

The Two Temples

dedicated to Sheridan Knowles

TEMPLE FIRST

"THIS is too bad," said I, "here have I tramped this blessed Sunday morning, all the way from the Battery, three long miles, for this express purpose, prayerbook under arm; here I am, I say, and, after all, I can't get in.

"Too bad. And how disdainful the great, fat-paunched, beadle-faced man looked, when, in answer to my humble petition, he said they had no galleries. Just the same as if he'd said, they didn't entertain poor folks. But I'll wager something that had my new coat been done last night, as the false tailor promised, and had I, arrayed therein this bright morning, tickled the fat-paunched, beadle-faced man's palm with a bank-note, then, gallery or no gallery, I would have had a fine seat in this marble-buttressed, stained-glassed, spic-and-span new temple.

"Well, here I am in the porch, very politely bowed out of the nave. I suppose I'm excommunicated; excluded, anyway.—That's a noble string of flashing carriages drawn up along the curb; those champing horses too have a haughty curve to their foam-flecked necks. Property of those 'miserable sinners' inside, I presume. I don't a bit wonder they unreservedly confess to such misery as *that*.—See the gold hat-bands, too, and other gorgeous trimmings, on those glossy groups of low-voiced gossipers near by. If I were in

149

England now, I should think those chaps a company of royal dukes, right honorable barons, etc. As it is, though, I guess they are only lackeys.—By the way, here I dodge about, as if I wanted to get into their aristocratic circle. In fact, it looks a sort of lackeyish to be idly standing outside a fine temple, cooling your heels, during service.—I had best move back to the Battery again, peeping into my prayer-book as I go.—But hold, don't I see a small door? Just in there, to one side, if I don't mistake, is a very low and very narrow vaulted door. No one seems to go that way. Ten to one, that identical door leads up into the tower. And now that I think of it, there is usually in these splendid, new-fashioned Gothic Temples, a curious little window high over the orchestra and everything else, away up among the gilded clouds of the ceiling's frescoes; and that little window, seems to me, if one could but get there, ought to command a glorious bird's-eye view of the entire field of operations below.—I guess I'll try it. No one in the porch now. The beadle-faced man is smoothing down some ladies' cushions, far up the broad aisle, I dare say. Softly now. If the small door ain't locked, I shall have stolen a march upon the beadle-faced man, and secured a humble seat in the sanctuary, in spite of him.—Good! Thanks for this! The door is not locked. Bell-ringer forgot to lock it, no doubt. Now, like any felt-footed grimalkin, up I steal among the leads."

Ascending some fifty stone steps along a very narrow curving stair-way, I found myself on a blank platform forming the second story of the huge square tower.

I seemed inside some magic-lantern. On three sides, three gigantic Gothic windows of richly dyed glass, filled the otherwise meagre place with all sorts of sunrises and sunsets, lunar and solar rainbows, falling stars, and other flaming fire-works and pyrotechnics. But after all, it was but a gorgeous dungeon; for I couldn't look out, any more than if I had been the occupant of a basement cell in "the Tombs." With some pains, and care not to do any serious harm, I contrived to scratch a minute opening in a great purple star forming the centre of the chief compartment of the middle window; when peeping through, as through goggles, I ducked my head in dismay. The beadle-faced man, with no hat on his head, was just in the act of driving three ragged little boys into the middle of the street; and how could I help trembling at the apprehension of his discovering a rebellious caitiff like me peering down on him from the tower? For, in stealing up here, I had set at naught his high authority. He whom he thought effectually ejected had burglariously returned. For a moment I was almost ready to bide my chance, and get to the sidewalk again with all dispatch. But another Jacob's ladder of lofty steps,— wooden ones, this time—allured me to another and still higher flight,—in sole hopes of gaining that one secret window where I might, at distance, take part in the proceedings.

Presently I noticed something which, owing to the first marvellous effulgence of the place, had remained unseen till now. Two strong ropes, dropping through holes in the rude ceiling high overhead, fell a sheer length of sixty feet, right through the center of the space, and dropped in coils upon the floor of the huge magic-lantern. Bell-ropes these, thought I, and quaked. For if the beadle-faced man should learn that a grimalkin was somewhere prowling about the edifice, how easy for him to ring the alarm. Hark!—ah, that's only the organ—yes—it's the *"Venite, exultemus Domine."* Though an insider in one respect, yet am I but an outsider in another. But for all that, I will not be defrauded of my natural rights. Uncovering my head, and taking out my book, I stood erect, midway up the tall Jacob's ladder, as if standing among the congregation; and in spirit, if not in place, participated in those devout exult-ings. That over, I continued my upward path; and after crossing sundry minor platforms and irregular landings all the while on a general ascent, at last I was delighted by catching sight of a small round window in the otherwise dead-wall side of the tower, where the tower attached itself to the main building. In front of the window was a rude narrow gallery, used as a bridge to cross from the lower stairs on one side to the upper stairs on the opposite.

As I drew nigh the spot, I well knew from the added clearness with which the sound of worship came to me, that the window did indeed look down upon the entire interior. But I was hardly prepared to find that no pane of glass, stained or unstained, was to stand between me and the far-under aisles and altar. For the purpose of ventilation, doubtless, the opening had been left unsupplied with sash of any sort. But a sheet of fine-woven, gauzy wire-work was in place of that. When, all eagerness, and open book in hand, I first advanced to stand before the window, I involuntarily shrank, as from before the mouth of a furnace, upon suddenly feeling a forceful puff of strange, heated air, blown, as by a blacksmith's bellows, full into my face and lungs. Yes, thought I, this window is doubtless for ventilation. Nor is it quite so comfortable as I fancied it might be. But beggars must not be choosers. The furnace which makes the people below there feel so snug and cosy in their padded pews, is to me, who stand here upon the naked gallery, cause of grievous trouble. Besides, though my face is scorched, my back is frozen. But I won't complain. Thanks for this much, anyway,—that by hollowing one hand to my ear, and standing a little sideways out of the more violent rush of the torrid current, I can at least hear the priest sufficiently to make my responses in the proper place. Little dream the good congregation away down there, that they have a faithful clerk away up here. Here, too, is a fitter place for sincere devotions, where,

though I see, I remain unseen. Depend upon it, no Pharisee would have my pew. I like it, and admire it, too, because it is so very high. Height, somehow, hath devotion
in it. The archangelic anthems are raised in a lofty place.
All the good shall go to such an one. Yes, Heaven is high.

As thus I mused, the glorious organ burst, like an earthquake, almost beneath my feet; and I heard the invoking
cry—"Govern them and *lift* them up forever!" Then down
I gazed upon the standing human mass, far, far below,
whose heads, gleaming in the many-colored window-stains,
showed like beds of spangled pebbles, flashing in a Cuban
sun. So, at least, I knew they needs would look, if but the
wire-woven screen were drawn aside. That wire-woven
screen had the effect of casting crape upon all I saw. Only
by making allowances for the crape, could I gain a right
idea of the scene disclosed.

Surprising, most surprising, too, it was. As said before,
the window was a circular one; the part of the tower where
I stood was dusky-dark; its height above the congregation-
floor could not have been less than ninety or a hundred
feet; the whole interior temple was lit by naught but glass
dimmed, yet glorified with all imaginable rich and russet
hues; the approach to my strange look-out, through perfect
solitude, and along rude and dusty ways, enhanced the
theatric wonder of the populous spectacle of this sumptu-
ous sanctuary. Book in hand, responses on my tongue,
standing in the very posture of devotion, I could not rid
my soul of the intrusive thought, that, through some
necromancer's glass, I looked down upon some sly enchanter's show.

At length the lessons being read, the chants chanted,
the white-robed priest, a noble-looking man, with a form
like the incomparable Talma's, gave out from the reading-
desk the hymn before the sermon, and then through a
side door vanished from the scene. In good time I saw the

same Talma-like and noble-looking man reappear through the same side door, his white apparel wholly changed for black.

By the melodious tone and persuasive gesture of the speaker, and the all-approving attention of the throng, I knew the sermon must be eloquent, and well adapted to an opulent auditory; but owing to the priest's changed position from the reading-desk, to the pulpit, I could not so distinctly hear him now as in the previous rites. The text, however,—repeated at the outset, and often after quoted,—I could not but plainly catch:—"Ye are the salt of the earth."

At length the benediction was pronounced over the mass of low-inclining foreheads; hushed silence, intense motionlessness followed for a moment, as if the congregation were one of buried, not of living men; when, suddenly, miraculously, like the general rising at the Resurrection, the whole host came to their feet, amid a simultaneous roll, like a great drum-beat, from the enrapturing, overpowering organ. Then, in three freshets—all gay sprightly nods and becks—the gilded brooks poured down the gilded aisles.

Time for me, too, to go, thought I, as snatching one last look upon the imposing scene, I clasped my book and put it in my pocket. The best thing I can do just now, is to slide out unperceived amid the general crowd. Hurrying down the great length of ladder, I soon found myself at the base of the last stone step of the final flight; but started aghast—the door was locked! The bell-ringer, or more probably that forever-prying suspicious-looking beadle-faced man has done this. He would not let me in at all at first, and now, with the greatest inconsistency, he will not let me out. But what is to be done? Shall I knock on the door? That will never do. It will only frighten the crowd streaming by, and no one can adequately respond to my summons, except the beadle-faced man; and if he sees me, he will recognize me, and perhaps roundly rate me—poor, humble worshipper—before the entire public. No, I won't knock. But what then?

Long time I thought, and thought, till at last all was hushed again. Presently a clicking sound admonished me that the church was being closed. In sudden desperation, I gave a rap on the door. But too late. It was not heard. I was left alone and solitary in a temple which but a moment before was more populous than many villages.

A strange trepidation of gloom and loneliness gradually stole over me. Hardly conscious of what I did, I reascended the stone steps: higher and higher still, and only paused, when once more I felt the hot-air blast from the wire-woven screen. Snatching another peep down into the vast arena, I started at its hushed desertness. The long ranges of grouped columns down the nave, and clusterings of them into copses about the corners of the transept; together with the subdued, dim-streaming light from the autumnal glasses; all assumed a secluded and deep-wooded air. I seemed gazing from Pisgah into the forests of old Canaan. A Puseyitish painting of a Madonna and Child, adorning a lower window, seemed showing to me the sole tenants of this painted wilderness—the true Hagar and her Ishmael.—

With added trepidation I stole softly back to the magic-lantern platform; and revived myself a little by peeping through the scratch, upon the unstained light of open day.—But what is to be done, thought I, again.

I descended to the door; listened there; heard nothing. A third time climbing the stone steps, once more I stood in the magic-lantern, while the full nature of the more than awkwardness of my position came over me.

The first persons who will re-enter the temple, mused I, will doubtless be the beadle-faced man, and the bell-ringer. And the first man to come up here, where I am, will be the latter. Now what will be his natural impressions upon first descrying an unknown prowler here? Rather disadvantageous to said prowler's moral character. Explanations will be vain. Circumstances are against me. True, I may hide, till he retires again. But how do I know, that he will then leave the door unlocked? Besides, in a position of affairs like this, it is generally best, I think, to anticipate discovery, and by magnanimously announcing yourself, forestall an inglorious detection. But how announce myself? Already have I knocked, and no response. That moment, my eye, impatiently ranging roundabout, fell upon the bell-ropes. They suggested the usual signal made at dwelling-houses to convey tidings of a stranger's presence. But I was not an outside caller; alas, I was an inside prowler.— But one little touch of that bell-rope would be sure to bring relief. I have an appointment at three o'clock. The beadle-faced man must naturally reside very close by the church. He well knows the peculiar ring of his own bell. The slightest possible hum would bring him flying to the rescue. Shall I, or shall I not?—But I may alarm the neighborhood. Oh no; the merest tinkle, not by any means a loud vociferous peal. Shall I? Better voluntarily bring the beadle-faced man to me, than be involuntarily dragged out from this most suspicious hiding-place. I have to face him, first or last. Better now than later.—Shall I?—

No more. Creeping to the rope, I gave it a cautious twitch. No sound. A little less warily. All was dumb. Still more strongly. Horrors! my hands, instinctively clapped to my ears, only served to condense the appalling din. Some undreamed-of mechanism seemed to have been touched. The bell must have thrice revolved on its thunderous axis, multiplying the astounding reverberation.

My business is effectually done, this time, thought I, all in a tremble. Nothing will serve me now but the reckless confidence of innocence reduced to desperation.

In less than five minutes, I heard a running noise beneath me; the lock of the door clicked, and up rushed the beadle-faced man, the perspiration starting from his cheeks.

"You! Is it *you?* The man I turned away this very morning, skulking here? *You* dare to touch that bell? Scoundrel!"

And ere I could defend myself, seizing me irresistibly in his powerful grasp, he tore me along by the collar, and dragging me down the stairs, thrust me into the arms of three policemen, who, attracted by the sudden toll of the bell, had gathered curiously about the porch.

All remonstrances were vain. The beadle-faced man was bigoted against me. Represented as a lawless violator, and a remorseless disturber of the Sunday peace, I was conducted to the Halls of Justice. Next morning, my rather gentlemanly appearance procured me a private hearing from the judge. But the beadle-faced man must have made a Sunday night call on him. Spite of my coolest explanations, the circumstances of the case were deemed so exceedingly suspicious, that only after paying a round fine, and receiving a stinging reprimand, was I permitted to go at large, and pardoned for having humbly indulged myself in the luxury of public worship.

TEMPLE SECOND

A STRANGER in London on Saturday night, and without a copper! What hospitalities may such an one expect? What shall I do with myself this weary night? My landlady won't receive me in her parlor. I owe her money. She looks like flint on me. So in this monstrous rabblement must I crawl about till, say ten o'clock, and then slink home to my unlighted bed.

The case was this: The week following my inglorious expulsion from the transatlantic temple, I had packed up my trunks and damaged character, and repaired to the paternal, loving town of Philadelphia. There chance threw into my way an interesting young orphan lady and her aunt-duenna; the lady rich as Cleopatra, but not as beautiful; the duenna lovely as Charmian, but not so young. For the lady's health, prolonged travel had been prescribed. Maternally connected in old England, the lady chose London for her primal port. But ere securing their passage, the two were looking round for some young physician, whose disengagement from pressing business might induce him to accept, on a moderate salary, the post of private Æsculapius and knightly companion to the otherwise unprotected pair. The more necessary was this, as not only the voyage to England was intended, but an extensive European tour, to follow.

Enough. I came; I saw; I was made the happy man. We sailed. We landed on the other side; when, after two weeks of agonized attendance on the vacillations of the lady, I was very cavalierly dismissed, on the score, that the lady's maternal relations had persuaded her to try, through the winter, the salubrious climate of the foggy Isle of Wight, in preference to the fabulous blue atmosphere of the Ionian Isles. So much for national prejudice. (Nota Bene: The lady was in a sad decline.)

Having, ere sailing, been obliged to anticipate nearly a quarter's pay to foot my outfit bills, I was dismally cut adrift in Fleet Street without a solitary shilling. By disposing, at certain pawnbrokers, of some of my less indispensable apparel, I had managed to stave off the more slaughterous onsets of my landlady, while diligently looking about for any business that might providentially appear.

So on I drifted amid those indescribable crowds which every seventh night pour and roar through each main artery and block the by-veins of great London, the Leviathan. Saturday Night it was; and the markets and the shops, and every stall and counter were crushed with the one unceasing tide. A whole Sunday's victualling for three millions of human bodies, was going on. Few of them equally hungry with my own, as through my spent lassitude, the unscrupulous human whirlpools eddied me aside at corners, as any straw is eddied in the Norway Maelstrom. What dire suckings into oblivion must such swirling billows know. Better perish mid myriad sharks in mid-Atlantic, than die a penniless stranger in Babylonian London. Forlorn, outcast, without a friend, I staggered on through three millions of my own human kind. The fiendish gas-lights, shooting their Tartarean rays across the muddy, sticky streets, lit up the pitiless and pitiable scene.

Well, well, if this were but Sunday now, I might conciliate some kind female pew-opener, and rest me in some inn-like chapel, upon some stranger's outside bench. But it is Saturday night. The end of the weary week, and all but the end of weary me.

Disentangling myself at last from those skeins of Pandemonian lanes which snarl one part of the metropolis between Fleet Street and Holborn, I found myself at last in a wide and far less noisy street, a short and shopless one, leading up from the Strand, and terminating at its junction with a crosswise avenue. The comparative quietude of the place was inexpressively soothing. It was like emerging upon the green enclosure surrounding some Cathedral church, where sanctity makes all things still. Two lofty brilliant lights attracted me in this tranquil street. Thinking it might prove some moral or religious meeting, I hurried towards the spot; but was surprised to see two tall placards announcing the appearance that night of the stately Macready in the part of Cardinal Richelieu. Very few loiterers hung about the place, the hour being rather late, and the play-bill hawkers mostly departed, or keeping entirely quiet. This theatre, indeed, as I afterwards discovered, was not

only one of the best in point of acting, but likewise one of
the most decorous in its general management, inside and
out. In truth, the whole neighborhood, as it seemed to me—
issuing from the jam and uproar of those turbulent tides
against which, or borne on irresistibly by which, I had so
long been swimming—the whole neighborhood, I say, of
this pleasing street seemed in good keeping with the character imputed to its theatre.

Glad to find one blessed oasis of tranquillity, I stood leaning against a column of the porch, and striving to lose my
sadness in running over one of the huge placards. No one
molested me. A tattered little girl, to be sure, approached,
with a hand-bill extended, but marking me more narrowly,
retreated; her strange skill in physiognomy at once enabling
her to determine that I was penniless. As I read, and read
—for the placard, of enormous dimensions, contained minute particulars of each successive scene in the enacted play
—gradually a strong desire to witness this celebrated Macready in this his celebrated part stole over me. By one act,
I might rest my jaded limbs, and more than jaded spirits.
Where else could I go for rest, unless I crawled into my
cold and lonely bed far up in an attic of Craven Street,
looking down upon the muddy Phlegethon of the Thames.
Besides, what I wanted was not merely rest, but cheer; the
making one of many pleased and pleasing human faces;
the getting into a genial humane assembly of my kind; such
as, at its best and highest, is to be found in the unified multitude of a devout congregation. But no such assemblies
were accessible that night, even if my unbefriended and
rather shabby air would overcome the scruples of those
fastidious gentry with red gowns and long gilded staves,
who guard the portals of the first-class London tabernacles
from all profanation of a poor forlorn and fainting wanderer
like me. Not inns, but ecclesiastical hotels, where the pews
are the rented chambers.

No use to ponder, thought I, at last; it is Saturday night, not Sunday; and so, a theatre only can receive me. So powerfully in the end did the longing to get into the edifice come over me, that I almost began to think of pawning my overcoat for admittance. But from this last infatuation I was providentially withheld by a sudden cheery summons, in a voice unmistakably benevolent. I turned, and saw a man who seemed to be some sort of a working-man.

"Take it," said he, holding a plain red ticket towards me, full in the gas-light. "You want to go in; I know you do. Take it. I am suddenly called home. There—hope you'll enjoy yourself. Good-bye."

Blankly and mechanically, I had suffered the ticket to be thrust into my hand, and now stood quite astonished, bewildered, and for the time, ashamed. The plain fact was, I had received charity; and for the first time in my life. Often in the course of my strange wanderings I had needed charity, but never had asked it, and certainly never, ere this blessed night, had been offered it. And a stranger, and in the very maw of the roaring London, too! Next moment my sense of foolish shame departed, and I felt a queer feeling in my left eye, which, as sometimes is the case with people, was the weaker one; probably from being on the same side with the heart.

I glanced round eagerly. But the kind giver was no longer in sight. I looked upon the ticket. I understood. It was one of those checks given to persons inside a theatre when for any cause they desire to step out a moment. Its presentation ensures unquestioned readmittance.

"Shall I use it?" mused I.—What? It's charity.—But if it be gloriously right to do a charitable deed, can it be ingloriously wrong to receive its benefit?—No one knows you; go boldly in.—Charity.—Why these unvanquishable scruples? All your life, naught but charity sustains you, and all others in the world. Maternal charity nursed you as a babe; paternal charity fed you as a child; friendly charity got you your profession; and to the charity of every man you meet this night in London, are you indebted for your unattempted life. Any knife, any hand of all the millions of knives and hands in London, has you this night at its mercy. You, and all ınortals, live but by sufferance of your charitable kind; charitable by omission, not performance.— Stush for your self-upbraidings, and pitiful, poor, shabby pride, you friendless man without a purse.—Go in.

Debate was over. Marking the direction from which the stranger had accosted me, I stepped that way; and soon saw a low-vaulted, inferior-looking door on one side of the edifice. Entering, I wandered on and up, and up and on again, through various doubling stairs and wedge-like, ill-lit passages, whose bare boards much reminded me of my ascent of the Gothic tower on the ocean's far-other side. At last I gained a lofty platform, and saw a fixed human countenance facing me from a mysterious window of a sort of sentry-box or closet. Like some saint in a shrine, the countenance was illuminated by two smoky candles. I divined the man. I exhibited my diploma, and he nodded me to a little door beyond; while a sudden burst of orchestral music admonished me I was now very near my destination, and also revived the memory of the organ-anthems I had heard while on the ladder of the tower at home.

Next moment, the wire-woven gauzy screen of the venti-lating window in that same tower seemed enchantedly re-produced before me. The same hot blast of stifling air once more rushed into my lungs. From the same dizzy altitude, through the same fine-spun, vapory crapey air; far, far down upon just such a packed mass of silent human beings; lis-tening to just such grand harmonies; I stood within the topmost gallery of the temple. But hardly alone and silently as before. This time I had company. Not of the first circles, and certainly not of the dress-circle; but most acceptable, right welcome, cheery company, to otherwise uncompanioned me. Quiet, well-pleased working-men, and their glad wives and sisters, with here and there an aproned urchin, with all-absorbed, bright face, vermilioned by the excitement and the heated air, hovering like a painted cherub over the vast human firmament below. The height of the gallery was in truth appalling. The rail was low. I thought of deep-sea-leads, and the mariner in the vessel's chains, drawing up the line, with his long-drawn musical accompaniment. And, like beds of glittering coral, through the deep sea of azure smoke, there, far down, I saw the jewelled necks and white sparkling arms of crowds of ladies in the semicirque. But, in the interval of two acts, again the orchestra was heard; some inspiring national anthem now was played. As the volumed sound came undulating up, and broke in showery spray and foam of melody against our gallery rail, my head involuntarily was bowed, my hand instinctively sought my pocket. Only by a second thought did I check my momentary lunacy and remind myself that this time I had no small morocco book with me, and that this was not the house of prayer.

Quickly was my wandering mind—preternaturally affected by the sudden translation from the desolate street to this bewildering and blazing spectacle—arrested in its wanderings, by feeling at my elbow a meaning nudge; when turning suddenly, I saw a sort of coffee-pot, and pewter mug hospitably presented to me by a ragged, but good-natured looking boy.

"Thank you," said I, "I won't take any coffee, I guess."

"Coffee?—I guess?—ain't you a Yankee?"

"Aye, boy; true blue."

"Well, dad's gone to Yankee-land, a-seekin' of his fortin; so take a penny mug of ale, do, Yankee, for poor dad's sake."

Out from the tilted coffee-pot-looking can, came a coffee-colored stream, and a small mug of humming ale was in my hand.

"I don't want it, boy. The fact is, my boy, I have no penny by me. I happened to leave my purse at my lodgings."

"Never do you mind, Yankee; drink to honest dad."

"With all my heart, you generous boy; here's immortal life to him!"

He stared at my strange burst, smiled merrily, and left me, offering his coffee-pot in all directions, and not in vain.

'Tis not always poverty to be poor, mused I; one may fare well without a penny. A ragged boy may be a prince-like benefactor.

Because that unpurchased penny-worth of ale revived my drooping spirits strangely. Stuff was in that barley malt; a most sweet bitterness in those blessed hops. God bless the glorious boy!

The more I looked about me in this lofty gallery, the more was I delighted with its occupants. It was not spacious. It was, if anything, rather contracted, being the very cheapest portion of the house, where very limited attendance was expected; embracing merely the very crown of the topmost semicircle; and so commanding, with a sovereign outlook, and imperial downlook, the whole theatre, with the expanded stage directly opposite, though some hundred feet below. As at the tower, peeping into the transatlantic temple, so stood I here, at the very main-mast-head of all the interior edifice.

Such was the decorum of this special theatre, that nothing objectionable was admitted within its walls. With an unhurt eye of perfect love, I sat serenely in the gallery, gazing upon the pleasing scene, around me and below. Neither did it abate from my satisfaction, to remember, that Mr. Macready, the chief actor of the night, was an amiable gentleman, combining the finest qualities of social and Christian respectability, with the highest excellence in his particular profession; for which last he had conscientiously done much, in many ways, to refine, elevate, and chasten.

But now the curtain rises, and the robed Cardinal advances. How marvellous this personal resemblance! He looks every inch to be the self-same, stately priest I saw irradiated by the glow-worm dyes of the pictured windows from my high tower-pew. And shining as he does, in the rosy reflexes of these stained walls and gorgeous galleries, the mimic priest down there; he too seems lit by Gothic blazonings.—Hark! The same measured, courtly, noble tone. See! the same imposing attitude. Excellent actor is this Richelieu!

He disappears behind the scenes. He slips, no doubt, into the Green Room. He reappears somewhat changed in his habiliments. Do I dream, or is it genuine memory that recalls some similar thing seen through the woven wires?

The curtain falls. Starting to their feet, the enraptured thousands sound their responses, deafeningly; unmistakably sincere. Right from the undoubted heart. I have no duplicate in my memory of this. In earnestness of response, this second temple stands unmatched. And hath mere mimicry done this? What is it then to act a part?

But now the music surges up again, and borne by that rolling billow, I, and all the gladdened crowd, are harmoniously attended to the street.

I went home to my lonely lodging, and slept not much that night, for thinking of the First Temple and the Second Temple; and how that, a stranger in a strange land, I found sterling charity in the one; and at home, in my own land, was thrust out from the other.

Poor Man's Pudding and Rich Man's Crumbs

Poor Man's Pudding

Y ou see," said poet Blandmour, enthusiastically—as some forty years ago we walked along the road in a soft, moist snow-fall, toward the end of March —"you see, my friend, that the blessed almoner, Nature, is in all things beneficent; and not only so, but considerate in her charities, as any discreet human philanthropist might be. This snow, now, which seems so unseasonable, is in fact just what a poor husbandman needs. Rightly is this soft March snow, falling just before seed-time, rightly is it called 'Poor Man's Manure.' Distilling from kind heaven upon the soil, by a gentle penetration it nourishes every clod, ridge, and furrow. To the poor farmer it is as good as the rich farmer's farm-yard enrichments. And the poor man has no trouble to spread it, while the rich man has to spread his."

"Perhaps so," said I, without equal enthusiasm, brushing some of the damp flakes from my chest. "It may be as you say, dear Blandmour. But tell me, how is it that the wind drives yonder drifts of 'Poor Man's Manure' off poor Coulter's two-acre patch here, and piles it up yonder on rich Squire Teamster's twenty-acre field?"

"Ah! to be sure—yes—well; Coulter's field, I suppose, is sufficiently moist without further moistenings. Enough is as good as a feast, you know."

"Yes," replied I, "of this sort of damp fare," shaking another shower of the damp flakes from my person. "But tell me, this warm spring-snow may answer very well, as you say; but how is it with the cold snows of the long, long winters here?"

"Why, do you not remember the words of the Psalmist? —'The Lord giveth snow like wool;' meaning not only that snow is white as wool, but warm, too, as wool. For the only reason, as I take it, that wool is comfortable, is because air is entangled, and therefore warmed among its fibres. Just so, then, take the temperature of a December field when covered with this snow-fleece, and you will no doubt find it several degrees above that of the air. So, you see, the winter's snow *itself* is beneficent; under the pretense of frost— a sort of gruff philanthropist—actually warming the earth, which afterward is to be fertilizingly moistened by these gentle flakes of March."

"I like to hear you talk, dear Blandmour; and, guided by your benevolent heart, can only wish to poor Coulter plenty of this 'Poor Man's Manure.' "

"But that is not all," said Blandmour, eagerly. "Did you never hear of the 'Poor Man's Eye-water?' "

"Never."

"Take this soft March snow, melt it, and bottle it. It keeps pure as alcohol. The very best thing in the world for weak eyes. I have a whole demijohn of it myself. But the poorest man, afflicted in his eyes, can freely help himself to this same all-bountiful remedy. Now, what a kind provision is that!"

"Then 'Poor Man's Manure' is 'Poor Man's Eye-water' too?"

"Exactly. And what could be more economically contrived? One thing answering two ends—ends so very distinct."

"Very distinct, indeed."

"Ah! that is your way. Making sport of earnest. But never mind. We have been talking of snow; but common rain-water—such as falls all the year round—is still more kindly. Not to speak of its known fertilizing quality as to fields, consider it in one of its minor lights. Pray, did you ever hear of a 'Poor Man's Egg?' "

"Never. What is that, now?"

"Why, in making some culinary preparations of meal and flour, where eggs are recommended in the receipt-book, a substitute for the eggs may be had in a cup of cold rain water, which acts as leaven. And so a cup of cold rain-water thus used is called by housewives a 'Poor Man's Egg.' And many rich men's housekeepers sometimes use it."

"But only when they are out of hen's eggs, I presume, dear Blandmour. But your talk is—I sincerely say it—most agreeable to me. Talk on."

"Then there's 'Poor Man's Plaster' for wounds and other bodily harms; an alleviative and curative, compounded of simple, natural things; and so, being very cheap, is accessible to the poorest of sufferers. Rich men often use 'Poor Man's Plaster.' "

"But not without the judicious advice of a fee'd physician, dear Blandmour."

"Doubtless, they first consult the physician; but that may be an unnecessary precaution."

"Perhaps so. I do not gainsay it. Go on."

"Well, then, did you ever eat of a 'Poor Man's Pudding?' "

"I never so much as heard of it before."

"Indeed! Well, now you shall eat of one; and you shall eat it, too, as made, unprompted, by a poor man's wife, and you shall eat it at a poor man's table, and in a poor man's house. Come now, and if after this eating, you do not say that a 'Poor Man's Pudding' is as relishable as a rich man's, I will give up the point altogether; which briefly is: that.

through kind Nature, the poor, out of their very poverty, extract comfort."

Not to narrate any more of our conversations upon this subject (for we had several—I being at that time the guest of Blandmour in the country, for the benefit of my health), suffice it that, acting upon Blandmour's hint, I introduced myself into Coulter's house on a wet Monday noon (for the snow had thawed), under the innocent pretense of craving a pedestrian's rest and refreshment for an hour or two.

I was greeted, not without much embarrassment—owing, I suppose, to my dress—but still with unaffected and honest kindness. Dame Coulter was just leaving the wash-tub to get ready her one o'clock meal against her good man's return from a deep wood about a mile distant among the hills, where he was chopping by day's-work—seventy-five cents per day—and found himself. The washing being done outside the main building, under an infirm-looking old shed, the dame stood upon a half-rotten, soaked board to protect her feet, as well as might be, from the penetrating damp of the bare ground; hence she looked pale and chill. But her paleness had still another and more secret cause— the paleness of a mother to be. A quiet, fathomless heart-trouble, too, couched beneath the mild, resigned blue of her soft and wife-like eye. But she smiled upon me, as apologizing for the unavoidable disorder of a Monday and a washing-day, and, conducting me into the kitchen, set me down in the best seat it had—an old-fashioned chair of an enfeebled constitution.

I thanked her; and sat rubbing my hands before the ineffectual low fire, and—unobservantly as I could—glancing now and then about the room, while the good woman, throwing on more sticks, said she was sorry the room was no warmer. Something more she said, too—not repiningly, however—of the fuel, as old and damp; picked-up sticks in Squire Teamster's forest, where her husband was chopping the sappy logs of the living tree for the Squire's fires. It needed not her remark, whatever it was, to convince me of the inferior quality of the sticks; some being quite mossy and toad-stooled with long lying bedded among the accumulated dead leaves of many autumns. They made a sad hissing, and vain spluttering enough.

"You must rest yourself here till dinner-time, at least," said the dame; "what I have you are heartily welcome to."

I thanked her again, and begged her not to heed my presence in the least, but go on with her usual affairs.

I was struck by the aspect of the room. The house was old, and constitutionally damp. The window-sills had beads of exuded dampness upon them. The shriveled sashes shook in their frames, and the green panes of glass were clouded with the long thaw. On some little errand the dame passed into an adjoining chamber, leaving the door partly open. The floor of that room was carpetless, as the kitchen's was. Nothing but bare necessaries were about me; and those not of the best sort. Not a print on the wall; but an old volume of Doddridge lay on the smoked chimney-shelf.

"You must have walked a long way, sir; you sigh so with weariness."

"No, I am not nigh so weary as yourself, I dare say."

"Oh, but *I* am accustomed to that; *you* are not, I should think," and her soft, sad blue eye ran over my dress. "But I must sweep these shavings away; husband made him a new axe-helve this morning before sunrise, and I have been so busy washing, that I have had no time to clear up. But now they are just the thing I want for the fire. They'd be much better though, were they not so green."

Now if Blandmour were here, thought I to myself, he would call those green shavings "Poor Man's Matches," or "Poor Man's Tinder," or some pleasant name of that sort.

"I do not know," said the good woman, turning round to

me again—as she stirred among her pots on the smoky
fire—"I do not know how you will like our pudding. It
is only rice, milk, and salt boiled together."

"Ah, what they call 'Poor Man's Pudding,' I suppose
you mean."

A quick flush, half resentful, passed over her face.

"*We* do not call it so, sir," she said, and was silent.

Upbraiding myself for my inadvertence, I could not
but again think to myself what Blandmour would have
said, had he heard those words and seen that flush.

At last a slow, heavy footfall was heard; then a scraping
at the door, and another voice said, "Come, wife; come,
come—I must be back again in a jiff—if you say I *must*
take all my meals at home, you must be speedy; because the
Squire—Good day, sir," he exclaimed, now first catching
sight of me as he entered the room. He turned toward his
wife, inquiringly, and stood stock-still, while the moisture
oozed from his patched boots to the floor.

"This gentleman stops here awhile to rest and refresh:
he will take dinner with us, too. All will be ready now in
a trice; so sit down on the bench, husband, and be patient,
I pray. You see, sir," she continued, turning to me, "William
there wants, of mornings, to carry a cold meal into
the woods with him, to save the long one o'clock walk
across the fields to and fro. But I won't let him. A warm
dinner is more than pay for the long walk."

"I don't know about that," said William, shaking his
head. "I have often debated in my mind whether it really
paid. There's not much odds, either way, between a wet
walk after hard work, and a wet dinner before it. But I
like to oblige a good wife like Martha. And you know,
sir, that women will have their whimsies."

"I wish they all had as kind whimsies as your wife has,"
said I.

"Well, I've heard that some women ain't all maple-sugar;

but, content with dear Martha, I don't know much about others."

"You find rare wisdom in the woods," mused I.

"Now, husband, if you ain't too tired, just lend a hand to draw the table out."

"Nay," said I, "let him rest, and let me help."

"No," said William, rising.

"Sit still," said his wife to me.

The table set, in due time we all found ourselves with plates before us.

"You see what we have," said Coulter—"salt pork, rye-bread, and pudding. Let me help you. I got this pork of the Squire; some of his last year's pork, which he let me have on account. It isn't quite so sweet as this year's would be; but I find it hearty enough to work on, and that's all I eat for. Only let the rheumatiz and other sicknesses keep clear of me, and I ask no flavors or favors from any. But you don't eat of the pork!"

"I see," said the wife, gently and gravely, "that the gentleman knows the difference between this year's and last year's pork. But perhaps he will like the pudding."

I summoned up all my self-control, and smilingly assented to the proposition of the pudding, without by my looks casting any reflections upon the pork. But, to tell the truth, it was quite impossible for me (not being ravenous, but only a little hungry at the time) to eat of the latter. It had a yellowish crust all round it, and was rather rankish, I thought, to the taste. I observed, too, that the dame did not eat of it, though she suffered some to be put on her plate, and pretended to be busy with it when Coulter looked that way. But she ate of the rye-bread, and so did I.

"Now, then, for the pudding," said Coulter. "Quick, wife; the Squire sits in his sitting-room window, looking far out across the fields. His time-piece is true."

"He don't play the spy on you, does he?" said I.

"Oh, no!—I don't say that. He's a good enough man. He gives me work. But he's particular. Wife, help the gentleman. You see, sir, if I lose the Squire's work, what will become of—" and, with a look for which I honored humanity, with sly significance he glanced toward his wife; then, a little changing his voice, instantly continued—"that fine horse I am going to buy."

"I guess," said the dame, with a strange, subdued sort of inefficient pleasantry—"I guess that fine horse you sometimes so merrily dream of will long stay in the Squire's stall. But sometimes his man gives me a Sunday ride."

"A Sunday ride!" said I.

"You see," resumed Coulter, "wife loves to go to church; but the nighest is four miles off, over yon snowy hills. So she can't walk it; and I can't carry her in my arms, though I have carried her up-stairs before now. But, as she says, the Squire's man sometimes gives her a lift on the road; and for this cause it is that I speak of a horse I am going to have one of these fine sunny days. And already, before having it, I have christened it 'Martha.' But what am I about? Come, come, wife! the pudding! Help the gentleman, do! The Squire! the Squire!—think of the Squire! and help round the pudding. There, one—two—three mouthfuls must do me. Good-bye, wife. Good-bye, sir. I'm off."

And, snatching his soaked hat, the noble Poor Man hurriedly went out into the soak and the mire.

I suppose now, thinks I to myself, that Blandmour would poetically say, He goes to take a Poor Man's Saunter.

"You have a fine husband," said I to the woman, as we were now left together.

"William loves me this day as on the wedding-day, sir. Some hasty words, but never a harsh one. I wish I were better and stronger for his sake. And, oh! sir, both for his sake and mine," (and the soft, blue, beautiful eyes turned into two well-springs) "how I wish little William and Martha lived—it is so lonely-like now. William named after him, and Martha for me."

When a companion's heart of itself overflows, the best one can do is to do nothing. I sat looking down on my as yet untasted pudding.

"You should have seen little William, sir. Such a bright, manly boy, only six years old—cold, cold now!"

Plunging my spoon into the pudding, I forced some into my mouth to stop it.

"And little Martha—Oh! sir, she was the beauty! Bitter, bitter! but needs must be borne."

The mouthful of pudding now touched my palate, and touched it with a mouldy, briny taste. The rice, I knew, was of that damaged sort sold cheap; and the salt from the last year's pork barrel.

"Ah, sir, if those little ones yet to enter the world were the same little ones which so sadly have left it; returning friends, not strangers, strangers, always strangers! Yet does a mother soon learn to love them; for certain, sir, they come from where the others have gone. Don't you believe that, sir? Yes, I know all good people must. But, still, still—and I fear it is wicked, and very black-hearted, too—still, strive how I may to cheer me with thinking of little William and Martha in heaven, and with reading Dr. Doddridge there —still, still does dark grief leak in, just like the rain through our roof. I am left so lonesome now; day after day, all the day long, dear William is gone; and all the damp day long grief drizzles and drizzles down on my soul. But I pray to God to forgive me for this; and for the rest, manage it as well as I may."

Bitter and mouldy is the "Poor Man's Pudding," groaned I to myself, half choked with but one little mouthful of it, which would hardly go down.

I could stay no longer to hear of sorrows for which the

sincerest sympathies could give no adequate relief; of a fond persuasion, to which there could be furnished no further proof than already was had—a persuasion, too, of that sort which much speaking is sure more or less to mar; of causeless self-upbraidings, which no expostulations could have dispelled. I offered no pay for hospitalities gratuitous and honorable as those of a prince. I knew that such offerings would have been more than declined; charity resented.

The native American poor never lose their delicacy or pride; hence, though unreduced to the physical degradation of the European pauper, they yet suffer more in mind than the poor of any other people in the world. Those peculiar social sensibilities nourished by our own peculiar political principles, while they enhance the true dignity of a prosperous American, do but minister to the added wretchedness of the unfortunate; first, by prohibiting their acceptance of what little random relief charity may offer; and, second, by furnishing them with the keenest appreciation of the smarting distinction between their ideal of universal equality and their grindstone experience of the practical misery and infamy of poverty—a misery and infamy which is, ever has been, and ever will be, precisely the same in India, England, and America.

Under pretense that my journey called me forthwith, I bade the dame good-bye; shook her cold hand; looked my last into her blue, resigned eye, and went out into the wet. But cheerless as it was, and damp, damp, damp—the heavy atmosphere charged with all sorts of incipiencies—I yet became conscious, by the suddenness of the contrast, that the house air I had quitted was laden down with that peculiar deleterious quality, the height of which—insufferable to some visitants—will be found in a poor-house ward.

This ill-ventilation in winter of the rooms of the poor—a thing, too, so stubbornly persisted in—is usually charged upon them as their disgraceful neglect of the most simple means to health. But the instinct of the poor is wiser than we think. The air which ventilates, likewise *cools*. And to any shiverer, ill-ventilated warmth is better than well-ventilated cold. Of all the preposterous assumptions of humanity over humanity, nothing exceeds most of the criticisms made on the habits of the poor by the well-housed, well-warmed, and well-fed.

* * *

"Blandmour," said I that evening, as after tea I sat on his comfortable sofa, before a blazing fire, with one of his two ruddy little children on my knee, "you are not what may rightly be called a rich man; you have a fair competence; no more. Is it not so? Well, then, I do not include *you*, when I say, that if ever a Rich Man speaks prosperously to me of a Poor Man, I shall set it down as—I won't mention the word."

PICTURE SECOND

Rich Man's Crumbs

IN THE year 1814, during the summer following my first taste of the "Poor Man's Pudding," a sea-voyage was recommended to me by my physician. The Battle of Waterloo having closed the long drama of Napoleon's wars, many strangers were visiting Europe. I arrived in London at the time the victorious princes were there assembled enjoying the Arabian Nights' hospitalities of a grateful and gorgeous aristocracy, and the courtliest of gentlemen and kings—George the Prince Regent.

I had declined all letters but one to my banker. I wandered about for the best reception an adventurous traveler can have—the reception, I mean, which unsolicited chance and accident throw in his venturous way.

But I omit all else to recount one hour's hap under the lead of a very friendly man, whose acquaintance I made in the open street of Cheapside. He wore a uniform, and was some sort of a civic subordinate; I forget exactly what. He was off duty that day. His discourse was chiefly of the noble charities of London. He took me to two or three, and made admiring mention of many more.

"But," said he, as we turned into Cheapside again, "if you are at all curious about such things, let me take you— if it be not too late—to one of the most interesting of all— our Lord Mayor's Charities, sir; nay, the charities not only of a Lord Mayor, but, I may truly say, in this one instance, of emperors, regents, and kings. You remember the event of yesterday?"

"That sad fire on the river-side, you mean, unhousing so many of the poor?"

"No. The grand Guildhall Banquet to the princes. Who can forget it? Sir, the dinner was served on nothing but solid silver and gold plate, worth at the least £200,000— that is, 1,000,000 of your dollars; while the mere expenditure of meats, wines, attendance and upholstery, etc., can not be footed under £25,000—125,000 dollars of your hard cash."

"But, surely, my friend, you do not call that charity— feeding kings at that rate?"

"No. The feast came first—yesterday; and the charity after—to-day. How else would you have it, where princes are concerned? But I think we shall be quite in time— come; here we are at King Street, and down there is Guildhall. Will you go?"

"Gladly, my good friend. Take me where you will. I came but to roam and see."

Avoiding the main entrance of the hall, which was barred, he took me through some private way, and we found ourselves in a rear blind-walled place in the open air. I looked round amazed. The spot was grimy as a back-yard in the Five Points. It was packed with a mass of lean, famished, ferocious creatures, struggling and fighting for some mysterious precedency, and all holding soiled blue tickets in their hands.

"There is no other way," said my guide; "we can only get in with the crowd. Will you try it? I hope you have not on your drawing-room suit? What do you say? It will be well worth your sight. So noble a charity does not often offer. The one following the annual banquet of Lord Mayor's day—fine a charity as that certainly is—is not to be mentioned with what will be seen to-day. Is it, aye?"

As he spoke, a basement door in the distance was thrown open, and the squalid mass made a rush for the dark vault beyond.

I nodded to my guide, and sideways we joined in with the rest. Ere long we found our retreat cut off by the yelping crowd behind, and I could not but congratulate myself on having a civic, as well as civil guide; one, too, whose uniform made evident his authority.

It was just the same as if I were pressed by a mob of cannibals on some pagan beach. The beings round me roared with famine. For in this mighty London misery but maddens. In the country it softens. As I gazed on the meagre, murderous pack, I thought of the blue eye of the gentle wife of poor Coulter. Some sort of curved, glittering steel thing (not a sword; I know not what it was), before worn in his belt, was now flourished overhead by my guide, menacing the creatures to forbear offering the stranger violence.

As we drove, slow and wedge-like, into the gloomy vault, the howls of the mass reverberated. I seemed seething in the Pit with the Lost. On and on through the dark and the damp, and then up a stone stairway to a wide portal; when, diffusing, the pestiferous mob poured in bright day between painted walls and beneath a painted dome. I thought of the anarchic sack of Versailles.

A few moments more and I stood bewildered among the beggars in the famous Guildhall.

Where I stood—where the thronged rabble stood, less than twelve hours before sat His Imperial Majesty, Alexander of Russia; His Royal Majesty, Frederic William, King of Prussia; His Royal Highness, George, Prince Regent of England; His world-renowned Grace, the Duke of Wellington; with a mob of magnificoes, made up of conquering field-marshals, earls, counts, and innumerable other nobles of mark.

The walls swept to and fro, like the foliage of a forest, with blazonings of conquerors' flags. Naught outside the hall was visible. No windows were within four-and-twenty feet of the floor. Cut off from all other sights, I was hemmed in by one splendid spectacle—splendid, I mean, everywhere but as the eye fell toward the floor. *That* was foul as a hovel's—as a kennel's; the naked boards being strewed with the smaller and more wasteful fragments of the feast, while the two long parallel lines, up and down the hall, of now unrobed, shabby, dirty pine-tables were piled with less trampled wrecks. The dyed banners were in keeping with the last night's kings; the floor suited the beggars of to-day. The banners looked down upon the floor as from his balcony Dives upon Lazarus. A line of liveried men kept back with their staves the impatient jam of the mob, who, otherwise, might have instantaneously converted the Charity into a Pillage. Another body of gowned and gilded officials distributed the broken meats—the cold victuals and crumbs of kings. One after another the beggars held up their dirty blue tickets, and were served with the plundered wreck of a pheasant, or the rim of a pasty—like the detached crown of an old hat—the solids and meats stolen out.

"What a noble charity!" whispered my guide. "See that

pasty now, snatched by that pale girl; I dare say the Emperor of Russia ate of that last night."

"Very probably," murmured I; "it looks as though some omnivorous Emperor or other had had a finger in that pie."

"And see yon pheasant, too—there—*that* one—the boy in the torn shirt has it now—look! The Prince Regent might have dined off that."

The two breasts were gouged ruthlessly out, exposing the bare bones, embellished with the untouched pinions and legs.

"Yes, who knows!" said my guide, "his Royal Highness the Prince Regent might have eaten of that identical pheasant."

"I don't doubt it," murmured I, "he is said to be uncommonly fond of the breast. But where is Napoleon's head in a charger? I should fancy *that* ought to have been the principal dish."

"You are merry. Sir, even Cossacks are charitable here in Guildhall. Look! the famous Platoff, the Hetman himself—(he was here last night with the rest)—no doubt he thrust a lance into yon fat pork-pie there. Look! the old shirtless man has it now. How he licks his chops over it, little thinking of or thanking the good, kind Cossack that left it him! Ah! another—a stouter—has grabbed it. It falls; bless my soul!—the dish is quite empty—only a bit of the hacked crust."

"The Cossacks, my friend, are said to be immoderately fond of fat," observed I. "The Hetman was hardly so charitable as you thought."

"A noble charity, upon the whole, for all that. See, even Gog and Magog yonder, at the other end of the hall, fairly laugh out their delight at the scene."

"But don't you think, though," hinted I, "that the sculptor, whoever he was, carved the laugh too much into a grin —a sort of sardonical grin?"

"Well, that's as you take it, sir. But see—now I'd wager a guinea the Lord Mayor's lady dipped her golden spoon into yonder golden-hued jelly. See, the jelly-eyed old body has slipped it, in one broad gulp, down his throat!"

"Peace to that jelly!" breathed I.

"What a generous, noble, magnanimous charity this is! Unheard of in any country but England, which feeds her very beggars with golden-hued jellies."

"But not three times every day, my friend. And do you really think that jellies are the best sort of relief you can furnish to beggars? Would not plain beef and bread, with something to do, and be paid for, be better?"

"But plain beef and bread were not eaten here. Emperors, and prince-regents, and kings, and field-marshals don't often dine on plain beef and bread. So the leavings are according. Tell me, can you expect that the crumbs of kings can be like the crumbs of squirrels?"

"*You!* I mean *you!* stand aside, or else be served and away! Here, take this pasty, and be thankful that you taste of the same dish with Her Grace the Duchess of Devonshire. Graceless ragamuffin, do you hear?"

These words were bellowed at me through the din by a red-gowned official nigh the board.

"Surely he does not mean *me*," said I to my guide; "he has not confounded *me* with the rest."

"One is known by the company he keeps," smiled my guide. "See! not only stands your hat awry and bunged on your head, but your coat is fouled and torn. Nay," he cried to the red-gown, "this is an unfortunate friend; a simple spectator, I assure you."

"Ah! is that you, old lad?" responded the red-gown, in familiar recognition of my guide—a personal friend, as it seemed. "Well, convey your friend out forthwith. Mind the grand crash; it will soon be coming; hark! now! away with him!"

Too late. The last dish had been seized. The yet un-glutted mob raised a fierce yell, which wafted the banners like a strong gust, and filled the air with a reek as from sewers. They surged against the tables, broke through all barriers, and billowed over the hall—their bare tossed arms like the dashed ribs of a wreck. It seemed to me as if a sud-den impotent fury of fell envy possessed them. That one half-hour's peep at the mere remnants of the glories of the Banquets of Kings, the unsatisfying mouthfuls of dis-embowelled pasties, plundered pheasants, and half-sacked jellies, served to remind them of the intrinsic contempt of the alms. In this sudden mood, or whatever mysterious thing it was that now seized them, these Lazaruses seemed ready to spew up in repentant scorn the contumelious crumbs of Dives.

"This way, this way! stick like a bee to my back," intensely whispered my guide. "My friend there has answered my beck, and thrown open yon private door for us two. Wedge —wedge in—quick—there goes your bunged hat—never stop for your coat-tail—hit that man—strike him down! hold! jam! now! now! wrench along for your life! ha! here we breathe freely; thank God! You faint. Ho!"

"Never mind. This fresh air revives me."

I inhaled a few more breaths of it, and felt ready to pro-ceed.

"And now conduct me, my good friend, by some front passage into Cheapside, forthwith. I must home."

"Not by the sidewalk though. Look at your dress. I must get a hack for you."

"Yes, I suppose so," said I, ruefully eying my tatters, and then glancing in envy at the close-bodied coat and flat cap of my guide, which defied all tumblings and tearings.

"There, now, sir," said the honest fellow, as he put me into the hack, and tucked in me and my rags, "when you get back to your own country, you can say you have witnessed the greatest of all England's noble charities. Of course, you will make reasonable allowances for the unavoidable jam. Good-bye. Mind, Jehu"—addressing the driver on the box—"this is a *gentleman* you carry. He is just from the Guildhall Charity, which accounts for his appearance. Go on now. London Tavern, Fleet Street, remember, is the place."

* * *

"Now, Heaven in its kind mercy save me from the noble charities of London," sighed I, as that night I lay bruised and battered on my bed; "and Heaven save me equally from the 'Poor Man's Pudding' and the 'Rich Man's Crumbs.' "

The Paradise of Bachelors and The Tartarus of Maids

I

The Paradise of Bachelors

I T LIES not far from Temple Bar.

Going to it, by the usual way, is like stealing from a heated plain into some cool, deep glen, shady among harboring hills.

Sick with the din and soiled with the mud of Fleet Street —where the Benedick tradesmen are hurrying by, with ledger-lines ruled along their brows, thinking upon rise of bread and fall of babies—you adroitly turn a mystic corner —not a street—glide down a dim, monastic way, flanked by dark, sedate, and solemn piles, and still wending on, give the whole care-worn world the slip, and, disentangled, stand beneath the quiet cloisters of the Paradise of Bachelors.

Sweet are the oases in Sahara; charming the isle-groves of August prairies; delectable pure faith amidst a thousand perfidies; but sweeter, still more charming, most delectable, the dreamy Paradise of Bachelors, found in the stony heart of stunning London.

In mild meditation pace the cloisters; take your pleasure, sip your leisure, in the garden waterward; go linger in the ancient library; go worship in the sculptured chapel; but little have you seen, just nothing do you know, not the sweet kernel have you tasted, till you dine among the banded Bachelors, and see their convivial eyes and glasses sparkle. Not dine in bustling commons, during term-time, in the hall; but tranquilly, by private hint, at a private table; some fine Templar's hospitably invited guest.

Templar? That's a romantic name. Let me see. Brian de Bois-Guilbert was a Templar, I believe. Do we understand you to insinuate that those famous Templars still survive in modern London? May the ring of their armed heels be heard, and the rattle of their shields, as in mailed prayer the monk-knights kneel before the consecrated Host? Surely a monk-knight were a curious sight picking his way along the Strand, his gleaming corselet and snowy surcoat spattered by an omnibus. Long-bearded, too, according to his order's rule; his face fuzzy as a pard's; how would the grim ghost look among the crop-haired, close-shaven citizens? We know indeed—sad history recounts it—that a moral blight tainted at last this sacred Brotherhood. Though no sworded foe might outskill them in the fence, yet the worm of luxury crawled beneath their guard, gnawing the core of knightly troth, nibbling the monastic vow, till at last the monk's austerity relaxed to wassailing, and the sworn knights-bachelors grew to be but hypocrites and rakes.

But for all this, quite unprepared were we to learn that Knights-Templars (if at all in being) were so entirely secularized as to be reduced from carving out immortal fame in glorious battling for the Holy Land, to the carving of roast-mutton at a dinner-board. Like Anacreon, do these degenerate Templars now think it sweeter far to fall in banquet than in war? Or, indeed, how can there be any survival of that famous order? Templars in modern London! Templars in their red-cross mantles smoking cigars at the Divan! Templars crowded in a railway train, till, stacked with steel helmet, spear, and shield, the whole train looks like one elongated locomotive!

No. The genuine Templar is long since departed. Go view the wondrous tombs in the Temple Church; see there the rigidly-haughty forms stretched out, with crossed arms upon their stilly hearts, in everlasting and undreaming rest. Like the years before the flood, the bold Knights-Templars are no more. Nevertheless, the name remains, and the nominal society, and the ancient grounds, and some of the ancient edifices. But the iron heel is changed to a boot of patent-leather; the long two-handed sword to a one-handed quill; the monk-giver of gratuitous ghostly counsel now counsels for a fee; the defender of the sarcophagus (if in good practice with his weapon) now has more than one case to defend; the vowed opener and clearer of all highways leading to the Holy Sepulchre, now has it in particular charge to check, to clog, to hinder, and embarrass all the courts and avenues of Law; the knight-combatant of the Saracen, breasting spear-points at Acre, now fights law-points in Westminster Hall. The helmet is a wig. Struck by Time's enchanter's wand, the Templar is to-day a Lawyer.

But, like many others tumbled from proud glory's height —like the apple, hard on the bough but mellow on the ground—the Templar's fall has but made him all the finer fellow.

I dare say those old warrior-priests were but gruff and grouty at the best; cased in Birmingham hardware, how could their crimped arms give yours or mine a hearty shake? Their proud, ambitious, monkish souls clasped shut, like horn-book missals; their very faces clapped in bomb-shells; what sort of genial men were these? But best of comrades, most affable of hosts, capital diner is the modern Templar. His wit and wine are both of sparkling brands.

The church and cloisters, courts and vaults, lanes and passages, banquet-halls, refectories, libraries, terraces, gardens, broad walks, domiciles, and dessert-rooms, covering a very large space of ground, and all grouped in central neighborhood, and quite sequestered from the old city's surrounding din; and everything about the place being kept in most bachelor-like particularity, no part of London offers to a quiet wight so agreeable a refuge.

The Temple is, indeed, a city by itself. A city with all

the best appurtenances, as the above enumeration shows. A city with a park to it, and flower-beds, and a river-side— the Thames flowing by as openly, in one part, as by Eden's primal garden flowed the mild Euphrates. In what is now the Temple Garden the old Crusaders used to exercise their steeds and lances; the modern Templars now lounge on the benches beneath the trees, and, switching their patent-leather boots, in gay discourse exercise at repartee.

Long lines of stately portraits in the banquet-halls, show what great men of mark—famous nobles, judges, and Lord Chancellors—have in their time been Templars. But all Templars are not known to universal fame; though, if the having warm hearts and warmer welcomes, full minds and fuller cellars, and giving good advice and glorious dinners, spiced with rare divertisements of fun and fancy, merit immortal mention, set down, ye muses, the names of R. F. C. and his imperial brother.

Though to be a Templar, in the one true sense, you must needs be a lawyer, or a student at the law, and be ceremoniously enrolled as member of the order, yet as many such, though Templars, do not reside within the Temple's precincts, though they may have their offices there, just so, on the other hand, there are many residents of the hoary old domiciles who are not admitted Templars. If being, say, a lounging gentleman and bachelor, or a quiet, unmarried, literary man, charmed with the soft seclusion of the spot, you much desire to pitch your shady tent among the rest in this serene encampment, then you must make some special friend among the order, and procure him to rent, in his name but at your charge, whatever vacant chamber you may find to suit.

Thus, I suppose, did Dr. Johnson, that nominal Benedick and widower but virtual bachelor, when for a space he resided here. So, too, did that undoubted bachelor and rare good soul, Charles Lamb. And hundreds more, of sterling spirits, Brethren of the Order of Celibacy, from time to time have dined, and slept, and tabernacled here. Indeed, the place is all a honey-comb of offices and domiciles. Like any cheese, it is quite perforated through and through in all directions with the snug cells of bachelors. Dear, delightful spot! Ah! when I bethink me of the sweet hours there passed, enjoying such genial hospitalities beneath those time-honored roofs, my heart only finds due utterance through poetry; and, with a sigh, I softly sing, "Carry me back to old Virginny!"

Such then, at large, is the Paradise of Bachelors. And such I found it one pleasant afternoon in the smiling month of May, when, sallying from my hotel in Trafalgar Square, I went to keep my dinner-appointment with that fine Barrister, Bachelor, and Bencher, R. F. C. (he *is* the first and second, and *should be* the third; I hereby nominate him), whose card I kept fast pinched between my gloved forefinger and thumb, and every now and then snatched still another look at the pleasant address inscribed beneath the name, "No —, Elm Court, Temple."

At the core he was a right bluff, care-free, right comfortable, and most companionable Englishman. If on a first acquaintance he seemed reserved, quite icy in his air—patience; this Champagne will thaw. And if it never do, better frozen Champagne than liquid vinegar.

There were nine gentlemen, all bachelors, at the dinner. One was from "No. —, King's Bench Walk, Temple"; a second, third, and fourth, and fifth, from various courts or passages christened with some similarly rich resounding syllables. It was, indeed, a sort of Senate of the Bachelors, sent to this dinner from widely scattered districts, to represent the general celibacy of the Temple. Nay, it was, by representation, a Grand Parliament of the best Bachelors in universal London; several of those present being from distant quarters of the town, noted immemorial seats of lawyers and unmarried men—Lincoln's Inn, Furnival's Inn; and one gentleman, upon whom I looked with a sort of collateral awe, hailed from the spot where Lord Verulam once abode a bachelor—Gray's Inn.

The apartment was well up toward heaven. I know not how many strange old stairs I climbed to get to it. But a good dinner, with famous company, should be well earned. No doubt our host had his dining-room so high with a view to secure the prior exercise necessary to the due relishing and digesting of it.

The furniture was wonderfully unpretending, old, and snug. No new shining mahogany, sticky with undried varnish; no uncomfortably luxurious ottomans, and sofas too fine to use, vexed you in this sedate apartment. It is a thing which every sensible American should learn from every sensible Englishman, that glare and glitter, gim-cracks and gewgaws, are not indispensable to domestic solacement. The American Benedick snatches, down-town, a tough chop in a gilded show-box; the English bachelor leisurely dines at home on that incomparable South Down of his, off a plain deal board.

The ceiling of the room was low. Who wants to dine under the dome of St. Peter's? High ceilings! If that is your demand, and the higher the better, and you be so very tall, then go dine out with the topping giraffe in the open air.

In good time the nine gentlemen sat down to nine covers, and soon were fairly under way.

If I remember right, ox-tail soup inaugurated the affair. Of a rich russet hue, its agreeable flavor dissipated my first confounding of its main ingredient with teamsters' gads and the raw-hides of ushers. (By way of interlude, we here drank a little claret.) Neptune's was the next tribute rendered—turbot coming second; snow-white, flaky, and just gelatinous enough, not too turtleish in its unctuousness.

(At this point we refreshed ourselves with a glass of sherry.) After these light skirmishers had vanished, the heavy artillery of the feast marched in, led by that well-known English generalissimo, roast beef. For aides-de-camp we had a saddle of mutton, a fat turkey, a chicken-pie, and endless other savory things; while for avant-couriers came nine silver flagons of humming ale. This heavy ordnance having departed on the track of the light skirmishers, a picked brigade of game-fowl encamped upon the board, their camp-fires lit by the ruddiest of decanters.

Tarts and puddings followed, with innumerable niceties; then cheese and crackers. (By way of ceremony, simply, only to keep up good old fashions, we here each drank a glass of good old port.)

The cloth was now removed; and, like Blucher's army coming in at the death on the field of Waterloo, in marched a fresh detachment of bottles, dusty with their hurried march.

All these manœuvrings of the forces were superintended by a surprising old field-marshal (I can not school myself to call him by the inglorious name of waiter), with snowy hair and napkin, and a head like Socrates. Amidst all the hilarity of the feast, intent on important business, he disdained to smile. Venerable man!

I have above endeavored to give some slight schedule of the general plan of operations. But any one knows that a good, genial dinner is a sort of pell-mell, indiscriminate affair, quite baffling to detail in all particulars. Thus, I spoke of taking a glass of claret, and a glass of sherry, and a glass of port, and a mug of ale—all at certain specific periods and times. But those were merely the state bumpers, so to speak. Innumerable impromptu glasses were drained between the periods of those grand imposing ones.

The nine bachelors seemed to have the most tender concern for each other's health. All the time, in flowing wine, they most earnestly expressed their sincerest wishes for the entire well-being and lasting hygiene of the gentleman on the right and on the left. I noticed that when one of these kind bachelors desired a little more wine (just for his stomach's sake, like Timothy), he would not help himself to it unless some other bachelor would join him. It seemed held something indelicate, selfish, and unfraternal, to be seen taking a lonely, unparticipated glass. Meantime, as the wine ran apace, the spirits of the company grew more and more to perfect genialness and unconstraint. They related all sorts of pleasant stories. Choice experiences in their private lives were now brought out, like choice brands of Moselle or Rhenish, only kept for particular company. One told us how mellowly he lived when a student at Oxford; with various spicy anecdotes of most frank-hearted noble lords, his liberal companions. Another bachelor, a gray-headed man, with a sunny face, who, by his own account, embraced every opportunity of leisure to cross over into the Low Countries, on sudden tours of inspection of the fine old Flemish architecture there—this learned, white-haired, sunny-faced old bachelor excelled in his descriptions of the elaborate splendors of those old guild-halls, town-halls, and stadthold-houses, to be seen in the land of the ancient Flemings. A third was a great frequenter of the British Museum, and knew all about scores of wonderful antiquities, of Oriental manuscripts, and costly books without a duplicate. A fourth had lately returned from a trip to Old Granada, and, of course, was full of Saracenic scenery. A fifth had a funny case in law to tell. A sixth was erudite in wines. A seventh had a strange characteristic anecdote of the private life of the Iron Duke, never printed, and never before announced in any public or private company. An eighth had lately been amusing his evenings, now and then, with translating

a comic poem of Pulci's. He quoted for us the more amusing passages.

And so the evening slipped along, the hours told, not
by a water-clock, like King Alfred's, but a wine-chronome-
ter. Meantime the table seemed a sort of Epsom Heath; a
regular ring, where the decanters galloped round. For
fear one decanter should not with sufficient speed reach
his destination, another was sent express after him to
hurry him; and then a third to hurry the second; and so
on with a fourth and fifth. And throughout all this nothing
loud, nothing unmannerly, nothing turbulent. I am quite
sure, from the scrupulous gravity and austerity of his air,
that had Socrates, the field-marshal, perceived aught of
indecorum in the company he served, he would have
forthwith departed without giving warning. I afterward
learned that, during the repast, an invalid bachelor in an
adjoining chamber enjoyed his first sound refreshing slumber in three long, weary weeks.

It was the very perfection of quiet absorption of good living, good drinking, good feeling, and good talk. We were a
band of brothers. Comfort—fraternal, household comfort,
was the grand trait of the affair. Also, you could plainly see
that these easy-hearted men had no wives or children to
give an anxious thought. Almost all of them were travelers,
too: for bachelors alone can travel freely, and without any
twinges of their consciences touching desertion of the fire-
side.

The thing called pain, the bugbear styled trouble—those
two legends seemed preposterous to their bachelor imaginations. How could men of liberal sense, ripe scholarship in
the world, and capacious philosophical and convivial un-
derstandings—how could they suffer themselves to be imposed upon by such monkish fables? Pain! Trouble! As
well talk of Catholic miracles. No such thing.—Pass the

sherry, sir.—Pooh, pooh! Can't be!—The port, sir, if you please. Nonsense; don't tell me so.—The decanter stops with you, sir, I believe.

And so it went.

Not long after the cloth was drawn our host glanced significantly upon Socrates, who, solemnly stepping to a stand, returned with an immense convolved horn, a regular Jericho horn, mounted with polished silver, and otherwise chased and curiously enriched; not omitting two life-like goats' heads, with four more horns of solid silver, projecting from opposite sides of the mouth of the noble main horn.

Not having heard that our host was a performer on the bugle, I was surprised to see him lift this horn from the table, as if he were about to blow an inspiring blast. But I was relieved from this, and set quite right as touching the purposes of the horn, by his now inserting his thumb and forefinger into its mouth; whereupon a slight aroma was stirred up, and my nostrils were greeted with the smell of some choice Rappee. It was a mull of snuff. It went the rounds. Capital idea this, thought I, of taking snuff about this juncture. This goodly fashion must be introduced among my countrymen at home, further ruminated I.

The remarkable decorum of the nine bachelors—a decorum not to be affected by any quantity of wine—a decorum unassailable by any degree of mirthfulness—this was again set in a forcible light to me, by now observing that, though they took snuff very freely, yet not a man so far violated the proprieties, or so far molested the invalid bachelor in the adjoining room as to indulge himself in a sneeze. The snuff was snuffed silently, as if it had been some fine innoxious powder brushed off the wings of butterflies.

But fine though they be, bachelors' dinners, like bachelors' lives, can not endure forever. The time came for breaking up. One by one the bachelors took their hats, and two by two, and arm-in-arm they descended, still conversing, to the flagging of the court; some going to their neighboring chambers to turn over the *Decameron* ere retiring for the night; some to smoke a cigar, promenading in the garden on the cool river-side; some to make for the street, call a hack, and be driven snugly to their distant lodgings.

I was the last lingerer.

"Well," said my smiling host, "what do you think of the Temple here, and the sort of life we bachelors make out to live in it?"

"Sir," said I, with a burst of admiring candor—"Sir, this is the very Paradise of Bachelors!"

II

The Tartarus of Maids

IT LIES not far from Woedolor Mountain in New England. Turning to the East, right out from among bright farms and sunny meadows, nodding in early June with odorous grasses, you enter ascendingly among bleak hills. These gradually close in upon a dusky pass, which, from the violent Gulf Stream of air unceasingly driving between its cloven walls of haggard rock, as well as from the tradition of a crazy spinster's hut having long ago stood somewhere hereabouts, is called the Mad Maid's Bellows-pipe.

Winding along at the bottom of the gorge is a dangerously narrow wheel-road, occupying the bed of a former torrent. Following this road to its highest point, you stand as within a Dantean gateway. From the steepness of the walls here, their strangely ebon hue, and the sudden contraction of the gorge, this particular point is called the Black Notch. The ravine now expandingly descends into a great, purple, hopper-shaped hollow, far sunk among many Plutonian, shaggy-wooded mountains. By the country people this hollow is called the Devil's Dungeon. Sounds of torrents fall on all sides upon the ear. These rapid waters unite at last in one turbid brick-colored stream, boiling through a flume among enormous boulders. They call this strange-colored torrent Blood River. Gaining a dark precipice it wheels suddenly to the West, and makes one maniac spring of sixty feet into the arms of a stunted wood of gray-haired pines, between which it thence eddies on its further way down to the invisible low-lands.

Conspicuously crowning a rocky bluff high to one side, at the cataract's verge, is the ruin of an old saw-mill, built in those primitive times when vast pines and hemlocks superabounded throughout the neighboring region. The black-mossed bulk of those immense, rough-hewn, and spike-knotted logs, here and there tumbled all together, in long abandonment and decay, or left in solitary, perilous projection over the cataract's gloomy brink, impart to this rude wooden ruin not only much of the aspect of one of rough-quarried stone, but also a sort of feudal, Rhineland, and Thurmberg look, derived from the pinnacled wildness of the neighboring scenery.

Not far from the bottom of the Dungeon stands a large whitewashed building, relieved, like some great whited sepulchre, against the sullen background of mountain-side firs, and other hardy evergreens, inaccessibly rising in grim terraces for some two thousand feet.

The building is a paper-mill.

Having embarked on a large scale in the seedsman's business (so extensively and broadcast, indeed, that at length my seeds were distributed through all the Eastern and Northern States, and even fell into the far soil of Missouri and the Carolinas), the demand for paper at my place became so great, that the expenditure soon amounted to a most important item in the general account. It need hardly be hinted how paper comes into use with seedsmen, as envelopes. These are mostly made of yellowish paper, folded square; and when filled, are all but flat, and being stamped, and superscribed with the nature of the seeds contained, assume not a little the appearance of business-letters ready for the mail. Of these small envelopes I used an incredible quantity—several hundreds of thousands in a year. For a time I had purchased my paper from the wholesale dealers in a neighboring town. For economy's sake, and partly for the adventure of the trip, I now resolved to cross the mountains, some sixty miles, and order my future paper at the Devil's Dungeon paper-mill.

The sleighing being uncommonly fine toward the end of January, and promising to hold so for no small period, in spite of the bitter cold I started one gray Friday noon in my pung, well fitted with buffalo and wolf robes; and, spending one night on the road, next noon came in sight of Woedolor Mountain.

The far summit fairly smoked with frost; white vapors curled up from its white-wooded top, as from a chimney. The intense congelation made the whole country look like one petrifaction. The steel shoes of my pung craunched and gritted over the vitreous, chippy snow, as if it had been broken glass. The forests here and there skirting the route, feeling the same all-stiffening influence, their inmost fibres penetrated with the cold, strangely groaned—not in the swaying branches merely, but likewise in the vertical trunk—as the fitful gusts remorselessly swept through them. Brittle with excessive frost, many colossal tough-grained maples, snapped in twain like pipestems, cumbered the unfeeling earth.

Flaked all over with frozen sweat, white as a milky ram, his nostrils at each breath sending forth two horn-shaped shoots of heated respiration, Black, my good horse, but six years old, started at a sudden turn, where, right across the track—not ten minutes fallen—an old distorted hemlock lay, darkly undulatory as an anaconda.

Gaining the Bellows-pipe, the violent blast, dead from behind, all but shoved my high-backed pung up-hill. The gust shrieked through the shivered pass, as if laden with lost spirits bound to the unhappy world. Ere gaining the summit, Black, my horse, as if exasperated by the cutting wind, slung out with his strong hind legs, tore the light pung straight up-hill, and sweeping grazingly through the narrow notch, sped downward madly past the ruined saw-mill. Into the Devil's Dungeon horse and cataract rushed together.

With might and main, quitting my seat and robes, and standing backward, with one foot braced against the dash-board, I rasped and churned the bit, and stopped him just in time to avoid collision, at a turn, with the bleak nozzle of a rock, couchant like a lion in the way—a road-side rock.

At first I could not discover the paper-mill.

The whole hollow gleamed with the white, except, here and there, where a pinnacle of granite showed one wind-swept angle bare. The mountains stood pinned in shrouds—a pass of Alpine corpses. Where stands the mill? Suddenly a whirring, humming sound broke upon my ear. I looked, and there, like an arrested avalanche, lay the large white-washed factory. It was subordinately surrounded by a cluster of other and smaller buildings, some of which, from their cheap, blank air, great length, gregarious windows, and comfortless expression, no doubt were boarding-houses of the operatives. A snow-white hamlet amidst the snows. Various rude, irregular squares and courts resulted from the somewhat picturesque clusterings of these build-ings, owing to the broken, rocky nature of the ground, which forbade all method in their relative arrangement. Several narrow lanes and alleys, too, partly blocked with snow fallen from the roof, cut up the hamlet in all directions.

When, turning from the traveled highway, jingling with bells of numerous farmers—who, availing themselves of the fine sleighing, were dragging their wood to market—and frequently diversified with swift cutters dashing from inn to inn of the scattered villages—when, I say, turning from that bustling main-road, I by degrees wound into the Mad Maid's Bellows-pipe, and saw the grim Black Notch beyond, then something latent, as well as something obvious in the time and scene, strangely brought back to my mind my first sight of dark and grimy Temple Bar. And when Black, my horse, went darting through the Notch, perilously grazing its rocky wall, I remembered being in a runaway London omnibus, which in much the same sort of style, though by no means at an equal rate, dashed through the ancient arch of Wren. Though the two objects did by no means completely correspond, yet this partial inadequacy but served to tinge the similitude not less with the vividness than the disorder of a dream. So that, when upon reining up at the protruding rock I at last caught sight of the quaint groupings of the factory-buildings, and with the traveled highway and the Notch behind, found myself all alone, silently and privily stealing through deep-cloven passages into this sequestered spot, and saw the long, high-gabled main factory edifice, with a rude tower—for hoisting heavy boxes—at one end, standing among its crowded outbuildings and boarding-houses, as the Temple Church amidst the surrounding offices and dormitories, and when the marvelous retirement of this mysterious mountain nook fastened its whole spell upon me, then, what memory lacked, all tributary imagination furnished, and I said to myself, "This is the very counterpart of the

Paradise of Bachelors, but snowed upon, and frost-painted to a sepulchre."

Dismounting and warily picking my way down the dangerous declivity—horse and man both sliding now and then upon the icy ledges—at length I drove, or the blast drove me, into the largest square, before one side of the main edifice. Piercingly and shrilly the shotted blast blew by the corner; and redly and demoniacally boiled Blood River at one side. A long wood-pile, of many scores of cords, all glittering in mail of crusted ice, stood crosswise in the square. A row of horse-posts, their north sides plastered with adhesive snow, flanked the factory wall. The bleak frost packed and paved the square as with some ringing metal.

The inverted similitude recurred—"The sweet, tranquil Temple garden, with the Thames bordering its green beds," strangely meditated I.

But where are the gay bachelors?

Then, as I and my horse stood shivering in the wind-spray, a girl ran from a neighboring dormitory door, and throwing her thin apron over her bare head, made for the opposite building.

"One moment, my girl; is there no shed hereabouts which I may drive into?"

Pausing, she turned upon me a face pale with work, and blue with cold; an eye supernatural with unrelated misery.

"Nay," faltered I, "I mistook you. Go on; I want nothing."

Leading my horse close to the door from which she had come, I knocked. Another pale, blue girl appeared, shivering in the doorway as, to prevent the blast, she jealously held the door ajar.

"Nay, I mistake again. In God's name shut the door. But hold, is there no man about?"

That moment a dark-complexioned, well-wrapped personage passed, making for the factory door, and spying him coming, the girl rapidly closed the other one.

"Is there no horse-shed here, sir?"

"Yonder, to the wood-shed," he replied, and disappeared inside the factory.

With much ado I managed to wedge in horse and pung between the scattered piles of wood all sawn and split Then, blanketing my horse, and piling my buffalo on the blanket's top, and tucking in its edges well around the breast-band and breeching, so that the wind might not strip him bare, I tied him fast, and ran lamely for the factory door, stiff with frost, and cumbered with my driver's dread-naught.

Immediately I found myself standing in a spacious place, intolerably lighted by long rows of windows, focusing inward the snowy scene without.

At rows of blank-looking counters sat rows of blank-looking girls, with blank, white folders in their blank hands, all blankly folding blank paper.

In one corner stood some huge frame of ponderous iron, with a vertical thing like a piston periodically rising and falling upon a heavy wooden block. Before it—its tame minister—stood a tall girl, feeding the iron animal with half-quires of rose-hued note-paper which, at every downward dab of the piston-like machine, received in the corner the impress of a wreath of roses. I looked from the rosy paper to the pallid cheek, but said nothing.

Seated before a long apparatus, strung with long, slender strings like any harp, another girl was feeding it with foolscap sheets which, so soon as they curiously traveled from her on the cords, were withdrawn at the opposite end of the machine by a second girl. They came to the first girl blank; they went to the second girl ruled.

I looked upon the first girl's brow, and saw it was young

and fair; I looked upon the second girl's brow, and saw it was ruled and wrinkled. Then, as I still looked, the two—for some small variety to the monotony—changed places; and where had stood the young, fair brow, now stood the ruled and wrinkled one.

Perched high upon a narrow platform, and still higher upon a high stool crowning it, sat another figure serving some other iron animal; while below the platform sat her mate in some sort of reciprocal attendance.

Not a syllable was breathed. Nothing was heard but the low, steady overruling hum of the iron animals. The human voice was banished from the spot. Machinery—that vaunted slave of humanity—here stood menially served by human beings, who served mutely and cringingly as the slave serves the Sultan. The girls did not so much seem accessory wheels to the general machinery as mere cogs to the wheels.

All this scene around me was instantaneously taken in at one sweeping glance—even before I had proceeded to unwind the heavy fur tippet from around my neck. But as soon as this fell from me, the dark-complexioned man, standing close by, raised a sudden cry, and seizing my arm, dragged me out into the open air, and without pausing for a word instantly caught up some congealed snow and began rubbing both my cheeks.

"Two white spots like the whites of your eyes," he said; "man, your cheeks are frozen."

"That may well be," muttered I; " 'tis some wonder the frost of the Devil's Dungeon strikes in no deeper. Rub away."

Soon a horrible, tearing pain caught at my reviving cheeks. Two gaunt blood-hounds, one on each side, seemed mumbling them. I seemed Actæon.

Presently, when all was over, I re-entered the factory, made known my business, concluded it satisfactorily, and then begged to be conducted throughout the place to view it.

"Cupid is the boy for that," said the dark-complexioned man. "Cupid!" and by this odd fancy-name calling a dimpled, red-cheeked, spirited-looking, forward little fellow, who was rather impudently, I thought, gliding about among the passive-looking girls—like a gold-fish through hueless waves—yet doing nothing in particular that I could see, the man bade him lead the stranger through the edifice.

"Come first and see the water-wheel," said this lively lad, with the air of boyishly-brisk importance.

Quitting the folding-room, we crossed some damp, cold boards, and stood beneath a great wet shed, incessantly showering with foam, like the green barnacled bow of some East Indiaman in a gale. Round and round here went the enormous revolutions of the dark colossal water-wheel, grim with its one immutable purpose.

"This sets our whole machinery a-going, sir; in every part of all these buildings; where the girls work and all."

I looked, and saw that the turbid waters of Blood River had not changed their hue by coming under the use of man.

"You make only blank paper; no printing of any sort, I suppose? All blank paper, don't you?"

"Certainly; what else should a paper-factory make?"

The lad here looked at me as if suspicious of my common-sense.

"Oh, to be sure!" said I, confused and stammering; "it only struck me as so strange that red waters should turn out pale chee—paper, I mean."

He took me up a wet and rickety stair to a great light room, furnished with no visible thing but rude, manger-like receptacles running all round its sides; and up to these mangers, like so many mares haltered to the rack, stood rows of girls. Before each was vertically thrust up a long, glittering scythe, immovably fixed at bottom to the manger-edge. The curve of the scythe, and its having no snath to it, made it look exactly like a sword. To and fro, across the sharp edge, the girls forever dragged long strips of rags, washed white, picked from baskets at one side; thus ripping asunder every seam, and converting the tatters almost into lint. The air swam with the fine, poisonous particles, which from all sides darted, subtilely, as motes in sunbeams, into the lungs.

"This is the rag-room," coughed the boy.

"You find it rather stifling here," coughed I, in answer; "but the girls don't cough."

"Oh, they are used to it."

"Where do you get such hosts of rags?" picking up a handful from a basket.

"Some from the country round about; some from far over sea—Leghorn and London."

" 'Tis not unlikely, then," murmured I, "that among these heaps of rags there may be some old shirts, gathered from the dormitories of the Paradise of Bachelors. But the buttons are all dropped off. Pray, my lad, do you ever find any bachelors' buttons hereabouts?"

"None grow in this part of the country. The Devil's Dungeon is no place for flowers."

"Oh! you mean the *flowers* so called—the Bachelor's Buttons?"

"And was not that what you asked about? Or did you mean the gold bosom-buttons of our boss, Old Bach, as our whispering girls all call him?"

"The man, then, I saw below is a bachelor, is he?"

"Oh, yes, he's a Bach."

"The edges of those swords, they are turned outward from the girls, if I see right; but their rags and fingers fly so, I can not distinctly see."

"Turned outward."

Yes, murmured I to myself; I see it now; turned outward; and each erected sword is so borne, edge-outward.

before each girl. If my reading fails me not, just so, of old, condemned state-prisoners went from the hall of judgment to their doom: an officer before, bearing a sword, its edge turned outward, in significance of their fatal sentence. So, through consumptive pallors of this blank, raggy life, go these white girls to death.

"Those scythes look very sharp," again turning toward the boy.

"Yes; they have to keep them so. Look!"

That moment two of the girls, dropping their rags, plied each a whet-stone up and down the sword-blade. My unaccustomed blood curdled at the sharp shriek of the tormented steel.

Their own executioners; themselves whetting the very swords that slay them; meditated I.

"What makes those girls so sheet-white, my lad?"

"Why"—with a roguish twinkle, pure ignorant drollery, not knowing heartlessness—"I suppose the handling of such white bits of sheets all the time makes them so sheety."

"Let us leave the rag-room now, my lad."

More tragical and more inscrutably mysterious than any mystic sight, human or machine, throughout the factory, was the strange innocence of cruel-heartedness in this usage-hardened boy.

"And now," said he, cheerily, "I suppose you want to see our great machine, which cost us twelve thousand dollars only last autumn. That's the machine that makes the paper, too. This way, sir."

Following him, I crossed a large, bespattered place, with two great round vats in it, full of a white, wet, woolly-looking stuff, not unlike the albuminous part of an egg, soft-boiled.

"There," said Cupid, tapping the vats carelessly, "these are the first beginnings of the paper, this white pulp you see. Look how it swims bubbling round and round, moved by the paddle here. From hence it pours from both vats into that one common channel yonder, and so goes, mixed up and leisurely, to the great machine. And now for that."

He led me into a room, stifling with a strange, blood-like, abdominal heat, as if here, true enough, were being finally developed the germinous particles lately seen.

Before me, rolled out like some long Eastern manuscript, lay stretched one continuous length of iron frame-work— multitudinous and mystical, with all sorts of rollers, wheels, and cylinders, in slowly-measured and unceasing motion.

"Here first comes the pulp now," said Cupid, pointing to the nighest end of the machine. "See; first it pours out and spreads itself upon this wide, sloping board; and then— look—slides, thin and quivering, beneath the first roller there. Follow on now, and see it as it slides from under that to the next cylinder. There; see how it has become just a very little less pulpy now. One step more, and it grows still more to some slight consistence. Still another cylinder, and it is so knitted—though as yet mere dragon-fly wing— that it forms an air-bridge here, like a suspended cobweb, between two more separated rollers; and flowing over the last one, and under again, and doubling about there out of sight for a minute among all those mixed cylinders you indistinctly see, it reappears here, looking now at last a little less like pulp and more like paper, but still quite delicate and defective yet awhile. But—a little further onward, sir, if you please—here now, at this further point, it puts on something of a real look, as if it might turn out to be something you might possibly handle in the end. But it's not yet done, sir. Good way to travel yet, and plenty more of cylinders must roll it."

"Bless my soul!" said I, amazed at the elongation, inter- minable convolutions, and deliberate slowness of the machine; "it must take a long time for the pulp to pass from end to end, and come out paper."

"Oh! not so long," smiled the precocious lad, with a superior and patronizing air; "only nine minutes. But look; you may try it for yourself. Have you a bit of paper? Ah! here's a bit on the floor. Now mark that with any word you please, and let me dab it on here, and we'll see how long before it comes out at the other end."

"Well, let me see," said I, taking out my pencil; "come, I'll mark it with your name."

Bidding me take out my watch, Cupid adroitly dropped the inscribed slip on an exposed part of the incipient mass.

Instantly my eye marked the second-hand on my dial-plate.

Slowly I followed the slip, inch by inch; sometimes pausing for full half a minute as it disappeared beneath inscrutable groups of the lower cylinders, but only gradually to emerge again; and so, on, and on, and on—inch by inch; now in open sight, sliding along like a freckle on the quivering sheet; and then again wholly vanished; and so, on, and on, and on—inch by inch; all the time the main sheet growing more and more to final firmness—when, suddenly, I saw a sort of paper-fall, not wholly unlike a water-fall; a scissory sound smote my ear, as of some cord being snapped; and down dropped an unfolded sheet of perfect foolscap, with my "Cupid" half faded out of it, and still moist and warm.

My travels were at an end, for here was the end of the machine.

"Well, how long was it?" said Cupid.

"Nine minutes to a second," replied I, watch in hand. "I told you so."

For a moment a curious emotion filled me, not wholly unlike that which one might experience at the fulfillment of some mysterious prophecy. But how absurd, thought I again; the thing is a mere machine, the essence of which is unvarying punctuality and precision.

Previously absorbed by the wheels and cylinders, my attention was now directed to a sad-looking woman standing by.

"That is rather an elderly person so silently tending the machine-end here. She would not seem wholly used to it either."

"Oh," knowingly whispered Cupid, through the din, "she only came last week. She was a nurse formerly. But the business is poor in these parts, and she's left it. But look at the paper she is piling there."

"Aye, foolscap," handling the piles of moist, warm sheets, which continually were being delivered into the woman's waiting hands. "Don't you turn out anything but foolscap at this machine?"

"Oh, sometimes, but not often, we turn out finer work— cream-laid and royal sheets, we call them. But foolscap being in chief demand, we turn out foolscap most."

It was very curious. Looking at that blank paper continually dropping, dropping, dropping, my mind ran on in wonderings of those strange uses to which those thousand sheets eventually would be put. All sorts of writings would be writ on those now vacant things—sermons, lawyers' briefs, physicians' prescriptions, love-letters, marriage certificates, bills of divorce, registers of births, death-warrants, and so on, without end. Then, recurring back to them as they here lay all blank, I could not but bethink me of that celebrated comparison of John Locke, who, in demonstration of his theory that man had no innate ideas, compared the human mind at birth to a sheet of blank paper; something destined to be scribbled on, but what sort of characters no soul might tell.

Pacing slowly to and fro along the involved machine, still humming with its play, I was struck as well by the inevitability as the evolvement-power in all its motions.

"Does that thin cobweb there," said I, pointing to the

sheet in its more imperfect stage, "does that never tear or break? It is marvelous fragile, and yet this machine it passes through is so mighty."

"It never is known to tear a hair's point."

"Does it never stop—get clogged?"

"No. It *must* go. The machinery makes it go just *so;* just that very way, and at that very pace you there plainly *see* it go. The pulp can't help going."

Something of awe now stole over me, as I gazed upon this inflexible iron animal. Always, more or less, machinery of this ponderous, elaborate sort strikes, in some moods, strange dread into the human heart, as some living, panting Behemoth might. But what made the thing I saw so specially terrible to me was the metallic necessity, the unbudging fatality which governed it. Though, here and there, I could not follow the thin, gauzy vail of pulp in the course of its more mysterious or entirely invisible advance, yet it was indubitable that, at those points where it eluded me, it still marched on in unvarying docility to the autocratic cunning of the machine. A fascination fastened on me. I stood spell-bound and wandering in my soul. Before my eyes—there, passing in slow procession along the wheeling cylinders, I seemed to see, glued to the pallid incipience of the pulp, the yet more pallid faces of all the pallid girls I had eyed that heavy day. Slowly, mournfully, beseechingly, yet unresistingly, they gleamed along, their agony dimly outlined on the imperfect paper, like the print of the tormented face on the handkerchief of Saint Veronica.

"Halloa! the heat of the room is too much for you," cried Cupid, staring at me.

"No—I am rather chill, if anything."

"Come out, sir—out—out," and, with the protecting air of a careful father, the precocious lad hurried me outside.

In a few moments, feeling revived a little, I went into the folding-room—the first room I had entered, and where the desk for transacting business stood, surrounded by the blank counters and blank girls engaged at them.

"Cupid here has led me a strange tour," said I to the dark-complexioned man before mentioned, whom I had ere this discovered not only to be an old bachelor, but also the principal proprietor. "Yours is a most wonderful factory. Your great machine is a miracle of inscrutable intricacy."

"Yes, all our visitors think it so. But we don't have many. We are in a very out-of-the-way corner here. Few inhabitants, too. Most of our girls come from far-off villages."

"The girls," echoed I, glancing round at their silent forms. "Why is it, sir, that in most factories, female operatives, of whatever age, are indiscriminately called girls, never women?"

"Oh! as to that—why, I suppose, the fact of their being generally unmarried—that's the reason, I should think. But it never struck me before. For our factory here, we will not have married women; they are apt to be off-and-on too much. We want none but steady workers: twelve hours to the day, day after day, through the three hundred and sixty-five days, excepting Sundays, Thanksgiving, and Fast-days. That's our rule. And so, having no married women, what females we have are rightly enough called girls."

"Then these are all maids," said I, while some pained homage to their pale virginity made me involuntarily bow.

"All maids."

Again the strange emotion filled me.

"Your cheeks look whitish yet, sir," said the man, gazing at me narrowly. "You must be careful going home. Do they pain you at all now? It's a bad sign, if they do."

"No doubt, sir," answered I, "when once I have got out of the Devil's Dungeon, I shall feel them mending."

"Ah, yes; the winter air in valleys, or gorges, or any sunken place, is far colder and more bitter than elsewhere.

You would hardly believe it now, but it is colder here than at the top of Woedolor Mountain."

"I dare say it is, sir. But time presses me; I must depart."

With that, remuffling myself in dread-naught and tippet, thrusting my hands into my huge seal-skin mittens, I sallied out into the nipping air, and found poor Black, my horse, all cringing and doubled up with the cold.

Soon, wrapped in furs and meditations, I ascended from the Devil's Dungeon.

At the Black Notch I paused, and once more bethought me of Temple Bar. Then, shooting through the pass, all alone with inscrutable nature, I exclaimed—Oh! Paradise of Bachelors! and oh! Tartarus of Maids!

The Lightning-Rod Man

WHAT grand irregular thunder, thought I, standing on my hearth-stone among the Acroceraunian hills, as the scattered bolts boomed overhead, and crashed down among the valleys, every bolt followed by zigzag irradiations, and swift slants of sharp rain, which audibly rang, like a charge of spear-points, on my low shingled roof. I suppose, though, that the mountains hereabouts break and churn up the thunder, so that it is far more glorious here than on the plain. Hark!—some one at the door. Who is this that chooses a time of thunder for making calls? And why don't he, man-fashion, use the knocker, instead of making that doleful undertaker's clatter with his fist against the hollow panel? But let him in. Ah, here he comes. "Good day, sir:" an entire stranger. "Pray be seated." What is that strange-looking walking-stick he carries: "A fine thunder-storm, sir."

"Fine?—Awful!"

"You are wet. Stand here on the hearth before the fire."

"Not for worlds!"

The stranger still stood in the exact middle of the cottage, where he had first planted himself. His singularity impelled a closer scrutiny. A lean, gloomy figure. Hair dark and lank, mattedly streaked over his brow. His sunken pitfalls of eyes were ringed by indigo halos, and played with an innocuous sort of lightning: the gleam without the bolt.

The whole man was dripping. He stood in a puddle on the bare oak floor: his strange walking-stick vertically resting at his side.

It was a polished copper rod, four feet long, lengthwise attached to a neat wooden staff, by insertion into two balls of greenish glass, ringed with copper bands. The metal rod terminated at the top tripodwise, in three keen tines, brightly gilt. He held the thing by the wooden part alone.

"Sir," said I, bowing politely, "have I the honor of a visit from that illustrious god, Jupiter Tonans? So stood he in the Greek statue of old, grasping the lightning-bolt. If you be he, or his viceroy, I have to thank you for this noble storm you have brewed among our mountains. Listen: that was a glorious peal. Ah, to a lover of the majestic, it is a good thing to have the Thunderer himself in one's cottage. The thunder grows finer for that. But pray be seated. This old rush-bottomed arm-chair, I grant, is a poor substitute for your evergreen throne on Olympus; but, condescend to be seated."

While I thus pleasantly spoke, the stranger eyed me, half in wonder, and half in a strange sort of horror; but did not move a foot.

"Do, sir, be seated; you need to be dried ere going forth again."

I planted the chair invitingly on the broad hearth, where a little fire had been kindled that afternoon to dissipate the dampness, not the cold; for it was early in the month of September.

But without heeding my solicitation, and still standing in the middle of the floor, the stranger gazed at me portentously and spoke.

"Sir," said he, "excuse me; but instead of my accepting your invitation to be seated on the hearth there, I solemnly warn *you*, that you had best accept *mine*, and stand with me in the middle of the room. Good Heavens!" he cried, starting—"there is another of those awful crashes. I warn you, sir, quit the hearth."

"Mr. Jupiter Tonans," said I, quietly rolling my body on the stone, "I stand very well here."

"Are you so horridly ignorant, then," he cried, "as not to know, that by far the most dangerous part of a house, during such a terrific tempest as this, is the fire-place?"

"Nay, I did not know that," involuntarily stepping upon the first board next to the stone.

The stranger now assumed such an unpleasant air of successful admonition, that—quite involuntarily again—I stepped back upon the hearth, and threw myself into the erectest, proudest posture I could command. But I said nothing.

"For Heaven's sake," he cried, with a strange mixture of alarm and intimidation—"for Heaven's sake, get off the hearth! Know you not, that the heated air and soot are conductors;—to say nothing of those immense iron fire-dogs? Quit the spot—I conjure—I command you."

"Mr. Jupiter Tonans, I am not accustomed to be commanded in my own house."

"Call me not by that pagan name. You are profane in this time of terror."

"Sir, will you be so good as to tell me your business? If you seek shelter from the storm, you are welcome, so long as you be civil; but if you come on business, open it forthwith. Who are you?"

"I am a dealer in lightning-rods," said the stranger, softening his tone; "my special business is——— Merciful Heaven! what a crash!—Have you ever been struck—your premises, I mean? No? It's best to be provided,"—significantly rattling his metallic staff on the floor,—"by nature, there are no castles in thunder-storms; yet, say but the word, and of this cottage I can make a Gibraltar by a few waves of this wand. Hark, what Himalayas of concussions!"

"You interrupted yourself; your special business you were about to speak of."

"My special business is to travel the country for orders for lightning-rods. This is my specimen rod;" tapping his staff; "I have the best of references"—fumbling in his pockets. "In Criggan last month, I put up three-and-twenty rods on only five buildings."

"Let me see. Was it not at Criggan last week, about midnight on Saturday, that the steeple, the big elm, and the assembly-room cupola were struck? Any of your rods there?"

"Not on the tree and cupola, but the steeple."

"Of what use is your rod, then?"

"Of life-and-death use. But my workman was heedless. In fitting the rod at top to the steeple, he allowed a part of the metal to graze the tin sheeting. Hence the accident. Not my fault, but his. Hark!"

"Never mind. That clap burst quite loud enough to be heard without finger-pointing. Did you hear of the event at Montreal last year? A servant girl struck at her bed-side with a rosary in her hand; the beads being metal. Does your beat extend into the Canadas?"

"No. And I hear that there, iron rods only are in use. They should have *mine*, which are copper. Iron is easily fused. Then they draw out the rod so slender, that it has not body enough to conduct the full electric current. The metal melts; the building is destroyed. My copper rods never act so. Those Canadians are fools. Some of them knob the rod at the top, which risks a deadly explosion, instead of imperceptibly carrying down the current into the earth, as this sort of rod does. *Mine* is the only true rod. Look at it. Only one dollar a foot."

"This abuse of your own calling in another might make one distrustful with respect to yourself."

"Hark! The thunder becomes less muttering. It is nearing us, and nearing the earth, too. Hark! One crammed crash! All the vibrations made one by nearness. Another flash. Hold."

"What do you?" I said, seeing him now instantaneously relinquishing his staff, lean intently forward towards the window, with his right fore and middle fingers on his left wrist.

But ere the words had well escaped me, another exclamation escaped him.

"Crash! only three pulses—less than a third of a mile off—yonder, somewhere in that wood. I passed three stricken oaks there, ripped out new and glittering. The oak draws lightning more than other timber, having iron in solution in its sap. Your floor here seems oak."

"Heart-of-oak. From the peculiar time of your call upon me, I suppose you purposely select stormy weather for your journeys. When the thunder is roaring, you deem it an hour peculiarly favorable for producing impressions favorable to your trade."

"Hark!—Awful!"

"For one who would arm others with fearlessness, you seem unbeseemingly timorous yourself. Common men choose fair weather for their travels: you choose thunderstorms; and yet ———"

"That I travel in thunder-storms, I grant; but not without particular precautions, such as only a lightning-rod man may know. Hark! Quick—look at my specimen rod. Only one dollar a foot."

"A very fine rod, I dare say. But what are these particular precautions of yours? Yet first let me close yonder shutters; the slanting rain is beating through the sash. I will bar up."

"Are you mad? Know you not that yon iron bar is a swift conductor? Desist."

"I will simply close the shutters, then, and call my boy to bring me a wooden bar. Pray, touch the bell-pull there."

"Are you frantic? That bell-wire might blast you. Never touch bell-wire in a thunder-storm, nor ring a bell of any sort."

"Nor those in belfries? Pray, will you tell me where and how one may be safe in a time like this? Is there any part of my house I may touch with hopes of my life?"

"There is; but not where you now stand. Come away from the wall. The current will sometimes run down a wall, and—a man being a better conductor than a wall—it would leave the wall and run into him. Swoop! *That* must have fallen very nigh. That must have been globular lightning."

"Very probably. Tell me at once, which is, in your opinion, the safest part of this house?"

"This room, and this one spot in it where I stand. Come hither."

"The reasons first."

"Hark!—after the flash the gust—the sashes shiver— the house, the house!—Come hither to me!"

"The reasons, if you please."

"Come hither to me!"

"Thank you again, I think I will try my old stand—the hearth. And now, Mr. Lightning-rod-man, in the pauses of the thunder, be so good as to tell me your reasons for esteeming this one room of the house the safest, and your own one stand-point there the safest spot in it."

There was now a little cessation of the storm for a while. The Lightning-rod man seemed relieved, and replied:—

"Your house is a one-storied house, with an attic and a cellar; this room is between. Hence its comparative safety. Because lightning sometimes passes from the clouds to the earth, and sometimes from the earth to the clouds. Do you comprehend?—and I choose the middle of the room, because, if the lightning should strike the house at all, it would come down the chimney or walls; so, obviously, the further you are from them, the better. Come hither to me, now."

"Presently. Something you just said, instead of alarming me, has strangely inspired confidence."

"What have I said?"

"You said that sometimes lightning flashes from the earth to the clouds."

"Aye, the returning-stroke, as it is called; when the earth, being overcharged with the fluid, flashes its surplus upward."

"The returning-stroke; that is, from earth to sky. Better and better. But come here on the hearth and dry yourself."

"I am better here, and better wet."

"How?"

"It is the safest thing you can do—Hark, again!—to get yourself thoroughly drenched in a thunder-storm. Wet clothes are better conductors than the body; and so, if the lightning strike, it might pass down the wet clothes without touching the body. The storm deepens again. Have you a rug in the house? Rugs are non-conductors. Get one, that I may stand on it here, and you, too. The skies blacken—it is dusk at noon. Hark!—the rug, the rug!"

I gave him one; while the hooded mountains seemed closing and tumbling into the cottage.

"And now, since our being dumb will not help us," said I, resuming my place, "let me hear your precautions in traveling during thunder-storms."

"Wait till this one is passed."

"Nay, proceed with the precautions. You stand in the safest possible place according to your own account. Go on."

"Briefly, then. I avoid pine-trees, high houses, lonely

barns, upland pastures, running water, flocks of cattle and sheep, a crowd of men. If I travel on foot—as to-day— I do not walk fast; if in my buggy, I touch not its back or sides; if on horseback, I dismount and lead the horse. But of all things, I avoid tall men."

"Do I dream? Man avoid man? and in danger-time, too."

"Tall men in a thunder-storm I avoid. Are you so grossly ignorant as not to know, that the height of a six-footer is sufficient to discharge an electric cloud upon him? Are not lonely Kentuckians, ploughing, smit in the unfinished furrow? Nay, if the six-footer stand by running water, the cloud will sometimes *select* him as its conductor to that running water. Hark! Sure, yon black pinnacle is split. Yes, a man is a good conductor. The lightning goes through and through a man, but only peels a tree. But sir, you have kept me so long answering your questions, that I have not yet come to business. Will you order one of my rods? Look at this specimen one? See: it is of the best of copper. Copper's the best conductor. Your house is low; but being upon the mountains, that lowness does not one whit depress it. You mountaineers are most exposed. In mountainous countries the lightning-rod man should have most business. Look at the specimen, sir. One rod will answer for a house so small as this. Look over these recommendations. Only one rod, sir; cost, only twenty dollars. Hark! There go all the granite Taconics and Hoosics dashed together like pebbles. By the sound, that must have struck something. An elevation of five feet above the house, will protect twenty feet radius all about the rod. Only twenty dollars, sir—a dollar a foot. Hark!—Dreadful!—Will you order? Will you buy? Shall I put down your name? Think of being a heap of charred offal, like a haltered horse burnt in his stall; and all in one flash!"

"You pretended envoy extraordinary and minister pleni-potentiary to and from Jupiter Tonans," laughed I; "you mere man who come here to put you and your pipestem between clay and sky, do you think that because you can strike a bit of green light from the Leyden jar, that you can thoroughly avert the supernal bolt? Your rod rusts, or breaks, and where are you? Who has empowered you, you Tetzel, to peddle round your indulgences from divine ordinations? The hairs of our heads are numbered, and the days of our lives. In thunder as in sunshine, I stand at ease in the hands of my God. False negotiator, away! See, the scroll of the storm is rolled back; the house is unharmed; and in the blue heavens I read in the rainbow, that the Deity will not, of purpose, make war on man's earth."

"Impious wretch!" foamed the stranger, blackening in the face as the rainbow beamed, "I will publish your infidel notions."

"Begone! move quickly! if quickly you can, you that shine forth into sight in moist times like the worm."

The scowl grew blacker on his face; the indigo-circles enlarged round his eyes as the storm-rings round the midnight moon. He sprang upon me, his tri-forked thing at my heart.

I seized it; I snapped it; I dashed it; I trod it; and dragging the dark lightning-king out of my door, flung his elbowed, copper sceptre after him.

But spite of my treatment, and spite of my dissuasive talk of him to my neighbors, the Lightning-rod man still dwells in the land; still travels in storm-time, and drives a brave trade with the fears of man.

The Happy Failure:
A Story of the River Hudson

THE appointment was that I should meet my elderly
uncle at the river-side, precisely at nine in the
morning. The skiff was to be ready, and the apparatus to be brought down by his grizzled old black man.
As yet, the nature of the wonderful experiment remained
a mystery to all but the projector.

I was first on the spot. The village was high up the river,
and the inland summer sun was already oppressively warm.
Presently I saw my uncle advancing beneath the trees, hat
off, and wiping his brow; while far behind staggered poor
old Yorpy, with what seemed one of the gates of Gaza
on his back.

"Come, hurrah, stump along, Yorpy!" cried my uncle,
impatiently turning round every now and then.

Upon the black's staggering up to the skiff, I perceived
that the great gate of Gaza was transformed into a huge,
shabby, oblong box, hermetically sealed. The sphinx-like
blankness of the box quadrupled the mystery in my mind.

"Is *this* the wonderful apparatus?" said I, in amazement.
"Why, it's nothing but a battered old dry-goods box, nailed
up. And is *this* the thing, uncle, that is to make you a
million of dollars ere the year be out? What a forlorn-
looking, lack-lustre, old ash-box it is."

"Put it into the skiff!" roared my uncle to Yorpy, without
heeding my boyish disdain. "Put it in, you grizzle-headed

223

cherub—put it in carefully, carefully! If that box bursts, my everlasting fortune collapses."

"Bursts?—collapses?" cried I, in alarm. "It ain't full of combustibles? Quick! let me go to the further end of the boat!"

"Sit still, you simpleton!" cried my uncle again. "Jump in, Yorpy, and hold on to the box like grim death while I shove off. Carefully! carefully! you dunderheaded black! Mind t'other side of the box, I say! Do you mean to destroy the box?"

"Duyvel take de pox!" muttered old Yorpy, who was a sort of Dutch African. "De pox has been my cuss for de ten long 'ear."

"Now, then, we're off—take an oar, youngster; you, Yorpy, clinch the box fast. Here we go now. Carefully! carefully! You, Yorpy, stop shaking the box! Easy! easy! there's a big snag. Pull now. Hurrah! deep water at last! Now give way, youngster, and away to the island."

"The island!" said I. "There's no island hereabouts."

"There is ten miles above the bridge, though," said my uncle, determinately.

"Ten miles off! Pull that old dry-goods box ten miles up the river in this blazing sun!"

"All that I have to say," said my uncle, firmly, "is that we are bound to Quash Island."

"Mercy, uncle! If I had known of this great long pull of ten mortal miles in this fiery sun, you wouldn't have juggled *me* into the skiff so easy. What's *in* that box?— paving-stones? See how the skiff settles down under it. I won't help pull a box of paving-stones ten miles. What's the use of pulling 'em?"

"Look you, simpleton," quoth my uncle, pausing upon his suspended oar. "Stop rowing, will ye! Now then, if you don't want to share in the glory of my experiment; if you are wholly indifferent to halving its immortal renown; I say, sir,

if you care not to be present at the first trial of my Great
Hydraulic-Hydrostatic Apparatus for draining swamps and
marshes, and converting them, at the rate of one acre the
hour, into fields more fertile than those of the Genessee;
if you care not, I repeat, to have this proud thing to tell—
in far future days, when poor old I shall have been long
dead and gone, boy—to your children, and your children's
children; in that case, sir, you are free to land forthwith."

"Oh, uncle! I did not mean—"

"No words, sir! Yorpy, take his oar, and help pull him
ashore."

"But, my dear uncle; I declare to you that—"

"Not a syllable, sir; you have cast open scorn upon the
Great Hydraulic-Hydrostatic Apparatus. Yorpy, put him
ashore, Yorpy. It's shallow here again. Jump out, Yorpy, and
wade with him ashore."

"Now, my dear, good, kind uncle, do but pardon me this
one time, and I will say just nothing about the apparatus."

"Say nothing about it! When it is my express end and aim
it shall be famous! Put him ashore, Yorpy."

"Nay, uncle, I *will* not give up my oar. I have an oar in
this matter, and I mean to keep it. You shall not cheat me
out of my share of your glory."

"Ah, now there—that's sensible. You may stay, youngster.
Pull again now."

We were all silent for a time, steadily plying our way. At
last I ventured to break water once more.

"I am glad, dear uncle, you have revealed to me at last
the nature and end of your great experiment. It is the
effectual draining of swamps; an attempt, dear uncle, in
which, if you do but succeed (as I know you will), you
will earn the glory denied to a Roman emperor. He tried
to drain the Pontine marsh, but failed."

"The world has shot ahead the length of its own diameter
since then," quoth my uncle, proudly. "If that Roman

emperor were here, I'd show him what can be done in the present enlightened age."

Seeing my good uncle so far mollified now as to be quite self-complacent, I ventured another remark.

"This is a rather severe, hot pull, dear uncle."

"Glory is not to be gained, youngster, without pulling hard for it—against the stream, too, as we do now. The natural tendency of man, in the mass, is to go down with the universal current into oblivion."

"But why pull so far, dear uncle, upon the present occasion? Why pull ten miles for it? You do but propose, as I understand it, to put to the actual test this admirable invention of yours. And could it not be tested almost anywhere?"

"Simple boy," quoth my uncle, "would you have some malignant spy steal from me the fruits of ten long years of high-hearted, persevering endeavor? Solitary in my scheme, I go to a solitary place to test it. If I fail—for all things are possible—no one out of the family will know it. If I succeed, secure in the secrecy of my invention, I can boldly demand any price for its publication."

"Pardon me, dear uncle; you are wiser than I."

"One would think years and gray hairs should bring wisdom, boy."

"Yorpy there, dear uncle; think you his grizzled locks thatch a brain improved by long life?"

"Am I Yorpy, boy? Keep to your oar!"

Thus padlocked again, I said no further word till the skiff grounded on the shallows, some twenty yards from the deep-wooded isle.

"Hush!" whispered my uncle, intensely; "not a word now!" and he sat perfectly still, slowly sweeping with his glance the whole country around, even to both banks of the here wide-expanded stream.

"Wait till that horseman, yonder, passes!" he whispered

again, pointing to a speck moving along a lofty river-side road, which perilously wound on midway up a long line of broken bluffs and cliffs. "There—he's out of sight now, behind the copse. Quick! Yorpy! Carefully, though! Jump overboard, and shoulder the box, and—Hold!"

We were all mute and motionless again.

"Ain't that a boy, sitting like Zacchæus in yonder tree of the orchard on the other bank? Look, youngster—young eyes are better than old—don't you see him?"

"Dear uncle, I see the orchard, but I can't see any boy."

"He's a spy—I know he is," suddenly said my uncle, disregardful of my answer, and intently gazing, shading his eyes with his flattened hand. "Don't touch the box, Yorpy. Crouch! crouch down, all of ye!"

"Why, uncle—there—see—the boy is only a withered white bough. I see it very plainly now."

"You don't see the tree I mean," quoth my uncle, with a decided air of relief, "but never mind; I defy the boy. Yorpy, jump out, and shoulder the box. And now then, youngster, off with your shoes and stockings, roll up your trowsers legs, and follow me. Carefully, Yorpy, carefully. That's more precious than a box of gold, mind."

"Heavy as de gelt, anyhow," growled Yorpy, staggering and splashing in the shallows beneath it.

"There, stop under the bushes there—in among the flags—so—gently, gently—there, put it down just there. Now, youngster, are you ready? Follow—tiptoes, tiptoes!"

"I can't wade in this mud and water on my tiptoes, uncle; and I don't see the need of it either."

"Go ashore, sir—instantly!"

"Why, uncle, I *am* ashore."

"Peace! follow me, and no more."

Crouching in the water in complete secrecy, beneath the bushes and among the tall flags, my uncle now stealthily produced a hammer and wrench from one of his enormous pockets, and presently tapped the box. But the sound alarmed him.

"Yorpy," he whispered, "go you off to the right, behind the bushes, and keep watch. If you see anyone coming, whistle softly. Youngster, you do the same to the left."

We obeyed; and presently, after considerable hammering and supplemental tinkering, my uncle's voice was heard in the utter solitude, loudly commanding our return.

Again we obeyed, and now found the cover of the box removed. All eagerness, I peeped in, and saw a surprising multiplicity of convoluted metal pipes and syringes of all sorts and varieties, all sizes and calibres, inextricably interwreathed together in one gigantic coil. It looked like a huge nest of anacondas and adders.

"Now then, Yorpy," said my uncle, all animation, and flushed with the foretaste of glory, "do you stand this side, and be ready to tip when I give the word. And do you, youngster, stand ready to do as much for the other side. Mind, don't budge it the fraction of a barley-corn till I say the word. All depends on a proper adjustment."

"No fear, uncle. I will be careful as a lady's tweezers."

"I s'ant lift de heavy pox," growled old Yorpy, "till de wort pe given; no fear o' dat."

"Oh boy," said my uncle now, upturning his face devotionally, while a really noble gleam irradiated his gray eyes, locks, and wrinkles; "oh boy! this, *this* is the hour which for ten long years has, in the prospect, sustained me through all my painstaking obscurity. Fame will be the sweeter because it comes at the last; the truer, because it comes to an old man like me, not to a boy like you. Sustainer! I glorify Thee."

He bowed over his venerable head, and—as I live— something like a shower-drop somehow fell from my face into the shallows.

"Tip!"

We tipped.

"A little more!"

We tipped a little more.

"A *leetle* more!"

We tipped a *leetle* more.

"Just a *leetle*, very *leetle* bit more."

With great difficulty we tipped just a *leetle*, very *leetle* more.

All this time my uncle was diligently stooping over, and striving to peep in, up, and under the box where the coiled anacondas and adders lay; but the machine being now fairly immersed, the attempt was wholly vain.

He rose erect, and waded slowly all round the box; his countenance firm and reliant, but not a little troubled and vexed.

It was plain something or other was going wrong. But as I was left in utter ignorance as to the mystery of the contrivance, I could not tell where the difficulty lay, or what was the proper remedy.

Once more, still more slowly, still more vexedly, my uncle waded round the box, the dissatisfaction gradually deepening, but still controlled, and still with hope at the bottom of it.

Nothing could be more sure than that some anticipated effect had, as yet, failed to develop itself. Certain I was, too, that the waterline did not lower about my legs.

"Tip it a *leetle* bit—very *leetle* now."

"Dear uncle, it is tipped already as far as it can be. Don't you see it rests now square on its bottom?"

"You, Yorpy, take your black hoof from under the box!"

This gust of passion on the part of my uncle made the matter seem still more dubious and dark. It was a bad symptom, I thought.

"Surely you *can* tip it just a *leetle* more!"

"Not a hair, uncle."

"Blast and blister the cursed box, then!" roared my uncle, in a terrific voice, sudden as a squall. Running at the box, he dashed his bare foot into it, and with astonishing power all but crushed in the side. Then, seizing the whole box, he disemboweled it of all its anacondas and adders, and, tearing and wrenching them, flung them right and left over the water.

"Hold, hold, my dear, dear uncle!—do, for Heaven's sake, desist. Don't destroy so, in one frantic moment, all your long calm years of devotion to one darling scheme. Hold, I conjure!"

Moved by my vehement voice and uncontrollable tears, he paused in his work of destruction, and stood steadfastly eying me, or rather blankly staring at me, like one demented.

"It is not yet wholly ruined, dear uncle; come put it together now. You have hammer and wrench; put it together again, and try it once more. While there is life there is hope."

"While there is life hereafter there is *despair*," he howled.

"Do, do now, dear uncle—here, here, put these pieces together; or, if that can't be done without more tools, try a *section* of it—that will do just as well. Try it once; try, uncle."

My persistent persuasiveness told upon him. The stubborn stump of hope, plowed at and uprooted in vain, put forth one last miraculous green sprout.

Steadily and carefully culling out of the wreck some of the more curious-looking fragments, he mysteriously involved them together, and then, clearing out the box, slowly inserted them there, and ranging Yorpy and me as before, bade us tip the box once again.

We did so; and as no perceptible effect yet followed, I was each moment looking for the previous command to tip the box over yet more, when, glancing into my uncle's face, I started aghast. It seemed pinched, shriveled into mouldy whiteness, like a mildewed grape. I dropped the box, and sprang toward him just in time to prevent his fall.

Leaving the woeful box where we had dropped it, Yorpy and I helped the old man into the skiff, and silently pulled from Quash Isle.

How swiftly the current now swept us down! How hardly before had we striven to stem it! I thought of my poor uncle's saying, not an hour gone by, about the universal drift of the mass of humanity toward utter oblivion.

"Boy!" said my uncle at last, lifting his head.

I looked at him earnestly, and was gladdened to see that the terrible blight of his face had almost departed.

"Boy, there's not much left in an old world for an old man to invent."

I said nothing.

"Boy, take my advice, and never try to invent anything but—happiness."

I said nothing.

"Boy, about ship, and pull back for the box."

"Dear uncle!"

"It will make a good wood-box, boy. And faithful old Yorpy can sell the old iron for tobacco-money."

"Dear massa! dear old massa! dat be very fust time in de ten long 'ear yoo hab mention kindly old Yorpy. I tank yoo, dear old massa; I tank yoo so kindly. Yoo is yourself again in de ten long 'ear."

"Aye, long ears enough," sighed my uncle; "Æsopian ears. But it's all over now. Boy, I'm glad I've failed. I say, boy, failure has made a good old man of me. It was horrible at first, but I'm glad I've failed. Praise be to God for the failure!"

His face kindled with a strange, rapt earnestness. I have never forgotten that look. If the event made my uncle a good old man, as he called it, it made me a wise young one. Example did for me the work of experience.

When some years had gone by, and my dear old uncle began to fail, and, after peaceful days of autumnal content, was gathered gently to his fathers—faithful old Yorpy closing his eyes—as I took my last look at his venerable face, the pale resigned lips seemed to move. I seemed to hear again his deep, fervent cry—"Praise be to God for the failure!"

The Fiddler

So my poem is damned, and immortal fame is not for
me! I am nobody forever and ever. Intolerable fate!
Snatching my hat, I dashed down the criticism,
and rushed out into Broadway, where enthusiastic throngs
were crowding to a circus in a side-street near by, very
recently started, and famous for a capital clown.

Presently my old friend Standard rather boisterously
accosted me.

"Well met, Helmstone, my boy! Ah! what's the matter?
Haven't been committing murder? Ain't flying justice?
You look wild!"

"You have seen it, then?" said I, of course referring to
the criticism.

"Oh yes; I was there at the morning performance. Great
clown, I assure you. But here comes Hautboy. Hautboy—
Helmstone."

Without having time or inclination to resent so mortify-
ing a mistake, I was instantly soothed as I gazed on the
face of the new acquaintance so unceremoniously introduced. His person was short and full, with a juvenile,
animated cast to it. His complexion rurally ruddy; his eye
sincere, cheery, and gray. His hair alone betrayed that he
was not an overgrown boy. From his hair I set him down
as forty or more.

"Come, Standard," he gleefully cried to my friend, "are

you not going to the circus? The clown is inimitable, they say. Come; Mr. Helmstone, too—come both; and circus over, we'll take a nice stew and punch at Taylor's."

The sterling content, good humor, and extraordinary ruddy, sincere expression of this most singular new acquaintance acted upon me like magic. It seemed mere loyalty to human nature to accept an invitation from so unmistakably kind and honest a heart.

During the circus performance I kept my eye more on Hautboy than on the celebrated clown. Hautboy was the sight for me. Such genuine enjoyment as his struck me to the soul with a sense of the reality of the thing called happiness. The jokes of the clown he seemed to roll under his tongue as ripe magnum bonums. Now the foot, now the hand, was employed to attest his grateful applause. At any hit more than ordinary, he turned upon Standard and me to see if his rare pleasure was shared. In a man of forty I saw a boy of twelve; and this too without the slightest abatement of my respect. Because all was so honest and natural, every expression and attitude so graceful with genuine good-nature, that the marvelous juvenility of Hautboy assumed a sort of divine and immortal air, like that of some forever youthful god of Greece.

But much as I gazed upon Hautboy, and much as I admired his air, yet that desperate mood in which I had first rushed from the house had not so entirely departed as not to molest me with momentary returns. But from these relapses I would rouse myself, and swiftly glance round the broad amphitheatre of eagerly interested and all-applauding human faces. Hark! claps, thumps, deafening huzzas; the vast assembly seemed frantic with acclamation; and what, mused I, has caused all this? Why, the clown only comically grinned with one of his extra grins.

Then I repeated in my mind that sublime passage in my poem, in which Cleothemes the Argive vindicates the justice of the war. Aye, aye, thought I to myself, did I now leap into the ring there, and repeat that identical passage, nay, enact the whole tragic poem before them, would they applaud the poet as they applaud the clown? No! They would hoot me, and call me doting or mad. Then what does this prove? Your infatuation or their insensibility? Perhaps both; but indubitably the first. But why wail? Do you seek admiration from the admirers of a buffoon? Call to mind the saying of the Athenian, who, when the people vociferously applauded in the forum, asked his friend in a whisper, what foolish thing had he said?

Again my eye swept the circus, and fell on the ruddy radiance of the countenance of Hautboy. But its clear honest cheeriness disdained my disdain. My intolerant pride was rebuked. And yet Hautboy dreamed not what magic reproof to a soul like mine sat on his laughing brow. At the very instant I felt the dart of the censure, his eye twinkled, his hand waved, his voice was lifted in jubilant delight at another joke of the inexhaustible clown.

Circus over, we went to Taylor's. Among crowds of others, we sat down to our stews and punches at one of the small marble tables. Hautboy sat opposite to me. Though greatly subdued from its former hilarity, his face still shone with gladness. But added to this was a quality not so prominent before: a certain serene expression of leisurely, deep good sense. Good sense and good humor in him joined hands. As the conversation proceeded between the brisk Standard and him—for I said little or nothing—I was more and more struck with the excellent judgment he evinced. In most of his remarks upon a variety of topics Hautboy seemed intuitively to hit the exact line between enthusiasm and apathy. It was plain that while Hautboy saw the world pretty much as it was, yet he did not theoretically espouse its bright side nor its dark side. Rejecting all solutions, he but acknowledged facts. What was sad in the world he did not superficially gainsay; what was glad in it he did not cynically slur; and all which was to him personally enjoyable, he gratefully took to his heart. It was plain, then—so it seemed at that moment, at least—that his extraordinary cheerfulness did not arise either from deficiency of feeling or thought.

Suddenly remembering an engagement, he took up his hat, bowed pleasantly, and left us.

"Well, Helmstone," said Standard, inaudibly drumming on the slab, "what do you think of your new acquaintance?"

The two last words tingled with a peculiar and novel significance.

"New acquaintance indeed," echoed I. "Standard, I owe you a thousand thanks for introducing me to one of the most singular men I have ever seen. It needed the optical sight of such a man to believe in the possibility of his existence."

"You rather like him, then," said Standard, with ironical dryness.

"I hugely love and admire him, Standard. I wish I were Hautboy."

"Ah? That's a pity, now. There's only one Hautboy in the world."

This last remark set me to pondering again, and somehow it revived my dark mood.

"His wonderful cheerfulness, I suppose," said I, sneering with spleen, "originates not less in a felicitous fortune than in a felicitous temper. His great good sense is apparent; but great good sense may exist without sublime endowments. Nay, I take it, in certain cases, that good sense is simply owing to the absence of those. Much more, cheerfulness. Unpossessed of genius, Hautboy is eternally blessed."

"Ah? You would not think him an extraordinary genius, then?"

"Genius? What! such a short, fat fellow a genius! Genius, like Cassius, is lank."

"Ah? But could you not fancy that Hautboy might formerly have had genius, but luckily getting rid of it, at last fatted up?"

"For a genius to get rid of his genius is as impossible as for a man in the galloping consumption to get rid of that."

"Ah? You speak very decidedly."

"Yes, Standard," cried I, increasing in spleen, "your cheery Hautboy, after all, is no pattern, no lesson for you and me. With average abilities; opinions clear, because circumscribed; passions docile, because they are feeble; a temper hilarious, because he was born to it—how can your Hautboy be made a reasonable example to a heady fellow like you, or an ambitious dreamer like me? Nothing tempts him beyond common limit; in himself he has nothing to restrain. By constitution he is exempted from all moral harm. Could ambition but prick him; had he but once heard applause, or endured contempt, a very different man would your Hautboy be. Acquiescent and calm from the cradle to the grave, he obviously slides through the crowd."

"Ah?"

"Why do you say *Ah* to me so strangely whenever I speak?"

"Did you ever hear of Master Betty?"

"The great English prodigy, who long ago ousted the Siddons and the Kembles from Drury Lane, and made the whole town run mad with acclamation?"

"The same," said Standard, once more inaudibly drumming on the slab.

I looked at him perplexed. He seemed to be holding the master-key of our theme in mysterious reserve; seemed to be throwing out his Master Betty, too, to puzzle me only the more.

"What under heaven can Master Betty, the great genius and prodigy, an English boy twelve years old, have to do with the poor commonplace plodder, Hautboy, an American of forty?"

"Oh, nothing in the least. I don't imagine that they ever saw each other. Besides, Master Betty must be dead and buried long ere this."

"Then why cross the ocean, and rifle the grave to drag his remains into this living discussion?"

"Absent-mindedness, I suppose. I humbly beg pardon. Proceed with your observations on Hautboy. You think he never had genius, quite too contented, and happy and fat for that—ah? You think him no pattern for men in general? affording no lesson of value to neglected merit, genius ignored, or impotent presumption rebuked?—all of which three amount to much the same thing. You admire his cheerfulness, while scorning his commonplace soul. Poor Hautboy, how sad that your very cheerfulness should, by a by-blow, bring you despite!"

"I don't say I scorn him; you are unjust. I simply declare that he is no pattern for me."

A sudden noise at my side attracted my ear. Turning, I saw Hautboy again, who very blithely reseated himself on the chair he had left.

"I was behind time with my engagement," said Hautboy, "so thought I would run back and rejoin you. But come, you have sat long enough here. Let us go to my rooms. It is only a five minutes' walk."

"If you will promise to fiddle for us, we will," said Standard.

Fiddle! thought I—he's a jiggumbob *fiddler*, then? No wonder genius declines to measure its pace to a fiddler's bow. My spleen was very strong on me now.

"I will gladly fiddle you your fill," replied Hautboy to Standard. "Come on."

In a few minutes we found ourselves in the fifth story of a sort of storehouse, in a lateral street to Broadway. It was curiously furnished with all sorts of odd furniture which seemed to have been obtained, piece by piece, at auctions of old-fashioned household stuff. But all was charmingly clean and cozy.

Pressed by Standard, Hautboy forthwith got out his dented old fiddle and, sitting down on a tall rickety stool, played away right merrily at "Yankee Doodle" and other off-handed, dashing, and disdainfully care-free airs. But common as were the tunes, I was transfixed by something miraculously superior in the style. Sitting there on the old stool, his rusty hat sideways cocked on his head, one foot dangling adrift, he plied the bow of an enchanter. All my moody discontent, every vestige of peevishness, fled. My whole splenetic soul capitulated to the magical fiddle.

"Something of an Orpheus, ah?" said Standard, archly nudging me beneath the left rib.

"And I, the charmed Bruin," murmured I.

The fiddle ceased. Once more, with redoubled curiosity, I gazed upon the easy, indifferent Hautboy. But he entirely baffled inquisition.

When, leaving him, Standard and I were in the street once more, I earnestly conjured him to tell me who, in sober truth, this marvelous Hautboy was.

"Why, haven't you seen him? And didn't you yourself lay his whole anatomy open on the marble slab at Taylor's? What more can you possibly learn? Doubtless, your own masterly insight has already put you in possession of all."

"You mock me, Standard. There is some mystery here. Tell me, I entreat you, who is Hautboy?"

"An extraordinary genius, Helmstone," said Standard, with sudden ardor, "who in boyhood drained the whole flagon of glory; whose going from city to city was a going from triumph to triumph. One who has been an object of wonder to the wisest, been caressed by the loveliest, received the open homage of thousands on thousands of the rabble. But to-day he walks Broadway and no man knows him. With you and me, the elbow of the hurrying clerk, and the pole of the remorseless omnibus, shove him. He who has a hundred times been crowned with laurels, now wears, as you see, a bunged beaver. Once fortune poured showers of gold into his lap, as showers of laurel leaves upon his brow. To-day, from house to house he hies, teaching fiddling for a living. Crammed once with fame, he is now hilarious without it. *With* genius and *without* fame, he is happier than a king. More a prodigy now than ever."

"His true name?"

"Let me whisper it in your ear."

"What! Oh, Standard, myself, as a child, have shouted myself hoarse applauding that very name in the theatre."

"I have heard your poem was not very handsomely received," said Standard, now suddenly shifting the subject.

"Not a word of that, for Heaven's sake!" cried I. "If Cicero, traveling in the East, found sympathetic solace for his grief in beholding the arid overthrow of a once gorgeous city, shall not my petty affair be as nothing, when I behold in Hautboy the vine and the rose climbing the shattered shafts of his tumbled temple of Fame?"

Next day I tore all my manuscripts, bought me a fiddle, and went to take regular lessons of Hautboy.

Jimmy Rose

A TIME ago, no matter how long precisely, I, an old man, removed from the country to the city, having become unexpected heir to a great old house in a narrow street of one of the lower wards, once the haunt of style and fashion, full of gay parlors and bridal chambers; but now, for the most part, transformed into counting-rooms and warehouses. There bales and boxes usurp the place of sofas; day-books and ledgers are spread where once the delicious breakfast toast was buttered. In those old wards the glorious old soft-waffle days are over.

Nevertheless, in this old house of mine, so strangely spared, some monument of departed days survived. Nor was this the only one. Amidst the warehouse ranges some few other dwellings likewise stood. The street's transmutation was not yet complete. Like those old English friars and nuns, long haunting the ruins of their retreats after they had been despoiled, so some few strange old gentlemen and ladies still lingered in the neighborhood, and would not, could not, might not quit it. And I thought that when, one spring, emerging from my white-blossoming orchard, my own white hairs and white ivory-headed cane were added to their loitering census, that those poor old souls insanely fancied the ward was looking up—the tide of fashion setting back again.

For many years the old house had been unoccupied by

an owner; those into whose hands it from time to time had passed having let it out to various shifting tenants; decayed old towns-people, mysterious recluses, or transient, ambiguous-looking foreigners.

While from certain cheap furbishings to which the exterior had been subjected, such as removing a fine old pulpit-like porch crowning the summit of six lofty steps, and set off with a broad-brimmed sounding-board overshadowing the whole, as well as replacing the original heavy window-shutters (each pierced with a crescent in the upper panel to admit an Oriental and moony light into the otherwise shut-up rooms of a sultry morning in July) with frippery Venetian blinds; while, I repeat, the front of the house hereby presented an incongruous aspect, as if the graft of modernness had not taken in its ancient stock; still, however it might fare without, within little or nothing had been altered. The cellars were full of great grim, arched bins of blackened brick, looking like the ancient tombs of Templars, while overhead were shown the first-floor timbers, huge, square, and massive, all red oak, and through long eld, of a rich and Indian color. So large were those timbers, and so thickly ranked, that to walk in those capacious cellars was much like walking along a line-of-battle ship's gun-deck.

All the rooms in each story remained just as they stood ninety years ago, with all their heavy-molded, wooden cornices, paneled wainscots, and carved and inaccessible mantels of queer horticultural and zoological devices. Dim with longevity, the very covering of the walls still preserved the patterns of the times of Louis XVI. In the largest parlor (the drawing-room, my daughters called it, in distinction from two smaller parlors, though I did not think the distinction indispensable) the paper hangings were in the most gaudy style. Instantly we knew such paper could

only have come from Paris—genuine Versailles paper—
the sort of paper that might have hung in Marie Antoinette's
boudoir. It was of great diamond lozenges, divided by massive festoons of roses (onions, Biddy the girl said they were,
but my wife soon changed Biddy's mind on that head); and
in those lozenges, one and all, as in an over-arbored garden-
cage, sat a grand series of gorgeous illustrations of the
natural history of the most imposing Parisian-looking birds:
parrots, macaws, and peacocks, but mostly peacocks. Real
Prince Esterhazys of birds: all rubies, diamonds, and Orders
of the Golden Fleece. But, alas! the north side of this old
apartment presented a strange look: half mossy and half
mildew, something as ancient forest trees on their north
sides, to which particular side the moss most clings, and
where, they say, internal decay first strikes. In short, the
original resplendence of the peacocks had been sadly
dimmed on that north side of the room, owing to a small
leak in the eaves, from which the rain had slowly trickled
its way down the wall, clean down to the first floor. This
leak the irreverent tenants, at that period occupying the
premises, did not see fit to stop, or rather, did not think it
worth their while, seeing that they only kept their fuel and
dried their clothes in the parlor of the peacocks. Hence
many of the once glowing birds seemed as if they had their
princely plumage bedraggled in a dusty shower. Most
mournfully their starry trains were blurred. Yet so patiently
and so pleasantly, nay, here and there so ruddily did they
seem to bide their bitter doom, so much of real elegance
still lingered in their shapes, and so full, too, seemed they
of a sweet engaging pensiveness, meditating all day long,
for years and years, among their faded bowers, that though
my family repeatedly adjured me (especially my wife, who, I
fear, was too young for me) to destroy the whole hen-
roost, as Biddy called it, and cover the walls with a beauti-

ful, nice, genteel, cream-colored paper, despite all entreaties, I could not be prevailed upon, however submissive in other things.

But chiefly would I permit no violation of the old parlor of the peacocks or room of roses (I call it by both names), on account of its long association in my mind with one of the original proprietors of the mansion—the gentle Jimmy Rose.

Poor Jimmy Rose!

He was among my earliest acquaintances. It is not many years since he died; and I and two other tottering old fellows took hack, and in sole procession followed him to his grave.

Jimmy was born a man of moderate fortune. In his prime he had an uncommonly handsome person: large and manly, with bright eyes of blue, brown curling hair, and cheeks that seemed painted with carmine, but it was health's genuine bloom, deepened by the joy of life. He was by nature a great ladies' man, and like most deep adorers of the sex, never tied up his freedom of general worship by making one willful sacrifice of himself at the altar.

Adding to his fortune by a large and princely business, something like that of the great Florentine trader, Cosmo the Magnificent, he was enabled to entertain on a grand scale. For a long time his dinners, suppers, and balls, were not to be surpassed by any given in the party-giving city of New York. His uncommon cheeriness; the splendor of his dress; his sparkling wit; radiant chandeliers; infinite fund of small-talk; French furniture; glowing welcomes to his guests; his bounteous heart and board; his noble graces and his glorious wine; what wonder if all these drew crowds to Jimmy's hospitable abode? In the winter assemblies he figured first on the manager's list. James Rose, Esq., too, was the man to be found foremost in all presentations of plate to highly successful actors at the Park, or of swords and guns to highly successful generals in the field. Often, also, was he chosen to present the gift on account of his fine gift of finely saying fine things.

"Sir," said he, in a great drawing-room in Broadway, as he extended toward General G— a brace of pistols set with turquoise, "Sir," said Jimmy with a Castilian flourish and a rosy smile, "there would have been more turquoise here set, had the names of your glorious victories left room."

Ah, Jimmy, Jimmy! Thou didst excel in compliments. But it was inwrought with thy inmost texture to be affluent in all things which give pleasure. And who shall reproach thee with borrowed wit on this occasion, though borrowed indeed it was? Plagiarize otherwise as they may, not often are the men of this world plagiarists in praise.

But times changed. Time, true plagiarist of the seasons.

Sudden and terrible reverses in business were made mortal by mad prodigality on all hands. When his affairs came to be scrutinized, it was found that Jimmy could not pay more than fifteeen shillings in the pound. And yet in time the deficiency might have been made up—of course, leaving Jimmy penniless—had it not been that in one winter gale two vessels of his from China perished off Sandy Hook, perished at the threshold of their port.

Jimmy was a ruined man.

It was years ago. At that period I resided in the country, but happened to be in the city on one of my annual visits. It was but four or five days since seeing Jimmy at his house the centre of all eyes, and hearing him, at the close of the entertainment, toasted by a brocaded lady, in these well-remembered words: "Our noble host; the bloom on his cheek, may it last long as the bloom in his heart!" And they, the sweet ladies and gentlemen there, they drank that toast so gaily and frankly off; and Jimmy, such a kind, proud, grateful tear stood in his honest eye, angelically glancing round at the sparkling faces, and equally sparkling, and equally feeling, decanters.

Ah! poor, poor Jimmy—God guard us all—poor Jimmy Rose!

Well, it was but four or five days after this that I heard a clap of thunder—no, a clap of bad news. I was crossing the Bowling Green in a snow-storm not far from Jimmy's house on the Battery, when I saw a gentleman come sauntering along, whom I remembered at Jimmy's table as having been the first to spring to his feet in eager response to the lady's toast. Not more brimming the wine in his lifted glass than the moisture in his eye on that happy occasion.

Well, this good gentleman came sailing across the Bowling Green, swinging a silver-headed rattan; seeing me, he paused, "Ah, lad, that was rare wine Jimmy gave us the other night. Shan't get any more, though. Heard the news? Jimmy's burst. Clean smash, I assure you. Come along down to the Coffee-house and I'll tell you more. And if you say so, we'll arrange over a bottle of claret for a sleighing party to Cato's to-night. Come along."

"Thank you," said I, "I—I—I am engaged."

Straight as an arrow I went to Jimmy's. Upon inquiring for him, the man at the door told me that his master was not in; nor did he know where he was; nor had his master been in the house for forty-eight hours.

Walking up Broadway again, I questioned passing acquaintances; but though each man verified the report, no man could tell where Jimmy was, and no one seemed to care, until I encountered a merchant, who hinted that probably Jimmy, having scraped up from the wreck a snug lump of coin, had prudently betaken himself off to parts unknown. The next man I saw, a great nabob he was, too, foamed at the mouth when I mentioned Jimmy's name. "Rascal; regular scamp, sir, is Jimmy Rose! But there are keen fellows after him." I afterward heard that this indignant gentleman had lost the sum of seventy-five dollars and seventy-five cents indirectly through Jimmy's failure. And yet I dare say the share of the dinners he had eaten at Jimmy's might more than have balanced that sum, considering that he was something of a wine-bibber, and such wines as Jimmy imported cost a plum or two. Indeed, now that I bethink me, I recall how I had more than once observed this same middle-aged gentleman, and how that toward the close of one of Jimmy's dinners he would sit at the table pretending to be earnestly talking with beaming Jimmy, but all the while, with a half-furtive sort of tremulous eagerness and hastiness, pour down glass after glass of noble wine, as if now, while Jimmy's bounteous sun was at meridian, was the time to make his selfish hay.

At last I met a person famed for his peculiar knowledge of whatever was secret or withdrawn in the histories and habits of noted people. When I inquired of this person where Jimmy could possibly be, he took me close to Trinity Church rail, out of the jostling of the crowd, and whispered me, that Jimmy had the evening before entered an old house of his (Jimmy's), in C— Street, which old house had been for a time untenanted. The inference seemed to be that perhaps Jimmy might be lurking there now. So getting the precise locality, I bent my steps in that direction, and at last halted before the house containing the room of roses. The shutters were closed, and cobwebs were spun in their crescents. The whole place had a dreary, deserted air. The snow lay unswept, drifted in one billowy heap against the porch, no footprint tracking it. Whoever was within, surely that lonely man was an abandoned one. Few or no people were in the street; for even at that period the fashion of the street had departed from it, while trade had not as yet occupied what its rival had renounced.

Looking up and down the sidewalk a moment, I softly

knocked at the door. No response. I knocked again, and louder. No one came. I knocked and rung both; still without effect. In despair I was going to quit the spot, when, as a last resource, I gave a prolonged summons, with my utmost strength, upon the heavy knocker, and then again stood still; while from various strange old windows up and down the street, various strange old heads were thrust out in wonder at so clamorous a stranger. As if now frightened from its silence, a hollow, husky voice addressed me through the keyhole.

"Who are you?" it said.

"A friend."

"Then shall you not come in," replied the voice, more hollowly than before.

"Great Heaven! this is not Jimmy Rose," thought I, starting. This is the wrong house. I have been misdirected. But still, to make all sure, I spoke again.

"Is James Rose within there?"

No reply.

Once more I spoke:

"I am William Ford; let me in."

"Oh, I can not, I can not! I am afraid of everyone."

It *was* Jimmy Rose!

"Let me in, Rose; let me in, man. I am your friend."

"I will not. I can trust no man now."

"Let me in, Rose; trust at least one, in me."

"Quit the spot, or—"

With that I heard a rattling against the huge lock, not made by any key, as if some small tube were being thrust into the keyhole. Horrified, I fled fast as feet could carry me.

I was a young man then, and Jimmy was not more than forty. It was five-and-twenty years ere I saw him again. And what a change. He whom I expected to behold—if behold at all—dry, shrunken, meagre, cadaverously fierce with misery and misanthropy—amazement! the old Persian roses bloomed in his cheeks. And yet poor as any rat; poor in the last dregs of poverty; a pauper beyond alms-house pauperism; a promenading pauper in a thin, thread-bare, careful coat; a pauper with wealth of polished words; a courteous, smiling, shivering gentleman.

Ah, poor, poor Jimmy—God guard us all—poor Jimmy Rose!

Though at the first onset of his calamity, when creditors, once fast friends, pursued him as carrion for jails; though then, to avoid their hunt, as well as the human eye, he had gone and denned in the old abandoned house; and there, in his loneliness, had been driven half mad, yet time and tide had soothed him down to sanity. Perhaps at bottom Jimmy was too thoroughly good and kind to be made from any cause a man-hater. And doubtless it at last seemed irreligious to Jimmy even to shun mankind.

Sometimes sweet sense of duty will entice one to bitter doom. For what could be more bitter than now, in abject need, to be seen of those—nay, crawl and visit them in an humble sort, and be tolerated as an old eccentric, wandering in their parlors—who once had known him richest of the rich, and gayest of the gay? Yet this Jimmy did. Without rudely breaking him right down to it, fate slowly bent him more and more to the lowest deep. From an unknown quarter he received an income of some seventy dollars, more or less. The principal he would never touch, but, by various modes of eking it out, managed to live on the interest. He lived in an attic, where he supplied himself with food. He took but one regular repast a day—meal and milk—and nothing more, unless procured at others' tables. Often, about the tea-hour, he would drop in upon some old acquaintance, clad in his neat, forlorn frock coat, with worn velvet sewed upon the edges of the cuffs, and a similar device upon the hems of his pantaloons, to hide that dire look of having been grated off by rats. On Sunday he made a point of always dining at some fine house or other.

It is evident that no man could with impunity be allowed to lead this life unless regarded as one who, free from vice, was by fortune brought so low that the plummet of pity alone could reach him. Not much merit redounded to his entertainers because they did not thrust the starving gentleman forth when he came for his poor alms of tea and toast. Some merit had been theirs had they clubbed together and provided him, at small cost enough, with a sufficient income to make him, in point of necessaries, independent of the daily dole of charity; charity not sent to him, either, but charity for which he had to trudge round to their doors.

But the most touching thing of all were those roses in his cheeks; those ruddy roses in his nipping winter. How they bloomed; whether meal and milk, and tea and toast could keep them flourishing; whether now he painted them; by what strange magic they were made to blossom so; no son of man might tell. But there they bloomed. And besides the roses, Jimmy was rich in smiles. He smiled ever. The lordly door which received him to his eleemosynary teas, knew no such smiling guest as Jimmy. In his prosperous days the smile of Jimmy was famous far and wide. It should have been trebly famous now.

Wherever he went to tea, he had all of the news of the town to tell. By frequenting the reading-rooms, as one privileged through harmlessness, he kept himself informed of European affairs and the last literature, foreign and domestic. And of this, when encouragement was given, he would largely talk. But encouragement was not always given. At certain houses, and not a few, Jimmy would drop in about ten minutes before the tea-hour, and drop out again about ten minutes after it; well knowing that his further presence was not indispensable to the contentment or felicity of his host.

How forlorn it was to see him so heartily drinking the generous tea, cup after cup, and eating the flavorous bread and butter, piece after piece, when, owing to the lateness of the dinner hour with the rest, and the abundance of that one grand meal with them, no one besides Jimmy touched the bread and butter, or exceeded a single cup of Souchong. And knowing all this very well, poor Jimmy would try to hide his hunger, and yet gratify it, too, by striving hard to carry on a sprightly conversation with his hostess, and throwing in the eagerest mouthfuls with a sort of absent-minded air, as if he ate merely for custom's sake, and not starvation's.

Poor, poor Jimmy—God guard us all—poor Jimmy Rose!

Neither did Jimmy give up his courtly ways. Whenever there were ladies at the table, sure were they of some fine word; though, indeed, toward the close of Jimmy's life, the young ladies rather thought his compliments somewhat musty, smacking of cocked hats and small-clothes—nay, of old pawnbrokers' shoulder-lace and sword belts. For there still lingered in Jimmy's address a subdued sort of martial air; he having in his palmy days been, among other things, a general of the State militia. There seems a fatality in these militia generalships. Alas! I can recall more than two or three gentlemen who from militia generals became paupers. I am afraid to think why this is so. Is it that this military leaning in a man of an unmilitary heart—that is, a gentle, peaceable heart—is an indication of some weak love of vain display? But ten to one it is not so. At any rate, it is unhandsome, if not unchristian, in the happy, too much to moralize on those who are not so.

So numerous were the houses that Jimmy visited, or so cautious was he in timing his less welcome calls, that at certain mansions he only dropped in about once a year or so. And annually, upon seeing at that house the blooming Miss Frances or Miss Arabella, he would profoundly bow in his forlorn old coat, and with his soft, white hand take hers in gallant wise, saying, "Ah, Miss Arabella, these jewels here are bright upon these fingers; but brighter would they look were it not for those still brighter diamonds of your eyes!"

Though in thy own need thou hadst no pence to give the poor, thou, Jimmy, still hadst alms to give the rich. For not the beggar chattering at the corner pines more after bread than the vain heart after compliment. The rich in their craving glut, as the poor in their craving want, we have with us always. So, I suppose, thought Jimmy Rose.

But all women are not vain, or if a little grain that way inclined, more than redeem it all with goodness. Such was the sweet girl that closed poor Jimmy's eyes. The only daughter of an opulent alderman, she knew Jimmy well, and saw to him in his declining days. During his last sickness, with her own hands she carried him jellies and blancmange; made tea for him in his attic, and turned the poor old gentleman in his bed. And well hadst thou deserved it, Jimmy, at that fair creature's hands; well merited to have thy old eyes closed by woman's fairy fingers, who through life, in riches and in poverty, was still woman's sworn champion and devotee.

I hardly know that I should mention here one little incident connected with this young lady's ministrations, and poor Jimmy's reception of them. But it is harm to neither; I will tell it.

Chancing to be in town, and hearing of Jimmy's illness, I went to see him. And there in his lone attic I found the lovely ministrant. Withdrawing upon seeing another visitor, she left me alone with him. She had brought some little delicacies, and also several books, of such a sort as are sent by serious-minded well-wishers to invalids in a serious crisis. Now whether it was repugnance at being considered next door to death, or whether it was but the natural peevishness brought on by the general misery of his state; however it was, as the gentle girl withdrew, Jimmy, with what small remains of strength were his, pitched the books into the furthest corner, murmuring, "Why will she bring me this sad old stuff? Does she take me for a pauper? Thinks she to salve a gentleman's heart with Poor Man's Plaster?"

Poor, poor Jimmy—God guard us all—poor Jimmy Rose!

Well, well, I am an old man, and I suppose these tears I drop are driblets from my dotage. But Heaven be praised, Jimmy needs no man's pity now.

Jimmy Rose is dead!

Meantime, as I sit within the parlor of the peacocks—that chamber from which his husky voice had come ere threatening me with the pistol—I still must meditate upon his strange example, whereof the marvel is, how after that gay, dashing, nobleman's career, he could be content to crawl through life, and peep about among the marbles and mahoganies for contumelious tea and toast, where once like a very Warwick he had feasted the huzzaing world with Burgundy and venison.

And every time I look at the wilted resplendence of those proud peacocks on the wall, I bethink me of the withering change in Jimmy's once resplendent pride of state. But still again, every time I gaze upon those festoons of perpetual roses, mid which the faded peacocks hang, I bethink me of those undying roses which bloomed in ruined Jimmy's cheek.

Transplanted to another soil, all the unkind past forgot, God grant that Jimmy's roses may immortally survive!

Benito Cereno

I N THE year 1799, Captain Amasa Delano, of Duxbury, in Massachusetts, commanding a large sealer and general trader, lay at anchor with a valuable cargo, in the harbor of Santa Maria—a small, desert, uninhabited island toward the southern extremity of the long coast of Chile. There he had touched for water.

On the second day, not long after dawn, while lying in his berth, his mate came below, informing him that a strange sail was coming into the bay. Ships were then not so plenty in those waters as now. He rose, dressed, and went on deck.

The morning was one peculiar to that coast. Everything was mute and calm; everything gray. The sea, though undulated into long roods of swells, seemed fixed, and was sleeked at the surface like waved lead that has cooled and set in the smelter's mold. The sky seemed a gray surtout. Flights of troubled gray fowl, kith and kin with flights of troubled gray vapors among which they were mixed, skimmed low and fitfully over the waters, as swallows over meadows before storms. Shadows present, foreshadowing deeper shadows to come.

To Captain Delano's surprise, the stranger, viewed through the glass, showed no colors; though to do so upon entering a haven, however uninhabited in its shores, where but a single other ship might be lying, was the custom among peaceful seamen of all nations. Considering the lawlessness and loneliness of the spot, and the sort of stories, at that day, associated with those seas, Captain Delano's surprise might have deepened into some uneasiness had he not been a person of a singularly undistrustful good-nature, not liable, except on extraordinary and repeated incentives, and hardly then, to indulge in personal alarms, any way involving the imputation of malign evil in man. Whether, in view of what humanity is capable, such a trait implies, along with a benevolent heart, more than ordinary quickness and accuracy of intellectual perception, may be left to the wise to determine.

But whatever misgivings might have obtruded on first seeing the stranger, would almost, in any seaman's mind, have been dissipated by observing that, the ship, in navigating into the harbor, was drawing too near the land; a sunken reef making out off her bow. This seemed to prove her a stranger, indeed, not only to the sealer, but the island; consequently, she could be no wonted freebooter on that ocean. With no small interest, Captain Delano continued to watch her—a proceeding not much facilitated by the vapors partly mantling the hull, through which the far matin light from her cabin streamed equivocally enough; much like the sun—by this time hemisphered on the rim of the horizon, and, apparently, in company with the strange ship entering the harbor—which, wimpled by the same low, creeping clouds, showed not unlike a Lima intriguante's one sinister eye peering across the Plaza from the Indian loop-hole of her dusk *saya-y-manto*.

It might have been but a deception of the vapors, but, the longer the stranger was watched the more singular appeared her manœuvres. Ere long it seemed hard to decide whether she meant to come in or no—what she wanted, or what she was about. The wind, which had breezed up a little during the night, was now extremely light and baffling, which the more increased the apparent uncertainty of her movements.

Surmising, at last, that it might be a ship in distress, Captain Delano ordered his whale-boat to be dropped, and, much to the wary opposition of his mate, prepared to board her, and, at the least, pilot her in. On the night previous, a fishing party of the seamen had gone a long distance to some detached rocks out of sight from the sealer, and, an hour or two before daybreak, had returned, having met with no small success. Presuming that the stranger might have been long off soundings, the good captain put several baskets of the fish, for presents, into his boat, and so pulled away. From her continuing too near the sunken reef, deeming her in danger, calling to his men, he made all haste to apprise those on board of their situation. But, some time ere the boat came up, the wind, light though it was, having shifted, had headed the vessel off, as well as partly broken the vapors from about her.

Upon gaining a less remote view, the ship, when made signally visible on the verge of the leaden-hued swells, with the shreds of fog here and there raggedly furring her, appeared like a whitewashed monastery after a thunder-storm, seen perched upon some dun cliff among the Pyrenees. But it was no purely fanciful resemblance which now, for a moment, almost led Captain Delano to think that nothing less than a ship-load of monks was before him. Peering over the bulwarks were what really seemed, in the hazy distance, throngs of dark cowls; while, fitfully revealed through the open port-holes, other dark moving figures were dimly descried, as of Black Friars pacing the cloisters.

Upon a still nigher approach, this appearance was modified, and the true character of the vessel was plain—a Spanish merchantman of the first class, carrying negro slaves, amongst other valuable freight, from one colonial port to another. A very large, and, in its time, a very fine vessel, such as in those days were at intervals encountered along that main; sometimes superseded Acapulco treasure-ships, or retired frigates of the Spanish king's navy, which, like superannuated Italian palaces, still, under a decline of masters, preserved signs of former state.

As the whale-boat drew more and more nigh, the cause of the peculiar pipe-clayed aspect of the stranger was seen in the slovenly neglect pervading her. The spars, ropes, and great part of the bulwarks, looked woolly, from long unacquaintance with the scraper, tar, and the brush. Her keel seemed laid, her ribs put together, and she launched, from Ezekiel's Valley of Dry Bones.

In the present business in which she was engaged, the ship's general model and rig appeared to have undergone no material change from their original warlike and Froissart pattern. However, no guns were seen.

The tops were large, and were railed about with what had once been octagonal net-work, all now in sad disrepair. These tops hung overhead like three ruinous aviaries, in one of which was seen perched, on a ratlin, a white noddy, a strange fowl, so called from its lethargic, somnambulistic character, being frequently caught by hand at sea. Battered and mouldy, the castellated forecastle seemed some ancient turret, long ago taken by assault, and then left to decay. Toward the stern, two high-raised quarter galleries—the balustrades here and there covered with dry, tindery sea-moss—opening out from the unoccupied state-cabin, whose dead-lights, for all the mild weather, were hermetically closed and calked—these tenantless balconies hung over the sea as if it were the grand Venetian canal. But the principal relic of faded grandeur was the ample oval of the shield-like stern-piece, intricately carved with the arms of Castile and Leon, medallioned about by groups of mythological or symbolical devices; uppermost and central of which was a dark satyr in a mask, holding his foot on the prostrate neck of a writhing figure, likewise masked.

Whether the ship had a figure-head, or only a plain beak, was not quite certain, owing to canvas wrapped about that part, either to protect it while undergoing a refurbishing, or else decently to hide its decay. Rudely painted or chalked, as in a sailor freak, along the forward side of a sort of pedestal below the canvas, was the sentence, "*Seguid vuestro jefe*," (follow your leader); while upon the tarnished headboards, near by, appeared, in stately capitals, once gilt, the ship's name, "San Dominick," each letter streakingly corroded with tricklings of copper-spike rust; while, like mourning weeds, dark festoons of sea-grass slimily swept to and fro over the name, with every hearse-like roll of the hull.

As, at last, the boat was hooked from the bow along toward the gangway amidship, its keel, while yet some inches separated from the hull, harshly grated as on a sunken coral reef. It proved a huge bunch of conglobated barnacles adhering below the water to the side like a wen—a token of baffling airs and long calms passed somewhere in those seas.

Climbing the side, the visitor was at once surrounded by a clamorous throng of whites and blacks, but the latter outnumbering the former more than could have been expected, negro transportation-ship as the stranger in port was. But, in one language, and as with one voice, all poured out a common tale of suffering; in which the negresses, of whom there were not a few, exceeded the others in their dolorous vehemence. The scurvy, together with the fever, had swept off a great part of their number, more especially the Spaniards. Off Cape Horn they had narrowly escaped shipwreck; then, for days together, they had lain tranced without wind; their provisions were low; their water next to none; their lips that moment were baked.

While Captain Delano was thus made the mark of all eager tongues, his one eager glance took in all faces, with every other object about him.

Always upon first boarding a large and populous ship at sea, especially a foreign one, with a nondescript crew such as Lascars or Manila men, the impression varies in a peculiar way from that produced by first entering a strange house with strange inmates in a strange land. Both house and ship—the one by its walls and blinds, the other by its high bulwarks like ramparts—hoard from view their interiors till the last moment; but in the case of the ship there is this addition: that the living spectacle it contains, upon its sudden and complete disclosure, has, in contrast with the blank ocean which zones it, something of the effect of enchantment. The ship seems unreal; these strange costumes, gestures, and faces, but a shadowy tableau just emerged from the deep, which directly must receive back what it gave.

Perhaps it was some such influence, as above is attempted to be described, which, in Captain Delano's mind, heightened whatever, upon a staid scrutiny, might have seemed unusual; especially the conspicuous figures of four elderly grizzled negroes, their heads like black, doddered willow tops, who, in venerable contrast to the tumult below them, were couched, sphynx-like, one on the starboard cat-head, another on the larboard, and the remaining pair face to face on the opposite bulwarks above the main-chains. They each had bits of unstranded old junk in their hands, and, with a sort of stoical self-content, were picking the junk into oakum, a small heap of which lay by their sides. They accompanied the task with a continuous, low, monotonous chant; droning and drooling away like so many gray-headed bag-pipers playing a funeral march.

The quarter-deck rose into an ample elevated poop, upon the forward verge of which, lifted, like the oakum-pickers, some eight feet above the general throng, sat along in a row, separated by regular spaces, the cross-legged figures of six other blacks; each with a rusty hatchet in his hand, which, with a bit of brick and a rag, he was engaged like a scullion in scouring; while between each two was a small stack of hatchets, their rusted edges turned forward awaiting a like operation. Though occasionally the four oakum-pickers would briefly address some person or persons in the crowd below, yet the six hatchet-polishers neither spoke to others, nor breathed a whisper among themselves, but sat intent upon their task, except at intervals, when, with the peculiar love in negroes of uniting industry with pastime, two and two they sideways clashed their hatchets together, like cymbals, with a barbarous din. All six, unlike the generality, had the raw aspect of unsophisticated Africans.

But that first comprehensive glance which took in those ten figures, with scores less conspicuous, rested but an instant upon them, as, impatient of the hubbub of voices, the visitor turned in quest of whomsoever it might be that commanded the ship.

But as if not unwilling to let nature make known her own case among his suffering charge, or else in despair of restraining it for the time, the Spanish captain, a gentlemanly, reserved-looking, and rather young man to a stranger's eye, dressed with singular richness, but bearing plain traces of recent sleepless cares and disquietudes, stood passively by, leaning against the main-mast, at one moment casting a dreary, spiritless look upon his excited people, at the next an unhappy glance toward his visitor. By his side stood a black of small stature, in whose rude face, as occasionally, like a shepherd's dog, he mutely turned it up into the Spaniard's, sorrow and affection were equally blended.

Struggling through the throng, the American advanced to the Spaniard, assuring him of his sympathies, and offering to render whatever assistance might be in his power.

To which the Spaniard returned for the present but grave and ceremonious acknowledgments, his national formality dusked by the saturnine mood of ill-health.

But losing no time in mere compliments, Captain Delano, returning to the gangway, had his baskets of fish brought up; and as the wind still continued light, so that some hours at least must elapse ere the ship could be brought to the anchorage, he bade his men return to the sealer, and fetch back as much water as the whale-boat could carry, with whatever soft bread the steward might have, all the remaining pumpkins on board, with a box of sugar, and a dozen of his private bottles of cider.

Not many minutes after the boat's pushing off, to the vexation of all, the wind entirely died away, and the tide turning, began drifting back the ship helplessly seaward. But trusting this would not long last, Captain Delano sought, with good hopes, to cheer up the strangers, feeling no small satisfaction that, with persons in their condition, he could—thanks to his frequent voyages along the Spanish main—converse with some freedom in their native tongue.

While left alone with them, he was not long in observing some things tending to heighten his first impressions; but surprise was lost in pity, both for the Spaniards and blacks, alike evidently reduced from scarcity of water and provisions; while long-continued suffering seemed to have brought out the less good-natured qualities of the negroes, besides, at the same time, impairing the Spaniard's authority over them. But, under the circumstances, precisely this condition of things was to have been anticipated. In armies, navies, cities, or families, in nature herself, nothing more relaxes good order than misery. Still, Captain Delano was not without the idea, that had Benito Cereno been a man of greater energy, misrule would hardly have come to the present pass. But the debility, constitutional or induced by hardships, bodily and mental, of the Spanish captain, was too obvious to be overlooked. A prey to settled dejection, as if long mocked with hope he would not now indulge it, even when it had ceased to be a mock, the prospect of that day, or evening at furthest, lying at anchor, with plenty of water for his people, and a brother captain to counsel and befriend, seemed in no perceptible degree to encourage him. His mind appeared unstrung, if not still more seriously affected. Shut up in these oaken walls, chained to one dull round of command, whose unconditionality cloyed him, like some hypochondriac abbot he moved slowly about, at times suddenly pausing, starting, or staring, biting his lip, biting his finger-nail, flushing, paling, twitching his beard, with other symptoms of an absent or moody mind. This distempered spirit was lodged, as before hinted, in as distempered a frame. He was rather tall, but seemed never to have been robust, and now with nervous suffering was almost worn to a skeleton. A tendency to some pulmonary complaint appeared to have been lately confirmed. His voice was like that of one with lungs half gone—hoarsely suppressed, a husky whisper. No wonder that, as in this state he tottered about, his private servant apprehensively followed him. Sometimes the negro gave his master his arm, or took his handkerchief out of his pocket for him; performing these and similar offices with that affectionate zeal which transmutes into something filial or fraternal acts in themselves but menial; and which has gained for the negro the repute of making the most pleasing body-servant in the world; one, too, whom a master need be on no stiffly superior terms with, but may treat with familiar trust; less a servant than a devoted companion.

Marking the noisy indocility of the blacks in general, as well as what seemed the sullen inefficiency of the whites it was not without humane satisfaction that Captain Delano witnessed the steady good conduct of Babo

But the good conduct of Babo, hardly more than the ill-behavior of others, seemed to withdraw the half-lunatic Don Benito from his cloudy languor. Not that such precisely was the impression made by the Spaniard on the mind of his visitor. The Spaniard's individual unrest was, for the present, but noted as a conspicuous feature in the ship's general affliction. Still, Captain Delano was not a little concerned at what he could not help taking for the time to be Don Benito's unfriendly indifference towards himself. The Spaniard's manner, too, conveyed a sort of sour and gloomy disdain, which he seemed at no pains to disguise. But this the American in charity ascribed to the harassing effects of sickness, since, in former instances, he had noted that there are peculiar natures on whom prolonged physical suffering seems to cancel every social instinct of kindness; as if, forced to black bread themselves, they deemed it but equity that each person coming nigh them should, indirectly, by some slight or affront, be made to partake of their fare.

But ere long Captain Delano bethought him that, indulgent as he was at the first, in judging the Spaniard, he might not, after all, have exercised charity enough. At bottom it was Don Benito's reserve which displeased him; but the same reserve was shown towards all but his faithful personal attendant. Even the formal reports which, according to sea-usage, were, at stated times, made to him by some petty underling, either a white, mulatto or black, he hardly had patience enough to listen to, without betraying contemptuous aversion. His manner upon such occasions was, in its degree, not unlike that which might be supposed to have been his imperial countryman's, Charles V, just previous to the anchoritish retirement of that monarch from the throne.

This splenetic disrelish of his place was evinced in almost every function pertaining to it. Proud as he was moody, he condescended to no personal mandate. Whatever special orders were necessary, their delivery was delegated to his body-servant, who in turn transferred them to their ultimate destination, through runners, alert Spanish boys or slave boys, like pages or pilot-fish within easy call continually hovering round Don Benito. So that to have beheld this undemonstrative invalid gliding about, apathetic and mute, no landsman could have dreamed that in him was lodged a dictatorship beyond which, while at sea, there was no earthly appeal.

Thus, the Spaniard, regarded in his reserve, seemed the involuntary victim of mental disorder. But, in fact, his reserve might, in some degree, have proceeded from design. If so, then here was evinced the unhealthy climax of that icy though conscientious policy, more or less adopted by all commanders of large ships, which, except in signal emergencies, obliterates alike the manifestation of sway with every trace of sociality; transforming the man into a block, or rather into a loaded cannon, which, until there is call for thunder, has nothing to say.

Viewing him in this light, it seemed but a natural token of the perverse habit induced by a long course of such hard self-restraint, that, notwithstanding the present condition of his ship, the Spaniard should still persist in a demeanor, which, however harmless, or, it may be, appropriate, in a well-appointed vessel, such as the *San Dominick* might have been at the outset of the voyage, was anything but judicious now. But the Spaniard, perhaps, thought that it was with captains as with gods: reserve, under all events, must still be their cue. But probably this appearance of slumbering dominion might have been but an attempted disguise to conscious imbecility—not deep policy, but shallow device. But be all this as it might, whether Don Benito's manner was designed or not, the more Captain Delano noted its pervading reserve, the less he felt uneasiness at any particular manifestation of that reserve towards himself.

Neither were his thoughts taken up by the captain alone. Wonted to the quiet orderliness of the sealer's comfortable family of a crew, the noisy confusion of the *San Dominick's* suffering host repeatedly challenged his eye. Some prominent breaches, not only of discipline but of decency, were observed. These Captain Delano could not but ascribe, in the main, to the absence of those subordinate deck-officers to whom, along with higher duties, is intrusted what may be styled the police department of a populous ship. True, the old oakum-pickers appeared at times to act the part of monitorial constables to their countrymen, the blacks; but though occasionally succeeding in allaying trifling outbreaks now and then between man and man, they could do little or nothing toward establishing general quiet. The *San Dominick* was in the condition of a transatlantic emigrant ship, among whose multitude of living freight are some individuals, doubtless, as little troublesome as crates and bales; but the friendly remonstrances of such with their ruder companions are of not so much avail as the unfriendly arm of the mate. What the *San Dominick* wanted was, what the emigrant ship has, stern superior officers. But on these decks not so much as a fourth-mate was to be seen.

The visitor's curiosity was roused to learn the particulars of those mishaps which had brought about such absenteeism, with its consequences; because, though deriving some inkling of the voyage from the wails which at the first moment had greeted him, yet of the details no clear understanding had been had. The best account would, doubtless, be given by the captain. Yet at first the visitor was loth to ask it, unwilling to provoke some distant rebuff. But plucking up courage, he at last accosted Don Benito, renewing the expression of his benevolent interest, adding, that did he (Captain Delano) but know the particulars of the ship's misfortunes, he would, perhaps, be better able in the end to relieve them. Would Don Benito favor him with the whole story?

Don Benito faltered; then, like some somnambulist suddenly interfered with, vacantly stared at his visitor, and ended by looking down on the deck. He maintained this posture so long, that Captain Delano, almost equally disconcerted, and involuntarily almost as rude, turned suddenly from him, walking forward to accost one of the Spanish seamen for the desired information. But he had hardly gone five paces, when, with a sort of eagerness, Don Benito invited him back, regretting his momentary absence of mind, and professing readiness to gratify him.

While most part of the story was being given, the two captains stood on the after part of the main-deck, a privileged spot, no one being near but the servant.

"It is now a hundred and ninety days," began the Spaniard, in his husky whisper, "that this ship, well officered and well manned, with several cabin passengers—some fifty Spaniards in all—sailed from Buenos Ayres bound to Lima, with a general cargo, hardware, Paraguay tea and the like —and," pointing forward, "that parcel of negroes, now not more than a hundred and fifty, as you see, but then numbering over three hundred souls. Off Cape Horn we had heavy gales. In one moment, by night, three of my best officers, with fifteen sailors, were lost, with the main-yard; the spar snapping under them in the slings, as they sought, with heavers, to beat down the icy sail. To lighten the hull, the heavier sacks of maté were thrown into the sea, with most of the water-pipes lashed on deck at the time. And this last necessity it was, combined with the prolonged detentions afterwards experienced, which eventually brought about our chief causes of suffering. When——"

Here there was a sudden fainting attack of his cough, brought on, no doubt, by his mental distress. His servant sustained him, and drawing a cordial from his pocket placed it to his lips. He a little revived. But unwilling to leave him unsupported while yet imperfectly restored, the black with one arm still encircled his master, at the same time keeping his eye fixed on his face, as if to watch for the first sign of complete restoration, or relapse, as the event might prove.

The Spaniard proceeded, but brokenly and obscurely, as one in a dream.

—"Oh, my God! rather than pass through what I have, with joy I would have hailed the most terrible gales; but——"

His cough returned and with increased violence; this subsiding, with reddened lips and closed eyes he fell heavily against his supporter.

"His mind wanders. He was thinking of the plague that followed the gales," plaintively sighed the servant; "my poor, poor master!" wringing one hand, and with the other wiping the mouth. "But be patient, Señor," again turning to Captain Delano, "these fits do not last long; master will soon be himself."

Don Benito reviving, went on; but as this portion of the story was very brokenly delivered, the substance only will here be set down.

It appeared that after the ship had been many days tossed in storms off the Cape, the scurvy broke out, carrying off numbers of the whites and blacks. When at last they had worked round into the Pacific, their spars and sails were so damaged, and so inadequately handled by the surviving mariners, most of whom were become invalids, that, unable to lay her northerly course by the wind, which was powerful, the unmanageable ship, for successive days and nights, was blown northwestward, where the breeze suddenly deserted her, in unknown waters, to sultry calms. The absence of the water-pipes now proved as fatal to life as before their presence had menaced it. Induced, or at least aggravated, by the more than scanty allowance of water, a malignant fever followed the scurvy; with the excessive heat of the lengthened calm, making such short work of it as to sweep away, as by billows, whole families of the Africans, and a yet larger number, proportionably, of the Spaniards, including, by a luckless fatality, every remaining officer on board. Consequently, in the smart west winds eventually following the calm, the already rent sails, having to be simply dropped, not furled, at need, had been gradually reduced to the beggars' rags they were now. To procure substitutes for his lost sailors, as well as supplies of water and sails, the captain, at the earliest opportunity, had made for Valdivia, the southernmost civilized port of Chile and South America; but upon nearing the coast the thick weather had prevented him from so much as sighting that harbor. Since which period, almost without a crew, and almost without canvas and almost without water, and, at intervals, giving its added dead to the sea, the *San Dominick* had been battledored about by contrary winds, inveigled by currents, or grown weedy in calms. Like a man lost in woods, more than once she had doubled upon her own track.

"But throughout these calamities," huskily continued Don Benito, painfully turning in the half embrace of his servant, "I have to thank those negroes you see, who, though to your inexperienced eyes appearing unruly, have, indeed, conducted themselves with less of restlessness than even their owner could have thought possible under such circumstances."

Here he again fell faintly back. Again his mind wandered; but he rallied, and less obscurely proceeded.

"Yes, their owner was quite right in assuring me that no fetters would be needed with his blacks; so that while, as is wont in this transportation, those negroes have always remained upon deck—not thrust below, as in the Guinea-men—they have, also, from the beginning, been freely permitted to range within given bounds at their pleasure."

Once more the faintness returned—his mind roved—but, recovering, he resumed:

"But it is Babo here to whom, under God, I owe not only my own preservation, but likewise to him, chiefly, the merit is due, of pacifying his more ignorant brethren, when at intervals tempted to murmurings."

"Ah, master," sighed the black, bowing his face, "don't speak of me; Babo is nothing; what Babo has done was but duty."

"Faithful fellow!" cried Captain Delano. "Don Benito, I envy you such a friend; slave I cannot call him."

As master and man stood before him, the black uphold-ing the white, Captain Delano could not but bethink him of the beauty of that relationship which could present such a spectacle of fidelity on the one hand and confidence on the other. The scene was heightened by the contrast in dress, denoting their relative positions. The Spaniard wore a loose Chile jacket of dark velvet; white small-clothes and stockings, with silver buckles at the knee and instep; a high-crowned sombrero, of fine grass; a slender sword, silver mounted, hung from a knot in his sash—the last being an almost invariable adjunct, more for utility than ornament, of a South American gentleman's dress to this hour. Ex-cepting when his occasional nervous contortions brought about disarray, there was a certain precision in his attire curiously at variance with the unsightly disorder around; especially in the belittered Ghetto, forward of the main-mast, wholly occupied by the blacks.

The servant wore nothing but wide trowsers, apparently, from their coarseness and patches, made out of some old topsail; they were clean, and confined at the waist by a bit of unstranded rope. which, with his composed, deprecatory

air at times, made him look something like a begging friar
of St. Francis.

However unsuitable for the time and place, at least in
the blunt-thinking American's eyes, and however strangely
surviving in the midst of all his afflictions, the toilette of
Don Benito might not, in fashion at least, have gone beyond the style of the day among South Americans of his
class. Though on the present voyage sailing from Buenos
Ayres, he had avowed himself a native and resident of
Chile, whose inhabitants had not so generally adopted the
plain coat and once plebeian pantaloons; but, with a becoming modification, adhered to their provincial costume, picturesque as any in the world. Still, relatively to the pale
history of the voyage, and his own pale face, there seemed
something so incongruous in the Spaniard's apparel, as
almost to suggest the image of an invalid courtier tottering
about London streets in the time of the plague.

The portion of the narrative which, perhaps, most excited interest, as well as some surprise, considering the latitudes in question, was the long calms spoken of, and more
particularly the ship's so long drifting about. Without communicating the opinion, of course, the American could not
but impute at least part of the detentions both to clumsy
seamanship and faulty navigation. Eying Don Benito's
small, yellow hands, he easily inferred that the young captain had not got into command at the hawse-hole, but the
cabin-window; and if so, why wonder at incompetence, in
youth, sickness, and gentility united?

But drowning criticism in compassion, after a fresh repetition of his sympathies, Captain Delano, having heard out
his story, not only engaged, as in the first place, to see Don
Benito and his people supplied in their immediate bodily
needs, but, also, now further promised to assist him in
procuring a large permanent supply of water, as well as
some sails and rigging; and, though it would involve no

small embarrassment to himself, yet he would spare three of his best seamen for temporary deck-officers; so that without delay the ship might proceed to Concepcion, there fully to refit for Lima, her destined port.

Such generosity was not without its effect, even upon the invalid. His face lighted up; eager and hectic, he met the honest glance of his visitor. With gratitude he seemed overcome.

"This excitement is bad for master," whispered the servant, taking his arm, and with soothing words gently drawing him aside.

When Don Benito returned, the American was pained to observe that his hopefulness, like the sudden kindling in his cheek, was but febrile and transient.

Ere long, with a joyless mien, looking up towards the poop, the host invited his guest to accompany him there, for the benefit of what little breath of wind might be stirring.

As during the telling of the story, Captain Delano had once or twice started at the occasional cymballing of the hatchet-polishers, wondering why such an interruption should be allowed, especially in that part of the ship, and in the ears of an invalid; and moreover, as the hatchets had anything but an attractive look, and the handlers of them still less so, it was, therefore, to tell the truth, not without some lurking reluctance, or even shrinking, it may be, that Captain Delano, with apparent complaisance, acquiesced in his host's invitation. The more so, since, with an untimely caprice of punctilio, rendered distressing by his cadaverous aspect, Don Benito, with Castilian bows, solemnly insisted upon his guest's preceding him up the ladder leading to the elevation; where, one on each side of the last step, sat for armorial supporters and sentries two of the ominous file. Gingerly enough stepped good Captain Delano between them, and in the instant of leaving them behind, like one running the gauntlet, he felt an apprehensive twitch in the calves of his legs.

But when, facing about, he saw the whole file, like so many organ-grinders, still stupidly intent on their work, unmindful of everything beside, he could not but smile at his late fidgety panic.

Presently, while standing with his host, looking forward upon the decks below, he was struck by one of those instances of insubordination previously alluded to. Three black boys, with two Spanish boys, were sitting together on the hatches, scraping a rude wooden platter, in which some scanty mess had recently been cooked. Suddenly, one of the black boys, enraged at a word dropped by one of his white companions, seized a knife, and, though called to forbear by one of the oakum-pickers, struck the lad over the head, inflicting a gash from which blood flowed.

In amazement, Captain Delano inquired what this meant. To which the pale Don Benito dully muttered, that it was merely the sport of the lad.

"Pretty serious sport, truly," rejoined Captain Delano. "Had such a thing happened on board the *Bachelor's Delight*, instant punishment would have followed."

At these words the Spaniard turned upon the American one of his sudden, staring, half-lunatic looks; then, relapsing into his torpor, answered, "Doubtless, doubtless, Señor."

Is it, thought Captain Delano, that this hapless man is one of those paper captains I've known, who by policy wink at what by power they cannot put down? I know no sadder sight than a commander who has little of command but the name.

"I should think, Don Benito," he now said, glancing towards the oakum-picker who had sought to interfere with the boys, "that you would find it advantageous to keep all your blacks employed, especially the younger ones, no matter at what useless task, and no matter what happens to the ship. Why, even with my little band, I find such a course indispensable. I once kept a crew on my quarter-deck thrumming mats for my cabin, when, for three days, I had given up my ship—mats, men, and all—for a speedy loss, owing to the violence of a gale, in which we could do nothing but helplessly drive before it."

"Doubtless, doubtless," muttered Don Benito.

"But," continued Captain Delano, again glancing upon the oakum-pickers and then at the hatchet-polishers, near by, "I see you keep some, at least, of your host employed."

"Yes," was again the vacant response.

"Those old men there, shaking their pows from their pulpits," continued Captain Delano, pointing to the oakum-pickers, "seem to act the part of old dominies to the rest, little heeded as their admonitions are at times. Is this voluntary on their part, Don Benito, or have you appointed them shepherds to your flock of black sheep?"

"What posts they fill, I appointed them," rejoined the Spaniard, in an acrid tone, as if resenting some supposed satiric reflection.

"And these others, these Ashantee conjurors here," continued Captain Delano, rather uneasily eying the brandished steel of the hatchet-polishers, where, in spots, it had been brought to a shine, "this seems a curious business they are at, Don Benito?"

"In the gales we met," answered the Spaniard, "what of our general cargo was not thrown overboard was much damaged by the brine. Since coming into calm weather, I have had several cases of knives and hatchets daily brought up for overhauling and cleaning."

"A prudent idea, Don Benito. You are part owner of ship and cargo, I presume; but none of the slaves, perhaps?"

"I am owner of all you see," impatiently returned Don Benito, "except the main company of blacks, who belonged to my late friend, Alexandro Aranda."

As he mentioned this name, his air was heart-broken; his knees shook; his servant supported him.

Thinking he divined the cause of such unusual emotion, to confirm his surmise, Captain Delano, after a pause, said: "And may I ask, Don Benito, whether—since a while ago you spoke of some cabin passengers—the friend, whose loss so afflicts you, at the outset of the voyage accompanied his blacks?"

"Yes."

"But died of the fever?"

"Died of the fever. Oh, could I but——" Again quivering, the Spaniard paused.

"Pardon me," said Captain Delano, lowly, "but I think that, by a sympathetic experience, I conjecture, Don Benito, what it is that gives the keener edge to your grief. It was once my hard fortune to lose, at sea, a dear friend, my own brother, then supercargo. Assured of the welfare of his spirit, its departure I could have borne like a man; but that honest eye, that honest hand—both of which had so often met mine—and that warm heart; all, all—like scraps to the dogs—to throw all to the sharks! It was then I vowed never to have for fellow-voyager a man I loved, unless, unbeknown to him, I had provided every requisite, in case of a fatality, for embalming his mortal part for interment on shore. Were your friend's remains now on board this ship, Don Benito, not thus strangely would the mention of his name affect you."

"On board this ship?" echoed the Spaniard. Then, with horrified gestures, as directed against some spectre, he unconsciously fell into the ready arms of his attendant, who, with a silent appeal toward Captain Delano, seemed beseeching him not again to broach a theme so unspeakably distressing to his master.

This poor fellow now, thought the pained American, is the victim of that sad superstition which associates gob lins with the deserted body of man, as ghosts with an abandoned house. How unlike are we made! What to me, in like case, would have been a solemn satisfaction, the bare suggestion, even, terrifies the Spaniard into this trance. Poor Alexandro Aranda! what would you say could you here see your friend—who, on former voyages, when you, for months, were left behind, has, I dare say, often longed, and longed, for one peep at you—now transported with terror at the least thought of having you anyway nigh him.

At this moment, with a dreary grave-yard toll, betokening a flaw, the ship's forecastle bell, smote by one of the grizzled oakum-pickers, proclaimed ten o'clock, through the leaden calm; when Captain Delano's attention was caught by the moving figure of a gigantic black, emerging from the general crowd below, and slowly advancing towards the elevated poop. An iron collar was about his neck, from which depended a chain, thrice wound round his body; the terminating links padlocked together at a broad band of iron, his girdle.

"How like a mute Atufal moves," murmured the servant.

The black mounted the steps of the poop, and, like a brave prisoner, brought up to receive sentence, stood in unquailing muteness before Don Benito, now recovered from his attack.

At the first glimpse of his approach, Don Benito had started, a resentful shadow swept over his face; and, as with the sudden memory of bootless rage, his white lips glued together.

This is some mulish mutineer, thought Captain Delano, surveying, not without a mixture of admiration, the colossal form of the negro.

"See, he waits your question, master," said the servant.

Thus reminded, Don Benito, nervously averting his glance, as if shunning, by anticipation, some rebellious response, in a disconcerted voice, thus spoke:—

"Atufal, will you ask my pardon, now?"

The black was silent.

"Again, master," murmured the servant, with bitter up-braiding eying his countryman, "Again, master; he will bend to master yet."

"Answer," said Don Benito, still averting his glance, "say but the one word, *pardon*, and your chains shall be off."

Upon this, the black, slowly raising both arms, let them lifelessly fall, his links clanking, his head bowed; as much as to say, "No, I am content."

"Go," said Don Benito, with inkept and unknown emotion.

Deliberately as he had come, the black obeyed.

"Excuse me, Don Benito," said Captain Delano, "but this scene surprises me; what means it, pray?"

"It means that that negro alone, of all the band, has given me peculiar cause of offense. I have put him in chains; I ——"

Here he paused; his hand to his head, as if there were a swimming there, or a sudden bewilderment of memory had come over him; but meeting his servant's kindly glance seemed reassured, and proceeded:—

"I could not scourge such a form. But I told him he must ask my pardon. As yet he has not. At my command, every two hours he stands before me."

"And how long has this been?"

"Some sixty days."

"And obedient in all else? And respectful?"

"Yes."

"Upon my conscience, then," exclaimed Captain Delano, impulsively, "he has a royal spirit in him, this fellow."

"He may have some right to it," bitterly returned Don Benito, "he says he was king in his own land."

"Yes," said the servant, entering a word, "those slits in Atufal's ears once held wedges of gold; but poor Babo here, in his own land, was only a poor slave; a black man's slave was Babo, who now is the white's."

Somewhat annoyed by these conversational familiarities, Captain Delano turned curiously upon the attendant, then glanced inquiringly at his master; but, as if long wonted to these little informalities, neither master nor man seemed to understand him.

"What, pray, was Atufal's offense, Don Benito?" asked Captain Delano; "if it was not something very serious, take a fool's advice, and, in view of his general docility, as well as in some natural respect for his spirit, remit him his penalty."

"No, no, master never will do that," here murmured the servant to himself, "proud Atufal must first ask master's pardon. The slave there carries the padlock, but master here carries the key."

His attention thus directed, Captain Delano now noticed for the first, that, suspended by a slender silken cord, from Don Benito's neck, hung a key. At once, from the servant's muttered syllables, divining the key's purpose, he smiled and said:—"So, Don Benito—padlock and key—significant symbols, truly."

Biting his lip, Don Benito faltered.

Though the remark of Captain Delano, a man of such native simplicity as to be incapable of satire or irony, had been dropped in playful allusion to the Spaniard's singularly evidenced lordship over the black; yet the hypochondriac seemed some way to have taken it as a malicious reflection upon his confessed inability thus far to break down, at least, on a verbal summons, the entrenched will of the slave. Deploring this supposed misconception, yet despairing of correcting it, Captain Delano shifted the subject; but finding his companion more than ever withdrawn, as if still sourly digesting the lees of the presumed affront above-mentioned, by and by Captain Delano likewise became less talkative, oppressed, against his own will, by what seemed the secret vindictiveness of the morbidly sensitive Spaniard. But the good sailor, himself of a quite contrary disposition, refrained, on his part, alike from the appearance as from the feeling of resentment, and if silent, was only so from contagion.

Presently the Spaniard, assisted by his servant, somewhat discourteously crossed over from his guest; a procedure which, sensibly enough, might have been allowed to pass for idle caprice of ill-humor, had not master and man, lingering round the corner of the elevated skylight, begun whispering together in low voices. This was unpleasing. And more: the moody air of the Spaniard, which at times had not been without a sort of valetudinarian stateliness, now seemed anything but dignified; while the menial familiarity of the servant lost its original charm of simple-hearted attachment.

In his embarrassment, the visitor turned his face to the other side of the ship. By so doing, his glance accidentally fell on a young Spanish sailor, a coil of rope in his hand, just stepped from the deck to the first round of the mizzen-rigging. Perhaps the man would not have been particularly noticed, were it not that, during his ascent to one of the yards, he, with a sort of covert intentness, kept his eye fixed on Captain Delano, from whom, presently, it passed, as if by a natural sequence, to the two whisperers.

His own attention thus redirected to that quarter, Captain Delano gave a slight start. From something in Don Benito's manner just then, it seemed as if the visitor had, at least partly, been the subject of the withdrawn consultation going on—a conjecture as little agreeable to the guest as it was little flattering to the host.

The singular alternations of courtesy and ill-breeding in the Spanish captain were unaccountable, except on one of two suppositions—innocent lunacy, or wicked imposture

But the first idea, though it might naturally have oc
curred to an indifferent observer, and, in some respect, had
not hitherto been wholly a stranger to Captain Delano's
mind, yet, now that, in an incipient way, he began to regard the stranger's conduct something in the light of an
intentional affront, of course the idea of lunacy was virtually vacated. But if not a lunatic, what then? Under the
circumstances, would a gentleman, nay, any honest boor,
act the part now acted by his host? The man was an im-
poster. Some low-born adventurer, masquerading as an
oceanic grandee; yet so ignorant of the first requisites of
mere gentlemanhood as to be betrayed into the present remarkable indecorum. That strange ceremoniousness, too,
at other times evinced, seemed not uncharacteristic of one
playing a part above his real level. Benito Cereno—Don
Benito Cereno—a sounding name. One, too, at that period,
not unknown, in the surname, to super-cargoes and sea
captains trading along the Spanish Main, as belonging to
one of the most enterprising and extensive mercantile
families in all those provinces; several members of it having
titles; a sort of Castilian Rothschild, with a noble brother,
or cousin, in every great trading town of South America.
The alleged Don Benito was in early manhood, about
twenty-nine or thirty. To assume a sort of roving cadetship
in the maritime affairs of such a house, what more likely
scheme for a young knave of talent and spirit? But the
Spaniard was a pale invalid. Never mind. For even to the
degree of simulating mortal disease, the craft of some trick-
sters had been known to attain. To think that, under the
aspect of infantile weakness, the most savage energies might
be couched—those velvets of the Spaniard but the silky
paw to his fangs.

From no train of thought did these fancies come; not
from within, but from without; suddenly, too, and in one
throng, like hoar frost; yet as soon to vanish as the mild

sun of Captain Delano's good-nature regained its meridian.

Glancing over once more towards his host—whose side-face, revealed above the skylight, was now turned towards him—he was struck by the profile, whose clearness of cut was refined by the thinness, incident to ill-health, as well as ennobled about the chin by the beard. Away with suspicion. He was a true off-shoot of a true hidalgo Cereno.

Relieved by these and other better thoughts, the visitor, lightly humming a tune, now began indifferently pacing the poop, so as not to betray to Don Benito that he had at all mistrusted incivility, much less duplicity; for such mistrust would yet be proved illusory, and by the event; though, for the present, the circumstance which had provoked that distrust remained unexplained. But when that little mystery should have been cleared up, Captain Delano thought he might extremely regret it, did he allow Don Benito to become aware that he had indulged in ungenerous surmises. In short, to the Spaniard's black-letter text, it was best, for a while, to leave open margin.

Presently, his pale face twitching and overcast, the Spaniard, still supported by his attendant, moved over towards his guest, when, with even more than his usual embarrassment, and a strange sort of intriguing intonation in his husky whisper, the following conversation began:—

"Señor, may I ask how long you have lain at this isle?"

"Oh, but a day or two, Don Benito."

"And from what port are you last?"

"Canton."

"And there, Señor, you exchanged your sealskins for teas and silks, I think you said?"

"Yes. Silks, mostly."

"And the balance you took in specie, perhaps?"

Captain Delano, fidgeting a little, answered—

"Yes; some silver; not a very great deal, though."

"Ah—well. May I ask how many men have you, Señor?"

Captain Delano slightly started, but answered—

"About five-and-twenty, all told."

"And at present, Señor, all on board, I suppose?"

"All on board, Don Benito," replied the Captain, now with satisfaction.

"And will be to-night, Señor?"

At this last question, following so many pertinacious ones, for the soul of him Captain Delano could not but look very earnestly at the questioner, who, instead of meeting the glance, with every token of craven discomposure dropped his eyes to the deck; presenting an unworthy contrast to his servant, who, just then, was kneeling at his feet, adjusting a loose shoe-buckle; his disengaged face meantime, with humble curiosity, turned openly up into his master's downcast one.

The Spaniard, still with a guilty shuffle, repeated his question:

"And—and will be to-night, Señor?"

"Yes, for aught I know," returned Captain Delano—"but nay," rallying himself into fearless truth, "some of them talked of going off on another fishing party about midnight."

"Your ships generally go—go more or less armed, I believe, Señor?"

"Oh, a six-pounder or two, in case of emergency," was the intrepidly indifferent reply, "with a small stock of muskets, sealing-spears, and cutlasses, you know."

As he thus responded, Captain Delano again glanced at Don Benito, but the latter's eyes were averted; while abruptly and awkwardly shifting the subject, he made some peevish allusion to the calm, and then, without apology, once more, with his attendant, withdrew to the opposite bulwarks, where the whispering was resumed.

At this moment, and ere Captain Delano could cast a cool thought upon what had just passed, the young Spanish sailor, before mentioned, was seen descending from the rigging. In act of stooping over to spring inboard to the deck, his voluminous, unconfined frock, or shirt, of coarse woolen, much spotted with tar, opened out far down the chest, revealing a soiled under-garment of what seemed the finest linen, edged, about the neck, with a narrow blue ribbon, sadly faded and worn. At this moment the young sailor's eye was again fixed on the whisperers, and Captain Delano thought he observed a lurking significance in it, as if silent signs, of some Freemason sort, had that instant been interchanged.

This once more impelled his own glance in the direction of Don Benito, and, as before, he could not but infer that himself formed the subject of the conference. He paused. The sound of the hatchet-polishing fell on his ears. He cast another swift side-look at the two. They had the air of conspirators. In connection with the late questionings, and the incident of the young sailor, these things now begat such return of involuntary suspicion, that the singular guilelessness of the American could not endure it. Plucking up a gay and humorous expression, he crossed over to the two rapidly, saying:—"Ha, Don Benito, your black here seems high in your trust; a sort of privy-counselor, in fact."

Upon this, the servant looked up with a good-natured grin, but the master started as from a venomous bite. It was a moment or two before the Spaniard sufficiently recovered himself to reply; which he did, at last, with cold constraint:—"Yes, Señor, I have trust in Babo."

Here Babo, changing his previous grin of mere animal humor into an intelligent smile, not ungratefully eyed his master.

Finding that the Spaniard now stood silent and reserved, as if involuntarily, or purposely giving hint that his guest's proximity was inconvenient just then, Captain Delano, unwilling to appear uncivil even to incivility itself, made some trivial remark and moved off; again and again turning over in his mind the mysterious demeanor of Don Benito Cereno.

He had descended from the poop, and, wrapped in thought, was passing near a dark hatchway, leading down into the steerage, when, perceiving motion there, he looked to see what moved. The same instant there was a sparkle in the shadowy hatchway, and he saw one of the Spanish sailors, prowling there, hurriedly placing his hand in the bosom of his frock, as if hiding something. Before the man could have been certain who it was that was passing, he slunk below out of sight. But enough was seen of him to make it sure that he was the same young sailor before noticed in the rigging.

What was that which so sparkled? thought Captain Delano. It was no lamp—no match—no live coal. Could it have been a jewel? But how come sailors with jewels?— or with silk-trimmed under-shirts either? Has he been robbing the trunks of the dead cabin-passengers? But if so, he would hardly wear one of the stolen articles on board ship here. Ah, ah—if, now, that was, indeed, a secret sign I saw passing between this suspicious fellow and his captain awhile since; if I could only be certain that, in my uneasiness, my senses did not deceive me, then——

Here, passing from one suspicious thing to another, his mind revolved the strange questions put to him concerning his ship.

By a curious coincidence, as each point was recalled, the black wizards of Ashantee would strike up with their hatchets, as in ominous comment on the white stranger's thoughts. Pressed by such enigmas and portents, it would have been almost against nature, had not, even into the least distrustful heart, some ugly misgivings obtruded.

Observing the ship, now helplessly fallen into a current, with enchanted sails, drifting with increased rapidity seaward; and noting that, from a lately intercepted projection of the land, the sealer was hidden, the stout mariner began to quake at thoughts which he barely durst confess to himself. Above all, he began to feel a ghostly dread of Don Benito. And yet, when he roused himself, dilated his chest, felt himself strong on his legs, and coolly considered it—what did all these phantoms amount to?

Had the Spaniard any sinister scheme, it must have reference not so much to him (Captain Delano) as to his ship (the *Bachelor's Delight*). Hence the present drifting away of the one ship from the other, instead of favoring any such possible scheme, was, for the time, at least, opposed to it. Clearly any suspicion, combining such contradictions, must need be delusive. Besides, was it not absurd to think of a vessel in distress—a vessel by sickness almost dismanned of her crew—a vessel whose inmates were parched for water—was it not a thousand times absurd that such a craft should, at present, be of a piratical character; or her commander, either for himself or those under him, cherish any desire but for speedy relief and refreshment? But then, might not general distress, and thirst in particular, be affected? And might not that same undiminished Spanish crew, alleged to have perished off to a remnant, be at that very moment lurking in the hold? On heartbroken pretense of entreating a cup of cold water, fiends in human form had got into lonely dwellings, nor retired until a dark deed had been done. And among the Malay pirates, it was no unusual thing to lure ships after them into their treacherous harbors, or entice boarders from a declared enemy at sea, by the spectacle of thinly manned or vacant decks, beneath which prowled a hundred spears with yellow arms ready to upthrust them through the mats. Not that Captain Delano had entirely credited such things. He had heard of them—and now, as stories, they recurred. The present destination of the ship was the anchorage.

There she would be near his own vessel. Upon gaining that vicinity, might not the *San Dominick*, like a slumbering volcano, suddenly let loose energies now hid?

He recalled the Spaniard's manner while telling his story. There was a gloomy hesitancy and subterfuge about it. It was just the manner of one making up his tale for evil purposes, as he goes. But if that story was not true, what was the truth? That the ship had unlawfully come into the Spaniard's possession? But in many of its details, especially in reference to the more calamitous parts, such as the fatalities among the seamen, the consequent prolonged beating about, the past sufferings from obstinate calms, and still continued suffering from thirst; in all these points, as well as others, Don Benito's story had corroborated not only the wailing ejaculations of the indiscriminate multitude, white and black, but likewise—what seemed impossible to be counterfeit—by the very expression and play of every human feature, which Captain Delano saw. If Don Benito's story was, throughout, an invention, then every soul on board, down to the youngest negress, was his carefully drilled recruit in the plot: an incredible inference. And yet, if there was ground for mistrusting his veracity, that inference was a legitimate one.

But those questions of the Spaniard. There, indeed, one might pause. Did they not seem put with much the same object with which the burglar or assassin, by day-time, reconnoitres the walls of a house? But, with ill purposes, to solicit such information openly of the chief person endangered, and so, in effect, setting him on his guard; how unlikely a procedure was that? Absurd, then, to suppose that those questions had been prompted by evil designs. Thus, the same conduct, which, in this instance, had raised the alarm, served to dispel it. In short, scarce any suspicion or uneasiness, however apparently reasonable at the time, which was not now, with equally apparent reason, dismissed.

At last he began to laugh at his former forebodings; and laugh at the strange ship for, in its aspect, someway siding with them, as it were; and laugh, too, at the odd-looking blacks, particularly those old scissors-grinders, the Ashantees; and those bed-ridden old knitting women, the oakumpickers; and almost at the dark Spaniard himself, the central hobgoblin of all.

For the rest, whatever in a serious way seemed enigmatical, was now good-naturedly explained away by the thought that, for the most part, the poor invalid scarcely knew what he was about; either sulking in black vapors, or putting idle questions without sense or object. Evidently, for the present, the man was not fit to be intrusted with the ship. On some benevolent plea withdrawing the command from him, Captain Delano would yet have to send her to Concepcion, in charge of his second mate, a worthy person and good navigator—a plan not more convenient for the *San Dominick* than for Don Benito; for, relieved from all anxiety, keeping wholly to his cabin, the sick man, under the good nursing of his servant, would, probably, by the end of the passage, be in a measure restored to health, and with that he should also be restored to authority.

Such were the American's thoughts. They were tranquilizing. There was a difference between the idea of Don Benito's darkly pre-ordaining Captain Delano's fate, and Captain Delano's lightly arranging Don Benito's. Nevertheless, it was not without something of relief that the good seaman presently perceived his whale-boat in the distance. Its absence had been prolonged by unexpected detention at the sealer's side, as well as its returning trip lengthened by the continual recession of the goal.

The advancing speck was observed by the blacks. Their shouts attracted the attention of Don Benito, who, with a return of courtesy, approaching Captain Delano, expressed satisfaction at the coming of some supplies, slight and temporary as they must necessarily prove.

Captain Delano responded; but while doing so, his attention was drawn to something passing on the deck below: among the crowd climbing the landward bulwarks, anxiously watching the coming boat, two blacks, to all appearances accidentally incommoded by one of the sailors, violently pushed him aside, which the sailor someway resenting, they dashed him to the deck, despite the earnest cries of the oakum-pickers.

"Don Benito," said Captain Delano quickly, "do you see what is going on there? Look!"

But, seized by his cough, the Spaniard staggered, with both hands to his face, on the point of falling. Captain Delano would have supported him, but the servant was more alert, who, with one hand sustaining his master, with the other applied the cordial. Don Benito restored, the black withdrew his support, slipping aside a little, but dutifully remaining within call of a whisper. Such discretion was here evinced as quite wiped away, in the visitor's eyes, any blemish of impropriety which might have attached to the attendant, from the indecorous conferences before mentioned; showing, too, that if the servant were to blame, it might be more the master's fault than his own, since, when left to himself, he could conduct thus well.

His glance called away from the spectacle of disorder to the more pleasing one before him, Captain Delano could not avoid again congratulating his host upon possessing such a servant, who, though perhaps a little too forward now and then, must upon the whole be invaluable to one in the invalid's situation.

"Tell me, Don Benito," he added, with a smile—"I

should like to have your man here, myself—what will you take for him? Would fifty doubloons be any object?"

"Master wouldn't part with Babo for a thousand doubloons," murmured the black, overhearing the offer, and taking it in earnest, and, with the strange vanity of a faithful slave, appreciated by his master, scorning to hear so paltry a valuation put upon him by a stranger. But Don Benito, apparently hardly yet completely restored, and again interrupted by his cough, made but some broken reply.

Soon his physical distress became so great, affecting his mind, too, apparently, that, as if to screen the sad spectacle, the servant gently conducted his master below.

Left to himself, the American, to while away the time till his boat should arrive, would have pleasantly accosted some one of the few Spanish seamen he saw; but recalling something that Don Benito had said touching their ill conduct, he refrained; as a shipmaster indisposed to countenance cowardice or unfaithfulness in seamen.

While, with these thoughts, standing with eye directed forward towards that handful of sailors, suddenly he thought that one or two of them returned the glance and with a sort of meaning. He rubbed his eyes, and looked again; but again seemed to see the same thing. Under a new form, but more obscure than any previous one, the old suspicions recurred, but, in the absence of Don Benito, with less of panic than before. Despite the bad account given of the sailors, Captain Delano resolved forthwith to accost one of them. Descending the poop, he made his way through the blacks, his movement drawing a queer cry from the oakum-pickers, prompted by whom, the negroes, twitching each other aside, divided before him; but, as if curious to see what was the object of this deliberate visit to their Ghetto, closing in behind, in tolerable order, followed the white stranger up. His progress thus proclaimed as by mounted kings-at-arms, and escorted as by a Kaffir guard of honor, Captain Delano, assuming a good-humored, off-handed air, continued to advance; now and then saying a blithe word to the negroes, and his eye curiously surveying the white faces, here and there sparsely mixed in with the blacks, like stray white pawns venturously involved in the ranks of the chess-men opposed.

While thinking which of them to select for his purpose, he chanced to observe a sailor seated on the deck engaged in tarring the strap of a large block, a circle of blacks squatted round him inquisitively eying the process.

The mean employment of the man was in contrast with something superior in his figure. His hand, black with continually thrusting it into the tar-pot held for him by a negro, seemed not naturally allied to his face, a face which would have been a very fine one but for its haggardness. Whether this haggardness had aught to do with criminality, could not be determined; since, as intense heat and cold, though unlike, produce like sensations, so innocence and guilt, when, through casual association with mental pain, stamping any visible impress, use one seal—a hacked one.

Not again that this reflection occurred to Captain Delano at the time, charitable man as he was. Rather another idea. Because observing so singular a haggardness combined with a dark eye, averted as in trouble and shame, and then again recalling Don Benito's confessed ill opinion of his crew, insensibly he was operated upon by certain general notions which, while disconnecting pain and abashment from virtue, invariably link them with vice.

If, indeed, there be any wickedness on board this ship, thought Captain Delano, be sure that man there has fouled his hand in it, even as now he fouls it in the pitch. I don't like to accost him. I will speak to this other, this old Jack here on the windlass.

He advanced to an old Barcelona tar, in ragged red

breeches and dirty night-cap, cheeks trenched and bronzed, whiskers dense as thorn hedges. Seated between two sleepy-looking Africans, this mariner, like his younger shipmate, was employed upon some rigging—splicing a cable—the sleepy-looking blacks performing the inferior function of holding the outer parts of the ropes for him.

Upon Captain Delano's approach, the man at once hung his head below its previous level; the one necessary for business. It appeared as if he desired to be thought absorbed, with more than common fidelity, in his task. Being addressed, he glanced up, but with what seemed a furtive, diffident air, which sat strangely enough on his weather-beaten visage, much as if a grizzly bear, instead of growling and biting, should simper and cast sheep's eyes. He was asked several questions concerning the voyage—questions purposely referring to several particulars in Don Benito's narrative, not previously corroborated by those impulsive cries greeting the visitor on first coming on board. The questions were briefly answered, confirming all that remained to be confirmed of the story. The negroes about the windlass joined in with the old sailor; but, as they became talkative, he by degrees became mute, and at length quite glum, seemed morosely unwilling to answer more questions, and yet, all the while, this ursine air was somehow mixed with his sheepish one.

Despairing of getting into unembarrassed talk with such a centaur, Captain Delano, after glancing round for a more promising countenance, but seeing none, spoke pleasantly to the blacks to make way for him; and so, amid various grins and grimaces, returned to the poop, feeling a little strange at first, he could hardly tell why, but upon the whole with regained confidence in Benito Cereno.

How plainly, thought he, did that old whiskerando yonder betray a consciousness of ill desert. No doubt, when he saw me coming, he dreaded lest I, apprised by his captain of the crew's general misbehavior, came with sharp words for him, and so down with his head. And yet—and yet, now that I think of it, that very old fellow, if I err not, was one of those who seemed so earnestly eying me here awhile since. Ah, these currents spin one's head round almost as much as they do the ship. Ha, there now's a pleasant sort of sunny sight; quite sociable, too.

His attention had been drawn to a slumbering negress, partly disclosed through the lacework of some rigging, lying, with youthful limbs carelessly disposed, under the lee of the bulwarks, like a doe in the shade of a woodland rock. Sprawling at her lapped breasts, was her wide-awake fawn, stark naked, its black little body half lifted from the deck, crosswise with its dam's; its hands, like two paws, clambering upon her; its mouth and nose ineffectually rooting to get at the mark; and meantime giving a vexatious half-grunt, blending with the composed snore of the negress.

The uncommon vigor of the child at length roused the mother. She started up, at a distance facing Captain Delano. But as if not at all concerned at the attitude in which she had been caught, delightedly she caught the child up, with maternal transports, covering it with kisses.

There's naked nature, now; pure tenderness and love, thought Captain Delano, well pleased.

This incident prompted him to remark the other negresses more particularly than before. He was gratified with their manners: like most uncivilized women, they seemed at once tender of heart and tough of constitution; equally ready to die for their infants or fight for them. Unsophisticated as leopardesses; loving as doves. Ah! thought Captain Delano, these, perhaps, are some of the very women whom Ledyard saw in Africa, and gave such a noble account of.

These natural sights somehow insensibly deepened his confidence and ease. At last he looked to see how his boat was getting on; but it was still pretty remote. He turned to see if Don Benito had returned; but he had not.

To change the scene, as well as to please himself with a leisurely observation of the coming boat, stepping over into the mizzen-chains, he clambered his way into the starboard quarter-gallery—one of those abandoned Venetian-looking water-balconies previously mentioned—retreats cut off from the deck. As his foot pressed the half-damp, half-dry sea-mosses matting the place, and a chance phantom cats-paw —an islet of breeze, unheralded, unfollowed—as this ghostly cats-paw came fanning his cheek; as his glance fell upon the row of small, round dead-lights—all closed like coppered eyes of the coffined—and the state-cabin door, once connecting with the gallery, even as the dead-lights had once looked out upon it, but now calked fast like a sarcophagus lid; and to a purple-black, tarred-over panel, threshold, and post; and he bethought him of the time, when that state-cabin and this state-balcony had heard the voices of the Spanish king's officers, and the forms of the Lima viceroy's daughters had perhaps leaned where he stood—as these and other images flitted through his mind, as the cats-paw through the calm, gradually he felt rising a dreamy inquietude, like that of one who alone on the prairie feels unrest from the repose of the noon.

He leaned against the carved balustrade, again looking off toward his boat; but found his eye falling upon the ribbon grass, trailing along the ship's water-line, straight as a border of green box; and parterres of sea-weed, broad ovals and crescents, floating nigh and far, with what seemed long formal alleys between, crossing the terraces of swells, and sweeping round as if leading to the grottoes below. And overhanging all was the balustrade by his arm, which, partly stained with pitch and partly embossed with moss, seemed the charred ruin of some summer-house in a grand garden long running to waste.

Trying to break one charm, he was but becharmed anew. Though upon the wide sea, he seemed in some far inland country; prisoner in some deserted château, left to stare at empty grounds, and peer out at vague roads, where never wagon or wayfarer passed.

But these enchantments were a little disenchanted as his eye fell on the corroded main-chains. Of an ancient style, massy and rusty in link, shackle and bolt, they seemed even more fit for the ship's present business than the one for which she had been built.

Presently he thought something moved nigh the chains. He rubbed his eyes, and looked hard. Groves of rigging were about the chains; and there, peering from behind a great stay, like an Indian from behind a hemlock, a Spanish sailor, a marlingspike in his hand, was seen, who made what seemed an imperfect gesture towards the balcony, but immediately, as if alarmed by some advancing step along the deck within, vanished into the recesses of the hempen forest, like a poacher.

What meant this? Something the man had sought to communicate, unbeknown to any one, even to his captain. Did the secret involve aught unfavorable to his captain? Were those previous misgivings of Captain Delano's about to be verified? Or, in his haunted mood at the moment, had some random, unintentional motion of the man, while busy with the stay, as if repairing it, been mistaken for a significant beckoning?

Not unbewildered, again he gazed off for his boat. But it was temporarily hidden by a rocky spur of the isle. As with some eagerness he bent forward, watching for the first shooting view of its beak, the balustrade gave way before him like charcoal. Had he not clutched an outreaching rope he would have fallen into the sea. The crash, though feeble, and the fall, though hollow, of the rotten fragments, must have been overheard. He glanced up.

With sober curiosity peering down upon him was one of the old oakum-pickers, slipped from his perch to an outside boom; while below the old negro, and, invisible to him, reconnoitering from a port-hole like a fox from the mouth of its den, crouched the Spanish sailor again. From something suddenly suggested by the man's air, the mad idea now darted into Captain Delano's mind, that Don Benito's plea of indisposition, in withdrawing below, was but a pretense: that he was engaged there maturing his plot, of which the sailor, by some means gaining an inkling, had a mind to warn the stranger against; incited, it may be, by gratitude for a kind word on first boarding the ship. Was it from foreseeing some possible interference like this, that Don Benito had, beforehand, given such a bad character of his sailors, while praising the negroes; though, indeed, the former seemed as docile as the latter the contrary? The whites, too, by nature, were the shrewder race. A man with some evil design, would he not be likely to speak well of that stupidity which was blind to his depravity, and malign that intelligence from which it might not be hidden? Not unlikely, perhaps. But if the whites had dark secrets concerning Don Benito, could then Don Benito be any way in complicity with the blacks? But they were too stupid. Besides, who ever heard of a white so far a renegade as to apostatize from his very species almost, by leaguing in against it with negroes? These difficulties recalled former ones. Lost in their mazes, Captain Delano, who had now regained the deck, was uneasily advancing along it, when he observed a new face; an aged sailor seated cross-legged near the main hatchway. His skin was shrunk up with wrinkles like a pelican's empty pouch; his hair frosted; his countenance grave and composed. His hands were full of ropes, which he was working into a large knot. Some blacks were about him obligingly dipping the strands for him, here and there, as the exigencies of the operation demanded.

Captain Delano crossed over to him, and stood in silence surveying the knot; his mind, by a not uncongenial transition, passing from its own entanglements to those of the hemp. For intricacy, such a knot he had never seen in an American ship, nor indeed any other. The old man looked like an Egyptian priest, making Gordian knots for the temple of Ammon. The knot seemed a combination of double-bowline-knot, treble-crown-knot, back-handed-well-knot, knot-in-and-out-knot, and jamming-knot.

At last, puzzled to comprehend the meaning of such a knot, Captain Delano addressed the knotter:—

"What are you knotting there, my man?"

"The knot," was the brief reply, without looking up.

"So it seems; but what is it for?"

"For some one else to undo," muttered back the old man, plying his fingers harder than ever, the knot being now nearly completed.

While Captain Delano stood watching him, suddenly the old man threw the knot towards him, saying in broken English—the first heard in the ship—something to this effect: "Undo it, cut it, quick." It was said lowly, but with such condensation of rapidity, that the long, slow words in Spanish, which had preceded and followed, almost operated as covers to the brief English between.

For a moment, knot in hand, and knot in head, Captain Delano stood mute; while, without further heeding him, the old man was now intent upon other ropes. Presently there was a slight stir behind Captain Delano. Turning, he saw the chained negro, Atufal, standing quietly there. The next moment the old sailor rose, muttering, and, followed by his subordinate negroes, removed to the forward part of the ship, where in the crowd he disappeared.

An elderly negro, in a clout like an infant's, and with a pepper and salt head, and a kind of attorney air, now approached Captain Delano. In tolerable Spanish, and with a good-natured, knowing wink, he informed him that the old knotter was simple-witted, but harmless; often playing his odd tricks. The negro concluded by begging the knot, for of course the stranger would not care to be troubled with it. Unconsciously, it was handed to him. With a sort of congé, the negro received it, and, turning his back, ferreted into it like a detective custom-house officer after smuggled laces. Soon, with some African word, equivalent to pshaw, he tossed the knot overboard.

All this is very queer now, thought Captain Delano, with a qualmish sort of emotion; but, as one feeling incipient sea-sickness, he strove, by ignoring the symptoms, to get rid of the malady. Once more he looked off for his boat. To his delight, it was now again in view, leaving the rocky spur astern.

The sensation here experienced, after at first relieving his uneasiness, with unforeseen efficacy soon began to remove it. The less distant sight of that well-known boat— showing it, not as before, half blended with the haze, but with outline defined, so that its individuality, like a man's, was manifest; that boat, *Rover* by name, which, though now in strange seas, had often pressed the beach of Captain Delano's home, and, brought to its threshold for repairs, had familiarly lain there, as a Newfoundland dog; the sight of that household boat evoked a thousand trustful associations, which, contrasted with previous suspicions, filled him not only with lightsome confidence, but somehow with half humorous self-reproaches at his former lack of it.

"What, I, Amasa Delano—Jack of the Beach, as they called me when a lad—I, Amasa; the same that, duck-satchel in hand, used to paddle along the water-side to the school-house made from the old hulk—I, little Jack of the Beach, that used to go berrying with cousin Nat and the rest; I to be murdered here at the ends of the earth, on board a haunted pirate-ship by a horrible Spaniard? Too nonsensical to think of! Who would murder Amasa Delano? His conscience is clean. There is some one above. Fie, fie, Jack of the Beach! you are a child indeed; a child of the second childhood, old boy; you are beginning to dote and drool, I'm afraid."

Light of heart and foot, he stepped aft, and there was met by Don Benito's servant, who, with a pleasing expression, responsive to his own present feelings, informed him that his master had recovered from the effects of his coughing fit, and had just ordered him to go present his compliments to his good guest, Don Amasa, and say that he (Don Benito) would soon have the happiness to rejoin him.

There now, do you mark that? again thought Captain Delano, walking the poop. What a donkey I was. This kind gentleman who here sends me his kind compliments, he, but ten minutes ago, dark-lantern in hand, was dodging round some old grindstone in the hold, sharpening a hatchet for me, I thought. Well, well; these long calms have a morbid effect on the mind, I've often heard, though I never believed it before. Ha! glancing towards the boat; there's *Rover*; good dog; a white bone in her mouth. A pretty big bone though, seems to me.—What? Yes, she has fallen afoul of the bubbling tide-rip there. It sets her the other way, too, for the time. Patience.

It was now about noon, though, from the grayness of everything, it seemed to be getting towards dusk.

The calm was confirmed. In the far distance, away from the influence of land, the leaden ocean seemed laid out and leaded up, its course finished, soul gone, defunct. But the current from landward, where the ship was, increased; silently sweeping her further and further towards the tranced waters beyond.

Still, from his knowledge of those latitudes, cherishing hopes of a breeze, and a fair and fresh one, at any moment,

Captain Delano, despite present prospects, buoyantly counted upon bringing the *San Dominick* safely to anchor ere night. The distance swept over was nothing; since, with a good wind, ten minutes' sailing would retrace more than sixty minutes' drifting. Meantime, one moment turning to mark *Rover* fighting the tide-rip, and the next to see Don Benito approaching, he continued walking the poop.

Gradually he felt a vexation arising from the delay of his boat; this soon merged into uneasiness; and at last—his eye falling continually, as from a stage-box into the pit, upon the strange crowd before and below him, and, by and by, recognizing there the face—now composed to indifference—of the Spanish sailor who had seemed to beckon from the main-chains—something of his old trepidations returned.

Ah, thought he—gravely enough—this is like the ague: because it went off, it follows not that it won't come back.

Though ashamed of the relapse, he could not altogether subdue it; and so, exerting his good-nature to the utmost, insensibly he came to a compromise.

Yes, this is a strange craft; a strange history, too, and strange folks on board. But—nothing more.

By way of keeping his mind out of mischief till the boat should arrive, he tried to occupy it with turning over and over, in a purely speculative sort of way, some lesser peculiarities of the captain and crew. Among others, four curious points recurred:

First, the affair of the Spanish lad assailed with a knife by the slave boy; an act winked at by Don Benito. Second, the tyranny in Don Benito's treatment of Atufal, the black; as if a child should lead a bull of the Nile by the ring in his nose. Third, the trampling of the sailor by the two negroes; a piece of insolence passed over without so much as a reprimand. Fourth, the cringing submission to their master, of all the ship's underlings, mostly blacks; as if by the least inadvertence they feared to draw down his despotic displeasure.

Coupling these points, they seemed somewhat contradictory. But what then, thought Captain Delano, glancing towards his now nearing boat—what then? Why, Don Benito is a very capricious commander. But he is not the first of the sort I have seen; though it's true he rather exceeds any other. But as a nation—continued he in his reveries—these Spaniards are all an odd set; the very word Spaniard has a curious, conspirator, Guy-Fawkish twang to it. And yet, I dare say, Spaniards in the main are as good folks as any in Duxbury, Massachusetts. Ah good! At last *Rover* has come.

As, with its welcome freight, the boat touched the side, the oakum-pickers, with venerable gestures, sought to restrain the blacks, who, at the sight of three gurried water-casks in its bottom, and a pile of wilted pumpkins in its bow, hung over the bulwarks in disorderly raptures.

Don Benito, with his servant, now appeared; his coming, perhaps, hastened by hearing the noise. Of him Captain Delano sought permission to serve out the water, so that all might share alike, and none injure themselves by unfair excess. But sensible, and, on Don Benito's account, kind as this offer was, it was received with what seemed impatience; as if aware that he lacked energy as a commander, Don Benito, with the true jealousy of weakness, resented as an affront any interference. So, at least, Captain Delano inferred.

In another moment the casks were being hoisted in, when some of the eager negroes accidentally jostled Captain Delano, where he stood by the gangway; so that, unmindful of Don Benito, yielding to the impulse of the moment, with good-natured authority he bade the blacks stand back; to enforce his words making use of a half-mirth-ful, half-menacing gesture. Instantly the blacks paused, just where they were, each negro and negress suspended in his or her posture, exactly as the word had found them —for a few seconds continuing so—while, as between the responsive posts of a telegraph, an unknown syllable ran from man to man among the perched oakum-pickers. While the visitor's attention was fixed by this scene, suddenly the hatchet-polishers half rose, and a rapid cry came from Don Benito.

Thinking that at the signal of the Spaniard he was about to be massacred, Captain Delano would have sprung for his boat, but paused, as the oakum-pickers, dropping down into the crowd with earnest exclamations, forced every white and every negro back, at the same moment, with gestures friendly and familiar, almost jocose, bidding him, in substance, not be a fool. Simultaneously the hatchet-polishers resumed their seats, quietly as so many tailors, and at once, as if nothing had happened, the work of hoisting in the casks was resumed, whites and blacks singing at the tackle.

Captain Delano glanced towards Don Benito. As he saw his meagre form in the act of recovering itself from reclining in the servant's arms, into which the agitated invalid had fallen, he could not but marvel at the panic by which himself had been surprised, on the darting supposition that such a commander, who, upon a legitimate occasion, so trivial, too, as it now appeared, could lose all self-command, was, with energetic iniquity, going to bring about his murder.

The casks being on deck, Captain Delano was handed a number of jars and cups by one of the steward's aids, who, in the name of his captain, entreated him to do as he had proposed—dole out the water. He complied, with republican impartiality as to this republican element, which always seeks one level, serving the oldest white no better than the youngest black; excepting, indeed, poor Don Benito, whose condition, if not rank, demanded an extra allowance. To him, in the first place, Captain Delano presented a fair pitcher of the fluid; but, thirsting as he was for it, the Spaniard quaffed not a drop until after several grave bows and salutes. A reciprocation of courtesies which the sight-loving Africans hailed with clapping of hands.

Two of the less wilted pumpkins being reserved for the cabin table, the residue were minced up on the spot for the general regalement. But the soft bread, sugar, and bottled cider, Captain Delano would have given the whites alone, and in chief Don Benito; but the latter objected; which disinterestedness not a little pleased the American; and so mouthfuls all around were given alike to whites and blacks; excepting one bottle of cider, which Babo insisted upon setting aside for his master.

Here it may be observed that as, on the first visit of the boat, the American had not permitted his men to board the ship, neither did he now; being unwilling to add to the confusion of the decks.

Not uninfluenced by the peculiar good-humor at present prevailing, and for the time oblivious of any but benevolent thoughts, Captain Delano, who, from recent indications, counted upon a breeze within an hour or two at furthest, dispatched the boat back to the sealer, with orders for all the hands that could be spared immediately to set about rafting casks to the watering-place and filling them. Likewise he bade word be carried to his chief officer, that if, against present expectation, the ship was not brought to anchor by sunset, he need be under no concern; for as there was to be a full moon that night, he (Captain Delano) would remain on board ready to play the pilot, come the wind soon or late.

As the two Captains stood together, observing the departing boat—the servant, as it happened, having just spied a spot on his master's velvet sleeve, and silently engaged rubbing it out—the American expressed his regrets that the *San Dominick* had no boats; none, at least, but the un-seaworthy old hulk of the long-boat, which, warped as a camel's skeleton in the desert, and almost as bleached, lay pot-wise inverted amid-ships, one side a little tipped, fur-nishing a subterraneous sort of den for family groups of the blacks, mostly women and small children; who, squatting on old mats below, or perched above in the dark dome, on the elevated seats, were descried, some distance within, like a social circle of bats, sheltering in some friendly cave; at intervals, ebon flights of naked boys and girls, three or four years old, darting in and out of the den's mouth.

"Had you three or four boats now, Don Benito," said Captain Delano, "I think that, by tugging at the oars, your negroes here might help along matters some. Did you sail from port without boats, Don Benito?"

"They were stove in the gales, Señor."

"That was bad. Many men, too, you lost then. Boats and men. Those must have been hard gales, Don Benito."

"Past all speech," cringed the Spaniard.

"Tell me, Don Benito," continued his companion with increased interest, "tell me, were these gales immediately off the pitch of Cape Horn?"

"Cape Horn?—who spoke of Cape Horn?"

"Yourself did, when giving me an account of your voy-age," answered Captain Delano, with almost equal aston-ishment at this eating of his own words, even as he ever seemed eating his own heart, on the part of the Spaniard. "You yourself, Don Benito, spoke of Cape Horn," he em-phatically repeated.

The Spaniard turned, in a sort of stooping posture, paus-ing an instant, as one about to make a plunging exchange of elements, as from air to water.

At this moment a messenger-boy, a white, hurried by,

in the regular performance of his function carrying the last
expired half-hour forward to the forecastle, from the cabin
time-piece, to have it struck at the ship's large bell.

"Master," said the servant, discontinuing his work on
the coat sleeve, and addressing the rapt Spaniard with a
sort of timid apprehensiveness, as one charged with a duty,
the discharge of which, it was foreseen, would prove irksome to the very person who had imposed it, and for whose
benefit it was intended, "master told me never mind where
he was, or how engaged, always to remind him, to a minute,
when shaving-time comes. Miguel has gone to strike the
half-hour afternoon. It is *now*, master. Will master go into
the cuddy?"

"Ah—yes," answered the Spaniard, starting, as from
dreams into realities; then turning upon Captain Delano, he
said that ere long he would resume the conversation.

"Then if master means to talk more to Don Amasa,"
said the servant, "why not let Don Amasa sit by master in
the cuddy, and master can talk, and Don Amasa can listen,
while Babo here lathers and strops."

"Yes," said Captain Delano, not unpleased with this
sociable plan, "yes, Don Benito, unless you had rather not,
I will go with you."

"Be it so, Señor."

As the three passed aft, the American could not but
think it another strange instance of his host's capriciousness,
this being shaved with such uncommon punctuality in the
middle of the day. But he deemed it more than likely that
the servant's anxious fidelity had something to do with the
matter; inasmuch as the timely interruption served to rally
his master from the mood which had evidently been coming
upon him.

The place called the cuddy was a light deck-cabin
formed by the poop, a sort of attic to the large cabin below.
Part of it had formerly been the quarters of the officers;

but since their death all the partitionings had been thrown down, and the whole interior converted into one spacious and airy marine hall; for absence of fine furniture and picturesque disarray of odd appurtenances, somewhat answering to the wide, cluttered hall of some eccentric bachelor-squire in the country, who hangs his shooting-jacket and tobacco-pouch on deer antlers, and keeps his fishing-rod, tongs, and walking-stick in the same corner.

The similitude was heightened, if not originally suggested, by glimpses of the surrounding sea; since, in one aspect, the country and the ocean seem cousins-german.

The floor of the cuddy was matted. Overhead, four or five old muskets were stuck into horizontal holes along the beams. On one side was a claw-footed old table lashed to the deck; a thumbed missal on it, and over it a small, meagre crucifix attached to the bulk-head. Under the table lay a dented cutlass or two, with a hacked harpoon, among some melancholy old rigging, like a heap of poor friars' girdles. There were also two long, sharp-ribbed settees of Malacca cane, black with age, and uncomfortable to look at as inquisitors' racks, with a large, misshapen arm-chair, which, furnished with a rude barber's crotch at the back, working with a screw, seemed some grotesque engine of torment. A flag-locker was in one corner, open, exposing various colored bunting, some rolled up, others half unrolled, still others tumbled. Opposite was a cumbrous washstand, of black mahogany, all of one block, with a pedestal, like a font, and over it a railed shelf, containing combs, brushes, and other implements of the toilet. A torn hammock of stained grass swung near; the sheets tossed, and the pillow wrinkled up like a brow, as if whoever slept here slept but illy, with alternate visitations of sad thoughts and bad dreams.

The further extremity of the cuddy, overhanging the ship's stern, was pierced with three openings, windows or port-holes, according as men or cannon might peer, socially or unsocially, out of them. At present neither men nor cannon were seen, though huge ring-bolts and other rusty iron fixtures of the wood-work hinted of twenty-four-pounders.

Glancing towards the hammock as he entered, Captain Delano said, "You sleep here, Don Benito?"

"Yes, Señor, since we got into mild weather."

"This seems a sort of dormitory, sitting-room, sail-loft, chapel, armory, and private closet all together, Don Benito," added Captain Delano, looking round.

"Yes, Señor; events have not been favorable to much order in my arrangements."

Here the servant, napkin on arm, made a motion as if waiting his master's good pleasure. Don Benito signified his readiness, when, seating him in the Malacca arm-chair, and for the guest's convenience drawing opposite one of the settees, the servant commenced operations by throwing back his master's collar and loosening his cravat.

There is something in the negro which, in a peculiar way, fits him for avocations about one's person. Most negroes are natural valets and hair-dressers; taking to the comb and brush congenially as to the castanets, and flourishing them apparently with almost equal satisfaction. There is, too, a smooth tact about them in this employment, with a marvelous, noiseless, gliding briskness, not ungraceful in its way, singularly pleasing to behold, and still more so to be the manipulated subject of. And above all is the great gift of good-humor. Not the mere grin or laugh is here meant. Those were unsuitable. But a certain easy cheerfulness, harmonious in every glance and gesture; as though God had set the whole negro to some pleasant tune.

When to this is added the docility arising from the unaspiring contentment of a limited mind, and that susceptibility of blind attachment sometimes inhering in indisputable inferiors, one readily perceives why those hypochondriacs, Johnson and Byron—it may be, something like the hypochondriac Benito Cereno—took to their hearts, almost to the exclusion of the entire white race, their serving men, the negroes, Barber and Fletcher. But if there be that in the negro which exempts him from the inflicted sourness of the morbid or cynical mind, how, in his most prepossessing aspects, must he appear to a benevolent one? When at ease with respect to exterior things, Captain Delano's nature was not only benign, but familiarly and humorously so. At home, he had often taken rare satisfaction in sitting in his door, watching some free man of color at his work or play. If on a voyage he chanced to have a black sailor, invariably he was on chatty and half-gamesome terms with him. In fact, like most men of a good, blithe heart, Captain Delano took to negroes, not philanthropically, but genially, just as other men to Newfoundland dogs.

Hitherto, the circumstances in which he found the *San Dominick* had repressed the tendency. But in the cuddy, relieved from his former uneasiness, and, for various reasons, more sociably inclined than at any previous period of the day, and seeing the colored servant, napkin on arm, so debonair about his master, in a business so familiar as that of shaving, too, all his old weakness for negroes returned.

Among other things, he was amused with an odd instance of the African love of bright colors and fine shows, in the black's informally taking from the flag-locker a great piece of bunting of all hues, and lavishly tucking it under his master's chin for an apron.

The mode of shaving among the Spaniards is a little different from what it is with other nations. They have a basin, specifically called a barber's basin, which on one side is scooped out, so as accurately to receive the chin, against which it is closely held in lathering; which is done, not with a brush, but with soap dipped in the water of the basin and rubbed on the face.

In the present instance salt-water was used for lack of better; and the parts lathered were only the upper lip, and low down under the throat, all the rest being cultivated beard.

The preliminaries being somewhat novel to Captain Delano, he sat curiously eying them, so that no conversation took place, nor, for the present, did Don Benito appear disposed to renew any.

Setting down his basin, the negro searched among the razors, as for the sharpest, and having found it, gave it an additional edge by expertly stropping it on the firm, smooth, oily skin of his open palm; he then made a gesture as if to begin, but midway stood suspended for an instant, one hand elevating the razor, the other professionally dabbling among the bubbling suds on the Spaniard's lank neck. Not unaffected by the close sight of the gleaming steel, Don Benito nervously shuddered; his usual ghastliness was heightened by the lather, which lather, again, was intensified in its hue by the contrasting sootiness of the negro's body. Altogether the scene was somewhat peculiar, at least to Captain Delano, nor, as he saw the two thus postured, could he resist the vagary, that in the black he saw a headsman, and in the white a man at the block. But this was one of those antic conceits, appearing and vanishing in a breath, from which, perhaps, the best regulated mind is not always free.

Meantime the agitation of the Spaniard had a little loosened the bunting from around him, so that one broad fold swept curtain-like over the chair-arm to the floor, revealing, amid a profusion of armorial bars and ground-colors—black, blue, and yellow—a closed castle in a blood-red field diagonal with a lion rampant in a white.

"The castle and the lion," exclaimed Captain Delano—
"why, Don Benito, this is the flag of Spain you use here.
It's well it's only I, and not the King, that sees this," he
added, with a smile, "but"—turning towards the black—
"it's all one, I suppose, so the colors be gay," which playful remark did not fail somewhat to tickle the negro.

"Now, master," he said, readjusting the flag, and pressing
the head gently further back into the crotch of the chair;
"now, master," and the steel glanced nigh the throat.

Again Don Benito faintly shuddered.

"You must not shake so, master. See, Don Amasa,
master always shakes when I shave him. And yet master
knows I never yet have drawn blood, though it's true, if
master will shake so, I may some of these times. Now,
master," he continued. "And now, Don Amasa, please go
on with your talk about the gale, and all that; master can
hear, and, between times, master can answer."

"Ah yes, these gales," said Captain Delano; "but the
more I think of your voyage, Don Benito, the more I wonder, not at the gales, terrible as they must have been, but
at the disastrous interval following them. For here, by your
account, have you been these two months and more getting
from Cape Horn to Santa Maria, a distance which I myself,
with a good wind, have sailed in a few days. True, you had
calms, and long ones, but to be becalmed for two months,
that is, at least, unusual. Why, Don Benito, had almost any
other gentleman told me such a story, I should have been
half disposed to a little incredulity."

Here an involuntary expression came over the Spaniard,
similar to that just before on the deck, and whether it was
the start he gave, or a sudden gawky roll of the hull in the
calm, or a momentary unsteadiness of the servant's hand,
however it was, just then the razor drew blood, spots of
which stained the creamy lather under the throat: immediately the black barber drew back his steel, and, remain-

ing in his professional attitude, back to Captain Delano, and face to Don Benito, held up the trickling razor, saying, with a sort of half humorous sorrow, "See, master—you shook so—here's Babo's first blood."

No sword drawn before James the First of England, no assassination in that timid King's presence, could have produced a more terrified aspect than was now presented by Don Benito.

Poor fellow, thought Captain Delano, so nervous he can't even bear the sight of barber's blood; and this unstrung, sick man, is it credible that I should have imagined he meant to spill all my blood, who can't endure the sight of one little drop of his own? Surely, Amasa Delano, you have been beside yourself this day. Tell it not when you get home, sappy Amasa. Well, well, he looks like a murderer, doesn't he? More like as if himself were to be done for. Well, well, this day's experience shall be a good lesson.

Meantime, while these things were running through the honest seaman's mind, the servant had taken the napkin from his arm, and to Don Benito had said—"But answer Don Amasa, please, master, while I wipe this ugly stuff off the razor, and strop it again."

As he said the words, his face was turned half round, so as to be alike visible to the Spaniard and the American, and seemed, by its expression, to hint, that he was desirous, by getting his master to go on with the conversation, considerately to withdraw his attention from the recent annoying accident. As if glad to snatch the offered relief, Don Benito resumed, rehearsing to Captain Delano, that not only were the calms of unusual duration, but the ship had fallen in with obstinate currents; and other things he added, some of which were but repetitions of former statements, to explain how it came to pass that the passage from Cape Horn to Santa Maria had been so exceedingly long; now and then mingling with his words, incidental praises, less qualified than before, to the blacks, for their general good conduct. These particulars were not given consecutively, the servant, at convenient times, using his razor, and so, between the intervals of shaving, the story and panegyric went on with more than usual huskiness.

To Captain Delano's imagination, now again not wholly at rest, there was something so hollow in the Spaniard's manner, with apparently some reciprocal hollowness in the servant's dusky comment of silence, that the idea flashed across him, that possibly master and man, for some unknown purpose, were acting out, both in word and deed, nay, to the very tremor of Don Benito's limbs, some juggling play before him. Neither did the suspicion of collusion lack apparent support, from the fact of those whispered conferences before mentioned. But then, what could be the object of enacting this play of the barber before him? At last, regarding the notion as a whimsy, insensibly suggested, perhaps, by the theatrical aspect of Don Benito in his harlequin ensign, Captain Delano speedily banished it.

The shaving over, the servant bestirred himself with a small bottle of scented waters, pouring a few drops on the head, and then diligently rubbing; the vehemence of the exercise causing the muscles of his face to twitch rather strangely.

His next operation was with comb, scissors, and brush; going round and round, smoothing a curl here, clipping an unruly whisker-hair there, giving a graceful sweep to the temple-lock, with other impromptu touches evincing the hand of a master; while, like any resigned gentleman in barber's hands, Don Benito bore all, much less uneasily, at least, than he had done the razoring; indeed, he sat so pale and rigid now, that the negro seemed a Nubian sculptor finishing off a white statue-head.

All being over at last, the standard of Spain removed, tumbled up, and tossed back into the flag-locker, the negro's warm breath blowing away any stray hair which might have lodged down his master's neck; collar and cravat readjusted; a speck of lint whisked off the velvet lapel; all this being done, backing off a little space, and pausing with an expression of subdued self-complacency, the servant for a moment surveyed his master, as, in toilet at least, the creature of his own tasteful hands.

Captain Delano playfully complimented him upon his achievement; at the same time congratulating Don Benito.

But neither sweet waters, nor shampooing, nor fidelity, nor sociality, delighted the Spaniard. Seeing him relapsing into forbidding gloom, and still remaining seated, Captain Delano, thinking that his presence was undesired just then, withdrew, on pretense of seeing whether, as he had prophesied, any signs of a breeze were visible.

Walking forward to the main-mast, he stood awhile thinking over the scene, and not without some undefined misgivings, when he heard a noise near the cuddy, and turning, saw the negro, his hand to his cheek. Advancing, Captain Delano perceived that the cheek was bleeding. He was about to ask the cause, when the negro's wailing soliloquy enlightened him.

"Ah, when will master get better from his sickness; only the sour heart that sour sickness breeds made him serve Babo so; cutting Babo with the razor, because, only by accident, Babo had given master one little scratch; and for the first time in so many a day, too. Ah, ah, ah," holding his hand to his face.

Is is possible, thought Captain Delano; was it to wreak in private his Spanish spite against this poor friend of his, that Don Benito, by his sullen manner, impelled me to withdraw? Ah, this slavery breeds ugly passions in man.— Poor fellow!

He was about to speak in sympathy to the negro, but with a timid reluctance he now re-entered the cuddy.

Presently master and man came forth; Don Benito leaning on his servant as if nothing had happened.

But a sort of love-quarrel, after all, thought Captain Delano.

He accosted Don Benito, and they slowly walked together. They had gone but a few paces, when the steward—a tall, rajah-looking mulatto, orientally set off with a pagoda turban formed by three or four Madras handkerchiefs wound about his head, tier on tier—approaching with a salaam, announced lunch in the cabin.

On their way thither, the two captains were preceded by the mulatto, who, turning round as he advanced, with continual smiles and bows, ushered them on, a display of elegance which quite completed the insignificance of the small bare-headed Babo, who, as if not unconscious of inferiority, eyed askance the graceful steward. But in part, Captain Delano imputed his jealous watchfulness to that peculiar feeling which the full-blooded African entertains for the adulterated one. As for the steward, his manner, if not bespeaking much dignity of self-respect, yet evidenced his extreme desire to please; which is doubly meritorious, as at once Christian and Chesterfieldian.

Captain Delano observed with interest that while the complexion of the mulatto was hybrid, his physiognomy was European—classically so.

"Don Benito," whispered he, "I am glad to see this usher-of-the-golden-rod of yours; the sight refutes an ugly remark once made to me by a Barbados planter; that when a mulatto has a regular European face, look out for him; he is a devil. But see, your steward here has features more regular than King George's of England; and yet there he nods, and bows, and smiles; a king, indeed—the king of kind hearts and polite fellows. What a pleasant voice he has, too."

"He has, señor."

"But tell me, has he not, so far as you have known him,

always proved a good, worthy fellow?" said Captain Delano, pausing, while with a final genuflexion the steward disappeared into the cabin; "come, for the reason just mentioned, I am curious to know."

"Francesco is a good man," a sort of sluggishly responded Don Benito, like a phlegmatic appreciator, who would neither find fault nor flatter.

"Ah, I thought so. For it were strange, indeed, and not very creditable to us white-skins, if a little of our blood mixed with the African's, should, far from improving the latter's quality, have the sad effect of pouring vitriolic acid into black broth; improving the hue, perhaps, but not the wholesomeness."

"Doubtless, doubtless, Señor, but"—glancing at Babo—"not to speak of negroes, your planter's remark I have heard applied to the Spanish and Indian intermixtures in our provinces. But I know nothing about the matter," he listlessly added.

And here they entered the cabin.

The lunch was a frugal one. Some of Captain Delano's fresh fish and pumpkins, biscuit and salt beef, the reserved bottle of cider, and the *San Dominick's* last bottle of Canary.

As they entered, Francesco, with two or three colored aids, was hovering over the table giving the last adjustments. Upon perceiving their master they withdrew, Francesco making a smiling congé, and the Spaniard, without condescending to notice it, fastidiously remarking to his companion that he relished not superfluous attendance.

Without companions, host and guest sat down, like a childless married couple, at opposite ends of the table, Don Benito waving Captain Delano to his place, and, weak as he was, insisting upon that gentleman being seated before himself.

The negro placed a rug under Don Benito's feet, and a cushion behind his back, and then stood behind, not his master's chair, but Captain Delano's. At first, this a little surprised the latter. But it was soon evident that, in taking his position, the black was still true to his master; since by facing him he could the more readily anticipate his slightest want.

"This is an uncommonly intelligent fellow of yours, Don Benito," whispered Captain Delano across the table.

"You say true, Señor."

During the repast, the guest again reverted to parts of Don Benito's story, begging further particulars here and there. He inquired how it was that the scurvy and fever should have committed such wholesale havoc upon the whites, while destroying less than half of the blacks. As if this question reproduced the whole scene of plague before the Spaniard's eyes, miserably reminding him of his solitude in a cabin where before he had had so many friends and officers round him, his hand shook, his face became hueless, broken words escaped; but directly the sane memory of the past seemed replaced by insane terrors of the present. With starting eyes he stared before him at vacancy. For nothing was to be seen but the hand of his servant pushing the Canary over towards him. At length a few sips served partially to restore him. He made random reference to the different constitution of races, enabling one to offer more resistance to certain maladies than another. The thought was new to his companion.

Presently Captain Delano, intending to say something to his host concerning the pecuniary part of the business he had undertaken for him, especially—since he was strictly accountable to his owners—with reference to the new suit of sails, and other things of that sort; and naturally preferring to conduct such affairs in private, was desirous that the servant should withdraw; imagining that Don Benito for a few minutes could dispense with his attendance. He, however, waited awhile; thinking that, as the conversation proceeded, Don Benito, without being prompted, would perceive the propriety of the step.

But it was otherwise. At last catching his host's eye, Captain Delano, with a slight backward gesture of his thumb, whispered, "Don Benito, pardon me, but there is an interference with the full expression of what I have to say to you."

Upon this the Spaniard changed countenance; which was imputed to his resenting the hint, as in some way a reflection upon his servant. After a moment's pause, he assured his guest that the black's remaining with them could be of no disservice; because since losing his officers he had made Babo (whose original office, it now appeared, had been captain of the slaves) not only his constant attendant and companion, but in all things his confidant.

After this, nothing more could be said; though, indeed, Captain Delano could hardly avoid some little tinge of irritation upon being left ungratified in so inconsiderable a wish, by one, too, for whom he intended such solid services. But it is only his querulousness, thought he; and so filling his glass he proceeded to business.

The price of the sails and other matters was fixed upon. But while this was being done, the American observed that, though his original offer of assistance had been hailed with hectic animation, yet now, when it was reduced to a business transaction, indifference and apathy were betrayed. Don Benito, in fact, appeared to submit to hearing the details more out of regard to common propriety, than from any impression that weighty benefit to himself and his voyage was involved.

Soon, his manner became still more reserved. The effort was vain to seek to draw him into social talk. Gnawed by his splenetic mood, he sat twitching his beard, while to little purpose the hand of his servant, mute as that on the wall, slowly pushed over the Canary.

Lunch being over, they sat down on the cushioned transom; the servant placing a pillow behind his master. The long continuance of the calm had now affected the atmosphere. Don Benito sighed heavily, as if for breath.

"Why not adjourn to the cuddy?" said Captain Delano. "There is more air there." But the host sat silent and motionless.

Meantime his servant knelt before him, with a large fan of feathers. And Francesco coming in on tiptoes, handed the negro a little cup of aromatic waters, with which at intervals he chafed his master's brow; smoothing the hair along the temples as a nurse does a child's. He spoke no word. He only rested his eye on his master's, as if, amid all Don Benito's distress, a little to refresh his spirit by the silent sight of fidelity.

Presently the ship's bell sounded two o'clock; and through the cabin windows a slight rippling of the sea was discerned; and from the desired direction.

"There," exclaimed Captain Delano, "I told you so, Don Benito, look!"

He had risen to his feet, speaking in a very animated tone, with a view the more to rouse his companion. But though the crimson curtain of the stern-window near him that moment fluttered against his pale cheek, Don Benito seemed to have even less welcome for the breeze than the calm.

Poor fellow, thought Captain Delano, bitter experience has taught him that one ripple does not make a wind, any more than one swallow a summer. But he is mistaken for once. I will get his ship in for him, and prove it.

Briefly alluding to his weak condition, he urged his host to remain quietly where he was, since he (Captain Delano) would with pleasure take upon himself the responsibility of making the best use of the wind.

Upon gaining the deck, Captain Delano started at the

unexpected figure of Atufal, monumentally fixed at the threshold, like one of those sculptured porters of black marble guarding the porches of Egyptian tombs.

But this time the start was, perhaps, purely physical. Atufal's presence, singularly attesting docility even in sullenness, was contrasted with that of the hatchet-polishers, who in patience evinced their industry; while both spectacles showed, that lax as Don Benito's general authority might be, still, whenever he chose to exert it, no man so savage or colossal but must, more or less, bow.

Snatching a trumpet which hung from the bulwarks, with a free step Captain Delano advanced to the forward edge of the poop, issuing his orders in his best Spanish. The few sailors and many negroes, all equally pleased, obediently set about heading the ship towards the harbor.

While giving some directions about setting a lower stu'n-sail, suddenly Captain Delano heard a voice faithfully repeating his orders. Turning, he saw Babo, now for the time acting, under the pilot, his original part of captain of the slaves. This assistance proved valuable. Tattered sails and warped yards were soon brought into some trim. And no brace or halyard was pulled but to the blithe songs of the inspirited negroes.

Good fellows, thought Captain Delano, a little training would make fine sailors of them. Why see, the very women pull and sing too. These must be some of those Ashantee negresses that make such capital soldiers, I've heard. But who's at the helm? I must have a good hand there.

He went to see.

The *San Dominick* steered with a cumbrous tiller, with large horizontal pulleys attached. At each pulley-end stood a subordinate black, and between them, at the tiller-head, the responsible post, a Spanish seaman, whose countenance evinced his due share in the general hopefulness and confidence at the coming of the breeze.

He proved the same man who had behaved with so shame-faced an air on the windlass.

"Ah,—it is you, my man," exclaimed Captain Delano— "well, no more sheep's eyes now;—look straight forward and keep the ship so. Good hand, I trust? And want to get into the harbor, don't you?"

The man assented with an inward chuckle, grasping the tiller-head firmly. Upon this, unperceived by the American, the two blacks eyed the sailor intently.

Finding all right at the helm, the pilot went forward to the forecastle, to see how matters stood there.

The ship now had way enough to breast the current. With the approach of evening, the breeze would be sure to freshen.

Having done all that was needed for the present, Captain Delano, giving his last orders to the sailors, turned aft to report affairs to Don Benito in the cabin; perhaps additionally incited to rejoin him by the hope of snatching a moment's private chat while the servant was engaged upon deck.

From opposite sides, there were, beneath the poop, two approaches to the cabin; one further forward than the other, and consequently communicating with a longer passage. Marking the servant still above, Captain Delano, taking the nighest entrance—the one last named, and at whose porch Atufal still stood—hurried on his way, till, arrived at the cabin threshold, he paused an instant, a little to recover from his eagerness. Then, with the words of his intended business upon his lips, he entered. As he advanced toward the seated Spaniard, he heard another footstep, keeping time with his. From the opposite door, a salver in hand, the servant was likewise advancing.

"Confound the faithful fellow," thought Captain Delano; "what a vexatious coincidence."

Possibly, the vexation might have been something different, were it not for the brisk confidence inspired by the breeze. But even as it was, he felt a slight twinge, from a sudden indefinite association in his mind of Babo with Atufal.

"Don Benito," said he, "I give you joy; the breeze will hold, and will increase. By the way, your tall man and time-piece, Atufal, stands without. By your order, of course?"

Don Benito recoiled, as if at some bland satirical touch, delivered with such adroit garnish of apparent good breeding as to present no handle for retort.

He is like one flayed alive, thought Captain Delano; where may one touch him without causing a shrink?

The servant moved before his master, adjusting a cushion; recalled to civility, the Spaniard stiffly replied: "You are right. The slave appears where you saw him, according to my command; which is, that if at the given hour I am below, he must take his stand and abide my coming."

"Ah now, pardon me, but that is treating the poor fellow like an ex-king indeed. Ah, Don Benito," smiling, "for all the license you permit in some things, I fear lest, at bottom, you are a bitter hard master."

Again Don Benito shrank; and this time, as the good sailor thought, from a genuine twinge of his conscience.

Again conversation became constrained. In vain Captain Delano called attention to the now perceptible motion of the keel gently cleaving the sea; with lack-lustre eye, Don Benito returned words few and reserved.

By and by, the wind having steadily risen, and still blowing right into the harbor, bore the *San Dominick* swiftly on. Rounding a point of land, the sealer at distance came into open view.

Meantime Captain Delano had again repaired to the deck, remaining there some time. Having at last altered the ship's course, so as to give the reef a wide berth, he returned for a few moments below.

I will cheer up my poor friend, this time, thought he.

"Better and better, Don Benito," he cried as he blithely re-entered: "there will soon be an end to your cares, at least for a while. For when, after a long, sad voyage, you know, the anchor drops into the haven, all its vast weight seems lifted from the captain's heart. We are getting on famously, Don Benito. My ship is in sight. Look through this side-light here; there she is; all a-taunt-o! The *Bachelor's Delight*, my good friend. Ah, how this wind braces one up. Come, you must take a cup of coffee with me this evening. My old steward will give you as fine a cup as ever any sultan tasted. What say you, Don Benito, will you?"

At first, the Spaniard glanced feverishly up, casting a longing look towards the sealer, while with mute concern his servant gazed into his face. Suddenly the old ague of coldness returned, and dropping back to his cushions he was silent.

"You do not answer. Come, all day you have been my host; would you have hospitality all on one side?"

"I cannot go," was the response.

"What? It will not fatigue you. The ships will lie together as near as they can, without swinging foul. It will be little more than stepping from deck to deck; which is but as from room to room. Come, come, you must not refuse me."

"I cannot go," decisively and repulsively repeated Don Benito.

Renouncing all but the last appearance of courtesy, with a sort of cadaverous sullenness, and biting his thin nails to the quick, he glanced, almost glared, at his guest, as if impatient that a stranger's presence should interfere with the full indulgence of his morbid hour. Meantime the sound of the parted waters came more and more gurglingly and merrily in at the windows; as reproaching him for his dark spleen; as telling him that, sulk as he might, and go mad with it, nature cared not a jot; since, whose fault was it, pray?

But the foul mood was now at its depth, as the fair wind at its height.

There was something in the man so far beyond any mere unsociality or sourness previously evinced, that even the forbearing good-nature of his guest could no longer endure it. Wholly at a loss to account for such demeanor, and deeming sickness with eccentricity, however extreme, no adequate excuse, well satisfied, too, that nothing in his own conduct could justify it, Captain Delano's pride began to be roused. Himself became reserved. But all seemed one to the Spaniard. Quitting him, therefore, Captain Delano once more went to the deck.

The ship was now within less than two miles of the sealer. The whale-boat was seen darting over the interval.

To be brief, the two vessels, thanks to the pilot's skill, ere long in neighborly style lay anchored together.

Before returning to his own vessel, Captain Delano had intended communicating to Don Benito the smaller details of the proposed services to be rendered. But, as it was, unwilling anew to subject himself to rebuffs, he resolved, now that he had seen the *San Dominick* safely moored, immediately to quit her, without further allusion to hospitality or business. Indefinitely postponing his ulterior plans, he would regulate his future actions according to future circumstances. His boat was ready to receive him; but his host still tarried below. Well, thought Captain Delano, if he has little breeding, the more need to show mine. He descended to the cabin to bid a ceremonious, and, it may be, tacitly rebukeful adieu. But to his great satisfaction, Don Benito, as if he began to feel the weight of that treatment with which his slighted guest had, not indecorously, retaliated upon him, now supported by his servant, rose to his feet, and grasping Captain Delano's hand, stood tremu lous; too much agitated to speak. But the good augury hence drawn was suddenly dashed, by his resuming all his previous reserve, with augmented gloom, as, with half-averted eyes, he silently reseated himself on his cushions. With a corresponding return of his own chilled feelings, Captain Delano bowed and withdrew.

He was hardly midway in the narrow corridor, dim as a tunnel, leading from the cabin to the stairs, when a sound, as of the tolling for execution in some jail-yard, fell on his ears. It was the echo of the ship's flawed bell, striking the hour, drearily reverberated in this subterranean vault. Instantly, by a fatality not to be withstood, his mind, responsive to the portent, swarmed with superstitious suspicions. He paused. In images far swifter than these sentences, the minutest details of all his former distrusts swept through him.

Hitherto, credulous good-nature had been too ready to furnish excuses for reasonable fears. Why was the Spaniard, so superfluously punctilious at times, now heedless of common propriety in not accompanying to the side his depart ing guest? Did indisposition forbid? Indisposition had not forbidden more irksome exertion that day. His last equivo cal demeanor recurred. He had risen to his feet, grasped his guest's hand, motioned toward his hat; then, in an instant, all was eclipsed in sinister muteness and gloom. Did this imply one brief, repentant relenting at the final moment, from some iniquitous plot, followed by remorseless return to it? His last glance seemed to express a calamitous, yet acquiescent farewell to Captain Delano forever. Why decline the invitation to visit the sealer that evening? Or was the Spaniard less hardened than the Jew, who refrained not from supping at the board of him whom the same night he meant to betray? What imported all those day-long enigmas and contradictions, except they were intended to mystify, preliminary to some stealthy blow? Atufal, the pretended rebel, but punctual shadow, that moment lurked by the threshold without. He seemed a sentry, and more. Who, by his own confession, had stationed him there? Was the negro now lying in wait?

The Spaniard behind—his creature before: to rush from darkness to light was the involuntary choice.

The next moment, with clenched jaw and hand, he passed Atufal, and stood unharmed in the light. As he saw his trim ship lying peacefully at anchor, and almost within ordinary call; as he saw his household boat, with familiar faces in it, patiently rising and falling on the short waves by the *San Dominick's* side; and then, glancing about the decks where he stood, saw the oakum-pickers still gravely plying their fingers; and heard the low, buzzing whistle and industrious hum of the hatchet-polishers, still bestirring themselves over their endless occupation; and more than all, as he saw the benign aspect of nature, taking her innocent repose in the evening; the screened sun in the quiet camp of the west shining out like the mild light from Abraham's tent; as charmed eye and ear took in all these, with the chained figure of the black, clenched jaw and hand relaxed. Once again he smiled at the phantoms which had mocked him, and felt something like a tinge of remorse, that, by harboring them even for a moment, he should, by implication, have betrayed an atheist doubt of the ever-watchful Providence above.

There was a few minutes' delay, while, in obedience to his orders, the boat was being hooked along to the gangway. During this interval, a sort of saddened satisfaction stole over Captain Delano, at thinking of the kindly offices he had that day discharged for a stranger. Ah, thought he, after good actions one's conscience is never ungrateful, however much so the benefited party may be.

Presently, his foot, in the first act of descent into the boat, pressed the first round of the side-ladder, his face presented inward upon the deck. In the same moment, he heard his name courteously sounded; and, to his pleased surprise, saw Don Benito advancing—an unwonted energy in his air, as if, at the last moment, intent upon making amends for his recent discourtesy. With instinctive good feeling, Captain Delano, withdrawing his foot, turned and reciprocally advanced. As he did so, the Spaniard's nervous eagerness increased, but his vital energy failed; so that, the better to support him, the servant, placing his master's hand on his naked shoulder, and gently holding it there, formed himself into a sort of crutch.

When the two captains met, the Spaniard again fervently took the hand of the American, at the same time casting an earnest glance into his eyes, but, as before, too much overcome to speak.

I have done him wrong, self-reproachfully thought Captain Delano; his apparent coldness has deceived me; in no instance has he meant to offend.

Meantime, as if fearful that the continuance of the scene might too much unstring his master, the servant seemed anxious to terminate it. And so still presenting himself as a crutch, and walking between the two captains, he advanced with them towards the gangway; while still, as if full of kindly contrition, Don Benito would not let go the hand of Captain Delano, but retained it in his, across the black's body.

Soon they were standing by the side, looking over into the boat, whose crew turned up their curious eyes. Waiting a moment for the Spaniard to relinquish his hold, the now embarrassed Captain Delano lifted his foot, to overstep the threshold of the open gangway; but still Don Benito would not let go his hand. And yet, with an agitated tone, he said, "I can go no further; here I must bid you adieu.

Adieu, my dear, dear Don Amasa. Go—go!" suddenly tearing his hand loose, "go, and God guard you better than me, my best friend."

Not unaffected, Captain Delano would now have lingered; but catching the meekly admonitory eye of the servant, with a hasty farewell he descended into his boat, followed by the continual adieus of Don Benito, standing rooted in the gangway.

Seating himself in the stern, Captain Delano, making a last salute, ordered the boat shoved off. The crew had their oars on end. The bowsmen pushed the boat a sufficient distance for the oars to be lengthwise dropped. The instant that was done, Don Benito sprang over the bulwarks, falling at the feet of Captain Delano; at the same time calling towards his ship, but in tones so frenzied, that none in the boat could understand him. But, as if not equally obtuse, three sailors, from three different and distant parts of the ship, splashed into the sea, swimming after their captain, as if intent upon his rescue.

The dismayed officer of the boat eagerly asked what this meant. To which, Captain Delano, turning a disdainful smile upon the unaccountable Spaniard, answered that, for his part, he neither knew nor cared; but it seemed as if Don Benito had taken it into his head to produce the impression among his people that the boat wanted to kidnap him. "Or else—give way for your lives," he wildly added, starting at a clattering hubbub in the ship, above which rang the tocsin of the hatchet-polishers; and seizing Don Benito by the throat he added, "this plotting pirate means murder!" Here, in apparent verification of the words, the servant, a dagger in his hand, was seen on the rail overhead, poised, in the act of leaping, as if with desperate fidelity to befriend his master to the last; while, seemingly to aid the black, the three white sailors were trying to clamber into the hampered bow. Meantime, the whole host of negroes, as if inflamed at the sight of their jeopardized captain, impended in one sooty avalanche over the bulwarks.

All this, with what preceded, and what followed, occurred with such involutions of rapidity, that past, present, and future seemed one.

Seeing the negro coming, Captain Delano had flung the Spaniard aside, almost in the very act of clutching him, and, by the unconscious recoil, shifting his place, with arms thrown up, so promptly grappled the servant in his descent, that with dagger presented at Captain Delano's heart, the black seemed of purpose to have leaped there as to his mark. But the weapon was wrenched away, and the assailant dashed down into the bottom of the boat, which now, with disentangled oars, began to speed through the sea.

At this juncture, the left hand of Captain Delano, on one side, again clutched the half-reclining Don Benito, heedless that he was in a speechless faint, while his right foot, on the other side, ground the prostrate negro; and his right arm pressed for added speed on the after oar, his eye bent forward, encouraging his men to their utmost.

But here, the officer of the boat, who had at last succeeded in beating off the towing sailors, and was now, with face turned aft, assisting the bowsman at his oar, suddenly called to Captain Delano, to see what the black was about; while a Portuguese oarsman shouted to him to give heed to what the Spaniard was saying.

Glancing down at his feet, Captain Delano saw the freed hand of the servant aiming with a second dagger— a small one, before concealed in his wool—with this he was snakishly writhing up from the boat's bottom, at the heart of his master, his countenance lividly vindictive, expressing the centred purpose of his soul; while the Spaniard, half-choked, was vainly shrinking away, with husky words, incoherent to all but the Portuguese.

That moment, across the long-benighted mind of Captain Delano, a flash of revelation swept, illuminating, in unanticipated clearness, his host's whole mysterious demeanor, with every enigmatic event of the day, as well as the entire past voyage of the *San Dominick*. He smote Babo's hand down, but his own heart smote him harder. With infinite pity he withdrew his hold from Don Benito. Not Captain Delano, but Don Benito, the black, in leaping into the boat, had intended to stab.

Both the black's hands were held, as, glancing up towards the *San Dominick*, Captain Delano, now with scales dropped from his eyes, saw the negroes, not in misrule, not in tumult, not as if frantically concerned for Don Benito, but with mask torn away, flourishing hatchets, and knives, in ferocious piratical revolt. Like delirious black dervishes, the six Ashantees danced on the poop. Prevented by their foes from springing into the water, the Spanish boys were hurrying up to the topmost spars, while such of the few Spanish sailors, not already in the sea, less alert, were descried, helplessly mixed in, on deck, with the blacks.

Meantime Captain Delano hailed his own vessel, ordering the ports up, and the guns run out. But by this time the cable of the *San Dominick* had been cut; and the fag-end, in lashing out, whipped away the canvas shroud about the beak, suddenly revealing, as the bleached hull swung round towards the open ocean, death for the figure-head, in a human skeleton; chalky comment on the chalked words below, *"Follow your leader."*

At the sight, Don Benito, covering his face, wailed out: " 'Tis he, Aranda! my murdered, unburied friend!"

Upon reaching the sealer, calling for ropes, Captain Delano bound the negro, who made no resistance, and had him hoisted to the deck. He would then have assisted the now almost helpless Don Benito up the side; but Don Benito, wan as he was, refused to move, or be moved, until the negro should have been first put below out of view. When, presently assured that it was done, he no more shrank from the ascent.

The boat was immediately dispatched back to pick up the three swimming sailors. Meantime, the guns were in readiness, though, owing to the *San Dominick* having glided somewhat astern of the sealer, only the aftermost one could be brought to bear. With this, they fired six times; thinking to cripple the fugitive ship by bringing down her spars. But only a few inconsiderable ropes were shot away. Soon the ship was beyond the gun's range, steering broad out of the bay; the blacks thickly clustering round the bowsprit, one moment with taunting cries towards the whites, the next with upthrown gestures hailing the now dusky moors of ocean—cawing crows escaped from the hand of the fowler.

The first impulse was to slip the cables and give chase. But, upon second thoughts, to pursue with whale-boat and yawl seemed more promising.

Upon inquiring of Don Benito what fire-arms they had on board the *San Dominick*, Captain Delano was answered that they had none that could be used; because, in the earlier stages of the mutiny, a cabin-passenger, since dead, had secretly put out of order the locks of what few muskets there were. But with all his remaining strength, Don Benito entreated the American not to give chase, either with ship or boat; for the negroes had already proved themselves such desperadoes, that, in case of a present assault, nothing but a total massacre of the whites could be looked for. But, regarding this warning as coming from one whose spirit had been crushed by misery, the American did not give up his design.

The boats were got ready and armed. Captain Delano

ordered his men into them. He was going himself when Don Benito grasped his arm.

"What! have you saved my life, Señor, and are you now going to throw away your own?"

The officers also, for reasons connected with their interests and those of the voyage, and a duty owing to the owners, strongly objected against their commander's going. Weighing their remonstrances a moment, Captain Delano felt bound to remain; appointing his chief mate—an athletic and resolute man, who had been a privateer's-man—to head the party. The more to encourage the sailors, they were told, that the Spanish captain considered his ship good as lost; that she and her cargo, including some gold and silver, were worth more than a thousand doubloons. Take her, and no small part should be theirs. The sailors replied with a shout.

The fugitives had now almost gained an offing. It was nearly night; but the moon was rising. After hard, prolonged pulling, the boats came up on the ship's quarters, at a suitable distance laying upon their oars to discharge their muskets. Having no bullets to return, the negroes sent their yells. But, upon the second volley, Indian-like, they hurled their hatchets. One took off a sailor's fingers. Another struck the whale-boat's bow, cutting off the rope there, and remaining stuck in the gunwale like a woodman's axe. Snatching it, quivering from its lodgment, the mate hurled it back. The returned gauntlet now stuck in the ship's broken quarter-gallery, and so remained.

The negroes giving too hot a reception, the whites kept a more respectful distance. Hovering now just out of reach of the hurtling hatchets, they, with a view to the close encounter which must soon come, sought to decoy the blacks into entirely disarming themselves of their most murderous weapons in a hand-to-hand fight, by foolishly flinging them, as missiles, short of the mark, into the sea.

But, ere long, perceiving the stratagem, the negroes desisted, though not before many of them had to replace their lost hatchets with handspikes; an exchange which, as counted upon, proved, in the end, favorable to the assailants.

Meantime, with a strong wind, the ship still clove the water; the boats alternately falling behind, and pulling up, to discharge fresh volleys.

The fire was mostly directed towards the stern, since there, chiefly, the negroes, at present, were clustering. But to kill or maim the negroes was not the object. To take them, with the ship, was the object. To do it, the ship must be boarded; which could not be done by boats while she was sailing so fast.

A thought now struck the mate. Observing the Spanish boys still aloft, high as they could get, he called to them to descend to the yards, and cut adrift the sails. It was done. About this time, owing to causes hereafter to be shown, two Spaniards, in the dress of sailors, and conspicuously showing themselves, were killed; not by volleys, but by deliberate marksman's shots; while, as it afterwards appeared, by one of the general discharges, Atufal, the black, and the Spaniard at the helm likewise were killed. What now, with the loss of the sails, and loss of leaders, the ship became unmanageable to the negroes.

With creaking masts, she came heavily round to the wind; the prow slowly swinging into view of the boats, its skeleton gleaming in the horizontal moonlight, and casting a gigantic ribbed shadow upon the water. One extended arm of the ghost seemed beckoning the whites to avenge it.

"Follow your leader!" cried the mate; and, one on each bow, the boats boarded. Sealing-spears and cutlasses crossed hatchets and hand-spikes. Huddled upon the long-boat amidships, the negresses raised a wailing chant, whose chorus was the clash of the steel.

For a time, the attack wavered; the negroes wedging

themselves to beat it back; the half-repelled sailors, as yet unable to gain a footing, fighting as troopers in the saddle, one leg sideways flung over the bulwarks, and one without, plying their cutlasses like carters' whips. But in vain. They were almost overborne, when, rallying themselves into a squad as one man, with a huzza, they sprang inboard, where, entangled, they involuntarily separated again. For a few breaths' space, there was a vague, muffled, inner sound, as of submerged sword-fish rushing hither and thither through shoals of black-fish. Soon, in a reunited band, and joined by the Spanish seamen, the whites came to the surface, irresistibly driving the negroes toward the stern. But a barricade of casks and sacks, from side to side, had been thrown up by the main-mast. Here the negroes faced about, and though scorning peace or truce, yet fain would have had respite. But, without pause, overleaping the barrier, the unflagging sailors again closed. Exhausted, the blacks now fought in despair. Their red tongues lolled, wolf-like, from their black mouths. But the pale sailors' teeth were set; not a word was spoken; and in five minutes more, the ship was won.

Nearly a score of the negroes were killed. Exclusive of those by the balls, many were mangled; their wounds— mostly inflicted by the long-edged sealing-spears, resembling those shaven ones of the English at Preston Pans, made by the poled scythes of the Highlanders. On the other side, none were killed, though several were wounded; some severely, including the mate. The surviving negroes were temporarily secured, and the ship, towed back into the harbor at midnight, once more lay anchored.

Omitting the incidents and arrangements ensuing, suffice it that, after two days spent in refitting, the ships sailed in company for Concepcion, in Chile, and thence for Lima, in Peru; where, before the vice-regal courts, the whole affair, from the beginning, underwent investigation.

Though, midway on the passage, the ill-fated Spaniard, relaxed from constraint, showed some signs of regaining health with free-will; yet, agreeably to his own foreboding, shortly before arriving at Lima, he relapsed, finally becoming so reduced as to be carried ashore in arms. Hearing of his story and plight, one of the many religious institutions of the City of Kings opened an hospitable refuge to him, where both physician and priest were his nurses, and a member of the order volunteered to be his one special guardian and consoler, by night and by day.

The following extracts, translated from one of the official Spanish documents, will, it is hoped, shed light on the preceding narrative, as well as, in the first place, reveal the true port of departure and true history of the *San Dominick's* voyage, down to the time of her touching at the island of Santa Maria.

But, ere the extracts come, it may be well to preface them with a remark.

The document selected, from among many others, for partial translation, contains the deposition of Benito Cereno; the first taken in the case. Some disclosures therein were, at the time, held dubious for both learned and natural reasons. The tribunal inclined to the opinion that the deponent, not undisturbed in his mind by recent events, raved of some things which could never have happened. But subsequent depositions of the surviving sailors, bearing out the revelations of their captain in several of the strangest particulars, gave credence to the rest. So that the tribunal, in its final decision, rested its capital sentences upon statements which, had they lacked confirmation, it would have deemed it but duty to reject.

I, Don José de Abos and Padilla, *His Majesty's Notary for the Royal Revenue, and Register of this Province, and Notary Public of the Holy Crusade of this Bishoprick, &c.*

Do certify and declare, as much as is requisite in law, that, in the criminal cause commenced the twenty-fourth of the month of September, in the year seventeen hundred and ninety-nine, against the negroes of the ship San Dominick, *the following declaration before me was made:*

Declaration of the first Witness, DON BENITO CERENO.

The same day and month and year, His Honor, Doctor Juan Martinez de Rozas, Councilor of the Royal Audience of this Kingdom, and learned in the law of this Intendency, ordered the captain of the ship San Dominick, *Don Benito Cereno, to appear; which he did in his litter, attended by the monk Infelez; of whom he received the oath, which he took by God, our Lord, and a Sign of the Cross; under which he promised to tell the truth of whatever he should know and should be asked;—and being interrogated agreeably to the tenor of the act, commencing the process, he said, that on the twentieth of May last, he set sail with his ship from the port of Valparaiso, bound to that of Callao; loaded with the produce of the country beside thirty cases of hardware and one hundred and sixty blacks, of both sexes, mostly belonging to Don Alexandro Aranda, gentleman, of the City of Mendoza; that the crew of the ship consisted of thirty-six men, beside the persons who went as passengers; that the negroes were in part as follows:*

[Here, in the original, follows a list of some fifty names, descriptions, and ages, compiled from certain recovered documents of Aranda's and also from recollections of the deponent, from which portions only are extracted.]

*—One, from about eighteen to nineteen years, named José, and this was the man that waited upon his master, Don Alexandro, and who speaks well the Spanish, having served him four or five years; * * * a mulatto, named Francesco, the cabin steward, of a good person and voice, having*

sung in the Valparaiso churches, native of the province of
Buenos Ayres, aged about thirty-five years. * * * A smart
negro, named Dago, who had been for many years a grave-
digger among the Spaniards, aged forty-six years. * * *
Four old negroes, born in Africa, from sixty to seventy, but
sound, calkers by trade, whose names are as follows:—the
first was named Mure, and he was killed (as was also his son
named Diamelo); the second, Nacta; the third, Yola, likewise killed; the fourth, Ghofan; and six full-grown negroes,
aged from thirty to forty-five, all raw, and born among the
Ashantees—Matinqui, Yau, Lecbe, Mapenda, Yambaio,
Akim; four of whom were killed; * * * a powerful negro
named Atufal, who being supposed to have been a chief in
Africa, his owner set great store by him. * * * And a small
negro of Senegal, but some years among the Spaniards, aged
about thirty, which negro's name was Babo; * * * that he
does not remember the names of the others, but that still
expecting the residue of Don Alexandro's papers will be
found, will then take due account of them all, and remit to
the court; * * * and thirty-nine women and children of all
ages.

[The catalogue over, the deposition goes on:]

* * * That all the negroes slept upon deck, as is customary in this navigation, and none wore fetters, because the
owner, his friend Aranda, told him that they were all tract-
able; * * * that on the seventh day after leaving port, at
three o'clock in the morning, all the Spaniards being asleep
except the two officers on the watch, who were the boatswain, Juan Robles, and the carpenter, Juan Bautista Ga-
yete, and the helmsman and his boy, the negroes revolted
suddenly, wounded dangerously the boatswain and the carpenter, and successively killed eighteen men of those who
were sleeping upon deck, some with hand-spikes and
hatchets, and others by throwing them alive overboard,

after tying them; that of the Spaniards upon deck, they left about seven, as he thinks, alive and tied, to manœuvre the ship, and three or four more, who hid themselves, remained also alive. Although in the act of revolt the negroes made themselves masters of the hatchway, six or seven wounded went through it to the cockpit, without any hindrance on their part; that during the act of revolt, the mate and another person, whose name he does not recollect, attempted to come up through the hatchway, but being quickly wounded, were obliged to return to the cabin; that the deponent resolved at break of day to come up the companion-way, where the negro Babo was, being the ringleader, and Atufal, who assisted him, and having spoken to them, exhorted them to cease committing such atrocities, asking them, at the same time, what they wanted and intended to do, offering, himself, to obey their commands; that notwithstanding this, they threw, in his presence, three men, alive and tied, overboard; that they told the deponent to come up, and that they would not kill him; which having done, the negro Babo asked him whether there were in those seas any negro countries where they might be carried, and he answered them, No; that the negro Babo afterwards told him to carry them to Senegal, or to the neighboring islands of St. Nicholas; and he answered, that this was impossible, on account of the great distance, the necessity involved of rounding Cape Horn, the bad condition of the vessel, the want of provisions, sails, and water; but that the negro Babo replied to him he must carry them in any way; that they would do and conform themselves to everything the deponent should require as to eating and drinking; that after a long conference, being absolutely compelled to please them, for they threatened to kill all the whites if they were not, at all events, carried to Senegal, he told them that what was most wanting for the voyage was water; that they would go near the coast to take it, and thence they would proceed on their course; that the negro Babo agreed to it; and the deponent steered towards the intermediate ports, hoping to meet some Spanish or foreign vessel that would save them; that within ten or eleven days they saw the land, and continued their course by it in the vicinity of Nasca; that the deponent observed that the negroes were now restless and mutinous, because he did not effect the taking in of water, the negro Babo having required, with threats, that it should be done, without fail, the following day; he told him he saw plainly that the coast was steep, and the rivers designated in the maps were not to be found, with other reasons suitable to the circumstances; that the best way would be to go to the island of Santa Maria, where they might water easily, it being a solitary island, as the foreigners did; that the deponent did not go to Pisco, that was near, nor make any other port of the coast, because the negro Babo had intimated to him several times, that he would kill all the whites the very moment he should perceive any city, town, or settlement of any kind on the shores to which they should be carried: that having determined to go to the island of Santa Maria, as the deponent had planned, for the purpose of trying whether, on the passage or near the island itself, they could find any vessel that should favor them, or whether he could escape from it in a boat to the neighboring coast of Arauco, to adopt the necessary means he immediately changed his course, steering for the island; that the negroes Babo and Atufal held daily conferences, in which they discussed what was necessary for their design of returning to Senegal, whether they were to kill all the Spaniards, and particularly the deponent; that eight days after parting from the coast of Nasca, the deponent being on the watch a little after day-break, and soon after the negroes had their meeting, the negro Babo came to the place where the deponent was, and told him that he had determined to kill his master, Don Alexandro Aranda, both

because he and his companions could not otherwise be sure
of their liberty, and that to keep the seamen in subjection,
he wanted to prepare a warning of what road they should
be made to take did they or any of them oppose him; and
that, by means of the death of Don Alexandro, that warning
would best be given; but, that what this last meant, the deponent did not at the time comprehend, nor could not, further than that the death of Don Alexandro was intended;
and moreover the negro Babo proposed to the deponent to
call the mate Raneds, who was sleeping in the cabin, before
the thing was done, for fear, as the deponent understood it,
that the mate, who was a good navigator, should not be killed
with Don Alexandro and the rest; that the deponent, who
was the friend, from youth, of Don Alexandro, prayed and
conjured, but all was useless; for the negro Babo answered
him that the thing could not be prevented, and that all the
Spaniards risked their death if they should attempt to frustrate his will in this matter, or any other; that, in this conflict, the deponent called the mate, Raneds, who was forced
to go apart, and immediately the negro Babo commanded
the Ashantee Matinqui and the Ashantee Lecbe to go and
commit the murder; that those two went down with hatchets
to the berth of Don Alexandro; that, yet half alive and
mangled, they dragged him on deck; that they were going
to throw him overboard in that state, but the negro Babo
stopped them, bidding the murder be completed on the deck
before him, which was done, when, by his orders, the body
was carried below, forward; that nothing more was seen of
it by the deponent for three days; * * * that Don Alonzo
Sidonia, an old man, long resident at Valparaiso, and lately
appointed to a civil office in Peru, whither he had taken
passage, was at the time sleeping in the berth opposite Don
Alexandro's; that awakening at his cries, surprised by them,
and at the sight of the negroes with their bloody hatchets in
their hands, he threw himself into the sea through a window

which was near him, and was drowned, without it being in the power of the deponent to assist or take him up; * * * that a short time after killing Aranda, they brought upon deck his cousin-german, of middle-age, Don Francisco Masa, of Mendoza, and the young Don Joaquin, Marques de Aramboalaza, then lately from Spain, with his Spanish servant Ponce, and the three young clerks of Aranda, José Morairi, Lorenzo Bargas, and Hermenegildo Gandix, all of Cadiz; that Don Joaquin and Hermenegildo Gandix, the negro Babo, for purposes hereafter to appear, preserved alive; but Don Francisco Masa, José Morairi, and Lorenzo Bargas, with Ponce the servant, beside the boatswain, Juan Robles, the boatswain's mates, Manuel Viscaya and Roderigo Hurta, and four of the sailors, the negro Babo ordered to be thrown alive into the sea, although they made no resistance, nor begged for anything else but mercy; that the boatswain, Juan Robles, who knew how to swim, kept the longest above water, making acts of contrition, and, in the last words he uttered, charged this deponent to cause mass to be said for his soul to our Lady of Succor; * * * that, during the three days which followed, the deponent, uncertain what fate had befallen the remains of Don Alexandro, frequently asked the negro Babo where they were, and, if still on board, whether they were to be preserved for interment ashore, entreating him so to order it; that the negro Babo answered nothing till the fourth day, when at sunrise, the deponent coming on deck, the negro Babo showed him a skeleton, which had been substituted for the ship's proper figure-head—the image of Cristobal Colon, the discoverer of the New World; that the negro Babo asked him whose skeleton that was, and whether, from its whiteness, he should not think it a white's; that, upon discovering his face, the negro Babo, coming close, said words to this effect: "Keep faith with the blacks from here to Senegal, or you shall in spirit, as now in body, follow your leader," *pointing to the prow;* * * * *that the same morning the negro Babo took by succession each Spaniard forward, and asked him whose skeleton that was, and whether, from its whiteness, he should not think it a white's; that each Spaniard covered his face; that then to each the negro Babo repeated the words in the first place said to the deponent;* * * * *that they (the Spaniards), being then assembled aft, the negro Babo harangued them, saying that he had now done all; that the deponent (as navigator for the negroes) might pursue his course, warning him and all of them that they should, soul and body, go the way of Don Alexandro, if he saw them (the Spaniards) speak or plot anything against them (the negroes)—a threat which was repeated every day; that, before the events last mentioned, they had tied the cook to throw him overboard, for it is not known what thing they heard him speak, but finally the negro Babo spared his life, at the request of the deponent; that a few days after, the deponent, endeavoring not to omit any means to preserve the lives of the remaining whites, spoke to the negroes peace and tranquillity, and agreed to draw up a paper, signed by the deponent and the sailors who could write, as also by the negro Babo, for himself and all the blacks, in which the deponent obliged himself to carry them to Senegal, and they not to kill any more, and he formally to make over to them the ship, with the cargo, with which they were for that time satisfied and quieted.* * * * *But the next day, the more surely to guard against the sailors' escape, the negro Babo commanded all the boats to be destroyed but the long-boat, which was unseaworthy, and another, a cutter in good condition, which knowing it would yet be wanted for towing the water casks, he had it lowered down into the hold.* * * *

[Various particulars of the prolonged and perplexed navigation ensuing here follow, with incidents of a calamitous calm, from which portion one passage is extracted, to wit:]

—*That on the fifth day of the calm, all on board suffering much from the heat, and want of water, and five having died in fits, and mad, the negroes became irritable, and for a chance gesture, which they deemed suspicious—though it was harmless—made by the mate, Raneds, to the deponent in the act of handing a quadrant, they killed him; but that for this they afterwards were sorry, the mate being the only remaining navigator on board, except the deponent.*

* * *

—*That omitting other events, which daily happened, and which can only serve uselessly to recall past misfortunes and conflicts, after seventy-three days' navigation, reckoned from the time they sailed from Nasca, during which they navigated under a scanty allowance of water, and were afflicted with the calms before mentioned, they at last arrived at the island of Santa Maria, on the seventeenth of the month of August, at about six o'clock in the afternoon, at which hour they cast anchor very near the American ship,* Bachelor's Delight, *which lay in the same bay, commanded by the generous Captain Amasa Delano; but at six o'clock in the morning, they had already descried the port, and the negroes became uneasy, as soon as at distance they saw the ship, not having expected to see one there; that the negro Babo pacified them, assuring them that no fear need be had; that straightway he ordered the figure on the bow to be covered with canvas, as for repairs, and had the decks a little set in order; that for a time the negro Babo and the negro Atufal conferred; that the negro Atufal was for sailing away, but the negro Babo would not, and, by himself, cast about what to do; that at last he came to the deponent, proposing to him to say and do all that the deponent declares*

to have said and done to the American captain; * * * that
the negro Babo warned him that if he varied in the least,
or uttered any word, or gave any look that should give the
least intimation of the past events or present state, he would
instantly kill him, with all his companions, showing a
dagger, which he carried hid, saying something which, as
he understood it, meant that that dagger would be alert as
his eye; that the negro Babo then announced the plan to
all his companions, which pleased them; that he then, the
better to disguise the truth, devised many expedients, in
some of them uniting deceit and defense; that of this sort
was the device of the six Ashantees before named, who were
his bravoes; that them he stationed on the break of the
poop, as if to clean certain hatchets (in cases, which were
part of the cargo), but in reality to use them, and distribute
them at need, and at a given word he told them; that, among
other devices, was the device of presenting Atufal, his right
hand man, as chained, though in a moment the chains could
be dropped; that in every particular he informed the deponent what part he was expected to enact in every device,
and what story he was to tell on every occasion, always
threatening him with instant death if he varied in the least:
that, conscious that many of the negroes would be turbulent, the negro Babo appointed the four aged negroes, who
were calkers, to keep what domestic order they could on
the decks; that again and again he harangued the Spaniards
and his companions, informing them of his intent, and of
his devices, and of the invented story that this deponent
was to tell; charging them lest any of them varied from that
story; that these arrangements were made and matured during the interval of two or three hours, between their first
sighting the ship and the arrival on board of Captain
Amasa Delano; that this happened about half-past seven
o'clock in the morning, Captain Amasa Delano coming
in his boat, and all gladly receiving him; that the depo-

nent, as well as he could force himself, acting then the part of principal owner, and a free captain of the ship, told Captain Amasa Delano, when called upon, that he came from Buenos Ayres, bound to Lima, with three hundred negroes; that off Cape Horn, and in a subsequent fever, many negroes had died; that also, by similar casualties, all the sea-officers and the greatest part of the crew had died.

* * *

[And so the deposition goes on, circumstantially recounting the fictitious story dictated to the deponent by Babo, and through the deponent imposed upon Captain Delano; and also recounting the friendly offers of Captain Delano, with other things, but all of which is here omitted. After the fictitious story, etc., the deposition proceeds:]
—that the generous Captain Amasa Delano remained on board all the day, till he left the ship anchored at six o'clock in the evening, deponent speaking to him always of his pretended misfortunes, under the fore-mentioned principles, without having had it in his power to tell a single word, or give him the least hint, that he might know the truth and state of things; because the negro Babo, performing the office of an officious servant with all the appearance of submission of the humble slave, did not leave the deponent one moment; that this was in order to observe the deponent's actions and words, for the negro Babo understands well the Spanish; and besides, there were thereabout some others who were constantly on the watch, and likewise understood the Spanish; * * * that upon one occasion, while deponent was standing on the deck conversing with Amasa Delano, by a secret sign the negro Babo drew him (the deponent) aside, the act appearing as if originating with the deponent; that then, he being drawn aside, the negro Babo proposed to him to gain from Amasa Delano full particulars about his ship, and crew, and arms; that the deponent asked "For

what?" that the negro Babo answered he might conceive; that, grieved at the prospect of what might overtake the generous Captain Amasa Delano, the deponent at first refused to ask the desired questions, and used every argument to induce the negro Babo to give up this new design; that the negro Babo showed the point of his dagger; that, after the information had been obtained, the negro Babo again drew him aside, telling him that that very night he (the deponent) would be captain of two ships, instead of one, for that, great part of the American's ship's crew being to be absent fishing, the six Ashantees, without any one else, would easily take it; that at this time he said other things to the same purpose; that no entreaties availed; that, before Amasa Delano's coming on board, no hint had been given touching the capture of the American ship; that to prevent this project the deponent was powerless; * * * —that in some things his memory is confused, he cannot distinctly recall every event; * * *—that as soon as they had cast anchor at six o'clock in the evening, as has before been stated, the American Captain took leave, to return to his vessel; that upon a sudden impulse, which the deponent believes to have come from God and his angels, he, after the farewell had been said, followed the generous Captain Amasa Delano as far as the gunwale, where he stayed, under pretense of taking leave, until Amasa Delano should have been seated in his boat; that on shoving off, the deponent sprang from the gunwale into the boat, and fell into it, he knows not how, God guarding him; that—

[Here, in the original, follows the account of what further happened at the escape, and how the *San Dominick* was retaken, and of the passage to the coast; including in the recital many expressions of "eternal gratitude" to the "generous Captain Amasa Delano." The deposition then proceeds with recapitulatory remarks, and a partial renu

meration of the negroes, making record of their individual
part in the past events, with a view to furnishing, according
to command of the court, the data whereon to found the
criminal sentences to be pronounced. From this portion is
the following:]

—*That he believes that all the negroes, though not in the
first place knowing to the design of revolt, when it was
accomplished, approved it.* * * * *That the negro, José,
eighteen years old, and in the personal service of Don Alexandro, was the one who communicated the information to
the negro Babo about the state of things in the cabin,
before the revolt; that this is known, because, in the preceding nights, he used to come from his berth, which was under
his master's, in the cabin, to the deck where the ringleader
and his associates were, and had secret conversations with
the negro Babo, in which he was several times seen by the
mate; that, one night, the mate drove him away twice;
* * * that this same negro José was the one who, without
being commanded to do so by the negro Babo, as Lecbe
and Matinqui were, stabbed his master, Don Alexandro,
after he had been dragged half-lifeless to the deck; * * *
that the mulatto steward, Francesco, was of the first band
of revolters, that he was, in all things, the creature and tool
of the negro Babo; that, to make his court, he, just before
a repast in the cabin, proposed, to the negro Babo, poisoning
a dish for the generous Captain Amasa Delano; this is
known and believed, because the negroes have said it; but
that the negro Babo, having another design, forbade Francesco; * * * that the Ashantee Lecbe was one of the worst
of them; for that, on the day the ship was retaken, he
assisted in the defense of her, with a hatchet in each hand,
with one of which he wounded, in the breast, the chief
mate of Amasa Delano, in the first act of boarding; this all
knew; that, in sight of the deponent, Lecbe struck with a*

hatchet, Don Francisco Masa, when, by the negro Babo's orders, he was carrying him to throw him overboard alive, beside participating in the murder, before mentioned, of Don Alexandro Aranda, and others of the cabin-passengers; that, owing to the fury with which the Ashantees fought in the engagement with the boats, but this Lecbe and Yau survived; that Yau was bad as Lecbe; that Yau was the man who, by Babo's command, willingly prepared the skeleton of Don Alexandro, in a way the negroes afterwards told the deponent, but which he, so long as reason is left him, can never divulge; that Yau and Lecbe were the two who, in a calm by night, riveted the skeleton to the bow; this also the negroes told him; that the negro Babo was he who traced the inscription below it; that the negro Babo was the plotter from first to last; he ordered every murder, and was the helm and keel of the revolt; that Atufal was his lieutenant in all; but Atufal, with his own hand, committed no murder; nor did the negro Babo; * * * that Atufal was shot, being killed in the fight with the boats, ere boarding; * * * that the negresses of age, were knowing to the revolt, and testified themselves satisfied at the death of their master, Don Alexandro; that, had the negroes not restrained them, they would have tortured to death, instead of simply killing, the Spaniards slain by command of the negro Babo; that the negresses used their utmost influence to have the deponent made away with; that, in the various acts of murder, they sang songs and danced—not gaily, but solemnly; and before the engagement with the boats, as well as during the action, they sang melancholy songs to the negroes, and that this melancholy tone was more inflaming than a different one would have been, and was so intended; that all this is believed, because the negroes have said it; —that of the thirty-six men of the crew, exclusive of the passengers (all of whom are now dead), which the deponent had knowledge of, six only remained alive, with four cabin-

*boys and ship-boys, not included with the crew; * * *
—that the negroes broke an arm of one of the cabin-boys
and gave him strokes with hatchets.*

[Then follow various random disclosures referring to
various periods of time. The following are extracted:]

—*That during the presence of Captain Amasa Delano on
board, some attempts were made by the sailors, and one by
Hermenegildo Gandix, to convey hints to him of the true
state of affairs; but that these attempts were ineffectual,
owing to fear of incurring death, and, furthermore, owing
to the devices which offered contradictions to the true state
of affairs, as well as owing to the generosity and piety
of Amasa Delano incapable of sounding such wickedness;
* * * that Luys Galgo, a sailor about sixty years of age, and
formerly of the King's navy, was one of those who sought to
convey tokens to Captain Amasa Delano; but his intent,
though undiscovered, being suspected, he was, on a pretense, made to retire out of sight, and at last into the hold,
and there was made away with. This the negroes have since
said; * * * that one of the ship-boys feeling, from Captain
Amasa Delano's presence, some hopes of release, and not
having enough prudence, dropped some chance word respecting his expectations, which being overheard and
understood by a slave-boy with whom he was eating at the
time, the latter struck him on the head with a knife, inflicting a bad wound, but of which the boy is now healing; that
likewise, not long before the ship was brought to anchor,
one of the seamen, steering at the time, endangered himself
by letting the blacks remark some expression in his countenance, arising from a cause similar to the above; but this
sailor, by his heedful after conduct, escaped; * * * that these
statements are made to show the court that from the beginning to the end of the revolt, it was impossible for the*

deponent and his men to act otherwise than they did; * * *
—that the third clerk, Hermenegildo Gandix, who before
had been forced to live among the seamen, wearing a sea-
man's habit, and in all respects appearing to be one for
the time, he, Gandix, was killed by a musket ball fired
through mistake from the boats before boarding; having in
his fright run up the mizzen-rigging, calling to the boats—
"don't board," lest upon their boarding the negroes should
kill him; that this inducing the Americans to believe he
some way favored the cause of the negroes, they fired two
balls at him, so that he fell wounded from the rigging, and
was drowned in the sea; * * *—that the young Don Joa-
quin, Marques de Aramboalaza, like Hermenegildo Gan-
dix, the third clerk, was degraded to the office and appear-
ance of a common seaman; that upon one occasion when
Don Joaquin shrank, the negro Babo commanded the
Ashantee Lecbe to take tar and heat it, and pour it upon
Don Joaquin's hands; * * *—that Don Joaquin was killed
owing to another mistake of the Americans, but one impos-
sible to be avoided, as upon the approach of the boats, Don
Joaquin, with a hatchet tied edge out and upright to his
hand, was made by the negroes to appear on the bulwarks;
whereupon, seen with arms in his hands and in a ques-
tionable attitude, he was shot for a renegade seaman; * * *
—that on the person of Don Joaquin was found secreted a
jewel, which, by papers that were discovered, proved to
have been meant for the shrine of our Lady of Mercy in
Lima; a votive offering, beforehand prepared and guarded,
to attest his gratitude, when he should have landed in
Peru, his last destination, for the safe conclusion of his
entire voyage from Spain; * * *—that the jewel, with the
other effects of the late Don Joaquin, is in the custody of the
brethren of the Hospital de Sacerdotes, awaiting the dis-
position of the honorable court; * * *—that, owing to the
condition of the deponent, as well as the haste in which the

boats departed for the attack, the Americans were not fore-warned that there were, among the apparent crew, a passenger and one of the clerks disguised by the negro Babo; * * *—that, beside the negroes killed in the action, some were killed after the capture and re-anchoring at night, when shackled to the ring-bolts on deck; that these deaths were committed by the sailors, ere they could be prevented. That so soon as informed of it, Captain Amasa Delano used all his authority, and, in particular with his own hand, struck down Martinez Gola, who, having found a razor in the pocket of an old jacket of his, which one of the shackled negroes had on, was aiming it at the negro's throat; that the noble Captain Amasa Delano also wrenched from the hand of Bartholomew Barlo a dagger, secreted at the time of the massacre of the whites, with which he was in the act of stabbing a shackled negro, who, the same day, with another negro, had thrown him down and jumped upon him; * * *—that, for all the events, befalling through so long a time, during which the ship was in the hands of the negro Babo, he cannot here give account; but that, what he has said is the most substantial of what occurs to him at present, and is the truth under the oath which he has taken, which declaration he affirmed and ratified, after hearing it read to him.

He said that he is twenty-nine years of age, and broken in body and mind; that when finally dismissed by the court, he shall not return home to Chile, but betake himself to the monastery on Mount Agonia without; and signed with his honor, and crossed himself, and, for the time, departed as he came, in his litter, with the monk Infelez, to the Hospital de Sacerdotes. Benito Cereno.

Doctor Rozas.

If the Deposition have served as the key to fit into the lock of the complications which precede it, then, as a vault whose door has been flung back, the *San Dominick's* hull lies open to-day.

Hitherto the nature of this narrative, besides rendering the intricacies in the beginning unavoidable, has more or less required that many things, instead of being set down in the order of occurrence, should be retrospectively, or irregularly given; this last is the case with the following passages, which will conclude the account:

During the long, mild voyage to Lima, there was, as before hinted, a period during which the sufferer a little recovered his health, or, at least in some degree, his tranquillity. Ere the decided relapse which came, the two captains had many cordial conversations—their fraternal unreserve in singular contrast with former withdrawments.

Again and again it was repeated, how hard it had been to enact the part forced on the Spaniard by Babo.

"Ah, my dear friend," Don Benito once said, "at those very times when you thought me so morose and ungrateful, nay, when, as you now admit, you have thought me plotting your murder, at those very times my heart was frozen; I could not look at you, thinking of what, both on board this ship and your own, hung, from other hands, over my kind benefactor. And as God lives, Don Amasa, I know not whether desire for my own safety alone could have nerved me to that leap into your boat, had it not been for the thought that, did you, unenlightened, return to your ship, you, my best friend, with all who might be with you, stolen upon, that night, in your hammocks, would never in this world have wakened again. Do but think how you walked this deck, how you sat in this cabin, every inch of ground mined into honey-combs under you. Had I dropped the least hint, made the least advance towards an understanding between us, death, explosive death—yours as mine—would have ended the scene."

"True, true," cried Captain Delano, starting, "you have

saved my life, Don Benito, more than I yours; saved it, too, against my knowledge and will."

"Nay, my friend," rejoined the Spaniard, courteous even to the point of religion, "God charmed your life, but you saved mine. To think of some things you did—those smilings and chattings, rash pointings and gesturings. For less than these, they slew my mate, Raneds; but you had the Prince of Heaven's safe-conduct through all ambuscades."

"Yes, all is owing to Providence, I know: but the temper of my mind that morning was more than commonly pleasant, while the sight of so much suffering, more apparent than real, added to my good-nature, compassion, and charity, happily interweaving the three. Had it been otherwise, doubtless, as you hint, some of my interferences might have ended unhappily enough. Besides, those feelings I spoke of enabled me to get the better of momentary distrust, at times when acuteness might have cost me my life, without saving another's. Only at the end did my suspicions get the better of me, and you know how wide of the mark they then proved."

"Wide, indeed," said Don Benito, sadly; "you were with me all day; stood with me, sat with me, talked with me, looked at me, ate with me, drank with me; and yet, your last act was to clutch for a monster, not only an innocent man, but the most pitiable of all men. To such degree may malign machinations and deceptions impose. So far may even the best man err, in judging the conduct of one with the recesses of whose condition he is not acquainted. But you were forced to it; and you were in time undeceived. Would that, in both respects, it was so ever, and with all men."

"You generalize, Don Benito; and mournfully enough. But the past is passed; why moralize upon it? Forget it. See, yon bright sun has forgotten it all, and the blue sea, and the blue sky; these have turned over new leaves."

"Because they have no memory," he dejectedly replied; "because they are not human."

"But these mild trades that now fan your cheek, do they not come with a human-like healing to you? Warm friends, steadfast friends are the trades."

"With their steadfastness they but waft me to my tomb, Señor," was the foreboding response.

"You are saved," cried Captain Delano, more and more astonished and pained; "you are saved: what has cast such a shadow upon you?"

"The negro."

There was silence, while the moody man sat, slowly and unconsciously gathering his mantle about him, as if it were a pall.

There was no more conversation that day.

But if the Spaniard's melancholy sometimes ended in muteness upon topics like the above, there were others upon which he never spoke at all; on which, indeed, all his old reserves were piled. Pass over the worst, and, only to elucidate, let an item or two of these be cited. The dress, so precise and costly, worn by him on the day whose events have been narrated, had not willingly been put on. And that silver-mounted sword, apparent symbol of despotic command, was not, indeed, a sword, but the ghost of one. The scabbard, artificially stiffened, was empty.

As for the black—whose brain, not body, had schemed and led the revolt, with the plot—his slight frame, inadequate to that which it held, had at once yielded to the superior muscular strength of his captor, in the boat. Seeing all was over, he uttered no sound, and could not be forced to. His aspect seemed to say, since I cannot do deeds, I will not speak words. Put in irons in the hold, with the rest, he was carried to Lima. During the passage, Don

Benito did not visit him. Nor then, nor at any time after, would he look at him. Before the tribunal he refused. When pressed by the judges he fainted. On the testimony of the sailors alone rested the legal identity of Babo.

Some months after, dragged to the gibbet at the tail of a mule, the black met his voiceless end. The body was burned to ashes; but for many days, the head, that hive of subtlety, fixed on a pole in the Plaza, met, unabashed, the gaze of the whites; and across the Plaza looked towards St. Bartholomew's church, in whose vaults slept then, as now, the recovered bones of Aranda: and across the Rimac bridge looked towards the monastery, on Mount Agonia without; where, three months after being dismissed by the court, Benito Cereno, borne on the bier, did, indeed, follow his leader.

The Bell-Tower

Like negroes, these powers own man sullenly;
mindful of their higher master; while serving,
plot revenge

The world is apoplectic with high-living of
ambition; and apoplexy has its fall.

Seeking to conquer a larger liberty, man but
extends the empire of necessity.

from a private MS.

IN THE south of Europe, nigh a once frescoed capital, now with dank mould cankering its bloom, central in a plain, stands what, at distance, seems the black mossed stump of some immeasurable pine, fallen, in forgotten days, with Anak and the Titan.

As all along where the pine tree falls, its dissolution leaves a mossy mound—last-flung shadow of the perished trunk; never lengthening, never lessening; unsubject to the fleet falsities of the sun; shade immutable, and true gauge which cometh by prostration—so westward from what seems the stump, one steadfast spear of lichened ruin veins the plain.

From that tree-top, what birded chimes of silver throats had rung. A stone pine; a metallic aviary in its crown: the Bell-Tower, built by the great mechanician, the unblest foundling, Bannadonna.

Like Babel's, its base was laid in a high hour of renovated earth, following the second deluge, when the waters of th⸱⸱

Dark Ages had dried up, and once more the green appeared. No wonder that, after so long and deep submersion, the jubilant expectation of the race should, as with Noah's sons, soar into Shinar aspiration.

In firm resolve, no man in Europe at that period went beyond Bannadonna. Enriched through commerce with the Levant, the state in which he lived voted to have the noblest Bell-Tower in Italy. His repute assigned him to be architect.

Stone by stone, month by month, the tower rose. Higher, higher, snail-like in pace, but torch or rocket in its pride.

After the masons would depart, the builder, standing alone upon its ever-ascending summit, at close of every day, saw that he overtopped still higher walls and trees. He would tarry till a late hour there, wrapped in schemes of other and still loftier piles. Those who of saints' days thronged the spot—hanging to the rude poles of scaffolding, like sailors on yards, or bees on boughs, unmindful of lime and dust, and falling chips of stone—their homage not the less inspirited him to self-esteem.

At length the holiday of the Tower came. To the sound of viols, the climax-stone slowly rose in air, and, amid the firing of ordnance, was laid by Bannadonna's hands upon the final course. Then mounting it, he stood erect, alone, with folded arms, gazing upon the white summits of blue inland Alps, and whiter crests of bluer Alps off-shore—sights invisible from the plain. Invisible, too, from thence was that eye he turned below, when, like the cannon booms, came up to him the people's combustions of applause.

That which stirred them so was, seeing with what serenity the builder stood three hundred feet in air, upon an unrailed perch. This none but he durst do. But his periodic standing upon the pile, in each stage of its growth —such discipline had its last result.

Little remained now but the bells. These, in all respects, must correspond with their receptacle.

The minor ones were prosperously cast. A highly enriched one followed, of a singular make, intended for suspension in a manner before unknown. The purpose of this bell, its rotary motion, and connection with the clock-work, also executed at the time, will, in the sequel, receive mention.

In the one erection, bell-tower and clock-tower were united, though, before that period, such structures had commonly been built distinct; as the Campanile and Torre dell' Orologio of St. Mark to this day attest.

But it was upon the great state-bell that the founder lavished his more daring skill. In vain did some of the less elated magistrates here caution him; saying that though truly the tower was Titanic, yet limit should be set to the dependent weight of its swaying masses. But undeterred, he prepared his mammoth mold, dented with mythological devices; kindled his fires of balsamic firs; melted his tin and copper, and, throwing in much plate, contributed by the public spirit of the nobles, let loose the tide.

The unleashed metals bayed like hounds. The workmen shrunk. Through their fright, fatal harm to the bell was dreaded. Fearless as Shadrach, Bannadonna, rushing through the glow, smote the chief culprit with his ponderous ladle. From the smitten part, a splinter was dashed into the seething mass, and at once was melted in.

Next day a portion of the work was heedfully uncovered. All seemed right. Upon the third morning, with equal satisfaction, it was bared still lower. At length, like some old Theban king, the whole cooled casting was disinterred. All was fair except in one strange spot. But as he suffered no one to attend him in these inspections, he concealed the blemish by some preparation which none knew better to devise.

The casting of such a mass was deemed no small triumph for the caster; one, too, in which the state might not scorn to share. The homicide was overlooked. By the charitable that deed was but imputed to sudden transports of esthetic passion, not to any flagitious quality. A kick from an Arabian charger; not sign of vice, but blood.

His felony remitted by the judge, absolution given him by the priest, what more could even a sickly conscience have desired!

Honoring the tower and its builder with another holiday, the republic witnessed the hoisting of the bells and clock-work amid shows and pomps superior to the former.

Some months of more than usual solitude on Banna-donna's part ensued. It was not unknown that he was engaged upon something for the belfry, intended to complete it, and surpass all that had gone before. Most people imagined that the design would involve a casting like the bells. But those who thought they had some further insight, would shake their heads, with hints, that not for nothing did the mechanician keep so secret. Meantime, his seclusion failed not to invest his work with more or less of that sort of mystery pertaining to the forbidden.

Ere long he had a heavy object hoisted to the belfry, wrapped in a dark sack or cloak—a procedure sometimes had in the case of an elaborate piece of sculpture, or statue, which, being intended to grace the front of a new edifice, the architect does not desire exposed to critical eyes, till set up, finished, in its appointed place. Such was the impression now. But, as the object rose, a statuary present observed, or thought he did, that it was not entirely rigid, but was, in a manner, pliant. At last, when the hidden thing had attained its final height, and, obscurely seen from below, seemed almost of itself to step into the belfry, as if with little assistance from the crane, a shrewd old black-smith present ventured the suspicion that it was but a living man. This surmise was thought a foolish one, while the general interest failed not to augment.

Not without demur from Bannadonna, the chief-magistrate of the town, with an associate—both elderly men—followed what seemed the image up the tower. But, arrived at the belfry, they had little recompense. Plausibly entrenching himself behind the conceded mysteries of his art, the mechanician withheld present explanation. The magistrates glanced toward the cloaked object, which, to their surprise, seemed now to have changed its attitude, or else had before been more perplexingly concealed by the violent muffling action of the wind without. It seemed now seated upon some sort of frame, or chair, contained within the domino. They observed that nigh the top, in a sort of square, the web of the cloth, either from accident or design, had its warp partly withdrawn, and the cross threads plucked out here and there, so as to form a sort of woven grating. Whether it were the low wind or no, stealing through the stone lattice-work, or only their own perturbed imaginations, is uncertain, but they thought they discerned a slight sort of fitful, spring-like motion, in the domino. Nothing, however incidental or insignificant, escaped their uneasy eyes. Among other things, they pried out, in a corner, an earthen cup, partly corroded and partly encrusted, and one whispered to the other, that this cup was just such a one as might, in mockery, be offered to the lips of some brazen statue, or, perhaps, still worse.

But, being questioned, the mechanician said, that the cup was simply used in his founder's business, and described the purpose; in short, a cup to test the condition of metals in fusion. He added, that it had got into the belfry by the merest chance.

Again, and again, they gazed at the domino, as at some suspicious incognito at a Venetian masque. All sorts of vague apprehensions stirred them. They even dreaded lest, when they should descend, the mechanician, though without a flesh and blood companion, for all that, would not be left alone.

Affecting some merriment at their disquietude, he begged to relieve them, by extending a coarse sheet of workman's canvas between them and the object.

Meantime he sought to interest them in his other work; nor, now that the domino was out of sight, did they long remain insensible to the artistic wonders lying round them; wonders hitherto beheld but in their unfinished state; because, since hoisting the bells, none but the caster had entered within the belfry. It was one trait of his, that, even in details, he would not let another do what he could, without too great loss of time, accomplish for himself. So, for several preceding weeks, whatever hours were unemployed in his secret design, had been devoted to elaborating the figures on the bells.

The clock-bell, in particular, now drew attention. Under a patient chisel, the latent beauty of its enrichments, before obscured by the cloudings incident to casting, that beauty in its shyest grace, was now revealed. Round and round the bell, twelve figures of gay girls, garlanded, hand-in-hand, danced in a choral ring—the embodied hours.

"Bannadonna," said the chief, "this bell excels all else. No added touch could here improve. Hark!" hearing a sound, "was that the wind?"

"The wind, Excellenza," was the light response. "But the figures, they are not yet without their faults. They need some touches yet. When those are given, and the —— block yonder," pointing towards the canvas screen, "when Haman there, as I merrily call him,—him? *it*, I mean—— when Haman is fixed on this, his lofty tree, then, gentlemen, will I be most happy to receive you here again."

The equivocal reference to the object caused some return of restlessness. However, on their part, the visitors forbore further allusion to it, unwilling, perhaps, to let the foundling see how easily it lay within his plebeian art to stir the placid dignity of nobles.

"Well, Bannadonna," said the chief, "how long ere you are ready to set the clock going, so that the hour shall be sounded? Our interest in you, not less than in the work itself, makes us anxious to be assured of your success. The people, too,—why, they are shouting now. Say the exact hour when you will be ready."

"To-morrow, Excellenza, if you listen for it,—or should you not, all the same—strange music will be heard. The stroke of one shall be the first from yonder bell," pointing to the bell, adorned with girls and garlands, "that stroke shall fall there, where the hand of Una clasps Dua's. The stroke of one shall sever that loved clasp. To-morrow, then, at one o'clock, as struck here, precisely here," advancing and placing his finger upon the clasp, "the poor mechanic will be most happy once more to give you liege audience, in this his littered shop. Farewell till then, illustrious magnificoes, and hark ye for your vassal's stroke."

His still, Vulcanic face hiding its burning brightness like a forge, he moved with ostentatious deference towards the scuttle, as if so far to escort their exit. But the junior magistrate, a kind-hearted man, troubled at what seemed to him a certain sardonical disdain, lurking beneath the foundling's humble mien, and in Christian sympathy more distressed at it on his account than on his own, dimly surmising what might be the final fate of such a cynic solitaire, nor perhaps uninfluenced by the general strangeness of surrounding things, this good magistrate had glanced sadly, sideways from the speaker, and thereupon his foreboding eye had started at the expression of the unchanging face of the Hour Una.

"How is this, Bannadonna?" he lowly asked, "Una looks unlike her sisters."

"In Christ's name, Bannadonna," impulsively broke in the chief, his attention, for the first attracted to the figure, by his associate's remark, "Una's face looks just like that of Deborah, the prophetess, as painted by the Florentine, Del Fonca."

"Surely, Bannadonna," lowly resumed the milder magistrate, "you meant the twelve should wear the same jocundly abandoned air. But see, the smile of Una seems but a fatal one. 'Tis different."

While his mild associate was speaking, the chief glanced, inquiringly, from him to the caster, as if anxious to mark how the discrepancy would be accounted for. As the chief stood, his advanced foot was on the scuttle's curb.

Bannadonna spoke:

"Excellenza, now that, following your keener eye, I glance upon the face of Una, I do, indeed perceive some little variance. But look all round the bell, and you will find no two faces entirely correspond. Because there is a law in art—— but the cold wind is rising more; these lattices are but a poor defense. Suffer me, magnificoes, to conduct you, at least, partly on your way. Those in whose well-being there is a public stake, should be heedfully attended."

"Touching the look of Una you were saying, Bannadonna, that there was a certain law in art," observed the chief, as the three now descended the stone shaft, "pray, tell me, then——."

"Pardon; another time, Excellenza;—the tower is damp."

"Nay, I must rest, and hear it now. Here,—here is a wide landing, and through this leeward slit, no wind, but ample light. Tell us of your law; and at large."

"Since, Excellenza, you insist, know that there is a law in art, which bars the possibility of duplicates. Some years ago, you may remember, I graved a small seal for your republic, bearing, for its chief device, the head of your own ancestor, its illustrious founder. It becoming necessary, for the customs' use, to have innumerable impressions for bales and boxes, I graved an entire plate, containing one hundred of the seals. Now, though, indeed, my object was to have those hundred heads identical, and though, I dare say, people think them so, yet, upon closely scanning an uncut impression from the plate, no two of those five-score faces, side by side, will be found alike. Gravity is the air of all; but, diversified in all. In some, benevolent; in some, ambiguous; in two or three, to a close scrutiny, all but incipiently malign, the variation of less than a hair's breadth in the linear shadings round the mouth sufficing to all this. Now, Excellenza, transmute that general gravity into joyousness, and subject it to twelve of those variations I have described, and tell me, will you not have my hours here, and Una one of them? But I like ———."

"Hark! is that—a footfall above?"

"Mortar, Excellenza; sometimes it drops to the belfry-floor from the arch where the stonework was left undressed. I must have it seen to. As I was about to say: for one, I like this law forbidding duplicates. It evokes fine personalities. Yes, Excellenza, that strange, and—to you—uncertain smile, and those fore-looking eyes of Una, suit Bannadonna very well."

"Hark!—sure we left no soul above?"

"No soul, Excellenza; rest assured, no *soul*.—Again the mortar."

"It fell not while we were there."

"Ah, in your presence, it better knew its place, Excellenza," blandly bowed Bannadonna.

"But, Una," said the milder magistrate, "she seemed intently gazing on you; one would have almost sworn that she picked you out from among us three."

"If she did, possibly, it might have been her finer apprehension, Excellenza."

"How, Bannadonna? I do not understand you."

"No consequence, no consequence, Excellenza—but the shifted wind is blowing through the slit. Suffer me to escort you on; and then, pardon, but the toiler must to his tools."

"It may be foolish, Signor," said the milder magistrate, as, from the third landing, the two now went down unescorted, "but, somehow, our great mechanician moves me strangely. Why, just now, when he so superciliously replied, his walk seemed Sisera's, God's vain foe, in Del Fonca's painting. And that young, sculptured Deborah, too. Aye, and that——."

"Tush, tush, Signor!" returned the chief. "A passing whim. Deborah?—Where's Jael, pray?"

"Ah," said the other, as they now stepped upon the sod, "Ah, Signor, I see you leave your fears behind you with the chill and gloom; but mine, even in this sunny air, remain. Hark!"

It was a sound from just within the tower door, whence they had emerged. Turning, they saw it closed.

"He has slipped down and barred us out." smiled the chief; "but it is his custom."

Proclamation was now made, that the next day, at one hour after meridian, the clock would strike, and—thanks to the mechanician's powerful art—with unusual accompaniments. But what those should be, none as yet could say. The announcement was received with cheers.

By the looser sort, who encamped about the tower all night, lights were seen gleaming through the topmost blind-work, only disappearing with the morning sun. Strange sounds, too, were heard, or were thought to be, by those whom anxious watching might not have left mentally undisturbed—sounds, not only of some ringing implement,

but also—so they said—half-suppressed screams and plain-
ings, such as might have issued from some ghostly engine,
overplied.

Slowly the day drew on; part of the concourse chasing
the weary time with songs and games, till, at last, the great
blurred sun rolled, like a football, against the plain.

At noon, the nobility and principal citizens came from
the town in cavalcade; a guard of soldiers, also, with music,
the more to honor the occasion.

Only one hour more. Impatience grew. Watches were
held in hands of feverish men, who stood, now scrutinizing
their small dial-plates, and then, with neck thrown back,
gazing toward the belfry, as if the eye might foretell that
which could only be made sensible to the ear; for, as yet,
there was no dial to the tower-clock.

The hour-hands of a thousand watches now verged
within a hair's breadth of the figure I. A silence, as of the
expectation of some Shiloh, pervaded the swarming plain.
Suddenly a dull, mangled sound—naught ringing in it;
scarcely audible, indeed, to the outer circles of the people
—that dull sound dropped heavily from the belfry. At the
same moment, each man stared at his neighbor blankly.
All watches were upheld. All hour-hands were at—had
passed—the figure I. No bell-stroke from the tower. The
multitude became tumultuous.

Waiting a few moments, the chief magistrate, commanding silence, hailed the belfry, to know what thing unforeseen had happened there.

No response.

He hailed again and yet again.

All continued hushed.

By his order, the soldiers burst in the tower-door; when,
stationing guards to defend it from the now surging mob,
the chief, accompanied by his former associate, climbed the
winding stairs. Half-way up, they stopped to listen. No

sound. Mounting faster, they reached the belfry; but, at the threshold, started at the spectacle disclosed. A spaniel, which, unbeknown to them, had followed them thus far, stood shivering as before some unknown monster in a brake: or, rather, as if it snuffed footsteps leading to some other world.

Bannadonna lay, prostrate and bleeding, at the base of the bell which was adorned with girls and garlands. He lay at the feet of the hour Una; his head coinciding, in a vertical line, with her left hand, clasped by the hour Dua. With downcast face impending over him, like Jael over nailed Sisera in the tent, was the domino; now no more becloaked.

It had limbs, and seemed clad in a scaly mail, lustrous as a dragon-beetle's. It was manacled, and its clubbed arms were uplifted, as if, with its manacles, once more to smite its already smitten victim. One advanced foot of it was inserted beneath the dead body, as if in the act of spurning it.

Uncertainty falls on what now followed.

It were but natural to suppose that the magistrates would, at first, shrink from immediate personal contact with what they saw. At the least, for a time, they would stand in involuntary doubt; it may be, in more or less of horrified alarm. Certain it is, that an arquebuss was called for from below. And some add, that its report, followed by a fierce whiz, as of the sudden snapping of a main-spring, with a steely din, as if a stack of sword-blades should be dashed upon a pavement, these blended sounds came ringing to the plain, attracting every eye far upward to the belfry, whence, through the lattice-work, thin wreaths of smoke were curling.

Some averred that it was the spaniel, gone mad by fear, which was shot. This, others denied. True it was, the spaniel never more was seen; and, probably, for some unknown reason, it shared the burial now to be related of the domino. For, whatever the preceding circumstances may have been, the first instinctive panic over, or else all ground of reasonable fear removed, the two magistrates, by themselves, quickly rehooded the figure in the dropped cloak wherein it had been hoisted. The same night, it was secretly lowered to the ground, smuggled to the beach, pulled far out to sea, and sunk. Nor to any after urgency, even in free convivial hours, would the twain ever disclose the full secrets of the belfry.

From the mystery unavoidably investing it, the popular solution of the foundling's fate involved more or less of supernatural agency. But some few less unscientific minds pretended to find little difficulty in otherwise accounting for it. In the chain of circumstantial inferences drawn, there may, or may not, have been some absent or defective links. But, as the explanation in question is the only one which tradition has explicitly preserved, in dearth of better, it will here be given. But, in the first place, it is requisite to present the supposition entertained as to the entire motive and mode, with their origin, of the secret design of Bannadonna; the minds above-mentioned assuming to penetrate as well into his soul as into the event. The disclosure will indirectly involve reference to peculiar matters, none of the clearest, beyond the immediate subject.

At that period, no large bell was made to sound otherwise than as at present, by agitation of a tongue within, by means of ropes, or percussion from without, either from cumbrous machinery, or stalwart watchmen, armed with heavy hammers, stationed in the belfry, or in sentry-boxes on the open roof, according as the bell was sheltered or exposed.

It was from observing these exposed bells, with their watchmen, that the foundling, as was opined, derived the first suggestion of his scheme. Perched on a great mast or spire, the human figure, viewed from below, undergoes such a reduction in its apparent size, as to obliterate its intelligent features. It evinces no personality. Instead of bespeaking volition, its gestures rather resemble the automatic ones of the arms of a telegraph.

Musing, therefore, upon the purely Punchinello aspect of the human figure thus beheld, it had indirectly occurred to Bannadonna to devise some metallic agent, which should strike the hour with its mechanic hand, with even greater precision than the vital one. And, moreover, as the vital watchman on the roof, sallying from his retreat at the given periods, walked to the bell with uplifted mace, to smite it, Bannadonna had resolved that his invention should likewise possess the power of locomotion, and, along with that, the appearance, at least, of intelligence and will.

If the conjectures of those who claimed acquaintance with the intent of Bannadonna be thus far correct, no unenterprising spirit could have been his. But they stopped not here; intimating that though, indeed, his design had, in the first place, been prompted by the sight of the watchman, and confined to the devising of a subtle substitute for him: yet, as is not seldom the case with projectors, by insensible gradations, proceeding from comparatively pigmy aims to Titanic ones, the original scheme had, in its anticipated eventualities, at last, attained to an unheard-of degree of daring. He still bent his efforts upon the locomotive figure for the belfry, but only as a partial type of an ulterior creature, a sort of elephantine Helot, adapted to further, in a degree scarcely to be imagined, the universal conveniences and glories of humanity; supplying nothing less than a supplement to the Six Days' Work; stocking the earth with a new serf, more useful than the ox, swifter than the dolphin, stronger than the lion, more cunning than the ape, for industry an ant, more fiery than serpents, and yet, in patience, another ass. All excellences of all God-made creatures, which served man, were here to receive advancement, and then to be combined in one. Talus was to have been the all-accomplished Helot's name. Talus, iron slave to Bannadonna, and, through him, to man.

Here, it might well be thought that, were these last conjectures as to the foundling's secrets not erroneous, then must he have been hopelessly infected with the craziest chimeras of his age; far outgoing Albert Magus and Cornelius Agrippa. But the contrary was averred. However marvelous his design, however apparently transcending not alone the bounds of human invention, but those of divine creation, yet the proposed means to be employed were alleged to have been confined within the sober forms of sober reason. It was affirmed that, to a degree of more than skeptic scorn, Bannadonna had been without sympathy for any of the vain-glorious irrationalities of his time. For example, he had not concluded, with the visionaries among the metaphysicians, that between the finer mechanic forces and the ruder animal vitality some germ of correspondence might prove discoverable. As little did his scheme partake of the enthusiasm of some natural philosophers, who hoped, by physiological and chemical inductions, to arrive at a knowledge of the source of life, and so qualify themselves to manufacture and improve upon it. Much less had he aught in common with the tribe of alchemists, who sought, by a species of incantations, to evoke some surprising vitality from the laboratory. Neither had he imagined, with certain sanguine theosophists, that, by faithful adoration of the Highest, unheard-of powers would be vouchsafed to man. A practical materialist, what Bannadonna had aimed at was to have been reached, not by logic, not by crucible, not by conjuration, not by altars; but by plain vice-bench and hammer. In short, to solve nature, to steal into her, to intrigue beyond her, to procure some one else to bind her to his hand;—these, one and all, had not been his objects; but, asking no favors from any element or any being, of himself, to rival her, outstrip her, and rule her. He stooped to conquer. With him, common sense was theurgy; machinery, miracle; Prometheus, the heroic name for machinist; man, the true God.

Nevertheless, in his initial step, so far as the experimental automaton for the belfry was concerned, he allowed fancy some little play; or, perhaps, what seemed his fancifulness was but his utilitarian ambition collaterally extended. In figure, the creature for the belfry should not be likened after the human pattern, nor any animal one, nor after the ideals, however wild, of ancient fable, but equally in aspect as in organism be an original production; the more terrible to behold, the better.

Such, then, were the suppositions as to the present scheme, and the reserved intent. How, at the very threshold, so unlooked-for a catastrophe overturned all, or rather, what was the conjecture here, is now to be set forth.

It was thought that on the day preceding the fatality, his visitors having left him, Bannadonna had unpacked the belfry image, adjusted it, and placed it in the retreat provided—a sort of sentry-box in one corner of the belfry; in short, throughout the night, and for some part of the ensuing morning, he had been engaged in arranging everything connected with the domino; the issuing from the sentry-box each sixty minutes; sliding along a grooved way, like a railway; advancing to the clock-bell, with uplifted manacles; striking it at one of the twelve junctions of the four-and-twenty hands; then wheeling, circling the bell, and retiring to its post, there to bide for another sixty minutes, when the same process was to be repeated; the bell, by a cunning mechanism, meantime turning on its vertical axis, so as to present, to the descending mace, the clasped hands of the next two figures, when it would strike two, three, and so on, to the end. The musical metal in this time-bell being so managed in the fusion, by some art, perishing with its originator, that each of the clasps of the four-and-twenty hands should give forth its own peculiar resonance when parted.

But on the magic metal, the magic and metallic stranger never struck but that one stroke, drove but that one nail, severed but that one clasp, by which Bannadonna clung to his ambitious life. For, after winding up the creature in the sentry-box, so that, for the present, skipping the intervening hours, it should not emerge till the hour of one, but should then infallibly emerge, and, after deftly oiling the grooves whereon it was to slide, it was surmised that the mechanician must then have hurried to the bell, to give his final touches to its sculpture. True artist, he here became absorbed; and absorption still further intensified, it may be, by his striving to abate that strange look of Una; which, though, before others, he had treated with such unconcern, might not, in secret, have been without its thorn.

And so, for the interval, he was oblivious of his creature; which, not oblivious of him, and true to its creation, and true to its heedful winding up, left its post precisely at the given moment; along its well-oiled route, slid noiselessly towards its mark; and, aiming at the hand of Una, to ring one clangorous note, dully smote the intervening brain of Bannadonna, turned backwards to it; the manacled arms then instantly up-springing to their hovering poise. The falling body clogged the thing's return; so there it stood, still impending over Bannadonna, as if whispering some post-mortem terror. The chisel lay dropped from the hand, but beside the hand; the oil-flask spilled across the iron track.

In his unhappy end, not unmindful of the rare genius of the mechanician, the republic decreed him a stately funeral. It was resolved that the great bell—the one whose casting had been jeopardized through the timidity of the ill-starred workman—should be rung upon the entrance of the bier into the cathedral. The most robust man of the country round was assigned the office of bell-ringer.

But as the pall-bearers entered the cathedral porch, naught but a broken and disastrous sound, like that of some lone Alpine land-slide, fell from the tower upon their ears. And then, all was hushed.

Glancing backwards, they saw the groined belfry crashed sideways in. It afterwards appeared that the powerful peasant, who had the bell-rope in charge, wishing to test at once the full glory of the bell, had swayed down upon the rope with one concentrate jerk. The mass of quaking metal, too ponderous for its frame, and strangely feeble somewhere at its top, loosed from its fastening, tore sideways down, and tumbling in one sheer fall, three hundred feet to the soft sward below, buried itself inverted and half out of sight.

Upon its disinterment, the main fracture was found to have started from a small spot in the ear; which, being scraped, revealed a defect, deceptively minute, in the casting; which defect must subsequently have been pasted over with some unknown compound.

The remolten metal soon reassumed its place in the tower's repaired superstructure. For one year the metallic choir of birds sang musically in its belfry-bough-work of sculptured blinds and traceries. But on the first anniversary of the tower's completion—at early dawn, before the concourse had surrounded it—an earthquake came; one loud crash was heard. The stone-pine, with its bower of songsters, lay overthrown upon the plain.

So the blind slave obeyed its blinder lord; but, in obedience, slew him. So the creator was killed by the creature. So the bell was too heavy for the tower. So the bell's main weakness was where man's blood had flawed it. And so pride went before the fall.

I and My Chimney

I and My Chimney

I AND my chimney, two gray-headed old smokers, reside in the country. We are, I may say, old settlers here; particularly my old chimney, which settles more and more every day.

Though I always say, *I and my chimney,* as Cardinal Wolsey used to say, *I and my King,* yet this egotistic way of speaking, wherein I take precedence of my chimney, is hardly borne out by the facts; in everything, except the above phrase, my chimney taking precedence of me.

Within thirty feet of the turf-sided road, my chimney—a huge, corpulent old Harry VIII of a chimney—rises full in front of me and all my possessions. Standing well up a hill-side, my chimney, like Lord Rosse's monster telescope, swung vertical to hit the meridian moon, is the first object to greet the approaching traveler's eye, nor is it the last which the sun salutes. My chimney, too, is before me in receiving the first-fruits of the seasons. The snow is on its head ere on my hat; and every spring, as in a hollow beech tree, the first swallows build their nests in it.

But it is within doors that the pre-eminence of my chimney is most manifest. When in the rear room, set apart for that object, I stand to receive my guests (who, by the way, call more, I suspect, to see my chimney than me), I then stand, not so much before, as, strictly speaking, behind my chimney, which is, indeed, the true host. Not that I demur. In the presence of my betters, I hope I know my place.

From this habitual precedence of my chimney over me, some even think that I have got into a sad rearward way altogether; in short, from standing behind my old-fashioned chimney so much, I have got to be quite behind the age, too, as well as running behind-hand in everything else. But to tell the truth, I never was a very forward old fellow, nor what my farming neighbors call a forehanded one. Indeed, those rumors about my behindhandedness are so far correct, that I have an odd sauntering way with me sometimes of going about with my hands behind my back. As for my belonging to the rear-guard in general, certain it is, I bring up the rear of my chimney—which, by the way, is this moment before me—and that, too, both in fancy and fact. In brief, my chimney is my superior; my superior by I know not how many heads and shoulders; my superior, too, in that humbly bowing over with shovel and tongs, I much minister to it; yet never does it minister, or incline over to me; but, if anything, in its settlings, rather leans the other way.

My chimney is grand seignior here—the one great domineering object, not more of the landscape, than of the house; all the rest of which house, in each architectural arrangement, as may shortly appear, is, in the most marked manner, accommodated, not to my wants, but to my chimney's, which, among other things, has the centre of the house to himself. leaving but the odd holes and corners to me.

But I and my chimney must explain; and, as we are both rather obese, we may have to expatiate.

In those houses which are strictly double houses—that is, where the hall is in the middle—the fire-places usually are on opposite sides; so that while one member of the household is warming himself at a fire built into a recess of the north wall, say another member, the former's own brother, perhaps, may be holding his feet to the blaze before a hearth in the south wall—the two thus fairly sitting back to back. Is this well? Be it put to any man who has a proper fraternal feeling. Has it not a sort of sulky appearance? But very probably this style of chimney building originated with some architect afflicted with a quarrelsome family.

Then again, almost every modern fire-place has its separate flue—separate throughout, from hearth to chimney-top. At least such an arrangement is deemed desirable. Does not this look egotistical, selfish? But still more, all these separate flues, instead of having independent masonry establishments of their own, or instead of being grouped together in one federal stock in the middle of the house—instead of this, I say, each flue is surreptitiously honey-combed into the walls; so that these last are here and there, or indeed almost anywhere, treacherously hollow, and, in consequence, more or less weak. Of course, the main reason of this style of chimney building is to economize room. In cities, where lots are sold by the inch, small space is to spare for a chimney constructed on magnanimous principles; and, as with most thin men, who are generally tall, so with such houses, what is lacking in breadth must be made up in height. This remark holds true even with regard to many very stylish abodes, built by the most stylish of gentlemen. And yet, when that stylish gentleman, Louis le Grand of France, would build a palace for his lady friend, Madame de Maintenon, he built it but one story high—in fact, in the cottage style. But then, how uncommonly quadrangular, spacious, and broad—horizontal acres, not vertical ones. Such is the palace which, in all its one-storied magnificence of Languedoc marble, in the garden of Versailles, still remains to this day. Any man can buy a square foot of land and plant a liberty-pole on it; but it takes a king to set apart whole acres for a grand Trianon.

But nowadays it is different; and furthermore, what originated in a necessity has been mounted into a vaunt. In
towns there is large rivalry in building tall houses. If one
gentleman builds his house four stories high, and another
gentleman comes next door and builds five stories high, then
the former, not to be looked down upon that way, immediately sends for his architect and claps a fifth and a sixth
story on top of his previous four. And, not till the gentleman
has achieved his aspiration, not till he has stolen over the
way by twilight and observed how his sixth story soars
beyond his neighbor's fifth—not till then does he retire to
his rest with satisfaction.

Such folks, it seems to me, need mountains for neighbors, to take this emulous conceit of soaring out of them.

If, considering that mine is a very wide house, and by
no means lofty, aught in the above may appear like interested pleading, as if I did but fold myself about in the
cloak of a general proposition, cunningly to tickle my individual vanity beneath it, such misconception must vanish
upon my frankly conceding, that land adjoining my alder
swamp was sold last month for ten dollars an acre, and
thought a rash purchase at that; so that for wide houses
hereabouts there is plenty of room, and cheap. Indeed, so
cheap—dirt cheap—is the soil, that our elms thrust out
their roots in it, and hang their great boughs over it, in the
most lavish and reckless way. Almost all our crops, too, are
sown broadcast, even peas and turnips. A farmer among us,
who should go about his twenty-acre field, poking his finger
into it here and there, and dropping down a mustard seed,
would be thought a penurious, narrow-minded husbandman. The dandelions in the river-meadows, and the forget-
me-nots along the mountain roads, you see at once they are
put to no economy in space. Some seasons, too, our rye
comes up, here and there a spear, sole and single like a
church-spire. It doesn't care to crowd itself where it knows

there is such a deal of room. The world is wide, the world is all before us, says the rye. Weeds, too, it is amazing how they spread. No such thing as arresting them—some of our pastures being a sort of Alsatia for the weeds. As for the grass, every spring it is like Kossuth's rising of what he calls the peoples. Mountains, too, a regular camp-meeting of them. For the same reason, the same all-sufficiency of room, our shadows march and countermarch, going through their various drills and masterly evolutions, like the old imperial guard on the Champs de Mars. As for the hills, especially where the roads cross them, the supervisors of our various towns have given notice to all concerned, that they can come and dig them down and cart them off, and never a cent to pay, no more than for the privilege of picking blackberries. The stranger who is buried here, what liberal-hearted landed proprietor among us grudges him his six feet of rocky pasture?

Nevertheless, cheap, after all, as our land is, and much as it is trodden under foot, I, for one, am proud of it for what it bears; and chiefly for its three great lions—the Great Oak, Ogg Mountain, and my chimney.

Most houses here, are but one and a half stories high; few exceed two. That in which I and my chimney dwell, is in width nearly twice its height, from sill to eaves—which accounts for the magnitude of its main content—besides, showing that in this house, as in this country at large, there is abundance of space, and to spare, for both of us.

The frame of the old house is of wood—which but the more sets forth the solidity of the chimney, which is of brick. And as the great wrought nails, binding the clapboards, are unknown in these degenerate days, so are the huge bricks in the chimney walls. The architect of the chimney must have had the pyramid of Cheops before him; for, after that famous structure, it seems modeled, only its rate of decrease towards the summit is considerably less, and it is truncated. From the exact middle of the mansion it soars from the cellar, right up through each successive floor, till, four feet square, it breaks water from the ridge-pole of the roof, like an anvil-headed whale, through the crest of a billow. Most people, though, liken it, in that part, to a razeed observatory, masoned up.

The reason for its peculiar appearance above the roof touches upon rather delicate ground. How shall I reveal that, forasmuch as many years ago the original gable roof of the old house had become very leaky, a temporary proprietor hired a band of woodmen, with their huge, cross-cut saws, and went to sawing the old gable roof clean off. Off it went, with all its birds' nests, and dormer windows. It was replaced with a modern roof, more fit for a railway wood-house than an old country gentleman's abode. This operation—razeeing the structure some fifteen feet—was, in effect upon the chimney, something like the falling of the great spring tides. It left uncommon low water all about the chimney—to abate which appearance, the same person now proceeds to slice fifteen feet off the chimney itself, actually beheading my royal old chimney—a regicidal act which, were it not for the palliating fact that he was a poulterer by trade, and, therefore, hardened to such neck-wringings, should send that former proprietor down to posterity in the same cart with Cromwell.

Owing to its pyramidal shape, the reduction of the chimney inordinately widened its razeed summit. Inordinately, I say, but only in the estimation of such as have no eye to the picturesque. What care I, if, unaware that my chimney, as a free citizen of this free land, stands upon an independent basis of its own, people passing it wonder how such a brick-kiln, as they call it, is supported upon mere joists and rafters? What care I? I will give a traveler a cup of switchel, if he want it; but am I bound to supply him with a sweet taste? Men of cultivated minds see, in my old house and chimney, a goodly old elephant-and-castle.

All feeling hearts will sympathize with me in what I am now about to add. The surgical operation, above referred to, necessarily brought into the open air a part of the chimney previously under cover, and intended to remain so and, therefore, not built of what are called weather-bricks. In consequence, the chimney, though of a vigorous constitution, suffered not a little from so naked an exposure; and, unable to acclimate itself, ere long began to fail—showing blotchy symptoms akin to those in measles. Whereupon travelers, passing my way, would wag their heads, laughing: "See that wax nose—how it melts off!" But what cared I? The same travelers would travel across the sea to view Kenilworth peeling away, and for a very good reason: that of all artists of the picturesque, decay wears the palm—I would say, the ivy. In fact, I've often thought that the proper place for my old chimney is ivied old England.

In vain my wife—with what probable ulterior intent will, ere long, appear—solemnly warned me, that unless something were done, and speedily, we should be burnt to the ground, owing to the holes crumbling through the aforesaid blotchy parts, where the chimney joined the roof. "Wife," said I, "far better that my house should burn down, than that my chimney should be pulled down, though but a few feet. They call it a wax nose; very good; not for me to tweak the nose of my superior." But at last the man who has a mortgage on the house dropped me a note, reminding me that, if my chimney was allowed to stand in that invalid condition, my policy of insurance would be void. This was a sort of hint not to be neglected. All the world over, the picturesque yields to the pocketesque. The mortgagor cared not, but the mortgagee did.

So another operation was performed. The wax nose was taken off, and a new one fitted on. Unfortunately for the expression—being put up by a squint-eyed mason who, at the time, had a bad stitch in the same side—the new nose stands a little awry, in the same direction.

Of one thing, however, I am proud. The horizontal dimensions of the new part are unreduced.

Large as the chimney appears upon the roof, that is nothing to its spaciousness below. At its base in the cellar, it is precisely twelve feet square; and hence covers precisely one hundred and forty-four superficial feet. What an appropriation of terra firma for a chimney, and what a huge load for this earth! In fact, it was only because I and my chimney formed no part of his ancient burden, that that stout peddler, Atlas of old, was enabled to stand up so bravely under his pack. The dimensions given may, perhaps, seem fabulous. But, like those stones at Gilgal, which Joshua set up for a memorial of having passed over Jordan, does not my chimney remain, even unto this day?

Very often I go down into my cellar, and attentively survey that vast square of masonry. I stand long, and ponder over, and wonder at it. It has a druidical look, away down in the umbrageous cellar there, whose numerous vaulted passages, and far glens of gloom, resemble the dark, damp depths of primeval woods. So strongly did this conceit steal over me, so deeply was I penetrated with wonder at the chimney, that one day—when I was a little out of my mind, I now think—getting a spade from the garden, I set to work, digging round the foundation, especially at the corners thereof, obscurely prompted by dreams of striking upon some old, earthen-worn memorial of that by-gone day when, into all this gloom, the light of heaven entered, as the masons laid the foundation-stones, peradventure sweltering under an August sun, or pelted by a March storm. Plying my blunted spade, how vexed was I by that ungracious interruption of a neighbor who, calling to see me upon

some business, and being informed that I was below, said
I need not be troubled to come up, but he would go down
to me; and so, without ceremony, and without my having
been forewarned, suddenly discovered me, digging in my
cellar.

"Gold digging, sir?"

"Nay, sir," answered I, starting, "I was merely—ahem!
—merely—I say I was merely digging—round my
chimney."

"Ah, loosening the soil, to make it grow. Your chimney,
sir, you regard as too small, I suppose; needing further
development, especially at the top?"

"Sir!" said I, throwing down the spade, "do not be
personal. I and my chimney—"

"Personal?"

"Sir, I look upon this chimney less as a pile of masonry
than as a personage. It is the king of the house. I am but
a suffered and inferior subject."

In fact, I would permit no gibes to be cast at either myself or my chimney; and never again did my visitor refer
to it in my hearing, without coupling some compliment
with the mention. It well deserves a respectful consideration. There it stands, solitary and alone—not a council-of-
ten flues, but, like his sacred majesty of Russia, a unit of an
autocrat.

Even to me, its dimensions, at times, seem incredible. It
does not look so big—no, not even in the cellar. By the mere
eye, its magnitude can be but imperfectly comprehended,
because only one side can be received at one time; and said
side can only present twelve feet, linear measure. But then,
each other side also is twelve feet long; and the whole
obviously forms a square; and twelve times twelve is one
hundred and forty-four. And so, an adequate conception of
the magnitude of this chimney is only to be got at by a sort

of process in the higher mathematics, by a method somewhat akin to those whereby the surprising distances of fixed
stars are computed.

It need hardly be said, that the walls of my house are
entirely free from fire-places. These all congregate in the
middle—in the one grand central chimney, upon all four
sides of which are hearths—two tiers of hearths—so that
when, in the various chambers, my family and guests are
warming themselves of a cold winter's night, just before
retiring, then, though at the time they may not be thinking
so, all their faces mutually look towards each other, yea,
all their feet point to one centre; and, when they go to
sleep in their beds, they all sleep round one warm chimney,
like so many Iroquois Indians, in the woods, round their
one heap of embers. And just as the Indians' fire serves, not
only to keep them comfortable, but also to keep off wolves,
and other savage monsters, so my chimney, by its obvious
smoke at top, keeps off prowling burglars from the towns—
for what burglar or murderer would dare break into an
abode from whose chimney issues such a continual smoke—
betokening that if the inmates are not stirring, at least
fires are, and in case of an alarm, candles may readily be
lighted, to say nothing of muskets.

But stately as is the chimney—yea, grand high altar as
it is, right worthy for the celebration of high mass before
the Pope of Rome, and all his cardinals—yet what is there
perfect in this world? Caius Julius Caesar, had he not been
so inordinately great, they say that Brutus, Cassius, Antony,
and the rest, had been greater. My chimney, were it not so
mighty in its magnitude, my chambers had been larger.
How often has my wife ruefully told me, that my chimney,
like the English aristocracy, casts a contracting shade all
round it. She avers that endless domestic inconveniences
arise—more particularly from the chimney's stubborn central locality. The grand objection with her is, that it stands

midway in the place where a fine entrance-hall ought to be. In truth, there is no hall whatever to the house—nothing but a sort of square landing-place, as you enter from the wide front door. A roomy enough landing-place, I admit, but not attaining to the dignity of a hall. Now, as the front door is precisely in the middle of the front of the house, inwards it faces the chimney. In fact, the opposite wall of the landing-place is formed solely by the chimney; and hence—owing to the gradual tapering of the chimney—is a little less than twelve feet in width. Climbing the chimney in this part, is the principal stair-case—which, by three abrupt turns, and three minor landing-places, mounts to the second floor, where, over the front door, runs a sort of narrow gallery, something less than twelve feet long, leading to chambers on either hand. This gallery, of course, is railed; and so, looking down upon the stairs, and all those landing-places together, with the main one at bottom, resembles not a little a balcony for musicians, in some jolly old abode, in times Elizabethan. Shall I tell a weakness? I cherish the cobwebs there, and many a time arrest Biddy in the act of brushing them with her broom, and have many a quarrel with my wife and daughters about it.

Now the ceiling, so to speak, of the place where you enter the house, that ceiling is, in fact, the ceiling of the second floor, not the first. The two floors are made one here; so that ascending this turning stairs, you seem going up into a kind of soaring tower, or light-house. At the second landing, midway up the chimney, is a mysterious door, entering to a mysterious closet; and here I keep mysterious cordials, of a choice, mysterious flavor, made so by the constant nurturing and subtle ripening of the chimney's gentle heat, distilled through that warm mass of masonry. Better for wines is it than voyages to the Indias; my chimney itself a tropic. A chair by my chimney in a November day is as good for an invalid as a long season spent in Cuba. Often I think how grapes might ripen against my chimney. How my wife's geraniums bud there! Bud in December. Her eggs, too—can't keep them near the chimney, on account of hatching. Ah, a warm heart has my chimney.

How often my wife was at me about that projected grand entrance-hall of hers, which was to be knocked clean through the chimney, from one end of the house to the other, and astonish all guests by its generous amplitude. "But, wife," said I, "the chimney—consider the chimney: if you demolish the foundation, what is to support the superstructure?" "Oh, that will rest on the second floor." The truth is, women know next to nothing about the realities of architecture. However, my wife still talked of running her entries and partitions. She spent many long nights elaborating her plans; in imagination building her boasted hall through the chimney, as though its high mightiness were a mere spear of sorrel-top. At last, I gently reminded her that, little as she might fancy it, the chimney was a fact—a sober, substantial fact, which, in all her plannings, it would be well to take into full consideration. But this was not of much avail.

And here, respectfully craving her permission, I must say a few words about this enterprising wife of mine. Though in years nearly old as myself, in spirit she is young as my little sorrel mare, Trigger, that threw me last fall. What is extraordinary, though she comes of a rheumatic family, she is straight as a pine, never has any aches; while for me with the sciatica, I am sometimes as crippled up as any old apple tree. But she has not so much as a toothache. As for her hearing—let me enter the house in my dusty boots, and she away up in the attic. And for her sight—Biddy, the housemaid, tells other people's housemaids, that her mistress will spy a spot on the dresser straight through the pewter platter, put up on purpose to hide it. Her faculties are alert as her limbs and her senses. No danger of my spouse dying of torpor. The longest night in the year I've known her lie awake, planning her campaign for the morrow. She is a natural projector. The maxim, "Whatever is, is right," is not hers. Her maxim is, Whatever is, is wrong; and what is more, must be altered; and what is still more, must be altered right away. Dreadful maxim for the wife of a dozy old dreamer like me, who dote on seventh days as days of rest, and, out of a sabbatical horror of industry, will, on a week-day, go out of my road a quarter of a mile, to avoid the sight of a man at work.

That matches are made in heaven, may be, but my wife would have been just the wife for Peter the Great, or Peter the Piper. How she would have set in order that huge littered empire of the one, and with indefatigable painstaking picked the peck of pickled peppers for the other.

But the most wonderful thing is, my wife never thinks of her end. Her youthful incredulity, as to the plain theory, and still plainer fact of death, hardly seems Christian. Advanced in years, as she knows she must be, my wife seems to think that she is to teem on, and be inexhaustible forever. She doesn't believe in old age. At that strange promise in the plain of Mamre, my old wife, unlike old Abraham's, would not have jeeringly laughed within herself.

Judge how to me, who, sitting in the comfortable shadow of my chimney, smoking my comfortable pipe, with ashes not unwelcome at my feet, and ashes not unwelcome all but in my mouth; and who am thus in a comfortable sort of not unwelcome, though, indeed, ashy enough way, reminded of the ultimate exhaustion even of the most fiery life; judge how to me this unwarrantable vitality in my wife must come, sometimes, it is true, with a moral and a calm, but oftener with a breeze and a ruffle.

If the doctrine be true, that in wedlock contraries attract, by how cogent a fatality must I have been drawn to my wife! While spicily impatient of present and past, like a glass of ginger-beer she overflows with her schemes; and, with like energy as she puts down her foot, puts down her preserves and her pickles, and lives with them in a continual future; or ever full of expectations both from time and space, is ever restless for newspapers, and ravenous for letters. Content with the years that are gone, taking no thought for the morrow, and looking for no new thing from any person or quarter whatever, I have not a single scheme or expectation on earth, save in unequal resistance of the undue encroachment of hers.

Old myself, I take to oldness in things; for that cause mainly loving old Montaigne, and old cheese, and old wine; and eschewing young people, hot rolls, new books, and early potatoes, and very fond of my old claw-footed chair, and old club-footed Deacon White, my neighbor, and that still nigher old neighbor, my betwisted old grape-vine, that of a summer evening leans in his elbow for cosy company at my window-sill, while I, within doors, lean over mine to meet his; and above all, high above all, am fond of my high-manteled old chimney. But she, out of that infatuate juvenility of hers, takes to nothing but newness; for that cause mainly, loving new cider in autumn, and in spring, as if she were own daughter of Nebuchadnezzar, fairly raving after all sorts of salads and spinaches, and more particularly green cucumbers (though all the time nature rebukes such unsuitable young hankerings in so elderly a person, by never permitting such things to agree with her), and has an itch after recently-discovered fine prospects (so no grave-yard be in the background), and also after Swedenborgianism, and the Spirit Rapping philosophy, with other new views, alike in things natural and unnatural; and immortally hopeful, is forever making new flower-beds even on the north side of the house, where the bleak mountain wind would scarce allow the wiry weed called hard-hack to gain

a thorough footing; and on the road-side sets out mere
pipestems of young elms; though there is no hope of any
shade from them, except over the ruins of her great grand-
daughters' grave-stones; and won't wear caps, but plaits her
gray hair; and takes the Ladies' Magazine for the fashions;
and always buys her new almanac a month before the new
year; and rises at dawn; and to the warmest sunset turns a
cold shoulder; and still goes on at odd hours with her new
course of history, and her French, and her music; and likes
young company; and offers to ride young colts; and sets out
young suckers in the orchard; and has a spite against my
elbowed old grape-vine, and my club-footed old neighbor,
and my claw-footed old chair, and above all, high above all,
would fain persecute, unto death, my high-manteled old
chimney. By what perverse magic, I a thousand times think,
does such a very autumnal old lady have such a very vernal
young soul? When I would remonstrate at times, she spins
round on me with, "Oh, don't you grumble, old man (she
always calls me old man), it's I, young I, that keep you from
stagnating." Well, I suppose it is so. Yea, after all, these
things are well ordered. My wife, as one of her poor relations, good soul, intimates, is the salt of the earth, and none
the less the salt of my sea, which otherwise were unwholesome. She is its monsoon, too, blowing a brisk gale over it,
in the one steady direction of my chimney.

Not insensible of her superior energies, my wife has frequently made me propositions to take upon herself all the
responsibilities of my affairs. She is desirous that, domes-
tically, I should abdicate; that, renouncing further rule,
like the venerable Charles V, I should retire into some sort
of monastery. But indeed, the chimney excepted, I have
little authority to lay down. By my wife's ingenious application of the principle that certain things belong of right to
female jurisdiction, I find myself, through my easy com-
pliances, insensibly stripped by degrees of one masculine

prerogative after another. In a dream I go about my fields, a sort of lazy, happy-go-lucky, good-for-nothing, loafing, old Lear. Only by some sudden revelation am I reminded who is over me; as year before last, one day seeing in one corner of the premises fresh deposits of mysterious boards and timbers, the oddity of the incident at length begat serious meditation. "Wife," said I, "whose boards and timbers are those I see near the orchard there? Do you know anything about them, wife? Who put them there? You know I do not like the neighbors to use my land that way; they should ask permission first."

She regarded me with a pitying smile.

"Why, old man, don't you know I am building a new barn? Didn't you know that, old man?"

This is the poor old lady that was accusing me of tyrannizing over her.

To return now to the chimney. Upon being assured of the futility of her proposed hall, so long as the obstacle remained, for a time my wife was for a modified project. But I could never exactly comprehend it. As far as I could see through it, it seemed to involve the general idea of a sort of irregular archway, or elbowed tunnel, which was to penetrate the chimney at some convenient point under the stair-case, and carefully avoiding dangerous contact with the fire-places, and particularly steering clear of the great interior flue, was to conduct the enterprising traveler from the front door all the way into the dining-room in the remote rear of the mansion. Doubtless it was a bold stroke of genius, that plan of hers, and so was Nero's when he schemed his grand canal through the Isthmus of Corinth. Nor will I take oath, that, had her project been accomplished, then, by help of lights hung at judicious intervals through the tunnel, some Belzoni or other might have succeeded in future ages in penetrating through the masonry, and actually emerging into the dining-room, and once there, it would have been inhospitable treatment of such a traveler to have denied him a recruiting meal.

But my bustling wife did not restrict her objections, nor in the end confine her proposed alterations to the first floor. Her ambition was of the mounting order. She ascended with her schemes to the second floor, and so to the attic. Perhaps there was some small ground for her discontent with things as they were. The truth is, there was no regular passage-way up stairs or down, unless we again except that little orchestra-gallery before mentioned. And all this was owing to the chimney, which my gamesome spouse seemed despitefully to regard as the bully of the house. On all its four sides, nearly all the chambers sidled up to the chimney for the benefit of a fire-place. The chimney would not go to them; they must needs go to it. The consequence was, almost every room, like a philosophical system, was in itself an entry, or passage-way to other rooms, and systems of rooms—a whole suite of entries, in fact. Going through the house, you seem to be forever going somewhere, and getting nowhere. It is like losing one's self in the woods; round and round the chimney you go, and if you arrive at all, it is just where you started, and so you begin again, and again get nowhere. Indeed—though I say it not in the way of fault-finding at all—never was there so labyrinthine an abode. Guests will tarry with me several weeks and every now and then, be anew astonished at some unforeseen apartment.

The puzzling nature of the mansion, resulting from the chimney, is peculiarly noticeable in the dining-room, which has no less than nine doors, opening in all directions, and into all sorts of places. A stranger, for the first time entering this dining-room, and naturally taking no special heed at what door he entered, will, upon rising to depart, commit the strangest blunders. Such, for instance, as opening the first door that comes handy, and finding himself stealing up stairs by the back passage. Shutting that door, he will proceed to another, and be aghast at the cellar yawning at his feet. Trying a third, he surprises the housemaid at her work. In the end, no more relying on his own unaided efforts, he procures a trusty guide in some passing person, and in good time successfully emerges. Perhaps as curious a blunder as any, was that of a certain stylish young gentleman, a great exquisite, in whose judicious eyes my daughter Anna had found especial favor. He called upon the young lady one evening, and found her alone in the dining room at her needle-work. He stayed rather late; and after abundance of superfine discourse, all the while retaining his hat and cane, made his profuse adieus, and with repeated graceful bows proceeded to depart, after the fashion of courtiers from the Queen, and by so doing, opening a door at random, with one hand placed behind, very effectually succeeded in backing himself into a dark pantry, where he carefully shut himself up, wondering there was no light in the entry. After several strange noises as of a cat among the crockery, he reappeared through the same door, looking uncommonly crest-fallen, and, with a deeply embarrassed air, requested my daughter to designate at which of the nine he should find exit. When the mischievous Anna told me the story, she said it was surprising how unaffected and matter-of-fact the young gentleman's manner was after his reappearance. He was more candid than ever, to be sure; having inadvertently thrust his white kids into an open drawer of Havana sugar, under the impression, probably, that being what they call "a sweet fellow," his route might possibly lie in that direction.

Another inconvenience resulting from the chimney is the bewilderment of a guest in gaining his chamber, many strange doors lying between him and it. To direct him by finger-posts would look rather queer; and just as queer in him to be knocking at every door on his route, like London's city guest, the king, at Temple Bar.

Now, of all these things and many, many more, my family continually complained. At last my wife came out with her sweeping proposition—in toto to abolish the chimney.

"What!" said I, "abolish the chimney? To take out the back-bone of anything, wife, is a hazardous affair. Spines out of backs, and chimneys out of houses, are not to be taken like frosted lead-pipes from the ground. Besides," added I, "the chimney is the one grand permanence of this abode. If undisturbed by innovators, then in future ages, when all the house shall have crumbled from it, this chimney will still survive—a Bunker Hill monument. No, no, wife, I can't abolish my back-bone."

So said I then. But who is sure of himself, especially an old man, with both wife and daughters ever at his elbow and ear? In time, I was persuaded to think a little better of it; in short, to take the matter into preliminary consideration. At length it came to pass that a master-mason—a rough sort of architect—one Mr. Scribe, was summoned to a conference. I formally introduced him to my chimney. A previous introduction from my wife had introduced him to myself. He had been not a little employed by that lady, in preparing plans and estimates for some of her extensive operations in drainage. Having, with much ado, extorted from my spouse the promise that she would leave us to an unmolested survey, I began by leading Mr. Scribe down to the root of the matter, in the cellar. Lamp in hand, I descended; for though up stairs it was noon, below it was night.

We seemed in the pyramids; and I, with one hand holding my lamp overhead, and with the other pointing out, in the obscurity, the hoar mass of the chimney, seemed some

Arab guide, showing the cob-webbed mausoleum of the great god Apis.

"This is a most remarkable structure, sir," said the master-mason, after long contemplating it in silence, "a most remarkable structure, sir."

"Yes," said I, complacently, "every one says so."

"But large as it appears above the roof, I would not have inferred the magnitude of this foundation, sir," eying it critically.

Then taking out his rule, he measured it.

"Twelve feet square; one hundred and forty-four square feet! Sir, this house would appear to have been built simply for the accommodation of your chimney."

"Yes, my chimney and me. Tell me candidly, now," I added, "would you have such a famous chimney abolished?"

"I wouldn't have it in a house of mine, sir, for a gift," was the reply. "It's a losing affair altogether, sir. Do you know, sir, that in retaining this chimney, you are losing, not only one hundred and forty-four square feet of good ground, but likewise a considerable interest upon a considerable principal?"

"How?"

"Look, sir," said he, taking a bit of red chalk from his pocket, and figuring against a whitewashed wall, "twenty times eight is so and so; then forty-two times thirty-nine is so and so—ain't it, sir? Well, add those together, and subtract this here, then that makes so and so," still chalking away.

To be brief, after no small ciphering, Mr. Scribe informed me that my chimney contained, I am ashamed to say how many thousand and odd valuable bricks.

"No more," said I fidgeting. "Pray now, let us have a look above."

In that upper zone we made two more circumnavigations for the first and second floors. That done, we stood together at the foot of the stairway by the front door; my hand upon the knob, and Mr. Scribe hat in hand.

"Well, sir," said he, a sort of feeling his way, and, to help himself, fumbling with his hat, "well, sir, I think it can be done."

"What, pray, Mr. Scribe; *what* can be done?"

"Your chimney, sir; it can without rashness be removed, I think."

"*I* will think of it, too, Mr. Scribe," said I, turning the knob, and bowing him towards the open space without, "I will *think* of it, sir; it demands consideration; much obliged to ye; good morning, Mr. Scribe."

"It is all arranged, then," cried my wife with great glee, bursting from the nighest room.

"When will they begin?" demanded my daughter Julia.

"To-morrow?" asked Anna.

"Patience, patience, my dears," said I, "such a big chimney is not to be abolished in a minute."

Next morning it began again.

"You remember the chimney," said my wife.

"Wife," said I, "it is never out of my house, and never out of my mind."

"But when is Mr. Scribe to begin to pull it down?" asked Anna.

"Not to-day, Anna," said I.

"*When*, then?" demanded Julia, in alarm.

Now, if this chimney of mine was, for size, a sort of belfry, for ding-donging at me about it, my wife and daughters were a sort of bells, always chiming together, or taking up each other's melodies at every pause, my wife the key-clapper of all. A very sweet ringing, and pealing, and chiming, I confess; but then, the most silvery of bells may, sometimes, dismally toll, as well as merrily play. And as touching the subject in question, it became so now. Perceiving a strange relapse of opposition in me, wife and daughters began a soft and dirge-like, melancholy tolling over it.

At length my wife, getting much excited, declared to me, with pointed finger, that so long as that chimney stood, she should regard it as the monument of what she called my broken pledge. But finding this did not answer, the next day she gave me to understand that either she or the chimney must quit the house.

Finding matters coming to such a pass, I and my pipe philosophized over them awhile, and finally concluded between us, that little as our hearts went with the plan, yet for peace's sake, I might write out the chimney's death-warrant. and, while my hand was in, scratch a note to Mr. Scribe.

Considering that I, and my chimney, and my pipe, from having been so much together, were three great cronies, the facility with which my pipe consented to a project so fatal to the goodliest of our trio; or rather, the way in which I and my pipe, in secret, conspired together, as it were, against our unsuspicious old comrade—this may seem rather strange, if not suggestive of sad reflections upon us two. But, indeed, we sons of clay, that is my pipe and I, are no whit better than the rest. Far from us, indeed, to have volunteered the betrayal of our crony. We are of a peaceable nature, too. But that love of peace it was which made us false to a mutual friend, as soon as his cause demanded a vigorous vindication. But I rejoice to add, that better and braver thoughts soon returned, as will now briefly be set forth.

To my note, Mr. Scribe replied in person.

Once more we made a survey, mainly now with a view to a pecuniary estimate.

"I will do it for five hundred dollars," said Mr. Scribe at last, again hat in hand.

"Very well, Mr. Scribe, I will think of it," replied I, again bowing him to the door.

Not unvexed by this, for the second time, unexpected response, again he withdrew, and from my wife and daughters again burst the old exclamations.

The truth is, resolve how I would, at the last pinch I and my chimney could not be parted.

"So Holofernes will have his way, never mind whose heart breaks for it," said my wife next morning, at breakfast, in that half-didactic, half-reproachful way of hers, which is harder to bear than her most energetic assault. Holofernes, too, is with her a pet name for any fell domestic despot. So, whenever, against her most ambitious innovations, those which saw me quite across the grain, I, as in the present instance, stand with however little steadfastness on the defence, she is sure to call me Holofernes, and ten to one takes the first opportunity to read aloud, with a suppressed emphasis, of an evening, the first newspaper paragraph about some tyrannic day-laborer who, after being for many years the Caligula of his family, ends by beating his long-suffering spouse to death, with a garret door wrenched off its hinges, and then, pitching his little innocents out of the window, suicidally turns inward towards the broken wall scored with the butcher's and baker's bills, and so rushes headlong to his dreadful account.

Nevertheless, for a few days, not a little to my surprise, I heard no further reproaches. An intense calm pervaded my wife, but beneath which, as in the sea, there was no knowing what portentous movements might be going on. She frequently went abroad, and in a direction which I thought not unsuspicious; namely, in the direction of New Petra, a griffin-like house of wood and stucco, in the highest style of ornamental art, graced with four chimneys in the form of erect dragons spouting smoke from their nostrils;

the elegant modern residence of Mr. Scribe, which he had built for the purpose of a standing advertisement, not more of his taste as an architect, than his solidity as a master-mason.

At last, smoking my pipe one morning, I heard a rap at the door, and my wife, with an air unusually quiet for her, brought me a note. As I have no correspondents except Solomon, with who, in his sentiments, at least, I entirely correspond, the note occasioned me some little surprise, which was not diminished upon reading the following:

New Petra, April 1st.

Sir:—During my last examination of your chimney, possibly you may have noted that I frequently applied my rule to it in a manner apparently unnecessary. Possibly also, at the same time, you might have observed in me more or less of perplexity, to which, however, I refrained from giving any verbal expression.

I now feel it obligatory upon me to inform you of what was then but a dim suspicion, and as such would have been unwise to give utterance to, but which now, from various subsequent calculations assuming no little probability, it may be important that you should not remain in further ignorance of.

It is my solemn duty to warn you, sir, that there is architectural cause to conjecture that somewhere concealed in your chimney is a reserved space, hermetically closed, in short, a secret chamber, or rather closet. How long it has been there, it is for me impossible to say. What it contains is hid, with itself, in darkness. But probably a secret closet would not have been contrived except for some extraordinary object, whether for the concealment of treasure, or what other purpose, may be left to those better acquainted with the history of the house to guess.

But enough: in making this disclosure, sir, my conscience

is eased. *Whatever step you choose to take upon it is, of course, a matter of indifference to me; though, I confess, as respects the character of the closet, I cannot but share in a natural curiosity.*

Trusting that you may be guided aright, in determining whether it is Christian-like knowingly to reside in a house, hidden in which is a secret closet,

I remain,

With much respect,

Yours very humbly,

HIRAM SCRIBE

My first thought upon reading this note was, not of the alleged mystery of manner to which, at the outset, it alluded —for none such had I at all observed in the master-mason during his surveys—but of my late kinsman, Captain Julian Dacres, long a ship-master and merchant in the Indian trade, who, about thirty years ago, and at the ripe age of ninety, died a bachelor, and in this very house, which he had built. He was supposed to have retired into this country with a large fortune. But to the general surprise, after being at great cost in building himself this mansion, he settled down into a sedate, reserved, and inexpensive old age, which by the neighbors was thought all the better for his heirs; but lo! upon opening the will, his property was found to consist but of the house and grounds, and some ten thousand dollars in stocks; but the place, being found heavily mortgaged, was in consequence sold. Gossip had its day, and left the grass quietly to creep over the captain's grave, where he still slumbers in a privacy as unmolested as if the billows of the Indian Ocean, instead of the billows of inland verdure, rolled over him. Still, I remembered, long ago, hearing strange solutions whispered by the country people for the mystery involving his will, and, by reflex, himself; and that, too, as well in conscience as purse. But people who could circulate the report (which they did), that Captain Julian Dacres had, in his day, been a Borneo pirate, surely were not worthy of credence in their collateral notions. It is queer what wild whimsies of rumors will, like toadstools, spring up about any eccentric stranger who, settling down among a rustic population, keeps quietly to himself. With some, inoffensiveness would seem a prime cause of offense. But what chiefly had led me to scout at these rumors, particularly as referring to concealed treasure, was the circumstance, that the stranger (the same who razeed the roof and the chimney) into whose hands the estate had passed on my kinsman's death, was of that sort of character, that had there been the least ground for those reports, he would speedily have tested them, by tearing down and rummaging the walls.

Nevertheless, the note of Mr. Scribe, so strangely recalling the memory of my kinsman, very naturally chimed in with what had been mysterious, or at least unexplained, about him; vague flashings of ingots united in my mind with vague gleamings of skulls. But the first cool thought soon dismissed such chimeras; and, with a calm smile, I turned towards my wife, who, meantime, had been sitting near by, impatient enough, I dare say, to know who could have taken it into his head to write me a letter.

"Well, old man," said she, "who is it from, and what is it about?"

"Read it, wife," said I, handing it.

Read it she did, and then—such an explosion! I will not pretend to describe her emotions, or repeat her expressions. Enough that my daughters were quickly called in to share the excitement. Although they had never before dreamed of such a revelation as Mr. Scribe's, yet upon the first suggestion they instinctively saw the extreme likelihood of it. In corroboration, they cited first my kinsman, and second, my chimney; alleging that the profound mystery involving the former, and the equally profound masonry involving the latter, though both acknowledged facts, were alike preposterous on any other supposition than the secret closet.

But all this time I was quietly thinking to myself: Could it be hidden from me that my credulity in this instance would operate very favorably to a certain plan of theirs? How to get to the secret closet, or how to have any certainty about it at all, without making such fell work with the chimney as to render its set destruction superfluous? That my wife wished to get rid of the chimney, it needed no reflection to show; and that Mr. Scribe, for all his pretended disinterestedness, was not opposed to pocketing five hundred dollars by the operation, seemed equally evident. That my wife had, in secret, laid heads together with Mr. Scribe, I at present refrain from affirming. But when I consider her enmity against my chimney, and the steadiness with which at the last she is wont to carry out her schemes, if by hook or by crook she can, especially after having been once baffled, why, I scarcely knew at what step of hers to be surprised.

Of one thing only was I resolved, that I and my chimney should not budge.

In vain all protests. Next morning I went out into the road, where I had noticed a diabolical-looking old gander that, for its doughty exploits in the way of scratching into forbidden inclosures, had been rewarded by its master with a portentous, four-pronged, wooden decoration, in the shape of a collar of the Order of the Garotte. This gander I cornered, and rummaging out its stiffest quill, plucked it, took it home, and making a stiff pen, inscribed the following stiff note:

Chimney Side, April 2.

Mr. Scribe.

Sir:—*For your conjecture, we return you our joint thanks and compliments, and beg leave to assure you, that*

We shall remain,
Very faithfully,
The same,
I AND MY CHIMNEY.

Of course, for this epistle we had to endure some pretty sharp raps. But having at last explicitly understood from me that Mr. Scribe's note had not altered my mind one jot, my wife, to move me, among other things said, that if she remembered aright, there was a statute placing the keeping in private houses of secret closets on the same unlawful footing with the keeping of gunpowder. But it had no effect.

A few days after, my spouse changed her key.

It was nearly midnight, and all were in bed but ourselves, who sat up, one in each chimney-corner; she, needles in hand, indefatigably knitting a sock; I, pipe in mouth, indolently weaving my vapors.

It was one of the first of the chill nights in autumn. There was a fire on the hearth, burning low. The air without was torpid and heavy; the wood, by an oversight, of the sort called soggy.

"Do look at the chimney," she began; "can't you see that something must be in it?"

"Yes, wife. Truly there is smoke in the chimney, as in Mr. Scribe's note."

"Smoke? Yes, indeed, and in my eyes, too. How you two wicked old sinners do smoke!—this wicked old chimney and you."

"Wife," said I, "I and my chimney like to have a quiet

smoke together, it is true, but we don't like to be called names."

"Now, dear old man," said she, softening down, and a little shifting the subject, "when you think of that old kinsman of yours, you *know* there must be a secret closet in this chimney."

"Secret ash-hole, wife, why don't you have it? Yes, I dare say there is a secret ash-hole in the chimney; for where do all the ashes go to that we drop down the queer hole yonder?"

"I know where they go to; I've been there almost as many times as the cat."

"What devil, wife, prompted you to crawl into the ash-hole! Don't you know that St. Dunstan's devil emerged from the ash-hole? You will get your death one of these days, exploring all about as you do. But supposing there be a secret closet, what then?"

"What, then? why what should be in a secret closet but—"

"Dry bones, wife," broke in I with a puff, while the sociable old chimney broke in with another.

"There again! Oh, how this wretched old chimney smokes," wiping her eyes with her handkerchief. "I've no doubt the reason it smokes so is, because that secret closet interferes with the flue. Do see, too, how the jambs here keep settling; and it's down hill all the way from the door to this hearth. This horrid old chimney will fall on our heads yet; depend upon it, old man."

"Yes, wife, I do depend on it; yes, indeed, I place every dependence on my chimney. As for its settling, I like it. I, too, am settling, you know, in my gait. I and my chimney are settling together, and shall keep settling, too, till, as in a great feather-bed, we shall both have settled away clean out of sight. But this secret oven; I mean, secret closet of yours, wife; where exactly do you suppose that secret closet is?"

"That is for Mr. Scribe to say."

"But suppose he cannot say exactly; what, then?"

"Why, then he can prove, I am sure, that it must be somewhere or other in this horrid old chimney."

"And if he can't prove that; what, then?"

"Why, then, old man," with a stately air, "I shall say little more about it."

"Agreed, wife," returned I, knocking my pipe-bowl against the jamb, "and now, to-morrow, I will a third time send for Mr. Scribe. Wife, the sciatica takes me; be so good as to put this pipe on the mantel."

"If you get the step-ladder for me, I will. This shocking old chimney, this abominable old-fashioned old chimney's mantels are so high, I can't reach them."

No opportunity, however trivial, was overlooked for a subordinate fling at the pile.

Here, by way of introduction, it should be mentioned, that besides the fire-places all round it, the chimney was, in the most haphazard way, excavated on each floor for certain curious out-of-the-way cupboards and closets, of all sorts and sizes, clinging here and there, like nests in the crotches of some old oak. On the second floor these closets were by far the most irregular and numerous. And yet this should hardly have been so, since the theory of the chimney was, that it pyramidically diminished as it ascended. The abridgment of its square on the roof was obvious enough; and it was supposed that the reduction must be methodically graduated from bottom to top.

"Mr. Scribe," said I when, the next day, with an eager aspect, that individual again came, "my object in sending for you this morning is, not to arrange for the demolition of my chimney, nor to have any particular conversation about it, but simply to allow you every reasonable facility for verifying, if you can, the conjecture communicated in your note."

Though in secret not a little crestfallen, it may be, by my phlegmatic reception, so different from what he had looked for; with much apparent alacrity he commenced the survey; throwing open the cupboards on the first floor, and peering into the closets on the second; measuring one within, and then comparing that measurement with the measurement without. Removing the fire-boards, he would gaze up the flues. But no sign of the hidden work yet.

Now, on the second floor the rooms were the most rambling conceivable. They, as it were, dovetailed into each other. They were of all shapes; not one mathematically square room among them all—a peculiarity which by the master-mason had not been unobserved. With a significant, not to say portentous expression, he took a circuit of the chimney, measuring the area of each room around it; then going down stairs, and out of doors, he measured the entire ground area; then compared the sum total of all the areas of all the rooms on the second floor with the ground area; then, returning to me in no small excitement, announced that there was a difference of no less than two hundred and odd square feet—room enough, in all conscience, for a secret closet.

"But, Mr. Scribe," said I, stroking my chin, "have you allowed for the walls, both main and sectional? They take up some space, you know."

"Ah, I had forgotten that," tapping his forehead; "but," still ciphering on his paper, "that will not make up the deficiency."

"But, Mr. Scribe, have you allowed for the recesses of so many fire-places on a floor, and for the fire-walls, and the flues; in short, Mr. Scribe, have you allowed for the legitimate chimney itself—some one hundred and forty-four square feet or thereabouts, Mr. Scribe?"

"How unaccountable. That slipped my mind, too."

"Did it, indeed, Mr. Scribe?"

He faltered a little, and burst forth with, "But we must not allow one hundred and forty-four square feet for the legitimate chimney. My position is, that within those undue limits the secret closet is contained."

I eyed him in silence a moment; then spoke:

"Your survey is concluded, Mr. Scribe; be so good now as to lay your finger upon the exact part of the chimney wall where you believe this secret closet to be; or would a witch-hazel wand assist you, Mr. Scribe?"

"No, sir, but a crow-bar would," he, with temper, rejoined.

Here, now, thought I to myself, the cat leaps out of the bag. I looked at him with a calm glance, under which he seemed somewhat uneasy. More than ever now I suspected a plot. I remembered what my wife had said about abiding by the decision of Mr. Scribe. In a bland way, I resolved to buy up the decision of Mr. Scribe.

"Sir," said I, "really I am much obliged to you for this survey. It has quite set my mind at rest. And no doubt you, too, Mr. Scribe, must feel much relieved. Sir," I added, "you have made three visits to the chimney. With a business man, time is money. Here are fifty dollars, Mr. Scribe. Nay, take it. You have earned it. Your opinion is worth it. And by the way," as he modestly received the money—"have you any objections to give me a—a—little certificate—something, say, like a steam-boat certificate, certifying that you, a competent surveyor, have surveyed my chimney, and found no reason to believe any unsoundness; in short, any—any secret closet in it. Would you be so kind, Mr. Scribe?"

"But, but, sir," stammered he with honest hesitation.

"Here, here are pen and paper," said I, with entire assurance.

Enough.

That evening I had the certificate framed and hung over the dining-room fire-place, trusting that the continual sight of it would forever put at rest at once the dreams and stratagems of my household.

But, no. Inveterately bent upon the extirpation of that noble old chimney, still to this day my wife goes about it, with my daughter Anna's geological hammer, tapping the wall all over, and then holding her ear against it, as I have seen the physicians of life insurance companies tap a man's chest, and then incline over for the echo. Sometimes of nights she almost frightens one, going about on this phantom errand, and still following the sepulchral response of the chimney, round and round, as if it were leading her to the threshold of the secret closet.

"How hollow it sounds," she will hollowly cry. "Yes, I declare," with an emphatic tap, "there is a secret closet here. Here, in this very spot. Hark! How hollow!"

"Pshaw! wife, of course it is hollow. Who ever heard of a solid chimney?"

But nothing avails. And my daughters take after, not me, but their mother.

Sometimes all three abandon the theory of the secret closet, and return to the genuine ground of attack—the unsightliness of so cumbrous a pile, with comments upon the great addition of room to be gained by its demolition, and the fine effect of the projected grand hall, and the convenience resulting from the collateral running in one direction and another of their various partitions. Not more ruthlessly did the Three Powers partition away poor Poland, than my wife and daughters would fain partition away my chimney.

But seeing that, despite all, I and my chimney still smoke our pipes, my wife reoccupies the ground of the secret closet, enlarging upon what wonders are there, and what a shame it is, not to seek it out and explore it.

"Wife," said I, upon one of these occasions, "why speak more of that secret closet, when there before you hangs contrary testimony of a master-mason, elected by yourself to decide. Besides, even if there were a secret closet, secret it should remain, and secret it shall. Yes, wife, here for once I must say my say. Infinite sad mischief has resulted from the profane bursting open of secret recesses. Though standing in the heart of this house, though hitherto we have all nestled about it, unsuspicious of aught hidden within, this chimney may or may not have a secret closet. But if it have, it is my kinsman's. To break into that wall would be to break into his breast. And that wall-breaking wish of Momus I account the wish of a church-robbing gossip and knave. Yes, wife, a vile eaves-dropping varlet was Momus."

"Moses?—Mumps? Stuff with your mumps and your Moses!"

The truth is, my wife, like all the rest of the world, cares not a fig for my philosophical jabber. In dearth of other philosophical companionship, I and my chimney have to smoke and philosophize together. And sitting up so late as we do at it, a mighty smoke it is that we two smoky old philosophers make.

But my spouse, who likes the smoke of my tobacco as little as she does that of the soot, carries on her war against both. I live in continual dread lest, like the golden bowl, the pipes of me and my chimney shall yet be broken. To stay that mad project of my wife's, naught answers. Or, rather, she herself is incessantly answering, incessantly besetting me with her terrible alacrity for improvement, which is a softer name for destruction. Scarce a day I do not find her with her tape-measure, measuring for her grand hall, while Anna holds a yard-stick on one side, and Julia looks approvingly on from the other. Mysterious intimations appear in the nearest village paper, signed "Claude," to the effect that a certain structure, standing on a certain hill, is a sad blemish to an otherwise lovely landscape. Anonymous letters arrive, threatening me with I know not what, unless I remove my chimney. Is it my wife, too, or who, that sets up the neighbors to badgering me on the same subject, and hinting to me that my chimney, like a huge elm, absorbs all moisture from my garden? At night, also, my wife will start as from sleep, professing to hear ghostly noises from the secret closet. Assailed on all sides, and in all ways, small peace have I and my chimney.

Were it not for the baggage, we would together pack up, and remove from the country.

What narrow escapes have been ours! Once I found in a drawer a whole portfolio of plans and estimates. Another time, upon returning after a day's absence, I discovered my wife standing before the chimney in earnest conversation with a person whom I at once recognized as a meddlesome architectural reformer, who, because he had no gift for putting up anything, was ever intent upon pulling down; in various parts of the country having prevailed upon half-witted old folks to destroy their old-fashioned houses, particularly the chimneys.

But worst of all was, that time I unexpectedly returned at early morning from a visit to the city, and upon approaching the house, narrowly escaped three brickbats which fell, from high aloft, at my feet. Glancing up, what was my horror to see three savages, in blue jean overalls, in the very act of commencing the long-threatened attack. Aye, indeed, thinking of those three brickbats, I and my chimney have had narrow escapes.

It is now some seven years since I have stirred from home. My city friends all wonder why I don't come to see them, as in former times. They think I am getting sour and unsocial. Some say that I have become a sort of mossy old misanthrope, while all the time the fact is, I am simply standing guard over my mossy old chimney; for it is resolved between me and my chimney, that I and my chimney will never surrender.

The Apple-Tree Table OR
Original Spiritual Manifestations

WHEN I first saw the table, dingy and dusty, in the furthest corner of the old hopper-shaped garret, and set out with broken, be-crusted, old purple vials and flasks, and a ghostly, dismantled old quarto, it seemed just such a necromantic little old table as might have belonged to Friar Bacon. Two plain features it had, significant of conjurations and charms—the circle and tripod; the slab being round, supported by a twisted little pillar, which, about a foot from the bottom, sprawled out into three crooked legs, terminating in three cloven feet. A very satanic-looking little old table, indeed.

In order to convey a better idea of it, some account may as well be given of the place it came from. A very old garret of a very old house in an old-fashioned quarter of one of the oldest towns in America. This garret had been closed for years. It was thought to be haunted; a rumor, I confess, which, however absurd (in my opinion), I did not, at the time of purchasing, very vehemently contradict; since, not improbably, it tended to place the property the more conveniently within my means.

It was, therefore, from no dread of the reputed goblins aloft, that, for five years after first taking up my residence in the house, I never entered the garret. There was no special inducement. The roof was well slated, and thoroughly tight. The company that insured the house waived all visitation, of the garret; why, then, should the owner be over-anxious about it?—particularly as he had no use for it, the house having ample room below. Then the key of the stair-door leading to it was lost. The lock was a huge, old-fashioned one. To open it, a smith would have to be called; an unnecessary trouble, I thought. Besides, though I had taken some care to keep my two daughters in ignorance of the rumor above-mentioned, still, they had, by some means, got an inkling of it, and were well enough pleased to see the entrance to the haunted ground closed. It might have remained so for a still longer time, had it not been for my accidentally discovering, in a corner of our glen-like, old, terraced garden, a large and curious key, very old and rusty, which I, at once, concluded must belong to the garret-door—a supposition which, upon trial, proved correct. Now, the possession of a key to anything at once provokes a desire to unlock and explore; and this, too, from a mere instinct of gratification, irrespective of any particular benefit to accrue.

Behold me, then, turning the rusty old key, and going up, alone, into the haunted garret.

It embraced the entire area of the mansion. Its ceiling was formed by the roof, showing the rafters and boards on which the slates were laid. The roof shedding the water four ways from a high point in the centre, the space beneath was much like that of a general's marquee—only midway broken by a labyrinth of timbers, for braces, from which waved innumerable cobwebs that, of a summer's noon, shone like Bagdad tissues and gauzes. On every hand, some strange insect was seen, flying, or running, or creeping, on rafter and floor.

Under the apex of the roof was a rude, narrow, decrepit step-ladder, something like a Gothic pulpit-stairway, leading to a pulpit-like platform, from which a still narrower ladder—a sort of Jacob's ladder—led some ways higher to the lofty scuttle. The slide of this scuttle was about two feet square, all in one piece, furnishing a massive frame for a single small pane of glass, inserted into it like a bull's-eye. The light of the garret came from this sole source, filtrated through a dense curtain of cobwebs. Indeed, the whole stairs, and platform, and ladder, were festooned, and carpeted, and canopied with cobwebs; which, in funereal accumulations, hung, too, from the groined, murky ceiling, like the Carolina moss in the cypress forest. In these cobwebs swung, as in ærial catacombs, myriads of all tribes of mummied insects.

Climbing the stairs to the platform, and pausing there, to recover my breath, a curious scene was presented. The sun was about half-way up. Piercing the little sky-light, it slopingly bored a rainbowed tunnel clear across the darkness of the garret. Here, millions of butterfly moles were swarming. Against the sky-light itself, with a cymbal-like buzzing, thousands of insects clustered in a golden mob.

Wishing to shed a clearer light through the place, I sought to withdraw the scuttle-slide. But no sign of latch or hasp was visible. Only after long peering, did I discover a little padlock, imbedded, like an oyster at the bottom of the sea, amid matted masses of weedy webs, chrysalides, and insectivorous eggs. Brushing these away, I found it locked. With a crooked nail, I tried to pick the lock, when scores of small ants and flies, half-torpid, crawled forth from the key-hole and, feeling the warmth of the sun in the pane, began frisking around me. Others appeared. Presently, I was overrun by them. As if incensed at this invasion of their retreat, countless bands darted up from below, beating about my head like hornets. At last, with a sudden jerk, I burst open the scuttle. And ah! what a change. As from the gloom of the grave and the companionship of worms, man shall at last rapturously rise into the living greenness and glory immortal, so, from my cobwebbed old garret, I thrust forth my head into the balmy air, and found myself hailed by the verdant tops of great trees, growing in the little garden below—trees, whose leaves soared high above my topmost slate.

Refreshed by this outlook, I turned inward to behold the garret, now unwontedly lit up. Such humped masses of obsolete furniture. An old escritoire, from whose pigeon-holes sprang mice, and from whose secret drawers came subterranean squeakings, as from chipmunks' holes in the woods; and broken-down old chairs, with strange carvings, which seemed fit to seat a conclave of conjurors. And a rusty, iron-bound chest, lidless, and packed full of mildewed old documents; one of which, with a faded red ink-blot at the end, looked as if it might have been the original bond that Doctor Faust gave to Mephistopheles. And, finally, in the least lighted corner of all, where was a profuse litter of indescribable old rubbish—among which was a broken telescope, and a celestial globe staved in—stood the little old table, one hoofed foot, like that of the Evil One, dimly revealed through the cobwebs. What a thick dust, half paste, had settled upon the old vials and flasks; how their once liquid contents had caked, and how strangely looked the mouldy old book in the middle—Cotton Mather's *Magnalia*.

Table and book I removed below, and had the dislocations of the one and the tatters of the other repaired. I resolved to surround this sad little hermit of a table, so long banished from genial neighborhood, with all the kindly influences of warm urns, warm fires, and warm hearts; little dreaming what all this warm nursing would hatch.

I was pleased by the discovery that the table was not of the ordinary mahogany, but of apple-tree wood, which age had darkened nearly to walnut. It struck me as being quite an appropriate piece of furniture for our cedar-parlor—so called, from its being, after the old fashion, wainscoted with that wood. The table's round slab, or *orb*, was so contrived as to be readily changed from a horizontal to a perpendicular position; so that, when not in use, it could be snugly placed in a corner. For myself, wife, and two daughters, I thought it would make a nice little breakfast and tea-table. It was just the thing for a whist table, too. And I also pleased myself with the idea, that it would make a famous reading-table.

In these fancies, my wife, for one, took little interest. She disrelished the idea of so unfashionable and indigent-looking a stranger as the table intruding into the polished society of more prosperous furniture. But when, after seeking its fortune at the cabinet-maker's, the table came home, varnished over, bright as a guinea, no one exceeded my wife in a gracious reception of it. It was advanced to an honorable position in the cedar-parlor.

But, as for my daughter Julia, she never got over her strange emotions upon first accidentally encountering the table. Unfortunately, it was just as I was in the act of bringing it down from the garret. Holding it by the slab, I was carrying it before me, one cobwebbed hoof thrust out, which weird object, at a turn of the stairs, suddenly touched my girl, as she was ascending; whereupon, turning, and seeing no living creature—for I was quite hidden behind my shield—seeing nothing, indeed, but the apparition of the Evil One's foot, as it seemed, she cried out, and there is no knowing what might have followed, had I not immediately spoken.

From the impression thus produced, my poor girl, of a very nervous temperament, was long recovering. Superstitiously grieved at my violating the forbidden solitude above, she associated in her mind the cloven-footed table with the reputed goblins there. She besought me to give up the idea of domesticating the table. Nor did her sister fail to add her entreaties. Between my girls there was a constitutional sympathy. But my matter-of-fact wife had now declared in the table's favor. She was not wanting in firmness and energy. To her, the prejudices of Julia and Anna were simply ridiculous. It was her maternal duty, she thought, to drive such weakness away. By degrees, the girls, at breakfast and tea, were induced to sit down with us at the table. Continual proximity was not without effect. By and by, they would sit pretty tranquilly, though Julia, as much as possible, avoided glancing at the hoofed feet, and, when at this I smiled, she would look at me seriously—as much as to say, Ah, papa, you, too, may yet do the same. She prophesied that, in connection with the table, something strange would yet happen. But I would only smile the more, while my wife indignantly chided.

Meantime, I took particular satisfaction in my table, as a night reading-table. At a ladies' fair, I bought me a beautifully worked reading-cushion, and, with elbow leaning thereon, and hand shading my eyes from the light, spent many a long hour—nobody by, but the queer old book I had brought down from the garret.

All went well, till the incident now about to be given—an incident, be it remembered, which, like every other in this narration, happened long before the time of the "Fox Girls."

It was late on a Saturday night in December. In the little old cedar-parlor, before the little old apple-tree table, I was sitting up, as usual, alone. I had made more than one effort to get up and go to bed; but I could not. I was, in fact, under a sort of fascination. Somehow, too, certain reasonable opinions of mine seemed not so reasonable as before. I felt nervous. The truth was, that though, in my previous night-readings, Cotton Mather had but amused me, upon this particular night he terrified me. A thousand times I had laughed at such stories. Old wives' fables, I thought, however entertaining. But now, how different.

They began to put on the aspect of reality. Now, for the first time it struck me that this was no romantic Mrs. Radcliffe who had written the *Magnalia*, but a practical, hard-working, earnest, upright man, a learned doctor, too, as well as a good Christian and orthodox clergyman. What possible motive could such a man have to deceive? His style had all the plainness and unpoetic boldness of truth. In the most straightforward way, he laid before me detailed accounts of New England witchcraft, each important item corroborated by respectable townsfolk, and, of not a few of the most surprising, he himself had been eye-witness. Cotton Mather testified whereof he had seen. But, is it possible? I asked myself. Then I remembered that Dr. Johnson, the matter-of-fact compiler of a dictionary, had been a believer in ghosts, besides many other sound, worthy men. Yielding to the fascination, I read deeper and deeper into the night. At last, I found myself starting at the least chance sound, and yet wishing that it were not so very still.

A tumbler of warm punch stood by my side, with which beverage, in a moderate way, I was accustomed to treat myself every Saturday night; a habit, however, against which my good wife had long remonstrated; predicting that, unless I gave it up, I would yet die a miserable sot. Indeed, I may here mention that, on the Sunday mornings following my Saturday nights, I had to be exceedingly cautious how I gave way to the slightest impatience at any accidental annoyance; because such impatience was sure to be quoted against me as evidence of the melancholy consequence of over-night indulgence. As for my wife, she, never sipping punch, could yield to any little passing peevishness as much as she pleased.

But, upon the night in question, I found myself wishing that, instead of my usual mild mixture, I had concocted some potent draught. I felt the need of stimulus. I wanted something to hearten me against Cotton Mather—doleful, ghostly, ghastly Cotton Mather. I grew more and more nervous. Nothing but fascination kept me from fleeing the room. The candles burnt low, with long snuffs, and huge winding-sheets. But I durst not raise the snuffers to them. It would make too much noise. And yet, previously, I had been wishing for noise. I read on and on. My hair began to have a sensation. My eyes felt strained; they pained me. I was conscious of it. I knew I was injuring them. I knew I should rue this abuse of them next day; but I read on and on. I could not help it. The skinny hand was on me.

All at once—Hark!

My hair felt like growing grass.

A faint sort of inward rapping or rasping—a strange, inexplicable sound, mixed with a slight kind of woodpecking or ticking.

Tick! Tick!

Yes, it was a faint sort of ticking.

I looked up at my great Strasbourg clock in one corner. It was not that. The clock had stopped.

Tick! Tick!

Was it my watch?

According to her usual practice at night, my wife had, upon retiring, carried my watch off to our chamber to hang it up on its nail.

I listened with all my ears.

Tick! Tick!

Was it a death-tick in the wainscot?

With a tremulous step I went all round the room, holding my ear to the wainscot.

No; it came not from the wainscot.

Tick! Tick!

I shook myself. I was ashamed of my fright.

Tick! Tick!

It grew in precision and audibleness. I retreated from the wainscot. It seemed advancing to meet me.

I looked round and round, but saw nothing, only one cloven foot of the little apple-tree table.

Bless me, said I to myself, with a sudden revulsion, it must be very late; ain't that my wife calling me? Yes, yes; I must to bed. I suppose all is locked up. No need to go the rounds.

The fascination had departed, though the fear had increased. With trembling hands, putting Cotton Mather out of sight, I soon found myself, candle-stick in hand, in my chamber, with a peculiar rearward feeling, such as some truant dog may feel. In my eagerness to get well into the chamber, I stumbled against a chair.

"Do try and make less noise, my dear," said my wife from the bed. "You have been taking too much of that punch, I fear. That sad habit grows on you. Ah, that I should ever see you thus staggering at night into your chamber."

"Wife, wife," hoarsely whispered I, "there is—is something tick—ticking in the cedar-parlor."

"Poor old man—quite out of his mind—I knew it would be so. Come to bed; come and sleep it off."

"Wife, wife!"

"Do, do come to bed. I forgive you. I won't remind you of it to-morrow. But you must give up the punch-drinking, my dear. It quite gets the better of you."

"Don't exasperate me," I cried, now truly beside myself; "I will quit the house!"

"No, no! not in that state. Come to bed, my dear. I won't say another word."

The next morning, upon waking, my wife said nothing about the past night's affair, and, feeling no little embarrassment myself, especially at having been thrown into such a panic, I also was silent. Consequently, my wife must still have ascribed my singular conduct to a mind disordered, not by ghosts, but by punch. For my own part, as I lay in bed watching the sun in the panes, I began to think that much midnight reading of Cotton Mather was not good for man; that it had a morbid influence upon the nerves, and gave rise to hallucinations. I resolved to put Cotton Mather permanently aside. That done, I had no fear of any return of the ticking. Indeed, I began to think that what seemed the ticking in the room, was nothing but a sort of buzzing in my ear.

As is her wont, my wife having preceded me in rising, I made a deliberate and agreeable toilet. Aware that most disorders of the mind have their origin in the state of the body, I made vigorous use of the flesh-brush, and bathed my head with New England rum, a specific once recommended to me as good for buzzing in the ear. Wrapped in my dressing-gown, with cravat nicely adjusted, and finger-nails neatly trimmed, I complacently descended to the little cedar-parlor to breakfast.

What was my amazement to find my wife on her knees, rummaging about the carpet nigh the little apple-tree table, on which the morning meal was laid, while my daughters, Julia and Anna, were running about the apartment distracted.

"Oh, papa, papa!" cried Julia, hurrying up to me, "I knew it would be so. The table, the table!"

"Spirits! spirits!" cried Anna, standing far away from it, with pointed finger.

"Silence!" cried my wife. "How can I hear it, if you make such a noise? Be still. Come here, husband; was this the ticking you spoke of? Why don't you move? Was this it? Here, kneel down and listen to it. Tick, tick, tick!— don't you hear it now?"

"I do, I do," cried I, while my daughters besought us both to come away from the spot.

Tick, tick, tick!

Right from under the snowy cloth, and the cheerful urn, and the smoking milk-toast, the unaccountable ticking was heard.

"Ain't there a fire in the next room, Julia?" said I. "Let us breakfast there, my dear," turning to my wife—"let us go—leave the table—tell Biddy to remove the things."

And so saying, I was moving towards the door in high self-possession, when my wife interrupted me.

"Before I quit this room, I will see into this ticking," she said with energy. "It is something that can be found out, depend upon it. I don't believe in spirits, especially at breakfast-time. Biddy! Biddy! Here, carry these things back to the kitchen," handing the urn. Then, sweeping off the cloth, the little table lay bare to the eye.

"It's the table, the table!" cried Julia.

"Nonsense," said my wife. "Who ever heard of a ticking table? It's on the floor. Biddy! Julia! Anna! move everything out of the room—table and all. Where are the tack-hammers?"

"Heavens, mamma—you are not going to take up the carpet?" screamed Julia.

"Here's the hammers, marm," said Biddy, advancing tremblingly.

"Hand them to me, then," cried my wife; for poor Biddy was, at long gun-distance, holding them out as if her mistress had the plague.

"Now, husband, do you take up that side of the carpet, and I will this." Down on her knees she then dropped, while I followed suit.

The carpet being removed, and the ear applied to the naked floor, not the slightest ticking could be heard.

"The table—after all, it is the table," cried my wife. "Biddy, bring it back."

"Oh no, marm, not I, please, marm," sobbed Biddy.

"Foolish creature!—Husband, do you bring it."

"My dear," said I, "we have plenty of other tables; why be so particular?"

"Where is that table?" cried my wife, contemptuously, regardless of my gentle remonstrance.

"In the wood-house, marm. I put it away as far as ever I could, marm," sobbed Biddy.

"Shall I go to the wood-house for it, or will you?" said my wife, addressing me in a frightful, business-like manner.

Immediately I darted out of the door, and found the little apple-tree table, upside down, in one of my chip-bins. I hurriedly returned with it, and once more my wife examined it attentively. Tick, tick, tick! Yes, it was the table.

"Please, marm," said Biddy, now entering the room, with hat and shawl—"please, marm, will you pay me my wages?"

"Take your hat and shawl off directly," said my wife; "set this table again."

"Set it," roared I, in a passion, "set it, or I'll go for the police."

"Heavens! heavens!" cried my daughters, in one breath. "What will become of us!—Spirits! Spirits!"

"Will you set the table?" cried I, advancing upon Biddy.

"I will, I will—yes, marm—yes, master—I will, I will. Spirits!—Holy Vargin!"

"Now, husband," said my wife, "I am convinced that, whatever it is that causes this ticking, neither the ticking nor the table can hurt us; for we are all good Christians, I hope. I am determined to find out the cause of it, too, which time and patience will bring to light. I shall break-fast on no other table but this, so long as we live in this house. So, sit down, now that all things are ready again, and let us quietly breakfast. My dears," turning to Julia and

Anna, "go to your room, and return composed. Let me have no more of this childishness."

Upon occasion my wife was mistress in her house.

During the meal, in vain was conversation started again and again; in vain my wife said something brisk to infuse into others an animation akin to her own. Julia and Anna, with heads bowed over their tea-cups, were still listening for the tick. I confess, too, that their example was catching. But, for the time, nothing was heard. Either the ticking had died quite away, or else, slight as it was, the increasing uproar of the street, with the general hum of day, so contrasted with the repose of night and early morning, smothered the sound. At the lurking inquietude of her companions, my wife was indignant; the more so, as she seemed to glory in her own exemption from panic. When breakfast was cleared away she took my watch and, placing it on the table, addressed the supposed spirits in it, with a jocosely defiant air: "There, tick away, let us see who can tick loudest!"

All that day, while abroad, I thought of the mysterious table. Could Cotton Mather speak true? Were there spirits? And would spirits haunt a tea-table? Would the Evil One dare show his cloven hoof in the bosom of an innocent family? I shuddered when I thought that I myself, against the solemn warnings of my daughters, had wilfully introduced the cloven hoof there. Yea, three cloven feet. But, towards noon, this sort of feeling began to wear off. The continual rubbing against so many practical people in the street brushed such chimeras away from me. I remembered that I had not acquitted myself very intrepidly either on the previous night or in the morning. I resolved to regain the good opinion of my wife.

To evince my hardihood the more signally, when tea was dismissed, and the three rubbers of whist had been played, and no ticking had been heard—which the more encouraged me—I took my pipe and, saying that bedtime had arrived for the rest, drew my chair towards the fire, and, removing my slippers, placed my feet on the fender, looking as calm and composed as old Democritus in the tombs of Abdera, when one midnight the mischievous little boys of the town tried to frighten that sturdy philosopher with spurious ghosts.

And I thought to myself, that the worthy old gentleman had set a good example to all times in his conduct on that occasion. For, when at the dead hour, intent on his studies, he heard the strange sounds, he did not so much as move his eyes from his page, only simply said: "Boys, little boys, go home. This is no place for you. You will catch cold here." The philosophy of which words lies here: that they imply the foregone conclusion, that any possible investigation of any possible spiritual phenomena was absurd; that upon the first face of such things, the mind of a sane man instinctively affirmed them a humbug, unworthy the least attention; more especially if such phenomena appear in tombs, since tombs are peculiarly the place of silence, lifelessness, and solitude; for which cause, by the way, the old man, as upon the occasion in question, made the tombs of Abdera his place of study.

Presently I was alone, and all was hushed. I laid down my pipe, not feeling exactly tranquil enough now thoroughly to enjoy it. Taking up one of the newspapers, I began, in a nervous, hurried sort of way, to read by the light of a candle placed on a small stand drawn close to the fire. As for the apple-tree table, having lately concluded that it was rather too low for a reading-table, I thought best not to use it as such that night. But it stood not very distant in the middle of the room.

Try as I would, I could not succeed much at reading.

Somehow I seemed all ear and no eye; a condition of intense auricular suspense. But ere long it was broken.

Tick, tick, tick!

Though it was not the first time I had heard that sound; nay, though I had made it my particular business on this occasion to wait for that sound, nevertheless, when it came, it seemed unexpected, as if a cannon had boomed through the window.

Tick! tick! tick!

I sat stock-still for a time, thoroughly to master, if possible, my first discomposure. Then rising, I looked pretty steadily at the table; went up to it pretty steadily; took hold of it pretty steadily; but let it go pretty quickly; then paced up and down, stopping every moment or two, with ear pricked to listen. Meantime, within me, the contest between panic and philosophy remained not wholly decided.

Tick! tick! tick!

With appalling distinctness the ticking now rose on the night.

My pulse fluttered—my heart beat. I hardly know what might not have followed, had not Democritus just then come to the rescue. For shame, said I to myself, what is the use of so fine an example of philosophy, if it cannot be followed? Straightway I resolved to imitate it, even to the old sage's occupation and attitude.

Resuming my chair and paper, with back presented to the table, I remained thus for a time, as if buried in study; when, the ticking still continuing, I drawled out, in as indifferent and dryly jocose a way as I could: "Come, come, Tick, my boy, fun enough for to-night."

Tick! tick! tick!

There seemed a sort of jeering defiance in the ticking now. It seemed to exult over the poor affected part I was playing. But much as the taunt stung me, it only stung me into persistence. I resolved not to abate one whit in my mode of address.

"Come, come, you make more and more noise, Tick, my boy; too much of a joke—time to have done."

No sooner said than the ticking ceased. Never was responsive obedience more exact. For the life of me, I could not help turning round upon the table, as one would upon some reasonable being, when—could I believe my senses? I saw something moving, or wriggling, or squirming upon the slab of the table. It shone like a glow-worm. Unconsciously, I grasped the poker that stood at hand. But bethinking me how absurd to attack a glow-worm with a poker, I put it down. How long I sat spell-bound and staring there, with my body presented one way and my face another, I cannot say; but at length I rose, and, buttoning my coat up and down, made a sudden intrepid forced march full upon the table. And there, near the centre of the slab, as I live, I saw an irregular little hole, or, rather, a short nibbled sort of crack, from which (like a butterfly escaping its chrysalis) the sparkling object, whatever it might be, was struggling. Its motion was the motion of life. I stood becharmed. Are there, indeed, spirits, thought I; and is this one? No; I must be dreaming. I turned my glance off to the red fire on the hearth, then back to the pale lustre on the table. What I saw was no optical illusion, but a real marvel. The tremor was increasing, when, once again, Democritus befriended me. Supernatural coruscation as it appeared, I strove to look at the strange object in a purely scientific way. Thus viewed, it appeared some new sort of small shining beetle or bug, and, I thought, not without something of a hum to it, too.

I still watched it, and with still increasing self-possession. Sparkling and wriggling, it still continued its throes. In another moment it was just on the point of escaping its prison. A thought struck me. Running for a tumbler, I clapped it over the insect just in time to secure it.

After watching it a while longer under the tumbler, I left all as it was, and, tolerably composed, retired.

Now, for the soul of me, I could not, at that time, comprehend the phenomenon. A live bug come out of a dead table? A fire-fly bug come out of a piece of ancient lumber, for one knows not how many years stored away in an old garret? Was ever such a thing heard of, or even dreamed of? How got the bug there? Never mind. I bethought me of Democritus, and resolved to keep cool. At all events, the mystery of the ticking was explained. It was simply the sound of the gnawing and filing, and tapping of the bug, in eating its way out. It was satisfactory to think that there was an end forever to the ticking. I resolved not to let the occasion pass without reaping some credit from it.

"Wife," said I, next morning, "you will not be troubled with any more ticking in our table. I have put a stop to all that."

"Indeed, husband," said she, with some incredulity.

"Yes, wife," returned I, perhaps a little vain-gloriously. "I have put a quietus upon that ticking. Depend upon it, the ticking will trouble you no more."

In vain she besought me to explain myself. I would not gratify her; being willing to balance any previous trepidation I might have betrayed, by leaving room now for the imputation of some heroic feat whereby I had silenced the ticking. It was a sort of innocent deceit by implication, quite harmless, and, I thought, of utility.

But when I went to breakfast, I saw my wife kneeling at the table again, and my girls looking ten times more frightened than ever.

"Why did you tell me that boastful tale?" said my wife indignantly. "You might have known how easily it would be found out. See this crack, too; and here is the ticking again, plainer than ever."

"Impossible," I exclaimed; but upon applying my ear, sure enough, tick! tick! tick! The ticking was there.

Recovering myself the best way I might, I demanded the bug.

"Bug?" screamed Julia. "Good heavens, papa!"

"I hope, sir, you have been bringing no bugs into this house," said my wife, severely.

"The bug, the bug!" I cried; "the bug under the tumbler."

"Bugs in tumblers!" cried the girls; "not *our* tumblers, papa? You have not been putting bugs into our tumblers? Oh, what does—what *does* it all mean?"

"Do you see this hole, this crack here?" said I, putting my finger on the spot.

"That I do," said my wife, with high displeasure. "And how did it come there? What have you been doing to the table?"

"Do you see this crack?" repeated I, intensely.

"Yes, yes," said Julia; "that was what frightened me so; it looks so like witch-work."

"Spirits! spirits!" cried Anna.

"Silence!" said my wife. "Go on, sir, and tell us what you know of the crack."

"Wife and daughters," said I, solemnly, "out of that crack, or hole, while I was sitting all alone here last night, a wonderful—"

Here, involuntarily, I paused, fascinated by the expectant attitudes and bursting eyes of Julia and Anna.

"What, what?" cried Julia.

"A bug, Julia."

"A bug?" cried my wife. "A bug come out of this table? And what did you do with it?"

"Clapped it under a tumbler."

"Biddy! Biddy!" cried my wife, going to the door. "Did you see a tumbler here on this table when you swept the room?"

"Sure I did, marm, and a 'bomnable bug under it."

"And what did you do with it?" demanded I.

"Put the bug in the fire, sir, and rinsed out the tumbler ever so many times, marm."

"Where is that tumbler?" cried Anna. "I hope you scratched it—marked it some way. I'll never drink out of that tumbler; never put it before me, Biddy. A bug—a bug! Oh, Julia! Oh, mamma! I feel it crawling all over me, even now. Haunted table!"

"Spirits! spirits!" cried Julia.

"My daughters," said their mother, with authority in her eyes, "go to your chamber till you can behave more like reasonable creatures. Is it a bug—a bug that can frighten you out of what little wits you ever had? Leave the room. I am astonished. I am pained by such childish conduct."

"Now tell me," said she, addressing me, as soon as they had withdrawn, "now tell me truly, did a bug really come out of this crack in the table?"

"Wife, it is even so."

"Did you see it come out?"

"I did."

She looked earnestly at the crack, leaning over it.

"Are you sure?" said she, looking up, but still bent over.

"Sure, sure."

She was silent. I began to think that the mystery of the thing began to tell even upon her. Yes, thought I, I shall presently see my wife shaking and shuddering, and, who knows, calling in some old dominie to exorcise the table, and drive out the spirits.

"I'll tell you what we'll do," said she suddenly, and not without excitement.

"What, wife?" said I, all eagerness, expecting some mystical proposition; "what, wife?"

"We will rub this table all over with that celebrated roach powder I've heard of."

"Good gracious! Then you don't think it's spirits?"

"Spirits?"

The emphasis of scornful incredulity was worthy of Democritus himself.

"But this ticking—this ticking?" said I.

"I'll whip that out of it."

"Come, come, wife," said I, "you are going too far the other way, now. Neither roach powder nor whipping will cure this table. It's a queer table, wife; there's no blinking it."

"I'll have it rubbed, though," she replied, "well rubbed;" and calling Biddy, she bade her get wax and brush, and give the table a vigorous manipulation. That done, the cloth was again laid, and we sat down to our morning meal; but my daughters did not make their appearance. Julia and Anna took no breakfast that day.

When the cloth was removed, in a business-like way my wife went to work with a dark colored cement, and hermetically closed the little hole in the table.

My daughters looking pale, I insisted upon taking them out for a walk that morning, when the following conversation ensued:

"My worst presentiments about that table are being verified, papa," said Julia; "not for nothing was that intimation of the cloven foot on my shoulder."

"Nonsense," said I. "Let us go into Mrs. Brown's, and have an ice-cream."

The spirit of Democritus was stronger on me now. By a curious coincidence, it strengthened with the strength of the sunlight.

"But is it not miraculous," said Anna, "how a bug should come out of a table?"

"Not at all, my daughter. It is a very common thing for bugs to come out of wood. You yourself must have seen them coming out of the ends of the billets on the hearth."

"Ah, but that wood is almost fresh from the woodland. But the table is at least a hundred years old."

"What of that?" said I, gaily. "Have not live toads been found in the hearts of dead rocks, as old as creation?"

"Say what you will, papa, I feel it is spirits," said Julia. "Do, do now, my dear papa, have that haunted table removed from the house."

"Nonsense," said I.

By another curious coincidence, the more they felt frightened, the more I felt brave.

Evening came.

"This ticking," said my wife; "do you think that another bug will come of this continued ticking?"

Curiously enough, that had not occurred to me before. I had not thought of there being twins of bugs. But now, who knew—there might be even triplets.

I resolved to take precautions and, if there was to be a second bug, infallibly secure it. During the evening, the ticking was again heard. About ten o'clock I clapped a tumbler over the spot, as near as I could judge of it by my ear. Then we all retired, and locking the door of the cedar-parlor, I put the key in my pocket.

In the morning, nothing was to be seen, but the ticking was heard. The trepidation of my daughters returned. They wanted to call in the neighbors. But to this my wife was vigorously opposed. We should be the laughing-stock of the whole town. So it was agreed that nothing should be disclosed. Biddy received strict charges; and, to make sure, was not allowed that week to go to confession, lest she should tell the priest.

I stayed home all that day, every hour or two bending over the table, both eye and ear. Towards night, I thought the ticking grew more distinct, and seemed divided from my ear by a thinner and thinner partition of the wood. I thought, too, that I perceived a faint heaving up, or bulging of the wood, in the place where I had placed the tumbler. To put an end to the suspense, my wife proposed taking a knife and cutting into the wood there; but I had a less impatient plan; namely, that she and I should sit up with the table that night, as, from present symptoms, the bug would probably make its appearance before morning. For myself, I was curious to see the first advent of the thing—the first dazzle of the chick as it chipped the shell.

The idea struck my wife not unfavorably. She insisted that both Julia and Anna should be of the party, in order that the evidence of their senses should disabuse their minds of all nursery nonsense. For that spirits should tick, and that spirits should take unto themselves the form of bugs, was, to my wife, the most foolish of all foolish imaginations. True, she could not account for the thing; but she had all confidence that it could be, and would yet be, somehow explained, and that to her entire satisfaction. Without knowing it herself, my wife was a female Democritus. For my own part, my present feelings were of a mixed sort. In a strange and not unpleasing way, I gently oscillated between Democritus and Cotton Mather. But to my wife and daughters I assumed to be pure Democritus —a jeerer at all tea-table spirits whatever.

So, laying in a good supply of candles and crackers, all four of us sat up with the table, and at the same time sat round it. For a while my wife and I carried on an animated conversation. But my daughters were silent. Then my wife and I would have had a rubber of whist, but my daughters could not be prevailed upon to join. So we played whisɔ with two dummies, literally; my wife won the rubber, and, fatigued with victory, put away the cards.

Half past eleven o'clock. No sign of the bug. The candles began to burn dim. My wife was just in the act of snuffing them, when a sudden, violent, hollow, resounding, rumbling thumping was heard.

Julia and Anna sprang to their feet.

"All well!" cried a voice from the street. It was the watchman, first ringing down his club on the pavement,. and then following it up with this highly satisfactory verbaȝ announcement.

"All well! Do you hear that, my girls?" said I, gaily.

Indeed it was astonishing how brave as Bruce I felt in company with three women, and two of them half frightened out of their wits.

I rose for my pipe, and took a philosophic smoke.

Democritus forever, thought I.

In profound silence, I sat smoking, when lo!—pop! pop! pop!—right under the table, a terrible popping.

This time we all four sprang up, and my pipe was broken.

"Good heavens! what's that?"

"Spirits! spirits!" cried Julia.

"Oh, oh, oh!" cried Anna.

"Shame," said my wife, "it's that new bottled cider, in the cellar, going off. I told Biddy to wire the bottles to-day."

I shall here transcribe from memoranda, kept during part of the night:

One o'clock. No sign of the bug. Ticking continues. Wife getting sleepy.

Two o'clock. No sign of the bug. Ticking intermittent Wife fast asleep.

Three o'clock. No sign of the bug. Ticking pretty steady. Julia and Anna getting sleepy.

Four o'clock. No sign of the bug. Ticking regular, but not spirited. Wife, Julia, and Anna, all fast asleep in their chairs.

Five o'clock. No sign of the bug. Ticking faint. Myself feeling drowsy. The rest still asleep.

So far the journal.

—Rap! rap! rap!

A terrific, portentous rapping against a door.

Startled from our dreams, we started to our feet.

Rap! rap! rap!

Julia and Anna shrieked.

I cowered in the corner.

"You fools!" cried my wife, "it's the baker with the bread."

Six o'clock.

She went to throw back the shutters, but ere it was done, a cry came from Julia. There, half in and half out its crack, there wriggled the bug, flashing in the room's general dimness like a fiery opal.

Had this bug had a tiny sword by its side—a Damascus sword—and a tiny necklace round its neck—a diamond necklace—and a tiny gun in its claw—a brass gun—and a tiny manuscript in its mouth—a Chaldee manuscript—Julia and Anna could not have stood more charmed.

In truth, it was a beautiful bug—a Jew jeweler's bug—a bug like a sparkle of a glorious sunset.

Julia and Anna had never dreamed of such a bug. To them, bug had been a word synonymous with hideousness. But this was a seraphical bug; or, rather, all it had of the bug was the B, for it was beautiful as a butterfly.

Julia and Anna gazed and gazed. They were no more alarmed. They were delighted.

"But how got this strange, pretty creature into the table?" cried Julia.

"Spirits can get anywhere," replied Anna.

"Pshaw!" said my wife.

"Do you hear any more ticking?" said I.

They all applied their ears, but heard nothing.

"Well, then, wife and daughters, now that it is all over, this very morning I will go and make inquiries about it."

"Oh, do, papa," cried Julia, "do go and consult Madame Pazzi, the conjuress."

"Better go and consult Professor Johnson, the naturalist," said my wife.

"Bravo, Mrs. Democritus!" said I, "Professor Johnson is the man."

By good fortune I found the professor in. Informing him briefly of the incident, he manifested a cool, collected sort of interest, and gravely accompanied me home. The table was produced, the two openings pointed out, the bug displayed, and the details of the affair set forth; my wife and daughters being present.

"And now, Professor," said I, "what do you think of it?"

Putting on his spectacles, the learned professor looked hard at the table, and gently scraped with his pen-knife into the holes, but said nothing.

"Is it not an unusual thing, this?" anxiously asked Anna.

"Very unusual, Miss."

At which Julia and Anna exchanged significant glances.

"But is it not wonderful, very wonderful?" demanded Julia.

"Very wonderful, Miss."

My daughters exchanged still more significant glances, and Julia, emboldened, again spoke.

"And must you not admit, sir, that it is the work of—of—of sp—?"

"Spirits? No," was the crusty rejoinder.

"My daughters," said I, mildly, "you should remember that this is not Madame Pazzi, the conjuress, you put your questions to, but the eminent naturalist, Professor Johnson. And now, Professor," I added, "be pleased to explain. Enlighten our ignorance."

Without repeating all that the learned gentleman said— for, indeed, though lucid, he was a little prosy—let the following summary of his explication suffice.

The incident was not wholly without example. The wood of the table was apple-tree, a sort of tree much fancied by various insects. The bugs had come from eggs laid inside the bark of the living tree in the orchard. By careful examination of the position of the hole from which the last bug had emerged, in relation to the cortical layers of the slab, and then allowing for the inch and a half along the grain, ere the bug had eaten its way entirely out, and then computing the whole number of cortical layers in the slab, with a reasonable conjecture for the number cut off from the outside, it appeared that the egg must have been laid in the tree some ninety years, more or less, before the tree could have been felled. But between the felling of the tree and the present time, how long might that be? It was a very old-fashioned table. Allow eighty years for the age of the table, which would make one hundred and fifty years that the bug had lain in the egg. Such, at least, was Professor Johnson's computation.

"Now, Julia," said I, "after that scientific statement of the case (though, I confess, I don't exactly understand it), where are your spirits? It is very wonderful as it is, but where are your spirits?"

"Where, indeed?" said my wife.

"Why, now, she did not *really* associate this purely natural phenomenon with any crude, spiritual hypothesis, did she?" observed the learned professor, with a slight sneer.

"Say what you will," said Julia, holding up, in the covered tumbler, the glorious, lustrous, flashing live opal, "say what you will, if this beauteous creature be not a spirit, it yet teaches a spiritual lesson. For if, after one hundred and fifty years' entombment, a mere insect comes forth at last into light, itself an effulgence, shall there be no glorified resurrection for the spirit of man? Spirits! spirits!" she exclaimed, with rapture, "I still believe in spirits, only now I believe in them with delight, when before I but thought of them with terror."

The mysterious insect did not long enjoy its radiant life; it expired the next day. But my girls have preserved it. Embalmed in a silver vinaigrette, it lies on the little apple-tree table in the pier of the cedar-parlor.

And whatever lady doubts this story, my daughters will be happy to show her both the bug and the table, and point out to her, in the repaired slab of the latter, the two sealing-wax drops designating the exact place of the two holes made by the two bugs, something in the same way in which are marked the spots where the cannon balls struck Brattle Street Church.

The Piazza

"With fairest flowers,
Whilst summer lasts, and I live here, Fidele—"

W HEN I removed into the country, it was to occupy an old-fashioned farm-house, which had no piazza—a deficiency the more regretted, because not only did I like piazzas, as somehow combining the coziness of in-doors with the freedom of out-doors, and it is so pleasant to inspect your thermometer there, but the country round about was such a picture, that in berry time no boy climbs hill or crosses vale without coming upon easels planted in every nook, and sun-burnt painters painting there. A very paradise of painters. The circle of the stars cut by the circle of the mountains. At least, so looks it from the house; though, once upon the mountains, no circle of them can you see. Had the site been chosen five rods off, this charmed ring would not have been.

The house is old. Seventy years since, from the heart of the Hearth Stone Hills, they quarried the Kaaba, or Holy Stone, to which, each Thanksgiving, the social pilgrims used to come. So long ago, that, in digging for the foundation, the workmen used both spade and axe, fighting the Troglodytes of those subterranean parts—sturdy roots of a sturdy wood, encamped upon what is now a long land-slide of sleeping meadow, sloping away off from my poppy-bed. Of that knit wood, but one survivor stands— an elm, lonely through steadfastness.

Whoever built the house, he builded better than he

knew; or else Orion in the zenith flashed down his Dam-
ocles' sword to him some starry night, and said, "Build
there." For how, otherwise, could it have entered the
builder's mind, that, upon the clearing being made, such
a purple prospect would be his?—nothing less than Greylock, with all his hills about him, like Charlemagne among
his peers.

Now, for a house, so situated in such a country, to have
no piazza for the convenience of those who might desire
to feast upon the view, and take their time and ease about
it, seemed as much of an omission as if a picture-gallery
should have no bench; for what but picture-galleries are the
marble halls of these same limestone hills?—galleries hung,
month after month anew, with pictures ever fading into
pictures ever fresh. And beauty is like piety—you cannot
run and read it; tranquillity and constancy, with, now-a-
days, an easy chair, are needed. For though, of old, when
reverence was in vogue, and indolence was not, the devotees
of Nature, doubtless, used to stand and adore—just as, in
the cathedrals of those ages, the worshipers of a higher
Power did—yet, in these times of failing faith and feeble
knees, we have the piazza and the pew.

During the first year of my residence, the more leisurely
to witness the coronation of Charlemagne (weather permitting, they crown him every sunrise and sunset), I
chose me, on the hill-side bank near by, a royal lounge
of turf—a green velvet lounge, with long, moss-padded
back; while at the head, strangely enough, there grew (but,
I suppose, for heraldry) three tufts of blue violets in a
field-argent of wild strawberries; and a trellis, with honey-
suckle, I set for canopy. Very majestical lounge, indeed. So
much so, that here, as with the reclining majesty of Den-
mark in his orchard, a sly ear-ache invaded me. But, if
damps abound at times in Westminster Abbey, because

it is so old, why not within this monastery of mountains, which is older?

A piazza must be had.

The house was wide—my fortune narrow; so that, to build a panoramic piazza, one round and round, it could not be—although, indeed, considering the matter by rule and square, the carpenters, in the kindest way, were anxious to gratify my furthest wishes, at I've forgotten how much a foot.

Upon but one of the four sides would prudence grant me what I wanted. Now, which side?

To the east, that long camp of the Hearth Stone Hills, fading far away towards Quito; and every fall, a small white flake of something peering suddenly, of a coolish morning, from the topmost cliff—the season's new-dropped lamb, its earliest fleece; and then the Christmas dawn, draping those dun highlands with redbarred plaids and tartans—goodly sight from your piazza, that. Goodly sight; but, to the north is Charlemagne—can't have the Hearth Stone Hills with Charlemagne.

Well, the south side. Apple-trees are there. Pleasant, of a balmy morning, in the month of May, to sit and see that orchard, white-budded, as for a bridal; and, in October, one green arsenal yard; such piles of ruddy shot. Very fine, I grant; but, to the north is Charlemagne.

The west side, look. An upland pasture, alleying away into a maple wood at top. Sweet, in opening spring, to trace upon the hill-side, otherwise gray and bare—to trace, I say, the oldest paths by their streaks of earliest green. Sweet, indeed, I can't deny; but, to the north is Charlemagne.

So Charlemagne, he carried it. It was not long after 1848; and, somehow, about that time, all round the world, these kings, they had the casting vote, and voted for themselves.

No sooner was ground broken, than all the neighborhood, neighbor Dives, in particular, broke, too—into a laugh. Piazza to the north! Winter piazza! Wants, of winter midnights, to watch the Aurora Borealis, I suppose; hope he's laid in good store of Polar muffs and mittens.

That was in the lion month of March. Not forgotten are the blue noses of the carpenters, and how they scouted at the greenness of the cit, who would build his sole piazza to the north. But March don't last forever; patience, and August comes. And then, in the cool elysium of my northern bower, I, Lazarus in Abraham's bosom, cast down the hill a pitying glance on poor old Dives, tormented in the purgatory of his piazza to the south.

But, even in December, this northern piazza does not repel—nipping cold and gusty though it be, and the north wind, like any miller, bolting by the snow, in finest flour—for then, once more, with frosted beard, I pace the sleety deck, weathering Cape Horn.

In summer, too, Canute-like; sitting here, one is often reminded of the sea. For not only do long ground-swells roll the slanting grain, and little wavelets of the grass ripple over upon the low piazza, as their beach, and the blown down of dandelions is wafted like the spray, and the purple of the mountains is just the purple of the billows, and a still August noon broods upon the deep meadows, as a calm upon the Line; but the vastness and the lonesomeness are so oceanic, and the silence and the sameness, too, that the first peep of a strange house, rising beyond the trees, is for all the world like spying, on the Barbary coast, an unknown sail.

And this recalls my inland voyage to fairy-land. A true voyage; but, take it all in all, interesting as if invented.

From the piazza, some uncertain object I had caught, mysteriously snugged away, to all appearance, in a sort of purpled breast-pocket, high up in a hopper-like hollow,

or sunken angle, among the northwestern mountains—
yet, whether, really, it was on a mountain-side, or a mountain-top, could not be determined; because, though, viewed
from favorable points, a blue summit, peering up away
behind the rest, will, as it were, talk to you over their
heads, and plainly tell you, that, though he (the blue summit) seems among them, he is not of them (God forbid!),
and, indeed, would have you know that he considers himself—as, to say truth, he has good right—by several cubits
their superior, nevertheless, certain ranges, here and there
double-filed, as in platoons, so shoulder and follow up upon
one another, with their irregular shapes and heights, that,
from the piazza, a nigher and lower mountain will, in most
states of the atmosphere, effacingly shade itself away into
a higher and further one; that an object, bleak on the
former's crest, will, for all that, appear nested in the
latter's flank. These mountains, somehow, they play at hide-
and-seek, and all before one's eyes.

But, be that as it may, the spot in question was, at all
events, so situated as to be only visible, and then but
vaguely, under certain witching conditions of light and
shadow.

Indeed, for a year or more, I knew not there was such a
spot, and might, perhaps, have never known, had it not
been for a wizard afternoon in autumn—late in autumn—
a mad poet's afternoon; when the turned maple woods in
the broad basin below me, having lost their first vermilion
tint, dully smoked, like smouldering towns, when flames
expire upon their prey; and rumor had it, that this smoki-
ness in the general air was not all Indian summer—which
was not used to be so sick a thing, however mild—but, in
great part, was blown from far-off forests, for weeks on fire,
in Vermont; so that no wonder the sky was ominous as
Hecate's cauldron—and two sportsmen, crossing a red
stubble buck-wheat field, seemed guilty Macbeth and fore-

boding Banquo; and the hermit-sun, hutted in an Adullam cave, well towards the south, according to his season, did little else but, by indirect reflection of narrow rays shot down a Simplon pass among the clouds, just steadily paint one small, round, strawberry mole upon the wan cheek of Northwestern hills. Signal as a candle. One spot of radiance, where all else was shade.

Fairies there, thought I; some haunted ring where fairies dance.

Time passed; and the following May, after a gentle shower upon the mountains—a little shower islanded in misty seas of sunshine; such a distant shower—and sometimes two, and three, and four of them, all visible together in different parts—as I love to watch from the piazza, instead of thunder-storms, as I used to, which wrap old Greylock, like a Sinai, till one thinks swart Moses must be climbing among scathed hemlocks there; after, I say, that gentle shower, I saw a rainbow, resting its further end just where, in autumn, I had marked the mole. Fairies there, thought I; remembering that rainbows bring out the blooms, and that, if one can but get to the rainbow's end, his fortune is made in a bag of gold. Yon rainbow's end, would I were there, thought I. And none the less I wished it, for now first noticing what seemed some sort of glen, or grotto, in the mountain side; at least, whatever it was, viewed through the rainbow's medium, it glowed like the Potosi mine. But a work-a-day neighbor said, no doubt it was but some old barn—an abandoned one, its broadside beaten in, the acclivity its background. But I, though I had never been there, I knew better.

A few days after, a cheery sunrise kindled a golden sparkle in the same spot as before. The sparkle was of that vividness, it seemed as if it could only come from glass. The building, then—if building, after all, it was—could, at least, not be a barn, much less an abandoned one; stale hay ten years musting in it. No; if aught built by mortal, it must be a cottage; perhaps long vacant and dismantled, but this very spring magically fitted up and glazed.

Again, one noon, in the same direction, I marked, over dimmed tops of terraced foliage, a broader gleam, as of a silver buckler, held sunwards over some croucher's head; which gleam, experience in like cases taught, must come from a roof newly shingled. This, to me, made pretty sure the recent occupancy of that far cot in fairy-land.

Day after day, now, full of interest in my discovery, what time I could spare from reading the *Midsummer-Night's Dream*, and all about Titania, wishfully I gazed off towards the hills: but in vain. Either troops of shadows, an imperial guard, with slow pace and solemn, defiled along the steeps; or, routed by pursuing light, fled broadcast from east to west—old wars of Lucifer and Michael; or the mountains, though unvexed by these mirrored sham fights in the sky, had an atmosphere otherwise unfavorable for fairy views. I was sorry; the more so, because I had to keep my chamber for some time after—which chamber did not face those hills.

At length, when pretty well again, and sitting out, in the September morning, upon the piazza, and thinking to myself, when, just after a little flock of sheep, the farmer's banded children passed, a-nutting, and said, "How sweet a day"—it was, after all, but what their fathers call a weather-breeder—and, indeed, was become so sensitive through my illness, as that I could not bear to look upon a Chinese creeper of my adoption, and which, to my delight, climbing a post of the piazza, had burst out in starry bloom, but now, if you removed the leaves a little, showed millions of strange, cankerous worms, which, feeding upon those blossoms, so shared their blessed hue, as to make it unblessed evermore—worms, whose germs had doubtless lurked in the very bulb which, so hopefully, I had planted: in thi ingrate peevishness of my weary convalescence, was I sitting there; when, suddenly looking off, I saw the golden mountain-window, dazzling like a deep-sea dolphin. Fairies there, thought I, once more; the queen of fairies at her fairy window; at any rate, some glad mountain-girl; it will do me good, it will cure this weariness, to look on her. No more; I'll launch my yawl—ho, cheerly, heart! and push away for fairy-land—for rainbow's end, in fairy-land.

How to get to fairy-land, by what road, I did not know; nor could any one inform me; not even one Edmund Spenser, who had been there—so he wrote me—further than that to reach fairy-land, it must be voyaged to, and with faith. I took the fairy-mountain's bearings, and the first fine day, when strength permitted, got into my yawl—high-pommeled, leather one—cast off the fast, and away I sailed, free voyager as an autumn leaf. Early dawn; and, sallying westward, I sowed the morning before me.

Some miles brought me nigh the hills; but out of present sight of them. I was not lost; for road-side golden-rods, as guide-posts, pointed, I doubted not, the way to the golden window. Following them, I came to a lone and languid region, where the grass-grown ways were traveled but by drowsy cattle, that, less waked than stirred by day, seemed to walk in sleep. Browse, they did not—the enchanted never eat. At least, so says Don Quixote, that sagest sage that ever lived.

On I went, and gained at last the fairy-mountain's base, but saw yet no fairy ring. A pasture rose before me. Letting down five mouldering bars—so moistly green, they seemed fished up from some sunken wreck—a wigged old Aries, long-visaged, and with crumpled horn, came snuffing up; and then, retreating, decorously led on along a milky-way of white-weed, past dim-clustering Pleiades and Hyades, of small forget-me-nots; and would have led me further still his astral path, but for golden flights of yellow-birds—pilots, surely, to the golden window, to one side flying before me, from bush to bush, towards deep woods—which woods themselves were luring—and, somehow, lured, too, by their fence, banning a dark road, which, however dark, led up. I pushed through; when Aries, renouncing me now for some lost soul, wheeled, and went his wiser way. Forbidding and forbidden ground—to him.

A winter wood road, matted all along with winter-green. By the side of pebbly waters—waters the cheerier for their solitude; beneath swaying fir-boughs, petted by no season, but still green in all, on I journeyed—my horse and I; on, by an old saw-mill, bound down and hushed with vines, that his grating voice no more was heard; on, by a deep flume clove through snowy marble, vernal-tinted, where freshet eddies had, on each side, spun out empty chapels in the living rock; on, where Jacks-in-the-pulpit, like their Baptist namesake, preached but to the wilderness; on, where a huge, cross-grain block, fern-bedded, showed where, in forgotten times, man after man had tried to split it, but lost his wedges for his pains—which wedges yet rusted in their holes; on, where, ages past, in step-like ledges of a cascade, skull-hollow pots had been churned out by ceaseless whirling of a flintstone—ever wearing, but itself unworn; on, by wild rapids pouring into a secret pool, but soothed by circling there awhile, issued forth serenely; on, to less broken ground, and by a little ring, where, truly, fairies must have danced, or else some wheel-tire been heated—for all was bare; still on, and up, and out into a hanging orchard, where maidenly looked down upon me a crescent moon, from morning.

My horse hitched low his head. Red apples rolled before him; Eve's apples; seek-no-furthers. He tasted one, I another; it tasted of the ground. Fairy-land not yet, thought I, flinging my bridle to a humped old tree, that crooked out an arm to catch it. For the way now lay where path was none, and none might go but by himself, and only go by daring. Through blackberry brakes that tried to pluck me back, though I but strained towards fruitless growths of mountain-laurel; up slippery steeps to barren heights, where stood none to welcome. Fairy-land not yet, thought I, though the morning is here before me.

Foot-sore enough and weary, I gained not then my journey's end, but came ere long to a craggy pass, dipping towards growing regions still beyond. A zigzag road, half overgrown with blueberry bushes, here turned among the cliffs. A rent was in their ragged sides; through it a little track branched off, which, upwards threading that short defile, came breezily out above, to where the mountain-top, part sheltered northward, by a taller brother, sloped gently off a space, ere darkly plunging; and here, among fantastic rocks, reposing in a herd, the foot-track wound, half beaten, up to a little, low-storied, grayish cottage, capped, nun-like, with a peaked roof.

On one slope, the roof was deeply weather-stained, and, nigh the turfy eaves-trough, all velvet-napped; no doubt the snail-monks founded mossy priories there. The other slope was newly shingled. On the north side, doorless and windowless, the clapboards, innocent of paint, were yet green as the north side of lichened pines, or copperless hulls of Japanese junks, becalmed. The whole base, like those of the neighboring rocks, was rimmed about with shaded streaks of richest sod; for, with hearth-stones in fairy-land, the natural rock, though housed, preserves to the last, just as in open fields, its fertilizing charm; only, by necessity, working now at a remove, to the sward without. So, at least, says Oberon, grave authority in fairy lore. Though setting Oberon aside, certain it is, that, even in the common world, the soil, close up to farm-houses, as close up to pasture rocks, is, even though untended, ever richer than it is a few rods off—such gentle, nurturing heat is radiated there.

But with this cottage, the shaded streaks were richest in its front and about its entrance, where the ground-sill, and especially the door-sill had, through long eld, quietly settled down.

No fence was seen, no inclosure. Near by—ferns, ferns, ferns; further—woods, woods, woods; beyond—mountains, mountains, mountains; then—sky, sky, sky. Turned out in ærial commons, pasture for the mountain moon. Nature, and but nature, house and all; even a low cross-pile of silver birch, piled openly, to season; up among whose silvery sticks, as through the fencing of some sequestered grave, sprang vagrant raspberry bushes—willful assertors of their right of way.

The foot-track, so dainty narrow, just like a sheep-track, led through long ferns that lodged. Fairy-land at last, thought I; Una and her lamb dwell here. Truly, a small abode—mere palanquin, set down on the summit, in a pass between two worlds, participant of neither.

A sultry hour, and I wore a light hat, of yellow sinnet, with white duck trowsers—both relics of my tropic sea-going. Clogged in the muffling ferns, I softly stumbled, staining the knees a sea-green.

Pausing at the threshold, or rather where threshold once had been, I saw, through the open door-way, a lonely girl, sewing at a lonely window. A pale-cheeked girl, and fly-specked window, with wasps about the mended upper panes. I spoke. She shyly started, like some Tahiti girl, secreted for a sacrifice, first catching sight, through palms, of Captain Cook. Recovering, she bade me enter; with her apron brushed off a stool; then silently resumed her own. With thanks I took the stool; but now, for a space, I, too; was mute. This, then, is the fairy-mountain house, and here, the fairy queen sitting at her fairy window.

I went up to it. Downwards, directed by the tunneled pass, as through a leveled telescope, I caught sight of a far-off, soft, azure world. I hardly knew it, though I came from it.

"You must find this view very pleasant," said I, at last.

"Oh, sir," tears starting in her eyes, "the first time I looked out of this window, I said 'never, never shall I weary of this.' "

"And what wearies you of it now?"

"I don't know," while a tear fell; "but it is not the view, it is Marianna."

Some months back, her brother, only seventeen, had come hither, a long way from the other side, to cut wood and burn coal, and she, elder sister, had accompanied him. Long had they been orphans, and now, sole inhabitants of the sole house upon the mountain. No guest came, no traveler passed. The zigzag, perilous road was only used at seasons by the coal wagons. The brother was absent the entire day, sometimes the entire night. When at evening, fagged out, he did come home, he soon left his bench, poor fellow, for his bed; just as one, at last, wearily quits that, too, for still deeper rest. The bench, the bed, the grave.

Silent I stood by the fairy window, while these things were being told.

"Do you know," said she at last, as stealing from her story, "do you know who lives yonder?—I have never been down into that country—away off there, I mean; that house, that marble one," pointing far across the lower landscape; "have you not caught it? there, on the long hill-side: the field before, the woods behind; the white shines out against their blue; don't you mark it? the only house in sight."

I looked; and after a time, to my surprise, recognized, more by its position than its aspect, or Marianna's description, my own abode, glimmering much like this mountain one from the piazza. The mirage haze made it appear less a farm-house than King Charming's palace.

"I have often wondered who lives there; but it must be some happy one; again this morning was I thinking so."

"Some happy one," returned I, starting; "and why do you think that? You judge some rich one lives there?"

"Rich or not, I never thought; but it looks so happy, I can't tell how; and it is so far away. Sometimes I think I do but dream it is there. You should see it in a sunset."

"No doubt the sunset gilds it finely; but not more than the sunrise does this house, perhaps."

"This house? The sun is a good sun, but it never gilds this house. Why should it? This old house is rotting. That makes it so mossy. In the morning, the sun comes in at this old window, to be sure—boarded up, when first we came; a window I can't keep clean, do what I may—and half burns, and nearly blinds me at my sewing, besides setting the flies and wasps astir—such flies and wasps as only lone mountain houses know. See, here is the curtain—this apron —I try to shut it out with then. It fades it, you see. Sun gild this house? not that ever Marianna saw."

"Because when this roof is gilded most, then you stay here within."

"The hottest, weariest hour of day, you mean? Sir, the sun gilds not this roof. It leaked so, brother newly shingled all one side. Did you not see it? The north side, where the sun strikes most on what the rain has wetted. The sun is a good sun; but this roof, it first scorches, and then rots. An old house. They went West, and are long dead, they say, who built it. A mountain house. In winter no fox could den in it. That chimney-place has been blocked up with snow, just like a hollow stump."

"Yours are strange fancies, Marianna."

"They but reflect the things."

"Then I should have said, 'These are strange things,' rather than, 'Yours are strange fancies.'"

"As you will;" and took up her sewing.

Something in those quiet words, or in that quiet act, it made me mute again; while, noting, through the fairy window, a broad shadow stealing on, as cast by some gigantic condor, floating at brooding poise on outstretched wings, I marked how, by its deeper and inclusive dusk, it wiped away into itself all lesser shades of rock or fern.

"You watch the cloud," said Marianna.

"No, a shadow; a cloud's, no doubt—though that I cannot see. How did you know it? Your eyes are on your work."

"It dusked my work. There, now the cloud is gone, Tray comes back."

"How?"

"The dog, the shaggy dog. At noon, he steals off, of himself, to change his shape—returns, and lies down awhile, nigh the door. Don't you see him? His head is turned round at you; though, when you came, he looked before him."

"Your eyes rest but on your work; what do you speak of?"

"By the window, crossing."

"You mean this shaggy shadow—the nigh one? And, yes, now that I mark it, it is not unlike a large, black Newfoundland dog. The invading shadow gone, the invaded one returns. But I do not see what casts it."

"For that, you must go without."

"One of those grassy rocks, no doubt."

"You see his head, his face?"

"The shadow's? You speak as if *you* saw it, and all the time your eyes are on your work."

"Tray looks at you," still without glancing up; "this is his hour; I see him."

"Have you, then, so long sat at this mountain-window, where but clouds and vapors pass, that, to you, shadows are as things, though you speak of them as of phantoms; that, by familiar knowledge, working like a second sight, you can, without looking for them, tell just where they are, though, as having mice-like feet, they creep about, and come and go; that, to you, these lifeless shadows are as living friends, who, though out of sight, are not out of mind, even in their faces—is it so?"

"That way I never thought of it. But the friendliest one, that used to soothe my weariness so much, coolly quivering on the ferns, it was taken from me, never to return, as Tray did just now. The shadow of a birch. The tree was struck by lightning, and brother cut it up. You saw the cross-pile out-doors—the buried root lies under it; but not the shadow. That is flown, and never will come back, nor ever anywhere stir again."

Another cloud here stole along, once more blotting out the dog, and blackening all the mountain; while the stillness was so still, deafness might have forgot itself, or else believed that noiseless shadow spoke.

"Birds, Marianna, singing-birds, I hear none; I hear nothing. Boys and bob-o-links, do they never come a-berrying up here?"

"Birds, I seldom hear; boys, never. The berries mostly ripe and fall—few, but me, the wiser."

"But yellow-birds showed me the way—part way, at least."

"And then flew back. I guess they play about the mountain-side, but don't make the top their home. And no doubt you think that, living so lonesome here, knowing nothing, hearing nothing—little, at least, but sound of thunder and the fall of trees—never reading, seldom speaking, yet ever wakeful, this is what gives me my strange thoughts—for so you call them—this weariness and wakefulness together. Brother, who stands and works in open air, would I could rest like him; but mine is mostly but dull woman's work—sitting, sitting, restless sitting."

"But, do you not go walk at times? These woods are wide."

"And lonesome; lonesome, because so wide. Sometimes, 'tis true, of afternoons, I go a little way; but soon come back again. Better feel lone by hearth, than rock. The shadows hereabouts I know—those in the woods are strangers."

"But the night?"

"Just like the day. Thinking, thinking—a wheel I cannot stop; pure want of sleep it is that turns it."

"I have heard that, for this wakeful weariness, to say one's prayers, and then lay one's head upon a fresh hop pillow——"

"Look!"

Through the fairy window, she pointed down the steep to a small garden patch near by—mere pot of rifled loam, half rounded in by sheltering rocks—where, side by side, some feet apart, nipped and puny, two hop-vines climbed two poles, and, gaining their tip-ends, would have then joined over in an upward clasp, but the baffled shoots, groping awhile in empty air, trailed back whence they sprung.

"You have tried the pillow, then?"

"Yes."

"And prayer?"

"Prayer and pillow."

"Is there no other cure, or charm?"

"Oh, if I could but once get to yonder house, and but look upon whoever the happy being is that lives there! A foolish thought: why do I think it? Is it that I live so lonesome, and know nothing?"

"I, too, know nothing; and, therefore, cannot answer; but, for your sake, Marianna, well could wish that I were that happy one of the happy house you dream you see; for then you would behold him now, and, as you say, this weariness might leave you."

—Enough. Launching my yawl no more for fairy-land, I stick to the piazza. It is my box-royal; and this amphi-theatre, my theatre of San Carlo. Yes, the scenery is magical—the illusion so complete. And Madam Meadow Lark, my prima donna, plays her grand engagement here; and, drinking in her sunrise note, which, Memnon-like, seems struck from the golden window, how far from me the weary face behind it.

But, every night, when the curtain falls, truth comes in with darkness. No light shows from the mountain. To and fro I walk the piazza deck, haunted by Marianna's face, and many as real a story.

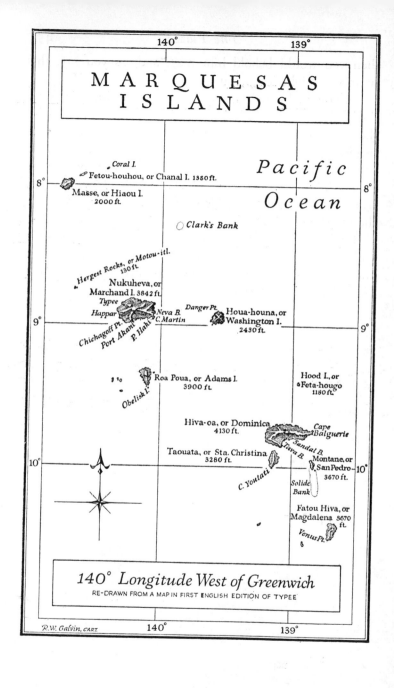

MARQUESAS ISLANDS

Pacific

Ocean

. Coral I.
Fetou-houhou, or Chanal I. 1380 ft.

Masse, or Hiaou I.
2000 ft.

8°

Clark's Bank

Hergest Rocks, or Motou-itl.
130 ft.

Nukuheva, or
Marchand I. 3842 ft.
Typee
Happar   Neva B.   Danger Pt.
Chichagoff Pt.   C. Martin   Houa-houna, or
Port Akam   P. Haki   Washington I.
2430 ft.

9°

Roa Poua, or Adams I.
3900 ft.

Obelisk I.

Hood I., or
Feta-hougo
1180 ft.

Hiva-oa, or Dominica
4130 ft.
Cape
Balguerie
Sandal B.

Taouata, or Sta. Christina
3280 ft.
Trava B.
Montane, or
San Pedro
3670 ft.

C. Youlati

10°

Solide
Bank

Fatou Hiva, or
Magdalena 3670
ft.
Venus Pt.

140° Longitude West of Greenwich

RE-DRAWN FROM A MAP IN FIRST ENGLISH EDITION OF TYPEE

R.W. Galvin, CART.

TYPEE

Preface

MORE than three years have elapsed since the occurrence of the events recorded in this volume. The interval, with the exception of the last few months, has been chiefly spent by the author tossing about on the wide ocean. Sailors are the only class of men who now-a-days see anything like stirring adventure; and many things which to fire-side people appear strange and romantic, to them seem as commonplace as a jacket out at elbows. Yet, notwithstanding the familiarity of sailors with all sorts of curious adventure, the incidents recorded in the following pages have often served, when "spun as a yarn," not only to relieve the weariness of many a night-watch at sea, but to excite the warmest sympathies of the author's shipmates. He has been therefore led to think that his story could scarcely fail to interest those who are less familiar than the sailor with a life of adventure.

In his account of the singular and interesting people among whom he was thrown, it will be observed that he chiefly treats of their more obvious peculiarities; and, in describing their customs, refrains in most cases from entering into explanations concerning their origin and purposes. As writers of travels among barbarous communities are generally very diffuse on these subjects, he deems it right to advert to what may be considered a culpable omission. No one can be more sensible than the author of his deficiencies in this and many other respects; but when the very peculiar circumstances in which he was placed are understood, he feels assured that all these omissions will be excused.

In very many published narratives no little degree of attention is bestowed upon dates; but as the author lost all knowledge of the days of the week, during the occurrence of the scenes herein related, he hopes that the reader will charitably pass over his shortcomings in this particular.

In the Polynesian words used in this volume—except in those cases where the spelling has been previously determined by others—that form of orthography has been employed, which might be supposed most easily to convey their sound to a stranger. In several works descriptive of the islands in the Pacific, many of the most beautiful combinations of vocal sounds have been altogether lost to the ear of the reader by an over-attention to the ordinary rules of spelling.

There are a few passages in the ensuing chapters which may be thought to bear rather hard upon a reverend order of men, the account of whose proceedings in different quarters of the globe—transmitted to us through their own hands —very generally, and often very deservedly, receives high commendation. Such passages will be found, however, to be based upon facts admitting of no contradiction, and which have come immediately under the writer's cognizance. The conclusions deduced from these facts are unavoidable, and in stating them the author has been influenced by no feeling of animosity, either to the individuals themselves or to that glorious cause which has not always been served by the proceedings of some of its advocates.

The great interest with which the important events lately occurring at the Sandwich, Marquesas, and Society Islands, have been regarded in America and England, and indeed throughout the world, will, he trusts, justify a few otherwise unwarrantable digressions.

There are some things related in the narrative which will be sure to appear strange, or perhaps entirely incomprehensible, to the reader; but they cannot appear more so to him than they did to the author at the time. He has stated such matters just as they occurred, and leaves every one to form his own opinion concerning them; trusting that his anxious desire to speak the unvarnished truth will gain for him the confidence of his readers.

Contents

CHAPTER I.

CHAPTER II.

CHAPTER III.

CHAPTER IV.

CHAPTER V.

CHAPTER VI.

CHAPTER VII.

CHAPTER VIII.

CHAPTER IX.

CHAPTER X.

CHAPTER XI.

462 *Contents*

CHAPTER XXXI.

CHAPTER XXXII.

CHAPTER XXXIII.

CHAPTER XXXIV.

APPENDIX.

Typee

CHAPTER I

The Sea—Longings for Shore—A Land-sick Ship—Destination of
the Voyagers—The Marquesas—Adventure of a Missionary's Wife
among the Savages—Characteristic Anecdote of the Queen of
Nukuheva.

SIX MONTHS at sea! Yes, reader, as I live, six months out
of sight of land; cruising after the sperm-whale beneath the scorching sun of the Line, and tossed on
the billows of the wide-rolling Pacific—the sky above, the
sea around, and nothing else! Weeks and weeks ago our
fresh provisions were all exhausted. There is not a sweet
potatoe left; not a single yam. Those glorious bunches of
banannas which once decorated our stern and quarter-deck
have, alas, disappeared! and the delicious oranges which
hung suspended from our tops and stays—they, too, are
gone! Yes, they are all departed, and there is nothing left
us but salt-horse and sea-biscuit. Oh! ye state-room sailors,
who make so much ado about a fourteen-days' passage
across the Atlantic; who so pathetically relate the priva-
tions and hardships of the sea, where, after a day of break-
fasting, lunching, dining off five courses, chatting, playing
whist, and drinking champaign-punch, it was your hard
lot to be shut up in little cabinets of mahogany and maple,
and sleep for ten hours, with nothing to disturb you but
"those good-for-nothing tars, shouting and tramping over
head,"—what would ye say to our six months out of sight
of land?

Oh! for a refreshing glimpse of one blade of grass—for a

snuff at the fragrance of a handful of the loamy earth! Is there nothing fresh around us? Is there no green thing to be seen? Yes, the inside of our bulwarks is painted green; but what a vile and sickly hue it is, as if nothing bearing even the semblance of verdure could flourish this weary way from land. Even the bark that once clung to the wood we use for fuel has been gnawed off and devoured by the captain's pig; and so long ago, too, that the pig himself has in turn been devoured.

There is but one solitary tenant in the chicken-coop, once a gay and dapper young cock, bearing him so bravely among the coy hens. But look at him now; there he stands, moping all the day long on that everlasting one leg of his. He turns with disgust from the mouldy corn before him, and the brackish water in his little trough. He mourns no doubt his lost companions, literally snatched from him one by one, and never seen again. But his days of mourning will be few; for Mungo, our black cook, told me yesterday that the word had at last gone forth, and poor Pedro's fate was sealed. His attenuated body will be laid out upon the captain's table next Sunday, and long before night will be buried with all the usual ceremonies beneath that worthy individual's vest. Who would believe that there could be any one so cruel as to long for the decapitation of the luckless Pedro; yet the sailors pray every minute, selfish fellows, that the miserable fowl may be brought to his end. They say the captain will never point the ship for the land so long as he has in anticipation a mess of fresh meat. This unhappy bird can alone furnish it; and when he is once devoured, the captain will come to his senses. I wish thee no harm, Peter; but as thou art doomed, sooner or later, to meet the fate of all thy race; and if putting a period to thy existence is to be the signal for our deliverance, why—truth to speak—I wish thy throat cut this very moment; for, oh! how I wish to see the living earth again! The old ship herself longs to look out upon the land from her hawse-holes once more, and Jack Lewis said right the other day when the captain found fault with his steering.

"Why, d'ye see, Captain Vangs," says bold Jack, "I'm as good a helmsman as ever put hand to spoke; but none of us can steer the old lady now. We can't keep her full and bye, sir: watch her ever so close, she will fall off; and then, sir, when I put the helm down so gently, and try like to coax her to the work, she won't take it kindly, but will fall round off again; and it's all because she knows the land is under the lee, sir, and she wont go any more to windward." Aye, and why should she, Jack? didn't every one of her stout timbers grow on shore, and hasn't she sensibilities as well as we?

Poor old ship! Her very looks denote her desires: how deplorably she appears! The paint on her sides, burnt up by the scorching sun, is puffed out and cracked. See the weeds she trails along with her, and what an unsightly bunch of those horrid barnacles has formed about her stern-piece; and every time she rises on a sea, she shows her copper torn away, or hanging in jagged strips.

Poor old ship! I say again: for six months she has been rolling and pitching about, never for one moment at rest. But courage, old lass, I hope to see thee soon within a biscuit's toss of the merry land, riding snugly at anchor in some green cove, and sheltered from the boisterous winds.

*   *   *   *   *

"Hurra, my lads! It's a settled thing; next week we shape our course to the Marquesas!" The Marquesas! What strange visions of outlandish things does the very name spirit up! Naked houris—cannibal banquets—groves of cocoa-nut—coral reefs—tatooed chiefs—and bamboo temples; sunny valleys planted with bread-fruit-trees—carved canoes dancing on the flashing blue waters—savage woodlands guarded by horrible idols—*heathenish rites and human sacrifices.*

Such were the strangely jumbled anticipations that haunted me during our passage from the cruising ground. I felt an irresistible curiosity to see those islands which the olden voyagers had so glowingly described.

The group for which we were now steering (although among the earliest of European discoveries in the South Seas, having been first visited in the year 1595) still continues to be tenanted by beings as strange and barbarous as ever. The missionaries, sent on a heavenly errand, had sailed by their lovely shores, and had abandoned them to their idols of wood and stone. How interesting the circumstances under which they were discovered! In the watery path of Mendanna, cruising in quest of some region of gold, these isles had sprung up like a scene of enchantment, and for a moment the Spaniard believed his bright dream was realised. In honour of the Marquess de Mendoza, then viceroy of Peru—under whose auspices the navigator sailed—he bestowed upon them the name which denoted the rank of his patron, and gave to the world on his return a vague and magnificent account of their beauty. But these islands, undisturbed for years, relapsed into their previous obscurity; and it is only recently that anything has been known concerning them. Once in the course of a half century, to be sure, some adventurous rover would break in upon their peaceful repose, and, astonished at the unusual scene, would be almost tempted to claim the merit of a new discovery.

Of this interesting group, but little account has ever been given, if we except the slight mention made of them in the sketches of South-Sea voyages. Cook, in his repeated circumnavigations of the globe, barely touched at their shores; and all that we know about them is from a few general narratives. Among these, there are two that claim particular notice. Porter's 'Journal of the Cruise of the U. S. frigate Essex, in the Pacific, during the late War,' is said to contain some interesting particulars concerning the islanders. This is a work, however, which I have never happened to meet with; and Stewart, the chaplain of the American sloop of war Vincennes, has likewise devoted a portion of his book, entitled 'A Visit to the South Seas,' to the same subject.

Within the last few years American and English vessels engaged in the extensive whale fisheries of the Pacific have occasionally, when short of provisions, put into the commo- dious harbour which there is in one of the islands; but a fear of the natives, founded on a recollection of the dread- ful fate which many white men have received at their hands, has deterred their crews from intermixing with the population sufficiently to gain any insight into their pecul- iar customs and manners.

The Protestant Missions appear to have despaired of reclaiming these islands from heathenism. The usage they have in every case received from the natives has been such as to intimidate the boldest of their number. Ellis, in his 'Polynesian Researches,' gives some interesting accounts of the abortive attempts made by the Tahiti Mission to estab- lish a branch Mission upon certain islands of the group. A short time before my visit to the Marquesas, a somewhat amusing incident took place in connection with these ef- forts, which I cannot avoid relating.

An intrepid missionary, undaunted by the ill-success that had attended all previous endeavours to conciliate the savages, and believing much in the efficacy of female in- fluence, introduced among them his young and beautiful wife, the first white woman who had ever visited their shores. The islanders at first gazed in mute admiration at so unusual a prodigy, and seemed inclined to regard it as some new divinity. But after a short time, becoming familiar with its charming aspect, and jealous of the folds which encircled its form, they sought to pierce the sacred veil of calico in which it was enshrined, and in the gratification of their curiosity so far overstepped the limits of good breeding, as deeply to offend the lady's sense of decorum. Her sex once ascertained, their idolatry was changed into contempt; and there was no end to the contumely showered upon her by the savages, who were exasperated at the deception which they conceived had been practised upon them. To the horror of her affectionate spouse, she was stripped of her garments, and given to understand that she could no longer carry on her deceits with impunity. The gentle dame was not sufficiently evangelised to endure this, and, fearful of further improprieties, she forced her husband to relinquish his undertaking, and together they returned to Tahiti.

Not thus shy of exhibiting her charms was the Island Queen herself, the beauteous wife of Mowanna, the king of Nukuheva. Between two and three years after the adventures recorded in this volume, I chanced, while aboard of a man-of-war, to touch at these islands. The French had then held possession of the Marquesas some time, and already prided themselves upon the beneficial effects of their jurisdiction, as discernible in the deportment of the natives. To be sure, in one of their efforts at reform they had slaughtered about a hundred and fifty of them at Whitihoo—but let that pass. At the time I mention, the French squadron was rendezvousing in the bay of Nukuheva, and during an interview between one of their captains and our worthy Commodore, it was suggested by the former, that we, as the flag-ship of the American squadron, should receive, in state, a visit from the royal pair. The French officer likewise represented, with evident satisfaction, that under their tuition the king and queen had imbibed proper notions of their elevated station, and on all ceremonious

occasions conducted themselves with suitable dignity. Ac·
cordingly, preparations were made to give their majesties
a reception on board in a style corresponding with their
rank.

One bright afternoon, a gig, gaily bedizened with streamers, was observed to shove off from the side of one of the
French frigates, and pull directly for our gangway. In the
stern sheets reclined Mowanna and his consort. As they
approached, we paid them all the honours due to royalty;
—manning our yards, firing a salute, and making a prodigious hubbub.

They ascended the accommodation ladder, were greeted
by the Commodore, hat in hand, and passing along the
quarterdeck, the marine guard presented arms, while the
band struck up 'The king of the Cannibal Islands.' So far
all went well. The French officers grimaced and smiled in
exceedingly high spirits, wonderfully pleased with the discreet manner in which these distinguished personages behaved themselves.

Their appearance was certainly calculated to produce an
effect. His majesty was arrayed in a magnificent military
uniform, stiff with gold lace and embroidery, while his
shaven crown was concealed by a huge chapeau bras, waving with ostrich plumes. There was one slight blemish,
however, in his appearance. A broad patch of tatooing
stretched completely across his face, in a line with his eyes,
making him look as if he wore a huge pair of goggles; and
royalty in goggles suggested some ludicrous ideas. But it
was in the adornment of the fair person of his dark-complexioned spouse that the tailors of the fleet had evinced
the gaiety of their national taste. She was habited in a
gaudy tissue of scarlet cloth, trimmed with yellow silk,
which, descending a little below the knees, exposed to view
her bare legs, embellished with spiral tatooing, and some
what resembling two miniature Trajan's columns. Upon

her head was a fanciful turban of purple velvet, figured with silver sprigs, and surmounted by a tuft of variegated feathers.

The ship's company crowding into the gangway to view the sight, soon arrested her majesty's attention. She singled out from their number an old *salt,* whose bare arms and feet, and exposed breast were covered with as many inscriptions in India ink as the lid of an Egyptian sarcophagus. Notwithstanding all the sly hints and remonstrances of the French officers, she immediately approached the man, and pulling further open the bosom of his duck frock, and rolling up the leg of his wide trowsers, she gazed with admiration at the bright blue and vermilion pricking, thus disclosed to view. She hung over the fellow, caressing him, and expressing her delight in a variety of wild exclamations and gestures. The embarrassment of the polite Gauls at such an unlooked-for occurrence may be easily imagined; but picture their consternation, when all at once the royal lady, eager to display the hieroglyphics on her own sweet form, bent forward for a moment, and turning sharply round, threw up the skirts of her mantle, and revealed a sight from which the aghast Frenchmen retreated precipitately, and tumbling into their boat, fled the scene of so shocking a catastrophe.

CHAPTER II

Passage from the Cruising Ground to the Marquesas—Sleepy times aboard Ship—South Sea Scenery—Land ho!—The French Squadron discovered at Anchor in the Bay of Nukuheva—Strange Pilot —Escort of Canoes—A Flotilla of Cocoa-nuts—Swimming Visitors —The Dolly boarded by them—State of affairs that ensue.

I can never forget the eighteen or twenty days during which the light trade-winds were silently sweeping us towards the islands. In pursuit of the sperm whale, we had been cruizing on the line some twenty degrees to the westward of the Gallipagos; and all that we had to do, when our course was determined on, was to square in the yards and keep the vessel before the breeze, and then the good ship and the steady gale did the rest between them. The man at the wheel never vexed the old lady with any superfluous steering, but comfortably adjusting his limbs at the tiller, would doze away by the hour. True to her work, the Dolly headed to her course, and like one of those characters who always do best when let alone, she jogged on her way like a veteran old sea-pacer as she was.

What a delightful, lazy, languid time we had whilst we were thus gliding along! There was nothing to be done; a circumstance that happily suited our disinclination to do anything. We abandoned the fore-peak altogether, and spreading an awning over the forecastle, slept, ate, and lounged under it the live-long day. Every one seemed to be under the influence of some narcotic. Even the officers aft, whose duty required them never to be seated while keeping a deck watch, vainly endeavoured to keep on their pins; and were obliged invariably to compromise the matter by leaning up against the bulwarks, and gazing abstractedly over the side. Reading was out of the question; take a book in your hand, and you were asleep in an instant.

Although I could not avoid yielding in a great measure to the general languor, still at times I contrived to shake off the spell, and to appreciate the beauty of the scene around me. The sky presented a clear expanse of the most delicate blue, except along the skirts of the horizon, where you might see a thin drapery of pale clouds which never varied their form or colour. The long, measured, dirge-like swell of the Pacific came rolling along, with its surface broken by little tiny waves, sparkling in the sunshine. Every now and then a shoal of flying fish, scared from the water under the bows, would leap into the air, and fall the next moment like a shower of silver into the sea. Then you would see the superb albicore, with his glittering sides, sailing aloft, and often describing an arc in his descent, disappear on the surface of the water. Far off, the lofty jet of the whale might be seen, and nearer at hand the prowling shark, that villainous footpad of the seas, would come skulking along, and, at a wary distance, regard us with his evil eye. At times, some shapeless monster of the deep, floating on the surface, would, as we approached, sink slowly into the blue waters, and fade away from the sight. But the most impressive feature of the scene was the almost unbroken silence that reigned over sky and water. Scarcely a sound could be heard but the occasional breathing of the grampus, and the rippling at the cut-water.

As we drew nearer the land, I hailed with delight the appearance of innumerable sea-fowl. Screaming and whirling in spiral tracks, they would accompany the vessel, and at times alight on our yards and stays. That piratical-looking fellow, appropriately named the man-of-war's hawk, with his blood-red bill and raven plumage, would come sweeping round us in gradually diminishing circles, till you could distinctly mark the strange flashings of his eye; and then, as if satisfied with his observation, would sail up into the air and disappear from the view. Soon, other evidences of our vicinity to the land were apparent, and it was not long before the glad announcement of its being in sight was heard from aloft,—given with that peculiar prolongation of sound that a sailor loves—"Land ho!"

The captain, darting on deck from the cabin, bawled lustily for his spy-glass; the mate in still louder accents hailed the mast-head with a tremendous "where-away?" The black cook thrust his woolly head from the galley, and Boatswain, the dog, leaped up between the knight-heads, and barked most furiously. Land ho! Aye, there it was. A hardly perceptible blue irregular outline, indicating the bold contour of the lofty heights of Nukuheva.

This island, although generally called one of the Marquesas, is by some navigators considered as forming one of a distinct cluster, comprising the islands of Ruhooka, Ropo, and Nukuheva; upon which three the appellation of the Washington Group has been bestowed. They form a triangle, and lie within the parallels of 8° 38″ and 9° 32″ South latitude, and 139° 20′ and 140° 10′ West longitude from Greenwich. With how little propriety they are to be regarded as forming a separate group will be at once apparent, when it is considered that they lie in the immediate vicinity of the other islands, that is to say, less than a degree to the north-west of them; that their inhabitants speak the Marquesan dialect, and that their laws, religion, and general customs are identical. The only reason why they were ever thus arbitrarily distinguished, may be attributed to the singular fact, that their existence was altogether unknown to the world until the year 1791, when they were discovered by Captain Ingraham, of Boston, Massachusetts, nearly two centuries after the discovery of the adjacent islands by the agent of the Spanish Viceroy. Notwithstanding this, I shall follow the example of most voyagers, and treat of them as forming part and parcel of the Marquesas.

Nukuheva is the most important of these islands, being the only one at which ships are much in the habit of touching, and is celebrated as being the place where the adventurous Captain Porter refitted his ships during the late war between England and the United States, and whence he sallied out upon the large whaling fleet then sailing under the enemy's flag in the surrounding seas. This island is about twenty miles in length and nearly as many in breadth. It has three good harbours on its coast; the largest and best of which is called by the people living in its vicinity 'Tyohee,' and by Captain Porter was denominated Massachusetts Bay. Among the adverse tribes dwelling about the shores of the other bays, and by all voyagers, it is generally known by the name bestowed upon the island itself —Nukuheva. Its inhabitants have become somewhat corrupted, owing to their recent commerce with Europeans; but so far as regards their peculiar customs and general mode of life, they retain their original primitive character, remaining very nearly in the same state of nature in which they were first beheld by white men. The hostile clans, residing in the more remote sections of the island, and very seldom holding any communication with foreigners, are in every respect unchanged from their earliest known condition.

In the bay of Nukuheva was the anchorage we desired to reach. We had perceived the loom of the mountains about sunset; so that after running all night with a very light breeze, we found ourselves close in with the island the next morning: but as the bay we sought lay on its farther side, we were obliged to sail some distance along the shore, catching, as we proceeded, short glimpses of blooming valleys, deep glens, waterfalls, and waving groves, hidden here and there by projecting and rocky headlands, every moment opening to the view some new and startling scene of beauty.

Those who for the first time visit the South Seas, generally are surprised at the appearance of the islands when beheld from the sea. From the vague accounts we sometimes have of their beauty, many people are apt to picture to themselves enamelled and softly swelling plains, shaded over with delicious groves, and watered by purling brooks, and the entire country but little elevated above the surrounding ocean. The reality is very different; bold rockbound coasts, with the surf beating high against the lofty cliffs, and broken here and there into deep inlets, which open to the view thickly-wooded valleys, separated by the spurs of mountains clothed with tufted grass, and sweeping down towards the sea from an elevated and furrowed interior, form the principal features of these islands.

Towards noon we drew abreast the entrance to the harbour, and at last we slowly swept by the intervening promontory, and entered the bay of Nukuheva. No description can do justice to its beauty; but that beauty was lost to me then, and I saw nothing but the tri-coloured flag of France trailing over the stern of six vessels, whose black hulls and bristling broadsides proclaimed their warlike character. There they were, floating in that lovely bay, the green eminences of the shore looking down so tranquilly upon them, as if rebuking the sternness of their aspect. To my eye nothing could be more out of keeping than the presence of these vessels; but we soon learnt what brought them there. The whole group of islands had just been taken possession of by Rear Admiral Du Petit Thouars, in the name of the invincible French nation.

This item of information was imparted to us by a most extraordinary individual, a genuine South-Sea vagabond, who came alongside of us in a whale-boat as soon as we entered the bay, and by the aid of some benevolent persons at the gangway was assisted on board, for our visitor was in that interesting stage of intoxication when a man is amiable and helpless. Although he was utterly unable to stand erect or to navigate his body across the deck, he still magnanimously proffered his services to pilot the ship to a good and secure anchorage. Our captain, however, rather distrusted his ability in this respect, and refused to recognise his claim to the character he assumed; but our gentleman was determined to play his part, for by dint of much scrambling he succeeded in getting into the weather-quarter boat, where he steadied himself by holding on to a shroud, and then commenced issuing his commands with amazing volubility and very peculiar gestures. Of course no one obeyed his orders; but as it was impossible to quiet him, we swept by the ships of the squadron with this strange fellow performing his antics in full view of all the French officers.

We afterwards learned that our eccentric friend had been a lieutenant in the English navy; but having disgraced his flag by some criminal conduct in one of the principal ports on the main, he had deserted his ship, and spent many years wandering among the islands of the Pacific, until accidentally being at Nukuheva when the French took possession of the place, he had been appointed pilot of the harbour by the newly constituted authorities.

As we slowly advanced up the bay, numerous canoes pushed off from the surrounding shores, and we were soon in the midst of quite a flotilla of them, their savage occupants struggling to get aboard of us, and jostling one another in their ineffectual attempts. Occasionally the projecting out-riggers of their slight shallops running foul of one another, would become entangled beneath the water, threatening to capsize the canoes, when a scene of confusion would ensue that baffles description. Such strange outcries and passionate gesticulations I never certainly heard or saw before. You would have thought the islanders were on the point of flying at one another's throats, whereas they were only amicably engaged in disentangling their boats.

Scattered here and there among the canoes might be seen numbers of cocoa nuts floating closely together in circular groups, and bobbing up and down with every wave. By some inexplicable means these cocoa nuts were all steadily approaching towards the ship. As I leaned curiously over the side endeavouring to solve their mysterious movements, one mass far in advance of the rest attracted my attention. In its centre was something I could take for nothing else than a cocoa nut, but which I certainly considered one of the most extraordinary specimens of the fruit I had ever seen. It kept twirling and dancing about among the rest in the most singular manner, and as it drew nearer I thought it bore a remarkable resemblance to the brown shaven skull of one of the savages. Presently it betrayed a pair of eyes, and soon I became aware that what I had supposed to have been one of the fruit was nothing else than the head of an islander, who had adopted this singular method of bringing his produce to market. The cocoa nuts were all attached to one another by strips of the husk, partly torn from the shell and rudely fastened together. Their proprietor inserting his head into the midst of them, impelled his necklace of cocoa nuts through the water by striking out beneath the surface with his feet.

I was somewhat astonished to perceive that among the number of natives that surrounded us not a single female was to be seen. At that time I was ignorant of the fact that by the operation of the "taboo" the use of canoes in all parts of the island is rigorously prohibited to the entire sex, for whom it is death even to be seen entering one when hauled on shore; consequently, whenever a Marquesan lady voyages by water, she puts in requisition the paddles of her own fair body.

We had approached within a mile and a half perhaps of the foot of the bay, when some of the islanders, who by this time had managed to scramble aboard of us at the risk of swamping their canoes, directed our attention to a singular commotion in the water ahead of the vessel. At first I imagined it to be produced by a shoal of fish sporting on the surface, but our savage friends assured us that it was caused by a shoal of "whinhenies" (young girls), who in this manner were coming off from the shore to welcome us. As they drew nearer, and I watched the rising and sinking of their forms, and beheld the uplifted right arm bearing above the water the girdle of tappa, and their long dark hair trailing beside them as they swam, I almost fancied they could be nothing else than so many mermaids:—and very like mermaids they behaved too.

We were still some distance from the beach, and under slow headway, when we sailed right into the midst of these swimming nymphs, and they boarded us at every quarter; many seizing hold of the chain-plates and springing into the chains; others, at the peril of being run over by the vessel in her course, catching at the bob-stays, and wreathing their slender forms about the ropes, hung suspended in the air. All of them at length succeeded in getting up the ship's side, where they clung dripping with the brine and glowing from the bath, their jet-black tresses streaming over their shoulders, and half enveloping their otherwise naked forms. There they hung, sparkling with savage vivacity, laughing gaily at one another, and chattering away with infinite glee. Nor were they idle the while, for each one performed the simple offices of the toilette for the other. Their luxuriant locks, wound up and twisted into the smallest possible compass, were freed from the briny element; the whole person carefully dried, and from a little round shell that passed from hand to hand, anointed with a fragrant oil: their adornments were completed by passing a few loose folds of white tappa, in a modest cincture, around the waist. Thus arrayed they no longer hesitated, but flung themselves lightly over the bulwarks, and were quickly frolicking about the decks. Many of them went forward, perching upon the head-rails or running out upon the bowsprit, while others seated themselves upon the taff-rail, or reclined at full length upon the boats. What a sight for us bachelor sailors! how avoid so dire a temptation? For who could think of tumbling these artless creatures overboard, when they had swam miles to welcome us?

Their appearance perfectly amazed me; their extreme youth, the light clear brown of their complexions, their delicate features, and inexpressibly graceful figures, their softly moulded limbs, and free unstudied action, seemed as strange as beautiful.

The 'Dolly' was fairly captured; and never I will say was vessel carried before by such a dashing and irresistible party of boarders! The ship taken, we could not do otherwise than yield ourselves prisoners, and for the whole period that she remained in the bay, the 'Dolly,' as well as her crew, were completely in the hands of the mermaids.

In the evening after we had come to an anchor the deck was illuminated with lanterns, and this picturesque band of sylphs, tricked out with flowers, and dressed in robes of variegated tappa, got up a ball in great style. These females are passionately fond of dancing, and in the wild grace and spirit of their style excel everything that I have ever seen. The varied dances of the Marquesan girls are beautiful in the extreme, but there is an abandoned voluptuousness in their character which I dare not attempt to describe.

Our ship was now wholly given up to every species of riot and debauchery. Not the feeblest barrier was interposed between the unholy passions of the crew and their unlimited gratification. The grossest licentiousness and the most shameful inebriety prevailed, with occasional and but short-lived interruptions, through the whole period of her stay. Alas for the poor savages when exposed to the influence of these polluting examples! Unsophisticated and confiding, they are easily led into every vice, and humanity weeps over the ruin thus remorselessly inflicted upon them by their European civilizers. Thrice happy are they who, inhabiting some yet undiscovered island in the midst of the ocean, have never been brought into contaminating contact with the white man.

CHAPTER III

Some Account of the late operations of the French at the Marquesas—Prudent Conduct of the Admiral—Sensation produced by
the Arrival of the Strangers—The first Horse seen by the Islanders—Reflections—Miserable Subterfuge of the French—Digression
concerning Tahiti—Seizure of the Island by the Admiral—Spirited Conduct of an English Lady.

.T WAS in the summer of 1842 that we arrived at the
islands; the French had then held possession of them for
several weeks. During this time they had visited some of
the principal places in the group, and had disembarked at
various points about five hundred troops. These were employed in constructing works of defence, and otherwise
providing against the attacks of the natives, who at any
moment might be expected to break out in open hostility.
The islanders looked upon the people who made this cava-
lier appropriation of their shores with mingled feelings of
fear and detestation. They cordially hated them; but the impulses of their resentment were neutralized by their dread
of the floating batteries, which lay with their fatal tubes
ostentatiously pointed, not at fortifications and redoubts,
but at a handful of bamboo sheds, sheltered in a grove of
cocoa-nuts! A valiant warrior doubtless, but a prudent
one too, was this same Rear-Admiral Du Petit Thouars.
Four heavy, double-banked frigates and three corvettes to
frighten a parcel of naked heathen into subjection! Sixty-
eight pounders to demolish huts of cocoa-nut boughs, and
Congreve rockets to set on fire a few canoe sheds!

At Nukuheva, there were about one hundred soldiers
ashore. They were encamped in tents, constructed of the
old sails and spare spars of the squadron, within the limits
of a redoubt mounted with a few nine-pounders, and surrounded with a fosse. Every other day, these troops were

marched out in martial array, to a level piece of ground in the vicinity, and there for hours went through all sorts of military evolutions, surrounded by flocks of the natives, who looked on with savage admiration at the show, and as savage a hatred of the actors. A regiment of the Old Guard, reviewed on a summer's day in the Champs Elysées, could not have made a more critically correct appearance. The officers' regimentals, resplendent with gold lace and embroidery, as if purposely calculated to dazzle the islanders, looked as if just unpacked from their Parisian cases.

The sensation produced by the presence of the strangers had not in the least subsided at the period of our arrival at the islands. Tht natives still flocked in numbers about the encampment, and watched with the liveliest curiosity everything that was going forward. A blacksmith's forge, which had been set up in the the shelter of a grove near the beach, attracted so great a crowd, that it required the utmost efforts of the sentries posted around to keep the inquisitive multitude at a sufficient distance to allow the workmen to ply their vocation. But nothing gained so large a share of admiration as a horse, which had been brought from Valparaiso by the Achille, one of the vessels of the squadron. The animal, a remarkably fine one, had been taken ashore and stabled in a hut of cocoa-nut boughs within the fortified enclosure. Occasionally it was brought out, and, being gaily caparisoned, was ridden by one of the officers at full speed over the hard sand beach. This performance was sure to be hailed with loud plaudits, and the "puarkee nuee" (big hog) was unanimously pronounced by the islanders to be the most extraordinary specimen of zoology that had ever come under their observation.

The expedition for the occupation of the Marquesas had sailed from Brest in the spring of 1842, and the secret of its destination was solely in the possession of its commander.

No wonder that those who contemplated such a signal infraction of the rights of humanity should have sought to veil the enormity from the eyes of the world. And yet, notwithstanding their iniquitous conduct in this and in other matters, the French have ever plumed themselves upon being the most humane and polished of nations. A high degree of refinement, however, does not seem to subdue our wicked propensities so much after all; and were civilization itself to be estimated by some of its results, it would seem perhaps better for what we call the barbarous part of the world to remain unchanged.

One example of the shameless subterfuges under which the French stand prepared to defend whatever cruelties they may hereafter think fit to commit in bringing the Marquesan natives into subjection is well worthy of being recorded. On some flimsy pretext or other Mowanna, the king of Nukuheva, whom the invaders by extravagant presents have cajoled over to their interests, and move about like a mere puppet, has been set up as the rightful sovereign of the entire island,—the alleged ruler by prescription of various clans who for ages perhaps have treated with each other as separate nations. To reinstate this much-injured prince in the assumed dignities of his ancestors, the disinterested strangers have come all the way from France: they are determined that his title shall be acknowledged. If any tribe shall refuse to recognise the authority of the French, by bowing down to the laced chapeau of Mowanna, let them abide the consequences of their obstinacy. Under cover of a similar pretence, have the outrages and massacres at Tahiti the beautiful, the queen of the South Seas, been perpetrated.

On this buccaneering expedition, Rear-Admiral Du Petit Thouars, leaving the rest of his squadron at the Marquesas—which had then been occupied by his forces about five months—set sail for the doomed island in the

Reine Blanche frigate. On his arrival, as an indemnity for alleged insults offered to the flag of his country, he demanded some twenty or thirty thousand dollars to be placed in his hands forthwith, and in default of payment, threatened to land and take possession of the place.

The frigate, immediately upon coming to an anchor, got springs on her cables, and with her guns cast loose and her men at their quarters, lay in the circular basin of Papeete, with her broadside bearing upon the devoted town; while her numerous cutters, hauled in order alongside, were ready to effect a landing, under cover of her batteries. She maintained this belligerent attitude for several days, during which time a series of informal negotiations were pending, and wide alarm spread over the island. Many of the Tahitians were at first disposed to resort to arms, and drive the invaders from their shores; but more pacific and feebler councils ultimately prevailed. The unfortunate queen, Pomarea, incapable of averting the impending calamity, terrified at the arrogance of the insolent Frenchman, and driven at last to despair, fled by night in a canoe to Emio.

During the continuance of the panic there occurred an instance of feminine heroism that I cannot omit to record.

In the grounds of the famous missionary consul, Pritchard, then absent in London, the consular flag of Britain waved as usual during the day, from a lofty staff planted within a few yards of the beach, and in full view of the frigate. One morning an officer, at the head of a party of men, presented himself at the verandah of Mr. Pritchard's house, and inquired in broken English for the lady his wife. The matron soon made her appearance; and the polite Frenchman, making one of his best bows, and playing gracefully with the aguilettes that danced upon his breast, proceeded in courteous accents to deliver his mission. "The admiral desired the flag to be hauled down—hoped it would be perfectly agreeable—and his men stood ready to perform the duty." "Tell the pirate your master," replied the spirited Englishwoman, pointing to the staff, "that if he wishes to strike those colours, he must come and perform the act himself; I will suffer no one else to do it." The lady then bowed haughtily and withdrew into the house. As the discomfited officer slowly walked away, he looked up to the flag, and perceived that the cord by which it was elevated to its place, led from the top of the staff, across the lawn, to an open upper window of the mansion, where sat the lady from whom he had just parted, tranquilly engaged in knitting. Was that flag hauled down? Mrs. Pritchard thinks not; and Rear Admiral Du Petit Thouars is believed to be of the same opinion.

CHAPTER IV

State of Affairs aboard the Ship—Contents of her Larder—Length of South Seamen's Voyages—Account of a Flying Whale-man—Determination to Leave the Vessel—The Bay of Nukuheva—The Typees—Invasion of their Valley by Porter—Reflections—Glen of Tior—Interview between the Old King and the French Admiral.

OUR ship had not been many days in the harbour of Nukuheva before I came to the determination of leaving her. That my reasons for resolving to take this step were numerous and weighty, may be inferred from the fact that I chose rather to risk my fortunes among the savages of the island than to endure another voyage on board the Dolly. To use the concise, point-blank phrase of the sailors, I had made up my mind to "run away." Now as a meaning is generally attached to these two words no way flattering to the individual to whom they are applied, it behoves me, for the sake of my own character, to offer some explanation of my conduct.

When I entered on board the Dolly, I signed as a matter of course the ship's articles, thereby voluntarily engaging and legally binding myself to serve in a certain capacity for the period of the voyage; and, special considerations apart, I was of course bound to fulfill the agreement. But in all contracts, if one party fail to perform his share of the compact, is not the other virtually absolved from his liability? Who is there who will not answer in the affirmative?

Having settled the principle, then, let me apply it to the particular case in question. In numberless instances had not only the implied but the specified conditions of the articles been violated on the part of the ship in which I served. The usage on board of her was tyrannical; the sick had been inhumanly neglected; the provisions had been doled out in scanty allowance; and her cruizes were unreasonably protracted. The captain was the author of these abuses; it was in vain to think that he would either remedy them, or alter his conduct, which was arbitrary and violent in the extreme. His prompt reply to all complaints and remonstrances was—the butt end of a handspike, so convincingly administered as effectually to silence the aggrieved party.

To whom could we apply for redress? We had left both law and equity on the other side of the Cape; and unfortunately, with a very few exceptions, our crew was composed of a parcel of dastardly and mean-spirited wretches, divided among themselves, and only united in enduring without resistance the unmitigated tyranny of the captain. It would have been mere madness for any two or three of the number, unassisted by the rest, to attempt making a stand against his ill usage. They would only have called down upon themselves the particular vengeance of this "Lord of the Plank," and subjected their shipmates to additional hardships.

But, after all, these things could have been endured awhile. had we entertained the hope of being speedily de

livered from them by the due completion of the term of
our servitude. But what a dismal prospect awaited us in
this quarter! The longevity of Cape Horn whaling voyages is proverbial, frequently extending over a period of
four or five years.

Some long-haired, bare-necked youths, who, forced by
the united influences of Captain Marryatt and hard times,
embark at Nantucket for a pleasure excursion to the
Pacific, and whose anxious mothers provide them with
bottled milk for the occasion, oftentimes return very respectable middle-aged gentlemen.

The very preparations made for one of these expeditions
are enough to frighten one. As the vessel carries out no
cargo, her hold is filled with provisions for her own consumption. The owners, who officiate as caterers for the
voyage, supply the larder with an abundance of dainties.
Delicate morsels of beef and pork, cut on scientific principles from every part of the animal, and of all conceivable
shapes and sizes, are carefully packed in salt, and stored
away in barrels; affording a never-ending variety in their
different degrees of toughness, and in the peculiarities of
their saline properties. Choice old water too, decanted into
stout six-barrel-casks, and two pints of which are allowed
every day to each soul on board; together with ample store
of sea-bread, previously reduced to a state of petrifaction,
with a view to preserve it either from decay or consumption in the ordinary mode, are likewise provided for the
nourishment and gastronomic enjoyment of the crew.

But not to speak of the quality of these articles of sailors'
fare, the abundance in which they are put on board a whaling vessel is almost incredible. Oftentimes, when we had
occasion to break out in the hold, and I beheld the successive tiers of casks and barrels, whose contents were all
destined to be consumed in due course by the ship's company, my heart has sunk within me.

Although, as a general case, a ship unlucky in falling in with whales continues to cruize after them until she has barely sufficient provisions remaining to take her home, turning round then quietly and making the best of her way to her friends, yet there are instances when even this natural obstacle to the further prosecution of the voyage is overcome by headstrong captains, who, bartering the fruits of their hard-earned toils for a new supply of provisions in some of the ports of Chili or Peru, begin the voyage afresh with unabated zeal and perseverance. It is in vain that the owners write urgent letters to him to sail for home, and for their sake to bring back the ship, since it appears he can put nothing in her. Not he. He has registered a vow: he will fill his vessel with good sperm oil, or failing to do so, never again strike Yankee soundings.

I heard of one whaler, which after many years' absence was given up for lost. The last that had been heard of her was a shadowy report of her having touched at some of those unstable islands in the far Pacific, whose eccentric wanderings are carefully noted in each new edition of the South-Sea charts. After a long interval, however, 'The Perseverance'—for that was her name—was spoken somewhere in the vicinity of the ends of the earth, cruizing along as leisurely as ever, her sails all bepatched and bequilted with rope-yarns, her spars fished with old pipe stores, and her rigging knotted and spliced in every possible direction. Her crew was composed of some twenty venerable Greenwich-pensioner-looking old salts, who just managed to hobble about deck. The ends of all the running ropes, with the exception of the signal halyards and poop-down-haul, were rove through snatch-blocks, and led to the capstan or windlass, so that not a yard was braced or a sail set without the assistance of machinery.

Her hull was incrusted with barnacles, which completely encased her. Three pet sharks followed in her wake, and every day came alongside to regale themselves from the contents of the cook's bucket, which were pitched over to them. A vast shoal of bonetas and albicores always kept her company.

Such was the account I heard of this vessel, and the remembrance of it always haunted me; what eventually became of her I never learned; at any rate she never reached home, and I suppose she is still regularly tacking twice in the twenty-four hours somewhere off Buggerry Island, or the Devil's-Tail Peak.

Having said thus much touching the usual length of these voyages, when I inform the reader that ours had as it were just commenced, we being only fifteen months out, and even at that time hailed as a late arrival, and boarded for news, he will readily perceive that there was little to encourage one in looking forward to the future, especially as I had always had a presentiment that we should make an unfortunate voyage, and our experience so far had justified the expectation.

I may here state, and on my faith as an honest man, that though more than three years have elapsed since I left this same identical vessel, she still continues in the Pacific, and but a few days since I saw her reported in the papers as having touched at the Sandwich Islands previous to going on the coast of Japan.

But to return to my narrative. Placed in these circumstances then, with no prospect of matters mending if I remained aboard the Dolly, I at once made up my mind to leave her: to be sure it was rather an inglorious thing to steal away privily from those at whose hands I had received wrongs and outrages that I could not resent; but how was such a course to be avoided when it was the only alternative left me? Having made up my mind, I proceeded to acquire all the information I could obtain relating to the island and its inhabitants, with a view of shaping my plans of escape accordingly. The result of these inquiries I will now state, in order that the ensuing narrative may be the better understood.

The bay of Nukuheva in which we were then lying is an expanse of water not unlike in figure the space included within the limits of a horse-shoe. It is, perhaps, nine miles in circumference. You approach it from the sea by a narrow entrance, flanked on either side by two small twin islets which soar conically to the height of some five hundred feet. From these the shore recedes on both hands, and describes a deep semicircle.

From the verge of the water the land rises uniformly on all sides, with green and sloping acclivities, until from gently rolling hill-sides and moderate elevations it insensibly swells into lofty and majestic heights, whose blue outlines, ranged all around, close in the view. The beautiful aspect of the shore is heightened by deep and romantic glens, which come down to it at almost equal distances, all apparently radiating from a common centre, and the upper extremities of which are lost to the eye beneath the shadow of the mountains. Down each of these little valleys flows a clear stream, here and there assuming the form of a slender cascade, then stealing invisibly along until it burst upon the sight again in larger and more noisy waterfalls, and at last demurely wanders along to the sea.

The houses of the natives, constructed of the yellow bamboo, tastefully twisted together in a kind of wicker-work, and thatched with the long tapering leaves of the palmetto, are scattered irregularly along these valleys beneath the shady branches of the cocoa-nut trees.

Nothing can exceed the imposing scenery of this bay. Viewed from our ship as she lay at anchor in the middle of the harbour, it presented the appearance of a vast natural amphitheatre in decay, and overgrown with vines, the deep glens that furrowed its sides appearing like enormous fissures caused by the ravages of time. Very often when lost in admiration at its beauty, I have experienced a pang of regret that a scene so enchanting should be hidden from the world in these remote seas, and seldom meet the eyes of devoted lovers of nature.

Besides this bay the shores of the island are indented by several other extensive inlets, into which descend broad and verdant valleys. These are inhabited by as many distinct tribes of savages, who, although speaking kindred dialects of a common language, and having the same religion and laws, have from time immemorial waged hereditary warfare against each other. The intervening mountains, generally two or three thousand feet above the level of the sea, geographically define the territories of each of these hostile tribes, who never cross them, save on some expedition of war or plunder. Immediately adjacent to Nukuheva, and only separated from it by the mountains seen from the harbour, lies the lovely valley of Happar, whose inmates cherish the most friendly relations with the inhabitants of Nukuheva. On the other side of Happar, and closely adjoining it, is the magnificent valley of the dreaded Typees, the unappeasable enemies of both these tribes.

These celebrated warriors appear to inspire the other islanders with unspeakable terrors. Their very name is a frightful one; for the word "Typee" in the Marquesan dialect signifies a lover of human flesh. It is rather singular that the title should have been bestowed upon them exclusively, inasmuch as the natives of all this group are irreclaimable cannibals. The name may, perhaps, have been given to denote the peculiar ferocity of this clan, and to convey a special stigma along with it.

These same Typees enjoy a prodigious notoriety all over the islands. The natives of Nukuheva would frequently recount in pantomime to our ship's company their terrible feats, and would show the marks of wounds they had received in desperate encounters with them. When ashore they would try to frighten us by pointing to one of their own number, and calling him a Typee, manifesting no little surprise that we did not take to our heels at so terrible an announcement. It was quite amusing, too, to see with what earnestness they disclaimed all cannibal propensities on their own part, while they denounced their enemies— the Typees—as inveterate gormandizers of human flesh; but this is a peculiarity to which I shall hereafter have occasion to allude.

Although I was convinced that the inhabitants of our bay were as arrant cannibals as any of the other tribes on the island, still I could not but feel a particular and most unqualified repugnance to the aforesaid Typees. Even before visiting the Marquesas, I had heard from men who had touched at the group on former voyages some revolting stories in connection with these savages; and fresh in my remembrance was the adventure of the master of the Katherine, who only a few months previous, imprudently venturing into this bay in an armed boat for the purpose of barter, was seized by the natives, carried back a little distance into their valley, and was only saved from a cruel death by the intervention of a young girl, who facilitated his escape by night along the beach to Nukuheva.

I had heard too of an English vessel that many years ago, after a weary cruize, sought to enter the bay of Nukuheva, and arriving within two or three miles of the land, was met by a large canoe filled with natives, who offered to lead the way to the place of their destination. The captain, unacquainted with the localities of the island, joyfully acceded to the proposition—the canoe paddled on and the ship followed. She was soon conducted to a beautiful inlet, and dropped her anchor in its waters beneath the shadows of the lofty shore. That same night the perfidious Typees, who had thus inveigled her into their fatal bay, flocked aboard the doomed vessel by hundreds, and at a given signal murdered every soul on board.

I shall never forget the observation of one of our crew as we were passing slowly by the entrance of this bay in our way to Nukuheva. As we stood gazing over the side at the verdant headlands, Ned, pointing with his hand in the direction of the treacherous valley, exclaimed, "There—there's Typee. Oh, the bloody cannibals, what a meal they'd make of us if we were to take it into our heads to land! but they say they don't like sailor's flesh, it's too salt. I say, maty, how should you like to be shoved ashore there, eh?" I little thought, as I shuddered at the question, that in the space of a few weeks I should actually be a captive in that self-same valley.

The French, although they had gone through the ceremony of hoisting their colours for a few hours at all the principal places of the group, had not as yet visited the bay of Typee, anticipating a fierce resistance on the part of the savages there, which for the present at least they wished to avoid. Perhaps they were not a little influenced in the adoption of this unusual policy from a recollection of the warlike reception given by the Typees to the forces of Captain Porter, about the year 1814, when that brave and accomplished officer endeavoured to subjugate the clan merely to gratify the mortal hatred of his allies the Nukuhevas and Happars.

On that occasion I have been told that a considerable detachment of sailors and marines from the frigate Essex, accompanied by at least two thousand warriors of Happar and Nukuheva, landed in boats and canoes at the head of the bay, and after penetrating a little distance into the valley, met with the stoutest resistance from its inmates. Valiantly, although with much loss, the Typees disputed every inch of ground, and after some hard fighting obliged their assailants to retreat and abandon their design of conquest.

The invaders, on their march back to the sea, consoled themselves for their repulse by setting fire to every house and temple in their route; and a long line of smoking ruins defaced the once-smiling bosom of the valley, and proclaimed to its pagan inhabitants the spirit that reigned in the breasts of Christian soldiers. Who can wonder at the deadly hatred of the Typees to all foreigners after such unprovoked atrocities?

Thus it is that they whom we denominate "savages" are made to deserve the title. When the inhabitants of some sequestered island first descry the "big canoe" of the European rolling through the blue waters towards their shores, they rush down to the beach in crowds, and with open arms stand ready to embrace the strangers. Fatal embrace! They fold to their bosoms the vipers whose sting is destined to poison all their joys; and the instinctive feeling of love within their breasts is soon converted into the bitterest hate.

The enormities perpetrated in the South Seas upon some of the inoffensive islanders wellnigh pass belief. These things are seldom proclaimed at home; they happen at the very ends of the earth; they are done in a corner, and there are none to reveal them. But there is, nevertheless, many a petty trader that has navigated the Pacific whose course from island to island might be traced by a series of cold-blooded robberies, kidnappings, and murders, the iniquity of which might be considered almost sufficient to sink her guilty timbers to the bottom of the sea.

Sometimes vague accounts of such things reach our firesides, and we coolly censure them as wrong, impolitic, needlessly severe, and dangerous to the crews of other vessels. How different is our tone when we read the highly-wrought description of the massacre of the crew of the Hobomak by the Feejees; how we sympathise for the unhappy victims, and with what horror do we regard the diabolical heathens, who, after all, have but avenged the unprovoked injuries which they have received. We breathe nothing but vengeance, and equip armed vessels to traverse thousands of miles of ocean in order to execute summary punishment upon the offenders. On arriving at their destination, they burn, slaughter, and destroy, according to the tenor of written instructions, and sailing away from the scene of devastation, call upon all Christendom to applaud their courage and their justice.

How often is the term "savages" incorrectly applied! None really deserving of it were ever yet discovered by voyagers or by travellers. They have discovered heathens and barbarians, whom by horrible cruelties they have exasperated into savages. It may be asserted without fear of contradiction, that in all the cases of outrages committed by Polynesians, Europeans have at some time or other been the aggressors, and that the cruel and bloodthirsty disposition of some of the islanders is mainly to be ascribed to the influence of such examples.

But to return. Owing to the mutual hostilities of the different tribes I have mentioned, the mountainous tracts which separate their respective territories remain altogether uninhabited; the natives invariably dwelling in the depths of the valleys, with a view of securing themselves from the predatory incursions of their enemies, who often lurk along their borders, ready to cut off any imprudent straggler, or make a descent upon the inmates of some sequestered habitation. I several times met with very aged men, who from this cause had never passed the confines of their native vale, some of them having never even ascended midway up the mountains in the whole course of their lives, and who, accordingly, had little idea of the appearance of any other part of the island, the whole of which is not perhaps more than sixty miles in circuit. The little space in which some of these clans pass away their days would seem almost incredible.

The glen of Tior will furnish a curious illustration of this. The inhabited part is not more than four miles in length, and varies in breadth from half a mile to less than a quarter. The rocky vine-clad cliffs on one side tower almost perpendicularly from their base to the height of at least fifteen hundred feet; while across the vale—in striking contrast to the scenery opposite—grass-grown elevations rise one above another in blooming terraces. Hemmed in by these stupendous barriers, the valley would be altogether shut out from the rest of the world, were it not that it is accessible from the sea at one end, and by a narrow defile at the other.

The impression produced upon my mind, when I first visited this beautiful glen, will never be obliterated.

I had come from Nukuheva by water in the ship's boat, and when we entered the bay of Tior it was high noon. The heat had been intense, as we had been floating upon the long smooth swell of the ocean, for there was but little wind. The sun's rays had expended all their fury upon us; and to add to our discomfort, we had omitted to supply ourselves with water previous to starting. What with heat and thirst together, I became so impatient to get ashore, that when at last we glided towards it, I stood up in the bow of the boat ready for a spring. As she shot two-thirds of her length high upon the beach, propelled by three or four strong strokes of the oars, I leaped among a parcel of juvenile savages, who stood prepared to give us a kind reception; and with them at my heels, yelling like so many imps, I rushed forward across the open ground in the vicinity of the sea, and plunged, diver fashion, into the recesses of the first grove that offered.

What a delightful sensation did I experience! I felt as if

floating in some new element, while all sort of gurgling, trickling, liquid sounds fell upon my ear. People may say what they will about the refreshing influences of a cold-water bath, but commend me when in a perspiration to the shade baths of Tior, beneath the cocoa-nut trees, and amidst the cool delightful atmosphere which surrounds them.

How shall I describe the scenery that met my eye, as I looked out from this verdant recess! The narrow valley, with its steep and close adjoining sides draperied with vines, and arched overhead with a fret-work of interlacing boughs, nearly hidden from view by masses of leafy verdure, seemed from where I stood like an immense arbour disclosing its vista to the eye, whilst as I advanced it insensibly widened into the loveliest vale eye ever beheld.

It so happened that the very day I was in Tior the French admiral, attended by all the boats of his squadron, came down in state from Nukuheva to take formal possession of the place. He remained in the valley about two hours, during which time he had a ceremonious interview with the king.

The patriarch-sovereign of Tior was a man very far advanced in years; but though age had bowed his form and rendered him almost decrepid, his gigantic frame retained all its original magnitude and grandeur of appearance. He advanced slowly and with evident pain, assisting his tottering steps with the heavy war-spear he held in his hand, and attended by a group of grey-bearded chiefs, on one of whom he occasionally leaned for support. The admiral came forward with head uncovered and extended hand, while the old king saluted him by a stately flourish of his weapon. The next moment they stood side by side, these two extremes of the social scale,—the polished, splendid Frenchman, and the poor tattooed savage. They were both tall and noble-looking men; but in other respects how strikingly contrasted! Du Petit Thouars exhibited upon his person all the paraphernalia of his naval rank. He wore a richly decorated admiral's frock-coat, a laced chapeau bras, and upon his breast were a variety of ribbons and orders; while the simple islander, with the exception of a slight cincture about his loins, appeared in all the nakedness of nature.

At what an immeasurable distance, thought I, are these two beings removed from each other. In the one is shown the result of long centuries of progressive civilization and refinement, which have gradually converted the mere creature into the semblance of all that is elevated and grand; while the other, after the lapse of the same period, has not advanced one step in the career of improvement. "Yet, after all," quoth I to myself, "insensible as he is to a thousand wants, and removed from harassing cares, may not the savage be the happier man of the two?" Such were the thoughts that arose in my mind as I gazed upon the novel spectacle before me. In truth it was an impressive one, and little likely to be effaced. I can recall even now with vivid distinctness every feature of the scene. The umbrageous shades where the interview took place—the glorious tropical vegetation around—the picturesque grouping of the mingled throng of soldiery and natives—and even the golden-hued bunch of banannas that I held in my hand at the time, and of which I occasionally partook while making the aforesaid philosophical reflections.

CHAPTER V

Thoughts previous to attempting an Escape—Toby, a Fellow Sailor, agrees to share the Adventure—Last Night aboard the Ship.

HAVING fully resolved to leave the vessel clandestinely, and having acquired all the knowledge concerning the bay that

I could obtain under the circumstances in which I was placed, I now deliberately turned over in my mind every plan of escape that suggested itself, being determined to act with all possible prudence in an attempt where failure would be attended with so many disagreeable consequences. The idea of being taken and brought back ignominiously to the ship was so inexpressibly repulsive to me, that I was determined by no hasty and imprudent measures to render such an event probable.

I knew that our worthy captain, who felt such a paternal solicitude for the welfare of his crew, would not willingly consent that one of his best hands should encounter the perils of a sojourn among the natives of a barbarous island; and I was certain that in the event of my disappearance, his fatherly anxiety would prompt him to offer, by way of a reward, yard upon yard of gaily printed calico for my apprehension. He might even have appreciated my services at the value of a musket, in which case I felt perfectly certain that the whole population of the bay would be immediately upon my track, incited by the prospect of so magnificent a bounty.

Having ascertained the fact before alluded to, that the islanders, from motives of precaution, dwelt altogether in the depths of the valleys, and avoided wandering about the more elevated portions of the shore, unless bound on some expedition of war or plunder, I concluded that if I could effect unperceived a passage to the mountains, I might easily remain among them, supporting myself by such fruits as came in my way until the sailing of the ship, an event of which I could not fail to be immediately apprised, as from my lofty position I should command a view of the entire harbour.

The idea pleased me greatly. It seemed to combine a great deal of practicability with no inconsiderable enjoyment in a quiet way; for how delightful it would be to look down upon the detested old vessel from the height of some thousand feet, and contrast the verdant scenery about me with the recollection of her narrow decks and gloomy forecastle! Why, it was really refreshing even to think of it; and so I straightway fell to picturing myself seated beneath a cocoa-nut tree on the brow of the mountain, with a cluster of plantains within easy reach, criticizing her nautical evolutions as she was working her way out of the harbour.

To be sure there was one rather unpleasant drawback to these agreeable anticipations—the possibility of falling in with a foraging party of these same bloody-minded Typees, whose appetites, edged perhaps by the air of so elevated a region, might prompt them to devour one. This, I must confess, was a most disagreeable view of the matter.

Just to think of a party of these unnatural gourmands taking it into their heads to make a convivial meal of a poor devil, who would have no means of escape or defence: however, there was no help for it. I was willing to encounter some risks in order to accomplish my object, and counted much upon my ability to elude these prowling cannibals amongst the many coverts which the mountains afforded. Besides, the chances were ten to one in my favour that they would none of them quit their own fastnesses.

I had determined not to communicate my design of withdrawing from the vessel to any of my shipmates, and least of all to solicit any one to accompany me in my flight. But it so happened one night, that being upon deck, revolving over in my mind various plans of escape, I perceived one of the ship's company leaning over the bulwarks, apparently plunged in a profound reverie. He was a young fellow about my own age, for whom I had all along entertained a great regard; and Toby, such was the name by which he went among us, for his real name he would never tell us, was every way worthy of it. He was active, ready, and obliging, of dauntless courage, and singularly open and fearless in the expression of his feelings. I had on more than one occasion got him out of scrapes into which this had led him; and I know not whether it was from this cause, or a certain congeniality of sentiment between us, that he had always shown a partiality for my society. We had battled out many a long watch together, beguiling the weary hours with chat, song, and story, mingled with a good many imprecations upon the hard destiny it seemed our common fortune to encounter.

Toby, like myself, had evidently moved in a different sphere of life, and his conversation at times betrayed this, although he was anxious to conceal it. He was one of that class of rovers you sometimes meet at sea, who never reveal their origin, never allude to home, and go rambling over the world as if pursued by some mysterious fate they cannot possibly elude.

There was much even in the appearance of Toby calculated to draw me towards him, for while the greater part of the crew were as coarse in person as in mind, Toby was endowed with a remarkably prepossessing exterior. Arrayed in his blue frock and duck trousers, he was as smart a looking sailor as ever stepped upon a deck; he was singularly small and slightly made, with great flexibility of limb. His naturally dark complexion had been deepened by exposure to the tropical sun, and a mass of jetty locks clustered about his temples, and threw a darker shade into his large black eyes. He was a strange wayward being, moody, fitful, and melancholy—at times almost morose. He had a quick and fiery temper too, which, when thoroughly roused, transported him into a state bordering on delirium.

It is strange the power that a mind of deep passion has over feebler natures. I have seen a brawny fellow, with no lack of ordinary courage, fairly quail before this slender stripling, when in one of his furious fits. But these paroxysms seldom occurred, and in them my big-hearted ship-mate vented the bile which more calm-tempered individuals get rid of by a continual pettishness at trivial annoyances.

No one ever saw Toby laugh; I mean in the hearty abandonment of broad-mouthed mirth. He did smile sometimes, it is true; and there was a good deal of dry, sarcastic humour about him, which told the more from the imperturbable gravity of his tone and manner.

Latterly I had observed that Toby's melancholy had greatly increased, and I had frequently seen him since our arrival at the island gazing wistfully upon the shore, when the remainder of the crew would be rioting below. I was aware that he entertained a cordial detestation of the ship, and believed that, should a fair chance of escape present itself, he would embrace it willingly. But the attempt was so perilous in the place where we then lay, that I supposed myself the only individual on board the ship who was sufficiently reckless to think of it. In this, however, I was mistaken.

When I perceived Toby leaning, as I have mentioned, against the bulwarks and buried in thought, it struck me at once that the subject of his meditations might be the same as my own. And if it be so, thought I, is he not the very one of all my shipmates whom I would choose for the partner of my adventure? and why should I not have some comrade with me to divide its dangers and alleviate its hardships? Perhaps I might be obliged to lie concealed among the mountains for weeks. In such an event what a solace would a companion be?

These thoughts passed rapidly through my mind, and I wondered why I had not before considered the matter in this light. But it was not too late. A tap upon the shoulder served to rouse Toby from his reverie; I found him ripe for the enterprise, and a very few words sufficed for a mutual understanding between us. In an hour's time we had arranged all the preliminaries, and decided upon our plan of action. We then ratified our engagement with an affectionate wedding of palms, and to elude suspicion repaired each to his hammock, to spend the last night on board the Dolly.

The next day the starboard watch, to which we both belonged, was to be sent ashore on liberty; and, availing ourselves of this opportunity, we determined, as soon after landing as possible, to separate ourselves from the rest of the men without exciting their suspicions, and strike back at once for the mountains. Seen from the ship, their summits appeared inaccessible, but here and there sloping spurs extended from them almost into the sea, buttressing the lofty elevations with which they were connected, and forming those radiating valleys I have before described. One of these ridges, which appeared more practicable than the rest, we determined to climb, convinced that it would conduct us to the heights beyond. Accordingly, we carefully observed its bearings and locality from the ship, so that when ashore we should run no chance of missing it.

In all this the leading object we had in view was to seclude ourselves from sight until the departure of the vessel; then to take our chance as to the reception the Nukuheva natives might give us; and after remaining upon the island as long as we found our stay agreeable, to leave it the first favourable opportunity that offered.

CHAPTER VI

A Specimen of Nautical Oratory—Criticisms of the Sailors—The Starboard Watch are given a Holiday—The Escape to the Mountains.

EARLY the next morning the starboard watch were mustered upon the quarter-deck, and our worthy captain, standing in the cabin gangway, harangued us as follows:—

"Now, men, as we are just off a six months' cruise, and have got through most all our work in port here, I suppose you want to go ashore. Well, I mean to give your watch liberty to-day, so you may get ready as soon as you please, and go; but understand this, I am going to give you liberty because I suppose you would growl like so many old quarter gunners if I didn't; at the same time, if you'll take my advice, every mother's son of you will stay aboard, and keep out of the way of the bloody cannibals altogether. Ten to one, men, if you go ashore, you will get into some infernal row, and that will be the end of you; for if those tattooed scoundrels get you a little ways back into their valleys, they'll nab you—that you may be certain of. Plenty of white men have gone ashore here and never been seen any more. There was the old Dido, she put in here about two years ago, and sent one watch off on liberty; they never were heard of again for a week—the natives swore they didn't know where they were—and only three of them ever got back to the ship again, and one with his face damaged for life, for the cursed heathens tattooed a broad patch clean across his figure-head. But it will be no use talking to you, for go you will, that I see plainly; so all I have to say is, that you need not blame me if the islanders make a meal of you. You may stand some chance of escaping them though, if you keep close about the French encampment, and are back to the ship again before sunset. Keep that much in your mind, if you forget all the rest I've been saying to you. There, go forward; bear a hand and rig yourselves, and stand by for a call. At two bells the boat will be manned to take you off, and the Lord have mercy on you!"

Various were the emotions depicted upon the countenances of the starboard watch whilst listening to this address; but on its conclusion there was a general move to

wards the forecastle, and we soon were all busily engaged
in getting ready for the holiday so auspiciously announced
by the skipper. During these preparations his harangue
was commented upon in no very measured terms; and
one of the party, after denouncing him as a lying old son
of a sea-cook who begrudged a fellow a few hours' liberty,
exclaimed with an oath, "But you don't bounce me out
of my liberty, old chap, for all your yarns; for I would go
ashore if every pebble on the beach was a live coal, and
every stick a gridiron, and the cannibals stood ready to
broil me on landing."

The spirit of this sentiment was responded to by all
hands, and we resolved that in spite of the captain's croak-
ings we would make a glorious day of it.

But Toby and I had our own game to play, and we
availed ourselves of the confusion which always reigns
among a ship's company preparatory to going ashore, to
confer together and complete our arrangements. As our
object was to effect as rapid a flight as possible to the mountains, we determined not to encumber ourselves with any
superfluous apparel; and accordingly, while the rest were
rigging themselves out with some idea of making a display,
we were content to put on new stout duck trousers, serviceable pumps, and heavy Havre-frocks, which with a Payta
hat completed our equipment.

When our shipmates wondered at this, Toby exclaimed
in his odd grave way that the rest might do as they liked,
but that he for one preserved his go-ashore traps for the
Spanish main, where the tie of a sailor's neckerchief might
make some difference; but as for a parcel of unbreeched
heathen, he wouldn't go to the bottom of his chest for any
of them, and was half disposed to appear among them in
buff himself. The men laughed at what they thought was
one of his strange conceits, and so we escaped suspicion.

It may appear singular that we should have been thus on

our guard with our own shipmates; but there were some among us who, had they possessed the least inkling of our project, would, for a paltry hope of reward, have immediately communicated it to the captain.

As soon as two bells were struck, the word was passed for the liberty-men to get into the boat. I lingered behind in the forecastle a moment to take a parting glance at its familiar features, and just as I was about to ascend to the deck my eye happened to light on the bread-barge and beef-kid, which contained the remnants of our last hasty meal. Although I had never before thought of providing anything in the way of food for our expedition, as I fully relied upon the fruits of the island to sustain us wherever we might wander, yet I could not resist the inclination I felt to provide luncheon from the relics before me. Accordingly I took a double handful of those small, broken, flinty bits of biscuit which generally go by the name of "midshipmen's nuts," and thrust them into the bosom of my frock; in which same ample receptacle I had previously stowed away several pounds of tobacco and a few yards of cotton cloth—articles with which I intended to purchase the good-will of the natives, as soon as we should appear among them after the departure of our vessel.

This last addition to my stock caused a considerable protuberance in front, which I abated in a measure by shaking the bits of bread around my waist, and distributing the plugs of tobacco among the folds of the garment.

Hardly had I completed these arrangements when my name was sung out by a dozen voices, and I sprung upon the deck, where I found all the party in the boat, and impatient to shove off. I dropped over the side and seated myself with the rest of the watch in the stern sheets, while the poor larboarders shipped their oars, and commenced pulling us ashore.

This happened to be the rainy season at the islands,

and the heavens had nearly the whole morning betokened one of those heavy showers which during this period so frequently occur. The large drops fell bubbling into the water shortly after our leaving the ship, and by the time we had effected a landing it poured down in torrents. We fled for shelter under cover of an immense canoe-house which stood hard by the beach, and waited for the first fury of the storm to pass.

It continued, however, without cessation; and the monotonous beating of the rain over head began to exert a drowsy influence upon the men, who, throwing themselves here and there upon the large war-canoes, after chatting awhile, all fell asleep.

This was the opportunity we desired, and Toby and I availed ourselves of it at once by stealing out of the canoe-house and plunging into the depths of an extensive grove that was in its rear. After ten minutes' rapid progress we gained an open space from which we could just descry the ridge we intended to mount looming dimly through the mists of the tropical shower, and distant from us, as we estimated, something more than a mile. Our direct course towards it lay through a rather populous part of the bay; but desirous as we were of evading the natives, and securing an unmolested retreat to the mountains, we determined, by taking a circuit through some extensive thickets, to avoid their vicinity altogether.

The heavy rain that still continued to fall without intermission favoured our enterprise, as it drove the islanders into their houses, and prevented any casual meeting with them. Our heavy frocks soon became completely saturated with water, and by their weight, and that of the articles we had concealed beneath them, not a little impeded our progress. But it was no time to pause when at any moment we might be surprised by a body of the savages, and forced at the very outset to relinquish our undertaking.

Since leaving the canoe-house we had scarcely exchanged a single syllable with one another; but when we
entered a second narrow opening in the wood, and again
caught sight of the ridge before us, I took Toby by the arm,
and pointing along its sloping outline to the lofty heights
at its extremity, said in a low tone, "Now Toby, not a word,
nor a glance backward, till we stand on the summit of
yonder mountain—so no more lingering, but let us shove
ahead while we can, and in a few hours' time we may laugh
aloud.—You are the lightest and the nimblest, so lead on,
and I will follow."

"All right, brother," said Toby, "quick's our play; only
let's keep close together, that's all;" and so saying, with a
bound like a young roe, he cleared a brook which ran across
our path, and rushed forward with a quick step.

When we arrived within a short distance of the ridge,
we were stopped by a mass of tall yellow reeds, growing
together as thickly as they could stand, and as tough and
stubborn as so many rods of steel; and we perceived, to our
chagrin, that they extended midway up the elevation we
purposed to ascend.

For a moment we gazed about us in quest of a more practicable route; it was, however, at once apparent that there
was no resource but to pierce this thicket of canes at all
hazards. We now reversed our order of march, I, being the
heaviest, taking the lead, with a view of breaking a path
through the obstruction, while Toby fell into the rear.

Two or three times I endeavoured to insinuate myself
between the canes, and by dint of coaxing and bending
them to make some progress; but a bull-frog might as well
have tried to work a passage through the teeth of a comb,
and I gave up the attempt in despair.

Half wild with meeting an obstacle we had so little anticipated, I threw myself desperately against it, crushing to
the ground the canes with which I came in contact; and,

rising to my feet again, repeated the action with like effect. Twenty minutes of this violent exercise almost exhausted me, but it carried us some way into the thicket; when Toby, who had been reaping the benefit of my labours by following close at my heels, proposed to become pioneer in turn, and accordingly passed ahead with a view of affording me a respite from my exertions. As however with his slight frame he made but bad work of it, I was soon obliged to resume my old place again.

On we toiled, the perspiration starting from our bodies in floods, our limbs torn and lacerated with the splintered fragments of the broken canes, until we had proceeded perhaps as far as the middle of the brake, when suddenly it ceased raining, and the atmosphere around us became close and sultry beyond expression. The elasticity of the reeds, quickly recovering from the temporary pressure of our bodies, caused them to spring back to their original position; so that they closed in upon us as we advanced, and prevented the circulation of the little air which might otherwise have reached us. Besides this, their great height completely shut us out from the view of surrounding objects, and we were not certain but that we might have been going all the time in a wrong direction.

Fatigued with my long-continued efforts, and panting for breath, I felt myself completely incapacitated for any further exertion. I rolled up the sleeve of my frock, and squeezed the moisture it contained into my parched mouth. But the few drops I managed to obtain gave me little relief, and I sunk down for a moment with a sort of dogged apathy, from which I was aroused by Toby, who had devised a plan to free us from the net in which we had become entangled.

He was laying about him lustily with his sheath-knife, lopping the canes right and left, like a reaper, and soon made quite a clearing around us. This sight reanimated me, and seizing my own knife, I hacked and hewed away without mercy. But alas! the farther we advanced, the thicker and taller, and apparently the more interminable, the reeds became.

I began to think we were fairly snared, and had almost made up my mind that without a pair of wings we should never be able to escape from the toils; when all at once I discerned a peep of daylight through the canes on my right, and, communicating the joyful tidings to Toby, we both fell to with fresh spirit, and speedily opening a passage towards it we found ourselves clear of perplexities, and in the near vicinity of the ridge.

After resting for a few moments we began the ascent, and after a little vigorous climbing found ourselves close to its summit. Instead however of walking along its ridge, where we should have been in full view of the natives in the vales beneath, and at a point where they could easily intercept us were they so inclined, we cautiously advanced on one side, crawling on our hands and knees, and screened from observation by the grass through which we glided, much in the fashion of a couple of serpents. After an hour employed in this unpleasant kind of locomotion, we started to our feet again and pursued our way boldly along the crest of the ridge.

This salient spur of the lofty elevations that encompassed the bay rose with a sharp angle from the valleys at its base, and presented, with the exception of a few steep acclivities, the appearance of a vast inclined plane, sweeping down towards the sea from the heights in the distance. We had ascended it near the place of its termination and at its lowest point, and now saw our route to the mountains distinctly defined along its narrow crest, which was covered with a soft carpet of verdure, and was in many parts only a few feet wide.

Elated with the success which had so far attended our

enterprise, and invigorated by the refreshing atmosphere we now inhaled, Toby and I in high spirits were making our way rapidly along the ridge, when suddenly from the valleys below which lay on either side of us we heard the distant shouts of the natives, who had just descried us, and to whom our figures, brought in bold relief against the sky, were plainly revealed.

Glancing our eyes into these valleys, we perceived their savage inhabitants hurrying to and fro, seemingly under the influence of some sudden alarm, and appearing to the eye scarcely bigger than so many pigmies; while their white thatched dwellings, dwarfed by the distance, looked like baby-houses. As we looked down upon the islanders from our lofty elevation, we experienced a sense of security; feeling confident that, should they undertake a pursuit, it would, from the start we now had, prove entirely fruitless, unless they followed us into the mountains, where we knew they cared not to venture.

However, we thought it as well to make the most of our time; and accordingly, where the ground would admit of it, we ran swiftly along the summit of the ridge, until we were brought to a stand by a steep cliff, which at first seemed to interpose an effectual barrier to our further advance. By dint of much hard scrambling however, and at some risk to our necks, we at last surmounted it, and continued our flight with unabated celerity.

We had left the beach early in the morning, and after an uninterrupted, though at times difficult and dangerous ascent, during which we had never once turned our faces to the sea, we found ourselves, about three hours before sunset, standing on the top of what seemed to be the highest land on the island, an immense overhanging cliff composed of basaltic rocks, hung round with parasitical plants. We must have been more than three thousand feet above the level of the sea, and the scenery viewed from this height was magnificent.

The lonely bay of Nukuheva, dotted here and there with the black hulls of the vessels composing the French squadron, lay reposing at the base of a circular range of elevations, whose verdant sides, perforated with deep glens or diversified with smiling valleys, formed altogether the loveliest view I ever beheld, and were I to live a hundred years, I should never forget the feeling of admiration which I then experienced.

CHAPTER VII

The other side of the Mountain—Disappointment—Inventory of Articles brought from the Ship—Division of the Stock of Bread—Appearance of the Interior of the Island—A Discovery—A Ravine and Waterfalls—A sleepless Night—Further Discoveries—My Illness—A Marquesan Landscape.

My CURIOSITY had been not a little raised with regard to the description of country we should meet on the other side of the mountains; and I had supposed, with Toby, that immediately on gaining the heights we should be enabled to view the large bays of Happar and Typee reposing at our feet on one side, in the same way that Nukuheva lay spread out below on the other. But here we were disappointed. Instead of finding the mountain we had ascended sweeping down in the opposite direction into broad and capacious valleys, the land appeared to retain its general elevation, only broken into a series of ridges and intervales, which as far as the eye could reach stretched away from us, with their precipitous sides covered with the brightest verdure, and waving here and there with the foliage of clumps of woodland; among which, however, we perceived none of those trees upon whose fruit we had relied with such certainty.

This was a most unlooked-for discovery, and one that promised to defeat our plans altogether, for we could not think of descending the mountain on the Nukuheva side in quest of food. Should we for this purpose be induced to retrace our steps, we should run no small chance of encountering the natives, who in that case, if they did nothing worse to us, would be certain to convey us back to the ship for the sake of the reward in calico and trinkets, which we had no doubt our skipper would hold out to them as an inducement to our capture.

What was to be done? The Dolly would not sail perhaps for ten days, and how were we to sustain life during this period? I bitterly repented our improvidence in not providing ourselves, as we easily might have done, with a supply of biscuit. With a rueful visage I now bethought me of the scanty handful of bread I had stuffed into the bosom of my frock, and felt somewhat desirous to ascertain what part of it had weathered the rather rough usage it had experienced in ascending the mountain. I accordingly proposed to Toby that we should enter into a joint examination of the various articles we had brought from the ship. With this intent we seated ourselves upon the grass; and a little curious to see with what kind of judgment my companion had filled his frock—which I remarked seemed about as well lined as my own—I requested him to commence operations by spreading out its contents.

Thrusting his hand, then, into the bosom of this capacious receptacle, he first brought to light about a pound of tobacco, whose component parts still adhered together, the whole outside being covered with soft particles of seabread. Wet and dripping, it had the appearance of having been just recovered from the bottom of the sea. But I paid slight attention to a substance of so little value to us in our present situation, as soon as I perceived the indications it gave of Toby's foresight in laying in a supply of food for the expedition.

I eagerly inquired what quantity he had brought with him, when, rummaging once more beneath his garment, he produced a small handful of something so soft, pulpy, and discoloured, that for a few moments he was as much puzzled as myself to tell by what possible instrumentality such a villainous compound had become engendered in his bosom. I can only describe it as a hash of soaked bread and bits of tobacco, brought to a doughy consistency by the united agency of perspiration and rain. But repulsive as it might otherwise have been, I now regarded it as an invaluable treasure, and proceeded with great care to transfer this paste-like mass to a large leaf which I had plucked from a bush beside me. Toby informed me that in the morning he had placed two whole biscuits in his bosom, with a view of munching them, should he feel so inclined, during our flight. These were now reduced to the equivocal substance which I had just placed on the leaf.

Another dive into the frock brought to view some four or five yards of calico print, whose tasteful pattern was rather disfigured by the yellow stains of the tobacco with which it had been brought in contact. In drawing this calico slowly from his bosom inch by inch, Toby reminded me of a juggler performing the feat of the endless ribbon. The next cast was a small one, being a sailor's little "ditty-bag," containing needles, thread, and other sewing utensils; then came a razor-case, followed by two or three separate plugs of negro-head, which were fished up from the bottom of the now empty receptacle. These various matters being inspected, I produced the few things that I had myself brought.

As might have been anticipated from the state of my companion's edible supplies, I found my own in a deplorable condition, and diminished to a quantity that would not have formed half a dozen mouthfuls for a hungry man who was partial enough to tobacco not to mind swallowing it. A few morsels of bread, with a fathom or two of white cotton cloth, and several pounds of choice pigtail, composed the extent of my possessions.

Our joint stock of miscellaneous articles was now made up into a compact bundle, which it was agreed we should carry alternately. But the sorry remains of the biscuit were not to be disposed of so summarily: the precarious circumstances in which we were placed made us regard them as something on which very probably depended the fate of our adventure. After a brief discussion, in which we both of us expressed our resolution of not descending into the bay until the ship's departure, I suggested to my companion that little of it as there was, we should divide the bread into six equal portions, each of which should be a day's allowance for both of us. This proposition he assented to; so I took the silk kerchief from my neck, and cutting it with my knife into half a dozen equal pieces, proceeded to make an exact division.

At first, Toby, with a degree of fastidiousness that seemed to me ill-timed, was for picking out the minute particles of tobacco with which the spongy mass was mixed; but against this proceeding I protested, as by such an operation we must have greatly diminished its quantity.

When the division was accomplished, we found that a day's allowance for the two was not a great deal more than what a table-spoon might hold. Each separate portion we immediately rolled up in the bit of silk prepared for it, and joining them altogether into a small package, I committed them, with solemn injunctions of fidelity, to the custody of Toby. For the remainder of that day we resolved to fast, as we had been fortified by a breakfast in the morning; and now starting again to our feet, we looked about us for a shelter during the night, which, from the appearance of the heavens, promised to be a dark and tempestuous one.

There was no place near us which would in any way answer our purpose; so turning our backs upon Nukuheva, we commenced exploring the unknown regions which lay upon the other side of the mountain.

In this direction, as far as our vision extended, not a sign of life, nor anything that denoted even the transient residence of man, could be seen. The whole landscape seemed one unbroken solitude, the interior of the island having apparently been untenanted since the morning of the creation; and as we advanced through this wilderness, our voices sounded strangely in our ears, as though human accents had never before disturbed the fearful silence of the place, interrupted only by the low murmurings of distant waterfalls.

Our disappointment, however, in not finding the various fruits with which we had intended to regale ourselves during our stay in these wilds, was a good deal lessened by the consideration that from this very circumstance we should be much less exposed to a casual meeting with the savage tribes about us, who we knew always dwelt beneath the shadows of those trees which supplied them with food.

We wandered along, casting eager glances into every bush we passed, until just as we had succeeded in mounting one of the many ridges that intersected the ground, I saw in the grass before me something like an indistinctly traced footpath, which appeared to lead along the top of the ridge, and to descend with it into a deep ravine about half a mile in advance of us.

Robinson Crusoe could not have been more startled at the footprint in the sand than we were at this unwelcome discovery. My first impulse was to make as rapid a retreat as possible, and bend our steps in some other direc·

tion; but our curiosity to see whither this path might lead, prompted us to pursue it. So on we went, the track becoming more and more visible the farther we proceeded, until it conducted us to the verge of the ravine, where it abruptly terminated.

"And so," said Toby, peering down into the chasm, "every one that travels this path takes a jump here, eh?"

"Not so," said I, "for I think they might manage to descend without it; what say you,—shall we attempt the feat?"

"And what, in the name of caves and coal-holes, do you expect to find at the bottom of that gulf but a broken neck —why it looks blacker than our ship's hold, and the roar of those waterfalls down there would batter one's brains to pieces."

"Oh, no, Toby," I exclaimed, laughing; "but there's something to be seen here, that's plain, or there would have been no path, and I am resolved to find out what it is."

"I will tell you what, my pleasant fellow," rejoined Toby quickly, "if you are going to pry into everything you meet with here that excites your curiosity, you will marvellously soon get knocked on the head; to a dead certainty you will come bang upon a party of these savages in the midst of your discovery-makings, and I doubt whether such an event would particularly delight you. Just take my advice for once, and let us 'bout ship and steer in some other direction; besides, it's getting late, and we ought to be mooring ourselves for the night."

"That is just the thing I have been driving at," replied I; "and I am thinking that this ravine will exactly answer our purpose, for it is roomy, secluded, well watered, and may shelter us from the weather."

"Aye, and from sleep too, and by the same token will give us sore throats and rheumatisms into the bargain," cried Toby, with evident dislike at the idea.

"Oh, very well then, my lad," said I, "since you will not

accompany me, here I go alone. You will see me in the morning;" and advancing to the edge of the cliff upon which we had been standing, I proceeded to lower myself down by the tangled roots which clustered about all the crevices of the rock. As I had anticipated, Toby, in spite of his previous remonstrances, followed my example, and dropping himself with the activity of a squirrel from point to point, he quickly outstripped me, and effected a landing at the bottom before I had accomplished two-thirds of the descent.

The sight that now greeted us was one that will ever be vividly impressed upon my mind. Five foaming streams, rushing through as many gorges, and swelled and turbid by the recent rains, united together in one mad plunge of nearly eighty feet, and fell with wild uproar into a deep black pool scooped out of the gloomy-looking rocks that lay piled around, and thence in one collected body dashed down a narrow sloping channel which seemed to penetrate into the very bowels of the earth. Overhead, vast roots of trees hung down from the sides of the ravine dripping with moisture, and trembling with the concussions produced by the fall. It was now sunset, and the feeble uncertain light that found its way into these caverns and woody depths heightened their strange appearance, and reminded us that in a short time we should find ourselves in utter darkness.

As soon as I had satisfied my curiosity by gazing at this scene, I fell to wondering how it was that what we had taken for a path should have conducted us to so singular a place, and began to suspect that after all I might have been deceived in supposing it to have been a track formed by the islanders. This was rather an agreeable reflection than otherwise, for it diminished our dread of accidentally meeting with any of them, and I came to the conclusion that perhaps we could not have selected a more secure

hiding-place than this very spot we had so accidentally
hit upon. Toby agreed with me in this view of the matter,
and we immediately began gathering together the limbs
of trees which lay scattered about, with the view of constructing a temporary hut for the night. This we were
obliged to build close to the foot of the cataract, for the current of water extended very nearly to the sides of the gorge.
The few moments of light that remained we employed in
covering our hut with a species of broad-bladed grass that
grew in every fissure of the ravine. Our hut, if it deserved
to be called one, consisted of six or eight of the straightest
branches we could find laid obliquely against the steep
wall of rock, with their lower ends within a foot of the
stream. Into the space thus covered over we managed to
crawl, and dispose our wearied bodies as best we could.

Shall I ever forget that horrid night? As for poor Toby,
I could scarcely get a word out of him. It would have been
some consolation to have heard his voice, but he lay shivering the live-long night like a man afflicted with the palsy,
with his knees drawn up to his head, while his back
was supported against the dripping side of the rock. During this wretched night there seemed nothing wanting to
complete the perfect misery of our condition. The rain descended in such torrents that our poor shelter proved a mere
mockery. In vain did I try to elude the incessant streams
that poured upon me; by protecting one part I only exposed
another, and the water was continually finding some new
opening through which to drench us.

I have had many a ducking in the course of my life, and
in general care little about it; but the accumulated horrors of
that night, the deathlike coldness of the place, the appalling darkness and the dismal sense of our forlorn condition,
almost unmanned me.

It will not be doubted that the next morning we were
early risers, and as soon as I could catch the faintest glimpse

of anything like daylight I shook my companion by the arm, and told him it was sunrise. Poor Toby lifted up his head, and after a moment's pause said, in a husky voice, "Then, shipmate, my toplights have gone out, for it appears darker now with my eyes open than it did when they were shut."

"Nonsense!" exclaimed I; "you are not awake yet."

"Awake!" roared Toby in a rage, "awake! You mean to insinuate I've been asleep, do you? It is an insult to a man to suppose he could sleep in such an infernal place as this."

By the time I had apologized to my friend for having misconstrued his silence, it had become somewhat more light, and we crawled out of our lair. The rain had ceased, but everything around us was dripping with moisture. We stripped off our saturated garments, and wrung them as dry as we could. We contrived to make the blood circulate in our benumbed limbs by rubbing them vigorously with our hands; and after performing our ablutions in the stream, and putting on our still wet clothes, we began to think it advisable to break our long fast, it being now twenty-four hours since we had tasted food.

Accordingly our day's ration was brought out, and seating ourselves on a detached fragment of rock, we proceeded to discuss it. First we divided it into two equal portions, and carefully rolling one of them up for our evening's repast, divided the remainder again as equally as possible, and then drew lots for the first choice. I could have placed the morsel that fell to my share upon the tip of my finger; but notwithstanding this I took care that it should be full ten minutes before I had swallowed the last crumb. What a true saying it is that "appetite furnishes the best sauce." There was a flavour and a relish to this small particle of food that under other circumstances it would have been impossible for the most delicate viands to have imparted. A copious draught of the pure water which flowed at our feet served to complete the meal, and after it we rose sensibly refreshed, and prepared for whatever might befall us.

We now carefully examined the chasm in which we had passed the night. We crossed the stream, and gaining the farther side of the pool I have mentioned, discovered proofs that the spot must have been visited by some one but a short time previous to our arrival. Further observation convinced us that it had been regularly frequented, and, as we afterwards conjectured from particular indications, for the purpose of obtaining a certain root, from which the natives obtain a kind of ointment.

These discoveries immediately determined us to abandon a place which had presented no inducement for us to remain, except the promise of security; and as we looked about us for the means of ascending again into the upper regions, we at last found a practicable part of the rock, and half an hour's toil carried us to the summit of the same cliff from which the preceding evening we had descended.

I now proposed to Toby that instead of rambling about the island, exposing ourselves to discovery at every turn, we should select some place as our fixed abode for as long a period as our food should hold out, build ourselves a comfortable hut, and be as prudent and circumspect as possible. To all this my companion assented, and we at once set about carrying the plan into execution.

With this view, after exploring without success a little glen near us, we crossed several of the ridges of which I have before spoken; and about noon found ourselves ascending a long and gradually rising slope, but still without having discovered any place adapted to our purpose. Low and heavy clouds betokened an approaching storm, and we hurried on to gain a covert in a clump of thick bushes which appeared to terminate the long ascent. We threw ourselves under the lee of these bushes, and pulling up the long grass that grew around, covered ourselves completely with it, and awaited the shower.

But it did not come as soon as we had expected, and before many minutes my companion was fast asleep, and I was rapidly falling into the same state of happy forgetfulness. Just at this juncture, however, down came the rain with a violence that put all thoughts of slumber to flight. Although in some measure sheltered, our clothes soon became as wet as ever: this, after all the trouble we had taken to dry them, was provoking enough: but there was no help for it; and I recommend all adventurous youths who abandon vessels in romantic islands during the rainy season to provide themselves with umbrellas.

After an hour or so the shower passed away. My companion slept through it all, or at least appeared so to do; and now that it was over I had not the heart to awaken him. As I lay on my back completely shrouded with verdure, the leafy branches drooping over me, and my limbs buried in grass, I could not avoid comparing our situation with that of the interesting babes in the wood. Poor little sufferers!—no wonder their constitutions broke down under the hardships to which they were exposed.

During the hour or two spent under the shelter of these bushes, I began to feel symptoms which I at once attributed to the exposure of the preceding night. Cold shiverings and a burning fever succeeded one another at intervals, while one of my legs was swelled to such a degree, and pained me so acutely, that I half suspected I had been bitten by some venomous reptile, the congenial inhabitant of the chasm from which we had lately emerged. I may here remark by the way—what I subsequently learned—that all the islands of Polynesia enjoy the reputation, in common with the Hibernian isle, of being free from the presence of any vipers; though whether Saint Patrick ever visited them, is a question I shall not attempt to decide.

As the feverish sensation increased upon me, I tossed about, still unwilling to disturb my slumbering companion, from whose side I removed two or three yards. I chanced to push aside a branch, and by so doing suddenly disclosed to my view a scene which even now I can recall with all the vividness of the first impression. Had a glimpse of the gardens of Paradise been revealed to me I could scarcely have been more ravished with the sight.

From the spot where I lay transfixed with surprise and delight, I looked straight down into the bosom of a valley, which swept away in long wavy undulations to the blue waters in the distance. Midway towards the sea, and peering here and there amidst the foliage, might be seen the palmetto-thatched houses of its inhabitants glistening in the sun that had bleached them to a dazzling whiteness. The vale was more than three leagues in length, and about a mile across at its greatest width.

On either side it appeared hemmed in by steep and green acclivities, which, uniting near the spot where I lay, formed an abrupt and semicircular termination of grassy cliffs and precipices hundreds of feet in height, over which flowed numberless small cascades. But the crowning beauty of the prospect was its universal verdure; and in this indeed consists, I believe, the peculiar charm of every Polynesian landscape. Everywhere below me, from the base of the precipice upon whose very verge I had been unconsciously reposing, the surface of the vale presented a mass of foliage, spread with such rich profusion that it was impossible to determine of what description of trees it consisted.

But perhaps there was nothing about the scenery I beheld more impressive than those silent cascades, whose slender threads of water, after leaping down the steep cliffs, were lost amidst the rich herbage of the valley.

Over all the landscape there reigned the most hushed repose, which I almost feared to break lest, like the enchanted gardens in the fairy tale, a single syllable might dissolve the spell. For a long time, forgetful alike of my own situation, and the vicinity of my still slumbering companion, I remained gazing around me, hardly able to comprehend by what means I had thus suddenly been made a spectator of such a scene.

CHAPTER VIII

The Important Question, Typee or Happar?—A Wild-Goose Chase —My Sufferings—Disheartening Situation—A Night in a Ravine —Morning Meal—Happy Idea of Toby—Journey towards the Valley.

RECOVERING from my astonishment at the beautiful scene before me, I quickly awakened Toby, and informed him of the discovery I had made. Together we now repaired to the border of the precipice, and my companion's admiration was equal to my own. A little reflection, however, abated our surprise at coming so unexpectedly upon this valley, since the large vales of Happar and Typee, lying upon this side of Nukuheva, and extending a considerable distance from the sea towards the interior, must necessarily terminate somewhere about this point.

The question now was as to which of those two places we were looking down upon. Toby insisted that it was the abode of the Happars, and I that it was tenanted by their enemies the ferocious Typees. To be sure I was not entirely convinced by my own arguments, but Toby's proposition to descend at once into the valley, and partake of the hospitality of its inmates, seemed to me to be risking so much upon the strength of a mere supposition, that I resolved to oppose it until we had more evidence to proceed upon.

The point was one of vital importance, as the natives of Happar were not only at peace with Nukuheva, but cultivated with its inhabitants the most friendly relations, and enjoyed beside a reputation for gentleness and humanity which led us to expect from them, if not a cordial reception, at least a shelter during the short period we should remain in their territory.

On the other hand, the very name of Typee struck a panic into my heart which I did not attempt to disguise. The thought of voluntarily throwing ourselves into the hands of these cruel savages, seemed to me an act of mere madness; and almost equally so the idea of venturing into the valley, uncertain by which of these two tribes it was inhabited. That the vale at our feet was tenanted by one of them, was a point that appeared to us past all doubt, since we knew that they resided in this quarter, although our information did not enlighten us further.

My companion, however, incapable of resisting the tempting prospect which the place held out of an abundant supply of food and other means of enjoyment, still clung to his own inconsiderate view of the subject, nor could all my reasoning shake it. When I reminded him that it was impossible for either of us to know anything with certainty, and when I dwelt upon the horrible fate we should encounter were we rashly to descend into the valley, and discover too late the error we had committed, he replied by detailing all the evils of our present condition, and the sufferings we must undergo should we continue to remain where we then were.

Anxious to draw him away from the subject, if possible —for I saw that it would be in vain to attempt changing his mind—I directed his attention to a long bright unwooded tract of land which, sweeping down from the elevations in the interior, descended into the valley before us. I then suggested to him that beyond this ridge might lie a capacious and untenanted valley, abounding with all manner of delicious fruits; for I had heard that there were several such upon the island, and proposed that we should endeavour to reach it, and if we found our expectations realised we should at once take refuge in it and remain there as long as we pleased.

He acquiesced in the suggestion; and we immediately, therefore, began surveying the country lying before us, with a view of determining upon the best route for us to pursue; but it presented little choice, the whole interval being broken into steep ridges, divided by dark ravines, extending in parallel lines at right angles to our direct course. All these we would be obliged to cross before we could hope to arrive at our destination.

A weary journey! But we decided to undertake it, though, for my own part, I felt little prepared to encounter its fatigues, shivering and burning by turns with the ague and fever; for I know not how else to describe the alternate sensations I experienced, and suffering not a little from the lameness which afflicted me. Added to this was the faintness consequent on our meagre diet—a calamity in which Toby participated to the same extent as myself.

These circumstances, however, only augmented my anxiety to reach a place which promised us plenty and repose, before I should be reduced to a state which would render me altogether unable to perform the journey. Accordingly we now commenced it by descending the almost perpendicular side of a steep and narrow gorge, bristling with a thick growth of reeds. Here there was but one mode for us to adopt. We seated ourselves upon the ground, and guided our descent by catching at the canes in our path. The velocity with which we thus slid down the side of the ravine soon brought us to a point where we could use our feet, and in a short time we arrived at the edge of the torrent, which rolled impetuously along the bed of the chasm.

After taking a refreshing draught from the water of the stream, we addressed ourselves to a much more difficult undertaking than the last. Every foot of our late descent had to be regained in ascending the opposite side of the gorge—an operation rendered the less agreeable from the consideration that in these perpendicular episodes we did not progress an hundred yards on our journey. But, ungrateful as the task was, we set about it with exemplary patience, and after a snail-like progress of an hour or more, had scaled perhaps one half of the distance, when the fever which had left me for awhile returned with such violence, and accompanied by so raging a thirst, that it required all the entreaties of Toby to prevent me from losing all the fruits of my late exertion, by precipitating myself madly down the cliffs we had just climbed, in quest of the water which flowed so temptingly at their base. At the moment all my hopes and fears appeared to be merged in this one desire, careless of the consequences that might result from its gratification. I am aware of no feeling, either of pleasure or of pain, that so completely deprives one of all power to resist its impulses, as this same raging thirst.

Toby earnestly conjured me to continue the ascent, assuring me that a little more exertion would bring us to the summit, and that then in less than five minutes we should find ourselves at the brink of the stream, which must necessarily flow on the other side of the ridge.

"Do not," he exclaimed, "turn back, now that we have proceeded thus far; for I tell you that neither of us will have the courage to repeat the attempt, if once more we find ourselves looking up to where we now are from the bottom of these rocks!"

I was not yet so perfectly beside myself as to be heedless of these representations, and therefore toiled on, ineffectually endeavouring to appease the thirst which consumed me, by thinking that in a short time I should be able to gratify it to my heart's content.

At last we gained the top of the second elevation, the loftiest of those I have described as extending in parallel lines between us and the valley we desired to reach. It commanded a view of the whole intervening distance; and, discouraged as I was by other circumstances, this prospect plunged me into the very depths of despair. Nothing but dark and fearful chasms, separated by sharp crested and perpendicular ridges as far as the eye could reach. Could we have stepped from summit to summit of these steep but narrow elevations we could easily have accomplished the distance; but we must penetrate to the bottom of every yawning gulf, and scale in succession every one of the eminences before us. Even Toby, although not suffering as I did, was not proof against the disheartening influences of the sight.

But we did not long stand to contemplate it, impatient as I was to reach the waters of the torrent which flowed beneath us. With an insensibility to danger which I cannot call to mind without shuddering, we threw ourselves down the depths of the ravine, startling its savage solitudes with the echoes produced by the falling fragments of rock we every moment dislodged from their places, careless of the insecurity of our footing, and reckless whether the slight roots and twigs we clutched at sustained us for the while, or treacherously yielded to our grasp. For my own part, I scarcely knew whether I was helplessly falling from the heights above, or whether the fearful rapidity with which I descended was an act of my own volition.

In a few minutes we reached the foot of the gorge, and kneeling upon a small ledge of dripping rocks, I bent over to the stream. What a delicious sensation was I now to experience! I paused for a second to concentrate all my capabilities of enjoyment, and then immerged my lips in the clear element before me. Had the apples of Sodom turned to ashes in my mouth, I could not have felt a more startling revulsion. A single drop of the cold fluid seemed to freeze every drop of blood in my body; the fever that had been

burning in my veins gave place on the instant to deathlike chills, which shook me one after another like so many
shocks of electricity, while the perspiration produced by
my late violent exertions congealed in icy beads upon my
forehead. My thirst was gone, and I fairly loathed the
water. Starting to my feet, the sight of those dank rocks,
oozing forth moisture at every crevice, and the dark stream
shooting along its dismal channel, sent fresh chills through
my shivering frame, and I felt as uncontrollable a desire
to climb up towards the genial sunlight as I before had to
descend the ravine.

After two hours' perilous exertions we stood upon the
summit of another ridge, and it was with difficulty I could
bring myself to believe that we had ever penetrated the
black and yawning chasm which then gaped at our feet.
Again we gazed upon the prospect which the height commanded, but it was just as depressing as the one which had
before met our eyes. I now felt that in our present situation it was in vain for us to think of ever overcoming the
obstacles in our way, and I gave up all thoughts of reaching the vale which lay beyond this series of impediments;
while at the same time I could not devise any scheme to
extricate ourselves from the difficulties in which we were
involved.

The remotest idea of returning to Nukuheva, unless
assured of our vessel's departure, never once entered my
mind, and indeed it was questionable whether we could
have succeeded in reaching it, divided as we were from the
bay by a distance we could not compute, and perplexed too
in our remembrance of localities by our recent wanderings. Besides, it was unendurable the thought of retracing
our steps and rendering all our painful exertions of no
avail.

There is scarcely anything when a man is in difficulties

that he is more disposed to look upon with abhorrence than a right-about retrograde movement—a systematic going over of the already trodden ground; and especially if he has a love of adventure, such a course appears indescribably repulsive, so long as there remains the least hope to be derived from braving untried difficulties.

It was this feeling that prompted us to descend the opposite side of the elevation we had just scaled, although with what definite object in view it would have been impossible for either of us to tell.

Without exchanging a syllable upon the subject, Toby and myself simultaneously renounced the design which had lured us thus far—perceiving in each other's countenances that desponding expression which speaks more eloquently than words.

Together we stood towards the close of this weary day in the cavity of the third gorge we had entered, wholly incapacitated for any further exertion, until restored to some degree of strength by food and repose.

We seated ourselves upon the least uncomfortable spot we could select, and Toby produced from the bosom of his frock the sacred package. In silence we partook of the small morsel of refreshment that had been left from the morning's repast, and without once proposing to violate the sanctity of our engagement with respect to the remainder, we rose to our feet, and proceeded to construct some sort of shelter under which we might obtain the sleep we so greatly needed.

Fortunately the spot was better adapted to our purpose than the one in which we had passed the last wretched night. We cleared away the tall reeds from a small but almost level bit of ground, and twisted them into a low basket-like hut, which we covered with a profusion of long thick leaves, gathered from a tree near at hand. We disposed them thickly all around, reserving only a slight opening that barely permitted us to crawl under the shelter we had thus obtained.

These deep recesses, though protected from the winds that assail the summits of their lofty sides, are damp and chill to a degree that one would hardly anticipate in such a climate; and being unprovided with anything but our woollen frocks and thin duck trousers to resist the cold of the place, we were the more solicitous to render our habitation for the night as comfortable as we could. Accordingly, in addition to what we had already done, we plucked down all the leaves within our reach and threw them in a heap over our little hut, into which we now crept, raking after us a reserved supply to form our couch.

That night nothing but the pain I suffered prevented me from sleeping most refreshingly. As it was, I caught two or three naps, while Toby slept away at my side as soundly as though he had been sandwiched between two Holland sheets. Luckily it did not rain, and we were preserved from the misery which a heavy shower would have occasioned us.

In the morning I was awakened by the sonorous voice of my companion ringing in my ears and bidding me rise. I crawled out from our heap of leaves, and was astonished at the change which a good night's rest had wrought in his appearance. He was as blithe and joyous as a young bird, and was staying the keenness of his morning's appetite by chewing the soft bark of a delicate branch he held in his hand, and he recommended the like to me as an admirable antidote against the gnawings of hunger.

For my own part, though feeling materially better than I had done the preceding evening, I could not look at the limb that had pained me so violently at intervals during the last twenty-four hours, without experiencing a sense of alarm that I strove in vain to shake off. Unwilling to disturb the flow of my comrade's spirits, I managed to stifle the complaints to which I might otherwise have given vent, and calling upon him good-humouredly to speed our banquet, I prepared myself for it by washing in the stream. This operation concluded, we swallowed, or rather absorbed, by a peculiar kind of slow sucking process, our respective morsels of nourishment, and then entered into a discussion as to the steps it was necessary for us to pursue.

"What's to be done now?" inquired I, rather dolefully.

"Descend into that same valley we descried yesterday," rejoined Toby, with a rapidity and loudness of utterance that almost led me to suspect he had been slyly devouring the broadside of an ox in some of the adjoining thickets. "What else," he continued, "remains for us to do but that, to be sure? Why, we shall both starve to a certainty if we remain here; and as to your fears of those Typees—depend upon it, it is all nonsense.

"It is impossible that the inhabitants of such a lovely place as we saw can be anything else but good fellows; and if you choose rather to perish with hunger in one of these soppy caverns, I for one prefer to chance a bold descent into the valley, and risk the consequences."

"And who is to pilot us thither," I asked, "even if we should decide upon the measure you propose? Are we to go again up and down those precipices that we crossed yesterday, until we reach the place we started from, and then take a flying leap from the cliffs to the valley?"

" 'Faith, I didn't think of that," said Toby; "sure enough, both sides of the valley appeared to be hemmed in by precipices, didn't they?"

"Yes," answered I, "as steep as the sides of a line-of-battle ship, and about a hundred times as high." My companion sank his head upon his breast and remained for a while in deep thought. Suddenly he sprang to his feet, while his eyes lighted up with that gleam of intelligence that marks the presence of some bright idea.

"Yes, yes," he exclaimed; "the streams all run in the same direction, and must necessarily flow into the valley before they reach the sea; all we have to do is just to follow this stream, and sooner or later it will lead us into the vale."

"You are right, Toby," I exclaimed, "you are right; it must conduct us thither, and quickly too; for, see with what a steep inclination the water descends."

"It does, indeed," burst forth my companion, overjoyed at my verification of his theory, "it does indeed; why, it is as plain as a pike-staff. Let us proceed at once; come, throw away all those stupid ideas about the Typees, and hurrah for the lovely valley of the Happars!"

"You will have it to be Happar, I see, my dear fellow; pray Heaven you may not find yourself deceived," observed I, with a shake of my head.

"Amen to all that, and much more," shouted Toby, rushing forward; "but Happar it is, for nothing else than Happar can it be. So glorious a valley—such forests of bread-fruit trees—such groves of cocoa-nut—such wildernesses of guava-bushes! Ah, shipmate! don't linger behind: in the name of all delightful fruits, I am dying to be at them. Come on, come on; shove ahead, there's a lively lad; never mind the rocks; kick them out of the way, as I do; and to-morrow, old fellow, take my word for it, we shall be in clover. Come on;" and so saying, he dashed along the ravine like a madman, forgetting my inability to keep up with him. In a few minutes, however, the exuberance of his spirits abated, and, pausing for a while, he permitted me to overtake him.

CHAPTER IX

Perilous Passage of the Ravine—Descent into the Valley.

THE fearless confidence of Toby was contagious, and I began to adopt the Happar side of the question. I could not, however, overcome a certain feeling of trepidation as we made our way along these gloomy solitudes. Our progress, at first comparatively easy, became more and more difficult. The bed of the watercourse was covered with fragments of broken rocks, which had fallen from above, offering so many obstructions to the course of the rapid stream, which vexed and fretted about them,—forming at intervals small waterfalls, pouring over into deep basins, or splashing wildly upon heaps of stones.

From the narrowness of the gorge, and the steepness of its sides, there was no mode of advancing but by wading through the water; stumbling every moment over the impediments which lay hidden under its surface, or tripping against the huge roots of trees. But the most annoying hindrance we encountered was from a multitude of crooked boughs, which, shooting out almost horizontally from the sides of the chasm, twisted themselves together in fantastic masses almost to the surface of the stream, affording us no passage except under the low arches which they formed. Under these we were obliged to crawl on our hands and feet, sliding along the oozy surface of the rocks, or slipping into the deep pools, and with scarce light enough to guide us. Occasionally we would strike our heads against some projecting limb of a tree; and while imprudently engaged in rubbing the injured part, would fall sprawling amongst flinty fragments, cutting and bruising ourselves, whilst the unpitying waters flowed over our prostrate bodies. Belzoni, worming himself through the subterranean passages of the Egyptian catacombs, could not have met with greater impediments than those we here encountered. But we struggled against them manfully, well knowing our only hope lay in advancing.

Towards sunset we halted at a spot where we made preparations for passing the night. Here we constructed a hut, in much the same way as before, and crawling into it, endeavoured to forget our sufferings. My companion, I believe, slept pretty soundly; but at daybreak, when we rolled out of our dwelling, I felt nearly disqualified for any further efforts. Toby prescribed as a remedy for my illness the contents of one of our little silk packages, to be taken at once in a single dose. To this species of medical treatment, however, I would by no means accede, much as he insisted upon it; and so we partook of our usual morsel, and silently resumed our journey. It was now the fourth day since we left Nukuheva, and the gnawings of hunger became painfully acute. We were fain to pacify them by chewing the tender bark of roots and twigs, which, if they did not afford us nourishment, were at least sweet and pleasant to the taste.

Our progress along the steep watercourse was necessarily slow, and by noon we had not advanced more than a mile. It was somewhere near this part of the day that the noise of falling waters, which we had faintly caught in the early morning, became more distinct; and it was not long before we were arrested by a rocky precipice of nearly a hundred feet in depth, that extended all across the channel, and over which the wild stream poured in an unbroken leap. On either hand the walls of the ravine presented their overhanging sides both above and below the fall, affording no means whatever of avoiding the cataract by taking a circuit round it.

"What's to be done now, Toby?" said I.

"Why," rejoined he, "as we cannot retreat, I suppose we must keep shoving along."

"Very true, my dear Toby; but how do you purpose accomplishing that desirable object?"

"By jumping from the top of the fall, if there be no other way," unhesitatingly replied my companion: "it will be much the quickest way of descent; but as you are not quite as active as I am, we will try some other way."

And, so saying, he crept cautiously along and peered over into the abyss, while I remained wondering by what possible means we could overcome this apparently insuperable obstruction. As soon as my companion had completed his survey, I eagerly inquired the result.

"The result of my observations you wish to know, do you?" began Toby, deliberately, with one of his odd looks: "well, my lad, the result of my observations is very quickly imparted. It is at present uncertain which of our two necks will have the honour to be broken first; but about a hundred to one would be a fair bet in favour of the man who takes the first jump."

"Then it is an impossible thing, is it?" inquired I, gloomily.

"No, shipmate; on the contrary, it is the easiest thing in life: the only awkward point is the sort of usage which our unhappy limbs may receive when we arrive at the bottom, and what sort of travelling trim we shall be in afterwards. But follow me now, and I will show you the only chance we have."

With this he conducted me to the verge of the cataract, and pointed along the side of the ravine to a number of curious looking roots, some three or four inches in thickness, and several feet long, which after twisting among the fissures of the rock, shot perpendicularly from it and ran tapering to a point in the air, hanging over the gulf like so many dark icicles. They covered nearly the entire surface of one side of the gorge, the lowest of them reaching even to the water. Many were moss-grown and decayed, with their extremities snapped short off, and those in the immediate vicinity of the fall were slippery with moisture.

Toby's scheme, and it was a desperate one, was to intrust ourselves to these treacherous-looking roots, and by slipping down from one to another to gain the bottom.

"Are you ready to venture it?" asked Toby, looking at me earnestly, but without saying a word as to the practicability of the plan.

"I am," was my reply; for I saw it was our only resource if we wished to advance, and as for retreating, all thoughts of that sort had been long abandoned.

After I had signified my assent, Toby, without uttering a single word, crawled along the dripping ledge until he gained a point from whence he could just reach one of the largest of the pendant roots; he shook it—it quivered in his grasp, and when he let it go it twanged in the air like a strong wire sharply struck. Satisfied by his scrutiny, my light-limbed companion swung himself nimbly upon it, and twisting his legs round it in sailor fashion, slipped down eight or ten feet, where his weight gave it a motion not unlike that of a pendulum. He could not venture to descend any further; so holding on with one hand, he with the other shook one by one all the slender roots around him, and at last, finding one which he thought trustworthy, shifted himself to it and continued his downward progress.

So far so well; but I could not avoid comparing my heavier frame and disabled condition with his light figure and remarkable activity; but there was no help for it, and in less than a minute's time I was swinging directly over his head. As soon as his upturned eyes caught a glimpse of me, he exclaimed in his usual dry tone, for the danger did not seem to daunt him in the least, "Mate, do me the kindness not to fall until I get out of your way;" and then swinging himself more on one side, he continued his descent. In the mean time I cautiously transferred myself from the limb down which I had been slipping to a couple of others that were near it, deeming two strings to my bow better than one, and taking care to test their strength before I trusted my weight to them.

On arriving towards the end of the second stage in this vertical journey, and shaking the long roots which were round me, to my consternation they snapped off one after another like so many pipe stems, and fell in fragments against the side of the gulf, splashing at last into the waters beneath.

As one after another the treacherous roots yielded to my grasp, and fell into the torrent, my heart sunk within me. The branches on which I was suspended over the yawning chasm swang to and fro in the air, and I expected them every moment to snap in twain. Appalled at the dreadful fate that menaced me, I clutched frantically at the only large root which remained near me, but in vain; I could not reach it, though my fingers were within a few inches of it. Again and again I tried to reach it, until at length, maddened with the thought of my situation, I swayed myself violently by striking my foot against the side of the rock, and at the instant that I approached the large root caught desperately at it, and transferred myself to it. It vibrated violently under the sudden weight, but fortunately did not give way.

My brain grew dizzy with the idea of the frightful risk I had just run, and I involuntarily closed my eyes to shut out the view of the depth beneath me. For the instant I was safe, and I uttered a devout ejaculation of thanksgiving for my escape.

"Pretty well done," shouted Toby underneath me; "you are nimbler than I thought you to be—hopping about up there from root to root like any young squirrel. As soon as you have diverted yourself sufficiently, I would advise you to proceed."

"Aye aye, Toby, all in good time: two or three more such famous roots as this, and I shall be with you."

The residue of my downward progress was comparatively easy; the roots were in greater abundance, and in one or two places jutting out points of rock assisted me greatly. In a few moments I was standing by the side of my companion.

Substituting a stout stick for the one I had thrown aside at the top of the precipice, we now continued our course along the bed of the ravine. Soon we were saluted by a sound in advance, that grew by degrees louder and louder, as the noise of the cataract we were leaving behind gradually died on our ears.

"Another precipice for us, Toby."

"Very good; we can descend them, you know—come on."

Nothing indeed appeared to depress or intimidate this intrepid fellow. Typees or Niagaras, he was as ready to engage one as the other, and I could not avoid a thousand times congratulating myself upon having such a companion in an enterprise like the present.

After an hour's painful progress, we reached the verge of another fall, still loftier than the preceding, and flanked both above and below with the same steep masses of rock, presenting, however, here and there narrow irregular ledges, supporting a shallow soil, on which grew a variety of bushes and trees, whose bright verdure contrasted beautifully with the foamy waters that flowed between them.

Toby, who invariably acted as pioneer, now proceeded to reconnoitre. On his return, he reported that the shelves of rock on our right would enable us to gain with little risk the bottom of the cataract. Accordingly, leaving the bed of the stream at the very point where it thundered down, we began crawling along one of these sloping ledges until it carried us to within a few feet of another that inclined downward at a still sharper angle, and upon which, by assisting each other, we managed to alight in safety. We warily crept along this, steadying ourselves by the naked roots of the shrubs that clung to every fissure. As we proceeded, the narrow path became still more contracted, rendering it difficult for us to maintain our footing, until suddenly, as we reached an angle of the wall of rock where we had expected it to widen, we perceived to our consternation that a yard or two farther on it abruptly terminated at a place we could not possibly hope to pass.

Toby as usual led the van, and in silence I waited to learn from him how he proposed to extricate us from this new difficulty.

"Well, my boy," I exclaimed, after the expiration of several minutes, during which time my companion had not uttered a word; "what's to be done now?"

He replied in a tranquil tone, that probably the best thing we could do in our present strait was to get out of it as soon as possible.

"Yes, my dear Toby, but tell me *how* we are to get out of it."

"Something in this sort of style," he replied; and at the same moment to my horror he slipped sideways off the rock, and as I then thought, by good fortune merely alighted among the spreading branches of a species of palm tree, that shooting its hardy roots along a ledge below, curved its trunk upwards into the air, and presented a thick mass of foliage about twenty feet below the spot where we had thus suddenly been brought to a stand still. I involuntarily held my breath, expecting to see the form of my companion, after being sustained for a moment by the branches of the tree, sink through their frail support, and fall headlong to the bottom. To my surprise and joy, however, he recovered himself, and disentangling his limbs from the fractured branches, he peered out from his leafy bed, and shouted lustily, "Come on, my hearty, there is no other alternative!" and with this he ducked beneath the foliage, and slipping down the trunk, stood in a moment at least fifty feet beneath me, upon the broad shelf of rock from which sprung the tree he had descended.

What would I not have given at that moment to have been by his side! The feat he had just accomplished seemed little less than miraculous, and I could hardly credit the evidence of my senses when I saw the wide distance that a single daring act had so suddenly placed between us.

Toby's animating "come on!" again sounded in my ears, and dreading to lose all confidence in myself if I remained meditating upon the step, I once more gazed down to assure myself of the relative bearing of the tree and my own position, and then closing my eyes and uttering one comprehensive ejaculation of prayer, I inclined myself over towards the abyss, and after one breathless instant fell with a crash into the tree, the branches snapping and crackling with my weight, as I sunk lower and lower among them, until I was stopped by coming in contact with a sturdy limb.

In a few moments I was standing at the foot of the tree, manipulating myself all over with a view of ascertaining the extent of the injuries I had received. To my surprise the only effects of my feat were a few slight contusions too trifling to care about. The rest of our descent was easily accomplished, and in half an hour after regaining the ravine we had partaken of our evening morsel, built our hut as usual, and crawled under its shelter.

The next morning, in spite of our debility and the agony of hunger under which we were now suffering, though neither of us confessed to the fact, we struggled along our dismal and still difficult and dangerous path, cheered by the hope of soon catching a glimpse of the valley before us, and towards evening the voice of a cataract which had for some time sounded like a low deep bass to the music of the smaller waterfalls, broke upon our ears in still louder tones, and assured us that we were approaching its vicinity.

That evening we stood on the brink of a precipice, over which the dark stream bounded in one final leap of full 300 feet. The sheer descent terminated in the region we so long had sought. On either side of the fall, two lofty and perpendicular bluffs buttressed the sides of the enormous cliff, and projected into the sea of verdure with which the valley waved, and a range of similar projecting eminences stood disposed in a half circle about the head of the vale. A thick canopy of traces hung over the very verge of the fall, leaving an arched aperture for the passage of the waters, which imparted a strange picturesqueness to the scene.

The valley was now before us; but instead of being conducted into its smiling bosom by the gradual descent of the deep watercourse we had thus far pursued, all our labours now appeared to have been rendered futile by its abrupt termination. But, bitterly disappointed, we did not entirely despair.

As it was now near sunset we determined to pass the night where we were, and on the morrow, refreshed by sleep and by eating at one meal all our stock of food, to accomplish a descent into the valley, or perish in the attempt.

We laid ourselves down that night on a spot, the recollection of which still makes me shudder. A small table of rock which projected over the precipice on one side of the stream, and was drenched by the spray of the fall, sustained a huge trunk of a tree which must have been deposited there by some heavy freshet. It lay obliquely, with one end resting on the rock and the other supported by the side of the ravine. Against it we placed in a sloping direction a number of the half decayed boughs that were strewn about, and covering the whole with twigs and leaves, awaited the morning's light beneath such shelter as it afforded.

During the whole of this night the continual roaring of the cataract—the dismal moaning of the gale through the trees—the pattering of the rain, and the profound darkness, affected my spirits to a degree which nothing had ever before produced. Wet, half famished, and chilled to the heart with the dampness of the place, and nearly wild with the pain I endured, I fairly cowered down to the earth under this multiplication of hardships, and abandoned myself to frightful anticipations of evil; and my companion, whose spirit at last was a good deal broken, scarcely uttered a word during the whole night.

At length the day dawned upon us, and rising from our miserable pallet, we stretched our stiffened joints, and after eating all that remained of our bread, prepared for the last stage of our journey.

I will not recount every hair breadth escape, and every fearful difficulty that occurred before we succeeded in reaching the bosom of the valley. As I have already described similar scenes, it will be sufficient to say that at length, after great toil and great dangers, we both stood with no limbs broken at the head of that magnificent vale which five days before had so suddenly burst upon my sight, and almost beneath the shadows of those very cliffs from whose summits we had gazed upon the prospect.

CHAPTER X

The Head of the Valley—Cautious Advance—A Path—Fruit—Discovery of Two of the Natives—Their singular Conduct—Approach towards the inhabited Parts of the Vale—Sensation produced by our Appearance—Reception at the House of one of the Natives.

How to obtain the fruit which we felt convinced must grow near at hand was our first thought.

Typee or Happar? A frightful death at the hands of the fiercest of cannibals, or a kindly reception from a gentler race of savages? Which? But it was too late now to discuss a question which would so soon be answered.

The part of the valley in which we found ourselves appeared to be altogether uninhabited. An almost impenetrable thicket extended from side to side, without presenting a single plant affording the nourishment we had confidently calculated upon; and with this object, we followed the course of the stream, casting quick glances as we proceeded into the thick jungles on either hand.

My companion—to whose solicitations I had yielded in descending into the valley—now that the step was taken, began to manifest a degree of caution I had little expected from him. He proposed that, in the event of our finding an adequate supply of fruit, we should remain in this unfrequented portion of the country—where we should run little chance of being surprised by its occupants, whoever they might be—until sufficiently recruited to resume our journey; when laying in a store of food equal to our wants, we might easily regain the bay of Nukuheva, after the lapse of a sufficient interval to ensure the departure of our vessel.

I objected strongly to this proposition, plausible as it was, as the difficulties of the route would be almost insurmountable, unacquainted as we were with the general bearings of the country, and I reminded my companion of the hardships which we had already encountered in our uncertain wanderings; in a word, I said that since we had deemed it advisable to enter the valley, we ought manfully to face the consequences, whatever they might be; the more especially as I was convinced there was no alternative left us but to fall in with the natives at once, and boldly risk the reception they might give us: and that as to myself, I felt the necessity of rest and shelter, and that until I had obtained them I should be wholly unable to encounter such sufferings as we had lately passed through. To the justice of these observations Toby somewhat reluctantly assented.

We were surprised that, after moving as far as we had along the valley, we should still meet with the same impervious thickets; and thinking that although the borders of the stream might be lined for some distance with them, yet beyond there might be more open ground, I requested Toby to keep a bright look-out upon one side, while I did the same on the other, in order to discover some opening in the bushes, and especially to watch for the slightest appearance of a path or anything else that might indicate the vicinity of the islanders.

What furtive and anxious glances we cast into those dim-looking shades! With what apprehensions we proceeded, ignorant at what moment we might be greeted by the javelin of some ambushed savage! At last my companion paused, and directed my attention to a narrow opening in the foliage. We struck into it and it soon brought us by an indistinctly traced path to a comparatively clear space, at the further end of which we descried a number of the trees, the native name of which is "annuee," and which bear a most delicious fruit.

What a race! I hobbling over the ground like some decrepid wretch, and Toby leaping forward like a greyhound. He quickly cleared one of the trees on which there were two or three of the fruit, but to our chagrin they proved to be much decayed; the rinds partly opened by the birds, and their hearts half devoured. However, we quickly despatched them, and no ambrosia could have been more delicious.

We looked about us uncertain whither to direct our steps, since the path we had so far followed appeared to be lost in the open space around us. At last we resolved to enter a grove near at hand, and had advanced a few rods when, just upon its skirts, I picked up a slender bread-fruit shoot perfectly green, and with the tender bark freshly stript from it. It was still slippery with moisture, and appeared as if it had been but that moment thrown aside. I said nothing, but merely held it up to Toby, who started at this undeniable evidence of the vicinity of the savages.

The plot was now thickening.—A short distance further lay a little faggot of the same shoots bound together with a strip of bark. Could it have been thrown down by some solitary native who, alarmed at seeing us, had hurried forward to carry the tidings of our approach to his countrymen?—Typee or Happar?—But it was too late to recede, so we moved on slowly, my companion in advance casting eager glances under the trees on either side, until all at once I saw him recoil as if stung by an adder. Sinking on his knee, he waved me off with one hand, while with the other he held aside some intervening leaves and gazed intently at some object.

Disregarding his injunction, I quickly approached him and caught a glimpse of two figures partly hidden by the dense foliage; they were standing close together, and were perfectly motionless. They must have previously perceived us, and withdrawn into the depths of the wood to elude our observation.

My mind was at once made up. Dropping my staff, and tearing open the package of things we had brought from the ship, I unrolled the cotton cloth, and holding it in one hand plucked with the other a twig from the bushes beside me, and telling Toby to follow my example, I broke through the covert and advanced, waving the branch in token of peace towards the shrinking forms before me.

They were a boy and girl, slender and graceful, and completely naked, with the exception of a slight girdle of bark, from which depended at opposite points two of the russet leaves of the bread-fruit tree. An arm of the boy, half screened from sight by her wild tresses, was thrown about the neck of the girl, while with the other he held one of her hands in his; and thus they stood together, their heads inclined forward, catching the faint noise we made in our progress, and with one foot in advance, as if half inclined to fly from our presence.

As we drew near their alarm evidently increased. Apprehensive that they might fly from us altogether, I stopped short and motioned them to advance and receive the gift I extended towards them, but they would not; I then uttered a few words of their language with which I was acquainted, scarcely expecting that they would understand me, but to show that we had not dropped from the clouds upon them. This appeared to give them a little confidence, so I approached nearer, presenting the cloth with one hand and holding the bough with the other, while they slowly retreated. At last they suffered us to approach so near to them that we were enabled to throw the cotton cloth across their shoulders, giving them to understand that it was theirs, and by a variety of gestures endeavouring to make them understand that we entertained the highest possible regard for them.

The frightened pair now stood still, whilst we endeavoured to make them comprehend the nature of our wants. In doing this Toby went through with a complete series of pantomimic illustrations—opening his mouth from ear to ear, and thrusting his fingers down his throat, gnashing his teeth and rolling his eyes about, till I verily believe the poor creatures took us for a couple of white cannibals who were about to make a meal of them. When, however, they understood us, they showed no inclination to relieve our wants. At this juncture it began to rain violently, and we motioned them to lead us to some place of shelter. With this request they appeared willing to comply, but nothing could evince more strongly the apprehension with which they regarded us, than the way in which, whilst walking before us, they kept their eyes constantly turned back to watch every movement we made, and even our very looks.

"Typee or Happar, Toby?" asked I as we walked after them.

"Of course Happar," he replied with a show of confidence which was intended to disguise his doubts.

"We shall soon know," I exclaimed; and at the same moment I stepped forward towards our guides, and pronouncing the two names interrogatively and pointing to the lowest part of the valley, endeavoured to come to the point at once. They repeated the words after me again and again, but without giving any peculiar emphasis to either, so that I was completely at a loss to understand them; for a couple of wilier young things than we afterwards found them to have been on this particular occasion never probably fell in any traveller's way.

More and more curious to ascertain our fate, I now threw together in the form of a question the words "Happar" and "Mortarkee," the latter being equivalent to the word "good." The two natives interchanged glances of peculiar meaning with one another at this, and manifested no little surprise; but on the repetition of the question, after some consultation together, to the great joy of Toby, they answered in the affirmative. Toby was now in ecstasies, especially as the young savages continued to reiterate their answer with great energy, as though desirous of impressing us with the idea that being among the Happars, we ought to consider ourselves perfectly secure.

Although I had some lingering doubts, I feigned great delight with Toby at this announcement, while my companion broke out into a pantomimic abhorrence of Typee, and immeasurable love for the particular valley in which we were; our guides all the while gazing uneasily at one another as if at a loss to account for our conduct.

They hurried on, and we followed them; until suddenly they set up a strange halloo, which was answered from beyond the grove through which we were passing, and the next moment we entered upon some open ground, at the extremity of which we descried a long, low hut, and in front of it were several young girls. As soon as they perceived us they fled with wild screams into the adjoining thickets, like so many startled fawns. A few moments after the whole valley resounded with savage outcries, and the natives came running towards us from every direction.

Had an army of invaders made an irruption into their territory they could not have evinced greater excitement. We were soon completely encircled by a dense throng, and in their eager desire to behold us they almost arrested our progress; an equal number surrounding our youthful guides, who with amazing volubility appeared to be detailing the circumstances which had attended their meeting with us. Every item of intelligence appeared to redouble the astonishment of the islanders, and they gazed at us with inquiring looks.

At last we reached a large and handsome building of bamboos, and were by signs told to enter it, the natives opening a lane for us through which to pass; on entering without ceremony, we threw our exhausted frames upon the mats that covered the floor. In a moment the slight tenement was completely full of people, whilst those who were unable to obtain admittance gazed at us through its open cane-work.

It was now evening, and by the dim light we could just discern the savage countenances around us, gleaming with wild curiosity and wonder; the naked forms and tattooed limbs of brawny warriors, with here and there the slighter figures of young girls, all engaged in a perfect storm of conversation, of which we were of course the one only theme; whilst our recent guides were fully occupied in answering the innumerable questions which every one put to them. Nothing can exceed the fierce gesticulation of these people when animated in conversation, and on this occasion they gave loose to all their natural vivacity, shouting and dancing about in a manner that well-nigh intimidated us.

Close to where we lay, squatting upon their haunches, were some eight or ten noble-looking chiefs—for such they subsequently proved to be—who, more reserved than the rest, regarded us with a fixed and stern attention, which not a little discomposed our equanimity. One of them in particular, who appeared to be the highest in rank, placed himself directly facing me; looking at me with a rigidity of aspect under which I absolutely quailed. He never once opened his lips, but maintained his severe expression of countenance, without turning his face aside for a single moment. Never before had I been subjected to so strange and steady a glance; it revealed nothing of the mind of the savage, but it appeared to be reading my own.

After undergoing this scrutiny till I grew absolutely nervous, with a view of diverting it if possible, and conciliating the good opinion of the warrior, I took some tobacco from the bosom of my frock and offered it to him. He quietly rejected the proffered gift, and, without speaking, motioned me to return it to its place.

In my previous intercourse with the natives of Nukuheva and Tior, I had found that the present of a small piece of tobacco would have rendered any of them devoted to my service. Was this act of the chief a token of his enmity? Typee or Happar? I asked within myself. I started, for at the same moment this identical question was asked by the strange being before me. I turned to Toby; the flickering light of a native taper showed me his countenance pale with trepidation at this fatal question. I paused for a second, and I know not by what impulse it was that I answered "Typee." The piece of dusky statuary nodded in approval, and then murmured "Mortarkee!" "Mortarkee," said I, without further hesitation—"Typee mortarkee."

What a transition! The dark figures around us leaped to their feet, clapped their hands in transport, and shouted again and again the talismanic syllables, the utterance of which appeared to have settled every thing.

When this commotion had a little subsided, the principal chief squatted once more before me, and throwing himself into a sudden rage, poured forth a string of philippics, which I was at no loss to understand, from the frequent recurrence of the word Happar, as being directed against the natives of the adjoining valley. In all these denunciations my companion and I acquiesced, while we extolled the character of the warlike Typees. To be sure our panegyrics were somewhat laconic, consisting in the repetition of that name, united with the potent adjective "mortarkee." But this was sufficient, and served to conciliate the good will of the natives, with whom our congeniality of sentiment on this point did more towards inspiring a friendly feeling than anything else that could have happened.

At last the wrath of the chief evaporated, and in a few moments he was as placid as ever. Laying his hand upon his breast, he now gave me to understand that his name was "Mehevi," and that, in return, he wished me to communicate my appellation. I hesitated for an instant, thinking that it might be difficult for him to pronounce my real name, and then with the most praiseworthy intentions intimated that I was known as "Tom." But I could not have made a worse selection; the chief could not master it: "Tommo," "Tomma," "Tommee," every thing but plain "Tom." As he persisted in garnishing the word with an additional syllable, I compromised the matter with him at the word "Tommo;" and by that name I went during the entire period of my stay in the valley. The same proceeding was gone through with Toby, whose mellifluous appellation was more easily caught.

An exchange of names is equivalent to a ratification of good will and amity among these simple people; and as we were aware of this fact, we were delighted that it had taken place on the present occasion.

Reclining upon our mats, we now held a kind of levee, giving audience to successive troops of the natives, who introduced themselves to us by pronouncing their respective names, and retired in high good humour on receiving ours in return. During this ceremony the greatest merriment prevailed, nearly every announcement on the part of the islanders being followed by a fresh sally of gaiety, which induced me to believe that some of them at least were innocently diverting the company at our expense, by bestowing upon themselves a string of absurd titles, of the humour of which we were of course entirely ignorant.

All this occupied about an hour, when the throng having a little diminished, I turned to Mehevi and gave him to understand that we were in need of food and sleep. Immediately the attentive chief addressed a few words to one of the crowd, who disappeared, and returned in a few moments with a calabash of "poee-poee," and two or three young cocoa-nuts stripped of their husks, and with their shells partly broken. We both of us forthwith placed one of these natural goblets to our lips, and drained it in a moment of the refreshing draught it contained. The poee-poee was then placed before us, and even famished as I was, I paused to consider in what manner to convey it to my mouth.

This staple article of food among the Marquese islanders is manufactured from the produce of the bread-fruit tree. It somewhat resembles in its plastic nature our book-binders' paste, is of a yellow colour, and somewhat tart to the taste.

Such was the dish, the merits of which I was now eager to discuss. I eyed it wistfully for a moment, and then unable any longer to stand on ceremony, plunged my hand into the yielding mass, and to the boisterous mirth of the natives drew it forth laden with the poee-poee, which adhered in lengthy strings to every finger. So stubborn was its consistency, that in conveying my heavily-freighted hand to my mouth, the connecting links almost raised the calabash from the mats on which it had been placed. This display of awkwardness—in which, by-the-bye, Toby kept me company—convulsed the bystanders with uncontrollable laughter.

As soon as their merriment had somewhat subsided, Mehevi, motioning us to be attentive, dipped the fore finger of his right hand in the dish, and giving it a rapid and scientific twirl, drew it out coated smoothly with the preparation. With a second peculiar flourish he prevented the poee-poee from dropping to the ground as he raised it to his mouth, into which the finger was inserted and drawn forth perfectly free from any adhesive matter. This performance was evidently intended for our instruction; so I again essayed the feat on the principles inculcated, but with very ill success.

A starving man, however, little heeds conventional proprieties, especially on a South-Sea Island, and accordingly Toby and I partook of the dish after our own clumsy fashion, beplastering our faces all over with the glutinous compound, and daubing our hands nearly to the wrist. This kind of food is by no means disagreeable to the palate of a European, though at first the mode of eating it may be. For my own part, after the lapse of a few days I became accustomed to its singular flavour, and grew remarkably fond of it.

So much for the first course; several other dishes followed it, some of which were positively delicious. We concluded our banquet by tossing off the contents of two more young cocoa-nuts, after which we regaled ourselves with the soothing fumes of tobacco, inhaled from a quaintly carved pipe which passed round the circle.

During the repast, the natives eyed us with intense curiosity, observing our minutest motions, and appearing to discover abundant matter for comment in the most trifling occurrence. Their surprise mounted the highest, when we began to remove our uncomfortable garments, which were saturated with rain. They scanned the whiteness of our limbs, and seemed utterly unable to account for the contrast they presented to the swarthy hue of our faces, embrowned from a six months' exposure to the scorching sun of the Line. They felt our skin, much in the same way that a silk mercer would handle a remarkably fine piece of satin; and some of them went so far in their investigation as to apply the olfactory organ.

Their singular behaviour almost led me to imagine that they never before had beheld a white man; but a few moments' reflection convinced me that this could not have been the case; and a more satisfactory reason for their conduct has since suggested itself to my mind.

Deterred by the frightful stories related of its inhabitants, ships never enter this bay, while their hostile relations with the tribes in the adjoining valleys prevent the Typees from visiting that section of the island where vessels occasionally lie. At long intervals, however, some intrepid captain will touch on the skirts of the bay, with two or three armed boats' crews, and accompanied by an interpreter. The natives who live near the sea descry the strangers long before they reach their waters, and aware of the purpose for which they come, proclaim loudly the news of their approach. By a species of vocal telegraph the intelligence reaches the inmost recesses of the vale in an inconceivably short space of time, drawing nearly its whole population down to the beach laden with every variety of fruit. The interpreter, who is invariably a "tabooed Kannaka," leaps ashore with the goods intended for barter, while the boats, with their oars shipped, and every man on his thwart, lie just outside the surf, heading off from the shore, in readiness at the first untoward event to escape to the open sea. As soon as the traffic is concluded, one of the boats pulls in under cover of the muskets of the others, the fruit is quickly thrown into her, and the transient visitors precipitately retire from what they justly consider so dangerous a vicinity.

The intercourse occuring with Europeans being so restricted, no wonder that the inhabitants of the valley manifested so much curiosity with regard to us, appearing as we did among them under such singular circumstances. I have no doubt that we were the first white men who ever penetrated thus far back into their territories, or at least the first who had ever descended from the head of the vale. What had brought us thither must have appeared a complete mystery to them, and from our ignorance of the language it was impossible for us to enlighten them. In answer to inquiries which the eloquence of their gestures enabled us to comprehend, all that we could reply was, that we had come from Nukuheva, a place, be it remembered, with which they were at open war. This intelligence appeared to affect them with the most lively emotions. "Nukuheva mortarkee?" they asked. Of course we replied most energetically in the negative.

They then plied us with a thousand questions, of which we could understand nothing more than that they had reference to the recent movements of the French, against whom they seemed to cherish the most fierce hatred. So eager were they to obtain information on this point, that they still continued to propound their queries long after we had shown that we were utterly unable to answer them. Occasionally we caught some indistinct idea of their meaning, when we would endeavour by every method in our power to communicate the desired intelligence. At such times their gratification was boundless, and they would redouble their efforts to make us comprehend them more perfectly. But all in vain; and in the end they looked at us despairingly, as if we were the receptacles of invaluable information; but how to come at it they knew not.

After a while the group around us gradually dispersed, and we were left about midnight (as we conjectured) with those who appeared to be permanent residents of the house. These individuals now provided us with fresh mats to lie upon, covered us with several folds of tappa, and then extinguishing the tapers that had been burning, threw themselves down beside us, and after a little desultory conversation were soon sound asleep.

CHAPTER XI

Midnight Reflections—Morning Visitors—A Warrior in Costume—
   A Savage Æsculapius—Practice of the Healing Art—Body Serv-
   ant—A Dwelling-house of the Valley described—Portraits of its
   Inmates.

VARIOUS and conflicting were the thoughts which oppressed me during the silent hours that followed the events related in the preceding chapter. Toby, wearied with the fatigues of the day, slumbered heavily by my side; but the pain under which I was suffering effectually prevented my sleeping, and I remained distressingly alive to all the fearful circumstances of our present situation. Was it possible that, after all our vicissitudes, we were really in the terrible valley of Typee, and at the mercy of its inmates, a fierce and unrelenting tribe of savages?

Typee or Happar? I shuddered when I reflected that there was no longer any room for doubt; and that, beyond all hope of escape, we were now placed in those very circumstances from the bare thought of which I had recoiled with such abhorrence but a few days before. What might not be our fearful destiny? To be sure, as yet we had been treated with no violence; nay, had been even kindly and hospitably entertained. But what dependence could be placed upon the fickle passions which sway the bosom of a savage? His inconstancy and treachery are proverbial. Might it not be that beneath these fair appearances the islanders covered some perfidious design, and that their friendly reception of us might only precede some horrible catastrophe? How strongly did these forebodings spring up in my mind as I lay restlessly upon a couch of mats, surrounded by the dimly revealed forms of those whom I so greatly dreaded.

From the excitement of these fearful thoughts I sank towards morning into an uneasy slumber; and on awaking, with a start, in the midst of an appalling dream, looked up into the eager countenances of a number of the natives, who were bending over me.

It was broad day; and the house was nearly filled with young females, fancifully decorated with flowers, who gazed upon me as I rose with faces in which childish delight and curiosity were vividly pourtrayed. After waking Toby, they seated themselves round us on the mats, and gave full play to that prying inquisitiveness which time out of mind has been attributed to the adorable sex.

As these unsophisticated young creatures were attended by no jealous duennas, their proceedings were altogether informal, and void of artificial restraint. Long and minute was the investigation with which they honoured us, and so uproarious their mirth, that I felt infinitely sheepish; and Toby was immeasurably outraged at their familiarity.

These lively young ladies were at the same time wonderfully polite and humane; fanning aside the insects that occasionally lighted on our brows; presenting us with food; and compassionately regarding me in the midst of my afflictions. But in spite of all their blandishments, my feelings of propriety were exceedingly shocked, for I could not but consider them as having overstepped the due limits of female decorum.

Having diverted themselves to their heart's content, our young visitants now withdrew, and gave place to successive troops of the other sex, who continued flocking towards the house until near noon; by which time I have no doubt that the greater part of the inhabitants of the valley had bathed themselves in the light of our benignant countenances.

At last, when their numbers began to diminish, a superb-looking warrior stooped the towering plumes of his head-dress beneath the low portal, and entered the house. I saw at once that he was some distinguished personage, the natives regarding him with the utmost deference, and making room for him as he approached. His aspect was imposing. The splendid long drooping tail-feathers of the tropical bird, thickly interspersed with the gaudy plumage of the cock, were disposed in an immense upright semicircle upon his head, their lower extremities being fixed in a crescent of guinea-beads which spanned the forehead. Around his neck were several enormous necklaces of boars' tusks, polished like ivory, and disposed in such a manner as that the longest and largest were upon his capacious chest. Thrust forward through the large apertures in his ears were two small and finely shaped sperm-whale teeth, presenting their cavities in front, stuffed with freshly-plucked leaves, and curiously wrought at the other end into strange little images and devices. These barbaric trinkets, garnished in this manner at their open extremities, and tapering and curving round to a point behind the ear, resembled not a little a pair of cornucopias.

The loins of the warrior were girt about with heavy folds of a dark-coloured tappa, hanging before and behind in clusters of braided tassels, while anklets and bracelets of curling human hair completed his unique costume. In his right hand he grasped a beautifully carved paddle-spear, nearly fifteen feet in length, made of the bright koar-wood, one end sharply pointed, and the other flattened like an oar-blade. Hanging obliquely from his girdle by a loop of sinnate was a richly decorated pipe; the slender reed forming its stem was coloured with a red pigment, and round it, as well as the idol-bowl, fluttered little streamers of the thinnest tappa.

But that which was most remarkable in the appearance of the splendid islander was the elaborated tattooing displayed on every noble limb. All imaginable lines and curves and figures were delineated over his whole body, and in their grotesque variety and infinite profusion I could only compare them to the crowded groupings of quaint patterns we sometimes see in costly pieces of lace-work. The most simple and remarkable of all these ornaments was that which decorated the countenance of the chief. Two broad stripes of tattooing, diverging from the centre of his shaven crown, obliquely crossed both eyes—staining the lids—to a little below either ear, where they united with another stripe which swept in a straight line along the lips and formed the base of the triangle. The warrior, from the excellence of his physical proportions, might certainly have been regarded as one of Nature's noblemen, and the lines drawn upon his face may possibly have denoted his exalted rank.

This warlike personage, upon entering the house, seated himself at some distance from the spot where Toby and myself reposed, while the rest of the savages looked alternately from us to him, as if in expectation of something they were disappointed in not perceiving. Regarding the chief attentively, I thought his lineaments appeared familiar to me. As soon as his full face was turned upon me, and I again beheld its extraordinary embellishment, and met the strange gaze to which I had been subjected the preceding night, I immediately, in spite of the alteration in his appearance, recognised the noble Mehevi. On addressing him, he advanced at once in the most cordial manner, and, greeting me warmly, seemed to enjoy not a little the effect his barbaric costume had produced upon me.

I forthwith determined to secure, if possible, the good will of this individual, as I easily perceived he was a man of great authority in his tribe, and one who might exert a powerful influence upon our subsequent fate. In the endeavour I was not repulsed; for nothing could surpass the friendliness he manifested towards both my companion and myself. He extended his sturdy limbs by our side, and endeavoured to make us comprehend the full extent of the kindly feelings by which he was actuated. The almost insuperable difficulty in communicating to one another our ideas affected the chief with no little mortification. He evinced a great desire to be enlightened with regard to the customs and peculiarities of the far-off country we had left behind us, and to which under the name of Maneeka he frequently alluded.

But that which more than any other subject engaged his attention was the late proceedings of the "Franee," as he called the French, in the neighbouring bay of Nukuheva.

This seemed a never-ending theme with him, and one concerning which he was never weary of interrogating us. All the information we succeeded in imparting to him on this subject was little more than that we had seen six men-of-war lying in the hostile bay at the time we had left it. When he received this intelligence, Mehevi, by the aid of his fingers, went through a long numerical calculation, as if estimating the number of Frenchmen the squadron might contain.

It was just after employing his faculties in this way that he happened to notice the swelling in my limb. He immediately examined it with the utmost attention, and after doing so despatched a boy who happened to be standing by with some message.

After the lapse of a few moments the stripling re-entered the house with an aged islander, who might have been taken for old Hippocrates himself. His head was as bald as the polished surface of a cocoa-nut shell, which article it precisely resembled in smoothness and colour, while a long silvery beard swept almost to his girdle of bark. Encircling his temples was a bandeau of the twisted leaves of the Omoo tree, pressed closely over the brows to shield his feeble vision from the glare of the sun. His tottering steps were supported by a long slim staff, resembling the wand with which a theatrical magician appears on the stage, and in one hand he carried a freshly plaited fan of the green leaflets of the cocoa-nut tree. A flowing robe of tappa, knotted over the shoulder, hung loosely round his stooping form, and heightened the venerableness of his aspect.

Mehevi, saluting this old gentleman, motioned him to a seat between us, and then uncovering my limb, desired him to examine it. The leech gazed intently from me to Toby, and then proceeded to business. After diligently observing the ailing member, he commenced manipulating it; and on the supposition probably that the complaint had deprived the leg of all sensation, began to pinch and hammer it in such a manner that I absolutely roared with the pain. Thinking that I was as capable of making an application of thumps and pinches to the part as any one else, I endeavoured to resist this species of medical treatment. But it was not so easy a matter to get out of the clutches of the old wizard; he fastened on the unfortunate limb as if it were something for which he had been long seeking, and muttering some kind of incantation continued his discipline, pounding it after a fashion that set me well nigh crazy; while Mehevi, upon the same principle which prompts an affectionate mother to hold a struggling child in a dentist's chair, restrained me in his powerful grasp, and actually encouraged the wretch in this infliction of torture.

Almost frantic with rage and pain, I yelled like a bedlamite; while Toby, throwing himself into all the attitudes of a posture-master, vainly endeavoured to expostulate with the natives by signs and gestures. To have looked at my companion, as, sympathising with my sufferings, he strove to put an end to them, one would have thought that he was the deaf and dumb alphabet incarnated. Whether my tormentor yielded to Toby's entreaties, or paused from sheer exhaustion, I do not know; but all at once he ceased his operations, and at the same time the chief relinquishing his hold upon me, I fell back, faint and breathless, with the agony I had endured.

My unfortunate limb was now left much in the same condition as a rump-steak after undergoing the castigating process which precedes cooking. My physician, having recovered from the fatigues of his exertions, as if anxious to make amends for the pain to which he had subjected me, now took some herbs out of a little wallet that was suspended from his waist, and moistening them in water, applied them to the inflamed part, stooping over it at the same time, and either whispering a spell, or having a little confidential chat with some imaginary demon located in the calf of my leg. My limb was now swathed in leafy bandages, and, grateful to Providence for the cessation of hostilities, I was suffered to rest.

Mehevi shortly after rose to depart; but before he went he spoke authoritatively to one of the natives whom he addressed as Kory-Kory; and from the little I could understand of what took place, pointed him out to me as a man whose peculiar business thenceforth would be to attend upon my person. I am not certain that I comprehended as much as this at the time, but the subsequent conduct of my trusty body-servant fully assured me that such must have been the case.

I could not but be amused at the manner in which the chief addressed me upon this occasion, talking to me for at least fifteen or twenty minutes as calmly as if I could understand every word that he said. I remarked this peculiarity very often afterwards in many other of the islanders.

Mehevi having now departed, and the family physician having likewise made his exit, we were left about sunset with the ten or twelve natives, who by this time I had ascertained composed the household of which Toby and I were members. As the dwelling to which we had been first introduced was the place of my permanent abode while I remained in the valley, and as I was necessarily placed upon the most intimate footing with its occupants, I may as well here enter into a little description of it and its inhabitants. This description will apply also to nearly all the other dwelling-places in the vale, and will furnish some idea of the generality of the natives.

Near one side of the valley, and about midway up the ascent of a rather abrupt rise of ground waving with the richest verdure, a number of large stones were laid in successive courses, to the height of nearly eight feet, and disposed in such a manner that their level surface corresponded in shape with the habitation which was perched upon it. A narrow space, however, was reserved in front of the dwelling, upon the summit of this pile of stones, (called by the natives a "pi-pi,") which being enclosed by a little picket of canes, gave it somewhat the appearance of a verandah. The frame of the house was constructed of large bamboos planted uprightly, and secured together at intervals by transverse stalks of the light wood of the habiscus, lashed with thongs of bark. The rear of the tenement—built up with successive ranges of cocoa-nut boughs bound one upon another, with their leaflets cunningly woven together—inclined a little from the vertical, and extended from the extreme edge of the "pi-pi" to about twenty feet from its surface; whence the shelving roof—thatched with the long tapering leaves of the palmetto—sloped steeply off to within about five feet of the floor; leaving the eaves drooping with tassel-like appendages over the front of the habitation. This was constructed of light and elegant canes, in a kind of open screen work, tastefully adorned with bindings of variegated sinnate, which served to hold together its various parts. The sides of the house were similarly built; thus presenting three quarters for the circulation of the air, while the whole was impervious to the rain.

In length this picturesque building was perhaps twelve yards, while in breadth it could not have exceeded as many feet. So much for the exterior; which with its wire-like reed-twisted sides, not a little reminded me of an immense aviary.

Stooping a little, you passed through a narrow aperture in its front; and facing you, on entering, lay two long, perfectly straight, and well-polished trunks of the cocoa-nut tree, extending the full length of the dwelling; one of them placed closely against the rear, and the other lying parallel with it some two yards distant, the interval between them being spread with a multitude of gaily-worked mats, nearly all of a different pattern. This space formed the common couch and lounging place of the natives, answering the purpose of a divan in Oriental countries. Here would they slumber through the hours of the night, and recline luxuriously during the greater part of the day. The remainder of the floor presented only the cool shining surfaces of the large stones of which the "pi-pi" was composed.

From the ridge-pole of the house hung suspended a number of large packages enveloped in coarse tappa; some of which contained festival dresses, and various other matters of the wardrobe, held in high estimation. These were easily accessible by means of a line, which, passing over the ridge-pole, had one end attached to a bundle, while with the other, which led to the side of the dwelling and was there secured, the package could be lowered or elevated at pleasure.

Against the farther wall of the house were arranged in tasteful figures a variety of spears and javelins, and other implements of savage warfare. Outside of the habitation, and built upon the piazza-like area in its front, was a little shed used as a sort of larder or pantry, and in which were stored various articles of domestic use and convenience. A few yards from the pi-pi was a large shed built of cocoanut boughs, where the process of preparing the "poee-poee" was carried on, and all culinary operations attended to.

Thus much for the house, and its appurtenances; and it will be readily acknowledged that a more commodious and appropriate dwelling for the climate and the people could not possibly be devised. It was cool, free to admit the air, scrupulously clean, and elevated above the dampness and impurities of the ground.

But now to sketch the inmates; and here I claim for my tried servitor and faithful valet Kory-Kory the precedence of a first description. As his character will be gradually unfolded in the course of my narrative, I shall for the present content myself with delineating his personal appearance. Kory-Kory, though the most devoted and best natured serving-man in the world, was, alas! a hideous object to look upon. He was some twenty-five years of age, and about six feet in height, robust and well made, and of the most extraordinary aspect. His head was carefully shaven, with the exception of two circular spots, about the size of a dollar, near the top of the cranium, where the hair, permitted to grow of an amazing length, was twisted up in two prominent knots, that gave him the appearance of being decorated with a pair of horns. His beard, plucked out by the roots from every other part of his face, was suffered to droop in hairy pendants, two of which garnished his upper lip, and an equal number hung from the extremity of his chin.

Kory-Kory, with a view of improving the handiwork of nature, and perhaps prompted by a desire to add to the engaging expression of his countenance, had seen fit to embellish his face with three broad longitudinal stripes of tattooing, which, like those country roads that go straight forward in defiance of all obstacles, crossed his nasal organ, descended into the hollow of his eyes, and even skirted the borders of his mouth. Each completely spanned his physiognomy; one extending in a line with his eyes, another crossing the face in the vicinity of the nose, and the third sweeping along his lips from ear to ear. His countenance thus triply hooped, as it were, with tattooing, always reminded me of those unhappy wretches whom I have sometimes observed gazing out sentimentally from behind the grated bars of a prison window; whilst the entire body of my savage valet, covered all over with representations of birds and fishes, and a variety of most unaccountable-looking creatures, suggested to me the idea of a pictorial museum of natural history, or an illustrated copy of 'Goldsmith's Animated Nature.'

But it seems really heartless in me to write thus of the poor islander, when I owe perhaps to his unremitting attentions the very existence I now enjoy. Kory-Kory, I mean thee no harm in what I say in regard to thy outward adornings; but they were a little curious to my unaccustomed sight, and therefore I dilate upon them. But to underrate or forget thy faithful services is something I could never be guilty of, even in the giddiest moment of my life.

The father of my attached follower was a native of gigantic frame, and had once possessed prodigious physical powers; but the lofty form was now yielding to the inroads of time, though the hand of disease seemed never to have been laid upon the aged warrior. Marheyo—for such was his name—appeared to have retired from all active participation in the affairs of the valley, seldom or never accompanying the natives in their various expeditions; and employing the greater part of his time in throwing up a little shed just outside the house, upon which he was engaged to my certain knowledge for four months, without appearing to make any sensible advance. I suppose the old gentleman was in his dotage, for he manifested in various ways the characteristics which mark this particular stage of life.

I remember in particular his having a choice pair of ear-ornaments, fabricated from the teeth of some sea-monster. These he would alternately wear and take off at least fifty times in the course of the day, going and coming from his little hut on each occasion with all the tranquillity imaginable. Sometimes slipping them through the slits in his ears, he would seize his spear—which in length and slightness resembled a fishing-pole—and go stalking beneath the shadows of the neighbouring groves, as if about to give a hostile meeting to some cannibal knight. But he would soon return again, and hiding his weapon under the projecting eaves of the house, and rolling his clumsy trinkets carefully in a piece of tappa, would resume his more pacific operations as quietly as if he had never interrupted them.

But despite his eccentricities, Marheyo was a most paternal and warm-hearted old fellow, and in this particular not a little resembled his son Kory-Kory. The mother of the latter was the mistress of the family, and a notable housewife, and a most industrious old lady she was. If she did not understand the art of making jellies, jams, custards, tea-cakes, and such like trashy affairs, she was profoundly skilled in the mysteries of preparing "amar," "poee-poee," and "kokoo," with other substantial matters. She was a genuine busy-body; bustling about the house like a country landlady at an unexpected arrival; for ever giving the young girls tasks to perform, which the little hussies as often neglected; poking into every corner, and rummaging over bundles of old tappa, or making a prodigious clatter among the calabashes. Sometimes she might have been seen squatting upon her haunches in front of a huge wooden basin, and kneading poee-poee with terrific vehemence, dashing the stone pestle about as if she would shiver the vessel into fragments; on other occasions, galloping about the valley in search of a particular kind of leaf, used in some of her recondite operations, and returning home, toiling and sweating, with a bundle of it, under which most women would have sunk.

To tell the truth, Kory-Kory's mother was the only industrious person in all the valley of Typee; and she could not have employed herself more actively had she been left an exceedingly muscular and destitute widow, with an inordinate supply of young children, in the bleakest part of the civilized world. There was not the slightest neces-

sity for the greater portion of the labour performed by
the old lady: but she seemed to work from some irresistible
impulse; her limbs continually swaying to and fro, as if
there were some indefatigable engine concealed within
her body which kept her in perpetual motion.

Never suppose that she was a termagant or a shrew for
all this; she had the kindliest heart in the world, and acted
towards me in particular in a truly maternal manner, occasionally putting some little morsel of choice food into
my hand, some outlandish kind of savage sweetmeat or
pastry, like a doting mother petting a sickly urchin with
tarts and sugar-plums. Warm indeed are my remembrances
of the dear, good, affectionate old Tinor!

Besides the individuals I have mentioned, there belonged to the household three young men, dissipated,
good-for-nothing, roystering blades of savages, who were
either employed in prosecuting love-affairs with the maidens of the tribe, or grew boozy on "arva" and tobacco in the
company of congenial spirits, the scapegraces of the valley.

Among the permanent inmates of the house were likewise several lovely damsels, who instead of thrumming
pianos and reading novels, like more enlightened young
ladies, substituted for these employments the manufacture
of a fine species of tappa; but for the greater portion of the
time were skipping from house to house, gadding and gos-
siping with their acquaintances.

From the rest of these, however, I must except the
beauteous nymph Fayaway, who was my peculiar favourite. Her free pliant figure was the very perfection of female
grace and beauty. Her complexion was a rich and mantling
olive, and when watching the glow upon her cheeks I could
almost swear that beneath the transparent medium there
lurked the blushes of a faint vermilion. The face of this
girl was a rounded oval, and each feature as perfectly

formed as the heart or imagination of man could desire. Her full lips, when parted with a smile, disclosed teeth of a dazzling whiteness; and when her rosy mouth opened with a burst of merriment, they looked like the milk-white seeds of the "arta," a fruit of the valley, which, when cleft in twain, shows them reposing in rows on either side, imbedded in the rich and juicy pulp. Her hair of the deepest brown, parted irregularly in the middle, flowed in natural ringlets over her shoulders, and whenever she chanced to stoop, fell over and hid from view her lovely bosom. Gazing into the depths of her strange blue eyes, when she was in a contemplative mood, they seemed most placid yet unfathomable; but when illuminated by some lively emotion, they beamed upon the beholder like stars. The hands of Fayaway were as soft and delicate as those of any countess; for an entire exemption from rude labour marks the girlhood and even prime of a Typee woman's life. Her feet, though wholly exposed, were as diminutive and fairly shaped as those which peep from beneath the skirts of a Lima lady's dress. The skin of this young creature, from continual ablutions and the use of mollifying ointments, was inconceivably smooth and soft.

I may succeed, perhaps, in particularising some of the individual features of Fayaway's beauty, but that general loveliness of appearance which they all contributed to produce I will not attempt to describe. The easy unstudied graces of a child of nature like this, breathing from infancy an atmosphere of perpetual summer, and nurtured by the simple fruits of the earth; enjoying a perfect freedom from care and anxiety, and removed effectually from all injurious tendencies, strike the eye in a manner which cannot be pourtrayed. This picture is no fancy sketch; it is drawn from the most vivid recollections of the person delineated.

Were I asked if the beauteous form of Fayaway was altogether free from the hideous blemish of tattooing, I should be constrain'd to answer that it was not. But the practitioners of the barbarous art, so remorseless in their inflictions upon the brawny limbs of the warriors of the tribe, seem to be conscious that it needs not the resources of their profession to augment the charms of the maidens of the vale.

The females are very little embellished in this way, and Fayaway, with all the other young girls of her age, were even less so than those of their sex more advanced in years. The reason of this peculiarity will be alluded to hereafter. All the tattooing that the nymph in question exhibited upon her person may be easily described. Three minute dots, no bigger than pinheads, decorated either lip, and at a little distance were not at all discernible. Just upon the fall of the shoulder were drawn two parallel lines half an inch apart, and perhaps three inches in length, the interval being filled with delicately executed figures. These narrow bands of tattooing, thus placed, always reminded me of those stripes of gold lace worn by officers in undress, and which were in lieu of epaulettes to denote their rank.

Thus much was Fayaway tattooed—the audacious hand which had gone so far in its desecrating work stopping short, apparently wanting the heart to proceed.

But I have omitted to describe the dress worn by this nymph of the valley.

Fayaway—I must avow the fact—for the most part clung to the primitive and summer garb of Eden. But how becoming the costume! It showed her fine figure to the best possible advantage; and nothing could have been better adapted to her peculiar style of beauty. On ordinary occasions she was habited precisely as I have described the two youthful savages whom we had met on first entering the valley. At other times, when rambling among the groves, or visiting at the houses of her acquaintances, she wore a tunic of white tappa, reaching from her waist to a little below the knees; and when exposed for any length of time to the sun, she invariably protected herself from its rays by a floating mantle of the same material, loosely gathered about the person. Her gala dress will be described hereafter.

As the beauties of our own land delight in bedecking themselves with fanciful articles of jewellery, suspending them from their ears, hanging them about their necks, and clasping them around their wrists; so Fayaway and her companions were in the habit of ornamenting themselves with similar appendages.

Flora was their jeweller. Sometimes they wore necklaces of small carnation flowers, strung like rubies upon a fibre of tappa, or displayed in their ears a single white bud, the stem thrust backward through the aperture, and showing in front the delicate petals folded together in a beautiful sphere, and looking like a drop of the purest pearl. Chaplets too, resembling in their arrangement the strawberry coronal worn by an English peeress, and composed of intertwined leaves and blossoms, often crowned their temples; and bracelets and anklets of the same tasteful pattern were frequently to be seen. Indeed, the maidens of the island were passionately fond of flowers, and never wearied of decorating their persons with them; a lovely trait in their character, and one that ere long will be more fully alluded to.

Though in my eyes, at least, Fayaway was indisputably the loveliest female I saw in Typee, yet the description I have given of her will in some measure apply to nearly all the youthful portion of her sex in the valley. Judge ye then, reader, what beautiful creatures they must have been.

CHAPTER XII

WHEN Mehevi had departed from the house, as related in the preceding chapter, Kory-Kory commenced the functions of the post assigned him. He brought us various kinds of food; and, as if I were an infant, insisted upon feeding me with his own hands. To this procedure I, of course, most earnestly objected, but in vain; and having laid a calabash of kokoo before me, he washed his fingers in a vessel of water, and then putting his hand into the dish and rolling the food into little balls, put them one after another into my mouth. All my remonstrances against this measure only provoked so great a clamour on his part, that I was obliged to acquiesce; and the operation of feeding being thus facilitated, the meal was quickly despatched. As for Toby, he was allowed to help himself after his own fashion.

The repast over, my attendant arranged the mats for repose, and, bidding me lie down, covered me with a large robe of tappa, at the same time looking approvingly upon me, and exclaiming, "Ki-Ki, muee muee, ah! moee moee mortarkee" (eat plenty, ah! sleep very good). The philosophy of this sentiment I did not pretend to question; for deprived of sleep for several preceding nights, and the pain in my limb having much abated, I now felt inclined to avail myself of the opportunity afforded me.

The next morning, on waking, I found Kory-Kory

stretched out on one side of me, while my companion lay upon the other. I felt sensibly refreshed after a night of sound repose, and immediately agreed to the proposition of my valet that I should repair to the water and wash, although dreading the suffering that the exertion might produce. From this apprehension, however, I was quickly relieved; for Kory-Kory, leaping from the pi-pi, and then backing himself up against it, like a porter in readiness to shoulder a trunk, with loud vociferations and a super-abundance of gestures, gave me to understand that I was to mount upon his back and be thus transported to the stream, which flowed perhaps two hundred yards from the house.

Our appearance upon the verandah in front of the habi-tation drew together quite a crowd, who stood looking on and conversing with one another in the most animated manner. They reminded one of a group of idlers gathered about the door of a village tavern when the equipage of some distinguished traveller is brought round previous to his departure. As soon as I clasped my arms about the neck of the devoted fellow, and he jogged off with me, the crowd —composed chiefly of young girls and boys—followed after, shouting and capering with infinite glee, and accompanied us to the banks of the stream.

On gaining it, Kory-Kory, wading up to his hips in the water, carried me half way across, and deposited me on a smooth black stone which rose a few inches above the sur-face. The amphibious rabble at our heels plunged in after us, and, climbing to the summit of the grass-grown rocks with which the bed of the brook was here and there broken, waited curiously to witness our morning ablutions.

Somewhat embarrassed by the presence of the female portion of the company, and feeling my cheeks burning with bashful timidity, I formed a primitive basin by join-ing my hands together, and cooled my blushes in the water it contained; then removing my frock, bent over and washed myself down to my waist in the stream. As soon as Kory-Kory comprehended from my motions that this was to be the extent of my performance, he appeared perfectly aghast with astonishment, and rushing towards me, poured out a torrent of words in eager deprecation of so limited an operation, enjoining me by unmistakeable signs to immerse my whole body. To this I was forced to consent; and the honest fellow regarding me as a froward, inexperienced child, whom it was his duty to serve at the risk of offending, lifted me from the rock, and tenderly bathed my limbs. This over, and resuming my seat, I could not avoid bursting into admiration of the scene around me.

From the verdant surfaces of the large stones that lay scattered about, the natives were now sliding off into the water, diving and ducking beneath the surface in all directions—the young girls springing buoyantly into the air, and revealing their naked forms to the waist, with their long tresses dancing about their shoulders, their eyes sparkling like drops of dew in the sun, and their gay laughter pealing forth at every frolicsome incident.

On the afternoon of the day that I took my first bath in the valley, we received another visit from Mehevi. The noble savage seemed to be in the same pleasant mood, and was quite as cordial in his manner as before. After remaining about an hour, he rose from the mats, and motioning to leave the house, invited Toby and myself to accompany him. I pointed to my leg; but Mehevi in his turn pointed to Kory-Kory, and removed that objection; so, mounting upon the faithful fellow's shoulders again—like the old man of the sea astride of Sindbad—I followed after the chief.

The nature of the route we now pursued struck me more forcibly than anything I had yet seen, as illustrating the indolent disposition of the islanders. The path was obviously the most beaten one in the valley, several others leading from either side into it, and perhaps for successive generations it had formed the principal avenue of the place. And yet, until I grew more familiar with its impediments, it seemed as difficult to travel as the recesses of a wilderness. Part of it swept round an abrupt rise of ground, the surface of which was broken by frequent inequalities, and thickly strewn with projecting masses of rocks, whose summits were often hidden from view by the drooping foliage of the luxuriant vegetation. Sometimes directly over, sometimes evading these obstacles with a wide circuit, the path wound along;—one moment climbing over a sudden eminence smooth with continued wear, then descending on the other side into a steep glen, and crossing the flinty channel of a brook. Here it pursued the depths of a glade, occasionally obliging you to stoop beneath vast horizontal branches; and now you stepped over huge trunks and boughs that lay rotting across the track.

Such was the grand thoroughfare of Typee. After proceeding a little distance along it—Kory-Kory panting and blowing with the weight of his burden—I dismounted from his back, and grasping the long spear of Mehevi in my hand, assisted my steps over the numerous obstacles of the road; preferring this mode of advance to one which, from the difficulties of the way, was equally painful to myself and my wearied servitor.

Our journey was soon at an end; for, scaling a sudden height, we came abruptly upon the place of our destination. I wish that it were possible to sketch in words this spot as vividly as I recollect it.

Here were situated the Taboo groves of the valley—the scene of many a prolonged feast, of many a horrid rite. Beneath the dark shadows of the consecrated bread-fruit trees there reigned a solemn twilight—a cathedral-like gloom. The frightful genius of pagan worship seemed to brood in silence over the place, breathing its spell upon every object around. Here and there, in the depths of these awful shades, half screened from sight by masses of over-hanging foliage, rose the idolatrous altars of the savages, built of enormous blocks of black and polished stone, placed one upon another, without cement, to the height of twelve or fifteen feet, and surmounted by a rustic open temple, en-closed with a low picket of canes, within which might be seen, in various stages of decay, offerings of bread-fruit and cocoa-nuts, and the putrefying relics of some recent sacri-fice.

In the midst of the wood was the hallowed "hoolah hoolah" ground—set apart for the celebration of the fan-tastic religious ritual of these people—comprising an ex-tensive oblong pi-pi, terminating at either end in a lofty terraced altar, guarded by ranks of hideous wooden idols, and with the two remaining sides flanked by ranges of bamboo sheds, opening towards the interior of the quad-rangle thus formed. Vast trees, standing in the middle of this space, and throwing over it an umbrageous shade, had their massive trunks built round with slight stages, elevated a few feet above the ground, and railed in with canes, forming so many rustic pulpits, from which the priests harangued their devotees.

This holiest of spots was defended from profanation by the strictest edicts of the all-pervading "taboo," which condemned to instant death the sacrilegious female who should enter or touch its sacred precincts, or even so much as press with her feet the ground made holy by the shadows that it cast.

Access was had to the enclosure through an embow-ered entrance on one side, facing a number of towering cocoa-nut trees, planted at intervals along a level area of a hundred yards. At the further extremity of this space was to be seen a building of considerable size, reserved for the habitation of the priests and religious attendants of the groves.

In its vicinity was another remarkable edifice, built as usual upon the summit of a pi-pi, and at least two hundred feet in length, though not more than twenty in breadth. The whole front of this latter structure was completely open, and from one end to the other ran a narrow veran-dah, fenced in on the edge of the pi-pi with a picket of canes. Its interior presented the appearance of an im-mense lounging-place, the entire floor being strewn with successive layers of mats, lying between parallel trunks of cocoa-nut trees, selected for the purpose from the straight-est and most symmetrical the vale afforded.

To this building, denominated in the language of the natives the "Ti," Mehevi now conducted us. Thus far we had been accompanied by a troop of the natives of both sexes; but as soon as we approached its vicinity, the fe-males gradually separated themselves from the crowd, and standing aloof, permitted us to pass on. The merciless prohibitions of the taboo extended likewise to this edifice, and were enforced by the same dreadful penalty that secured the Hoolah Hoolah ground from the imaginary pollution of a woman's presence.

On entering the house, I was surprised to see six muskets ranged against the bamboo on one side, from the barrels of which depended as many small canvas pouches, partly filled with powder. Disposed about these muskets, like the cutlasses that decorate the bulkhead of a man-of-war's cabin, were a great variety of rude spears and paddles, jave-lins, and war-clubs. This then, said I to Toby, must be the armory of the tribe.

As we advanced further along the building, we were struck with the aspect of four or five hideous old wretches, on whose decrepit forms time and tattooing seemed to have obliterated every trace of humanity. Owing to the continued operation of this latter process, which only terminates among the warriors of the island after all the figures stretched upon their limbs in youth have been blended together—an effect, however, produced only in cases of extreme longevity—the bodies of these men were of a uniform dull green colour—the hue which the tattooing gradually assumes as the individual advances in age. Their skin had a frightful scaly appearance, which, united with its singular colour, made their limbs not a little resemble dusty specimens of verde-antique. Their flesh, in parts, hung upon them in huge folds, like the overlapping plates on the flank of a rhinoceros. Their heads were completely bald, whilst their faces were puckered into a thousand wrinkles, and they presented no vestige of a beard. But the most remarkable peculiarity about them was the appearance of their feet; the toes, like the radiating lines of the mariner's compass, pointed to every quarter of the horizon. This was doubtless attributable to the fact, that during nearly a hundred years of existence the said toes never had been subjected to any artificial confinement, and in their old age, being averse to close neighbourhood, bid one another keep open order.

These repulsive-looking creatures appeared to have lost the use of their lower limbs altogether; sitting upon the floor cross-legged in a state of torpor. They never heeded us in the least, scarcely looking conscious of our presence, while Mehevi seated us upon the mats, and Kory-Kory gave utterance to some unintelligible gibberish.

In a few moments a boy entered with a wooden trencher of poee-poee; and in regaling myself with its contents I was obliged again to submit to the officious intervention of my indefatigable servitor. Various other dishes followed, the chief manifesting the most hospitable importunity in pressing us to partake, and to remove all bashfulness on our part, set us no despicable example in his own person.

The repast concluded, a pipe was lighted, which passed from mouth to mouth, and yielding to its soporific influence, the quiet of the place, and the deepening shadows of approaching night, my companion and I sank into a kind of drowsy repose, while the chief and Kory-Kory seemed to be slumbering beside us.

I awoke from an uneasy nap, about midnight, as I supposed; and, raising myself partly from the mat, became sensible that we were enveloped in utter darkness. Toby lay still asleep, but our late companions had disappeared. The only sound that interrupted the silence of the place was the asthmatic breathing of the old men I have mentioned, who reposed at a little distance from us. Beside them, as well as I could judge, there was no one else in the house.

Apprehensive of some evil, I roused my comrade, and we were engaged in a whispered conference concerning the unexpected withdrawal of the natives, when all at once, from the depths of the grove, in full view of us where we lay, shoots of flame were seen to rise, and in a few moments illuminated the surrounding trees, casting, by contrast, into still deeper gloom the darkness around us.

While we continued gazing at this sight, dark figures appeared moving to and fro before the flames; while others, dancing and capering about, looked like so many demons.

Regarding this new phenomenon with no small degree of trepidation, I said to my companion, "What can all this mean, Toby?"

"Oh, nothing," replied he; "getting the fire ready, I suppose."

"Fire!" exclaimed I, while my heart took to beating like a trip-hammer, "what fire?"

"Why, the fire to cook us, to be sure; what else would the cannibals be kicking up such a row about if it were not for that?"

"Oh, Toby! have done with your jokes; this is no time for them; something is about to happen, I feel confident."

"Jokes, indeed!" exclaimed Toby, indignantly. "Did you ever hear me joke? Why, for what do you suppose the devils have been feeding us up in this kind of style during the last three days, unless it were for something that you are too much frightened at to talk about? Look at that Kory-Kory there!—has he not been stuffing you with his confounded mushes, just in the way they treat swine before they kill them? Depend upon it, we will be eaten this blessed night, and there is the fire we shall be roasted by."

This view of the matter was not at all calculated to allay my apprehensions, and I shuddered when I reflected that we were indeed at the mercy of a tribe of cannibals, and that the dreadful contingency to which Toby had alluded was by no means removed beyond the bounds of possibility.

"There! I told you so! they are coming for us!" exclaimed my companion the next moment, as the forms of four of the islanders were seen in bold relief against the illuminated background, mounting the pi-pi and approaching towards us.

They came on noiselessly, nay stealthily, and glided along through the gloom that surrounded us as if about to spring upon some object they were fearful of disturbing before they should make sure of it.—Gracious heaven! the horrible reflections which crowded upon me that moment. —A cold sweat stood upon my brow, and spell-bound with terror I awaited my fate!

Suddenly the silence was broken by the well-remembered tones of Mehevi, and at the kindly accents of his voice my fears were immediately dissipated. "Tommo, Toby, ki ki!" (eat).—He had waited to address us until he had assured himself that we were both awake, at which he seemed somewhat surprised.

"Ki ki! is it?" said Toby in his gruff tones; "well, cook us first, will you?—but what's this?" he added, as another savage appeared, bearing before him a large trencher of wood, containing some kind of steaming meat, as appeared from the odours it diffused, and which he deposited at the feet of Mehevi. "A baked baby, I dare say! but I will have none of it, never mind what it is.—A pretty fool I should make of myself, indeed, waked up here in the middle of the night, stuffing and guzzling, and all to make a fat meal for a parcel of bloody-minded cannibals one of these mornings! —No, I see what they are at very plainly, so I am resolved to starve myself into a bunch of bones and gristle, and then, if they serve me up, they are welcome! But I say, Tommo, you are not going to eat any of that mess there, in the dark, are you? Why, how can you tell what it is?"

"By tasting it, to be sure," said I, masticating a morsel that Kory-Kory had just put in my mouth; "and excellently good it is too, very much like veal."

"A baked baby, by the soul of Captain Cook!" burst forth Toby, with amazing vehemence; "Veal! why there never was a calf on the island till you landed. I tell you you are bolting down mouthfuls from a dead Happar's carcass, as sure as you live, and no mistake!"

Emetics and lukewarm water! What a sensation in the abdominal regions! Sure enough, where could the fiends incarnate have obtained meat? But I resolved to satisfy myself at all hazards; and turning to Mehevi, I soon made the ready chief understand that I wished a light to be brought. When the taper came, I gazed eagerly into the vessel, and recognised the mutilated remains of a juvenile porker! "Puarkee!" exclaimed Kory-Kory, looking complacently at the dish; and from that day to this I have never forgotten that such is the designation of a pig in the Typee lingo.

The next morning, after being again abundantly feasted by the hospitable Mehevi, Toby and myself arose to depart. But the chief requested us to postpone our intention. "Abo, abo," (Wait, wait,) he said, and accordingly we resumed our seats, while, assisted by the zealous Kory-Kory, he appeared to be engaged in giving directions to a number of the natives outside, who were busily employed in making arrangements, the nature of which we could not comprehend. But we were not left long in our ignorance, for a few moments only had elapsed when the chief beckoned us to approach, and we perceived that he had been marshalling a kind of guard of honour to escort us on our return to the house of Marheyo.

The procession was led off by two venerable-looking savages, each provided with a spear, from the end of which streamed a pennon of milk-white tappa. After them went several youths, bearing aloft calabashes of poee-poee; and followed in their turn by four stalwart fellows, sustaining long bamboos, from the tops of which hung suspended, at least twenty feet from the ground, large baskets of green bread-fruit. Then came a troop of boys, carrying bunches of ripe banannas, and baskets made of the woven leaflets of cocoa-nut boughs, filled with the young fruit of the tree, the naked shells stripped of their husks peeping forth from the verdant wicker-work that surrounded them. Last of all came a burly islander, holding over his head a wooden trencher, in which lay disposed the remnants of our midnight feast, hidden from view, however, by a covering of bread-fruit leaves.

Astonished as I was at this exhibition, I could not avoid smiling at its grotesque appearance, and the associations it naturally called up. Mehevi, it seemed, was bent on replenishing old Marheyo's larder, fearful perhaps that without this precaution his guests might not fare as well as they could desire.

As soon as I descended from the pi-pi, the procession formed anew, enclosing us in its centre; where I remained part of the time, carried by Kory-Kory, and occasionally relieving him from his burden by limping along with a spear. When we moved off in this order, the natives struck up a musical recitative, which, with various alternations, they continued until we arrived at the place of our destination.

As we proceeded on our way, bands of young girls, darting from the surrounding groves, hung upon our skirts, and accompanied us with shouts of merriment and delight, which almost drowned the deep notes of the recitative. On approaching old Marheyo's domicile, its inmates rushed out to receive us; and while the gifts of Mehevi were being disposed of, the superannuated warrior did the honours of his mansion with all the warmth of hospitality evinced by an English squire when he regales his friends at some fine old patrimonial mansion.

CHAPTER XIII

Attempt to procure Relief from Nukuheva—Perilous Adventure of Toby in the Happar Mountain—Eloquence of Kory-Kory.

AMIDST these novel scenes a week passed away almost imperceptibly. The natives, actuated by some mysterious impulse, day after day redoubled their attentions to us. Their manner towards us was unaccountable. Surely, thought I, they would not act thus if they meant us any harm. But why this excess of deferential kindness, or what equivalent can they imagine us capable of rendering them for it?

We were fairly puzzled. But despite the apprehensions I could not dispel, the horrible character imputed to these Typees appeared to me wholly undeserved.

"Why, they are cannibals!" said Toby on one occasion when I eulogised the tribe. "Granted," I replied, "but a more humane, gentlemanly, and amiable set of epicures do not probably exist in the Pacific."

But, notwithstanding the kind treatment we received, I was too familiar with the fickle disposition of savages not to feel anxious to withdraw from the valley, and put myself beyond the reach of that fearful death which, under all these smiling appearances, might yet menace us. But here there was an obstacle in the way of doing so. It was idle for me to think of moving from the place until I should have recovered from the severe lameness that afflicted me; indeed my malady began seriously to alarm me; for, despite the herbal remedies of the natives, it continued to grow worse and worse. Their mild applications, though they soothed the pain, did not remove the disorder, and I felt convinced that without better aid I might anticipate long and acute suffering.

But how was this aid to be procured? From the surgeons of the French fleet, which probably still lay in the bay of Nukuheva, it might easily have been obtained, could I have made my case known to them. But how could that be effected?

At last, in the exigency to which I was reduced, I proposed to Toby that he should endeavour to go round to Nukuheva, and if he could not succeed in returning to the valley by water, in one of the boats of the squadron, and taking me off, he might at least procure me some proper medicines, and effect his return overland.

My companion listened to me in silence, and at first did not appear to relish the idea. The truth was, he felt impatient to escape from the place, and wished to avail himself of our present high favour with the natives to make good our retreat, before we should experience some sudden alteration in their behaviour. As he could not think of leaving me in my helpless condition, he implored me to be of good cheer, assured me that I should soon be better, and enabled in a few days to return with him to Nukuheva.

Added to this, he could not bear the idea of again returning to this dangerous place; and as for the expectation of persuading the Frenchmen to detach a boat's crew for the purpose of rescuing me from the Typees, he looked upon it as idle; and with arguments that I could not answer, urged the improbability of their provoking the hostilities of the clan by any such measure; especially as, for the purpose of quieting its apprehensions, they had as yet refrained from making any visit to the bay. "And even should they consent," said Toby, "they would only produce a commotion in the valley, in which we might both be sacrificed by these ferocious islanders." This was unanswerable; but still I clung to the belief that he might succeed in accomplishing the other part of my plan; and at last I overcame his scruples, and he agreed to make the attempt.

As soon as we succeeded in making the natives understand our intention, they broke out into the most vehement opposition to the measure, and for a while I almost despaired of obtaining their consent. At the bare thought of one of us leaving them, they manifested the most lively concern. The grief and consternation of Kory-Kory, in particular, was unbounded; he threw himself into a perfect paroxysm of gestures, which were intended to convey to us not only his abhorrence of Nukuheva and its uncivilized inhabitants, but also his astonishment that after becoming acquainted with the enlightened Typees, we should evince the least desire to withdraw, even for a time, from their agreeable society.

However, I overbore his objections by appealing to my lameness; from which I assured the natives I should speedily recover, if Toby were permitted to obtain the supplies I needed.

It was agreed that on the following morning my companion should depart, accompanied by some one or two of the household, who should point out to him an easy route, by which the bay might be reached before sunset.

At early dawn of the next day, our habitation was astir. One of the young men mounted into an adjoining cocoanut tree, and threw down a number of the young fruit, which old Marheyo quickly stripped of the green husks, and strung together upon a short pole. These were intended to refresh Toby on his route.

The preparations being completed, with no little emotion I bade my companion adieu. He promised to return in three days at farthest; and, bidding me keep up my spirits in the interval, turned round the corner of the pi-pi, and, under the guidance of the venerable Marheyo, was soon out of sight. His departure oppressed me with melancholy, and, re-entering the dwelling, I threw myself almost in despair upon the matting of the floor.

In two hours' time the old warrior returned, and gave me to understand that, after accompanying my companion a little distance, and showing him the route, he had left him journeying on his way.

It was about noon of this same day, a season which these people are wont to pass in sleep, that I lay in the house, surrounded by its slumbering inmates, and painfully affected by the strange silence which prevailed. All at once I thought I heard a faint shout, as if proceeding from some persons in the depth of the grove which extended in front of our habitation.

The sounds grew louder and nearer, and gradually the whole valley rang with wild outcries. The sleepers around me started to their feet in alarm, and hurried outside to discover the cause of the commotion. Kory-Kory, who had been the first to spring up, soon returned almost breathless, and nearly frantic with the excitement under which he seemed to be labouring. All that I could understand from him was that some accident had happened to Toby. Apprehensive of some dreadful calamity, I rushed out of the house, and caught sight of a tumultuous crowd, who, with shrieks and lamentations, were just emerging from the grove bearing in their arms some object, the sight of which produced all this transport of sorrow. As they drew near, the men redoubled their cries, while the girls, tossing their bare arms in the air, exclaimed plaintively, "Awha! awha! Toby muckee mooee!"—Alas! alas! Toby is killed!

In a moment the crowd opened, and disclosed the apparently lifeless body of my companion borne between two men, the head hanging heavily against the breast of the foremost. The whole face, neck, and bosom were covered with blood, which still trickled slowly from a wound behind the temple. In the midst of the greatest uproar and confusion the body was carried into the house and laid on a mat. Waving the natives off to give room and air, I bent eagerly over Toby, and, laying my hand upon the breast, ascertained that the heart still beat. Overjoyed at this, I seized a calabash of water, and dashed its contents upon his face, then wiping away the blood, anxiously examined the wound. It was about three inches long, and on removing the clotted hair from about it, showed the skull laid completely bare. Immediately with my knife I cut away the heavy locks, and bathed the part repeatedly in water.

In a few moments Toby revived, and opening his eyes for a second, closed them again without speaking. Kory-Kory, who had been kneeling beside me, now chafed his limbs gently with the palms of his hands, while a young girl at his head kept fanning him, and I still continued to moisten his lips and brow. Soon my poor comrade showed signs of animation, and I succeeded in making him swallow from a cocoa-nut shell a few mouthfuls of water.

Old Tinor now appeared, holding in her hand some simples she had gathered, the juice of which, she by signs besought me to squeeze into the wound. Having done so, I thought it best to leave Toby undisturbed until he should have had time to rally his faculties. Several times he opened his lips, but fearful for his safety I enjoined silence. In the course of two or three hours, however, he sat up, and was sufficiently recovered to tell me what had occurred.

"After leaving the house with Marheyo," said Toby, "we struck across the valley, and ascended the opposite heights. Just beyond them, my guide informed me, lay the valley of Happar, while along their summits, and skirting the head of the vale, was my route to Nukuheva. After mounting a little way up the elevation my guide paused, and gave me to understand that he could not accompany me any farther, and by various signs intimated that he was afraid to approach any nearer the territories of the enemies of his tribe. He however pointed out my path, which now lay clearly before me, and bidding me farewell hastily descended the mountain.

"Quite elated at being so near the Happars, I pushed up the acclivity, and soon gained its summit. It tapered up to a sharp ridge, from whence I beheld both the hostile valleys. Here I sat down and rested for a moment, refreshing myself with my cocoa-nuts. I was soon again pursuing my way along the height, when suddenly I saw three of the islanders, who must have just come out of Happar valley, standing in the path ahead of me. They were each armed with a heavy spear, and one from his appearance I took to be a chief. They sung out something, I could not understand what, and beckoned me to come on.

"Without the least hesitation I advanced towards them, and had approached within about a yard of the foremost, when, pointing angrily into the Typee valley, and uttering some savage exclamation, he wheeled round his weapon like lightning, and struck me in a moment to the ground.

The blow inflicted this wound, and took away my senses. As soon as I came to myself, I perceived the three islanders standing a little distance off, and apparently engaged in some violent altercation respecting me.

"My first impulse was to run for it; but, in endeavouring to rise, I fell back, and rolled down a little grassy precipice. The shock seemed to rally my faculties; so, starting to my feet, I fled down the path I had just ascended. I had no need to look behind me, for, from the yells I heard, I knew that my enemies were in full pursuit. Urged on by their fearful outcries, and heedless of the injury I had received —though the blood flowing from the wound trickled over into my eyes and almost blinded me—I rushed down the mountain side with the speed of the wind. In a short time I had descended nearly a third of the distance, and the savages had ceased their cries, when suddenly a terrific howl burst upon my ear, and at the same moment a heavy javelin darted past me as I fled, and stuck quivering in a tree close to me. Another yell followed, and a second spear and a third shot through the air within a few feet of my body, both of them piercing the ground obliquely in advance of me. The fellows gave a roar of rage and disappointment; but they were afraid, I suppose, of coming down further into the Typee valley, and so abandoned the chase. I saw them recover their weapons and turn back; and I continued my descent as fast as I could.

"What could have caused this ferocious attack on the part of these Happars I could not imagine, unless it were that they had seen me ascending the mountain with Marheyo, and that the mere fact of coming from the Typee valley was sufficient to provoke them.

"As long as I was in danger I scarcely felt the wound I had received; but when the chase was over I began to suffer from it. I had lost my hat in my flight, and the sun scorched my bare head. I felt faint and giddy; but, fearful

of falling to the ground beyond the reach of assistance, I
staggered on as well as I could, and at last gained the level
of the valley, and then down I sunk; and I knew nothing
more until I found myself lying upon these mats, and you
stooping over me with the calabash of water."

Such was Toby's account of this sad affair. I afterwards
learned that fortunately he had fallen close to a spot where
the natives go for fuel. A party of them caught sight of him
as he fell, and sounding the alarm, had lifted him up;
and after ineffectually endeavouring to restore him at the
brook, had hurried forward with him to the house.

This incident threw a dark cloud over our prospects. It
reminded us that we were hemmed in by hostile tribes,
whose territories we could not hope to pass, on our route
to Nukuheva, without encountering the effects of their
savage resentment. There appeared to be no avenue
opened to our escape but the sea, which washed the lower
extremity of the vale.

Our Typee friends availed themselves of the recent disaster of Toby to exhort us to a due appreciation of the
blessings we enjoyed among them; contrasting their own
generous reception of us with the animosity of their neigh-
bours. They likewise dwelt upon the cannibal propensities
of the Happars, a subject which they were perfectly aware
could not fail to alarm us; while at the same time they earnestly disclaimed all participation in so horrid a custom.
Nor did they omit to call upon us to admire the natural
loveliness of their own abode, and the lavish abundance
with which it produced all manner of luxuriant fruits; ex-
alting it in this particular above any of the surrounding
valleys.

Kory-Kory seemed to experience so heartfelt a desire to
infuse into our minds proper views on these subjects, that,
assisted in his endeavours by the little knowledge of the
language we had acquired, he actually succeeded in mak-

ing us comprehend a considerable part of what he said. To facilitate our correct apprehension of his meaning, he at first condensed his ideas into the smallest possible compass.

"Happar keekeeno nuee," he exclaimed; "nuee, nuee, ki ki kannaka!—ah! owle motarkee!" which signifies, "Terrible fellows those Happars!—devour an amazing quantity of men!—ah, shocking bad!" Thus far he explained himself by a variety of gestures, during the performance of which he would dart out of the house, and point abhorrently towards the Happar valley; running in to us again with a rapidity that showed he was fearful we would lose one part of his meaning before he could complete the other; and continuing his illustrations by seizing the fleshy part of my arm in his teeth, intimating by the operation that the people who lived over in that direction would like nothing better than to treat me in that manner.

Having assured himself that we were fully enlightened on this point, he proceeded to another branch of his subject. "Ah! Typee motarkee!—nuee, nuee mioree—nuee, nuee wai—nuee, nuee poee-poee—nuee, nuee kokoo—ah! nuee, nuee kiki—ah! nuee, nuee, nuee!" Which, literally interpreted as before, would imply, "Ah, Typee! isn't it a fine place though!—no danger of starving here, I tell you! —plenty of bread-fruit—plenty of water—plenty of pudding—ah! plenty of everything!—ah! heaps, heaps, heaps!" All this was accompanied by a running commentary of signs and gestures which it was impossible not to comprehend.

As he continued his harangue, however, Kory-Kory, in emulation of our more polished orators, began to launch out rather diffusely into other branches of his subject, enlarging, probably, upon the moral reflections it suggested; and proceeded in such a strain of unintelligible and stunning gibberish, that he actually gave me the headache for the rest of the day.

CHAPTER XIV

A great Event happens in the Valley—The Island Telegraph—
Something befalls Toby—Fayaway displays a tender heart—Melancholy reflections—Mysterious Conduct of the Islanders—Devotion of Kory-Kory—A rural Couch—A Luxury—Kory-Kory
strikes a Light *à la* Typee.

IN THE course of a few days Toby had recovered from the
effects of his adventure with the Happar warriors; the
wound on his head rapidly healing under the vegetable
treatment of the good Tinor. Less fortunate than my
companion, however, I still continued to languish under
a complaint the origin and nature of which were still a
mystery. Cut off as I was from all intercourse with the civilized world, and feeling the inefficiency of anything the
natives could do to relieve me; knowing too, that so long
as I remained in my present condition, it would be impossible for me to leave the valley, whatever opportunity might
present itself; and apprehensive that ere long we might
be exposed to some caprice on the part of the islanders, I
now gave up all hopes of recovery, and became a prey to
the most gloomy thoughts. A deep dejection fell upon me,
which neither the friendly remonstrances of my companion, the devoted attentions of Kory-Kory, nor all the soothing influences of Fayaway could remove.

One morning as I lay on the mats in the house, plunged
in melancholy reverie, and regardless of everything around
me, Toby, who had left me about an hour, returned in
haste, and with great glee told me to cheer up and be of
good heart; for he believed, from what was going on among
the natives, that there were boats approaching the bay.

These tidings operated upon me like magic. The hour
of our deliverance was at hand, and starting up, I was
soon convinced that something unusual was about to oc-

cur. The word "botee! botee!" was vociferated in all directions; and shouts were heard in the distance, at first feebly and faintly; but growing louder and nearer at each successive repetition, until they were caught up by a fellow in a cocoa-nut tree a few yards off, who sounding them in turn, they were reiterated from a neighbouring grove, and so died away gradually from point to point, as the intelligence penetrated into the farthest recesses of the valley. This was the vocal telegraph of the islanders; by means of which condensed items of information could be carried in a very few minutes from the sea to their remotest habitation, a distance of at least eight or nine miles. On the present occasion it was in active operation; one piece of information following another with inconceivable rapidity.

The greatest commotion now appeared to prevail. At every fresh item of intelligence the natives betrayed the liveliest interest, and redoubled the energy with which they employed themselves in collecting fruit to sell to the expected visitors. Some were tearing off the husks from cocoa-nuts; some perched in the trees were throwing down bread-fruit to their companions, who gathered them into heaps as they fell; while others were plying their fingers rapidly in weaving leafen baskets in which to carry the fruit.

There were other matters too going on at the same time. Here you would see a stout warrior polishing his spear with a bit of old tappa, or adjusting the folds of the girdle about his waist; and there you might descry a young damsel decorating herself with flowers, as if having in her eye some maidenly conquest; while, as in all cases of hurry and confusion in every part of the world, a number of individuals kept hurrying to and fro, with amazing vigour and perseverance, doing nothing themselves, and hindering others.

Never before had we seen the islanders in such a state of bustle and excitement; and the scene furnished abundant evidence of the fact—that it was only at long intervals any such events occur.

When I thought of the length of time that might intervene before a similar chance of escape would be presented, I bitterly lamented that I had not the power of availing myself effectually of the present opportunity.

From all that we could gather, it appeared that the natives were fearful of arriving too late upon the beach, unless they made extraordinary exertions. Sick and lame as I was, I would have started with Toby at once, had not Kory-Kory not only refused to carry me, but manifested the most invincible repugnance to our leaving the neighbourhood of the house. The rest of the savages were equally opposed to our wishes, and seemed grieved and astonished at the earnestness of my solicitations. I clearly perceived that while my attendant avoided all appearance of constraining my movements, he was nevertheless determined to thwart my wish. He seemed to me on this particular occasion, as well as often afterwards, to be executing the orders of some other person with regard to me, though at the same time feeling towards me the most lively affection.

Toby, who had made up his mind to accompany the islanders if possible, as soon as they were in readiness to depart, and who for that reason had refrained from showing the same anxiety that I had done, now represented to me that it was idle for me to entertain the hope of reaching the beach in time to profit by any opportunity that might then be presented.

"Do you not see," said he, "the savages themselves are fearful of being too late, and I should hurry forward myself at once did I not think that if I showed too much eagerness I should destroy all our hopes of reaping any benefit from this fortunate event. If you will only endeavour to appear tranquil or unconcerned, you will quiet their suspicions, and I have no doubt they will then let me go with them to the beach, supposing that I merely go out of curiosity. Should I succeed in getting down to the boats, I will make known the condition in which I have left you, and measures may then be taken to secure our escape."

In the expediency of this I could not but acquiesce; and as the natives had now completed their preparations, I watched with the liveliest interest the reception that Toby's application might meet with. As soon as they understood from my companion that I intended to remain, they appeared to make no objection to his proposition, and even hailed it with pleasure. Their singular conduct on this occasion not a little puzzled me at the time, and imparted to subsequent events an additional mystery.

The islanders were now to be seen hurrying along the path which led to the sea. I shook Toby warmly by the hand, and gave him my Payta hat to shield his wounded head from the sun, as he had lost his own. He cordially returned the pressure of my hand, and solemnly promising to return as soon as the boats should leave the shore, sprang from my side, and the next minute disappeared in a turn of the grove.

In spite of the unpleasant reflections that crowded upon my mind, I could not but be entertained by the novel and animated sight which now met my view. One after another the natives crowded along the narrow path, laden with every variety of fruit. Here, you might have seen one, who, after ineffectually endeavouring to persuade a surly porker to be conducted in leading strings, was obliged at last to seize the perverse animal in his arms, and carry him struggling against his naked breast, and squealing without intermission. There went two, who at a little distance might have been taken for the Hebrew spies, on their return to Moses with the goodly bunch of grapes. One trotted before the other at a distance of a couple of yards, while between them, from a pole resting on their shoulders, was suspended a huge cluster of banannas, which swayed to and fro with the rocking gait at which they proceeded. Here ran another, perspiring with his exertions, and bearing before him a quantity of cocoa-nuts, who, fearful of being too late, heeded not the fruit that dropped from his basket, and appeared solely intent upon reaching his destination, careless how many of his cocoa-nuts kept company with him.

In a short time the last straggler was seen hurrying on his way, and the faint shouts of those in advance died insensibly upon the ear. Our part of the valley now appeared nearly deserted by its inhabitants, Kory-Kory, his aged father, and a few decrepid old people being all that were left.

Towards sunset the islanders in small parties began to return from the beach, and among them, as they drew near to the house, I sought to descry the form of my companion. But one after another they passed the dwelling, and I caught no glimpse of him. Supposing, however, that he would soon appear with some of the members of the household, I quieted my apprehensions, and waited patiently to see him advancing in company with the beautiful Fayaway. At last, I perceived Tinor coming forward, followed by the girls and young men who usually resided in the house of Marheyo; but with them came not my comrade, and, filled with a thousand alarms, I eagerly sought to discover the cause of his delay.

My earnest questions appeared to embarrass the natives greatly. All their accounts were contradictory: one giving me to understand that Toby would be with me in a very short time; another that he did not know where he was; while a third, violently inveighing against him, assured me that he had stolen away, and would never come back. It appeared to me, at the time, that in making these various statements they endeavoured to conceal from me some terible disaster, lest the knowledge of it should overpower me.

Fearful lest some fatal calamity had overtaken him, I sought out young Fayaway, and endeavoured to learn from her, if possible, the truth.

This gentle being had early attracted my regard, not only from her extraordinary beauty, but from the attractive cast of her countenance, singularly expressive of intelligence and humanity. Of all the natives she alone seemed to appreciate the effect which the peculiarity of the circumstances in which we were placed had produced upon the minds of my companion and myself. In addressing me—especially when I lay reclining upon the mats suffering from pain—there was a tenderness in her manner which it was impossible to misunderstand or resist. Whenever she entered the house, the expression of her face indicated the liveliest sympathy for me; and moving towards the place where I lay, with one arm slightly elevated in a gesture of pity, and her large glistening eyes gazing intently into mine, she would murmur plaintively, "Awha! awha! Tommo," and seat herself mournfully beside me.

Her manner convinced me that she deeply compassionated my situation, as being removed from my country and friends, and placed beyond the reach of all relief. Indeed, at times I was almost led to believe that her mind was swayed by gentle impulses hardly to be anticipated from one in her condition; that she appeared to be conscious there were ties rudely severed, which had once bound us to our homes; that there were sisters and brothers anxiously looking forward to our return, who were, perhaps, never more to behold us.

In this amiable light did Fayaway appear in my eyes; and reposing full confidence in her candour and intelligence, I now had recourse to her, in the midst of my alarm, with regard to my companion.

My questions evidently distressed her. She looked round from one to another of the bystanders, as if hardly knowing what answer to give me. At last, yielding to my importunities, she overcame her scruples, and gave me to understand that Toby had gone away with the boats which had visited the bay, but had promised to return at the expiration of three days. At first I accused him of perfidiously deserting me; but as I grew more composed, I upbraided myself for imputing so cowardly an action to him, and tranquillized myself with the belief that he had availed himself of the opportunity to go round to Nukuheva, in order to make some arrangement by which I could be removed from the valley. At any rate, thought I, he will return with the medicines I require, and then, as soon as I recover, there will be no difficulty in the way of our departure.

Consoling myself with these reflections, I lay down that night in a happier frame of mind than I had done for some time. The next day passed without any allusion to Toby on the part of the natives, who seemed desirous of avoiding all reference to the subject. This raised some apprehensions in my breast; but when night came, I congratulated myself that the second day had now gone by, and that on the morrow Toby would again be with me. But the morrow came and went, and my companion did not appear. Ah! thought I, he reckons three days from the morning of his departure,—to-morrow he will arrive. But that weary day also closed upon me, without his return. Even yet I would not despair; I thought that something detained him —that he was waiting for the sailing of a boat, at Nukuheva, and that in a day or two at farthest I should see him again. But day after day of renewed disappointment passed by; at last hope deserted me, and I fell a victim to despair.

Yes, thought I, gloomily, he has secured his own escape, and cares not what calamity may befall his unfortunate comrade. Fool that I was, to suppose that any one would willingly encounter the perils of this valley, after having once got beyond its limits! He has gone, and has left me to combat alone all the dangers by which I am surrounded. Thus would I sometimes seek to derive a desperate consolation from dwelling upon the perfidy of Toby: whilst at other times I sunk under the bitter remorse which I felt as having by my own imprudence brought upon myself the fate which I was sure awaited me.

At other times I thought that perhaps after all these treacherous savages have made away with him, and thence the confusion into which they were thrown by my questions, and their contradictory answers, or he might be a captive in some other part of the valley; or, more dreadful still, might have met with that fate at which my very soul shuddered. But all these speculations were vain; no tidings of Toby ever reached me; he had gone never to return.

The conduct of the islanders appeared inexplicable. All reference to my lost comrade was carefully evaded, and if at any time they were forced to make some reply to my frequent inquiries on the subject, they would uniformly denounce him as an ungrateful runaway, who had deserted his friend, and taken himself off to that vile and detestable place Nukuheva.

But whatever might have been his fate, now that he was gone, the natives multiplied their acts of kindness and attention towards myself, treating me with a degree of deference which could hardly have been surpassed had I been some celestial visitant. Kory-Kory never for one moment left my side, unless it were to execute my wishes. The faithful fellow, twice every day, in the cool of the morning and in the evening, insisted upon carrying me to the stream, and bathing me in its refreshing water.

Frequently in the afternoon he would carry me to a particular part of the stream, where the beauty of the scene produced a soothing influence upon my mind. At this place the waters flowed between grassy banks, planted with enormous bread-fruit trees, whose vast branches interlacing overhead, formed a leafy canopy; near the stream were several smooth black rocks. One of these, projecting several feet above the surface of the water, had upon its summit a shallow cavity, which, filled with freshly-gathered leaves, formed a delightful couch.

Here I often lay for hours, covered with a gauze-like veil of tappa, while Fayaway, seated beside me, and holding in her hand a fan woven from the leaflets of a young cocoa-nut bough, brushed aside the insects that occasionally lighted on my face, and Kory-Kory, with a view of chasing away my melancholy, performed a thousand antics in the water before us.

As my eye wandered along this romantic stream, it would fall upon the half-immersed figure of a beautiful girl, standing in the transparent water, and catching in a little net a species of diminutive shell-fish, of which these people are extravagantly fond. Sometimes a chattering group would be seated upon the edge of a low rock in the midst of the brook, busily engaged in thinning and polishing the shells of cocoa-nuts, by rubbing them briskly with a small stone in the water, an operation which soon converts them into a light and elegant drinking vessel, somewhat resembling goblets made of tortoiseshell.

But the tranquillizing influences of beautiful scenery, and the exhibition of human life under so novel and charming an aspect, were not my only sources of consolation.

Every evening the girls of the house gathered about me on the mats, and after chasing away Kory-Kory from my side—who, nevertheless, retired only to a little distance and watched their proceedings with the most jealous attention—would anoint my whole body with a fragrant oil, squeezed from a yellow root, previously pounded between a couple of stones, and which in their language is denominated "aka." And most refreshing and agreeable are the juices of the "aka," when applied to one's limbs by the soft palms of sweet nymphs, whose bright eyes are beaming upon you with kindness; and I used to hail with delight the daily recurrence of this luxurious operation, in which I forgot all my troubles, and buried for the time every feeling of sorrow.

Sometimes in the cool of the evening my devoted servitor would lead me out upon the pi-pi in front of the house, and seating me near its edge, protect my body from the annoyances of the insects which occasionally hovered in the air, by wrapping me round with a large roll of tappa. He then bustled about, and employed himself at least twenty minutes in adjusting everything to secure my personal comfort.

Having perfected his arrangements, he would get my pipe, and, lighting it, would hand it to me. Often he was obliged to strike a light for the occasion, and as the mode he adopted was entirely different from what I had ever seen or heard of before, I will describe it.

A straight, dry, and partly decayed stick of the Habiscus, about six feet in length, and half as many inches in diameter, with a smaller bit of wood not more than a foot long, and scarcely an inch wide, is as invariably to be met with in every house in Typee as a box of lucifer matches in the corner of a kitchen cupboard at home.

The islander, placing the larger stick obliquely against some object, with one end elevated at an angle of forty-five degrees, mounts astride of it like an urchin about to gallop off upon a cane, and then grasping the smaller one firmly in both hands, he rubs its pointed end slowly up and down the extent of a few inches on the principal stick, until at last he makes a narrow groove in the wood, with an abrupt termination at the point furthest from him, where all the dusty particles which the friction creates are accumulated in a little heap.

At first Kory-Kory goes to work quite leisurely, but gradually quickens his pace, and waxing warm in the employment, drives the stick furiously along the smoking channel, plying his hands to and fro with amazing rapidity, the perspiration starting from every pore. As he approaches the climax of his effort, he pants and gasps for breath, and his eyes almost start from their sockets with the violence of his exertions. This is the critical stage of the operation; all his previous labours are vain if he cannot sustain the rapidity of the movement until the reluctant spark is produced. Suddenly he stops, becomes perfectly motionless. His hands still retain their hold of the smaller stick, which is pressed convulsively against the further end of the channel among the fine powder there accumulated, as if he had just pierced through and through some little viper that was wriggling and struggling to escape from his clutches. The next moment a delicate wreath of smoke curls spirally into the air, the heap of dusty particles glows with fire, and Kory-Kory almost breathless, dismounts from his steed.

This operation appeared to me to be the most laborious species of work performed in Typee; and had I possessed a sufficient intimacy with the language to have conveyed my ideas upon the subject, I should certainly have suggested to the most influential of the natives the expediency of establishing a college of vestals to be centrally located in the valley, for the purpose of keeping alive the indispensable article of fire; so as to supersede the necessity of such a vast outlay of strength and good temper, as were usually squandered on these occasions. There might, however, be special difficulties in carrying this plan into execution.

What a striking evidence does this operation furnish of the wide difference between the extreme of savage and civilized life. A gentleman of Typee can bring up a numerous family of children and give them all a highly respectable cannibal education, with infinitely less toil and anxiety than he expends in the simple process of striking a light; whilst a poor European artisan, who through the instrumentality of a lucifer performs the same operation in one second, is put to his wit's end to provide for his starving offspring that food which the children of a Polynesian father, without troubling their parent, pluck from the branches of every tree around them.

CHAPTER XV

Kindness of Marheyo and the rest of the Islanders—A full Description of the Bread-fruit Tree—Different Modes of preparing the Fruit.

ALL the inhabitants of the valley treated me with great kindness; but as to the household of Marheyo, with whom I was now permanently domiciled, nothing could surpass their efforts to minister to my comfort. To the gratification of my palate they paid the most unwearied attention. They continually invited me to partake of food, and when after eating heartily I declined the viands they continued to offer me, they seemed to think that my appetite stood in need of some piquant stimulant to excite its activity.

In pursuance of this idea, old Marheyo himself would hie him away to the sea-shore by the break of day, for the purpose of collecting various species of rare sea-weed; some of which among these people are considered a great luxury. After a whole day spent in this employment, he would return about nightfall with several cocoa-nut shells filled with different descriptions of kelp. In preparing these for use he manifested all the ostentation of a professed cook, although the chief mystery of the affair appeared to consist in pouring water in judicious quantities upon the slimy contents of his cocoa-nut shells.

The first time he submitted one of these saline salads to my critical attention I naturally thought that anything collected at such pains must possess peculiar merits; but one mouthful was a complete dose; and great was the consternation of the old warrior at the rapidity with which I ejected his Epicurean treat.

How true it is, that the rarity of any particular article enhances its value amazingly. In some part of the valley —I know not where, but probably in the neighbourhood of the sea—the girls were sometimes in the habit of procuring small quantities of salt, a thimble-full or so being the result of the united labours of a party of five or six employed for the greater part of the day. This precious commodity they brought to the house, enveloped in multitudinous folds of leaves; and as a special mark of the esteem in which they held me, would spread an immense leaf on the ground, and dropping one by one a few minute particles of the salt upon it, invite me to taste them.

From the extravagant value placed upon the article, I verily believe, that with a bushel of common Liverpool salt all the real estate in Typee might have been purchased. With a small pinch of it in one hand, and a quarter section of a bread-fruit in the other, the greatest chief in the valley would have laughed at all the luxuries of a Parisian table.

The celebrity of the bread-fruit tree, and the conspicuous place it occupies in a Typee bill of fare, induces me to give at some length a general description of the tree, and the various modes in which the fruit is prepared.

The bread-fruit tree, in its glorious prime, is a grand and towering object, forming the same feature in a Marquesan landscape that the patriarchal elm does in New

England scenery. The latter tree it not a little resembles in height, in the wide spread of its stalwart branches, and in its venerable and imposing aspect.

The leaves of the bread-fruit are of great size, and their edges are cut and scolloped as fantastically as those of a lady's lace collar. As they annually tend towards decay, they almost rival in the brilliant variety of their gradually changing hues the fleeting shades of the expiring dolphin. The autumnal tints of our American forests, glorious as they are, sink into nothing in comparison with this tree.

The leaf, in one particular stage, when nearly all the prismatic colours are blended on its surface, is often converted by the natives into a superb and striking head-dress. The principal fibre traversing its length being split open a convenient distance, and the elastic sides of the aperture pressed apart, the head is inserted between them, the leaf drooping on one side, with its forward half turned jauntily up on the brows, and the remaining part spreading laterally behind the ears.

The fruit somewhat resembles in magnitude and general appearance one of our citron melons of ordinary size; but, unlike the citron, it has no sectional lines drawn along the outside. Its surface is dotted all over with little conical prominences, looking not unlike the knobs on an antiquated church door. The rind is perhaps an eighth of an inch in thickness; and denuded of this, at the time when it is in the greatest perfection, the fruit presents a beautiful globe of white pulp, the whole of which may be eaten, with the exception of a slender core, which is easily removed.

The bread-fruit, however, is never used, and is indeed altogether unfit to be eaten, until submitted in one form or other to the action of fire.

The most simple manner in which this operation is performed, and I think, the best, consists in placing any number of the freshly plucked fruit, when in a particular stage of greenness, among the embers of a fire, in the same way that you would roast a potato. After the lapse of ten or fifteen minutes, the green rind embrowns and cracks, showing through the fissures in its sides the milk-white interior. As soon as it cools, the rind drops off, and you then have the soft round pulp in its purest and most delicious state. Thus eaten, it has a mild and pleasing flavour.

Sometimes, after having been roasted in the fire, the natives snatch it briskly from the embers, and permitting it to slip out of the yielding rind into a vessel of cold water, stir up the mixture, which they call "bo-a-sho." I never could endure this compound, and indeed the preparation is not greatly in vogue among the more polite Typees.

There is one form, however, in which the fruit is occasionally served, that renders it a dish fit for a king. As soon as it is taken from the fire the exterior is removed, the core extracted, and the remaining part is placed in a sort of shallow stone mortar, and briskly worked with a pestle of the same substance. While one person is performing this operation, another takes a ripe cocoa-nut, and breaking it in half, which they also do very cleverly, proceeds to grate the juicy meat into fine particles. This is done by means of a piece of mother-of-pearl shell, lashed firmly to the extreme end of a heavy stick, with its straight side accurately notched like a saw. The stick is sometimes a grotesquely-formed limb of a tree, with three or four branches twisting from its body like so many shapeless legs, and sustaining it two or three feet from the ground.

The native, first placing a calabash beneath the nose, as it were, of his curious-looking log-steed, for the purpose of receiving the grated fragments as they fall, mounts astride of it as if it were a hobby-horse, and twirling the inside of one of his hemispheres of cocoa-nut around the sharp teeth of the mother-of-pearl shell, the pure white meat falls in snowy showers into the receptacle provided. Having obtained a quantity sufficient for his purpose, he places it in a bag made of the net-like fibrous substance attached to all cocoa-nut trees, and compressing it over the bread-fruit, which being now sufficiently pounded, is put into a wooden bowl—extracts a thick creamy milk. The delicious liquid soon bubbles round the fruit, and leaves it at last just peeping above its surface.

This preparation is called "kokoo," and a most luscious preparation it is. The hobby-horse and the pestle and mortar were in great requisition during the time I remained in the house of Marheyo, and Kory-Kory had frequent occasion to show his skill in their use.

But the great staple articles of food into which the bread-fruit is converted by these natives are known respectively by the names of Amar and Poee-Poee.

At certain seasons of the year, when the fruit of the hundred groves of the valley has reached its maturity, and hangs in golden spheres from every branch, the islanders assemble in harvest groups, and garner in the abundance which surrounds them. The trees are stripped of their nodding burdens, which, easily freed from the rind and core, are gathered together in capacious wooden vessels, where the pulpy fruit is soon worked by a stone pestle, vigorously applied, into a blended mass of a doughy consistency, called by the natives "Tutao." This is then divided into separate parcels, which, after being made up into stout packages, enveloped in successive folds of leaves, and bound round with thongs of bark, are stored away in large receptacles hollowed in the earth, from whence they are drawn as occasion may require.

In this condition the Tutao sometimes remains for years, and even is thought to improve by age. Before it is fit to be eaten, however, it has to undergo an additional process. A primitive oven is scooped in the ground, and its bottom being loosely covered with stones, a large fire is kindled within it. As soon as the requisite degree of heat is attained, the embers are removed, and the surface of the stones being covered with thick layers of leaves, one of the larger packages of Tutao is deposited upon them, and overspread with another layer of leaves. The whole is then quickly heaped up with earth, and forms a sloping mound.

The Tutao thus baked is called "Amar;" the action of the oven having converted it into an amber-coloured caky substance, a little tart, but not at all disagreeable to the taste.

By another and final process the "Amar" is changed into "Poee-Poee." This transition is rapidly effected. The amar is placed in a vessel, and mixed with water until it gains a proper pudding-like consistency, when, without further preparation, it is in readiness for use. This is the form in which the "Tutao" is generally consumed. The singular mode of eating it I have already described.

Were it not that the bread-fruit is thus capable of being preserved for a length of time, the natives might be reduced to a state of starvation; for owing to some unknown cause the trees sometimes fail to bear fruit; and on such occasions the islanders chiefly depend upon the supplies they have been enabled to store away.

This stately tree, which is rarely met with upon the Sandwich Islands, and then only of a very inferior quality, and at Tahiti does not abound to a degree that renders its fruit the principal article of food, attains its greatest excellence in the genial climate of the Marquesan group, where it grows to an enormous magnitude, and flourishes in the utmost abundance.

CHAPTER XVI

Melancholy condition—Occurrence at the Ti—Anecdote of Marheyo
—Shaving the Head of a Warrior.

IN LOOKING back to this period, and calling to remembrance the numberless proofs of kindness and respect which I received from the natives of the valley, I can scarcely understand how it was that, in the midst of so many consolatory circumstances, my mind should still have been consumed by the most dismal forebodings, and have remained a prey to the profoundest melancholy. It is true that the suspicious circumstances which had attended the disappearance of Toby were enough of themselves to excite distrust with regard to the savages, in whose power I felt myself to be entirely placed, especially when it was combined with the knowledge that these very men, kind and respectful as they were to me, were, after all, nothing better than a set of cannibals.

But my chief source of anxiety, and that which poisoned every temporary enjoyment, was the mysterious disease in my leg, which still remained unabated. All the herbal applications of Tinor, united with the severer discipline of the old leech, and the affectionate nursing of Kory-Kory, had failed to relieve me. I was almost a cripple, and the pain I endured at intervals was agonizing. The unaccountable malady showed no signs of amendment; on the contrary, its violence increased day by day, and threatened the most fatal results, unless some powerful means were employed to counteract it. It seemed as if I were destined to sink under this grievous affliction, or at least that it would hinder me from availing myself of any opportunity of escaping from the valley.

An incident which occurred as nearly as I can estimate

about three weeks after the disappearance of Toby, convinced me that the natives, from some reason or other, would interpose every possible obstacle to my leaving them.

One morning there was no little excitement evinced by the people near my abode, and which I soon discovered proceeded from a vague report that boats had been seen at a great distance approaching the bay. Immediately all was bustle and animation. It so happened that day that the pain I suffered having somewhat abated, and feeling in much better spirits than usual, I had complied with Kory-Kory's invitation to visit the chief Mehevi at the place called the "Ti," which I have before described as being situated within the precincts of the Taboo Groves. These sacred recesses were at no great distance from Marheyo's habitation, and lay between it and the sea; the path that conducted to the beach passing directly in front of the Ti, and thence skirting along the border of the groves.

I was reposing upon the mats, within the sacred building, in company with Mehevi and several other chiefs, when the announcement was first made. It sent a thrill of joy through my whole frame;—perhaps Toby was about to return. I rose at once to my feet, and my instinctive impulse was to hurry down to the beach, equally regardless of the distance that separated me from it, and of my disabled condition. As soon as Mehevi noticed the effect the intelligence had produced upon me, and the impatience I betrayed to reach the sea, his countenance assumed that inflexible rigidity of expression which had so awed me on the afternoon of our arrival at the house of Marheyo. As I was proceeding to leave the Ti, he laid his hand upon my shoulder, and said gravely, "abo, abo" (wait, wait). Solely intent upon the one thought that occupied my mind, and heedless of his request, I was brushing past him, when suddenly he assumed a tone of authority, and told me to "moee" (sit down). Though struck by the alteration in his demeanor, the excitement under which I laboured was too strong to permit me to obey the unexpected command, and I was still limping towards the edge of the pi-pi with Kory-Kory clinging to one arm in his efforts to restrain me, when the natives around starting to their feet, ranged themselves along the open front of the building, while Mehevi looked at me scowlingly, and reiterated his commands still more sternly.

It was at this moment, when fifty savage countenances were glaring upon me, that I first truly experienced I was indeed a captive in the valley. The conviction rushed upon me with staggering force, and I was overwhelmed by this confirmation of my worst fears. I saw at once that it was useless for me to resist, and sick at heart, I reseated myself upon the mats, and for the moment abandoned myself to despair.

I now perceived the natives one after the other hurrying past the Ti and pursuing the route that conducted to the sea. These savages, thought I, will soon be holding communication with some of my own countrymen perhaps, who with ease could restore me to liberty did they know of the situation I was in. No language can describe the wretchedness which I felt; and in the bitterness of my soul I imprecated a thousand curses on the perfidious Toby, who had thus abandoned me to destruction. It was in vain that Kory-Kory tempted me with food, or lighted my pipe, or sought to attract my attention by performing the uncouth antics that had sometimes diverted me. I was fairly knocked down by this last misfortune, which, much as I had feared it, I had never before had the courage calmly to contemplate.

Regardless of every thing but my own sorrow, I remained in the Ti for several hours, until shouts proceeding at intervals from the groves beyond the house proclaimed the return of the natives from the beach.

Whether any boats visited the bay that morning or not, I never could ascertain. The savages assured me that there had not—but I was inclined to believe that by deceiving me in this particular they sought to allay the violence of my grief. However that might be, this incident showed plainly that the Typees intended to hold me a prisoner. As they still treated me with the same sedulous attention as before, I was utterly at a loss how to account for their singular conduct. Had I been in a situation to instruct them in any of the rudiments of the mechanic arts, or had I manifested a disposition to render myself in any way useful among them, their conduct might have been attributed to some adequate motive, but as it was the matter seemed to me inexplicable.

During my whole stay on the island there occurred but two or three instances where the natives applied to me with the view of availing themselves of my superior information. And these now appear so ludicrous that I cannot forbear relating them.

The few things we had brought from Nukuheva had been done up into a small bundle which we had carried with us in our descent to the valley. This bundle, the first night of our arrival, I had used as a pillow, but on the succeeding morning, opening it for the inspection of the natives, they gazed upon the miscellaneous contents as though I had just revealed to them a casket of diamonds, and they insisted that so precious a treasure should be properly secured. A line was accordingly attached to it, and the other end being passed over the ridge-pole of the house, it was hoisted up to the apex of the roof, where it hung suspended directly over the mats where I usually reclined. When I desired anything from it I merely raised my finger to a bamboo beside me, and taking hold of the string which was there fastened, lowered the package. This was exceedingly handy, and I took care to let the natives understand how much I applauded the invention. Of this package the chief contents were a razor with its case, a supply of needles and thread, a pound or two of tobacco, and a few yards of a bright-coloured calico.

I should have mentioned that shortly after Toby's disappearance, perceiving the uncertainty of the time I might be obliged to remain in the valley–if, indeed, I ever should escape from it—and considering that my whole wardrobe consisted of a shirt and a pair of trousers, I resolved to doff these garments at once, in order to preserve them in a suitable condition for wear should I again appear among civilized beings. I was consequently obliged to assume the Typee costume, a little altered, however, to suit my own views of propriety, and in which I have no doubt I appeared to as much advantage as a senator of Rome enveloped in the folds of his toga. A few folds of yellow tappa tucked about my waist, descended to my feet in the style of a lady's petticoat, only I did not have recourse to those voluminous paddings in the rear with which our gentle dames are in the habit of augmenting the sublime rotundity of their figures. This usually comprised my in-door dress: whenever I walked out, I superadded to it an ample robe of the same material, which completely enveloped my person, and screened it from the rays of the sun.

One morning I made a rent in this mantle; and to show the islanders with what facility it could be repaired, I lowered my bundle, and taking from it a needle and thread, proceeded to stitch up the opening. They regarded this wonderful application of science with intense admiration; and whilst I was stitching away, old Marheyo, who was one of the lookers-on, suddenly clapped his hand to his forehead, and rushing to a corner of the house, drew forth a soiled and tattered strip of faded calico—which he must have procured some time or other in traffic on the beach—and besought me eagerly to exercise a little of my art upon it. I willingly complied, though certainly so stumpy a needle as mine never took such gigantic strides over calico before. The repairs completed, old Marheyo gave me a paternal hug; and divesting himself of his "maro" (girdle), swathed the calico about his loins, and slipping the beloved ornaments into his ears, grasped his spear and sallied out of the house, like a valiant Templer arrayed in a new and costly suit of armour.

I never used my razor during my stay in the island, but, although a very subordinate affair, it had been vastly admired by the Typees; and Narmonee, a great hero among them, who was exceedingly precise in the arrangements of his toilet and the general adjustment of his person, being the most accurately tattooed and laboriously horrified individual in all the valley, thought it would be a great advantage to have it applied to the already shaven crown of his head.

The implement they usually employ is a shark's tooth, which is about as well adapted to the purpose as a one-pronged fork for pitching hay. No wonder, then, that the acute Narmonee perceived the advantage my razor possessed over the usual implement. Accordingly, one day he requested as a personal favour that I would just run over his head with the razor. In reply, I gave him to understand that it was too dull, and could not be used to any purpose without being previously sharpened. To assist my meaning, I went through an imaginary honing process on the palm of my hand. Narmonee took my meaning in an instant, and running out of the house, returned the next moment with a huge rough mass of rock as big as a milestone, and indicated to me that that was exactly the thing I wanted. Of course there was nothing left for me but to proceed to business, and I began scraping away at a great rate. He writhed and wriggled under the infliction, but, fully convinced of my skill, endured the pain like a martyr.

Though I never saw Narmonee in battle, I will, from what I then observed, stake my life upon his courage and fortitude. Before commencing operations, his head had presented a surface of short bristling hairs, and by the time I had concluded my unskilful operation it resembled not a little a stubble field after being gone over with a harrow. However, as the chief expressed the liveliest satisfaction at the result, I was too wise to dissent from his opinion.

CHAPTER XVII

Improvement in Health and Spirits—Felicity of the Typees—Their Enjoyments compared with those of more enlightened Communities—Comparative Wickedness of civilized and unenlightened People—A Skirmish in the Mountain with the Warriors of Happar.

DAY after day wore on, and still there was no perceptible change in the conduct of the islanders towards me. Gradually I lost all knowledge of the regular occurrence of the days of the week, and sunk insensibly into that kind of apathy which ensues after some violent outbreak of despair. My limb suddenly healed, the swelling went down, the pain subsided, and I had every reason to suppose I should soon completely recover from the affliction that had so long tormented me.

As soon as I was enabled to ramble about the valley in company with the natives, troops of whom followed me whenever I sallied out of the house, I began to experience an elasticity of mind which placed me beyond the reach of those dismal forebodings to which I had so lately been a prey. Received wherever I went with the most deferential kindness; regaled perpetually with the most delightful fruits; ministered to by dark-eyed nymphs; and enjoying besides all the services of the devoted Kory-Kory, I thought that for a sojourn among cannibals, no man could have well made a more agreeable one.

To be sure there were limits set to my wanderings. Toward the sea my progress was barred by an express prohibition of the savages; and after having made two or three ineffectual attempts to reach it, as much to gratify my curiosity as anything else, I gave up the idea. It was in vain to think of reaching it by stealth, since the natives escorted me in numbers wherever I went, and not for one single moment that I can recall to mind was I ever permitted to be alone.

The green and precipitous elevations that stood ranged around the head of the vale where Marheyo's habitation was situated effectually precluded all hope of escape in that quarter, even if I could have stolen away from the thousand eyes of the savages.

But these reflections now seldom obtruded upon me; I gave myself up to the passing hour, and if ever disagreeable thoughts arose in my mind, I drove them away. When I looked around the verdant recess in which I was buried, and gazed up to the summits of the lofty eminence that hemmed me in, I was well disposed to think that I was in the "Happy Valley," and that beyond those heights there was nought but a world of care and anxiety.

As I extended my wanderings in the valley and grew more familiar with the habits of its inmates, I was fain to confess that, despite the disadvantages of his condition, the Polynesian savage, surrounded by all the luxurious provisions of nature, enjoyed an infinitely happier, though certainly a less intellectual existence, than the self-complacent European.

The naked wretch who shivers beneath the bleak skies,

and starves among the inhospitable wilds of Terra-del-Fuego, might indeed be made happier by civilization, for it would alleviate his physical wants. But the voluptuous Indian, with every desire supplied, whom Providence has bountifully provided with all the sources of pure and natural enjoyment, and from whom are removed so many of the ills and pains of life—what has he to desire at the hands of Civilization? She may "cultivate his mind,"—may "elevate his thoughts,"—these I believe are the established phrases—but will he be the happier? Let the once smiling and populous Hawaiian islands, with their now diseased, starving, and dying natives, answer the question. The missionaries may seek to disguise the matter as they will, but the facts are incontrovertible; and the devoutest Christian who visits that group with an unbiased mind, must go away mournfully asking—"Are these, alas! the fruits of twenty-five years of enlightening?"

In a primitive state of society, the enjoyments of life, though few and simple, are spread over a great extent, and are unalloyed; but Civilization, for every advantage she imparts, holds a hundred evils in reserve;—the heart burnings, the jealousies, the social rivalries, the family dissensions, and the thousand self-inflicted discomforts of refined life, which make up in units the swelling aggregate of human misery, are unknown among these unsophisticated people.

But it will be urged that these shocking unprincipled wretches are cannibals. Very true; and a rather bad trait in their character it must be allowed. But they are such only when they seek to gratify the passion of revenge upon their enemies; and I ask whether the mere eating of human flesh so very far exceeds in barbarity that custom which only a few years since was practised in enlightened England:—a convicted traitor, perhaps a man found guilty of honesty, patriotism, and suchlike heinous crimes, had his head lopped off with a huge axe, his bowels dragged out and thrown into a fire; while his body, carved into four quarters, was with his head exposed upon pikes, and permitted to rot and fester among the public haunts of men!

The fiend-like skill we display in the invention of all manner of death-dealing engines, the vindictiveness with which we carry on our wars, and the misery and desolation that follow in their train, are enough of themselves to distinguish the white civilized man as the most ferocious animal on the face of the earth.

His remorseless cruelty is seen in many of the institutions of our own favoured land. There is one in particular lately adopted in one of the States of the Union, which purports to have been dictated by the most merciful considerations. To destroy our malefactors piece-meal, drying up in their veins, drop by drop, the blood we are too chicken-hearted to shed by a single blow which would at once put a period to their sufferings, is deemed to be infinitely preferable to the old-fashioned punishment of gibbeting—much less annoying to the victim, and more in accordance with the refined spirit of the age; and yet how feeble is all language to describe the horrors we inflict upon these wretches, whom we mason up in the cells of our prisons, and condemn to perpetual solitude in the very heart of our population.

But it is needless to multiply the examples of civilized barbarity; they far exceed in the amount of misery they cause the crimes which we regard with such abhorrence in our less enlightened fellow-creatures.

The term "Savage" is, I conceive, often misapplied, and indeed when I consider the vices, cruelties, and enormities of every kind that spring up in the tainted atmosphere of a feverish civilization, I am inclined to think that so far as the relative wickedness of the parties is concerned, four or five Marquesan Islanders sent to the United States as

Missionaries might be quite as useful as an equal number of Americans despatched to the Islands in a similar capacity.

I once heard it given as an instance of the frightful depravity of a certain tribe in the Pacific, that they had no word in their language to express the idea of virtue. The assertion was unfounded; but were it otherwise, it might be met by stating that their language is almost entirely destitute of terms to express the delightful ideas conveyed by our endless catalogue of civilized crimes.

In the altered frame of mind to which I have referred, every object that presented itself to my notice in the valley struck me in a new light, and the opportunities I now enjoyed of observing the manners of its inmates, tended to strengthen my favourable impressions. One peculiarity that fixed my admiration was the perpetual hilarity reigning through the whole extent of the vale. There seemed to be no cares, griefs, troubles, or vexations, in all Typee. The hours tripped along as gaily as the laughing couples down a country dance.

There were none of those thousand sources of irritation that the ingenuity of civilized man has created to mar his own felicity. There were no foreclosures of mortgages, no protested notes, no bills payable, no debts of honour in Typee; no unreasonable tailors and shoemakers, perversely bent on being paid; no duns of any description; no assault and battery attorneys, to foment discord, backing their clients up to a quarrel, and then knocking their heads together; no poor relations, everlastingly occupying the spare bed-chamber, and diminishing the elbow room at the family table; no destitute widows with their children starving on the cold charities of the world; no beggars; no debtors' prisons; no proud and hard-hearted nabobs in Typee; or to sum up all in one word—no Money! "That root of all evil" was not to be found in the valley.

In this secluded abode of happiness there were no cross

old women, no cruel step-dames, no withered spinsters, no love-sick maidens, no sour old bachelors, no inattentive husbands, no melancholy young men, no blubbering youngsters, and no squalling brats. All was mirth, fun, and high good humour. Blue devils, hypochondria, and doleful dumps, went and hid themselves among the nooks and crannies of the rocks.

Here you would see a parcel of children frolicking together the live-long day, and no quarreling, no contention, among them. The same number in our own land could not have played together for the space of an hour without biting or scratching one another. There you might have seen a throng of young females, not filled with envyings of each other's charms, nor displaying the ridiculous affectations of gentility, nor yet moving in whalebone corsets, like so many automatons, but free, inartificially happy, and unconstrained.

There were some spots in that sunny vale where they would frequently resort to decorate themselves with garlands of flowers. To have seen them reclining beneath the shadows of one of the beautiful groves; the ground about them strewn with freshly gathered buds and blossoms, employed in weaving chaplets and necklaces, one would have thought that all the train of Flora had gathered together to keep a festival in honour of their mistress.

With the young men there seemed almost always some matter of diversion or business on hand that afforded a constant variety of enjoyment. But whether fishing, or carving canoes, or polishing their ornaments, never was there exhibited the least sign of strife or contention among them.

As for the warriors, they maintained a tranquil dignity of demeanor, journeying occasionally from house to house, where they were always sure to be received with the attention bestowed upon distinguished guests. The old men, of whom there were many in the vale, seldom stirred from their mats, where they would recline for hours and hours, smoking and talking to one another with all the garrulity of age.

But the continual happiness, which so far as I was able to judge appeared to prevail in the valley, sprung principally from that all-pervading sensation which Rousseau has told us he at one time experienced, the mere buoyant sense of a healthful physical existence. And indeed in this particular the Typees had ample reason to felicitate themselves, for sickness was almost unknown. During the whole period of my stay I saw but one invalid among them; and on their smooth clear skins you observed no blemish or mark of disease.

The general repose, however, upon which I have just been descanting, was broken in upon about this time by an event which proved that the islanders were not entirely exempt from those occurrences which disturb the quiet of more civilized communities.

Having now been a considerable time in the valley, I began to feel surprised that the violent hostility subsisting between its inhabitants, and those of the adjoining bay of Happar, should never have manifested itself in any warlike encounter. Although the valiant Typees would often by gesticulations declare their undying hatred against their enemies, and the disgust they felt at their cannibal propensities; although they dilated upon the manifold injuries they had received at their hands, yet with a forbearance truly commendable, they appeared patiently to sit down under their grievances, and to refrain from making any reprisals. The Happars, entrenched behind their mountains, and never even showing themselves on their summits, did not appear to me to furnish adequate cause for that excess of animosity evinced towards them by the heroic tenants of our vale, and I was inclined to believe that the deeds of blood attributed to them had been greatly exaggerated.

On the other hand, as the clamours of war had not up to this period disturbed the serenity of the tribe, I began to distrust the truth of those reports which ascribed so fierce and belligerent a character to the Typee nation. Surely, thought I, all these terrible stories I have heard about the inveteracy with which they carried on the feud, their deadly intensity of hatred, and the diabolical malice with which they glutted their revenge upon the inanimate forms of the slain, are nothing more than fables, and I must confess that I experienced something like a sense of regret at having my hideous anticipations thus disappointed. I felt in some sort like a 'prentice-boy who, going to the play in the expectation of being delighted with a cut-and-thrust tragedy, is almost moved to tears of disappointment at the exhibition of a genteel comedy.

I could not avoid thinking that I had fallen in with a greatly traduced people, and I moralized not a little upon the disadvantage of having a bad name, which in this instance had given a tribe of savages, who were as pacific as so many lambkins, the reputation of a confederacy of giant-killers.

But subsequent events proved that I had been a little too premature in coming to this conclusion. One day about noon, happening to be at the Ti, I had lain down on the mats with several of the chiefs, and had gradually sunk into a most luxurious siesta, when I was awakened by a tremendous outcry, and starting up beheld the natives seizing their spears and hurrying out, while the most puissant of the chiefs, grasping the six muskets which were ranged against the bamboos, followed after, and soon disappeared in the groves. These movements were accompanied by wild shouts, in which "Happar, Happar," greatly predominated. The islanders were now to be seen running past the Ti, and striking across the valley to the Happar side. Presently I heard the sharp report of a musket from the adjoining hills, and then a burst of voices in the same direction. At this the women, who had congregated in the groves, set up the most violent clamours, as they invariably do here as elsewhere on every occasion of excitement and alarm, with a view of tranquillizing their own minds and disturbing other people. On this particular occasion they made such an outrageous noise, and continued it with such perseverance, that for awhile, had entire volleys of musketry been fired off in the neighbouring mountains, I should not have been able to have heard them.

When this female commotion had a little subsided I listened eagerly for further information. At last bang went another shot, and then a second volley of yells from the hills. Again all was quiet, and continued so for such a length of time that I began to think the contending armies had agreed upon a suspension of hostilities; when pop went a third gun, followed as before with a yell. After this, for nearly two hours nothing occurred worthy of comment, save some straggling shouts from the hill-side, sounding like the halloos of a parcel of truant boys who had lost themselves in the woods.

During this interval I had remained standing on the piazza of the "Ti," which directly fronted the Happar mountain, and with no one near me but Kory-Kory and the old superannuated savages I have before described. These latter never stirred from their mats, and seemed altogether unconscious that anything unusual was going on.

As for Kory-Kory, he appeared to think that we were in the midst of great events, and sought most zealously to impress me with a due sense of their importance. Every sound that reached us conveyed some momentous item of intelligence to him. At such times, as if he were gifted with second sight, he would go through a variety of pantomimic illustrations, showing me the precise manner in which the redoubtable Typees were at that very moment chastising the insolence of the enemy. "Mehevi hanna pippee nuee Happar," he exclaimed every five minutes, giving me to understand that under that distinguished captain the warriors of his nation were performing prodigies of valour.

Having heard only four reports from the muskets, I was led to believe that they were worked by the islanders in the same manner as the Sultan Solyman's ponderous artillery at the siege of Byzantium, one of them taking an hour or two to load and train. At last, no sound whatever proceeding from the mountains, I concluded that the contest had been determined one way or the other. Such appeared, indeed, to be the case, for in a little while a courier arrived at the "Ti," almost breathless with his exertions, and communicated the news of a great victory having been achieved by his countrymen: "Happar poo arva!—Happar poo arva!" (the cowards had fled). Kory-Kory was in ecstacies, and commenced a vehement harangue, which, so far as I understood it, implied that the result exactly agreed with his expectations, and which, moreover, was intended to convince me that it would be a perfectly useless undertaking, even for an army of fire-eaters, to offer battle to the irresistible heroes of our valley. In all this I of course acquiesced, and looked forward with no little interest to the return of the conquerors, whose victory I feared might not have been purchased without cost to themselves.

But here I was again mistaken; for Mehevi, in conducting his warlike operations, rather inclined to the Fabian than to the Bonapartean tactics, husbanding his resources and exposing his troops to no unnecessary hazards. The total loss of the victors in this obstinately contested affair was, in killed, wounded, and missing—one forefinger and part of a thumb-nail (which the late proprietor brought along with him in his hand), a severely contused arm, and a considerable effusion of blood flowing from the thigh of a chief, who had received an ugly thrust from a Happar spear. What the enemy had suffered I could not discover, but I presume they had succeeded in taking off with them the bodies of their slain.

Such was the issue of the battle, as far as its results came under my observation; and as it appeared to be considered an event of prodigious importance, I reasonably concluded that the wars of the natives were marked by no very sanguinary traits. I afterwards learned how the skirmish had originated. A number of the Happars had been discovered prowling for no good purpose on the Typee side of the mountain; the alarm was sounded, and the invaders, after a protracted resistance, had been chased over the frontier. But why had not the intrepid Mehevi carried the war into Happar? Why had he not made a descent into the hostile vale, and brought away some trophy of his victory —some materials for the cannibal entertainment which I had heard usually terminated every engagement? After all, I was much inclined to believe that such shocking festivals must occur very rarely among the islanders, if, indeed, they ever take place.

For two or three days the late event was the theme of general comment; after which the excitement gradually wore away, and the valley resumed its accustomed tranquillity.

CHAPTER XVIII

Swimming in company with the Girls of the Valley—A Canoe—Effects of the Taboo—A pleasure Excursion on the Pond—Beautiful Freak of Fayaway—Mantua-making—A Stranger arrives in the Valley—His mysterious conduct—Native Oratory—The Interview—Its Results—Departure of the Stranger.

RETURNING health and peace of mind gave a new interest to everything around me. I sought to diversify my time by as many enjoyments as lay within reach. Bathing in company with troops of girls formed one of my chief amusements. We sometimes enjoyed the recreation in the waters of a miniature lake, into which the central stream of the valley expanded. This lovely sheet of water was almost circular in figure, and about three hundred yards across. Its beauty was indescribable. All around its banks waved luxuriant masses of tropical foliage, soaring high above which were to be seen, here and there, the symmetrical shaft of the cocoa-nut tree, surmounted by its tuft of graceful branches, drooping in the air like so many waving ostrich plumes.

The ease and grace with which the maidens of the valley propelled themselves through the water, and their familiarity with the element, were truly astonishing. Sometimes they might be seen gliding along, just under the surface, without apparently moving hand or foot—then throwing themselves on their sides, they darted through the water, revealing glimpses of their forms, as, in the course of their rapid progress, they shot for an instant partly into the air—at one moment they dived deep down into the water and the next they rose bounding to the surface.

I remember upon one occasion plunging in among a parcel of these river-nymphs, and counting vainly upon my superior strength, sought to drag some of them under the water, but I quickly repented my temerity. The amphibious young creatures swarmed about me like a shoal of dolphins, and seizing hold of my devoted limbs, tumbled me about and ducked me under the surface, until from the strange noises which rang in my ears, and the supernatural visions dancing before my eyes, I thought I was in the land of spirits. I stood indeed as little chance among them as a cumbrous whale attacked on all sides by a legion of sword-fish. When at length they relinquished their hold of me, they swam away in every direction, laughing at my clumsy endeavours to reach them.

There was no boat on the lake; but at my solicitation and for my special use, some of the young men attached to Marheyo's household, under the direction of the indefatigable Kory-Kory, brought up a light and tastefully-carved canoe from the sea. It was launched upon the sheet of water, and floated there as gracefully as a swan. But, melancholy to relate, it produced an effect I had not anticipated. The sweet nymphs, who had sported with me before in the lake, now all fled its vicinity. The prohibited craft, guarded by the edicts of the "taboo," extended the prohibition to the waters in which it lay.

For a few days, Kory-Kory, with one or two other youths, accompanied me in my excursions to the lake, and while I paddled about in my light canoe, would swim after me shouting and gambolling in pursuit. But I was ever partial to what is termed in the 'Young Men's Own Book'—"the society of virtuous and intelligent young ladies;" and in the absence of the mermaids, the amusement became dull and insipid. One morning I expressed to my faithful servitor my desire for the return of the nymphs. The honest fellow looked at me bewildered for a moment, and then shook his head solemnly, and murmured *"taboo! taboo!"* giving me to understand that unless the canoe was removed, I could not expect to have the young ladies back again. But to this procedure I was averse; I not only wanted the canoe to stay where it was, but I wanted the beauteous Fayaway to get into it, and paddle with me about the lake. This latter proposition completely horrified Kory-Kory's notions of propriety. He inveighed against it, as something too monstrous to be thought of. It not only shocked their established notions of propriety, but was at variance with all their religious ordinances.

However, although the "taboo" was a ticklish thing to

meddle with, I determined to test its capabilities of resisting an attack. I consulted the chief Mehevi, who endeavoured to dissuade me from my object: but I was not to be repulsed; and accordingly increased the warmth of my solicitations. At last he entered into a long, and I have no doubt a very learned and eloquent exposition of the history and nature of the "taboo" as affecting this particular case; employing a variety of most extraordinary words, which, from their amazing length and sonorousness, I have every reason to believe were of a theological nature. But all that he said failed to convince me: partly, perhaps, because I could not comprehend a word that he uttered; but chiefly, that for the life of me I could not understand why a woman should not have as much right to enter a canoe as a man. At last he became a little more rational, and intimated that, out of the abundant love he bore me, he would consult with the priests and see what could be done.

How it was that the priesthood of Typee satisfied the affair with their consciences, I know not; but so it was, and Fayaway's dispensation from this portion of the taboo was at length procured. Such an event I believe never before had occurred in the valley; but it was high time the islanders should be taught a little gallantry, and I trust that the example I set them may produce beneficial effects. Ridiculous, indeed, that the lovely creatures should be obliged to paddle about in the water, like so many ducks, while a parcel of great strapping fellows skimmed over its surface in their canoes.

The first day after Fayaway's emancipation I had a delightful little party on the lake—the damsel, Kory-Kory, and myself. My zealous body-servant brought from the house a calabash of poee-poee, half a dozen young cocoa-nuts—stripped of their husks—three pipes, as many yams, and me on his back a part of the way. Something of a load; but

Kory-Kory was a very strong man for his size, and by no means brittle in the spine. We had a very pleasant day; my trusty valet plied the paddle and swept us gently along the margin of the water, beneath the shades of the overhanging thickets. Fayaway and I reclined in the stern of the canoe, on the very best terms possible with one another; the gentle nymph occasionally placing her pipe to her lip, and exhaling the mild fumes of the tobacco, to which her rosy breath added a fresh perfume. Strange as it may seem, there is nothing in which a young and beautiful female appears to more advantage than in the act of smoking. How captivating is a Peruvian lady, swinging in her gaily-woven hammock of grass, extended between two orange trees, and inhaling the fragrance of a choice cigarro! But Fayaway, holding in her delicately formed olive hand the long yellow reed of her pipe, with its quaintly carved bowl, and every few moments languishingly giving forth light wreaths of vapour from her mouth and nostrils, looked still more engaging.

We floated about thus for several hours, when I looked up to the warm, glowing, tropical sky, and then down into the transparent depths below; and when my eye, wandering from the bewitching scenery around, fell upon the grotesquely-tattooed form of Kory-Kory, and finally encountered the pensive gaze of Fayaway, I thought I had been transported to some fairy region, so unreal did everything appear.

This lovely piece of water was the coolest spot in all the valley, and I now made it a place of continual resort during the hottest period of the day. One side of it lay near the termination of a long gradually expanding gorge, which mounted to the heights that environed the vale. The strong trade wind, met in its course by these elevations, circled and eddied about their summits, and was sometimes driven down the steep ravine and swept across the valley, ruffling in its passage the otherwise tranquil surface of the lake.

One day, after we had been paddling about for some time, I disembarked Kory-Kory, and paddled the canoe to the windward side of the lake. As I turned the canoe, Fayaway, who was with me, seemed all at once to be struck with some happy idea. With a wild exclamation of delight, she disengaged from her person the ample robe of tappa which was knotted over her shoulder (for the purpose of shielding her from the sun), and spreading it out like a sail, stood erect with upraised arms in the head of the canoe. We American sailors pride ourselves upon our straight clean spars, but a prettier little mast than Fayaway made was never shipped a-board of any craft.

In a moment the tappa was distended by the breeze—the long brown tresses of Fayaway streamed in the air—and the canoe glided rapidly through the water, and shot towards the shore. Seated in the stern, I directed its course with my paddle until it dashed up the soft sloping bank, and Fayaway, with a light spring, alighted on the ground; whilst Kory-Kory, who had watched our manœuvres with admiration, now clapped his hands in transport, and shouted like a madman. Many a time afterwards was this feat repeated.

If the reader have not observed ere this that I was the declared admirer of Miss Fayaway, all I can say is that he is little conversant with affairs of the heart, and I certainly shall not trouble myself to enlighten him any farther. Out of the calico I had brought from the ship I made a dress for this lovely girl. In it she looked, I must confess, something like an opera dancer. The drapery of the latter damsel generally commences a little above the elbows, but my island beauty's began at the waist, and terminated sufficiently far above the ground to reveal the most bewitching ankle in the universe.

The day that Fayaway first wore this robe was rendered memorable by a new acquaintance being introduced to me. In the afternoon I was lying in the house, when I heard a great uproar outside; but being by this time pretty well accustomed to the wild halloos which were almost continually ringing through the valley, I paid little attention to it, until old Marheyo, under the influence of some strange excitement, rushed into my presence and communicated the astounding tidings, "Marnoo pemi!" which being interpreted, implied that an individual by the name of Marnoo was approaching. My worthy old friend evidently expected that this intelligence would produce a great effect upon me, and for a time he stood earnestly regarding me, as if curious to see how I should conduct myself, but as I remained perfectly unmoved, the old gentleman darted out of the house again, in as great a hurry as he had entered it.

"Marnoo, Marnoo," cogitated I, "I have never heard that name before. Some distinguished character, I presume, from the prodigious riot the natives are making;" the tumultuous noise drawing nearer and nearer every moment, while "Marnoo!—Marnoo!" was shouted by every tongue.

I made up my mind that some savage warrior of consequence, who had not yet enjoyed the honour of an audience, was desirous of paying his respects on the present occasion. So vain had I become by the lavish attention to which I had been accustomed, that I felt half inclined, as a punishment for such neglect, to give this Marnoo a cold reception, when the excited throng came within view, convoying one of the most striking specimens of humanity that I ever beheld.

The stranger could not have been more than twenty-five years of age, and was a little above the ordinary height; had he been a single hair's breadth taller, the matchless sym-

metry of his form would have been destroyed. His unclad
limbs were beautifully formed; whilst the elegant outline
of his figure, together with his beardless cheeks, might have
entitled him to the distinction of standing for the statue of
the Polynesian Apollo; and indeed the oval of his countenance and the regularity of every feature reminded me of
an antique bust. But the marble repose of art was supplied
by a warmth and liveliness of expression only to be seen in
the South Sea Islander under the most favourable devel-
opments of nature. The hair of Marnoo was a rich curling
brown, and twined about his temples and neck in little
close curling ringlets, which danced up and down continually when he was animated in conversation. His cheek was
of a feminine softness, and his face was free from the least
blemish of tattooing, although the rest of his body was
drawn all over with fanciful figures, which—unlike the
unconnected sketching usual among these natives—appeared to have been executed in conformity with some
general design.

The tattooing on his back in particular attracted my attention. The artist employed must indeed have excelled in
his profession. Traced along the course of the spine was
accurately delineated the slender, tapering, and diamond-
checkered shaft of the beautiful "artu" tree. Branching
from the stem on either side, and disposed alternately,
were the graceful branches drooping with leaves all correctly drawn, and elaborately finished. Indeed, this piece
of tattooing was the best specimen of the Fine Arts I had
yet seen in Typee. A rear view of the stranger might have
suggested the idea of a spreading vine tacked against a garden wall. Upon his breast, arms, and legs, were exhibited
an infinite variety of figures; every one of which, however,
appeared to have reference to the general effect sought to
be produced. The tattooing I have described was of the
brightest blue, and when contrasted with the light olive

colour of the skin, produced an unique and even elegant effect. A slight girdle of white tappa, scarcely two inches in width, but hanging before and behind in spreading tassels, composed the entire costume of the stranger.

He advanced surrounded by the islanders, carrying under one arm a small roll of the native cloth, and grasping in his other hand a long and richly decorated spear. His manner was that of a traveller conscious that he is approaching a comfortable stage in his journey. Every moment he turned good-humouredly to the throng around him, and gave some dashing sort of reply to their incessant queries, which appeared to convulse them with uncontrollable mirth.

Struck by his demeanour, and the peculiarity of his appearance, so unlike that of the shaven-crowned and face-tattooed natives in general, I involuntarily rose as he entered the house, and proffered him a seat on the mats beside me. But without deigning to notice the civility, or even the more incontrovertible fact of my existence, the stranger passed on, utterly regardless of me, and flung himself upon the further end of the long couch that traversed the sole apartment of Marheyo's habitation.

Had the belle of the season, in the pride of her beauty and power, been cut in a place of public resort by some supercilious exquisite, she could not have felt greater indignation than I did at this unexpected slight.

I was thrown into utter astonishment. The conduct of the savages had prepared me to anticipate from every new-comer the same extravagant expressions of curiosity and regard. The singularity of his conduct, however, only roused my desire to discover who this remarkable personage might be, who now engrossed the attention of every one.

Tinor placed before him a calabash of poee-poee, from which the stranger regaled himself, alternating every mouthful with some rapid exclamation which was eagerly caught up and echoed by the crowd that completely filled the house. When I observed the striking devotion of the natives to him, and their temporary withdrawal of all attention from myself, I felt not a little piqued. The glory of Tommo is departed, thought I, and the sooner he removes from the valley the better. These were my feelings at the moment, and they were prompted by that glorious principle inherent in all heroic natures—the strong-rooted determination to have the biggest share of the pudding or go without any of it.

Marnoo, this all-attractive personage, having satisfied his hunger, and inhaled a few whiffs from a pipe which was handed to him, launched out into an harangue which completely enchained the attention of his auditors.

Little as I understood of the language, yet from his animated gestures and the varying expression of his features —reflected as from so many mirrors in the countenances around him, I could easily discover the nature of those passions which he sought to arouse. From the frequent recurrence of the words "Nukuheva" and "Frannee" (French), and some others with the meaning of which I was acquainted, he appeared to be rehearsing to his auditors events which had recently occurred in the neighbouring bays. But how he had gained the knowledge of these matters I could not understand, unless it were that he had just come from Nukuheva—a supposition which his travel-stained appearance not a little supported. But, if a native of that region, I could not account for his friendly reception at the hands of the Typees.

Never, certainly, had I beheld so powerful an exhibition of natural eloquence as Marnoo displayed during the course of his oration. The grace of the attitudes into which he threw his flexible figure, the striking gestures of his naked arms, and above all, the fire which shot from his brilliant eyes, imparted an effect to the continually changing accents of his voice, of which the most accomplished orator might have been proud. At one moment reclining sideways upon the mat, and leaning calmly upon his bended arm, he related circumstantially the aggressions of the French—their hostile visits to the surrounding bays, enumerating each one in succession—Happar, Puerka, Nuku- heva, Tior,—and then starting to his feet and precipitating himself forward with clenched hands and a countenance distorted with passion, he poured out a tide of invectives. Falling back into an attitude of lofty command, he exorted the Typees to resist these encroachments; reminding them, with a fierce glance of exultation, that as yet the terror of their name had preserved them from attack, and with a scornful sneer he sketched in ironical terms the wondrous intrepidity of the French, who, with five war-canoes and hundreds of men, had not dared to assail the naked warriors of their valley.

The effect he produced upon his audience was electric; one and all they stood regarding him with sparkling eyes and trembling limbs, as though they were listening to the inspired voice of a prophet.

But it soon appeared that Marnoo's powers were as versatile as they were extraordinary. As soon as he had finished this vehement harangue, he threw himself again upon the mats, and, singling out individuals in the crowd, addressed them by name, in a sort of bantering style, the humour of which, though nearly hidden from me, filled the whole assembly with uproarious delight.

He had a word for everybody; and, turning rapidly from one to another, gave utterance to some hasty witticism, which was sure to be followed by peals of laughter. To the females, as well as to the men, he addressed his discourse. Heaven only knows what he said to them, but he caused smiles and blushes to mantle their ingenuous faces. I am, indeed, very much inclined to believe that Marnoo, with his handsome person and captivating manners, was a sad deceiver among the simple maidens of the island.

During all this time he had never, for one moment, deigned to regard me. He appeared, indeed, to be altogether unconscious of my presence. I was utterly at a loss how to account for this extraordinary conduct. I easily perceived that he was a man of no little consequence among the islanders; that he possessed uncommon talents; and was gifted with a higher degree of knowledge than the inmates of the valley. For these reasons, I therefore greatly feared lest having, from some cause or other, unfriendly feelings toward me, he might exert his powerful influence to do me mischief.

It seemed evident that he was not a permanent resident of the vale, and yet, whence could he have come? On all sides the Typees were girt in by hostile tribes, and how could he possibly, if belonging to any of these, be received with so much cordiality?

The personal appearance of the enigmatical stranger suggested additional perplexities. The face, free from tattooing, and the unshaven crown, were peculiarities I had never before remarked in any part of the island, and I had always heard that the contrary were considered the indispensable distinctions of a Marquesan warrior. Altogether the matter was perfectly incomprehensible to me, and I awaited its solution with no small degree of anxiety.

At length, from certain indications, I suspected that he was making me the subject of his remarks, although he appeared cautiously to avoid either pronouncing my name, or looking in the direction where I lay. All at once he rose from the mats where he had been reclining, and, still conversing, moved towards me, his eye purposely evading mine, and seated himself within less than a yard of me. I had hardly recovered from my surprise, when he suddenly turned round, and, with a most benignant countenance, extended his right hand gracefully towards me. Of course I accepted the courteous challenge, and, as soon as our palms met, he bent towards me, and murmured in musical accents,—"How you do?" "How long you been in this bay?" "You like this bay?"

Had I been pierced simultaneously by three Happar spears, I could not have started more than I did at hearing these simple questions! For a moment I was overwhelmed with astonishment, and then answered something I know not what; but as soon as I regained my self-possession, the thought darted through my mind that from this individual I might obtain that information regarding Toby which I suspected the natives had purposely withheld from me. Accordingly I questioned him concerning the disappearance of my companion, but he denied all knowledge of the matter. I then enquired from whence he had come? He replied, from Nukuheva. When I expressed my surprise, he looked at me for a moment, as if enjoying my perplexity, and then, with his strange vivacity, exclaimed,—"Ah! me taboo,—me go Nukuheva,—me go Tior,—me go Typee,—me go every where,—nobody harm me,—me taboo."

This explanation would have been altogether unintelligible to me, had it not recalled to my mind something I had previously heard concerning a singular custom among these islanders. Though the country is possessed by various tribes, whose mutual hostilities almost wholly preclude any intercourse between them; yet there are instances where a person having ratified friendly relations with some individual belonging to the valley, whose inmates are at war with his own, may, under particular restrictions, venture with impunity into the country of his friend, where, under other circumstances, he would have been treated as an enemy. In this light are personal friendships regarded among them, and the individual so protected is said to be "taboo," and his person, to a certain extent, is held as sa-

cred. Thus the stranger informed me he had access to all
the valleys in the island.

Curious to know how he had acquired his knowledge of
English, I questioned him on the subject. At first, for some
reason or other, he evaded the enquiry, but afterwards told
me that, when a boy, he had been carried to sea by the captain of a trading vessel, with whom he had staid three years,
living part of the time with him at Sydney, in Australia,
and that, at a subsequent visit to the island, the captain
had, at his own request, permitted him to remain among
his countrymen. The natural quickness of the savage had
been wonderfully improved by his intercourse with the
white men, and his partial knowledge of a foreign language
gave him a great ascendancy over his less accomplished
countrymen.

When I asked the now affable Marnoo why it was that
he had not previously spoken to me, he eagerly enquired
what I had been led to think of him from his conduct in
that respect. I replied, that I had supposed him to be some
great chief or warrior, who had seen plenty of white men
before, and did not think it worth while to notice a poor
sailor. At this declaration of the exalted opinion I had
formed of him, he appeared vastly gratified, and gave me to
understand that he had purposely behaved in that manner, in order to increase my astonishment, as soon as he
should see proper to address me.

Marnoo now sought to learn my version of the story as
to how I came to be an inmate of the Typee valley. When
I related to him the circumstances under which Toby and
I had entered it, he listened with evident interest; but as
soon as I alluded to the absence, yet unaccounted for, of
my comrade, he endeavoured to change the subject, as if
it were something he desired not to agitate. It seemed, indeed, as if everything connected with Toby was destined
to beget distrust and anxiety in my bosom. Notwithstand-

ing Marnoo's denial of any knowledge of his fate, I could not avoid suspecting that he was deceiving me; and this suspicion revived those frightful apprehensions with regard to my own fate, which, for a short time past, had subsided in my breast.

Influenced by these feelings, I now felt a strong desire to avail myself of the stranger's protection, and under his safeguard to return to Nukuheva. But as soon as I hinted at this, he unhesitatingly pronounced it to be entirely impracticable; assuring me that the Typees would never consent to my leaving the valley. Although what he said merely confirmed the impression which I had before entertained, still it increased my anxiety to escape from a captivity, which, however endurable, nay, delightful it might be in some respects, involved in its issues a fate marked by the most frightful contingencies.

I could not conceal from my mind that Toby had been treated in the same friendly manner as I had been, and yet all their kindness had terminated in his mysterious disappearance. Might not the same fate await me?—a fate too dreadful to think of. Stimulated by these considerations, I urged anew my request to Marnoo; but he only set forth in stronger colours the impossibility of my escape, and repeated his previous declaration that the Typees would never be brought to consent to my departure.

When I endeavoured to learn from him the motives which prompted them to hold me a prisoner, Marnoo again assumed that mysterious tone which had tormented me with apprehensions when I had questioned him with regard to the fate of my companion.

Thus repulsed, in a manner which only served, by arousing the most dreadful forebodings, to excite me to renewed attempts, I conjured him to intercede for me with the natives, and endeavour to procure their consent to my leaving them. To this he appeared strongly averse; but, yielding at last to my importunities, he addressed several of the chiefs, who with the rest had been eyeing us intently during the whole of our conversation. His petition, however, was at once met with the most violent disapprobation, manifesting itself in angry glances and gestures, and a perfect torrent of passionate words, directed to both him and myself. Marnoo, evidently repenting the step he had taken, earnestly deprecated the resentment of the crowd, and in a few moments succeeded in pacifying to some extent the clamours which had broken out as soon as his proposition had been understood.

With the most intense interest had I watched the reception his intercession might receive; and a bitter pang shot through my heart at the additional evidence, now furnished, of the unchangeable determination of the islanders. Marnoo told me, with evident alarm in his countenance, that although admitted into the bay on a friendly footing with its inhabitants, he could not presume to meddle with their concerns, as such a procedure, if persisted in, would at once absolve the Typees from the restraints of the "Taboo," although so long as he refrained from any such conduct, it screened him effectually from the consequences of the enmity they bore his tribe.

At this moment, Mehevi, who was present, angrily interrupted him; and the words which he uttered, in a commanding tone, evidently meant that he must at once cease talking to me, and withdraw to the other part of the house. Marnoo immediately started up, hurriedly enjoining me not to address him again, and, as I valued my safety, to refrain from all further allusion to the subject of my departure; and then, in compliance with the order of the determined chief, but not before it had again been angrily repeated, he withdrew to a distance.

I now perceived, with no small degree of apprehension,

the same savage expression in the countenance of the natives which had startled me during the scene at the Ti. They glanced their eyes suspiciously from Marnoo to me, as if distrusting the nature of an intercourse carried on, as it was, in a language they could not understand, and they seemed to harbour the belief that already we had concerted measures calculated to elude their vigilance.

The lively countenances of these people are wonderfully indicative of the emotions of the soul, and the imperfections of their oral language are more than compensated for by the nervous eloquence of their looks and gestures. I could plainly trace, in every varying expression of their faces, all those passions which had been thus unexpectedly roused in their bosoms.

It required no reflection to convince me, from what was going on, that the injunction of Marnoo was not to be rashly slighted; and accordingly, great as was the effort to suppress my feelings, I accosted Mehevi in a good-humoured tone, with a view of dissipating any ill impression he might have received. But the ireful, angry chief was not so easily mollified. He rejected my advances with that peculiarly stern expression I have before described, and took care by the whole of his behaviour towards me to show the displeasure and resentment which he felt.

Marnoo, at the other extremity of the house, apparently desirous of making a diversion in my favour, exerted himself to amuse with his pleasantries the crowd about him; but his lively attempts were not so successful as they had previously been, and, foiled in his efforts, he rose gravely to depart. No one expressed any regret at this movement, so seizing his roll of tappa, and grasping his spear, he advanced to the front of the pi-pi, and waving his hand in adieu to the now silent throng, cast upon me a glance of mingled pity and reproach, and flung himself into the path which led from the house. I watched his receding figure until it was lost in the obscurity of the grove, and then gave myself up to the most desponding reflections.

CHAPTER XIX

Reflections after Marnoo's Departure—Battle of the Pop-guns—
Strange conceit of Marheyo—Process of making Tappa.

THE knowledge I had now obtained as to the intention of the savages deeply affected me.

Marnoo, I perceived, was a man who, by reason of his superior acquirements, and the knowledge he possessed of the events which were taking place in the different bays of the island, was held in no little estimation by the inhabitants of the valley. He had been received with the most cordial welcome and respect. The natives had hung upon the accents of his voice, and had manifested the highest gratification at being individually noticed by him. And yet, despite all this, a few words urged in my behalf, with the intent of obtaining my release from captivity, had sufficed not only to banish all harmony and good-will; but, if I could believe what he told me, had gone nigh to endanger his own personal safety.

How strongly rooted, then, must be the determination of the Typees with regard to me, and how suddenly could they display the strongest passions! The mere suggestion of my departure had estranged from me, for the time at least, Mehevi, who was the most influential of all the chiefs, and who had previously exhibited so many instances of his friendly sentiments. The rest of the natives had likewise evinced their strong repugnance to my wishes, and even Kory-Kory himself seemed to share in the general disapprobation bestowed upon me.

In vain I racked my invention to find out some motive

for the strange desire these people manifested to retain me among them; but I could discover none.

But however this might be, the scene which had just occurred admonished me of the danger of trifling with the wayward and passionate spirits against whom it was vain to struggle, and might even be fatal to do so. My only hope was to induce the natives to believe that I was reconciled to my detention in the valley, and by assuming a tranquil and cheerful demeanour, to allay the suspicions which I had so unfortunately aroused. Their confidence revived, they might in a short time remit in some degree their watchfulness over my movements, and I should then be the better enabled to avail myself of any opportunity which presented itself for escape. I determined, therefore, to make the best of a bad bargain, and to bear up manfully against whatever might betide. In this endeavour I succeeded beyond my own expectations. At the period of Marnoo's visit, I had been in the valley, as nearly as I could conjecture, some two months. Although not completely recovered from my strange illness which still lingered about me, I was free from pain and able to take exercise. In short, I had every reason to anticipate a perfect recovery. Freed from apprehensions on this point, and resolved to regard the future without flinching, I flung myself anew into all the social pleasures of the valley, and sought to bury all regrets, and all remembrances of my previous existence, in the wild enjoyments it afforded.

In my various wanderings through the vale, and as I became better acquainted with the character of its inhabitants, I was more and more struck with the light-hearted joyousness that everywhere prevailed. The minds of these simple savages, unoccupied by matters of graver moment, were capable of deriving the utmost delight from circumstances which would have passed unnoticed in more intelligent communities. All their enjoyment, indeed, seemed to be made up of the little trifling incidents of the passing hour; but these diminutive items swelled altogether to an amount of happiness seldom experienced by more enlightened individuals, whose pleasures are drawn from more elevated but rarer sources.

What community, for instance, of refined and intellectual mortals would derive the least satisfaction from shooting pop-guns? The mere supposition of such a thing being possible would excite their indignation, and yet the whole population of Typee did little else for ten days but occupy themselves with that childish amusement, fairly screaming, too, with the delight it afforded them.

One day I was frolicking with a little spirited urchin, some six years old, who chased me with a piece of bamboo about three feet long, with which he occasionally belaboured me. Seizing the stick from him, the idea happened to suggest itself, that I might make for the youngster, out of the slender tube, one of those nursery muskets with which I had sometimes seen children playing. Accordingly, with my knife I made two parallel slits in the cane several inches in length, and cutting loose at one end the elastic strip between them, bent it back and slipped the point into a little notch made for the purpose. Any small substance placed against this would be projected with considerable force through the tube, by merely springing the bent strip out of the notch.

Had I possessed the remotest idea of the sensation this piece of ordnance was destined to produce, I should certainly have taken out a patent for the invention. The boy scampered away with it, half delirious with ecstacy, and in twenty minutes afterwards I might have been seen surrounded by a noisy crowd—venerable old greybeards—responsible fathers of families—valiant warriors—matrons—young men—girls and children, all holding in their hand bits of bamboo, and each clamouring to be served first.

For three or four hours I was engaged in manufacturing pop-guns, but at last made over my good-will and interest in the concern to a lad of remarkable quick parts, whom I soon initiated into the art and mystery.

Pop, Pop, Pop, Pop, now resounded all over the valley. Duels, skirmishes, pitched battles, and general engagements were to be seen on every side. Here, as you walked along a path which led through a thicket, you fell into a cunningly-laid ambush, and became a target for a body of musketeers whose tattooed limbs you could just see peeping into view through the foliage. There, you were assailed by the intrepid garrison of a house, who levelled their bamboo rifles at you from between the upright canes which composed its sides. Farther on you were fired upon by a detachment of sharpshooters, mounted upon the top of a pi-pi.

Pop, Pop, Pop, Pop! green guavas, seeds, and berries were flying about in every direction, and during this dangerous state of affairs I was half afraid that, like the man and his brazen bull, I should fall a victim to my own ingenuity. Like everything else, however, the excitement gradually wore away, though ever after occasional pop-guns might be heard at all hours of the day.

It was towards the close of the pop-gun war, that I was infinitely diverted with a strange freak of Marheyo's.

I had worn, when I quitted the ship, a pair of thick pumps, which, from the rough usage they had received in scaling precipices and sliding down gorges, were so dilapidated as to be altogether unfit for use—so, at least, would have thought the generality of people, and so they most certainly were, when considered in the light of shoes. But things unserviceable in one way, may with advantage be applied in another, that is, if one have genius enough for the purpose. This genius Marheyo possessed in a superlative degree, as he abundantly evinced by the use to which he put these sorely bruised and battered old shoes.

Every article, however trivial, which belonged to me, the natives appeared to regard as sacred; and I observed that for several days after becoming an inmate of the house, my pumps were suffered to remain, untouched, where I had first happened to throw them. I remembered, however, that after awhile I had missed them from their accustomed place; but the matter gave me no concern, supposing that Tinor—like any other tidy housewife, having come across them in some of her domestic occupations—had pitched the useless things out of the house. But I was soon undeceived.

One day I observed old Marheyo bustling about me with unusual activity, and to such a degree as almost to supersede Kory-Kory in the functions of his office. One moment he volunteered to trot off with me on his back to the stream; and when I refused, noways daunted by the repulse he continued to frisk about me like a superannuated house-dog. I could not for the life of me conjecture what possessed the old gentleman, until all at once, availing himself of the temporary absence of the household, he went through a variety of uncouth gestures, pointing eagerly down to my feet, and then up to a little bundle which swung from the ridge-pole overhead. At last I caught a faint idea of his meaning, and motioned him to lower the package. He executed the order in the twinkling of an eye, and unrolling a piece of tappa displayed to my astonished gaze the identical pumps which I thought had been destroyed long before.

I immediately comprehended his desires, and very generously gave him the shoes, which had become quite mouldy, wondering for what earthly purpose he could want them.

The same afternoon I descried the venerable warrior approaching the house, with a slow, stately gait, ear-rings in ears, and spear in hand, with this highly ornamental pair of shoes suspended from his neck by a strip of bark, and swinging backwards and forwards on his capacious chest. In the gala costume of the tasteful Marheyo, these calf-skin pendants ever after formed the most striking feature.

But to turn to something a little more important. Although the whole existence of the inhabitants of the valley seemed to pass away exempt from toil, yet there were some light employments which, although amusing rather than laborious as occupations, contributed to their comfort and luxury. Among these, the most important was the manufacture of the native cloth,—"tappa,"—so well known, under various modifications, throughout the whole Polynesian Archipelago. As is generally understood, this useful and sometimes elegant article is fabricated from the bark of different trees. But, as I believe that no description of its manufacture has ever been given, I shall state what I know regarding it.

In the manufacture of the beautiful white tappa generally worn on the Marquesa Islands, the preliminary operation consists in gathering a certain quantity of the young branches of the cloth-tree. The exterior green bark being pulled off as worthless, there remains a slender fibrous substance, which is carefully stripped from the stick, to which it closely adheres. When a sufficient quantity of it has been collected, the various strips are enveloped in a covering of large leaves, which the natives use precisely as we do wrapping-paper, and which are secured by a few turns of a line passed round them. The package is then laid in the bed of some running stream, with a heavy stone placed over it, to prevent its being swept away. After it has remained for two or three days in this state, it is drawn out, and exposed, for a short time, to the action of the air, every distinct piece being attentively inspected, with a view of ascertaining whether it has yet been sufficiently affected by the operation. This is repeated again and again, until the desired result is obtained.

When the substance is in a proper state for the next process, it betrays evidences of incipient decomposition; the fibres are relaxed and softened, and rendered perfectly malleable. The different strips are now extended, one by one, in successive layers, upon some smooth surface—generally the prostrate trunk of a cocoa-nut tree—and the heap thus formed is subjected, at every new increase, to a moderate beating, with a sort of wooden mallet, leisurely applied. The mallet is made of a hard heavy wood resembling ebony, is about twelve inches in length, and perhaps two in breadth, with a rounded handle at one end, and in shape is the exact counterpart of one of our four-sided razor-strops. The flat surfaces of the implement are marked with shallow parallel indentations, varying in depth on the different sides, so as to be adapted to the several stages of the operation. These marks produce the corduroy sort of stripes discernible in the tappa in its finished state. After being beaten in the manner I have described, the material soon becomes blended in one mass, which, moistened occasionally with water, is at intervals hammered out, by a kind of gold-beating process, to any degree of thinness required. In this way the cloth is easily made to vary in strength and thickness, so as to suit the numerous purposes to which it is applied.

When the operation last described has been concluded, the new-made tappa is spread out on the grass to bleach and dry, and soon becomes of a dazzling whiteness. Sometimes, in the first stages of the manufacture, the substance is impregnated with a vegetable juice, which gives it a permanent colour. A rich brown and a bright yellow are occasionally seen, but the simple taste of the Typee people inclines them to prefer the natural tint.

The notable wife of Kammahammaha, the renowned

conqueror and king of the Sandwich Islands, used to pride herself in the skill she displayed in dyeing her tappa with contrasting colours disposed in regular figures; and, in the midst of the innovations of the times, was regarded, towards the decline of her life, as a lady of the old school, clinging as she did to the national cloth, in preference to the frippery of the European calicoes. But the art of printing the tappa is unknown upon the Marquesan Islands.

In passing along the valley, I was often attracted by the noise of the mallet, which, when employed in the manufacture of the cloth, produces at every stroke of its hard, heavy wood, a clear, ringing, and musical sound, capable of being heard at a great distance. When several of these implements happen to be in operation at the same time, and near one another, the effect upon the ear of a person, at a little distance, is really charming.

CHAPTER XX

History of a Day as usually spent in the Typee Valley—Dances of the Marquesan Girls.

NOTHING can be more uniform and undiversified than the life of the Typees; one tranquil day of ease and happiness follows another in quiet succession; and with these unsophisticated savages the history of a day is the history of a life. I will, therefore, as briefly as I can, describe one of our days in the valley.

To begin with the morning. We were not very early risers—the sun would be shooting his golden spikes above the Happar mountain, ere I threw aside my tappa robe, and girding my long tunic about my waist, sallied out with Fayaway and Kory-Kory, and the rest of the household, and bent my steps towards the stream. Here we found congregated all those who dwelt in our section of the valley;

and here we bathed with them. The fresh morning air
and the cool flowing waters put both soul and body in a
glow, and after a half-hour employed in this recreation,
we sauntered back to the house—Tinor and Marheyo
gathering dry sticks by the way for fire-wood; some of the
young men laying the cocoa-nut trees under contribution
as they passed beneath them; while Kory-Kory played his
outlandish pranks for my particular diversion, and Fayaway and I, not arm in arm to be sure, but sometimes hand
in hand, strolled along, with feelings of perfect charity for
all the world, and especial good-will towards each other.

Our morning meal was soon prepared. The islanders
are somewhat abstemious at this repast; reserving the
more powerful efforts of their appetite to a later period of
the day. For my own part, with the assistance of my valet,
who, as I have before stated, always officiated as spoon on
these occasions, I ate sparingly from one of Tinor's trenchers of poee-poee; which was devoted exclusively for my own
use, being mixed with the milky meat of ripe cocoa-nut.
A section of a roasted bread-fruit, a small cake of "Amar,"
or a mess of "Kokoo," two or three bananas, or a Maw-
mee apple; an annuee, or some other agreeable and nutri-
cious fruit served from day to day to diversify the meal,
which was finished by tossing off the liquid contents of a
young cocoa-nut or two.

While partaking of this simple repast, the inmates of
Marheyo's house, after the style of the indolent Romans,
reclined in sociable groups upon the divan of mats, and
digestion was promoted by cheerful conversation.

After the morning meal was concluded, pipes were
lighted; and among them my own especial pipe, a present
from the noble Mehevi. The islanders, who only smoke a
whiff or two at a time, and at long intervals, and who
keep their pipes going from hand to hand continually, regarded my systematic smoking of four or five pipefuls of

tobacco in succession, as something quite wonderful. When two or three pipes had circulated freely, the company gradually broke up. Marheyo went to the little hut he was for ever building. Tinor began to inspect her rolls of tappa, or employed her busy fingers in plaiting grass-mats. The girls anointed themselves with their fragrant oils, dressed their hair, or looked over their curious finery, and compared together their ivory trinkets, fashioned out of boar's tusks or whale's teeth. The young men and warriors produced their spears, paddles, canoe-gear, battle-clubs, and war-conchs, and occupied themselves in carving all sorts of figures upon them with pointed bits of shell or flint, and adorning them, especially the war-conchs, with tassels of braided bark and tufts of human hair. Some, immediately after eating, threw themselves once more upon the inviting mats, and resumed the employment of the previous night, sleeping as soundly as if they had not closed their eyes for a week. Others sallied out into the groves, for the purpose of gathering fruit or fibres of bark and leaves; the last two being in constant requisition, and applied to a hundred uses. A few, perhaps, among the girls, would slip into the woods after flowers, or repair to the stream with small calabashes and cocoa-nut shells, in order to polish them by friction with a smooth stone in the water. In truth these innocent people seemed to be at no loss for something to occupy their time; and it would be no light task to enumerate all their employments, or rather pleasures.

My own mornings I spent in a variety of ways. Sometimes I rambled about from house to house, sure of receiving a cordial welcome wherever I went; or from grove to grove, and from one shady place to another, in company with Kory-Kory and Fayaway, and a rabble rout of merry young idlers. Sometimes I was too indolent for exercise, and accepting one of the many invitations I was continually receiving, stretched myself out on the mats of some hospitable dwelling, and occupied myself pleasantly either in watching the proceedings of those around me or taking part in them myself. Whenever I chose to do the latter, the delight of the islanders was boundless; and there was always a throng of competitors for the honour of instructing me in any particular craft. I soon became quite an accomplished hand at making tappa—could braid a grass sling as well as the best of them—and once, with my knife, carved the handle of a javelin so exquisitely, that I have no doubt, to this day, Karnoonoo, its owner, preserves it as a surprising specimen of my skill. As noon approached, all those who had wandered forth from our habitation, began to return; and when mid-day was fairly come scarcely a sound was to be heard in the valley: a deep sleep fell upon all. The luxurious siesta was hardly ever omitted, except by old Marheyo, who was so eccentric a character, that he seemed to be governed by no fixed principles whatever; but acting just according to the humour of the moment, slept, ate, or tinkered away at his little hut, without regard to the proprieties of time or place. Frequently he might have been seen taking a nap in the sun at noon-day, or a bath in the stream at midnight. Once I beheld him perched eighty feet from the ground, in the tuft of a cocoa-nut tree, smoking; and often I saw him standing up to the waist in water, engaged in plucking out the stray hairs of his beard, using a piece of muscle-shell for tweezers.

The noon-tide slumber lasted generally an hour and a half; very often longer; and after the sleepers had arisen from their mats they again had recourse to their pipes, and then made preperations for the most important meal of the day.

I, however, like those gentlemen of leisure who breakfast at home and dine at their club, almost invariably, during my intervals of health, enjoyed the afternoon repast with the bachelor chiefs of the Ti, who were always re-joiced to see me, and lavishly spread before me all the good things which their larder afforded. Mehevi generally produced among other dainties a baked pig, an article which I have every reason to suppose was provided for my sole gratification.

The Ti was a right jovial place. It did my heart, as well as my body, good to visit it. Secure from female intrusion, there was no restraint upon the hilarity of the warriors, who, like the gentlemen of Europe after the cloth is drawn and the ladies retire, freely indulged their mirth.

After spending a considerable portion of the afternoon at the Ti, I usually found myself, as the cool of the evening came on, either sailing on the little lake with Fayaway, or bathing in the waters of the stream with a number of the savages, who, at this hour, always repaired thither. As the shadows of night approached, Marheyo's household were once more assembled under his roof: tapers were lit, long and curious chants were raised, interminable stories were told (for which one present was little the wiser), and all sorts of social festivities served to while away the time.

The young girls very often danced by moonlight in front of their dwellings. There are a great variety of these dances, in which, however, I never saw the men take part. They all consist of active, romping, mischievous evolutions, in which every limb is brought into requisition. Indeed, the Marquesan girls dance all over, as it were; not only do their feet dance, but their arms, hands, fingers, ay, their very eyes, seem to dance in their heads. In good sooth, they so sway their floating forms, arch their necks, toss aloft their naked arms, and glide, and swim, and whirl, that it was almost too much for a quiet, sober-minded, modest young man like myself.

The damsels wear nothing but flowers and their compendious gala tunics; and when they plume themselves for the dance, they look like a band of olive-coloured Sylphides on the point of taking wing.

Unless some particular festivity was going forward, the inmates of Marheyo's house retired to their mats rather early in the evening; but not for the night, since, after slumbering lightly for a while, they rose again, relit their tapers, partook of the third and last meal of the day, at which poee-poee alone was eaten, and then, after inhaling a narcotic whiff from a pipe of tobacco, disposed themselves for the great business of night, sleep. With the Marquesans it might almost be styled the great business of life, for they pass a large portion of their time in the arms of Somnus. The native strength of their constitutions is no way shown more emphatically than in the quantity of sleep they can endure. To many of them, indeed, life is little else than an often interrupted and luxurious nap.

CHAPTER XXI

The Spring of Arva Wai—Remarkable Monumental Remains— Some ideas with regard to the History of the Pi-Pis found in the Valley.

ALMOST every country has its medicinal springs famed for their healing virtues. The Cheltenham of Typee is embosomed in the deepest solitude, and but seldom receives a visitor. It is situated remote from any dwelling, a little way up the mountain, near the head of the valley; and you approach it by a pathway shaded by the most beautiful foliage and adorned with a thousand fragrant plants.

The mineral waters of Arva Wai ooze forth from the crevices of a rock, and gliding down its mossy side, fall at last, in many clustering drops, into a natural basin of stone fringed round with grass and dewy-looking little violet-coloured flowers, as fresh and beautiful as the perpetual moisture they enjoy can make them.

The water is held in high estimation by the islanders, some of whom consider it an agreeable as well as a medicinal beverage; they bring it from the mountain in their calabashes, and store it away beneath heaps of leaves in some shady nook near the house. Old Marheyo had a great love for the waters of the spring. Every now and then he lugged off to the mountain a great round demijohn of a calabash, and, panting with his exertions, brought it back filled with his darling fluid.

The water tasted like a solution of a dozen disagreeable things, and was sufficiently nauseous to have made the fortune of the proprietor, had the spa been situated in the midst of any civilized community.

As I am no chemist, I cannot give a scientific analysis of the water. All I know about the matter is, that one day Marheyo in my presence poured out the last drop from his huge calabash, and I observed at the bottom of the vessel a small quantity of gravelly sediment very much resembling our common sand. Whether this is always found in the water, and gives it its peculiar flavour and virtues, or whether its presence was merely incidental, I was not able to ascertain.

One day in returning from this spring by a circuitous path, I came upon a scene which reminded me of Stonehenge and the architectural labours of the Druid.

At the base of one of the mountains, and surrounded on all sides by dense groves, a series of vast terraces of stone rises, step by step, for a considerable distance up the hill side. These terraces cannot be less than one hundred yards in length and twenty in width. Their magnitude, however, is less striking than the immense size of the blocks composing them. Some of the stones, of an oblong shape, are from ten to fifteen feet in length, and five or six feet thick. Their sides are quite smooth, but though square, and of pretty regular formation, they bear no mark of the chisel. They are laid together without cement, and here and there show gaps between. The topmost terrace and the lower one are somewhat peculiar in their construction. They have both a quadrangular depression in the centre, leaving the rest of the terrace elevated several feet above it. In the intervals of the stones immense trees have taken root, and their broad boughs stretching far over, and interlacing together, support a canopy almost impenetrable to the sun. Overgrowing the greater part of them, and climbing from one to another, is a wilderness of vines, in whose sinewy embrace many of the stones lie half hidden, while in some places a thick growth of bushes entirely covers them. There is a wild pathway which obliquely crosses two of these terraces; and so profound is the shade, so dense the vegetation, that a stranger to the place might pass along it without being aware of their existence.

These structures bear every indication of a very high antiquity, and Kory-Kory, who was my authority in all matters of scientific research, gave me to understand that they were coeval with the creation of the world; that the great gods themselves were the builders; and that they would endure until time shall be no more. Kory-Kory's prompt explanation, and his attributing the work to a divine origin, at once convinced me that neither he nor the rest of his countrymen knew anything about them.

As I gazed upon this monument, doubtless the work of an extinct and forgotten race, thus buried in the green nook of an island at the ends of the earth, the existence of which was yesterday unknown, a stronger feeling of awe came over me than if I had stood musing at the mighty base of the Pyramid of Cheops. There are no inscriptions, no sculpture, no clue, by which to conjecture its history: nothing but the dumb stones. How many generations of those majestic trees which overshadow them have grown and flourished and decayed since first they were erected!

These remains naturally suggest many interesting reflections. They establish the great age of the island, an opinion which the builders of theories concerning the creation of the various groups in the South Seas are not always inclined to admit. For my own part, I think it just as probable that human beings were living in the valleys of the Marquesas three thousand years ago as that they were inhabiting the land of Egypt. The origin of the island of Nukuheva cannot be imputed to the coral insect; for indefatigable as that wonderful creature is, it would be hardly muscular enough to pile rocks one upon the other more than three thousand feet above the level of the sea. That the land may have been thrown up by a submarine volcano is as possible as anything else. No one can make an affidavit to the contrary, and therefore I will say nothing against the supposition: indeed, were geologists to assert that the whole continent of America had in like manner been formed by the simultaneous explosion of a train of Etnas laid under the water all the way from the North Pole to the parallel of Cape Horn, I am the last man in the world to contradict them.

I have already mentioned that the dwellings of the islanders were almost invariably built upon massive stone foundations, which they call pi-pis. The dimensions of these, however, as well as of the stones composing them, are comparatively small: but there are other and larger erections of a similar description comprising the "morais," or burying-grounds, and festival-places, in nearly all the valleys of the island. Some of these piles are so extensive, and so great a degree of labour and skill must have been requisite in constructing them, that I can scarcely believe they were built by the ancestors of the present inhabitants. If indeed they were, the race has sadly deteriorated in their knowledge of the mechanic arts. To say nothing of their habitual indolence, by what contrivance within the reach of so simple a people could such enormous masses have been moved or fixed in their places? and how could they with their rude implements have chiselled and hammered them into shape?

All of these larger pi-pis—like that of the Hoolah Hoolah ground in the Typee valley—bore incontestable marks of great age; and I am disposed to believe that their erection may be ascribed to the same race of men who were the builders of the still more ancient remains I have just described.

According to Kory-Kory's account, the pi-pi upon which stands the Hoolah Hoolah ground was built a great many moons ago, under the direction of Monoo, a great chief and warrior, and, as it would appear, master-mason among the Typees. It was erected for the express purpose to which it is at present devoted, in the incredibly short period of one sun; and was dedicated to the immortal wooden idols by a grand festival, which lasted ten days and nights.

Among the smaller pi-pis, upon which stand the dwelling-houses of the natives, I never observed any which intimated a recent erection. There are in every part of the valley a great many of these massive stone foundations which have no houses upon them. This is vastly convenient, for whenever an enterprising islander chooses to emigrate a few hundred yards from the place where he was born, all he has to do in order to establish himself in some new locality, is to select one of the many unappropriated pi-pis, and without further ceremony pitch his bamboo tent upon it.

CHAPTER XXII

Preparations for a Grand Festival in the Valley—Strange doings in the Taboo Groves—Monument of Calabashes—Gala Costume of the Typee Damsels—Departure for the Festival.

FROM the time that my lameness had decreased, I had made a daily practice of visiting Mehevi at the Ti, who invariably gave me a most cordial reception. I was always accompanied in these excursions by Fayaway and the ever-present Kory-Kory. The former, as soon as we reached the vicinity of the Ti—which was rigorously tabooed to the whole female sex—withdrew to a neighbouring hut, as if her feminine delicacy restrained her from approaching a habitation which might be regarded as a sort of Bachelor's Hall.

And in good truth it might well have been so considered. Although it was the permanent residence of several distinguished chiefs, and of the noble Mehevi in particular, it was still at certain seasons the favourite haunt of all the jolly, talkative, and elderly savages of the vale, who resorted thither in the same way that similar characters frequent a tavern in civilized countries. There they would remain hour after hour, chatting, smoking, eating poee-poee, or busily engaged in sleeping for the good of their constitutions.

This building appeared to be the head-quarters of the valley, where all flying rumours concentrated; and to have seen it filled with a crowd of the natives, all males, conversing in animated clusters, while multitudes were continually coming and going, one would have thought it a kind of savage Exchange, where the rise and fall of Polynesian Stock was discussed.

Mehevi acted as supreme lord over the place, spending the greater portion of his time there: and often when, at particular hours of the day, it was deserted by nearly every one else except the verd-antique looking centenarians, who were fixtures in the building, the chief himself was sure to be found enjoying his "otium cum dignitate" upon the luxurious mats which covered the floor. Whenever I made my appearance he invariably rose, and, like a gentleman doing the honours of his mansion, invited me to repose myself wherever I pleased, and calling out "tammaree!" (boy), a little fellow would appear, and then retiring for an instant, return with some savoury mess, from which the chief would press me to regale myself. To tell the truth, Mehevi was indebted to the excellence of his viands for the honour of my repeated visits,—a matter which cannot appear singular, when it is borne in mind that bachelors, all the world over, are famous for serving up unexceptionable repasts.

One day, on drawing near to the Ti, I observed that extensive preparations were going forward, plainly betokening some approaching festival. Some of the symptoms reminded me of the stir produced among the scullions of a large hotel, where a grand jubilee dinner is about to be given. The natives were hurrying about hither and thither, engaged in various duties; some lugging off to the stream enormous hollow bamboos, for the purpose of filling them with water; others chasing furious-looking hogs through the bushes, in their endeavours to capture them; and numbers employed in kneading great mountains of poee-poee heaped up in huge wooden vessels.

After observing these lively indications for a while, I was attracted to a neighbouring grove by a prodigious squeaking which I heard there. On reaching the spot I found it proceeded from a large hog which a number of natives were forcibly holding to the earth, while a muscular fellow, armed with a bludgeon, was ineffectually aiming murderous blows at the skull of the unfortunate porker. Again and again he missed his writhing and struggling victim, but though puffing and panting with his exertions, he still continued them; and after striking a sufficient number of blows to have demolished an entire drove of oxen, with one crashing stroke he laid him dead at his feet.

Without letting any blood from the body, it was immediately carried to a fire which had been kindled near at hand, and four savages taking hold of the carcass by its legs, passed it rapidly to and fro in the flames. In a moment the smell of burning bristles betrayed the object of this procedure. Having got thus far in the matter, the body was removed to a little distance; and, being disembowelled, the entrails were laid aside as choice parts, and the whole carcass thoroughly washed with water. An ample thick green cloth, composed of the long thick leaves of a species of palm-tree, ingeniously tacked together with little pins of bamboo, was now spread upon the ground, in which the body being carefully rolled, it was borne to an oven previously prepared to receive it. Here it was at once laid upon the heated stones at the bottom, and covered with thick layers of leaves, the whole being quickly hidden from sight by a mound of earth raised over it.

Such is the summary style in which the Typees convert perverse-minded and rebellious hogs into the most docile and amiable pork; a morsel of which placed on the tongue melts like a soft smile from the lips of Beauty.

I commend their peculiar mode of proceeding to the consideration of all butchers, cooks, and housewives. The hapless porker whose fate I have just rehearsed, was not the only one who suffered on that memorable day. Many a dismal grunt, many an imploring squeak, proclaimed what was going on throughout the whole extent of the valley; and I verily believe the first-born of every litter perished before the setting of that fatal sun.

The scene around the Ti was now most animated. Hogs

and poee-poee were baking in numerous ovens, which, heaped up with fresh earth into slight elevations, looked like so many ant-hills. Scores of the savages were vigorously plying their stone pestles in preparing masses of poee-poee, and numbers were gathering green bread-fruit and young cocoa-nuts in the surrounding groves; while an exceeding great multitude, with a view of encouraging the rest in their labours, stood still, and kept shouting most lustily without intermission.

It is a peculiarity among these people, that when engaged in any employment they always make a prodigious fuss about it. So seldom do they ever exert themselves, that when they do work they seem determined that so meritorious an action shall not escape the observation of those around. If, for example, they have occasion to remove a stone to a little distance, which perhaps might be carried by two able-bodied men, a whole swarm gather about it, and, after a vast deal of palavering, lift it up among them, every one struggling to get hold of it, and bear it off yelling and panting as if accomplishing some mighty achievement. Seeing them on these occasions, one is reminded of an infinity of black ants clustering about and dragging away to some hole the leg of a deceased fly.

Having for some time attentively observed these demonstrations of good cheer, I entered the Ti, where Mehevi sat complacently looking out upon the busy scene, and occasionally issuing his orders. The chief appeared to be in an extraordinary flow of spirits, and gave me to understand that on the morrow there would be grand doings in the Groves generally, and at the Ti in particular; and urged me by no means to absent myself. In commemoration of what event, however, or in honour of what distinguished personage, the feast was to be given, altogether passed my comprehension. Mehevi sought to enlighten my ignorance, but he failed as signally as when he had endeavoured to initiate me into the perplexing arcana of the taboo.

On leaving the Ti, Kory-Kory, who had as a matter of course accompanied me, observing that my curiosity remained unabated, resolved to make every thing plain and satisfactory. With this intent, he escorted me through the Taboo Groves, pointing out to my notice a variety of objects, and endeavoured to explain them in such an indescribable jargon of words, that it almost put me in bodily pain to listen to him. In particular, he led me to a remarkable pyramidical structure some three yards square at the base, and perhaps ten feet in height, which had lately been thrown up, and occupied a very conspicuous position. It was composed principally of large empty calabashes, with a few polished cocoa-nut shells, and looked not unlike a cenotaph of skulls. My cicerone perceived the astonishment with which I gazed at this monument of savage crockery, and immediately addressed himself to the task of enlightening me: but all in vain; and to this hour the nature of the monument remains a complete mystery to me. As, however, it formed so prominent a feature in the approaching revels, I bestowed upon the latter, in my own mind, the title of the "Feast of Calabashes."

The following morning, awaking rather late, I perceived the whole of Marheyo's family busily engaged in preparing for the festival. The old warrior himself was arranging in round balls the two grey locks of hair that were suffered to grow from the crown of his head; his ear-rings and spear, both well polished, lay beside him, while the highly decorative pair of shoes hung suspended from a projecting cane against the side of the house. The young men were similarly employed; and the fair damsels, including Fayaway, were anointing themselves with "aka," arranging their long tresses, and performing other matters connected with the duties of the toilet.

Having completed their preparations, the girls now exhibited themselves in gala costume; the most conspicuous feature of which was a necklace of beautiful white flowers, with the stems removed, and strung closely together upon a single fibre of tappa. Corresponding ornaments were inserted in their ears, and woven garlands upon their heads. About their waist they wore a short tunic of spotless white tappa, and some of them superadded to this a mantle of the same material, tied in an elaborate bow upon the left shoulder, and falling about the figure in picturesque folds.

Thus arrayed, I would have matched the charming Fayaway against any beauty in the world.

People may say what they will about the taste evinced by our fashionable ladies in dress. Their jewels, their feathers, their silks, and their furbelows would have sunk into utter insignificance beside the exquisite simplicity of attire adopted by the nymphs of the vale on this festive occasion. I should like to have seen a gallery of coronation beauties, at Westminster Abbey, confronted for a moment by this band of Island girls; their stiffness, formality, and affectation contrasted with the artless vivacity and unconcealed natural graces of these savage maidens. It would be the Venus de' Medici placed beside a milliner's doll.

It was not long before Kory-Kory and myself were left alone in the house, the rest of its inmates having departed for the Taboo Groves. My valet was all impatience to follow them; and was as fidgety about my dilatory movements as a diner out waiting hat in hand at the bottom of the stairs for some lagging companion. At last, yielding to his importunities, I set out for the Ti. As we passed the houses peeping out from the groves through which our route lay, I noticed that they were entirely deserted by their inhabitants.

When we reached the rock that abruptly terminated the

path, and concealed from us the festive scene, wild shouts and a confused blending of voices assured me that the occasion, whatever it might be, had drawn together a great multitude. Kory-Kory, previous to mounting the elevation, paused for a moment, like a dandy at a ball-room door, to put a hasty finish to his toilet. During this short interval, the thought struck me that I ought myself perhaps to be taking some little pains with my appearance. But as I had no holiday raiment, I was not a little puzzled to devise some means of decorating myself. However, as I felt desirous to create a sensation, I determined to do all that lay in my power; and knowing that I could not delight the savages more than by conforming to their style of dress, I removed from my person the large robe of tappa which I was accustomed to wear over my shoulders whenever I sallied into the open air, and remained merely girt about with a short tunic descending from my waist to my knees.

My quick-witted attendant fully appreciated the compliment I was paying to the costume of his race, and began more sedulously to arrange the folds of the one only garment which remained to me. Whilst he was doing this, I caught sight of a knot of young lasses, who were sitting near us on the grass surrounded by heaps of flowers which they were forming into garlands. I motioned to them to bring some of their handywork to me; and in an instant a dozen wreaths were at my disposal. One of them I put round the apology for a hat which I had been forced to construct for myself out of palmetto-leaves, and some of the others I converted into a splendid girdle. These operations finished, with the slow and dignified step of a full-dressed beau I ascended the rock.

CHAPTER XXIII

The Feast of Calabashes.

THE whole population of the valley seemed to be gathered within the precincts of the grove. In the distance could be seen the long front of the Ti, its immense piazza swarming with men, arrayed in every variety of fantastic costume, and all vociferating with animated gestures; while the whole interval between it and the place where I stood was enlivened by groups of females fancifully decorated, dancing, capering, and uttering wild exclamations. As soon as they descried me they set up a shout of welcome; and a band of them came dancing towards me chanting as they approached some wild recitative. The change in my garb seemed to transport them with delight, and clustering about me on all sides, they accompanied me towards the Ti. When however we drew near it these joyous nymphs paused in their career, and parting on either side, permitted me to pass on to the now densely thronged building.

So soon as I mounted to the pi-pi I saw at a glance that the revels were fairly under way.

What lavish plenty reigned around!—Warwick feasting his retainers with beef and ale was a niggard to the noble Mehevi!—All along the piazza of the Ti were arranged elaborately carved canoe-shaped vessels, some twenty feet in length, filled with newly made poee-poee, and sheltered from the sun by the broad leaves of the bananna. At intervals were heaps of green bread-fruit, raised in pyramidical stacks, resembling the regular piles of heavy shot to be seen in the yard of an arsenal. Inserted into the interstices of the huge stones which formed the pi-pi were large boughs of trees; hanging from the branches of which, and screened from the sun by their foliage, were innumerable little packages with leafy coverings, containing the meat of the numerous hogs which had been slain, done up in this manner to make it more accessible to the crowd. Leaning against the railing of the piazza were an immense number of long, heavy bamboos, plugged at the lower end, and with their projecting muzzles stuffed with a wad of leaves. These were filled with water from the stream, and each of them might hold from four to five gallons.

The banquet being thus spread, nought remained but for every one to help himself at his pleasure. Accordingly not a moment passed but the transplanted boughs I have mentioned were rifled by the throng of the fruit they certainly had never borne before. Calabashes of poee-poee were continually being replenished from the extensive receptacle in which that article was stored, and multitudes of little fires were kindled about the Ti for the purpose of roasting the bread-fruit.

Within the building itself was presented a most extraordinary scene. The immense lounge of mats lying between the parallel rows of the trunks of cocoa-nut trees, and extending the entire length of the house, at least two hundred feet, was covered by the reclining forms of a host of chiefs and warriors, who were eating at a great rate, or soothing the cares of Polynesian life in the sedative fumes of tobacco. The smoke was inhaled from large pipes, the bowls of which, made out of small cocoa-nut shells, were curiously carved in strange heathenish devices. These were passed from mouth to mouth by the recumbent smokers, who, taking two or three prodigious whiffs, handed the pipe to his neighbour; sometimes for that purpose stretching indolently across the body of some dozing individual whose exertions at the dinner-table had already induced sleep.

The tobacco used among the Typees was of a very mild and pleasing flavour, and as I always saw it in leaves, and the natives appeared pretty well supplied with it, I was led to believe that it must have been the growth of the valley. Indeed Kory-Kory gave me to understand that this was the case; but I never saw a single plant growing on the island. At Nukuheva, and, I believe, in all the other valleys, the weed is very scarce, being only obtained in small quantities from foreigners, and smoking is consequently with the inhabitants of these places a very great luxury. How it was that the Typees were so well furnished with it I cannot divine. I should think them too indolent to devote any attention to its culture; and, indeed, as far as my observation extended, not a single atom of the soil was under any other cultivation than that of shower and sunshine. The tobacco-plant, however, like the sugar-cane, may grow wild in some remote part of the vale.

There were many in the Ti for whom the tobacco did not furnish a sufficient stimulus, and who accordingly had recourse to "arva," as a more powerful agent in producing the desired effect.

"Arva" is a root very generally dispersed over the South Seas, and from it is extracted a juice, the effects of which upon the system are at first stimulating in a moderate degree; but it soon relaxes the muscles, and exerting a narcotic influence produces a luxurious sleep. In the valley this beverage was universally prepared in the following way:—Some half-dozen young boys seated themselves in a circle around an empty wooden vessel, each one of them being supplied with a certain quantity of the roots of the "arva," broken into small bits and laid by his side. A cocoa-nut goblet of water was passed around the juvenile company, who rinsing their mouths with its contents, proceeded to the business before them. This merely consisted in thoroughly masticating the "arva," and throwing it mouthful after mouthful into the receptacle provided. When a sufficient quantity had been thus obtained water was poured upon the mass, and being stirred about with the forefinger of the right-hand, the preparation was soon in readiness for use. The "arva" has medicinal qualities.

Upon the Sandwich Islands it has been employed with no small success in the treatment of scrofulous affections, and in combating the ravages of a disease for whose frightful inroads the ill-starred inhabitants of that group are indebted to their foregn benefactors. But the tenants of the Typee valley, as yet exempt from these inflictions, generally employ the "arva" as a minister to social enjoyment, and a calabash of the liquid circulates among them as the bottle with us.

Mehevi, who was greatly delighted with the change in my costume, gave me a cordial welcome. He had reserved for me a most delectable mess of "kokoo," well knowing my partiality for that dish; and had likewise selected three or four young cocoa-nuts, several roasted bread-fruit, and a magnificent bunch of bananas, for my especial comfort and gratification. These various matters were at once placed before me; but Kory-Kory deemed the banquet entirely insufficient for my wants until he had supplied me with one of the leafy packages of pork, which, notwithstanding the somewhat hasty manner in which it had been prepared, possessed a most excellent flavour, and was surprisingly sweet and tender.

Pork is not a staple article of food among the people of the Marquesas, consequently they pay little attention to the *breeding* of the swine. The hogs are permitted to roam at large in the groves, where they obtain no small part of their nourishment from the cocoa-nuts which continually fall from the trees. But it is only after infinite labour and difficulty, that the hungry animal can pierce the husk and shell so as to get at the meat. I have frequently been amused at seeing one of them, after crunching the obstinate nut with his teeth for a long time unsuccessfully, get into a violent passion with it. He would then root furiously under the cocoa-nut, and, with a fling of his snout, toss it before him on the ground. Following it up, he would crunch at it again savagely for a moment, and the next knock it on one side, pausing immediately after, as if wondering how it could so suddenly have disappeared. In this way the persecuted cocoa-nuts were often chased half across the valley.

The second day of the Feast of Calabashes was ushered in by still more uproarious noises than the first. The skins of innumerable sheep seemed to be resounding to the blows of an army of drummers. Startled from my slumbers by the din, I leaped up, and found the whole household engaged in making preparations for immediate departure. Curious to discover of what strange events these novel sounds might be the precursors, and not a little desirous to catch a sight of the instruments which produced the terrific noise, I accompanied the natives as soon as they were in readiness to depart for the Taboo Groves.

The comparatively open space that extended from the Ti toward the rock, to which I have before alluded as forming the ascent to the place was, with the building itself, now altogether deserted by the men, the whole distance being filled by bands of females, shouting and dancing under the influence of some strange excitement.

I was amused at the appearance of four or five old women who, in a state of utter nudity, with their arms extended flatly down their sides, and holding themselves perfectly erect, were leaping stiffly into the air, like so many sticks bobbing to the surface, after being pressed perpendicularly into the water. They preserved the utmost gravity of countenance, and continued their extraordinary movements without a single moment's cessation. They did not appear to attract the observation of the crowd around them, but I must candidly confess that, for my own part, I stared at them most pertinaciously.

Desirous of being enlightened with regard to the meaning of this peculiar diversion, I turned inquiringly to Kory-Kory; that learned Typee immediately proceeded to explain the whole matter thoroughly. But all that I could comprehend from what he said was, that the leaping figures before me were bereaved widows, whose partners had been slain in battle many moons previously; and who, at every festival, gave public evidence in this manner of their calamities. It was evident that Kory-Kory considered this an all-sufficient reason for so indecorous a custom; but I must say that it did not satisfy me as to its propriety.

Leaving these afflicted females, we passed on to the Hoolah-Hoolah ground. Within the spacious quadrangle, the whole population of the valley seemed to be assembled, and the sight presented was truly remarkable. Beneath the sheds of bamboo which opened towards the interior of the square, reclined the principal chiefs and warriors, while a miscellaneous throng lay at their ease under the enormous trees which spread a majestic canopy overhead. Upon the terraces of the gigantic altars, at either end, were deposited green bread-fruit in baskets of cocoa-nut leaves, large rolls of tappa, bunches of ripe bananas, clusters of mammee-apples, the golden-hued fruit of the artu-tree, and baked hogs, laid out in large wooden trenchers, fancifully decorated with freshly plucked leaves, whilst a variety of rude implements of war were piled in confused heaps before the ranks of hideous idols. Fruits of various kinds were likewise suspended in leafen baskets, from the tops of poles planted uprightly, and at regular intervals, along the lower terraces of both altars. At their base were arranged two parallel rows of cumbersome drums, standing at least fifteen feet in height, and formed from the hollow trunks of large trees.

Their heads were covered with shark skins, and their barrels were elaborately carved with various quaint figures and devices. At regular intervals they were bound round by a species of sinnate of various colours, and strips of native cloth flattened upon them here and there. Behind these instruments were built slight platforms, upon which stood a number of young men who, beating violently with the palms of their hands upon the drum-heads, produced those outrageous sounds which had awakened me in the morning. Every few minutes these musical performers hopped down from their elevation into the crowd below, and their places were immediately supplied by fresh recruits. Thus an incessant din was kept up that might have startled Pandemonium.

Precisely in the middle of the quadrangle were placed perpendicularly in the ground, a hundred or more slender, fresh-cut poles, stripped of their bark, and decorated at the end with a floating pennon of white tappa; the whole being fenced about with a little picket of canes. For what purpose these singular ornaments were intended I in vain endeavoured to discover.

Another most striking feature of the performance was exhibited by a score of old men, who sat cross-legged in the little pulpits, which encircled the trunks of the immense trees growing in the middle of the enclosure. These venerable gentlemen, who I presume were the priests, kept up an uninterrupted monotonous chant, which was nearly drowned in the roar of drums. In the right hand they held a finely woven grass fan, with a heavy black wooden handle curiously chased: these fans they kept in continual motion.

But no attention whatever seemed to be paid to the drummers or to the old priests; the individuals who composed the vast crowd present being entirely taken up in chatting and laughing with one another, smoking, drinking arva, and eating. For all the observation it attracted, or the good it achieved, the whole savage orchestra might, with great advantage to its own members and the company in general, have ceased the prodigious uproar they were making.

In vain I questioned Kory-Kory and others of the natives, as to the meaning of the strange things that were going on; all their explanations were conveyed in such a mass of outlandish gibberish and gesticulation that I gave up the attempt in despair. All that day the drums resounded, the priests chanted, and the multitude feasted and roared till sunset, when the throng dispersed, and the Taboo Groves were again abandoned to quiet and repose. The next day the same scene was repeated until night, when this singular festival terminated.

CHAPTER XXIV

Ideas suggested by the Feast of Calabashes—Inaccuracy of certain published Accounts of the Islands—A Reason—Neglected State of Heathenism in the Valley—Effigy of a dead Warrior—A singular Superstition—The Priest Kolory and the God Moa Artua—Amazing Religious Observance—A delapidated Shrine—Kory-Kory and the Idol—An Inference.

ALTHOUGH I had been baffled in my attempts to learn the origin of the Feast of Calabashes, yet it seemed very plain to me that it was principally, if not wholly, of a religious character. As a religious solemnity, however, it had not at all corresponded with the horrible descriptions of Polynesian worship which we have received in some published narratives, and especally in those accounts of the evangelized islands with which the missionaries have favoured us. Did not the sacred character of these persons render the purity of their intentions unquestionable, I should certainly be led to suppose that they had exaggerated the evils of

Paganism, in order to enhance the merit of their own disinterested labours.

In a certain work incidentally treating of the 'Washington, or Northern Marquesas Islands,' I have seen the frequent immolation of human victims upon the altars of their gods, positively and repeatedly charged upon the inhabitants. The same work gives also a rather minute account of their religion,—enumerates a great many of their superstitions,—and makes known the particular designations of numerous orders of the priesthood. One would almost imagine from the long list that is given of cannibal primates, bishops, archdeacons, prebendaries, and other inferior ecclesiastics, that the sacerdotal order far outnumbered the rest of the population, and that the poor natives were more severely priest-ridden than even the inhabitants of the papal states. These accounts are likewise calculated to leave upon the reader's mind an impression that human victims are daily cooked and served up upon the altars; that heathenish cruelties of every description are continually practised; and that these ignorant Pagans are in a state of the extremest wretchedness in consequence of the grossness of their superstitions. Be it observed, however, that all this information is given by a man who, according to his own statement, was only at one of the islands and remained there but two weeks, sleeping every night on board his ship, and taking little kid-glove excursions ashore in the daytime, attended by an armed party.

Now, all I can say is, that in all my excursions through the valley of Typee, I never saw any of these alleged enormities. If any of them are practised upon the Marquesas Islands they must certainly have come to my knowledge while living for months with a tribe of savages, wholly unchanged from their original primitive condition, and reputed the most ferocious in the South Seas.

The fact is, that there is a vast deal of unintentional humbuggery in some of the accounts we have from scientific men concerning the religious institutions of Polynesia. These learned tourists generally obtain the greater part of their information from the retired old South-Sea rovers, who have domesticated themselves among the barbarous tribes of the Pacific. Jack, who has long been accustomed to the long-bow, and to spin tough yarns on a ship's forecastle, invariably officiates as showman of the island on which he has settled, and having mastered a few dozen words of the language, is supposed to know all about the people who speak it. A natural desire to make himself of consequence in the eyes of the strangers, prompts him to lay claim to a much greater knowledge of such matters than he actually possesses. In reply to incessant queries, he communicates not only all he knows but a good deal more, and if there be any information deficient still he is at no loss to supply it. The avidity with which his anecdotes are noted down tickles his vanity, and his powers of invention increase with the credulity of his auditors. He knows just the sort of information wanted, and furnishes it to any extent.

This is not a supposed case; I have met with several individuals like the one described, and I have been present at two or three of their interviews with strangers.

Now, when the scientific voyager arrives at home with his collection of wonders, he attempts, perhaps, to give a description of some of the strange people he has been visiting. Instead of representing them as a community of lusty savages, who are leading a merry, idle, innocent life, he enters into a very circumstantial and learned narrative of certain unaccountable superstitions and practices, about which he knows as little as the islanders do themselves. Having had little time, and scarcely any opportunity to become acquainted with the customs he pretends to describe, he writes them down one after another in an off-hand, haphazard style; and were the book thus produced to be translated into the tongue of the people of whom it purports to give the history, it would appear quite as wonderful to them as it does to the American public, and much more improbable.

For my own part, I am free to confess my almost entire inability to gratify any curiosity that may be felt with regard to the theology of the valley. I doubt whether the inhabitants themselves could do so. They are either too lazy or too sensible to worry themselves about abstract points of religious belief. While I was among them they never held any synods or councils to settle the principles of their faith by agitating them. An unbounded liberty of conscience seemed to prevail. Those who pleased to do so were allowed to repose implicit faith in an ill-favoured god with a large bottle nose and fat shapeless arms crossed upon his breast; whilst others worshipped an image which, having no likeness either in heaven or on earth, could hardly be called an idol. As the islanders always maintained a discreet reserve, with regard to my own peculiar views on religion, I thought it would be excessively ill-bred in me to pry into theirs.

But, although my knowledge of the religious faith of the Typees was unavoidably limited, one of their superstitious observances with which I became acquainted interested me greatly.

In one of the most secluded portions of the valley within a stone's cast of Fayaway's lake—for so I christened the scene of our island yachting—and hard by a growth of palms, which stood ranged in order along both banks of the stream, waving their green arms as if to do honour to its passage, was the mausoleum of a deceased warrior chief. Like all the other edifices of any note, it was raised upon a small pi-pi of stones, which, being of unusual height, was

a conspicuous object from a distance. A light thatching of
bleached palmetto leaves hung over it like a self-supported
canopy; for it was not until you came very near that you
saw it was supported by four slender columns of bamboo
rising at each corner to a little more than the height of a
man. A clear area of a few yards surrounded the pi-pi, and
was enclosed by four trunks of cocoa-nut trees resting at
the angles on massive blocks of stone. The place was sacred.
The sign of the inscrutable taboo was seen in the shape of
a mystic roll of white tappa, suspended by a twisted cord
of the same material from the top of a slight pole planted
within the enclosure. The sanctity of the spot appeared
never to have been violated. The stillness of the grave was
there, and the calm solitude around was beautiful and
touching. The soft shadows of those lofty palm-trees!—I
can see them now—hanging over the little temple, as if
to keep out the intrusive sun.

On all sides as you approached this silent spot you caught
sight of the dead chief's effigy, seated in the stern of a canoe,
which was raised on a light frame a few inches above the
level of the pi-pi. The canoe was about seven feet in
length; of a rich, dark coloured wood, handsomely carved
and adorned in many places with variegated bindings of
stained sinnate, into which were ingeniously wrought a
number of sparkling seashells, and a belt of the same shells
ran all round it. The body of the figure—of whatever material it might have been made—was effectually concealed
in a heavy robe of brown tappa, revealing only the hands
and head; the latter skilfully carved in wood, and surmounted by a superb arch of plumes. These plumes, in the
subdued and gentle gales which found access to this sequestered spot, were never for one moment at rest, but
kept nodding and waving over the chief's brow. The long
leaves of the palmetto dropped over the eaves, and through
them you saw the warrior holding his paddle with both

hands in the act of rowing, leaning forward and inclining his head, as if eager to hurry on his voyage. Glaring at him for ever, and face to face, was a polished human skull, which crowned the prow of the canoe. The spectral figure-head, reversed in its position, glancing backwards, seemed to mock the impatient attitude of the warrior.

When I first visited this singular place with Kory-Kory, he told me—or at least I so understood him—that the chief was paddling his way to the realms of bliss, and bread-fruit —the Polynesian heaven—where every moment the bread-fruit trees dropped their ripened spheres to the ground, and where there was no end to the cocoa-nuts and bananas: there they reposed through the livelong eternity upon mats much finer than those of Typee; and every day bathed their glowing limbs in rivers of cocoa-nut oil. In that happy land there were plenty of plumes and feathers, and boars'-tusks and sperm-whale teeth, far preferable to all the shining trinkets and gay tappa of the white men; and, best of all, women far lovelier than the daughters of earth were there in abundance. "A very pleasant place," Kory-Kory said it was; "but after all, not much pleasanter, he thought, than Typee." "Did he not then," I asked him, "wish to accompany the warrior?" "Oh, no: he was very happy where he was; but supposed that some time or other he would go in his own canoe."

Thus far, I think, I clearly comprehended Kory-Kory. But there was a singular expression he made use of at the time, enforced by as singular a gesture, the meaning of which I would have given much to penetrate. I am inclined to believe it must have been a proverb he uttered; for I afterwards heard him repeat the same words several times, and in what appeared to me to be a somewhat similar sense. Indeed, Kory-Kory had a great variety of short, smart-sounding sentences, with which he frequently enlivened his discourse; and he introduced them with an air which plainly intimated, that, in his opinion, they settled the matter in question, whatever it might be.

Could it have been then, that when I asked him whether he desired to go to this heaven of bread-fruit, cocoa-nuts, and young ladies, which he had been describing, he answered by saying something equivalent to our old adage—"A bird in the hand is worth two in the bush?"—if he did, Kory-Kory was a discreet and sensible fellow, and I cannot sufficently admire his shrewdness.

Whenever in the course of my rambles through the valley I happened to be near the chief's mausoleum, I always turned aside to visit it. The place had a peculiar charm for me; I hardly know why; but so it was. As I leaned over the railing and gazed upon the strange effigy and watched the play of the feathery head-dress, stirred by the same breeze which in low tones breathed amidst the lofty palm-trees, I loved to yield myself up to the fanciful superstition of the islanders, and could almost believe that the grim warrior was bound heavenward. In this mood when I turned to depart, I bade him "God speed, and a pleasant voyage." Aye, paddle away, brave chieftain, to the land of spirits! To the material eye thou makest but little progress; but with the eye of faith, I see thy canoe cleaving the bright waves, which die away on those dimly looming shores of Paradise.

This strange superstition affords another evidence of the fact, that however ignorant man may be, he still feels within him his immortal spirit yearning after the unknown future.

Although the religious theories of the islands were a complete mystery to me, their practical every-day operation could not be concealed. I frequently passed the little temples reposing in the shadows of the taboo groves and beheld the offerings—mouldy fruit spread out upon a rude altar, or hanging in half-decayed baskets around some uncouth jolly-looking image; I was present during the continuance of the festival; I daily beheld the grinning idols marshalled rank and file in the Hoolah Hoolah ground, and was often in the habit of meeting those whom I supposed to be the priests. But the temples seemed abandoned to solitude; the festival had been nothing more than a jovial mingling of the tribe; the idols were quite as harmless as any other logs of wood; and the priests were the merriest dogs in the valley.

In fact religious affairs in Typee were at a very low ebb: all such matters sat very lightly upon the thoughtless inhabitants; and, in the celebration of many of their strange rites, they appeared merely to seek a sort of childish amusement.

A curious evidence of this was given in a remarkable ceremony in which I frequently saw Mehevi and several other chiefs and warriors of note take part; but never a single female.

Among those whom I looked upon as forming the priesthood of the valley, there was one in particular who often attracted my notice, and whom I could not help regarding as the head of the order. He was a noble looking man, in the prime of his life, and of a most benignant aspect. The authority this man, whose name was Kolory, seemed to exercise over the rest, the episcopal part he took in the Feast of Calabashes, his sleek and complacent appearance, the mystic characters which were tattooed upon his chest, and above all the mitre he frequently wore, in the shape of a towering head-dress, consisting of part of a cocoa-nut branch, the stalk planted uprightly on his brow, and the leaflets gathered together and passed round the temples and behind the ears, all these pointed him out as Lord Primate of Typee. Kolory was a sort of Knight Templar—a soldier-priest; for he often wore the dress of a Marquesan warrior, and always carried a long spear, which, instead of terminat-

ing in a paddle at the lower end, after the general fashion
of these weapons, was curved into a heathenish-looking
little image. This instrument, however, might perhaps
have been emblematic of his double functions. With one
end in carnal combat he transfixed the enemies of his
tribe; and with the other as a pastoral crook he kept in
order his spiritual flock. But this is not all I have to say
about Kolory. His martial grace very often carried about
with him what seemed to me the half of a broken war-
club. It was swathed round with ragged bits of white tappa,
and the upper part, which was intended to represent a
human head, was embellished with a strip of scarlet cloth
of European manufacture. It required little observation to
discover that this strange object was revered as a god. By
the side of the big and lusty images standing sentinel over
the altars of the Hoolah Hoolah ground, it seemed a mere
pigmy in tatters. But appearances all the world over are
deceptive. Little men are sometimes very potent, and rags
sometimes cover very extensive pretensions. In fact, this
funny little image was the "crack" god of the island; lord-
ing it over all the wooden lubbers who looked so grim and
dreadful; its name was Moa Artua. And it was in honour of
Moa Artua, and for the entertainment of those who believe
in him, that the curious ceremony I am about to describe
was observed.

Mehevi and the chieftains of the Ti have just risen from
their noontide slumbers. There are no affairs of state to
dispose of; and having eaten two or three breakfasts in
the course of the morning, the magnates of the valley feel
no appetite as yet for dinner. How are their leisure moments to be occupied? They smoke, they chat, and at last
one of their number makes a proposition to the rest, who
joyfully acquiescing, he darts out of the house, leaps from
the pi-pi, and disappears in the grove. Soon you see him
returning with Kolory, who bears the god Moa Artua in

his arms, and carries in one hand a small trough, hollowed out in the likeness of a canoe. The priest comes along dandling his charge as if it were a lachrymose infant he was endeavouring to put into a good humour. Presently, entering the Ti, he seats himself on the mats as composedly as a juggler about to perform his sleight-of-hand tricks; and with the chiefs disposed in a circle around him, commences his ceremony.

In the first place he gives Moa Artua an affectionate hug, then caressingly lays him to his breast, and, finally, whispers something in his ear; the rest of the company listening eagerly for a reply. But the baby-god is deaf or dumb, —perhaps both, for never a word does he utter. At last Kolory speaks a little louder, and soon growing angry, comes boldly out with what he has to say and bawls to him. He put me in mind of a choleric fellow, who, after trying in vain to communicate a secret to a deaf man, all at once flies into a passion and screams it out so that every one may hear. Still Moa Artua remains as quiet as ever; and Kolory, seemingly losing his temper, fetches him a box over the head, strips him of his tappa and red cloth, and laying him in a state of nudity in the little trough, covers him from sight. At this proceeding all present loudly applaud and signify their approval by uttering the adjective "motarkee" with violent emphasis. Kolory, however, is so desirous his conduct should meet with unqualified approbation, that he inquires of each individual separately whether, under existing circumstances, he has not done perfectly right in shutting up Moa Artua. The invariable response is "Aa, Aa" (yes, yes), repeated over again and again in a manner which ought to quiet the scruples of the most conscientious. After a few moments Kolory brings forth his doll again, and while arraying it very carefully in the tappa and red cloth, alternately fondles and chides it. The toilet being completed, he once more speaks to it aloud. The whole company hereupon show the greatest interest; while the priest holding Moa Artua to his ear interprets to them what he pretends the god is confidentially communicating to him. Some items of intelligence appear to tickle all present amazingly; for one claps his hands in a rapture; another shouts with merriment; and a third leaps to his feet and capers about like a madman.

What under the sun Moa Artua on these occasions had to say to Kolory I never could find out; but I could not help thinking that the former showed a sad want of spirit in being disciplined into making those disclosures, which at first he seemed bent on withholding. Whether the priest honestly interpreted what he believed the divinity said to him, or whether he was not all the while guilty of a vile humbug, I shall not presume to decide. At any rate, whatever as coming from the god was imparted to those present seemed to be generally of a complimentary nature: a fact which illustrates the sagacity of Kolory, or else the time-serving disposition of this hardly used deity.

Moa Artua having nothing more to say, his bearer goes to nursing him again, in which occupation, however, he is soon interrupted by a question put by one of the warriors to the god. Kolory hereupon snatches it up to his ear again, and after listening attentively, once more officiates as the organ of communication. A multitude of questions and answers having passed between the parties, much to the satisfaction of those who propose them, the god is put tenderly to bed in the trough, and the whole company unite in a long chaunt, led off by Kolory. This ended, the ceremony is over; the chiefs rise to their feet in high good humour, and my Lord Archbishop, after chatting awhile, and regaling himself with a whiff or two from a pipe of tobacco, tucks the canoe under his arm and marches off with it.

The whole of these proceedings were like those of a parcel of children playing with dolls and baby houses.

For a youngster scarcely ten inches high, and with so few early advantages as he doubtless had had, Moa Artua was certainly a precocious little fellow if he really said all that was imputed to him; but for what reason this poor devil of a deity, thus cuffed about, cajoled and shut up in a box, was held in greater estimation than the full-grown and dignified personages of the Taboo Groves, I cannot divine. And yet Mehevi, and other chiefs of unquestionable veracity—to say nothing of the Primate himself—assured me over and over again that Moa Artua was the tutelary deity of Typee, and was more to be held in honour than a whole battalion of the clumsy idols in the Hoolah Hoolah grounds. Kory-Kory—who seemed to have devoted considerable attention to the study of theology, as he knew the names of all the graven images in the valley, and often repeated them over to me—likewise entertained some rather enlarged ideas with regard to the character and pretensions of Moa Artua. He once gave me to understand, with a gesture there was no misconceiving, that if he (Moa Artua) were so minded, he could cause a cocoa-nut tree to sprout out of his (Kory-Kory's) head; and that it would be the easiest thing in life for him (Moa Artua) to take the whole island of Nukuheva in his mouth and dive down to the bottom of the sea with it.

But in sober seriousness, I hardly knew what to make of the religion of the valley. There was nothing that so much perplexed the illustrious Cook, in his intercourse with the South Sea islanders, as their sacred rites. Although this prince of navigators was in many instances assisted by interpreters in the prosecution of his researches, he still frankly acknowledges that he was at a loss to obtain any thing like a clear insight into the puzzling arcana of their faith. A similar admission has been made by other eminent voyagers: by Carteret, Byron, Kotzebue, and Vancouver.

For my own part, although hardly a day passed while I remained upon the island that I did not witness some religious ceremony or other, it was very much like seeing a parcel of "Freemasons" making secret signs to each other; I saw everything, but could comprehend nothing.

On the whole, I am inclined to believe, that the islanders in the Pacific have no fixed and definite ideas whatever on the subject of religion. I am persuaded that Kolory himself would be effectually posed were he called upon to draw up the articles of his faith and pronounce the creed by which he hoped to be saved. In truth, the Typees, so far as their actions evince, submitted to no laws human or divine—always excepting the thrice mysterious taboo. The "independent electors" of the valley were not to be brow-beaten by chiefs, priests, idols, or devils. As for the luckless idols, they received more hard knocks than supplications. I do not wonder that some of them looked so grim, and stood so bolt upright as if fearful of looking to the right or the left lest they should give any one offence. The fact is, they had to carry themselves *"pretty straight,"* or suffer the consequences. Their worshippers were such a precious set of fickle-minded and irreverent heathens, that there was no telling when they might topple one of them over, break it to pieces, and making a fire with it on the very altar itself, fall to roasting the offerings of bread-fruit, and eat them in spite of its teeth.

In how little reverence these unfortunate deities were held by the natives was on one occasion most convincingly proved to me.—Walking with Kory-Kory through the deepest recesses of the groves, I perceived a curious looking image, about six feet in height, which originally had been placed upright against a low pi-pi, surmounted by a ruinous bamboo temple, but having become fatigued and weak in the knees, was now carelessly leaning against it. The idol was partly concealed by the foliage of a tree which stood near, and whose leafy boughs drooped over the pile of stones, as if to protect the rude fane from the decay to which it was rapidly hastening. The image itself was nothing more than a grotesquely shaped log, carved in the likeness of a portly naked man with the arms clasped over the head, the jaws thrown wide apart, and its thick shapeless legs bowed into an arch. It was much decayed. The lower part was overgrown with a bright silky moss. Thin spears of grass sprouted from the distended mouth and fringed the outline of the head and arms. His godship had literally attained a green old age. All its prominent points were bruised and battered, or entirely rotted away. The nose had taken its departure, and from the general appearance of the head it might have been supposed that the wooden divinity, in despair at the neglect of its worshippers, had been trying to beat its own brains out against the surrounding trees.

I drew near to inspect more closely this strange object of idolatry; but halted reverently at the distance of two or three paces, out of regard to the religious prejudices of my valet. As soon, however, as Kory-Kory perceived that I was in one of my inquiring, scientific moods, to my astonishment, he sprang to the side of the idol, and pushing it away from the stones against which it rested, endeavoured to make it stand upon its legs. But the divinity had lost the use of them altogether; and while Kory-Kory was trying to prop it up, by placing a stick between it and the pi-pi, the monster fell clumsily to the ground, and would infallibly have broken its neck had not Kory-Kory providentially broken its fall by receiving its whole weight on his own half-crushed back. I never saw the honest fellow in such a rage before. He leaped furiously to his feet, and seizing the stick, began beating the poor image: every moment or two pausing and talking to it in the most violent manner, as if upbraiding it for the accident. When his indignation had subsided a little he whirled the idol about most profanely, so as to give me an opportunity of examining it on all sides. I am quite sure I never should have presumed to have taken such liberties with the god myself, and I was not a little shocked at Kory-Kory's impiety.

This anecdote speaks for itself. When one of the inferior order of natives could show such contempt for a venerable and decrepit God of the Groves, what the state of religion must be among the people in general is easily to be imagined. In truth, I regard the Typees as a back-slidden generation. They are sunk in religious sloth, and require a spiritual revival. A long prosperity of bread-fruit and cocoa-nuts has rendered them remiss in the performance of their higher obligations. The wood-rot malady is spreading among the idols—the fruit upon their altars is becoming offensive—the temples themselves need re-thatching—the tattooed clergy are altogether too light-hearted and lazy—and their flocks are going astray.

CHAPTER XXV

General Information gathered at the Festival—Personal Beauty of the Typees—Their Superiority over the Inhabitants of the other Islands—Diversity of Complexion—A vegetable Cosmetic and Ointment—Testimony of Voyagers to the uncommon Beauty of the Marquesans—Few Evidences of Intercourse with civilized Beings—Dilapidated Musket—Primitive Simplicity of Government—Regal Dignity of Mehevi.

ALTHOUGH I had been unable during the late festival to obtain information on many interesting subjects which had much excited my curiosity, still that important event had not passed by without adding materially to my general knowledge of the islanders.

I was especially struck by the physical strength and beauty which they displayed, by their great superiority in these respects over the inhabitants of the neighbouring bay of Nukuheva, and by the singular contrasts they presented among themselves in their various shades of complexion.

In beauty of form they surpassed anything I had ever seen. Not a single instance of natural deformity was observable in all the throng attending the revels. Occasionally I noticed among the men the scars of wounds they had received in battle; and sometimes, though very seldom, the loss of a finger, an eye, or an arm, attributable to the same cause. With these exceptions, every individual appeared free from those blemishes which sometimes mar the effect of an otherwise perfect form. But their physical excellence did not merely consist in an exemption from these evils; nearly every individual of their number might have been taken for a sculptor's model.

When I remembered that these islanders derived no advantage from dress, but appeared in all the naked simplicity of nature, I could not avoid comparing them with the fine gentlemen and dandies who promenade such unexceptionable figures in our frequented thoroughfares. Stripped of the cunning artifices of the tailor, and standing forth in the garb of Eden,—what a sorry set of round-shouldered, spindle-shanked, crane-necked varlets would civilized men appear! Stuffed calves, padded breasts, and scientifically cut pantaloons would then avail them nothing, and the effect would be truly deplorable.

Nothing in the appearance of the islanders struck me more forcibly than the whiteness of their teeth. The novelist always compares the masticators of his heroine to ivory; but I boldly pronounce the teeth of the Typees to be far more beautiful than ivory itself. The jaws of the oldest greybeards among them were much better garnished than those of most of the youths of civilized countries; while the teeth of the young and middle-aged, in their purity and whiteness, were actually dazzling to the eye. This marvellous whiteness of the teeth is to be ascribed to the pure vegetable diet of these people, and the uninterrupted healthfulness of their natural mode of life.

The men, in almost every instance, are of lofty stature, scarcely ever less than six feet in height, while the other sex are uncommonly diminutive. The early period of life at which the human form arrives at maturity in this generous tropical climate, likewise deserves to be mentioned. A little creature, not more than thirteen years of age, and who in other particulars might be regarded as a mere child, is often seen nursing her own baby; whilst lads who, under less ripening skies, would be still at school, are here responsible fathers of families.

On first entering the Typee Valley, I had been struck with the marked contrast presented by its inhabitants with those of the bay I had previously left. In the latter place, I had not been favourably impressed with the personal appearance of the male portion of the population; although with the females, excepting in some truly melancholy instances, I had been wonderfully pleased. I had observed that even the little intercourse Europeans had carried on with the Nukuheva natives had not failed to leave its traces amongst them. One of the most dreadful curses under which humanity labours had commenced its havocks, and betrayed, as it ever does among the South Sea islanders, the most aggravated symptoms. From this, as from all other foreign inflictions, the yet uncontaminated tenants of the Typee Valley were wholly exempt; and long may they continue so. Better will it be for them for ever to remain the happy and innocent heathens and barbarians that they now are, than, like the wretched inhabitants of the Sandwich Islands, to enjoy the mere name of Christians without experiencing any of the vital operations of true religion, whilst, at the same time, they are made the victims of the worst vices and evils of civilized life.

Apart, however, from these considerations, I am inclined to believe that there exists a radical difference between the two tribes, if indeed they are not distinct races of men. To those who have merely touched at Nukuheva Bay, without visiting other portions of the island, it would hardly appear credible the diversities presented between the various small clans inhabiting so diminutive a spot. But the hereditary hostility which has existed between them for ages fully accounts for this.

Not so easy, however, is it to assign an adequate cause for the endless variety of complexions to be seen in the Typee Valley. During the festival, I had noticed several young females whose skins were almost as white as any Saxon damsel's; a slight dash of the mantling brown being all that marked the difference. This comparative fairness of complexion, though in a great degree perfectly natural, is partly the result of an artificial process, and of an entire exclusion from the sun. The juice of the "papa" root, found in great abundance at the head of the valley, is held in great esteem as a cosmetic, with which many of the females daily anoint their whole person. The habitual use of it whitens and beautifies the skin. Those of the young girls who resort to this method of heightening their charms, never expose themselves to the rays of the sun; an observance, however, that produces little or no inconvenience, since there are but few of the inhabited portions of the vale which are not shaded over with a spreading canopy of boughs, so that one may journey from house to house, scarcely deviating from the direct course, and yet never once see his shadow cast upon the ground.

The "papa," when used, is suffered to remain upon the skin for several hours; being of a light green colour, it consequently imparts for the time a similar hue to the complexion. Nothing, therefore, can be imagined more singular than the appearance of these nearly naked damsels immediately after the application of the cosmetic. To look at one of them you would almost suppose she was some vegetable in an unripe state; and that, instead of living in the shade for ever, she ought to be placed out in the sun to ripen.

All the islanders are more or less in the habit of anointing themselves; the women preferring the "aker" or "papa," and the men using the oil of the cocoa-nut. Mehevi was remarkably fond of mollifying his entire cuticle with this ointment. Sometimes he might be seen, with his whole body fairly reeking with the perfumed oil of the nut, looking as if he had just emerged from a soap-boiler's vat, or had undergone the process of dipping in a tallow-chandlery. To this cause perhaps, united to their frequent bathing and extreme cleanliness, is ascribable, in a great measure, the marvellous purity and smoothness of skin exhibited by the natives in general.

The prevailing tint among the women of the valley was a light olive, and of this style of complexion Fayaway afforded the most beautiful example. Others were still darker, while not a few were of a genuine golden colour, and some of a swarthy hue.

As agreeing with much previously mentioned in this narrative, I may here observe, that Mendanna, their discoverer, in his account of the Marquesas, described the natives as wondrously beautiful to behold, and as nearly resembling the people of southern Europe. The first of these islands seen by Mendanna was La Madelena, which is not far distant from Nukuheva; and its inhabitants in every respect resemble those dwelling on that and the other islands of the group. Figueroa, the chronicler of Mendanna's voyage, says, that on the morning the land was descried, when the Spaniards drew near the shore, there sallied forth, in rude procession, about seventy canoes, and at the same time many of the inhabitants (females, I presume) made towards the ships by swimming. He adds, that "in complexion they were nearly white; of good stature, and finely formed; and on their faces and bodies were delineated representations of fishes and other devices." The old Don then goes on to say, "There came, among others, two lads paddling their canoe, whose eyes were fixed on the ship: they had beautiful faces and the most promising animation of countenance; and were in all things so becoming, that the pilot-mayor Quiros affirmed, nothing in his life ever caused him so much regret as the leaving such fine creatures to be lost in that country." More than two hundred years have gone by since the passage of which the above is a translation was written; and it appears to me now, as I read it, as fresh and true as if written but yesterday. The islanders are still the same; and I have seen boys in the Typee Valley of whose "beautiful faces" and "promising animation of countenance" no one who has not beheld them can form any adequate idea. Cook, in the account of his voyages, pronounces the Marquesans as by far the most splendid islanders in the South Seas. Stewart, the chaplain of the U. S. ship Vincennes, in his "Scenes in the South Seas," expresses, in more than one place, his amazement at the surpassing loveliness of the women; and says that many of the Nukuheva damsels reminded him forcibly of the most celebrated beauties in his own land. Fanning, a Yankee mariner of some reputation, likewise records his lively impressions of the physical appearance of these people; and Commodore David Porter of the U. S. frigate Essex, is said to have been vastly smitten by the beauty of the ladies. Their great superiority over all other Polynesians cannot fail to attract the notice of those who visit the principal groups in the Pacific. The voluptuous Tahitians are the only people who at all deserve to be compared with them;

while the dark-hued Hawaiians and the woolly-headed Fee-
gees are immeasurably inferior to them. The distinguishing
characteristic of the Marquesan islanders, and that which
at once strikes you, is the European cast of their features
—a peculiarity seldom observable among other uncivilized
people. Many of their faces present a profile classically
beautiful, and in the valley of Typee, I saw several who,
like the stranger Marnoo, were in every respect models of
beauty.

Some of the natives present at the Feast of Calabashes
had displayed a few articles of European dress; disposed,
however, about their persons after their own peculiar fashion. Among these I perceived the two pieces of cotton-cloth
which poor Toby and myself had bestowed upon our
youthful guides the afternoon we entered the valley. They
were evidently reserved for gala days; and during those of
the festival they rendered the young islanders who wore
them very distinguished characters. The small number who
were similarly adorned, and the great value they appeared
to place upon the most common and most trivial articles,
furnished ample evidence of the very restricted intercourse
they held with vessels touching at the island. A few cotton
handkerchiefs, of a gay pattern, tied about the neck, and
suffered to fall over the shoulders; strips of fanciful calico,
swathed about the loins, were nearly all I saw.

Indeed, throughout the valley, there were few things of
any kind to be seen of European origin. All I ever saw, beside the articles just alluded to, were the six muskets preserved in the Ti, and three or four similar implements of
warfare hung up in other houses; some small canvas bags,
partly filled with bullets and powder, and half a dozen old
hatchet-heads, with the edges blunted and battered to such
a degree as to render them utterly useless. These last
seemed to be regarded as nearly worthless by the natives;
and several times they held up one of them before me, and

throwing it aside with a gesture of disgust, manifested their contempt for anything that could so soon become unserviceable.

But the muskets, the powder, and the bullets were held in most extravagant esteem. The former, from their great age and the peculiarities they exhibited, were well worthy a place in any antiquarian's armory. I remember in particular one that hung in the Ti, and which Mehevi—supposing as a matter of course that I was able to repair it—had put into my hands for that purpose. It was one of those clumsy, old-fashioned, English pieces known generally as Tower Hill muskets, and, for aught I know, might have been left on the island by Wallace, Carteret, Cook, or Vancouver. The stock was half rotten and worm-eaten; the lock was as rusty and about as well adapted to its ostensible purpose as an old door-hinge; the threading of the screws about the trigger was completely worn away; while the barrel shook in the wood. Such was the weapon the chief desired me to restore to its original condition. As I did not possess the accomplishments of a gunsmith, and was likewise destitute of the necessary tools, I was reluctantly obliged to signify my inability to perform the task. At this unexpected communication Mehevi regarded me, for a moment, as if he half suspected I was some inferior sort of white man, who after all did not know much more than a Typee. However, after a most laboured explanation of the matter, I succeeded in making him understand the extreme difficulty of the task. Scarcely satisfied with my apologies, however, he marched off with the superannuated musket in something of a huff, as if he would no longer expose it to the indignity of being manipulated by such unskilful fingers.

During the festival I had not failed to remark the simplicity of manner, the freedom from all restraint, and, to a certain degree, the equality of condition manifested by the natives in general. No one appeared to assume any arrogant pretensions. There was little more than a slight difference in costume to distinguish the chiefs from the other natives. All appeared to mix together freely, and without any reserve; although I noticed that the wishes of a chief, even when delivered in the mildest tone, received the same immediate obedience which elsewhere would have been only accorded to a peremptory command. What may be the extent of the authority of the chiefs over the rest of the tribe, I will not venture to assert; but from all I saw during my stay in the valley, I was induced to believe that in matters concerning the general welfare it was very limited. The required degree of deference towards them, however, was willingly and cheerfully yielded; and as all authority is transmitted from father to son, I have no doubt that one of the effects here, as elsewhere, of high birth, is to induce respect and obedience.

The civil institutions of the Marquesas Islands appear to be in this, as in other respects, directly the reverse of those of the Tahitian and Hawaiian groups, where the original power of the king and chiefs was far more despotic than that of any tyrant in civilized countries. At Tahiti it used to be death for one of the inferior orders to approach, without permission, under the shadow of the king's house; or to fail in paying the customary reverence when food destined for the king was borne past them by his messengers. At the Sandwich Islands, Kaahumanu, the gigantic old dowager queen—a woman of nearly four hundred pounds weight, and who is said to be still living at Mowee—was accustomed, in some of her terrific gusts of temper, to snatch up an ordinary sized man who had offended her, and snap his spine across her knee. Incredible as this may seem, it is a fact. While at Lahainaluna—the residence of this monstrous Jezebel—a humpbacked wretch was pointed out to me, who, some twenty-five years previously, had had the vertebræ of his back-bone very seriously discomposed by his gentle mistress.

The particular grades of rank existing among the chiefs of Typee, I could not in all cases determine. Previous to the Feast of Calabashes I had been puzzled what particular station to assign to Mehevi. But the important part he took upon that occasion convinced me that he had no superior among the inhabitants of the valley. I had invariably noticed a certain degree of deference paid to him by all with whom I had ever seen him brought in contact; but when I remembered that my wanderings had been confined to a limited portion of the valley, and that towards the sea a number of distinguished chiefs resided, some of whom had separately visited me at Marheyo's house, and whom, until the Festival, I had never seen in the company of Mehevi, I felt disposed to believe that his rank after all might not be particularly elevated.

The revels, however, had brought together all the warriors whom I had seen individually and in groups at different times and places. Among them Mehevi moved with an easy air of superiority which was not to be mistaken; and he whom I had only looked at as the hospitable host of the Ti, and one of the military leaders of the tribe, now assumed in my eyes the dignity of royal station. His striking costume, no less than his naturally commanding figure, seemed indeed to give him pre-eminence over the rest. The towering helmet of feathers that he wore raised him in height above all who surrounded him; and though some others were similarly adorned, the length and luxuriance of their plumes were far inferior to his.

Mehevi was in fact the greatest of the chiefs—the head of his clan—the sovereign of the valley; and the simplicity of the social institutions of the people could not have been more completely proved than by the fact, that after having been several weeks in the valley, and almost in daily inter-course with Mehevi, I should have remained until the time of the festival ignorant of his regal character. But a new light had now broken in upon me. The Ti was the palace —and Mehevi the king. Both the one and the other of a most simple and patriarchal nature it must be allowed, and wholly unattended by the ceremonious pomp which usu-ally surrounds the purple.

After having made this discovery I could not avoid con-gratulating myself that Mehevi had from the first taken me as it were under his royal protection, and that he still continued to entertain for me the warmest regard, as far at least as I was enabled to judge from appearances. For the future I determined to pay most assiduous court to him, hoping that eventually through his kindness I might ob-tain my liberty.

CHAPTER XXVI

King Mehevi—Allusion to his Hawaiian Majesty—Conduct of Mar-heyo and Mehevi in certain delicate matters—Peculiar system of Marriage—Number of Population—Uniformity—Embalming—Places of Sepulchre—Funeral obsequies at Nukuheva—Number of Inhabitants in Typee—Location of the Dwellings—Happiness enjoyed in the Valley—A Warning—Some ideas with regard to the Civilization of the Islands—Reference to the Present state of the Hawaiians—Story of a Missionary's Wife—Fashionable Equipages at Oahu—Reflections.

KING MEHEVI!—A goodly sounding title!—and why should I not bestow it upon the foremost man in the valley of Typee? The republican missionaries of Oahu cause to be gazetted in the Court Journal, published at Honolula, the most trivial movements of "his gracious majesty" King Kammehammaha III., and "their highnesses the princes of the blood royal."—And who is his "gracious majesty," and what the quality of this "blood royal"?—His "gracious majesty" is a fat, lazy, negro-looking blockhead, with as little character as power. He has lost the noble traits of the barbarian, without acquiring the redeeming graces of a civilized being; and, although a member of the Hawaiian Temperance Society, is a most inveterate dram-drinker.

The "blood royal" is an extremely thick, depraved fluid; formed principally of raw fish, bad brandy, and European sweetmeats, and is charged with a variety of eruptive humours, which are developed in sundry blotches and pimples upon the august face of "majesty itself," and the angelic countenances of the "princes and princesses of the blood-royal"!

Now, if the farcical puppet of a chief magistrate in the Sandwich Islands be allowed the title of King, why should it be withheld from the noble savage Mehevi, who is a thousand times more worthy of the appellation? All hail, therefore, Mehevi, King of the Cannibal Valley, and long life and prosperity to his Typeean majesty! May Heaven for many a year preserve him, the uncompromising foe of Nukuheva and the French, if a hostile attitude will secure his lovely domain from the remorseless inflictions of South Sea civilization.

Previously to seeing the Dancing Widows I had little idea that there were any matrimonial relations subsisting in Typee, and I should as soon have thought of a Platonic affection being cultivated between the sexes, as of the solemn connexion of man and wife. To be sure, there were old Marheyo and Tinor, who seemed to have a sort of nuptial understanding with one another; but for all that, I had sometimes observed a comical-looking old gentleman dressed in a suit of shabby tattooing, who had the audacity to take various liberties with the lady, and that too in the very presence of the old warrior her husband, who looked on, as good-naturedly as if nothing was happening. This behaviour, until subsequent discoveries enlightened me, puzzled me more than anything else I witnessed in Typee.

As for Mehevi, I had supposed him a confirmed bachelor, as well as most of the principal chiefs. At any rate, if they had wives and families, they ought to have been ashamed of themselves; for sure I am, they never troubled themselves about any domestic affairs. In truth, Mehevi seemed to be the president of a club of hearty fellows, who kept "Bachelor's Hall" in fine style at the Ti. I had no doubt but that they regarded children as odious incumbrances; and their ideas of domestic felicity were sufficiently shown in the fact, that they allowed no meddlesome housekeepers to turn topsy-turvy those snug little arrangements they had made in their comfortable dwelling. I strongly suspected, however, that some of these jolly bachelors were carrying on love intrigues with the maidens of the tribe; although they did not appear publicly to acknowledge them. I happened to pop upon Mehevi three or four times when he was romping—in a most undignified manner for a warrior king—with one of the prettiest little witches in the valley. She lived with an old woman and a young man, in a house near Marheyo's; and although in appearance a mere child herself, had a noble boy about a year old, who bore a marvellous resemblance to Mehevi, whom I should certainly have believed to have been the father, were it not that the little fellow had no triangle on his face—but on second thoughts, tattooing is not hereditary. Mehevi, however, was not the only person upon whom the damsel Moonoony smiled—the young fellow of fifteen, who permanently resided in the house with her, was decidedly in her good graces. I sometimes beheld both him and the chief making love at the same time. Is it possible, thought I, that the valiant warrior can consent to give up a corner in the thing he loves? This too was a mystery which, with others of the same kind, was afterwards satisfactorily explained.

During the second day of the Feast of Calabashes, Kory-Kory—being determined that I should have some understanding on these matters—had, in the course of his explanations, directed my attention to a peculiarity I had frequently remarked among many of the females;—principally those of a mature age and rather matronly appearance. This consisted in having the right hand and the left foot most elaborately tattooed; while the rest of the body was wholly free from the operation of the art, with the exception of the minutely dotted lips and slight marks on the shoulders, to which I have previously referred as comprising the sole tattooing exhibited by Fayaway, in common with other young girls of her age. The hand and foot thus embellished were, according to Kory-Kory, the distinguishing badge of wedlock, so far as that social and highly commendable institution is known among these people. It answers, indeed, the same purpose as the plain gold ring worn by our fairer spouses.

After Kory-Kory's explanation of the subject, I was for some time studiously respectful in the presence of all females thus distinguished, and never ventured to indulge in the slightest approach to flirtation with any of their number. Married women, to be sure!—I knew better than to offend them.

A further insight however into the peculiar domestic customs of the inmates of the valley did away in a measure with the severity of my scruples, and convinced me that I was deceived in some at least of my conclusions. A regular system of polygamy exists among the islanders; but of a most extraordinary nature,—a plurality of husbands, instead of wives; and this solitary fact speaks volumes for the gentle disposition of the male population. Where else, indeed, could such a practice exist, even for a single day? —Imagine a revolution brought about in a Turkish seraglio, and the harem rendered the abode of bearded men; or

conceive some beautiful woman in our own country running distracted at the sight of her numerous lovers murder-
ing one another before her eyes, out of jealousy for the
unequal distribution of her favours!—Heaven defend us
from such a state of things!—We are scarcely amiable and
forbearing enough to submit to it.

I was not able to learn what particular ceremony was observed in forming the marriage contract, but am inclined
to think that it must have been of a very simple nature.
Perhaps the mere "popping the question," as it is termed
with us, might have been followed by an immediate nuptial alliance. At any rate, I have more than one reason to
believe that tedious courtships are unknown in the valley
of Typee.

The males considerably outnumber the females. This
holds true of many of the islands of Polynesia, although the
reverse of what is the case in most civilized countries. The
girls are first wooed and won, at a very tender age, by some
stripling in the household in which they reside. This, however, is a mere frolic of the affections, and no formal engagement is contracted. By the time this first love has a
little subsided, a second suitor presents himself, of graver
years, and carries both boy and girl away to his own habitation. This disinterested and generous-hearted fellow now
weds the young couple—marrying damsel and lover at the
same time—and all three thenceforth live together as harmoniously as so many turtles. I have heard of some men
who in civilized countries rashly marry large families with
their wives, but had no idea that there was any place where
people married supplementary husbands with them. In-
fidelity on either side is very rare. No man has more than
one wife, and no wife of mature years has less than two
husbands,—sometimes she has three, but such instances
are not frequent. The marriage tie, whatever it may be,
does not appear to be indissoluble; for separations occa-

sionally happen. These, however, when they do take place, produce no unhappiness, and are preceded by no bickerings; for the simple reason, that an ill-used wife or a henpecked husband is not obliged to file a bill in Chancery to obtain a divorce. As nothing stands in the way of a separation, the matrimonial yoke sits easily and lightly, and a Typee wife lives on very pleasant and sociable terms with her husbands. On the whole wedlock, as known among these Typees, seems to be of a more distinct and enduring nature than is usually the case with barbarous people. A baneful promiscuous intercourse of the sexes is hereby avoided, and virtue, without being clamorously invoked, is, as it were, unconsciously practised.

The contrast exhibited between the Marquesas and other islanders of the Pacific in this respect, is worthy of being noticed. At Tahiti the marriage tie was altogether unknown; and the relation of husband and wife, father and son, could hardly be said to exist. The Arreory Society—one of the most singular institutions that ever existed in any part of the world—spread universal licentiousness over the island. It was the voluptuous character of these people which rendered the disease introduced among them by De Bougainville's ships, in 1768, doubly destructive. It visited them like a plague, sweeping them off by hundreds.

Notwithstanding the existence of wedlock among the Typees, the Scriptural injunction to increase and multiply seems to be but indifferently attended to. I never saw any of those large families in arithmetical or step-ladder progression which one often meets with at home. I never knew of more than two youngsters living together in the same home, and but seldom even that number. As for the women, it was very plain that the anxieties of the nursery but seldom disturbed the serenity of their souls; and they were never to be seen going about the valley with half a score of little ones tagging at their apron-strings, or rather at the bread-fruit-leaf they usually wore in the rear.

The ratio of increase among all the Polynesian nations is very small; and in some places as yet uncorrupted by intercourse with Europeans, the births would appear but very little to outnumber the deaths; the population in such instances remaining nearly the same for several successive generations, even upon those islands seldom or never desolated by wars, and among people with whom the crime of infanticide is altogether unknown. This would seem expressly ordained by Providence to prevent the overstocking of the islands with a race too indolent to cultivate the ground, and who, for that reason alone, would, by any considerable increase in their numbers, be exposed to the most deplorable misery. During the entire period of my stay in the valley of Typee, I never saw more than ten or twelve children under the age of six months, and only became aware of two births.

It is to the absence of the marriage tie that the late rapid decrease of the population of the Sandwich Islands and of Tahiti is in part to be ascribed. The vices and diseases introduced among these unhappy people annually swell the ordinary mortality of the islands, while, from the same cause, the originally small number of births is proportionally decreased. Thus the progress of the Hawaiians and Tahitians to utter extinction is accelerated in a sort of compound ratio.

I have before had occasion to remark that I never saw any of the ordinary signs of a place of sepulchre in the valley, a circumstance which I attributed, at the time, to my living in a particular part of it, and being forbidden to extend my rambles to any considerable distance towards the sea. I have since thought it probable, however, that the Typees, either desirous of removing from their sight the evidences of mortality, or prompted by a taste for rural beauty, may have some charming cemetery situated in the shadowy recesses along the base of the mountains. At Nukuheva, two or three large quadrangular "pi-pis," heavily flagged, enclosed with regular stone walls, and shaded over and almost hidden from view by the interlacing branches of enormous trees, were pointed out to me as burial-places. The bodies, I understood, were deposited in rude vaults beneath the flagging, and were suffered to remain there without being disinterred. Although nothing could be more strange and gloomy than the aspect of these places, where the lofty trees threw their dark shadows over rude blocks of stone, a stranger in looking at them would have discerned none of the ordinary evidences of a place of sepulture.

During my stay in the valley, as none of its inmates were so accommodating as to die and be buried in order to gratify my curiosity with regard to their funeral rites, I was reluctantly obliged to remain in ignorance of them. As I have reason to believe, however, that the observances of the Typees in these matters are the same with those of all the other tribes on the island, I will here relate a scene I chanced to witness at Nukuheva.

A young man had died, about daybreak, in a house near the beach. I had been sent ashore that morning, and saw a good deal of the preparations they were making for his obsequies. The body, neatly wrapped in new white tappa, was laid out in an open shed of cocoa-nut boughs, upon a bier constructed of elastic bamboos ingeniously twisted together. This was supported, about two feet from the ground, by large canes planted upright in the earth. Two females, of a dejected appearance, watched by its side, plaintively chanting and beating the air with large grass fans whitened with pipe-clay. In the dwelling-house adjoining a numerous company were assembled, and various articles of food were being prepared for consumption. Two or three individuals, distinguished by head-dresses of beautiful tappa, and wearing a great number of ornaments, appeared to officiate as masters of the ceremonies. By noon the entertainment had fairly begun, and we were told that it would last during the whole of the two following days. With the exception of those who mourned by the corpse, every one seemed disposed to drown the sense of the late bereavement in convivial indulgence. The girls, decked out in their savage finery, danced; the old men chanted; the warriors smoked and chatted; and the young and lusty, of both sexes, feasted plentifully, and seemed to enjoy themselves as pleasantly as they could have done had it been a wedding.

The islanders understand the art of embalming, and practise it with such success, that the bodies of their great chiefs are frequently preserved for many years in the very houses where they died. I saw three of these in my visit to the Bay of Tior. One was enveloped in immense folds of tappa, with only the face exposed, and hung erect against the side of the dwelling. The others were stretched out upon biers of bamboo, in open, elevated temples, which seemed consecrated to their memory. The heads of enemies killed in battle are invariably preserved and hung up as trophies in the house of the conqueror. I am not acquainted with the process which is in use, but believe that fumigation is the principal agency employed. All the remains which I saw presented the appearance of a ham after being suspended for some time in a smoky chimney.

But to return from the dead to the living. The late festival had drawn together, as I had every reason to believe, the whole population of the vale, and consequently I was enabled to make some estimate with regard to its numbers. I should imagine that there were about two thousand inhabitants in Typee; and no number could have been better adapted to the extent of the valley. The valley is some nine miles in length, and may average one in breadth; the houses being distributed at wide intervals throughout its whole extent, principally, however, towards the head of the vale. There are no villages: the houses stand here and there in the shadow of the groves, or are scattered along the banks of the winding stream; their golden-hued bamboo sides and gleaming white thatch forming a beautiful contrast to the perpetual verdure in which they are embowered. There are no roads of any kind in the valley— nothing but a labyrinth of foot-paths twisting and turning among the thickets without end.

The penalty of the Fall presses very lightly upon the valley of Typee; for, with the one solitary exception of striking a light, I scarcely saw any piece of work performed there which caused the sweat to stand upon a single brow. As for digging and delving for a livelihood, the thing is altogether unknown. Nature had planted the bread-fruit and the banana, and in her own good time she brings them to maturity, when the idle savage stretches forth his hand, and satisfies his appetite.

Ill-fated people! I shudder when I think of the change a few years will produce in their paradisaical abode; and probably when the most destructive vices, and the worst attendances on civilization, shall have driven all peace and happiness from the valley, the magnanimous French will proclaim to the world that the Marquesas Islands have been converted to Christianity! and this the Catholic world will doubtless consider as a glorious event. Heaven help the "Isles of the Sea!"—The sympathy which Christendom feels for them has, alas! in too many instances proved their bane.

How little do some of these poor islanders comprehend when they look around them, that no inconsiderable part of their disasters originate in certain tea-party excitements, under the influence of which benevolent-looking gentlemen in white cravats solicit alms, and old ladies in spectacles, and young ladies in sober russet low gowns, contribute sixpences towards the creation of a fund, the object of which is to ameliorate the spiritual condition of the Polynesians, but whose end has almost invariably been to accomplish their temporal destruction!

Let the savages be civilized, but civilize them with benefits, and not with evils; and let heathenism be destroyed, but not by destroying the heathen. The Anglo-Saxon hive have extirpated Paganism from the greater part of the North American continent; but with it they have likewise extirpated the greater portion of the Red race. Civilization is gradually sweeping from the earth the lingering vestiges of Paganism, and at the same time the shrinking forms of its unhappy worshippers.

Among the islands of Polynesia, no sooner are the images overturned, the temples demolished, and the idolaters converted into *nominal* Christians, then disease, vice, and premature death make their appearance. The depopulated land is then recruited from the rapacious hordes of enlightened individuals who settle themselves within its borders, and clamorously announce the progress of the Truth. Neat villas, trim gardens, shaven lawns, spires, and cupolas arise, while the poor savage soon finds himself an interloper in the country of his fathers, and that too on the very site of the hut where he was born. The spontaneous fruits of the earth, which God in his wisdom had ordained for the support of the indolent natives, remorselessly seized upon and appropriated by the stranger, are devoured before the eyes of the starving inhabitants, or sent on board the numerous vessels which now touch at their shores.

When the famished wretches are cut off in this manner from their natural supplies, they are told by their benefactors to work and earn their support by the sweat of their brows! But to no fine gentleman born to hereditary opulence does manual labour come more unkindly than to the luxurious Indian when thus robbed of the bounty of Heaven. Habituated to a life of indolence, he cannot and will not exert himself; and want, disease, and vice, all evils of foreign growth, soon terminate his miserable existence.

But what matters all this? Behold the glorious result!— The abominations of Paganism have given way to the pure rites of the Christian worship,—the ignorant savage has been supplanted by the refined European! Look at Honolulu, the metropolis of the Sandwich Islands!—A community of disinterested merchants, and devoted self-exiled heralds of the Cross, located on the very spot that twenty years ago was defiled by the presence of idolatry. What a subject for an eloquent Bible-meeting orator! Nor has such an opportunity for a display of missionary rhetoric been allowed to pass by unimproved!—But when these philanthropists send us such glowing accounts of one half of their labours, why does their modesty restrain them from publishing the other half of the good they have wrought?— Not until I visited Honolulu was I aware of the fact that the small remnant of the natives had been civilized into draught horses, and evangelized into beasts of burden. But so it is. They have been literally broken into the traces, and are harnessed to the vehicles of their spiritual instructors like so many dumb brutes!

Among a multitude of similar exhibitions that I saw, I shall never forget a robust, red-faced, and very lady-like personage, a missionary's spouse, who day after day for months together took her regular airings in a little go-cart drawn by two of the islanders, one an old grey-headed man, and the other a rogueish stripling, both being, with the exception of the fig-leaf, as naked as when they were born. Over a level piece of ground this pair of *draught* bipeds would go with a shambling, unsightly trot, the youngster hanging back all the tme like a knowing horse, while the old hack plodded on and did all the work.

Rattling along through the streets of the town in this stylish equipage, the lady looks about her as magnificently as any queen driven in state to her coronation. A sudden elevation, and a sandy road, however, soon disturb her serenity. The small wheels become imbedded in the loose soil,--the old stager stands tugging and sweating, while the young one frisks about and does nothing; not an inch does the chariot budge. Will the tender-hearted lady, who has left friends and home for the good of the souls of the poor heathen, will she think a little about their bodies and get out, and ease the wretched old man until the ascent is mounted? Not she; she could not dream of it. To be sure, she used to think nothing of driving the cows to pasture on the old farm in New England; but times have changed since then. So she retains her seat and bawls out, "Hookee! hookee!" (pull, pull.) The old gentleman, frightened at the sound, labours away harder than ever; and the younger one makes a great show of straining himself, but takes care to keep one eye on his mistress, in order to know when to dodge out of harm's way. At last the good lady loses all patience; "Hookee! hookee!" and rap goes the heavy handle of her huge fan over the naked skull of the old savage; while the young one shies to one side and keeps beyond its range. "Hookee! hookee!" again she cries—"Hookee tata kannaka!" (pull strong, men,)—but all in vain, and she is obliged in the end to dismount and, sad necessity! actually to walk to the top of the hill.

At the town where this paragon of humility resides, is a spacious and elegant American chapel, where divine service is regularly performed. Twice every Sabbath towards the close of the exercises may be seen a score or two of little waggons ranged along the railing in front of the edifice, with two squalid native footmen in the livery of nakedness standing by each, and waiting for the dismission of the congregation to draw their superiors home.

Lest the slightest misconception should arise from anything thrown out in this chapter, or indeed in any other part of the volume, let me here observe, that against the cause of missions in the abstract no Christian can possibly be opposed: it is in truth a just and holy cause. But if the great end proposed by it be spiritual, the agency employed to accomplish that end is purely earthly; and, although the object in view be the achievement of much good, that agency may nevertheless be productive of evil. In short, missionary undertaking, however it may be blessed of Heaven, is in itself but human; and subject, like everything else, to errors and abuses. And have not errors and abuses crept into the most sacred places, and may there not be unworthy or incapable missionaries abroad, as well as ecclesiastics of a similar character at home? May not the unworthiness or incapacity of those who assume apostolic functions upon the remote islands of the sea more easily escape detection by the world at large than if it were displayed in the heart of a city? An unwarranted confidence in the sanctity of its apostles—a proneness to regard them as incapable of guile—and an impatience of the least suspicion as to their rectitude as men or Christians, have ever been prevailing faults in the Church. Nor is this to be wondered at: for subject as Christianty is to the assaults of unprincipled foes, we are naturally disposed to regard everything like an exposure of ecclesiastical misconduct as the offspring of malevolence or irreligious feeling. Not even this last consideration, however, shall deter me from the honest expression of my sentiments.

There is something decidedly wrong in the practical operations of the Sandwich Island Missions. Those who from pure religious motives contribute to the support of this enterprise, should take care to ascertain that their donations, flowing through many devious channels, at last effect their legitimate object, the conversion of the Hawaiians. I urge this not because I doubt the moral probity of those who disburse these funds, but because I know that they are not rightly applied. To read pathetic accounts of missionary hardships, and glowing descriptions of conversions, and baptisms taking place beneath palm-trees, is one thing; and to go to the Sandwich Islands and see the missionaries dwelling in picturesque and prettily-furnished coral-rock villas, whilst the miserable natives are committing all sorts of immoralities around them, is quite another.

In justice to the missionaries, however, I will willingly admit, that whatever evils may have resulted from their collective mismanagement of the business of the mission, and from the want of vital piety evinced by some of their number, still the present deplorable condition of the Sandwich Islands is by no means wholly chargeable against them. The demoralising influence of a dissolute foreign population, and the frequent visits of all descriptions of vessels, have tended not a little to increase the evils alluded to. In a word, here, as in every case where Civilization has in any way been introduced among those whom we call savages, she has scattered her vices, and withheld her blessings.

As wise a man as Shakespeare has said, that the bearer of evil tidings hath but a losing office; and so I suppose will it prove with me, in communicating to the trusting friends of the Hawaiian Mission what has been disclosed in various portions of this narrative. I am persuaded, however, that as these disclosures will by their very nature attract attention, so they will lead to something which will not be without ultimate benefit to the cause of Christianity in the Sandwich Islands.

I have but one thing more to add in connection with this

subject—those things which I have stated as facts will remain facts, in spite of whatever the bigoted or incredulous may say or write against them. My reflections, however, on those facts may not be free from error. If such be the case, I claim no further indulgence than should be conceded to every man whose object is to do good.

CHAPTER XXVII

The social Condition and general Character of the Typees.

I HAVE already mentioned that the influence exerted over the people of the valley by their chiefs was mild in the extreme: and as to any general rule or standard of conduct by which the commonalty were governed in their intercourse with each other, so far as my observation extended, I should be almost tempted to say that none existed on the island, except, indeed, the mysterious "Taboo" be considered as such. During the time I lived among the Typees, no one was ever put upon his trial for any offence against the public. To all appearances there were no courts of law or equity. There was no municipal police for the purpose of apprehending vagrants and disorderly characters. In short, there were no legal provisions whatever for the well-being and conservation of society, the enlightened end of civilized legislation. And yet everything went on in the valley with a harmony and smoothness unparalleled, I will venture to assert, in the most select, refined, and pious associations of mortals in Christendom. How are we to explain this enigma? These islanders were heathens! savages! ay, cannibals! and how came they, without the aid of established law, to exhibit, in so eminent a degree, that social order which is the greatest blessing and highest pride of the social state?

It may reasonably be inquired, how were these people governed? how were their passions controlled in their everyday transactions? It must have been by an inherent principle of honesty and charity towards each other. They seemed to be governed by that sort of tacit common-sense law which, say what they will of the inborn lawlessness of the human race, has its precepts graven on every breast. The grand principles of virtue and honour, however they may be distorted by arbitrary codes, are the same all the world over: and where these principles are concerned, the right or wrong of any action appears the same to the uncultivated as to the enlightened mind. It is to this indwelling, this universally diffused perception of what is *just* and *noble,* that the integrity of the Marquesans in their intercourse with each other is to be attributed. In the darkest nights they slept securely, with all their worldly wealth around them, in houses the doors of which were never fastened. The disquieting ideas of theft or assassination never disturbed them. Each islander reposed beneath his own palmetto thatching, or sat under his own bread-fruit-tree, with none to molest or alarm him. There was not a padlock in the valley, nor anything that answered the purpose of one: still there was no community of goods. This long spear, so elegantly carved and highly polished, belongs to Wormoonoo: it is far handsomer than the one which old Marheyo so greatly prizes; it is the most valuable article belonging to its owner. And yet I have seen it leaning against a cocoa-nut tree in the grove, and there it was found when sought for. Here is a sperm-whale tooth, graven all over with cunning devices: it is the property of Karluna: it is the most precious of the damsel's ornaments. In her estimation its price is far above rubies—and yet there hangs the dental jewel by its cord of braided bark, in the girl's house, which is far back in the valley; the door is left open, and all the inmates have gone off to bathe in the stream.

So much for the respect in which "personal property" is held in Typee; how secure an investment of "real property" may be, I cannot take upon me to say. Whether the land of the valley was the joint property of its inhabitants, or whether it was parcelled out among a certain number of landed proprietors who allowed everybody to "squat" and "poach" as much as he or she pleased, I never could ascertain. At any rate, musty parchments and title deeds there were none on the island; and I am half inclined to believe that its inhabitants hold their broad valleys in fee simple from Nature herself; to have and to hold, so long as grass grows and water runs; or until their French visitors, by a summary mode of conveyancing, shall appropriate them to their own benefit and behoof.

Yesterday I saw Kory-Kory hie him away, armed with a long pole, with which, standing on the ground, he knocked down the fruit from the topmost boughs of the trees, and brought them home in his basket of cocoa-nut leaves. To-day I see an islander, whom I know to reside in a distant part of the valley, doing the self-same thing. On the sloping bank of the stream are a number of banana-trees. I have often seen a score or two of young people making a merry foray on the great golden clusters, and bearing them off, one after another, to different parts of the vale, shouting and tramping as they went. No churlish old curmudgeon could have been the owner of that grove of bread-fruit trees, or of these gloriously yellow bunches of bananas.

From what I have said it will be perceived that there is a vast difference between "personal property" and "real estate" in the valley of Typee. Some individuals, of course, are more wealthy than others. For example: the ridge-pole of Marheyo's house bends under the weight of many a huge package of tappa; his long couch is laid with mats placed one upon the other seven deep. Outside, Tinor has ranged along in her bamboo cupboard—or whatever the place may be called—a goodly array of calabashes and wooden trenchers. Now, the house just beyond the grove, and next to Marheyo's, occupied by Ruaruga, is not quite so well furnished. There are only three moderate-sized packages swinging overhead: there are only two layers of mats beneath, and the calabashes and trenchers are not so numerous, nor so tastefully stained and carved. But then, Ruaruga has a house—not so pretty a one, to be sure—but just as commodious as Marheyo's; and, I suppose, if he wished to vie with his neighbour's establishment, he could do so with very little trouble. These, in short, constituted the chief differences perceivable in the relative wealth of the people in Typee.

Civilization does not engross all the virtues of humanity: she has not even her full share of them. They flourish in greater abundance and attain greater strength among many barbarous people. The hospitality of the wild Arab, the courage of the North American Indian, and the faithful friendships of some of the Polynesian nations, far surpass any thing of a similar kind among the polished communities of Europe. If truth and justice, and the better principles of our nature, cannot exist unless enforced by the statute-book, how are we to account for the social condition of the Typees? So pure and upright were they in all the relations of life, that entering their valley, as I did, under the most erroneous impressions of their character, I was soon led to exclaim in amazement: "Are these the ferocious savages, the blood-thirsty cannibals of whom I have heard such frightful tales! They deal more kindly with each other, and are more humane, than many who study essays on virtue and benevolence, and who repeat every night that beautiful prayer breathed first by the lips of the divine and gentle Jesus." I will frankly declare, that after passing a few weeks in this valley of the Marquesas, I formed a higher estimate of human nature than I had ever before entertained. But alas! since then I have been one of the crew of a man-of-war, and the pent-up wickedness of five hundred men has nearly overturned all my previous theories.

There was one admirable trait in the general character of the Typees which, more than any thing else, secured my admiration: it was the unanimity of feeling they displayed on every occasion. With them there hardly appeared to be any difference of opinion upon any subject whatever. They all thought and acted alike. I do not conceive that they could support a debating society for a single night: there would be nothing to dispute about; and were they to call a convention to take into consideration the state of the tribe, its session would be a remarkably short one. They showed this spirit of unanimity in every action of life: every thing was done in concert and good fellowship. I will give an instance of this fraternal feeling.

One day, in returning with Kory-Kory from my accustomed visit to the Ti, we passed by a little opening in the grove; on one side of which, my attendant informed me, was that afternoon to be built a dwelling of bamboo. At least a hundred of the natives were bringing materials to the ground, some carrying in their hands one or two of the canes which were to form the sides, others slender rods of the habiscus, strung with palmetto leaves, for the roof. Every one contributed something to the work; and by the united, but easy, and even indolent, labours of all, the entire work was completed before sunset. The islanders, while employed in erecting this tenement, reminded me of a colony of beavers at work. To be sure, they were hardly as silent and demure as those wonderful creatures, nor were they by any means as diligent. To tell the truth, they were somewhat inclined to be lazy, but a perfect tumult of hilarity prevailed; and they worked together so unitedly, and seemed actuated by such an instinct of friendliness, that it was truly beautiful to behold.

Not a single female took part in this employment: and if the degree of consideration in which the ever-adorable sex is held by the men be—as the philosophers affirm—a just criterion of the degree of refinement among a people, then I may truly pronounce the Typees to be as polished a community as ever the sun shone upon. The religious restrictions of the taboo alone excepted, the women of the valley were allowed every possible indulgence. Nowhere are the ladies more assiduously courted; nowhere are they better appreciated as the contributors to our highest enjoyments; and nowhere are they more sensible of their power. Far different from their condition among many rude nations, where the women are made to perform all the work while their ungallant lords and masters lie buried in sloth, the gentle sex in the valley of Typee were exempt from toil, if toil it might be called that, even in that tropical climate, never distilled one drop of perspiration. Their light household occupations, together with the manufacture of tappa, the platting of mats, and the polishing of drinking-vessels, were the only employments pertaining to the women. And even these resembled those pleasant avocations which fill up the elegant morning leisure of our fashionable ladies at home. But in these occupations, slight and agreeable though they were, the giddy young girls very seldom engaged. Indeed these wilful, care-killing damsels were averse to all useful employment. Like so many spoiled beauties, they ranged through the groves—bathed in the stream—danced—flirted—played all manner of mischievous pranks, and passed their days in one merry round of thoughtless happiness.

During my whole stay on the island I never witnessed a single quarrel, nor any thing that in the slightest degree approached even to a dispute. The natives appeared to form one household, whose members were bound together by the ties of strong affection. The love of kindred I did not so much perceive, for it seemed blended in the general love; and where all were treated as brothers and sisters, it was hard to tell who were actually related to each other by blood.

Let it not be supposed that I have overdrawn this picture. I have not done so. Nor let it be urged, that the hostility of this tribe to foreigners, and the hereditary feuds they carry on against their fellow-islanders beyond the mountains, are facts which contradict me. Not so: these apparent discrepancies are easily reconciled. By many a legendary tale of violence and wrong, as well as by events which have passed before their eyes, these people have been taught to look upon white men with abhorrence. The cruel invasion of their country by Porter has alone furnished them with ample provocation; and I can sympathize in the spirit which prompts the Typee warrior to guard all the passes to his valley with the point of his levelled spear, and, standing upon the beach, with his back turned upon his green home, to hold at bay the intruding European.

As to the origin of the enmity of this particular clan towards the neighbouring tribes, I cannot so confidently speak. I will not say that their foes are the aggressors, nor will I endeavour to palliate their conduct. But surely, if our evil passions must find vent, it is far better to expend them on strangers and aliens, than in the bosom of the community in which we dwell. In many polished countries civil contentions, as well as domestic enmities, are prevalent, at the same time that the most atrocious foreign wars are waged. How much less guilty, then, are our islanders, who of these three sins are only chargeable with one, and that the least criminal!

The reader will ere long have reason to suspect that the Typees are not free from the guilt of cannibalism; and he will then, perhaps, charge me with admiring a people against whom so odious a crime is chargeable. But this only enormity in their character is not half so horrible as it is usually described. According to the popular fictions, the crews of vessels, shipwrecked on some barbarous coast, are eaten alive like so many dainty joints by the uncivil inhabitants; and unfortunate voyagers are lured into smiling and treacherous bays; knocked in the head with outlandish war-clubs; and served up without any preliminary dressing. In truth, so horrific and improbable are these accounts, that many sensible and well-informed people will not believe that any cannibals exist; and place every book of voyages which purports to give any account of them, on the same shelf with Blue Beard and Jack the Giant-Killer; while others, implicitly crediting the most extravagant fictions, firmly believe that there are people in the world with tastes so depraved that they would infinitely prefer a single mouthful of material humanity to a good dinner of roast beef and plum pudding. But here, Truth, who loves to be centrally located, is again found between the two extremes; for cannibalism to a certain moderate extent is practised among several of the primitive tribes in the Pacific, but it is upon the bodies of slain enemies alone; and horrible and fearful as the custom is, immeasurably as it is to be abhorred and condemned, still I assert that those who indulge in it are in other respects humane and virtuous.

CHAPTER XXVIII

Fishing Parties—Mode of distributing the Fish—Midnight Banquet—Timekeeping Tapers—Unceremonious style of eating the Fish.

THERE was no instance in which the social and kindly dispositions of the Typees were more forcibly evinced than in the manner they conducted their great fishing parties. Four times during my stay in the valley the young men assembled near the full of the moon, and went together on these excursions. As they were generally absent about forty-eight hours, I was led to believe that they went out towards the open sea, some distance from the bay. The Polynesians seldom use a hook and line, almost always employing large well-made nets, most ingeniously fabricated from the twisted fibres of a certain bark. I examined several of them which had been spread to dry upon the beach at Nuku-heva. They resemble very much our own seines, and I should think were very nearly as durable.

All the South Sea Islanders are passionately fond of fish; but none of them can be more so than the inhabitants of Typee. I could not comprehend, therefore, why they so seldom sought it in their waters, for it was only at stated times that the fishing parties were formed, and these occasions were always looked forward to with no small degree of interest.

During their absence the whole population of the place were in a ferment, and nothing was talked of but "pehee, pehee" (fish, fish). Towards the time when they were expected to return the vocal telegraph was put into operation—the inhabitants, who were scattered throughout the length of the valley, leaped upon rocks and into trees, shouting with delight at the thoughts of the anticipated treat. As soon as the approach of the party was announced, there was a general rush of the men towards the beach; some of them remaining, however, about the Ti, in order to get matters in readiness for the reception of the fish, which were brought to the Taboo groves in immense packages of leaves, each one of them being suspended from a pole carried on the shoulders of two men.

I was present at the Ti on one of these occasions, and

the sight was most interesting. After all the packages had arrived, they were laid in a row under the verandah of the building and opened. The fish were all quite small, generally about the size of a herring, and of every variety of colour. About one-eighth of the whole being reserved for the use of the Ti itself, the remainder was divided into numerous smaller packages, which were immediately dispatched in every direction to the remotest parts of the valley. Arrived at their destination, these were in turn portioned out, and equally distributed among the various houses of each particular district. The fish were under a strict Taboo, until the distribution was completed, which seemed to be effected in the most impartial manner. By the operation of this system every man, woman, and child in the vale were at one and the same time partaking of this favourite article of food.

Once I remember the party arrived at midnight; but the unseasonableness of the hour did not repress the impatience of the islanders. The carriers dispatched from the Ti were to be seen hurrying in all directions through the deep groves; each individual preceded by a boy bearing a flaming torch of dried cocoa-nut boughs, which from time to time was replenished from the materials scattered along the path. The wild glare of these enormous flambeaux, lighting up with a startling brilliancy the innermost recesses of the vale, and seen moving rapidly along beneath the canopy of leaves, the savage shout of the excited messengers sounding the news of their approach, which was answered on all sides, and the strange appearance of their naked bodies, seen against the gloomy background, produced altogether an effect upon my mind that I shall long remember.

It was on this same occasion that Kory-Kory awakened me at the dead hour of night, and in a sort of transport communicated the intelligence contained in the words "pehee perni" (fish come). As I happened to have been in a remarkably sound and refreshing slumber, I could not imagine why the information had not been deferred until morning; indeed, I felt very much inclined to fly into a passion and box my valet's ears; but on second thoughts I got quietly up, and on going outside the house was not a little interested by the moving illumination which I beheld.

When old Marheyo received his share of the spoils, immediate preparations were made for a midnight banquet; calabashes of poee-poee were filled to the brim; green bread-fruit were roasted; and a huge cake of "amar" was cut up with a sliver of bamboo and laid out on an immense banana-leaf.

At this supper we were lighted by several of the native tapers, held in the hands of young girls. These tapers are most ingeniously made. There is a nut abounding in the valley, called by the Typees "armor," closely resembling our common horse-chestnut. The shell is broken, and the contents extracted whole. Any number of these are strung at pleasure upon the long elastic fibre that traverses the branches of the cocoa-nut tree. Some of these tapers are eight and ten feet in length; but being perfectly flexible, one end is held in a coil, while the other is lighted. The nut burns with a fitful bluish flame, and the oil that it contains is exhausted in about ten minutes. As one burns down, the next becomes ignited, and the ashes of the former are knocked into a cocoa-nut shell kept for the purpose. This primitive candle requires continual attention, and must be constantly held in the hand. The person so employed marks the lapse of time by the number of nuts consumed, which is easily learned by counting the bits of tappa distributed at regular intervals along the string.

I grieve to state so distressing a fact, but the inhabitants of Typee were in the habit of devouring fish much in the same way that a civilized being would eat a radish, and without any more previous preparation. They eat it raw; scales, bones, gills, and all the inside. The fish is held by the tail, and the head being introduced into the mouth, the animal disappears with a rapidity that would at first nearly lead one to imagine it had been launched bodily down the throat.

Raw fish! Shall I ever forget my sensations when I first saw my island beauty devour one? Oh, heavens! Fayaway, how could you ever have contracted so vile a habit? However, after the first shock had subsided, the custom grew less odious in my eyes, and I soon accustomed myself to the sight. Let no one imagine, however, that the lovely Fayaway was in the habit of swallowing great vulgar-looking fishes: oh, no; with her beautiful small hand she would clasp a delicate, little, golden-hued love of a fish, and eat it as elegantly and as innocently as though it were a Naples biscuit. But, alas! it was after all a raw fish; and all I can say is, that Fayaway ate it in a more ladylike manner than any other girl of the valley.

When at Rome do as the Romans do, I held to be so good a proverb, that being in Typee I made a point of doing as the Typees did. Thus I ate poee-poee as they did; I walked about in a garb striking for its simplicity; and I reposed on a community of couches; besides doing many other things in conformity with their peculiar habits; but the farthest I ever went in the way of conformity, was on several occasions to regale myself with raw fish. These being remarkably tender, and quite small, the undertaking was not so disagreeable in the main, and after a few trials I positively began to relish them: however, I subjected them to a slight operation with my knife previously to making my repast.

CHAPTER XXIX

Natural History of the Valley—Golden Lizards—Tameness of the Birds—Mosquitos—Flies—Dogs—A solitary Cat—The Climate—The Cocoa-nut Tree—Singular modes of climbing it—An agile young Chief—Fearlessness of the Children—Too-Too and the Cocoa-nut Tree—The Birds of the Valley.

I THINK I must enlighten the reader a little about the natural history of the valley.

Whence, in the name of Count Buffon and Baron Cuvier, came those dogs that I saw in Typee? Dogs!—Big hairless rats rather; all with smooth, shining, speckled hides —fat sides, and very disagreeable faces. Whence could they have come? That they were not the indigenous production of the region, I am firmly convinced. Indeed they seemed aware of their being interlopers, looking fairly ashamed, and always trying to hide themselves in some dark corner. It was plain enough they did not feel at home in the vale— that they wished themselves well out of it, and back to the ugly country from which they must have come.

Scurvy curs! they were my abhorrence; I should have liked nothing better than to have been the death of every one of them. In fact, on one occasion, I intimated the propriety of a canine crusade to Mehevi; but the benevolent king would not consent to it. He heard me very patiently; but when I had finished, shook his head, and told me, in confidence, that they were "taboo."

As for the animal that made the fortune of the ex-lord-mayor Whittington: I shall never forget the day that I was lying in the house about noon, everybody else being fast asleep; and happening to raise my eyes, met those of a big black spectral cat, which sat erect in the doorway, looking at me with its frightful goggling green orbs, like one of those monstrous imps that torment some of Teniers' saints! I am one of those unfortunate persons to whom the sight of these animals is at any time an insufferable annoyance.

Thus constitutionally averse to cats in general, the unexpected apparition of this one in particular utterly confounded me. When I had a little recovered from the fascination of its glance, I started up; the cat fled, and emboldened by this, I rushed out of the house in pursuit; but it had disappeared. It was the only time I ever saw one in the valley, and how it got there I cannot imagine. It is just possible that it might have escaped from one of the ships at Nukuheva. It was in vain to seek information on the subject from the natives; since none of them had seen the animal, the appearance of which remains a mystery to me to this day.

Among the few animals which are to be met with in Typee, there were none which I looked upon with more interest than a beautiful golden-hued species of lizard. It measured perhaps five inches from head to tail, and was most gracefully proportioned. Numbers of these creatures were to be seen basking in the sunshine upon the thatching of the houses, and multitudes at all hours of the day showed their glittering sides as they ran frolicking between the spears of grass or raced in troops up and down the tall shafts of the cocoa-nut trees. But the remarkable beauty of these little animals and their lively ways were not their only claims upon my admiration. They were perfectly tame and insensible to fear. Frequently, after seating myself upon the ground in some shady place during the heat of the day, I would be completely overrun with them. If I brushed one off my arm, it would leap perhaps into my hair: when I tried to frighten it away by gently pinching its leg, it would turn for protection to the very hand that attacked it.

The birds are also remarkably tame. If you happened to see one perched upon a branch within reach of your arm, and advanced towards it, it did not fly away immediately, but waited quietly looking at you, until you could almost touch it, and then took wing slowly, less alarmed at your presence, it would seem, than desirous of removing itself from your path. Had salt been less scarce in the valley than it was, this was the very place to have gone birding with it.

I remember that once, on an uninhabited island of the Gallipagos, a bird alighted on my outstretched arm, while its mate chirped from an adjoining tree. Its tameness, far from shocking me, as a similar occurrence did Selkirk, imparted to me the most exquisite tnrill of delight I ever experienced; and with somewhat of the same pleasure did I afterwards behold the birds and lizards of the valley show their confidence in the kindliness of man.

Among the numerous afflictions which the Europeans have entailed upon some of the natives of the South Seas, is the accidental introduction among them of that enemy of all repose and ruffler of even tempers—the Mosquito. At the Sandwich Islands and at two or three of the Society group there are now thriving colonies of these insects, who promise ere long to supplant altogether the aboriginal sandflies. They sting, buzz, and torment, from one end of the year to the other, and by incessantly exasperating the natives materially obstruct the benevolent labours of the missionaries.

From this grievous visitation, however, the Typees are as yet wholly exempt; but its place is unfortunately in some degree supplied by the occasional presence of a minute species of fly, which, without stinging, is nevertheless productive of no little annoyance. The tameness of the birds and lizards is as nothing when compared to the fearless confidence of this insect. He will perch upon one of your eye-lashes, and go to roost there, if you do not disturb him, or force his way through your hair, or along the cavity of the nostril, till you almost fancy he is resolved to explore the very brain itself. On one occasion I was so inconsiderate as to yawn while a number of them were hovering around me. I never repeated the act. Some half-dozen darted into the open apartment, and began walking about its ceiling; the sensation was dreadful. I involuntarily closed my mouth, and the poor creatures being enveloped in inner darkness, must in their consternation have stumbled over my palate, and been precipitated into the gulf beneath. At any rate, though I afterwards charitably held my mouth open for at least five minutes, with a view of affording egress to the stragglers, none of them ever availed themselves of the opportunity.

There are no wild animals of any kind on the island, unless it be decided that the natives themselves are such. The mountains and the interior present to the eye nothing but silent solitudes, unbroken by the roar of beasts of prey, and enlivened by few tokens even of minute animated existence. There are no venomous reptiles, and no snakes of any description to be found in any of the valleys.

In a company of Marquesan natives the weather affords no topic of conversation. It can hardly be said to have any vicissitudes. The rainy season, it is true, brings frequent showers, but they are intermitting and refreshing. When an islander bound on some expedition rises from his couch in the morning, he is never solicitous to peep out and see how the sky looks, or ascertain from what quarter the wind blows. He is always sure of a "fine day," and the promise of a few genial showers he hails with pleasure. There is never any of that "remarkable weather" on the island which from time immemorial has been experienced in America, and still continues to call forth the wondering conversational exclamations of its elderly citizens. Nor do there even occur any of those eccentric meteorological changes which elsewhere surprise us. In the valley of Typee ice-creams would never be rendered less acceptable by sudden frosts, nor would picnic parties be deferred on account of inauspicious snow-storms: for there day follows day in one unvarying round of summer and sunshine, and the whole year is one long tropical month of June just melting into July.

It is this genial climate which causes the cocoa-nuts to flourish as they do. This invaluable fruit, brought to perfection by the rich soil of the Marquesas, and borne aloft on a stately column more than a hundred feet from the ground, would seem at first almost inaccessible to the simple natives. Indeed the slender, smooth, and soaring shaft, without a single limb or protuberance of any kind to assist one in mounting it, presents an obstacle only to be overcome by the surprising agility and ingenuity of the islanders. It might be supposed that their indolence would lead them patiently to await the period when the ripened nuts, slowly parting from their stems, fall one by one to the ground. This certainly would be the case, were it not that the young fruit, encased in a soft green husk, with the incipient meat adhering in a jelly-like pellicle to its sides, and containing a bumper of the most delicious nectar, is what they chiefly prize. They have at least twenty different terms to express as many progressive stages in the growth of the nut. Many of them reject the fruit altogether except at a particular period of its growth, which, incredible as it may appear, they seemed to me to be able to ascertain within an hour or two. Others are still more capricious in their tastes; and after gathering together a heap of the nuts of all ages, and ingeniously tapping them, will sip first from one and then from another, as fastidiously as some delicate wine-bibber experimenting glass in hand among his dusty demijohns of different vintages.

Some of the young men, with more flexible frames than their comrades, and perhaps with more courageous souls, had a way of walking up the trunk of the cocoa-nut trees which to me seemed little less than miraculous; and when looking at them in the act, I experienced that curious perplexity a child feels when he beholds a fly moving feet uppermost along a ceiling.

I will endeavour to describe the way in which Narnee, a noble young chief, sometimes performed this feat for my peculiar gratification; but his preliminary performances must also be recorded. Upon my signifying my desire that he should pluck me the young fruit of some particular tree, the handsome savage, throwing himself into a sudden attitude of surprise, feigns astonishment at the apparent absurdity of the request. Maintaining this position for a moment, the strange emotions depicted on his countenance soften down into one of humorous resignation to my will, and then looking wistfully up to the tufted top of the tree, he stands on tip-toe, straining his neck and elevating his arm, as though endeavouring to reach the fruit from the ground where he stands. As if defeated in this childish attempt, he now sinks to the earth despondingly, beating his breast in well-acted despair; and then, starting to his feet all at once, and throwing back his head, raises both hands, like a school-boy about to catch a falling ball. After continuing this for a moment or two, as if in expectation that the fruit was going to be tossed down to him by some good spirit in the tree-top, he turns wildly round in another fit of despair, and scampers off to the distance of thirty or forty yards. Here he remains awhile, eyeing the tree, the very picture of misery; but the next moment, receiving, as it were, a flash of inspiration, he rushes again towards it, and clasping both arms about the trunk, with one elevated a little above the other, he presses the soles of his feet close together against the tree, extending his legs from it until they are nearly horizontal, and his body becomes doubled into an arch; then, hand over hand and foot after foot, he rises from the earth with steady rapidity, and almost before you are aware of it, has gained the cradled and embowered nest of nuts, and with boisterous glee flings the fruit to the ground.

This mode of walking the tree is only practicable where the trunk declines considerably from the perpendicular. This, however, is almost always the case; some of the perfectly straight shafts of the trees leaning at an angle of thirty degrees.

The less active among the men, and many of the children of the valley, have another method of climbing. They take a broad and stout piece of bark, and secure either end of it to their ankles; so that when the feet thus confined are extended apart, a space of little more than twelve inches is left between them. This contrivance greatly facilitates the act of climbing. The band pressed against the tree, and closely embracing it, yields a pretty firm support; while with the arms clasped about the trunk, and at regular intervals sustaining the body, the feet are drawn up nearly a yard at a time, and a corresponding elevation of the hands immediately succeeds. In this way I have seen little children, scarcely five years of age, fearlessly climbing the slender pole of a young cocoa-nut tree, and while hanging perhaps fifty feet from the ground, receive the plaudits of their parents beneath, who clapped their hands, and encouraged them to mount still higher.

What, thought I, on first witnessing one of these exhibitions, would the nervous mothers of America and England say to a similar display of hardihood in any of their children? The Lacedemonian nations might have approved of it, but most modern dames would have gone into hysterics at the sight.

At the top of the cocoa-nut tree the numerous branches, radiating on all sides from a common centre, form a sort of green and waving basket, between the leaflets of which you just discern the nuts thickly clustering together, and on the loftier trees looking no bigger from the ground than bunches of grapes. I remember one adventurous little fellow—Too-Too was the rascal's name—who had built himself a sort of aerial baby-house in the picturesque tuft of a tree adjoining Marheyo's habitation. He used to spend hours there,—rustling among the branches, and shouting with delight every time the strong gusts of wind rushing down from the mountain's side swayed to and fro the tall and flexible column on which he was perched. Whenever I heard Too-Too's musical voice, sounding strangely to the ear from so great a height, and beheld him peeping down upon me from out his leafy covert, he always recalled to my mind Dibdin's lines—

> "There's a sweet little cherub that sits up aloft,
> To look out for the life of poor Jack."

Birds—bright and beautiful birds—fly over the valley of Typee. You see them perched aloft among the immovable boughs of the majestic bread-fruit trees, or gently swaying on the elastic branches of the Omoo; skimming over the palmetto thatching of the bamboo huts; passing like spirits on the wing through the shadows of the grove, and sometimes descending into the bosom of the valley in gleaming flights from the mountains. Their plumage is purple and azure, crimson and white, black and gold; with bills of every tint:—bright bloody-red, jet black, and ivory white; and their eyes are bright and sparkling; they go sailing through the air in starry throngs; but alas! the spell of dumbness is upon them all—there is not a single warbler in the valley!

I know not why it was, but the sight of these birds, generally the ministers of gladness, always oppressed me with melancholy. As in their dumb beauty they hovered by me whilst I was walking, or looked down upon me with steady curious eyes from out the foliage, I was almost inclined to fancy that they knew they were gazing upon a stranger, and that they commiserated his fate.

CHAPTER XXX

A Professor of the Fine Arts—His Persecutions—Something about Tattooing and Tabooing—Two Anecdotes in illustration of the latter—A few thoughts on the Typee Dialect.

In ONE of my strolls with Kory-Kory, in passing along the border of a thick growth of bushes, my attention was arrested by a singular noise. On entering the thicket I witnessed for the first time the operation of tattooing as performed by these islanders.

I beheld a man extended flat upon his back on the ground, and, despite the forced composure of his countenance, it was evident that he was suffering agony. His tormentor bent over him, working away for all the world like a stone-cutter with mallet and chisel. In one hand he held a short slender stick, pointed with a shark's tooth, on the upright end of which he tapped with a small hammer-like piece of wood, thus puncturing the skin, and charging it with the colouring matter in which the instrument was dipped. A cocoa-nut shell containing this fluid was placed upon the ground. It is prepared by mixing with a vegetable juice the ashes of the "armor," or candle-nut, always preserved for the purpose. Beside the savage, and spread out upon a piece of soiled tappa, were a great number of curious black-looking little implements of bone and wood, used in the various divisions of his art. A few terminated in a single fine point, and, like very delicate pencils, were employed in giving the finishing touches, or in operating upon the more sensitive portions of the body, as was the case in the present instance. Others presented several points distributed in a line, somewhat resembling the teeth of a saw.

These were employed in the coarser parts of the work, and particularly in pricking in straight marks. Some presented their points disposed in small figures, and being placed upon the body, were, by a single blow of the hammer, made to leave their indelible impression. I observed a few the handles of which were mysteriously curved, as if intended to be introduced into the orifice of the ear, with a view perhaps of beating the tattoo upon the tympanum. Altogether, the sight of these strange instruments recalled to mind that display of cruel-looking mother-of-pearl-handled things which one sees in their velvet-lined cases at the elbow of a dentist.

The artist was not at this time engaged on an original sketch, his subject being a venerable savage, whose tattooing had become somewhat faded with age and needed a few repairs, and accordingly he was merely employed in touching up the works of some of the old masters of the Typee school, as delineated upon the human canvas before him. The parts operated upon were the eyelids, where a longitudinal streak, like the one which adorned Kory-Kory, crossed the countenance of the victim.

In spite of all the efforts of the poor old man, sundry twitchings and screwings of the muscles of the face denoted the exquisite sensibility of these shutters to the windows of his soul, which he was now having repainted. But the artist, with a heart as callous as that of an army surgeon, continued his performance, enlivening his labours with a wild chant, tapping away the while as merrily as a woodpecker.

So deeply engaged was he in his work, that he had not observed our approach, until, after having enjoyed an unmolested view of the operation, I chose to attract his attention. As soon as he perceived me, supposing that I sought him in his professional capacity, he seized hold of me in a paroxysm of delight, and was all eagerness to begin the work. When, however, I gave him to understand that he had altogether mistaken my views, nothing could exceed his grief and disappointment. But recovering from this, he seemed determined not to credit my assertion, and grasping his implements, he flourished them about in fearful vicinity to my face, going through an imaginary performance of his art, and every moment bursting into some admiring exclamation at the beauty of his designs.

Horrified at the bare thought of being rendered hideous for life if the wretch were to execute his purpose upon me, I struggled to get away from him, while Kory-Kory, turning traitor, stood by, and besought me to comply with the outrageous request. On my reiterated refusals the excited artist got half beside himself, and was overwhelmed with sorrow at losing so noble an opportunity of distinguishing himself in his profession.

The idea of engrafting his tattooing upon my white skin filled him with all a painter's enthusiasm: again and again he gazed into my countenance, and every fresh glimpse seemed to add to the vehemence of his ambition. Not knowing to what extremities he might proceed, and shuddering at the ruin he might inflict upon my figure-head, I now endeavoured to draw off his attention from it, and holding out my arm in a fit of desperation, signed to him to commence operations. But he rejected the compromise indignantly, and still continued his attack on my face, as though nothing short of that would satisfy him. When his fore-finger swept across my features, in laying out the borders of those parallel bands which were to encircle my countenance, the flesh fairly crawled upon my bones. At last, half wild with terror and indignation, I succeeded in breaking away from the three savages, and fled towards old Marheyo's house, pursued by the indomitable artist, who ran after me, implements in hand. Kory-Kory, however, at last interfered, and drew him off from the chace.

This incident opened my eyes to a new danger; and I now felt convinced that in some luckless hour I should be disfigured in such a manner as never more to have the *face* to return to my countrymen, even should an opportunity offer.

These apprehensions were greatly increased by the desire which King Mehevi and several of the inferior chiefs now manifested that I should be tattooed. The pleasure of the king was first signified to me some three days after my casual encounter with Karky the artist. Heavens! what imprecations I showered upon that Karky! Doubtless he had plotted a conspiracy against me and my countenance, and would never rest until his diabolical purpose was accomplished. Several times I met him in various parts of the valley, and, invariably, whenever he descried me, he came running after me with his mallet and chisel, flourishing them about my face as if he longed to begin. What an object he would have made of me!

When the king first expressed his wish to me, I made known to him my utter abhorrence of the measure, and worked myself into such a state of excitement, that he absolutely stared at me in amazement. It evidently surpassed his majesty's comprehension how any sober-minded and sensible individual could entertain the least possible objection to so beautifying an operation.

Soon afterwards he repeated his suggestion, and meeting with a like repulse, showed some symptoms of displeasure at my obduracy. On his a third time renewing his request, I plainly perceived that something must be done, or my visage was ruined for ever; I therefore screwed up my courage to the sticking point, and declared my willingness to have both arms tattooed from just above the wrist to the shoulder. His majesty was greatly pleased at the proposition, and I was congratulating myself with having thus compromised the matter, when he intimated that as a thing of course my face was first to undergo the operation. I was fairly driven to despair; nothing but the utter ruin of my "face divine," as the poets call it, would, I perceived, satisfy the inexorable Mehevi and his chiefs, or rather, that infernal Karky, for he was at the bottom of it all.

The only consolation afforded me was a choice of patterns: I was at perfect liberty to have my face spanned by three horizontal bars, after the fashion of my servingman's; or to have as many oblique stripes slanting across it; or if, like a true courtier, I chose to model my style on that of royalty, I might wear a sort of freemason badge upon my countenance in the shape of a mystic triangle. However, I would have none of these, though the king most earnestly impressed upon my mind that my choice was wholly unrestricted. At last, seeing my unconquerable repugnance, he ceased to importune me.

But not so some other of the savages. Hardly a day passed but I was subjected to their annoying requests, until at last my existence became a burden to me; the pleasures I had previously enjoyed no longer afforded me delight, and all my former desire to escape from the valley now revived with additional force.

A fact which I soon afterwards learned augmented my apprehension. The whole system of tattooing was, I found, connected with their religion; and it was evident, therefore, that they were resolved to make a convert of me.

In the decoration of the chiefs it seems to be necessary to exercise the most elaborate pencilling; while some of the inferior natives looked as if they had been daubed over indiscriminately with a house-painter's brush. I remember one fellow who prided himself hugely upon a great oblong patch, placed high upon his back, and who always reminded me of a man with a blister of Spanish flies stuck between his shoulders. Another whom I frequently met had the hollow of his eyes tattooed in two regular squares, and his visual organs being remarkable brilliant, they gleamed forth from out this setting like a couple of diamonds inserted in ebony.

Although convinced that tattooing was a religious observance, still the nature of the connection between it and the superstitious idolatry of the people was a point upon which I could never obtain any information. Like the still more important system of the "Taboo," it always appeared inexplicable to me.

There is a marked similarity, almost an identity, between the religious institutions of most of the Polynesian islands, and in all exists the mysterious "Taboo," restricted in its uses to a greater or less extent. So strange and complex in its arrangements is this remarkable system, that I have in several cases met with individuals who, after residing for years among the islands in the Pacific, and acquiring a considerable knowledge of the language, have nevertheless been altogether unable to give any satisfactory account of its operations. Situated as I was in the Typee valley, I perceived every hour the effects of this all-controlling power, without in the least comprehending it. Those effects were, indeed, wide-spread and universal, pervading the most important as well as the minutest transactions of life. The savage, in short, lives in the continual observance of its dictates, which guide and control every action of his being.

For several days after entering the valley I had been saluted at least fifty times in the twenty-four hours with the talismanic word "Taboo" shrieked in my ears, at some gross violation of its provisions, of which I had unconsciously been guilty. The day after our arrival I happened to hand some tobacco to Toby over the head of a native who sat between us. He started up, as if stung by an adder; while the whole company, manifesting an equal degree of horror, simultaneously screamed out "taboo!" I never again perpetrated a similar piece of ill-manners, which, indeed,

was forbidden by the canons of good breeding, as well as
by the mandates of the taboo. But it was not always so easy
to perceive wherein you had contravened the spirit of this
institution. I was many times called to order, if I may use
the phrase, when I could not for the life of me conjecture
what particular offence I had committed.

One day I was strolling through a secluded portion of
the valley, and hearing the musical sound of the cloth-
mallet at a little distance, I turned down a path that conducted me in a few moments to a house where there were
some half-dozen girls employed in making tappa. This was
an operation I had frequently witnessed, and had handled
the bark in all the various stages of its preparation. On the
present occasion the females were intent upon their occupation, and after looking up and talking gaily to me for a
few moments, they resumed their employment. I regarded
them for awhile in silence, and then carelessly picking up
a handful of the material that lay around, proceeded unconsciously to pick it apart. While thus engaged, I was
suddenly startled by a scream, like that of a whole board-
ing-school of young ladies just on the point of going into
hysterics. Leaping up with the idea of seeing a score of
Happar warriors about to perform anew the Sabine atroc-
ity, I found myself confronted by the company of girls,
who, having dropped their work, stood before me with
starting eyes, swelling bosoms, and fingers pointed in horror towards me.

Thinking that some venomous reptile must be concealed
in the bark which I held in my hand, I began cautiously to
separate and examine it. Whilst I did so the horrified girls
redoubled their shrieks. Their wild cries and frightened
motions actually alarmed me, and throwing down the
tappa, I was about to rush from the house, when in the
same instant their clamours ceased, and one of them seizing me by the arm, pointed to the broken fibres that had

just fallen from my grasp, and screamed in my ears the fatal word Taboo!

I subsequently found out that the fabric they were engaged in making was of a peculiar kind, destined to be worn on the heads of the females, and through every stage of its manufacture was guarded by a vigorous taboo, which interdicted the whole masculine gender from even so much as touching it.

Frequently in walking through the groves I observed bread-fruit and cocoa-nut trees, with a wreath of leaves twined in a peculiar fashion about their trunks. This was the mark of the taboo. The trees themselves, their fruit, and even the shadows they cast upon the ground, were consecrated by its presence. In the same way a pipe, which the king had bestowed upon me, was rendered sacred in the eyes of the natives, none of whom could I ever prevail upon to smoke from it. The bowl was encircled by a woven band of grass, somewhat resembling those Turks' heads occasionally worked in the handles of our whip-stalks.

A similar badge was once braided about my wrist by the royal hand of Mehevi himself, who, as soon as he had concluded the operation, pronounced me "Taboo." This occurred shortly after Toby's disappearance; and were it not that from the first moment I had entered the valley the natives had treated me with uniform kindness, I should have supposed that their conduct afterwards was to be ascribed to the fact that I had received this sacred investiture.

The capricious operations of the taboo is not its least remarkable feature: to enumerate them all would be impossible. Black hogs—infants to a certain age—women in an interesting situation—young men while the operation of tattooing their faces is going on—and certain parts of the valley during the continuance of a shower—are alike fenced about by the operation of the taboo.

I witnessed a striking instance of its effects in the bay of

Tior, my visit to which place has been alluded to in a former part of this narrative. On that occasion our worthy captain formed one of the party. He was a most insatiable sportsman. Outward bound, and off the pitch of Cape Horn, he used to sit on the taffrail, and keep the steward loading three or four old fowling-pieces, with which he would bring down albatrosses, Cape pigeons, jays, petrels, and divers other marine fowl, who followed chattering in our wake. The sailors were struck aghast at his impiety, and one and all attributed our forty days' beating about that horrid headland to his sacrilegious slaughter of these inoffensive birds.

At Tior he evinced the same disregard for the religious prejudices of the islanders, as he had previously shown for the superstitions of the sailors. Having heard that there were a considerable number of fowls in the valley—the progeny of some cocks and hens accidentally left there by an English vessel, and which, being strictly tabooed, flew about almost in a wild state—he determined to break through all restraints, and be the death of them. Accordingly, he provided himself with a most formidable looking gun, and announced his landing on the beach by shooting down a noble cock that was crowing what proved to be his own funeral dirge, on the limb of an adjoining tree. "Taboo," shrieked the affrighted savages. "Oh, hang your taboo," says the nautical sportsman; "talk taboo to the marines;" and bang went the piece again, and down came another victim. At this the natives ran scampering through the groves, horror-struck at the enormity of the act.

All that afternoon the rocky sides of the valley rang with successive reports, and the superb plumage of many a beautiful fowl was ruffled by the fatal bullet. Had it not been that the French admiral, with a large party, were then in the glen, I have no doubt that the natives, although their tribe was small and dispirited, would have inflicted summary vengeance upon the man who thus outraged their most sacred institutions; as it was, they contrived to annoy him not a little.

Thirsting with his exertions, the skipper directed his steps to a stream; but the savages, who had followed at a little distance, perceiving his object, rushed towards him and forced him away from its bank—his lips would have polluted it. Wearied at last, he sought to enter a house, that he might rest for a while on the mats; its inmates gathered tumultuously about the door and denied him admittance. He coaxed and blustered by turns, but in vain; the natives were neither to be intimidated nor appeased, and as a final resort he was obliged to call together his boat's crew, and pull away from what he termed the most infernal place he ever stepped upon.

Lucky was it for him and for us that we were not honoured on our departure by a salute of stones from the hands of the exasperated Tiors. In this way, on the neighbouring island of Ropo, were killed, but a few weeks previously, and for a nearly similar offence, the master and three of the crew of the K——.

I cannot determine with anything approaching to certainty, what power it is that imposes the taboo. When I consider the slight disparity of condition among the islanders—the very limited and inconsiderable prerogatives of the king and chiefs—and the loose and indefinite functions of the priesthood, most of whom were hardly to be distinguished from the rest of their countrymen, I am wholly at a loss where to look for the authority which regulates this potent institution. It is imposed upon something to-day, and withdrawn to-morrow; while its operations in other cases are perpetual. Sometimes its restrictions only affect a single individual—sometimes a particular family—

sometimes a whole tribe; and in a few instances they extend not merely over the various clans on a single island, but over all the inhabitants of an entire group. In illustration of this latter peculiarity, I may cite the law which forbids a female to enter a canoe—a prohibition which prevails upon all the northern Marquesas Islands.

The word itself (taboo) is used in more than one signification. It is sometimes used by a parent to his child, when in the exercise of parental authority he forbids it to perform a particular action. Anything opposed to the ordinary customs of the islanders, although not expressly prohibited, is said to be "taboo."

The Typee language is one very difficult to be acquired; it bears a close resemblance to the other Polynesian dialects, all of which show a common origin. The duplication of words, as "lumee lumee," "poee poee," "muee muee," is one of their peculiar features. But another, and a more annoying one, is the different senses in which one and the same word is employed; its various meanings all have a certain connection, which only makes the matter more puzzling. So one brisk, lively little word is obliged, like a servant in a poor family, to perform all sorts of duties; for instance, one particular combination of syllables expresses the ideas of sleep, rest, reclining, sitting, leaning, and all other things anywise analogous thereto, the particular meaning being shown chiefly by a variety of gestures and the eloquent expression of the countenance.

The intricacy of these dialects is another peculiarity. In the Missionary College at Lahainaluna, or Mawee, one of the Sandwich Islands, I saw a tabular exhibition of a Hawaiian verb, conjugated through all its moods and tenses. It covered the side of a considerable apartment, and I doubt whether Sir William Jones himself would not have despaired of mastering it.

CHAPTER XXXI

Strange custom of the Islanders—Their Chanting, and the peculiarity of their Voice—Rapture of the King at first hearing a Song—A new Dignity conferred on the Author—Musical Instruments in the Valley—Admiration of the Savages at beholding a Pugilistic Performance—Swimming Infant—Beautiful Tresses of the Girls —Ointment for the Hair.

SADLY discursive as I have already been, I must still further entreat the reader's patience, as I am about to string together, without any attempt at order, a few odds and ends of things not hitherto mentioned, but which are either curious in themselves or peculiar to the Typees.

There was one singular custom, observed in old Marheyo's domestic establishment, which often excited my surprise. Every night, before retiring, the inmates of the house gathered together on the mats, and squatting upon their haunches, after the universal practice of these islanders, would commence a low, dismal, and monotonous chant, accompanying the voice with the instrumental melody produced by two small half-rotten sticks tapped slowly together, a pair of which were held in the hands of each person present. Thus would they employ themselves for an hour or two, sometimes longer. Lying in the gloom which wrapped the further end of the house, I could not avoid looking at them, although the spectacle suggested nothing but unpleasant reflections. The flickering rays of the "armor" nut just served to reveal their savage lineaments, without dispelling the darkness that hovered about them.

Sometimes when, after falling into a kind of doze, and awaking suddenly in the midst of these doleful chantings, my eye would fall upon the wild-looking group engaged in their strange occupation, with their naked tattooed limbs, and shaven heads disposed in a circle, I was almost tempted to believe that I gazed upon a set of evil beings in the act of working a frightful incantation.

What was the meaning or purpose of this custom, whether it was practised merely as a diversion, or whether it was a religious exercise, a sort of family prayers, I never could discover.

The sounds produced by the natives on these occasions were of a most singular description; and had I not actually been present, I never would have believed that such curious noises could have been produced by human beings.

To savages generally is imputed a guttural articulation. This, however, is not always the case, especially among the inhabitants of the Polynesian Archipelago. The labial melody with which the Typee girls carry on an ordinary conversation, giving a musical prolongation to the final syllable of every sentence, and chirping out some of the words with a liquid, bird-like accent, was singularly pleasing.

The men, however, are not quite so harmonious in their utterance, and when excited upon any subject, would work themselves up into a sort of wordy paroxysm, during which all descriptions of rough-sided sounds were projected from their mouths, with a force and rapidity which was absolutely astonishing.

*   *   *   *   *   *

Although these savages are remarkably fond of chanting, still they appear to have no idea whatever of singing, at least as that art is practised among other nations.

I never shall forget the first time I happened to roar out a stave in the presence of the noble Mehevi. It was a stanza from the "Bavarian broom-seller." His Typean majesty, with all his court, gazed upon me in amazement, as if I had displayed some preternatural faculty which Heaven had denied to them. The king was delighted with the verse; but the chorus fairly transported him. At his solicitation I sang it again and again, and nothing could be more ludicrous than his vain attempts to catch the air and the words. The royal savage seemed to think that by screwing all the features of his face into the end of his nose he might possibly succeed in the undertaking, but it failed to answer the purpose; and in the end he gave it up, and consoled himself by listening to my repetition of the sounds fifty times over.

Previous to Mehevi's making the discovery, I had never been aware that there was anything of the nightingale about me; but I was now promoted to the place of court-minstrel, in which capacity I was afterwards perpetually called upon to officiate.

*   *   *   *   *   *

Besides the sticks and the drums, there are no other musical instruments among the Typees, except one which might appropriately be denominated a nasal flute. It is somewhat longer than an ordinary fife; is made of a beautiful scarlet-coloured reed; and has four or five stops, with a large hole near one end, which latter is held just beneath the left nostril. The other nostril being closed by a peculiar movement of the muscles about the nose, the breath is forced into the tube, and produces a soft dulcet sound, which is varied by the fingers running at random over the stops. This is a favourite recreation with the females, and one in which Fayaway greatly excelled. Awkward as such an instrument may appear, it was, in Fayaway's delicate little hands, one of the most graceful I have ever seen. A young lady, in the act of tormenting a guitar strung about her neck by a couple of yards of blue ribbon, is not half so engaging.

*   *   *   *   *   *

Singing was not the only means I possessed of diverting the royal Mehevi and his easy-going subjects. Nothing afforded them more pleasure than to see me go through the attitude of pugilistic encounter. As not one of the natives had soul enough in him to stand up like a man, and allow me to hammer away at him, for my own personal gratification and that of the king, I was necessitated to fight with an imaginary enemy, whom I invariably made to knock under to my superior prowess. Sometimes when this sorely battered shadow retreated precipitately towards a group of the savages, and, following him up, I rushed among them, dealing my blows right and left, they would disperse in all directions, much to the enjoyment of Mehevi, the chiefs, and themselves.

The noble art of self-defence appeared to be regarded by them as the peculiar gift of the white man; and I make little doubt but that they supposed armies of Europeans were drawn up provided with nothing else but bony fists and stout hearts, with which they set to in column, and pummelled one another at the word of command.

*   *   *   *   *   *

One day, in company with Kory-Kory, I had repaired to the stream for the purpose of bathing, when I observed a woman sitting upon a rock in the midst of the current, and watching with the liveliest interest the gambols of something, which at first I took to be an uncommonly large species of frog that was sporting in the water near her. Attracted by the novelty of the sight, I waded towards the spot where she sat, and could hardly credit the evidence of my senses when I beheld a little infant, the period of whose birth could not have extended back many days, paddling about as if it had just risen to the surface, after being hatched into existence at the bottom. Occasionally the delighted parent reached out her hands towards it, when the little thing, uttering a faint cry, and striking out its tiny limbs, would sidle for the rock, and the next moment be clasped to its mother's bosom. This was repeated again and again, the baby remaining in the stream about a minute at a time. Once or twice it made wry faces at swallowing a mouthful of water, and choked and spluttered as if on the point of strangling. At such times, however, the mother snatched it up, and by a process scarcely to be mentioned obliged it to eject the fluid. For several weeks afterwards I observed this woman bringing her child down to the stream regularly every day, in the cool of the morning and evening, and treating it to a bath. No wonder that the South Sea Islanders are so amphibious a race, when they are thus launched into the water as soon as they see the light. I am convinced that it is as natural for a human being to swim as it is for a duck. And yet in civilized communities how many able-bodied individuals die, like so many drowning kittens, from the occurrence of the most trivial accidents!

* * * * * *

The long, luxuriant, and glossy tresses of the Typee damsels often attracted my admiration. A fine head of hair is the pride and joy of every woman's heart! Whether, against the express will of Providence, it is twisted up on the crown of the head and there coiled away like a rope on a ship's deck; whether it be stuck behind the ears and hangs down like the swag of a small window-curtain; or whether it be permitted to flow over the shoulders in natural ringlets, it is always the pride of the owner, and the glory of the toilette.

The Typee girls devote much of their time to the dressing of their fair and redundant locks. After bathing, as they sometimes do five or six times every day, the hair is carefully dried, and if they have been in the sea, invariably washed in fresh water, and anointed with a highly scented oil extracted from the meat of the cocoa-nut. This oil is obtained in great abundance by the following very simple process:

A large vessel of wood, with holes perforated in the bottom, is filled with the pounded meat, and exposed to the rays of the sun. As the oleaginous matter exudes, it falls in drops through the apertures into a wide-mouthed calabash placed underneath. After a sufficient quantity has been thus collected, the oil undergoes a purifying process, and is then poured into the small spherical shells of the nuts of the moo-tree, which are hollowed out to receive it. These nuts are then hermetically sealed with a resinous gum, and the vegetable fragrance of their green rind soon imparts to the oil a delightful odour. After the lapse of a few weeks the exterior shell of the nuts becomes quite dry and hard, and assumes a beautiful carnation tint; and when opened they are found to be about two-thirds full of an ointment of a light yellow colour, and diffusing the sweetest perfume. This elegant little odorous globe would not be out of place even upon the toilette of a queen. Its merits as a preparation for the hair are undeniable—it imparts to it a superb gloss and a silky fineness.

CHAPTER XXXII

Apprehensions of Evil—Frightful Discovery—Some remarks on Cannibalism—Second Battle with the Happars—Savage Spectacle —Mysterious Feast—Subsequent Disclosures.

FROM the time of my casual encounter with Karky the artist, my life was one of absolute wretchedness. Not a day passed but I was persecuted by the solicitations of some of the natives to subject myself to the odious operation of tattooing. Their importunities drove me half wild, for I felt how easily they might work their will upon me regarding this or anything else which they took into their heads. Still, however, the behaviour of the islanders towards me was as kind as ever. Fayaway was quite as engaging; Kory-Kory as devoted: and Mehevi the king just as gracious and condescending as before. But I had now been three months in their valley, as nearly as I could estimate; I had grown familiar with the narrow limits to which my wanderings had been confined; and I began bitterly to feel the state of captivity in which I was held. There was no one with whom I could freely converse; no one to whom I could communicate my thoughts; no one who could sympathise with my sufferings. A thousand times I thought how much more endurable would have been my lot had Toby still been with me. But I was left alone, and the thought was terrible to me. Still, despite my griefs, I did all in my power to appear composed and cheerful, well knowing that by manifesting any uneasiness, or any desire to escape, I should only frustrate my object.

It was during the period I was in this unhappy frame of mind that the painful malady under which I had been labouring—after having almost completely subsided—began again to show itself, and with symptoms as violent as ever. This added calamity nearly unmanned me; the recurrence of the complaint proved that without powerful remedial applications all hope of cure was futile; and when I reflected that just beyond the elevations which bound me in, was the medical relief I needed, and that, although so near, it was impossible for me to avail myself of it, the thought was misery.

In this wretched situation, every circumstance which evinced the savage nature of the beings at whose mercy I was, augmented the fearful apprehensions that consumed me. An occurrence which happened about this time affected me most powerfully.

I have already mentioned that from the ridge-pole of Marheyo's house were suspended a number of packages enveloped in tappa. Many of these I had often seen in the hands of the natives, and their contents had been examined in my presence. But there were three packages hanging very nearly over the place where I lay, which from their remarkable appearance had often excited my curiosity. Several times I had asked Kory-Kory to show me their contents; but my servitor, who in almost every other particular had acceded to my wishes, always refused to gratify me in this.

One day, returning unexpectedly from the "Ti," my arrival seemed to throw the inmates of the house into the greatest confusion. They were seated together on the mats, and by the lines which extended from the roof to the floor I immediately perceived that the mysterious packages were for some purpose or other under inspection. The evident alarm the savages betrayed filled me with forebodings of evil, and with an uncontrollable desire to penetrate the secret so jealously guarded. Despite the efforts of Marheyo and Kory-Kory to restrain me, I forced my way into the midst of the circle, and just caught a glimpse of three human heads, which others of the party were hurriedly enveloping in the coverings from which they had been taken.

One of the three I distinctly saw. It was in a state of perfect preservation, and, from the slight glimpse I had of it, seemed to have been subjected to some smoking operation which had reduced it to the dry, hard, and mummy-like appearance it presented. The two long scalp-locks were twisted up into balls upon the crown of the head in the same way that the individual had worn them during life. The sunken cheeks were rendered yet more ghastly by the rows of glistening teeth which protruded from between the lips, while the sockets of the eyes—filled with oval bits of mother-of-pearl shell, with a black spot in the centre—heightened the hideousness of its aspect.

Two of the three were heads of the islanders; but the third, to my horror, was that of a white man. Although it had been quickly removed from my sight, still the glimpse I had of it was enough to convince me that I could not be mistaken.

Gracious God! what dreadful thoughts entered my mind! In solving this mystery perhaps I had solved another, and the fate of my lost companion might be revealed in the shocking spectacle I had just witnessed. I longed to have torn off the folds of cloth, and satisfied the awful doubts under which I laboured. But before I had recovered from the consternation into which I had been thrown, the fatal packages were hoisted aloft and once more swung over my head. The natives now gathered round me tumultuously, and laboured to convince me that what I had just seen were the heads of three Happar warriors, who had been slain in battle. This glaring falsehood added to my alarm, and it was not until I reflected that I had observed the packages swinging from their elevation before Toby's disappearance, that I could at all recover my composure.

But although this horrible apprehension had been dispelled, I had discovered enough to fill me, in my present state of mind, with the most bitter reflections. It was plain that I had seen the last relic of some unfortunate wretch, who must have been massacred on the beach by the savages, in one of those perilous trading adventures which I have before described.

It was not, however, alone the murder of the stranger that overcame me with gloom. I shuddered at the idea of the subsequent fate his inanimate body might have met with. Was the same doom reserved for me? Was I destined to perish like him—like him, perhaps, to be devoured, and my head to be preserved as a fearful memento of the event?

My imagination ran riot in these horrid speculations, and I felt certain that the worst possible evils would befal me. But whatever were my misgivings, I studiously concealed them from the islanders, as well as the full extent of the discovery I had made.

Although the assurances which the Typees had often given me, that they never eat human flesh, had not convinced me that such was the case, yet, having been so long a time in the valley without witnessing anything which indicated the existence of the practice, I began to hope that it was an event of very rare occurrence, and that I should be spared the horror of witnessing it during my stay among them; but, alas! these hopes were soon destroyed.

It is a singular fact, that in all our accounts of cannibal tribes we have seldom received the testimony of an eye-witness to the revolting practice. The horrible conclusion has almost always been derived either from the second-hand evidence of Europeans, or else from the admissions of the savages themselves, after they have in some degree become civilized. The Polynesians are aware of the detestation in which Europeans hold this custom, and therefore invariably deny its existence, and, with the craft peculiar to savages, endeavour to conceal every trace of it.

The excessive unwillingness betrayed by the Sandwich Islanders, even at the present day, to allude to the unhappy fate of Cook, has been often remarked. And so well have they succeeded in covering that event with mystery, that to this very hour, despite all that has been said and written on the subject, it still remains doubtful whether they wreaked upon his murdered body the vengeance they sometimes inflicted upon their enemies.

At Karakikova, the scene of that tragedy, a strip of ship's copper nailed against an upright post in the ground used to inform the traveller that beneath reposed the "remains" of the great circumnavigator. But I am strongly inclined to believe not only that the corpse was refused Christian burial, but that the heart which was brought to Vancouver some time after the event, and which the Hawaiians stoutly maintained was that of Captain Cook, was no such thing; and that the whole affair was a piece of imposture which was sought to be palmed off upon the credulous Englishman.

A few years since there was living on the island of Mowee (one of the Sandwich group) an old chief, who, actuated by a morbid desire for notoriety, gave himself out among the foreign residents of the place as the living tomb of Captain Cook's big toe!—affirming, that at the cannibal entertainment which ensued after the lamented Briton's death, that particular portion of his body had fallen to his share. His indignant countrymen actually caused him to be prosecuted in the native courts, on a charge nearly equivalent to what we term defamation of character; but the old fellow persisting in his assertion, and no invalidating proof being adduced, the plaintiffs were cast in the suit, and the cannibal reputation of the defendant fully established. This result was the making of his fortune; ever afterwards he was in the habit of giving very profitable audiences to all curious travellers who were desirous of beholding the man who had eaten the great navigator's great toe.

About a week after my discovery of the contents of the mysterious packages, I happened to be at the Ti, when another war-alarm was sounded, and the natives rushing to their arms, sallied out to resist a second incursion of the Happar invaders. The same scene was again repeated, only that on this occasion I heard at least fifteen reports of muskets from the mountains during the time that the skirmish lasted. An hour or two after its termination, loud pæans chanted through the valley announced the approach of the victors. I stood with Kory-Kory leaning against the railing of the pi-pi awaiting their advance, when a tumultuous crowd of islanders emerged with wild clamours from the neighbouring groves. In the midst of them marched four men, one preceding the other at regular intervals of eight or ten feet, with poles of a corresponding length, extended from shoulder to shoulder, to which were lashed with thongs of bark three long narrow bundles, carefully wrapped in ample coverings of freshly plucked palm-leaves, tacked together with slivers of bamboo. Here and there upon these green winding-sheets might be seen the stains of blood, while the warriors who carried the frightful burdens displayed upon their naked limbs similar sanguinary marks. The shaven head of the foremost had a deep gash upon it, and the clotted gore which had flowed from the wound remained in dry patches around it. This savage seemed to be sinking under the weight he bore. The bright tattooing upon his body was covered with blood and dust; his inflamed eyes rolled in their sockets, and his whole appearance denoted extraordinary suffering and exertion; yet, sustained by some powerful impulse, he continued to advance, while the throng around him with wild cheers sought to encourage him. The other three men were marked about the arms and breasts with several slight wounds, which they somewhat ostentatiously displayed.

These four individuals, having been the most active in the late encounter, claimed the honour of bearing the bodies of their slain enemies to the Ti. Such was the conclusion I drew from my own observations, and, as far as I could understand, from the explanation which Kory-Kory gave me.

The royal Mehevi walked by the side of these heroes. He carried in one hand a musket, from the barrel of which was suspended a small canvass pouch of powder, and in the other he grasped a short javelin, which he held before him and regarded with fierce exultation. This javelin he had wrested from a celebrated champion of the Happars, who had ignominiously fled, and was pursued by his foe beyond the summit of the mountain.

When within a short distance of the Ti, the warrior with the wounded head, who proved to be Narmonee, tottered forward two or three steps, and fell helplessly to the ground; but not before another had caught the end of the pole from his shoulder, and placed it upon his own.

The excited throng of islanders, who surrounded the person of the king and the dead bodies of the enemy, approached the spot where I stood, brandishing their rude implements of warfare, many of which were bruised and broken, and uttering continual shouts of triumph. When the crowd drew up opposite the Ti, I set myself to watch their proceedings most attentively; but scarcely had they halted when my servitor, who had left my side for an instant, touched my arm, and proposed our returning to Marheyo's house. To this I objected; but, to my surprise, Kory-Kory reiterated his request, and with an unusual vehemence of manner. Still, however, I refused to comply, and was retreating before him, as in his importunity he pressed upon me, when I felt a heavy hand laid upon my shoulder, and turning round, encountered the bulky form of Mow-Mow, a one-eyed chief, who had just detached himself from the crowd below, and had mounted the rear of the pi-pi upon which we stood. His cheek had been pierced by the point of a spear, and the wound imparted a still more frightful expression to his hideously tattooed face, already deformed by the loss of an eye. The warrior, without uttering a syllable, pointed fiercely in the direction of Marheyo's house, while Kory-Kory, at the same time presenting his back, desired me to mount.

I declined this offer, but intimated my willingness to withdraw, and moved slowly along the piazza, wondering what could be the cause of this unusual treatment. A few minutes' consideration convinced me that the savages were about to celebrate some hideous rite in connection with their peculiar customs, and at which they were determined I should not be present. I descended from the pi-pi, and attended by Kory-Kory, who on this occasion did not show his usual commiseration for my lameness, but seemed only anxious to hurry me on, walked away from the place. As I passed through the noisy throng, which by this time completely environed the Ti, I looked with fearful curiosity at the three packages, which now were deposited upon the ground; but although I had no doubt as to their contents, still their thick coverings prevented my actually detecting the form of a human body.

The next morning, shortly after sunrise, the same thundering sounds which had awakened me from sleep on the second day of the Feast of Calabashes, assured me that the savages were on the eve of celebrating another, and, as I fully believed, a horrible solemnity.

All the inmates of the house, with the exception of Marheyo, his son, and Tinor, after assuming their gala dresses, departed in the direction of the Taboo Groves.

Although I did not anticipate a compliance with my request, still, with a view of testing the truth of my suspicions, I proposed to Kory-Kory that, according to our usual custom in the morning, we should take a stroll to the Ti: he positively refused; and when I renewed the request, he evinced his determination to prevent my going there; and, to divert my mind from the subject, he offered to accompany me to the stream. We accordingly went, and bathed. On our coming back to the house, I was surprised to find that all its inmates had returned, and were lounging upon the mats as usual, although the drums still sounded from the groves.

The rest of the day I spent with Kory-Kory and Fayaway, wandering about a part of the valley situated in an opposite direction from the Ti; and whenever I so much as looked towards that building, although it was hidden from view by intervening trees, and at the distance of more than a mile, my attendant would exclaim, "taboo, taboo!"

At the various houses where we stopped, I found many of the inhabitants reclining at their ease, or pursuing some light occupation, as if nothing unusual were going forward; but amongst them all I did not perceive a single chief or warrior. When I asked several of the people why they were not at the "Hoolah Hoolah" (the feast), they uniformly answered the question in a manner which implied that it was not intended for them, but for Mehevi, Narmonee, Mow-Mow, Kolor, Womonoo, Kalow—running over, in their desire to make me comprehend their meaning, the names of all the principal chiefs.

Everything, in short, strengthened my suspicions with regard to the nature of the festival they were now celebrating; and which amounted almost to a certainty. While in Nukuheva I had frequently been informed that the whole tribe were never present at these cannibal banquets; but the chiefs and priests only, and everything I now observed agreed with the account.

The sound of the drums continued, without intermission, the whole day, and falling continually upon my ear, caused me a sensation of horror which I am unable to describe. On the following day hearing none of those noisy indications of revelry, I concluded that the inhuman feast was terminated; and feeling a kind of morbid curiosity to discover whether the Ti might furnish any evidence of what had taken place there, I proposed to Kory-Kory to walk there. To this proposition he replied by pointing with his finger to the newly risen sun, and then up to the zenith, intimating that our visit must be deferred until noon. Shortly after that hour we accordingly proceeded to the Taboo Groves, and as soon as we entered their precincts, I looked fearfully round in quest of some memorial of the scenes which had so lately been acted there; but everything appeared as usual. On reaching the Ti, we found Mehevi and a few chiefs reclining on the mats, who gave me as friendly a reception as ever. No allusions of any kind were made by them to the recent events; and I refrained, for obvious reasons, from referring to them myself.

After staying a short time I took my leave. In passing along the piazza, previously to descending from the pi-pi, I observed a curiously carved vessel of wood, of considerable size, with a cover placed over it, of the same material, and which resembled in shape a small canoe. It was surrounded by a low railing of bamboos, the top of which was scarcely a foot from the ground. As the vessel had been placed in its present position since my last visit, I at once concluded that it must have some connection with the recent festival; and, prompted by a curiosity I could not repress, in passing it I raised one end of the cover; at the same moment the chiefs, perceiving my design, loudly ejaculated, "Taboo! taboo!" But the slight glimpse sufficed; my eyes fell upon the disordered members of a human skeleton, the bones still fresh with moisture, and with particles of flesh clinging to them here and there!

Kory-Kory, who had been a little in advance of me, attracted by the exclamations of the chiefs, turned round in time to witness the expression of horror on my countenance. He now hurried towards me, pointing at the same time to the canoe, and exclaiming rapidly, "Puarkee! puarkee!" (Pig, pig). I pretended to yield to the deception, and repeated the words after him several times, as though acquiescing in what he said. The other savages, either deceived by my conduct or unwilling to manifest their displeasure at what could not now be remedied, took no further notice of the occurrence, and I immediately left the Ti.

All that night I lay awake, revolving in my mind the

fearful situation in which I was placed. The last horrid revelation had now been made, and the full sense of my condition rushed upon my mind with a force I had never before experienced.

Where, thought I, desponding, is there the slightest prospect of escape? The only person who seemed to possess the ability to assist me was the stranger Marnoo; but would he ever return to the valley? and if he did, should I be permitted to hold any communication with him? It seemed as if I were cut off from every source of hope, and that nothing remained but passively to await whatever fate was in store for me. A thousand times I endeavoured to account for the mysterious conduct of the natives. For what conceivable purpose did they thus retain me a captive? What could be their object in treating me with such apparent kindness, and did it not cover some treacherous scheme? Or, if they had no other design than to hold me a prisoner, how should I be able to pass away my days in this narrow valley, deprived of all intercourse with civilized beings, and for ever separated from friends and home?

One only hope remained to me. The French could not long defer a visit to the bay, and if they should permanently locate any of their troops in the valley, the savages could not for any length of time conceal my existence from them. But what reason had I to suppose that I should be spared until such an event occurred—an event which might be postponed by a hundred different contingencies?

CHAPTER XXXIII

The Stranger again arrives in the Valley—Singular Interview with him—Attempt to Escape—Failure—Melancholy Situation—Sympathy of Marheyo.

"MARNOO, Marnoo pemi!" Such were the welcome sounds which fell upon my ear some ten days after the events related in the preceding chapter. Once more the approach of the stranger was heralded, and the intelligence operated upon me like magic. Again I should be able to converse with him in my own language; and I resolved at all hazards to concert with him some scheme, however desperate, to rescue me from a condition that had now become insupportable.

As he drew near, I remembered with many misgivings the inauspicious termination of our former interview; and when he entered the house, I watched with intense anxiety the reception he met with from its inmates. To my joy, his appearance was hailed with the liveliest pleasure; and accosting me kindly, he seated himself by my side, and entered into conversation with the natives around him. It soon appeared, however, that on this occasion he had not any intelligence of importance to communicate. I inquired of him from whence he had last come? He replied from Pueearka, his native valley, and that he intended to return to it the same day.

At once it struck me that, could I but reach that valley under his protection, I might easily from thence reach Nukuheva by water; and animated by the prospect which this plan held out, I disclosed it in a few brief words to the stranger, and asked him how it could be best accomplished. My heart sunk within me when in his broken English he answered me that it could never be effected. "Kannaka no let you go no where," he said; "you taboo. Why you no like to stay? Plenty moee-moee (sleep)—plenty ki-ki (eat)—plenty whihenee (young girls)—Oh, very good place Typee! Suppose you no like this bay, why you come? You no hear about Typee? All white men afraid Typee, so no white men come."

These words distressed me beyond belief; and when I again related to him the circumstances under which I had descended into the valley, and sought to enlist his sympathies in my behalf by appealing to the bodily misery I endured, he listened to me with impatience, and cut me short by exclaiming passionately, "Me no hear you talk any more; by by Kannaka get mad, kill you and me too. No you see he no want you to speak to me at all?—you see—ah! by by you no mind—you get well, he kill you, eat you, hang you head up there, like Happar Kannaka.—Now you listen —but no talk any more. By by I go;—you see way I go.—Ah! then some night Kannaka all moee-moee (sleep)—you run away, you come Pueearka. I speak Pueearka Kannaka—he no harm you—ah! then I take you my canoe Nukuheva— and you no run away ship no more." With these words, enforced by a vehemence of gesture I cannot describe, Marnoo started from my side, and immediately engaged in conversation with some of the chiefs who had entered the house.

It would have been idle for me to have attempted resuming the interview so peremptorily terminated by Marnoo, who was evidently little disposed to compromise his own safety by any rash endeavours to ensure mine. But the plan he had suggested struck me as one which might possibly be accomplished, and I resolved to act upon it as speedily as possible.

Accordingly, when he rose to depart, I accompanied him with the natives outside of the house, with a view of carefully noting the path he would take in leaving the valley. Just before leaping from the pi-pi he clasped my hand, and looking significantly at me, exclaimed, "Now you see—you do what I tell you—ah! then you do good;—you no do so —ah! then you die." The next moment he waved his spear in adieu to the islanders, and following the route that conducted to a defile in the mountains lying opposite the Happar side, was soon out of sight.

A mode of escape was now presented to me, but how was I to avail myself of it? I was continually surrounded by the savages; I could not stir from one house to another without being attended by some of them; and even during the hours devoted to slumber the slightest movement which I made seemed to attract the notice of those who shared the mats with me. In spite of these obstacles, however, I determined forthwith to make the attempt. To do so with any prospect of success, it was necessary that I should have at least two hours' start before the islanders should discover my absence; for with such facility was any alarm spread through the valley, and so familiar, of course, were the inhabitants with the intricacies of the groves, that I could not hope, lame and feeble as I was, and ignorant of the route, to secure my escape unless I had this advantage. It was also by night alone that I could hope to accomplish my object, and then only by adopting the utmost precaution.

The entrance to Marheyo's habitation was through a low narrow opening in its wicker-work front. This passage, for no conceivable reason that I could devise, was always closed after the household had retired to rest, by drawing a heavy slide across it, composed of a dozen or more bits of wood, ingeniously fastened together by seizings of sinnate. When any of the inmates chose to go outside, the noise occasioned by the removing of this rude door awakened every body else; and on more than one occasion I had remarked that the islanders were nearly as irritable as more civilized beings under similar circumstances.

The difficulty thus placed in my way I determined to obviate in the following manner. I would get up boldly in the course of the night, and drawing the slide, issue from the house, and pretend that my object was merely to procure a drink from the calabash, which always stood without the dwelling on the corner of the pi-pi. On re-entering I would purposely omit closing the passage after me, and trusting that the indolence of the savages would prevent them from repairing my neglect, would return to my mat, and waiting patiently until all were again asleep, I would then steal forth, and at once take the route to Pueearka.

The very night which followed Marnoo's departure, I proceeded to put this project into execution. About midnight, as I imagined, I rose and drew the slide. The natives, just as I had expected, started up, while some of them asked, "Arware poo awa, Tommo?" (where are you going, Tommo?) "Wai" (water) I laconically answered, grasping the calabash. On hearing my reply they sank back again, and in a minute or two I returned to my mat, anxiously awaiting the result of the experiment.

One after another the savages turning restlessly, appeared to· resume their slumbers, and rejoicing at the stillness which prevailed, I was about to rise again from my couch, when I heard a slight rustling—a dark form was intercepted between me and the doorway—the slide was drawn across it, and the individual, whoever he was, returned to his mat. This was a sad blow to me; but as it might have roused the suspicions of the islanders to have made another attempt that night, I was reluctantly obliged to defer it until the next. Several times after I repeated the same manœuvre, but with as little success as before. As my pretence for withdrawing from the house was to allay my thirst, Kory-Kory, either suspecting some design on my part, or else prompted by a desire to please me, regularly every evening placed a calabash of water by my side.

Even under these inauspicious circumstances I again and again renewed the attempt; but when I did so my valet always rose with me, as if determined I should not remove myself from his observation. For the present, therefore, I was obliged to abandon the attempt; but I endeavoured to console myself with the idea that by this mode I might yet effect my escape.

Shortly after Marnoo's visit I was reduced to such a state,

that it was with extreme difficulty I could walk, even with the assistance of a spear, and Kory-Kory, as formerly, was obliged to carry me daily to the stream.

For hours and hours during the warmest part of the day I lay upon my mat, and while those around me were nearly all dozing away in careless ease, I remained awake, gloomily pondering over the fate which it appeared now idle for me to resist, when I thought of the loved friends who were thousands and thousands of miles from the savage island in which I was held a captive, when I reflected that my dreadful fate would for ever be concealed from them, and that with hope deferred they might continue to await my return long after my inanimate form had blended with the dust of the valley—I could not repress a shudder of anguish.

How vividly is impressed upon my mind every minute feature of the scene which met my view during those long days of suffering and sorrow! At my request my mats were always spread directly facing the door, opposite which, and at a little distance, was the hut of boughs that Marheyo was building.

Whenever my gentle Fayaway and Kory-Kory, laying themselves down beside me, would leave me awhile to uninterrupted repose, I took a strange interest in the slightest movements of the eccentric old warrior. All alone during the stillness of the tropical mid-day, he would pursue his quiet work, sitting in the shade and weaving together the leaflets of his cocoa-nut branches, or rolling upon his knee the twisted fibres of bark to form the cords with which he tied together the thatching of his tiny house. Frequently suspending his employment, and noticing my melancholy eye fixed upon him, he would raise his hand with a gesture expressive of deep commiseration, and then moving towards me slowly would enter on tip-toes, fearful of disturbing the slumbering natives, and, taking the fan from my hand, would sit before me, swaying it gently to and fro, and gazing earnestly into my face.

Just beyond the pi-pi, and disposed in a triangle before the entrance of the house, were three magnificent bread-fruit trees. At this moment I can recall to my mind their slender shafts, and the graceful inequalities of their bark, on which my eye was accustomed to dwell day after day in the midst of my solitary musings. It is strange how inanimate objects will twine themselves into our affections, especially in the hour of affliction. Even now, amidst all the bustle and stir of the proud and busy city in which I am dwelling, the image of those three trees seems to come as vividly before my eyes as if they were actually present, and I still feel the soothing quiet pleasure which I then had in watching hour after hour their topmost boughs waving gracefully in the breeze.

CHAPTER XXXIV

The Escape.

NEARLY three weeks had elapsed since the second visit of Marnoo, and it must have been more than four months since I entered the valley, when one day about noon, and whilst everything was in profound silence, Mow-Mow, the one-eyed chief, suddenly appeared at the door, and leaning forward towards me as I lay directly facing him, said in a low tone, "Toby pemi ena" (Toby has arrived here). Gracious heaven! What a tumult of emotions rushed upon me at this startling intelligence! Insensible to the pain that had before distracted me, I leaped to my feet, and called wildly to Kory-Kory, who was reposing by my side. The startled islanders sprang from their mats; the news was quickly communicated to them; and the next moment I was making my way to the Ti on the back of Kory-Kory, and surrounded by the excited savages.

All that I could comprehend of the particulars which Mow-Mow rehearsed to his auditors as we proceeded, was that my long-lost companion had arrived in a boat which had just entered the bay. These tidings made me most anxious to be carried at once to the sea, lest some untoward circumstance should prevent our meeting; but to this they would not consent, and continued their course towards the royal abode. As we approached it, Mehevi and several chiefs showed themselves from the piazza, and called upon us loudly to come to them.

As soon as we had approached, I endeavoured to make them understand that I was going down to the sea to meet Toby. To this the king objected, and motioned Kory-Kory to bring me into the house. It was in vain to resist; and in a few moments I found myself within the Ti, surrounded by a noisy group engaged in discussing the recent intelligence. Toby's name was frequently repeated, coupled with violent exclamations of astonishment. It seemed as if they yet remained in doubt with regard to the fact of his arrival, and at every fresh report that was brought from the shore they betrayed the liveliest emotions.

Almost frenzied at being held in this state of suspense, I passionately besought Mehevi to permit me to proceed. Whether my companion had arrived or not, I felt a presentiment that my own fate was about to be decided. Again and again I renewed my petition to Mehevi. He regarded me with a fixed and serious eye, but at length yielding to my importunity, reluctantly granted my request.

Accompanied by some fifty of the natives, I now rapidly continued my journey; every few moments being transferred from the back of one to another, and urging my bearer forward all the while with earnest entreaties. As I thus hurried forward, no doubt as to the truth of the information I had received ever crossed my mind. I was alive only to the one overwhelming idea, that a chance of deliverance was now afforded me, if the jealous opposition of the savages could be overcome.

Having been prohibited from approaching the sea during the whole of my stay in the valley, I had always associated with it the idea of escape. Toby too—if indeed he had ever voluntarily deserted me—must have effected his flight by the sea; and now that I was drawing near to it myself, I indulged in hopes which I had never felt before. It was evident that a boat had entered the bay, and I saw little reason to doubt the truth of the report that it had brought my companion. Every time therefore that we gained an elevation, I looked eagerly around, hoping to behold him.

In the midst of an excited throng, who by their violent gestures and wild cries appeared to be under the influence of some excitement as strong as my own, I was now borne along at a rapid trot, frequently stooping my head to avoid the branches which crossed the path, and never ceasing to implore those who carried me to accelerate their already swift pace.

In this manner we had proceeded about four or five miles, when we were met by a party of some twenty islanders, between whom and those who accompanied me ensued an animated conference. Impatient of the delay occasioned by this interruption, I was beseeching the man who carried me to proceed without his loitering companions, when Kory-Kory, running to my side, informed me, in three fatal words, that the news had all proved false—that Toby had not arrived—"Toby owlee permi." Heaven only knows how, in the state of mind and body I then was, I ever sustained the agony which this intelligence caused me: not that the news was altogether unexpected; but I had trusted that the fact might not have been made known until we should have arrived upon the beach. As it was, I at once foresaw the course the savages would pursue. They had only yielded thus far to my entreaties, that I might give a joyful welcome to my long-absent comrade; but now that it was known he had not arrived, they would at once oblige me to turn back.

My anticipations were but too correct. In spite of the resistance I made, they carried me into a house which was near the spot, and left me upon the mats. Shortly afterwards several of those who had accompanied me from the Ti, detaching themselves from the others, proceeded in the direction of the sea. Those who remained—among whom were Marheyo, Mow-Mow, Kory-Kory, and Tinor—gathered about the dwelling and appeared to be awaiting their return.

This convinced me that strangers—perhaps some of my own countrymen—had for some cause or other entered the bay. Distracted at the idea of their vicinity, and reckless of the pain which I suffered, I heeded not the assurances of the islanders, that there were no boats at the beach, but starting to my feet endeavoured to gain the door. Instantly the passage was blocked up by several men, who commanded me to resume my seat. The fierce looks of the irritated savages admonished me that I could gain nothing by force, and that it was by entreaty alone that I could hope to compass my object.

Guided by this consideration, I turned to Mow-Mow, the only chief present whom I had been much in the habit of seeing, and carefully concealing my real design, tried to make him comprehend that I still believed Toby to have arrived on the shore, and besought him to allow me to go forward to welcome him. To all his repeated assertions, that my companion had not been seen, I pretended to turn a deaf ear: while I urged my solicitations with an eloquence of gesture which the one-eyed chief appeared unable to resist. He seemed indeed to regard me as a froward child, to whose wishes he had not the heart to oppose force, and whom he must consequently humour. He spoke a few words to the natives, who at once retreated from the door, and immediately passed out of the house.

Here I looked earnestly round for Kory-Kory; but that hitherto faithful servitor was nowhere to be seen. Unwilling to linger even for a single instant when every moment might be so important, I motioned to a muscular fellow near me to take me upon his back: to my surprise he angrily refused. I turned to another, but with a like result. A third attempt was as unsuccessful, and I immediately perceived what had induced Mow-Mow to grant my request and why the other natives conducted themselves in so strange a manner. It was evident that the chief had only given me liberty to continue my progress towards the sea because he supposed that I was deprived of the means of reaching it.

Convinced by this of their determination to retain me a captive, I became desperate; and almost insensible to the pain which I suffered, I seized a spear which was leaning against the projecting eaves of the house, and supporting myself with it, resumed the path that swept by the dwelling. To my surprise I was suffered to proceed alone, all the natives remaining in front of the house, and engaging in earnest conversation, which every moment became more loud and vehement; and to my unspeakable delight I perceived that some difference of opinion had arisen between them; that two parties, in short, were formed, and consequently that in their divided counsels there was some chance of my deliverance.

Before I had proceeded a hundred yards I was again surrounded by the savages, who were still in all the heat of argument, and appeared every moment as if they would come to blows. In the midst of this tumult old Marheyo came to my side, and I shall never forget the benevolent expression of his countenance. He placed his arm upon my shoulder, and emphatically pronounced the only two English words I had taught him—"Home" and "Mother." I at once understood what he meant, and eagerly expressed my thanks to him. Fayaway and Kory-Kory were by his side, both weeping violently; and it was not until the old man had twice repeated the command that his son could bring himself to obey him, and take me again upon his back. The one-eyed chief opposed his doing so, but he was overruled, and, as it seemed to me, by some of his own party.

We proceeded onwards, and never shall I forget the ecstacy I felt when I first heard the roar of the surf breaking upon the beach. Before long I saw the flashing billows themselves through the opening between the trees. Oh glorious sight and sound of ocean! with what rapture did I hail you as familiar friends! By this time the shouts of the crowd upon the beach were distinctly audible, and in the blended confusion of sounds I almost fancied I could distinguish the voices of my own countrymen.

When we reached the open space which lay between the groves and the sea, the first object that met my view was an English whale-boat, lying with her bow pointed from the shore, and only a few fathoms distant from it. It was manned by five islanders, dressed in short tunics of calico. My first impression was that they were in the very act of pulling out from the bay; and that, after all my exertions, I had come too late. My soul sunk within me: but a second glance convinced me that the boat was only hanging off to keep out of the surf; and the next moment I heard my own name shouted out by a voice from the midst of the crowd.

Looking in the direction of the sound, I perceived, to my

indescribable joy, the tall figure of Karakoee, an Oahu Kannaka, who had often been aboard the 'Dolly,' while she lay in Nukuheva. He wore the green shooting-jacket with gilt buttons, which had been given to him by an officer of the Reine Blanche—the French flag-ship—and in which I had always seen him dressed. I now remembered the Kannaka had frequently told me that his person was tabooed in all the valleys of the island, and the sight of him at such a moment as this filled my heart with a tumult of delight.

Karakoee stood near the edge of the water with a large roll of cotton-cloth thrown over one arm, and holding two or three canvass bags of powder; while with the other hand he grasped a musket, which he appeared to be proffering to several of the chiefs around him. But they turned with disgust from his offers, and seemed to be impatient at his presence, with vehement gestures waving him off to his boat, and commanding him to depart.

The Kannaka, however, still maintained his ground, and I at once perceived that he was seeking to purchase my freedom. Animated by the idea, I called upon him loudly to come to me; but he replied, in broken English, that the islanders had threatened to pierce him with their spears, if he stirred a foot towards me. At this time I was still advancing, surrounded by a dense throng of the natives, several of whom had their hands upon me, and more than one javelin was threateningly pointed at me. Still I perceived clearly that many of those least friendly towards me looked irresolute and anxious.

I was still some thirty yards from Karakoee when my farther progress was prevented by the natives, who compelled me to sit down upon the ground, while they still retained their hold upon my arms. The din and tumult now became tenfold, and I perceived that several of the priests were on the spot, all of whom were evidently urging Mow-Mow and the other chiefs to prevent my departure; and the detestable word "Roo-ne! Roo-ne!" which I had heard repeated a thousand times during the day, was now shouted out on every side of me. Still I saw that the Kannaka continued his exertions in my favour—that he was boldly debating the matter with the savages, and was striving to entice them by displaying his cloth and powder, and snapping the lock of his musket. But all he said or did appeared only to augment the clamours of those around him, who seemed bent upon driving him into the sea.

When I remembered the extravagant value placed by these people upon the articles which were offered to them in exchange for me, and which were so indignantly rejected, I saw a new proof of the same fixed determination of purpose they had all along manifested with regard to me, and in despair, and reckless of consequences, I exerted all my strength, and shaking myself free from the grasp of those who held me, I sprung upon my feet and rushed towards Karakoee.

The rash attempt nearly decided my fate; for, fearful that I might slip from them, several of the islanders now raised a simultaneous shout, and pressing upon Karakoee, they menaced him with furious gestures, and actually forced him into the sea. Appalled at their violence, the poor fellow, standing nearly to the waist in the surf, endeavoured to pacify them; but at length, fearful that they would do him some fatal violence, he beckoned to his comrades to pull in at once, and take him into the boat.

It was at this agonizing moment, when I thought all hope was ended, that a new contest arose between the two parties who had accompanied me to the shore; blows were struck, wounds were given, and blood flowed. In the interest excited by the fray, every one had left me except Marheyo, Kory-Kory, and poor dear Fayaway, who clung to me, sobbing indignantly. I saw that now or never was the moment. Clasping my hands together, I looked imploringly at Marheyo, and moved towards the now almost deserted beach. The tears were in the old man's eyes, but neither he nor Kory-Kory attempted to hold me, and I soon reached the Kannaka, who had been anxiously watching my movements; the rowers pulled in as near as they dared to the edge of the surf; I gave one parting embrace to Fayaway, who seemed speechless with sorrow, and the next instant I found myself safe in the boat, and Karakoee by my side, who told the rowers at once to give way. Marhyeo and Kory-Kory, and a great many of the women, followed me into the water, and I was determined, as the only mark of gratitude I could show, to give them the articles which had been brought as my ransom. I handed the musket to Kory-Kory, with a rapid gesture which was equivalent to a "Deed of Gift;" threw the roll of cotton to old Marheyo, pointing as I did so to poor Fayaway, who had retired from the edge of the water and was sitting down disconsolate on the shingles; and tumbled the powder-bags out to the nearest young ladies, all of whom were vastly willing to take them. This distribution did not occupy ten seconds, and before it was over the boat was under full way; the Kannaka all the while exclaiming loudly against what he considered a useless throwing away of valuable property.

Although it was clear that my movements had been noticed by several of the natives, still they had not suspended the conflict in which they were engaged, and it was not until the boat was above fifty yards from the shore that Mow-Mow and some six or seven other warriors rushed into the sea and hurled their javelins at us. Some of the weapons passed quite as close to us as was desirable, but no one was wounded, and the men pulled away gallantly. But although soon out of the reach of the spears, our progress was extremely slow; it blew strong upon the shore, and the tide was against us; and I saw Karakoee, who was steering the boat, give many a look towards a jutting point of the bay round which we had to pass.

For a minute or two after our departure, the savages, who had formed into different groups, remained perfectly motionless and silent. All at once the enraged chief showed by his gestures that he had resolved what course he would take. Shouting loudly to his companions, and pointing with his tomahawk towards the headland, he set off at full speed in that direction, and was followed by about thirty of the natives, among whom were several of the priests, all yelling out "Roo-ne! Roo-ne!" at the very top of their voices. Their intention was evidently to swim off from the headland and interrupt us in our course. The wind was freshening every minute, and was right in our teeth, and it was one of those chopping angry seas in which it is so difficult to row. Still the chances seemed in our favour, but when we came within a hundred yards of the point, the active savages were already dashing into the water, and we all feared that within five minutes' time we should have a score of the infuriated wretches around us. If so, our doom was sealed, for these savages, unlike the feeble swimmers of civilized countries, are, if anything, more formidable antagonists in the water than when on the land. It was all a trial of strength; our natives pulled till their oars bent again, and the crowd of swimmers shot through the water despite its roughness, with fearful rapidity.

By the time we had reached the headland, the savages were spread right across our course. Our rowers got out their knives and held them ready between their teeth, and I seized the boat-hook. We were well aware that if they succeeded in intercepting us they would practise upon us the manœuvre which has proved so fatal to many a boat's crew in these seas. They would grapple the oars, and seizing hold of the gunwale, capsize the boat, and then we should be entirely at their mercy.

After a few breathless moments I discerned Mow-Mow. The athletic islander, with his tomahawk between his teeth, was dashing the water before him till it foamed again. He was the nearest to us, and in another instant he would have seized one of the oars. Even at the moment I felt horror at the act I was about to commit; but it was no time for pity or compunction, and with a true aim, and exerting all my strength, I dashed the boat-hook at him. It struck him just below the throat, and forced him down-wards. I had no time to repeat my blow, but I saw him rise to the surface in the wake of the boat, and never shall I forget the ferocious expression of his countenance.

Only one other of the savages reached the boat. He seized the gunwale, but the knives of our rowers so mauled his wrists, that he was forced to quit his hold, and the next minute we were past them all, and in safety. The strong excitement which had thus far kept me up, now left me, and I fell back fainting into the arms of Karakoee.

　　　*　　　*　　　*　　　*　　　*　　　*

The circumstances connected with my most unexpected escape may be very briefly stated. The captain of an Australian vessel, being in distress for men in these remote seas, had put into Nukuheva in order to recruit his ship's company; but not a single man was to be obtained; and the barque was about to get under weigh, when she was boarded by Karakoee, who informed the disappointed Englishman that an American sailor was detained by the savages in the neighbouring bay of Typee; and he offered, if supplied with suitable articles of traffic, to undertake his release. The Kannaka had gained his intelligence from Marnoo, to whom, after all, I was indebted for my escape.

The proposition was acceded to; and Karakoee, taking with him five tabooed natives of Nukuheva, again repaired aboard the barque, which in a few hours sailed to that part of the island, and threw her main-top-sail aback right off the entrance to the Typee bay. The whale-boat, manned by the tabooed crew, pulled towards the head of the inlet, while the ship lay "off and on" awaiting its return.

The events which ensued have already been detailed, and little more remains to be related. On reaching the 'Julia' I was lifted over the side, and my strange appearance and remarkable adventure occasioned the liveliest interest. Every attention was bestowed upon me that humanity could suggest. But to such a state was I reduced, that three months elapsed before I recovered my health.

The mystery which hung over the fate of my friend and companion Toby has never been cleared up. I still remain ignorant whether he succeeded in leaving the valley, or perished at the hands of the islanders.

APPENDIX

THE author of this volume arrived at Tahiti the very day that the iniquitous designs of the French were consummated by inducing the subordinate chiefs, during the absence of their queen, to ratify an artfully drawn treaty, by which she was virtually deposed. Both menaces and caresses were employed on this occasion, and the 32-pounders which peeped out of the portholes of the frigate were the principal arguments adduced to quiet the scruples of the more conscientious islanders.

And yet this piratical seizure of Tahiti, with all the woe and desolation which resulted from it, created not half so great a sensation, at least in America, as was caused by the proceedings of the English at the Sandwich Islands. No transaction has ever been more grossly misrepresented than the events which occurred upon the arrival of Lord George Paulet at Oahu. During a residence of four months at Honolulu, the metropolis of the group, the author was in the confidence of an Englishman who was much employed by his lordship; and great was the author's astonishment on his arrival at Boston, in the autumn of 1844, to read the distorted accounts and fabrications which had produced in the United States so violent an outbreak of indignation against the English. He deems it, therefore, a mere act of justice towards a gallant officer briefly to state the leading circumstances connected with the event in question.

It is needless to rehearse all the abuse that for some time previous to the spring of 1843 had been heaped upon the British residents, especially upon Captain Charlton, her Britannic Majesty's consul-general, by the native authorities of the Sandwich Islands. High in the favour of the imbecile king at this time was one Dr. Judd, a sanctimonious apothecary-adventurer, who, with other kindred and influential spirits, were animated by an inveterate dislike to England. The ascendancy of a junto of ignorant and designing Methodist elders in the councils of a half-civilized king, ruling with absolute sway over a nation just poised between barbarism and civilization, and exposed by the peculiarities of its relations with foreign states to unusual difficulties, was not precisely calculated to impart a healthy tone to the policy of the government.

At last matters were brought to such an extremity, through the iniquitous maladministration of affairs, that the endurance of further insults and injuries on the part of the British consul was no longer to be borne. Captain Charlton, insultingly forbidden to leave the islands, clandestinely withdrew, and arriving at Valparaiso, conferred with Rear-Admiral Thomas, the English commander-in-chief on the Pacific station. In consequence of this communication, Lord George Paulet was despatched by the admiral in the Carysfort frigate, to enquire into and correct the alleged abuses. On arriving at his destination, he sent his first-lieutenant ashore with a letter to the king, couched in terms of the utmost courtesy, and soliciting the honour of an audience. The messenger was denied access to his Majesty, and Paulet was coolly referred to Doctor Judd, and informed that the apothecary was invested with plenary powers to treat with him. Rejecting this insolent proposition, his lordship again addressed the king by letter, and renewed his previous request; but he encountered another repulse. Justly indignant at this treatment, he penned a third epistle, enumerating the grievances to be redressed, and demanding a compliance with his requisitions, under penalty of immediate hostilities.

The government was now obliged to act, and an artful stroke of policy was decided upon by the despicable counsellors of the king to entrap the sympathies and rouse the indignation of Christendom. His Majesty was made to intimate to the British captain that he could not, as the conscientious ruler of his beloved people, comply with the arbitrary demands of his lordship, and in deprecation of the horrors of war, tendered to his acceptance the "provisional cession" of the islands, subject to the result of the negotiations then pending in London. Paulet, a bluff and straight-forward sailor, took the king at his word, and after some preliminary arrangements, entered upon the administration of Hawaiian affairs, in the same firm and benignant spirit which marked the discipline of his frigate, and which had rendered him the idol of his ship's company. He soon endeared himself to nearly all orders of the islanders; but the king and the chiefs, whose feudal sway over the common people is laboriously sought to be perpetuated by their missionary advisers, regarded all his proceedings with the most vigilant animosity. Jealous of his growing popularity, and unable to counteract it, they endeavoured to assail his reputation abroad by ostentatiously protesting against his acts, and appealing in Oriental phrase to the *wide universe* to witness and compassionate their *unparalleled wrongs*.

Heedless of their idle clamours, Lord George Paulet addressed himself to the task of reconciling the differences among the foreign residents, remedying their grievances, promoting their mercantile interests, and ameliorating as far as lay in his power the condition of the degraded natives. The iniquities he brought to light and instantly suppressed are too numerous to be here recorded; but one instance may be mentioned that will give some idea of the lamentable misrule to which these poor islanders are subjected.

It is well known that the laws at the Sandwich Islands are subject to the most capricious alterations, which, by confounding all ideas of right and wrong in the minds of the natives, produce the most pernicious effects. In no case is this mischief more plainly discernible than in the continually shifting regulations concerning licentiousness. At one time the most innocent freedoms between the sexes are punished with fine and imprisonment; at another the revocation of the statute is followed by the most open and undisguised profligacy.

It so happened that at the period of Paulet's arrival the Connecticut blue laws had been for at least three weeks steadily enforced. In consequence of this, the fort at Honolulu was filled with a great number of young girls, who were confined there doing penance for their slips from virtue. Paulet, although at first unwilling to interfere with regulations having reference solely to the natives themselves, was eventually, by the prevalence of certain reports, induced to institute a strict inquiry into the internal administration of General Kekuanoa, governor of the island of Oahu, one of the pillars of the Hawaiian church, and captain of the fort. He soon ascertained that numbers of the young females employed during the day at work intended for the benefit of the king, were at night smuggled over the ramparts of the fort—which on one side directly overhangs the sea—and were conveyed by stealth on board such vessels as had contracted with the General to be supplied with them. Before daybreak they returned to their quarters, and their own silence with regard to these secret excursions was purchased by a small portion of those wages of iniquity which were placed in the hands of Kekuanoa.

The vigour with which the laws concerning licentiousness were at that period enforced, enabled the General to monopolize in a great measure the detestable trade in which he was engaged, and there consequently flowed into his coffers—and some say into those of the government also—considerable sums of money. It is indeed a lamentable fact, that the principal revenue of the Hawaiian government is derived from the fines levied upon, or rather the licences taken out by Vice, the prosperity of which is linked with that of the government. Were the people to become virtuous the authorities would become poor; but from present indications there is little apprehension to be entertained on that score.

Some five months after the date of the cession, the Dublin frigate, carrying the flag of Rear-Admiral Thomas, entered the harbour of Honolulu. The excitement that her sudden appearance produced on shore was prodigious. Three days after her arrival an English sailor hauled down the red cross which had been flying from the heights of the fort, and the Hawaiian colours were again displayed upon the same staff. At the same moment the long 42-pounders upon Punchbowl Hill opened their iron throats in triumphant reply to the thunders of the five men-of-war in the harbour; and King Kammahamaha III., surrounded by a splendid group of British and American officers, unfurled the royal standard to assembled thousands of his subjects, who, attracted by the imposing military display of the foreigners, had flocked to witness the formal restoration of the islands to their ancient rulers.

The Admiral, after sanctioning the proceedings of his subaltern, had brought the authorities to terms; and so removed the necessity of acting any longer under the provisional cession.

The event was made an occasion of riotous rejoicing by the king and the principal chiefs, who easily secured a display of enthusiasm from the inferior orders, by remitting for a time the accustomed severity of the laws. Royal proclamations in English and Hawaiian were placarded in the streets of Honolulu, and posted up in the more populous villages of the group, in which his Majesty announced to his loving subjects the re-establishment of his throne, and called upon them to celebrate it by breaking through all moral, legal, and religious restraint for ten consecutive days, during which time all the laws of the land were solemnly declared to be suspended.

Who that happened to be at Honolulu during those ten memorable days will ever forget them! The spectacle of universal broad-day debauchery, which was then exhibited, beggars description. The natives of the surrounding islands flocked to Honolulu by hundreds, and the crews of two frigates, opportunely let loose like so many demons to swell the heathenish uproar, gave the crowning flourish to the scene. It was a sort of Polynesian saturnalia. Deeds too atrocious to be mentioned were done at noon-day in the open street, and some of the islanders caught in the very act of stealing from the foreigners, were, on being taken to the fort by the aggrieved party, suffered immediately to go at large and to retain the stolen property—Keku-anoa informing the white men, with a sardonic grin, that the laws were "hannapa" (tied up).

The history of these ten days reveals in their true colours the character of the Sandwich islanders, and furnishes an eloquent commentary on the results which have flowed from the labours of the missionaries. Freed from the restraints of severe penal laws, the natives almost to a man had plunged voluntarily into every species of wickedness and excess, and by their utter disregard of all decency plainly showed, that although they had been schooled into a seeming submission to the new order of things, they were in reality as depraved and vicious as ever.

Such were the events which produced in America so general an outbreak of indignation against the spirited and high-minded Paulet. He is not the first man who, in the fearless discharge of his duty, has awakened the senseless clamours of those whose narrow-minded suspicions blind them to a proper appreciation of measures which unusual exigencies may have rendered necessary.

It is almost needless to add that the British cabinet never had any idea of appropriating the islands; and it furnishes a sufficient vindication of the acts of Lord George Paulet, that he not only received the unqualified approbation of his own government, but that to this hour the great body of the Hawaiian people invoke blessings on his head, and look back with gratitude to the time when his liberal and paternal sway diffused peace and happiness among them.

THE

STORY OF

TOBY

A SEQUEL TO

"TYPEE"

BY THE AUTHOR OF THAT WORK

NOTE TO THE SEQUEL

The author was more than two years in the South Seas, after escaping from the valley, as recounted in the last chapter. Some time after returning home the foregoing narrative was published, though it was little thought at the time that this would be the means of revealing the existence of Toby, who had long been given up for lost. But so it proved.

The story of his escape supplies a natural sequel to the adventure, and as such it is now added to the volume. It was related to the author by Toby himself, not ten days since.

New York, July, 1846.

The Story of Toby

SEQUEL

THE morning my comrade left me, as related in the narrative, he was accompanied by a large party of the natives, some of them carrying fruit and hogs for the purposes of traffic, as the report had spread that boats had touched at the bay.

As they proceeded through the settled parts of the valley, numbers joined them from every side, running with animated cries from every pathway. So excited were the whole party, that eager as Toby was to gain the beach, it was almost as much as he could do to keep up with them. Making the valley ring with their shouts, they hurried along on a swift trot, those in advance pausing now and then, and flourishing their weapons to urge the rest forward.

Presently they came to a place where the path crossed a bend of the main stream of the valley. Here a strange sound came through the grove beyond, and the Islanders halted. It was Mow-Mow, the one-eyed chief, who had gone on before; he was striking his heavy lance against the hollow bough of a tree.

This was a signal of alarm;—for nothing was now heard but shouts of "Happar! Happar!"—the warriors tilting with their spears and brandishing them in the air, and the women and boys shouting to each other, and picking up the stones in the bed of the stream. In a moment or two Mow-Mow and two or three other chiefs ran out from the grove, and the din increased ten fold.

Now, thought Toby, for a fray; and being unarmed, he besought one of the young men domiciled with Marheyo for the loan of his spear. But he was refused; the youth roguishly telling him that the weapon was very good for him (the Typee), but that a white man could fight much better with his fists.

The merry humor of this young wag seemed to be shared by the rest, for in spite of their warlike cries and gestures, everybody was capering about and laughing, as if it was one of the funniest things in the world to be awaiting the flight of a score or two of Happar javelins from an ambush in the thickets.

While my comrade was in vain trying to make out the meaning of all this, a good number of the natives separated themselves from the rest and ran off into the grove on one side, the others now keeping perfectly still, as if awaiting the result. After a little while, however, Mow-Mow, who stood in advance, motioned them to come on stealthily, which they did, scarcely rustling a leaf. Thus they crept along for ten or fifteen minutes, every now and then pausing to listen.

Toby by no means relished this sort of skulking; if there was going to be a fight he wanted it to begin at once. But all in good time,—for just then, as they went prowling into the thickest of the wood, terrific howls burst upon them on all sides, and volleys of darts and stones flew across the path. Not an enemy was to be seen, and what was still more surprising, not a single man dropped, though the pebbles fell among the leaves like hail.

There was a moment's pause, when the Typees, with wild shrieks, flung themselves into the covert, spear in hand; nor was Toby behindhand. Coming so near getting his skull broken by the stones, and animated by an old grudge he bore the Happars, he was among the first to dash at them. As he broke his way through the underbrush, trying, as he did so, to wrest a spear from a young chief, the shouts of battle all of a sudden ceased, and the wood was as still as death. The next moment, the party who had left them so mysteriously rushed out from behind every bush and tree, and united with the rest in long and merry peals of laughter.

It was all a sham, and Toby, who was quite out of breath with excitement, was much incensed at being made a fool of.

It afterwards turned out that the whole affair had been concerted for his particular benefit, though with what precise view it would be hard to tell. My comrade was the more enraged at this boys' play, since it had consumed so much time, every moment of which might be precious. Perhaps, however, it was partly intended for this very purpose; and he was led to think so, because, when the natives started again, he observed that they did not seem to be in so great a hurry as before. At last, after they had gone some distance, Toby, thinking all the while that they never would get to the sea, two men came running towards them, and a regular halt ensued, followed by a noisy discussion, during which Toby's name was often repeated. All this made him more and more anxious to learn what was going on at the beach; but it was in vain that he now tried to push forward; the natives held him back.

In a few moments the conference ended, and many of them ran down the path in the direction of the water, the rest surrounding Toby, and entreating him to "Moee," or sit down and rest himself. As an additional inducement, several calabashes of food, which had been brought along, were now placed on the ground, and opened, and pipes also were lighted. Toby bridled his impatience a while, but at last sprang to his feet and dashed forward again. He was soon overtaken nevertheless, and again surrounded, but without further detention was then permitted to go down to the sea.

They came out upon a bright green space between the groves and the water, and close under the shadow of the Happar mountain, where a path was seen, winding out of sight through a gorge.

No sign of a boat, however, was beheld; nothing but a tumultuous crowd of men and women, and some one in their midst, earnestly talking to them. As my comrade advanced, this person came forward and proved to be no stranger. He was an old grizzled sailor, whom Toby and myself had frequently seen in Nukuheva, where he lived an easy devil-may-care life in the household of Mowanna the king, going by the name of "Jimmy." In fact he was the royal favorite, and had a good deal to say in his master's councils. He wore a Manilla hat and a sort of tappa morning gown, sufficiently loose and negligent to show the verse of a song tatooed upon his chest, and a variety of spirited cuts by native artists in other parts of his body. He sported a fishing rod in his hand, and carried a sooty old pipe slung about his neck.

This old rover having retired from active life, had resided in Nukuheva some time—could speak the language, and for that reason was frequently employed by the French as an interpreter. He was an arrant old gossip too; for ever coming off in his canoe to the ships in the bay, and regaling their crews with choice little morsels of court scandal —such, for instance, as a shameful intrigue of his majesty with a Happar damsel, a public dancer at the feasts—and otherwise relating some incredible tales about the Marquesas generally. I remember in particular his telling the Dolly's crew what proved to be literally a cock-and-bull story, about two natural prodigies which he said were then on the island. One was an old monster of a hermit, having a marvellous reputation for sanctity, and reputed a famous sorcerer, who lived away off in a den among the mountains, where he hid from the world a great pair of horns that grew out of his temples. Notwithstanding his reputation for piety, this horrid old fellow was the terror of all the island round, being reported to come out from his retreat, and go a man-hunting every dark night. Some anonymous Paul Pry, too, coming down the mountain, once got a peep at his den, and found it full of bones. In short, he was a most unheard-of monster.

The other prodigy Jimmy told us about, was the younger son of a chief, who, although but just turned of ten, had entered upon holy orders, because his superstitious countrymen thought him especially intended for the priesthood from the fact of his having a comb on his head like a rooster. But this was not all; for still more wonderful to relate, the boy prided himself upon this strange crest, being actually endowed with a cock's voice, and frequently crowing over his peculiarity.

But to return to Toby. The moment he saw the old rover on the beach, he ran up to him, the natives following after, and forming a circle round them.

After welcoming him to the shore, Jimmy went on to tell him how that he knew all about our having run away from the ship, and being among the Typees. Indeed, he had been urged by Mowanna to come over to the valley, and after visiting his friends there, to bring us back with him, his royal master being exceedingly anxious to share with him the reward which had been held out for our capture. He, however, assured Toby that he had indignantly spurned the offer.

All this astonished my comrade not a little, as neither of us had entertained the least idea that any white man ever visited the Typees sociably. But Jimmy told him that such was the case nevertheless, although he seldom came into the bay, and scarcely ever went back from the beach. One of the priests of the valley, in some way or other connected with an old tatooed divine in Nukuheva, was a friend of his, and through him he was "taboo."

He said, moreover, that he was sometimes employed to come round to the bay, and engage fruit for ships lying in Nukuheva. In fact, he was now on that very errand, according to his own account, having just come across the mountains by the way of Happar. By noon of the next day the fruit would be heaped up in stacks on the beach, in readiness for the boats which he then intended to bring into the bay.

Jimmy now asked Toby whether he wished to leave the island—if he did, there was a ship in want of men lying in the other harbor, and he would be glad to take him over, and see him on board that very day.

"No," said Toby, "I cannot leave the island unless my comrade goes with me. I left him up the valley because they would not let him come down. Let us go now and fetch him."

"But how is he to cross the mountain with us," replied Jimmy, "even if we get him down to the beach? Better let him stay till to-morrow, and I will bring him round to Nukuheva in the boats."

"That will never do," said Toby, "but come along with me now, and let us get him down here at any rate;" and yielding to the impulse of the moment, he started to hurry back into the valley. But hardly was his back turned, when a dozen hands were laid on him, and he learned that he could not go a step further.

It was in vain that he fought with them; they would not hear of his stirring from the beach. Cut to the heart at this unexpected repulse, Toby now conjured the sailor to go after me alone. But Jimmy replied, that in the mood the

Typees then were they would not permit him so to do, though at the same time he was not afraid of their offering him any harm.

Little did Toby then think, as he afterwards had good reason to suspect, that this very Jimmy was a heartless villain, who, by his arts, had just incited the natives to restrain him as he was in the act of going after me. Well must the old sailor have known, too, that the natives would never consent to our leaving together, and he therefore wanted to get Toby off alone, for a purpose which he afterwards made plain. Of all this, however, my comrade now knew nothing.

He was still struggling with the islanders when Jimmy again came up to him, and warned him against irritating them, saying that he was only making matters worse for both of us, and if they became enraged, there was no telling what might happen. At last he made Toby sit down on a broken canoe by a pile of stones, upon which was a ruinous little shrine supported by four upright paddles, and in front partly screened by a net. The fishing parties met there, when they came in from the sea, for their offerings were laid before an image, upon a smooth black stone within. This spot Jimmy said was strictly "taboo," and no one would molest or come near him while he stayed by its shadow. The old sailor then went off, and began speaking very earnestly to Mow-Mow and some other chiefs, while all the rest formed a circle round the taboo place, looking intently at Toby, and talking to each other without ceasing.

Now, notwithstanding what Jimmy had just told him, there presently came up to my comrade an old woman, who seated herself beside him on the canoe.

"Typee mortarkee?" said she. "Mortarkee nuee," said Toby.

She then asked him whether he was going to Nukuheva; he nodded yes; and with a plaintive wail and her eyes filling with tears she rose and left him.

This old woman, the sailor afterwards said, was the wife of an aged king of a small inland valley, communicating by a deep pass with the country of the Typees. The inmates of the two valleys were related to each other by blood, and were known by the same name. The old woman had gone down into the Typee valley the day before, and was now with three chiefs, her sons, on a visit to her kinsmen.

As the old king's wife left him, Jimmy again came up to Toby, and told him that he had just talked the whole matter over with the natives, and there was only one course for him to follow. They would not allow him to go back into the valley, and harm would certainly come to both him and me, if he remained much longer on the beach. "So," said he, "you and I had better go to Nukuheva now overland, and to-morrow I will bring Tommo, as they call him, by water; they have promised to carry him down to the sea for me early in the morning, so that there will be no delay."

"No, no," said Toby desperately, "I will not leave him that way; we must escape together."

"Then there is no hope for you," exclaimed the sailor, "for if I leave you here on the beach, as soon as I am gone you will be carried back into the valley, and then neither of you will ever look upon the sea again." And with many oaths he swore that if he would only go to Nukuheva with him that day, he would be sure to have me there the very next morning.

"But how do you know they will bring him down to the beach to-morrow, when they will not do so to-day?" said Toby. But the sailor had many reasons, all of which were so mixed up with the mysterious customs of the islanders, that he was none the wiser. Indeed, their conduct, especially in preventing him from returning into the valley, was absolutely unaccountable to him; and added to everything else, was the bitter reflection, that the old sailor, after all, might possibly be deceiving him. And then again he had to think of me, left alone with the natives, and by no means well. If he went with Jimmy, he might at least hope to procure some relief for me. But might not the savages who had acted so strangely, hurry me off somewhere before his return? Then, even if he remained, perhaps they would not let him go back into the valley where I was.

Thus perplexed was my poor comrade; he knew not what to do, and his courageous spirit was of no use to him now. There he was, all by himself, seated upon the broken canoe—the natives grouped around him at a distance, and eyeing him more and more fixedly.

"It is getting late," said Jimmy, who was standing behind the rest. "Nukuheva is far off, and I cannot cross the Happar country by night. You see how it is:—if you come along with me, all will be well; if you do not, depend upon it, neither of you will ever escape."

"There is no help for it," said Toby, at last, with a heavy heart, "I will have to trust you;" and he came out from the shadow of the little shrine, and cast a long look up the valley.

"Now keep close to my side," said the sailor, "and let us be moving quickly." Tinor and Fayaway here appeared; the kind-hearted old woman embracing Toby's knees, and giving way to a flood of tears; while Fayaway, hardly less moved, spoke some few words of English she had learned, and held up three fingers before him—in so many days he would return.

At last Jimmy pulled Toby out of the crowd, and after calling to a young Typee who was standing by with a young pig in his arms, all three started for the mountains.

"I have told them that you are coming back again," said

the old fellow, laughing, as they began the ascent, "but they'll have to wait a long time." Toby turned, and saw the natives all in motion—the girls waving their tappas in adieu, and the men their spears. As the last figure entered the grove with one arm raised, and the three fingers spread, his heart smote him.

As the natives had at last consented to his going, it might have been, that some of them, at least, really counted upon his speedy return; probably supposing, as indeed he had told them when they were coming down the valley, that his only object in leaving them was to procure the medicines I needed. This, Jimmy also must have told them. And as they had done before, when my comrade, to oblige me, started on his perilous journey to Nukuheva, they looked upon me, in his absence, as one of two inseparable friends who was a sure guaranty for the other's return. This is only my own supposition, however, for as to all their strange conduct, it is still a mystery.

"You see what sort of a taboo man I am," said the sailor, after for some time silently following the path which led up the mountain. "Mow-Mow made me a present of this pig here, and the man who carries it will go right through Happar, and down into Nukuheva with us. So long as he stays by me he is safe, and just so it will be with you, and to-morrow with Tommo. Cheer up, then, and rely upon me, you will see him in the morning."

The ascent of the mountain was not very difficult, owing to its being near to the sea, where the island ridges are comparatively low; the path, too, was a fine one, so that in a short time all three were standing on the summit with the two valleys at their feet. The white cascades marking the green head of the Typee valley first caught Toby's eye; Marheyo's house could easily be traced by them.

As Jimmy led the way along the ridge, Toby observed that the valley of the Happars did not extend near so far inland as that of the Typees. This accounted for our mistake in entering the latter valley as we had.

A path leading down from the mountain was soon seen, and, following it, the party were in a short time fairly in the Happar valley.

"Now," said Jimmy, as they hurried on, "we taboo men have wives in all the bays, and I am going to show you the two I have here."

So, when they came to the house where he said they lived,—which was close by the base of the mountain in a shady nook among the groves,—he went in, and was quite furious at finding it empty—the ladies had gone out. However, they soon made their appearance, and, to tell the truth, welcomed Jimmy quite cordially, as well as Toby, about whom they were very inquisitive. Nevertheless, as the report of their arrival spread, and the Happars began to assemble, it became evident that the appearance of a white stranger among them was not by any means deemed so wonderful an event as in the neighboring valley.

The old sailor now bade his wives prepare something to eat, as he must be in Nukuheva before dark. A meal of fish, bread-fruit, and bananas, was accordingly served up, the party regaling themselves on the mats, in the midst of a numerous company.

The Happars put many questions to Jimmy about Toby; and Toby himself looked sharply at them, anxious to recognize the fellow who gave him the wound from which he was still suffering. But this fiery gentleman, so handy with his spear, had the delicacy, it seemed, to keep out of view. Certainly the sight of him would not have been any added inducement to making a stay in the valley,—some of the afternoon loungers in Happar having politely urged Toby to spend a few days with them,—there was a feast coming on. He, however, declined.

All this while the young Typee stuck to Jimmy like his

shadow, and though as lively a dog as any of his tribe, he was now as meek as a lamb, never opening his mouth except to eat. Although some of the Happars looked queerly at him, others were more civil, and seemed desirous of taking him abroad and showing him the valley. But the Typee was not to be cajoled in that way. How many yards he would have to remove from Jimmy before the taboo would be powerless, it would be hard to tell, but probably he himself knew to a fraction.

On the promise of a red cotton handkerchief, and something else which he kept secret, this poor fellow had undertaken a rather ticklish journey, though, as far as Toby could ascertain, it was something that had never happened before.

The island-punch—arva—was brought in at the conclusion of the repast, and passed round in a shallow calabash.

Now my comrade, while seated in the Happar house, began to feel more troubled than ever at leaving me: indeed, so sad did he feel that he talked about going back to the valley, and wanted Jimmy to escort him as far as the mountains. But the sailor would not listen to him, and, by way of diverting his thoughts, pressed him to drink of the arva. Knowing its narcotic nature, he refused; but Jimmy said he would have something mixed with it, which would convert it into an innocent beverage that would inspirit them for the rest of their journey. So at last he was induced to drink of it, and its effects were just as the sailor had predicted; his spirits rose at once, and all his gloomy thoughts left him.

The old rover now began to reveal his true character, though he was hardly suspected at the time. "If I get you off to a ship," said he, "you will surely give a poor fellow something for saving you." In short, before they left the house, he made Toby promise that he would give him five Spanish dollars if he succeeded in getting any part of his wages advanced from the vessel, aboard of which they were going; Toby, moreover, engaging to reward him still further, as soon as my deliverance was accomplished.

A little while after this they started again, accompanied by many of the natives, and going up the valley, took a steep path near its head, which led to Nukuheva. Here the Happars paused, and watched them as they ascended the mountain, one group of bandit-looking fellows, shaking their spears and casting threatening glances at the poor Typee, whose heart as well as heels seemed much the lighter when he came to look down upon them.

On gaining the heights once more, their way led for a time along several ridges covered with enormous ferns. At last they entered upon a wooded tract, and here they overtook a party of Nukuheva natives, well armed, and carrying bundles of long poles. Jimmy seemed to know them all very well, and stopped for a while, and had a talk about the "Wee-Wees," as the people of Nukuheva call the Monsieurs.

The party with the poles were King Mowanna's men, and by his orders they had been gathering them in the ravines for his allies the French.

Leaving these fellows to trudge on with their loads, Toby and his companions now pushed forward again, as the sun was already low in the west. They came upon the valleys of Nukuheva on one side of the bay, where the highlands slope off into the sea. The men-of-war were still lying in the harbor, and as Toby looked down upon them, the strange events which had happened so recently, seemed all a dream.

They soon descended towards the beach, and found themselves in Jimmy's house before it was well dark. Here he received another welcome from his Nukuheva wives, and after some refreshments in the shape of cocoa-nut milk and poee-poee, they entered a canoe (the Typee of course going along) and paddled off to a whale ship which was anchored near the shore. This was the vessel in want of men. Our own had sailed some time before. The captain professed great pleasure at seeing Toby, but thought from his exhausted appearance that he must be unfit for duty. However, he agreed to ship him, as well as his comrade, as soon as he should arrive.

Toby begged hard for an armed boat, in which to go round to Typee and rescue me, notwithstanding the promises of Jimmy. But this the captain would not hear of, and told him to have patience, for the sailor would be faithful to his word. When, too, he demanded the five silver dollars for Jimmy, the captain was unwilling to give them. But Toby insisted upon it, as he now began to think that Jimmy might be a mere mercenary, who would be sure to prove faithless if not well paid. Accordingly he not only gave him the money, but took care to assure him, over and over again, that as soon as he brought me aboard he would receive a still larger sum.

Before sun-rise the next day, Jimmy and the Typee started in two of the ship's boats, which were manned by tabooed natives. Toby, of course, was all eagerness to go along, but the sailor told him that if he did, it would spoil all; so, hard as it was, he was obliged to remain.

Towards evening he was on the watch, and descried the boats turning the headland and entering the bay. He strained his eyes, and thought he saw me; but I was not there. Descending from the mast almost distracted, he grappled Jimmy as he struck the deck, shouting in a voice that startled him, "Where is Tommo?" The old fellow faltered, but soon recovering, did all he could to soothe him, assuring him that it had proved to be impossible to get me down to the shore that morning; assigning many plausible reasons, and adding that early on the morrow he was going to visit the bay again in a French boat, when, if he did not find me on the beach—as this time he certainly expected to —he would march right back into the valley, and carry me away at all hazards. He, however, again refused to allow Toby to accompany him.

Now, situated as Toby was, his sole dependence for the present was upon this Jimmy, and therefore he was fain to comfort himself as well as he could with what the old sailor told him.

The next morning, however, he had the satisfaction of seeing the French boat start with Jimmy in it. To-night, then, I will see him, thought Toby; but many a long day passed before he ever saw Tommo again. Hardly was the boat out of sight, when the captain came forward and ordered the anchor weighed; he was going to sea.

Vain were all Toby's ravings,—they were disregarded; and when he came to himself, the sails were set, and the ship fast leaving the land.

* * * Oh! said he to me at our meeting, what sleepless nights were mine. Often I started from my hammock, dreaming you were before me, and upbraiding me for leaving you on the island.

* * * * * *

There is little more to be related. Toby left this vessel at New Zealand, and after some further adventures, arrived home in less than two years after leaving the Marquesas. He always thought of me as dead—and I had every reason to suppose that he too was no more; but a strange meeting was in store for us, one which made Toby's heart all the lighter.

BILLY BUDD
FORETOPMAN

What befell him
in the year of the
Great Mutiny
etc.

Dedicated

to

Jack Chase

Englishman

Wherever that great heart may now be
here on Earth or harbored in Paradise
Captain of the main-top in the year 1843
in the U. S. Frigate "United States."

Preface

THE year 1797, the year of this narrative, belongs to a period which as every thinker now feels, involved a crisis for Christendom not exceeded in its undetermined momentousness at the time by any other era whereof there is record. The opening proposition made by the Spirit of that Age, involved the rectification of the Old World's hereditary wrongs. In France to some extent this was bloodily effected. But what then? Straightway the Revolution itself became a wrongdoer, one more oppressive than the kings. Under Napoleon it enthroned upstart kings, and initiated that prolonged agony of continual war whose final throe was Waterloo. During those years not the wisest could have foreseen that the outcome of all would be what to some thinkers apparently it has since turned out to be, a political advance along nearly the whole line for Europeans.

Now, as elsewhere hinted, it was something caught from the Revolutionary Spirit that at Spithead emboldened the man-of-war's men to rise against real abuses, longstanding ones, and afterwards at the Nore to make inordinate and aggressive demands, successful resistance to which was confirmed only when the ringleaders were hung for an admonitory spectacle to the anchored fleet. Yet in a way analogous to the operation of the Revolution at large the Great Mutiny, though by Englishmen naturally deemed monstrous at the time, doubtless gave the first latent prompting to most important reforms in the British Navy.

Billy Budd
Foretopman
(An inside narrative.)

I

IN THE time before steamships, or then more frequently than now, a stroller along the docks of any considerable seaport would occasionally have his attention arrested by a group of bronzed mariners, man-of-war's men or merchant-sailors in holiday attire ashore on liberty. In certain instances they would flank, or, like a body-guard quite surround some superior figure of their own class, moving along with them like Aldebaran among the lesser lights of his constellation. That signal object was the "Handsome Sailor" of the less prosaic time alike of the military and merchant navies. With no perceptible trace of the vainglorious about him, rather with the off-hand unaffectedness of natural regality, he seemed to accept the spontaneous homage of his shipmates. A somewhat remarkable instance recurs to me. In Liverpool, now half a century ago I saw under the shadow of the great dingy street-wall of Prince's Dock (an obstruction long since removed) a common sailor, so intensely black that he must needs have been a native African of the unadulterate blood of Ham. A symmetric figure much above the average height. The two ends of a gay silk handkerchief thrown loose about the neck danced upon the displayed ebony of his chest; in his ears were big hoops of gold, and a Scotch Highland bonnet with a tartan band set off his shapely head.

It was a hot noon in July; and his face, lustrous with perspiration, beamed with barbaric good humor. In jovial sallies right and left his white teeth flashing into view, he rollicked along, the center of a company of his shipmates. These were made up of such an assortment of tribes and complexions as would have well fitted them to be marched up by Anacharsis Cloots before the bar of the first French Assembly as Representatives of the Human Race. At each spontaneous tribute rendered by the wayfarers to this black pagod of a fellow—the tribute of a pause and stare, and less frequent an exclamation,—the motley retinue showed that they took that sort of pride in the evoker of it which the Assyrian priests doubtless showed from their grand sculptured Bull when the faithful prostrated themselves.

To return.

If in some cases a bit of a nautical Murat in setting forth his person ashore, the handsome sailor of the period in question evinced nothing of the dandified Billy-be-Damn, an amusing character all but extinct now, but occasionally to be encountered, and in a form yet more amusing than the original, at the tiller of the boats on the tempestuous Erie Canal or, more likely, vaporing in the groggeries along the tow-path. Invariably a proficient in his perilous calling, he was also more or less of a mighty boxer or wrestler. It was strength and beauty. Tales of his prowess were recited. Ashore he was the champion; afloat the spokesman; on every suitable occasion always foremost. Close-reefing topsails in a gale, there he was, astride the weather yard-arm-end, foot in the Flemish horse as "stirrup," both hands tugging at the "ear-ring" as at a bridle, in very much the attitude of young Alexander curbing the fiery Bucephalus. A superb figure, tossed up as by the horns of Taurus against the thunderous sky, cheerily hallooing to the strenuous file along the spar.

The moral nature was seldom out of keeping with the physical make. Indeed, except as toned by the former, the comeliness and power, always attractive in masculine con-

junction, hardly could have drawn the sort of honest homage the Handsome Sailor in some examples received from
his less gifted associates.

Such a cynosure, at least in aspect, and something such
too in nature, though with important variations made apparent as the story proceeds, was welkin-eyed Billy Budd,
or Baby Budd as more familiarly under circumstances hereafter to be given he at last came to be called aged twenty-
one, a foretopman of the British fleet toward the close of
the last decade of the eighteenth century. It was not very
long prior to the time of the narration that follows that
he had entered the King's Service, having been impressed
on the Narrow Seas from a homeward-bound English merchantman into a seventy-four outward-bound, *H.M.S. Indomitable;* which ship, as was not unusual in those hurried days having been obliged to put to sea short of her
proper complement of men. Plump upon Billy at first sight
in the gangway the boarding officer Lieutenant Ratcliffe
pounced, even before the merchantman's crew was formally mustered on the quarter-deck for his deliberate
inspection. And him only he elected. For whether it was
because the other men when ranged before him showed
to ill advantage after Billy, or whether he had some scruples in view of the merchantman being rather short-
handed, however it might be, the officer contented himself
with his first spontaneous choice. To the surprise of the
ship's company, though much to the Lieutenant's satisfaction Billy made no demur. But, indeed, any demur would
have been as idle as the protest of a goldfinch popped into
a cage.

Noting this uncomplaining acquiescence, all but cheerful one might say, the shipmates turned a surprised glance
of silent reproach at the sailor. The shipmaster was one of
those worthy mortals found in every vocation even the
humbler ones—the sort of person whom everybody agrees

in calling "a respectable man." And—nor so strange to report as it may appear to be—though a ploughman of the troubled waters, life-long contending with the intractable elements, there was nothing this honest soul at heart loved better than simple peace and quiet. For the rest, he was fifty or thereabouts, a little inclined to corpulence, a prepossessing face, unwhiskered, and of an agreeable color —a rather full face, humanely intelligent in expression. On a fair day with a fair wind and all going well, a certain musical chime in his voice seemed to be the veritable unobstructed outcome of the innermost man. He had much prudence, much conscientiousness, and there were occasions when these virtues were the cause of overmuch disquietude in him. On a passage, so long as his craft was in any proximity to land, no sleep for Captain Graveling. He took to heart those serious responsibilities not so heavily borne by some shipmasters.

Now while Billy Budd was down in the forecastle getting his kit together, the *Indomitable's* lieutenant, burly and bluff, nowise disconcerted by Captain Graveling's omitting to proffer the customary hospitalities on an occasion so unwelcome to him, an omission simply caused by preoccupation of thought, unceremoniously invited himself into the cabin, and also to a flask from the spirit-locker, a receptacle which his experienced eye instantly discovered. In fact he was one of those sea-dogs in whom all the hardship and peril of naval life in the great prolonged wars of his time never impaired the natural instinct for sensuous enjoyment. His duty he always faithfully did; but duty is sometimes a dry obligation, and he was for irrigating its aridity whensoever possible with a fertilizing decoction of strong waters. For the cabin's proprietor there was nothing left but to play the part of the enforced host with whatever grace and alacrity were practicable. As necessary adjuncts to the flask, he silently placed tumbler and water-jug before the irrepressible guest. But excusing himself from partaking just then, he dismally watched the unembarrassed officer deliberately diluting his grog a little, then tossing it off in three swallows, pushing the empty tumbler away, yet not so far as to be beyond easy reach, at the same time settling himself in his seat and smacking his lips with high satisfaction, looking straight at the host.

These proceedings over, the Master broke the silence; and there lurked a rueful reproach in the tone of his voice; "Lieutenant, you are going to take my best man from me, the jewel of 'em."

"Yes, I know" rejoined the other, immediately drawing back the tumbler preliminary to a replenishing; "Yes I know. Sorry."

"Beg pardon, but you don't understand, Lieutenant. See here now. Before I shipped that young fellow, my forecastle was a rat-pit of quarrels. It was black times, I tell you, aboard the *'Rights'* here. I was worried to that degree my pipe had no comfort for me. But Billy came; and it was like a Catholic priest striking peace in an Irish shindy. Not that he preached to them or said or did anything in particular; but a virtue went out of him, sugaring the sour ones. They took to him like hornets to treacle; all but the buffer of the gang, the big shaggy chap with the fire-red whiskers. He indeed out of envy, perhaps, of the newcomer, and thinking such a 'sweet and pleasant fellow,' as he mockingly designated him to the others, could hardly have the spirit of a game-cock, must needs bestir himself in trying to get up an ugly row with him. Billy forebore with him and reasoned with him in a pleasant way—he is something like myself, lieutenant, to whom aught like a quarrel is hateful —but nothing served. So, in the second dog-watch one day the Red Whiskers in presence of the others, under pretence of showing Billy just whence a sirloin steak was cut —for the fellow had once been a butcher—insultingly gave

him a dig under the ribs. Quick as lightning Billy let fly
his arm. I dare say he never meant to do quite as much as
he did, but anyhow he gave the burly fool a terrible drubbing. It took about half a minute, I should think. And,
Lord bless you, the lubber was astonished at the celerity.
And will you believe it, Lieutenant, the Red Whiskers now
really loves Billy—loves him, or is the biggest hypocrite
that ever I heard of. But they all love him. Some of 'em do
his washing, darn his old trousers for him; the carpenter
is at odd times making a pretty little chest of drawers for
him. Anybody will do anything for Billy Budd; and it's the
happy family here. But now Lieutenant, if that young fellow goes—I know how it will be aboard the '*Rights.*' Not
again very soon shall I, coming up from dinner, lean over
the capstan smoking a quiet pipe—no, not very soon again,
I think. Ay, Lieutenant, you are going to take away the
jewel of 'em; you are going to take away my peacemaker!"
And with that the good soul had really some ado in check-
ing a rising sob.

"Well," said the officer who had listened with amused
interest to all this, and now waxing merry with his tipple;
"Well, blessed are the peacemakers especially the fighting
peacemakers! And such are the seventy-four beauties some
of which you see poking their noses out of the port-holes
of yonder warship lying-to for me" pointing through the
cabin window at the *Indomitable*. "But courage! don't look
so downhearted, man. Why, I pledge you in advance the
royal approbation. Rest assured that His Majesty will be
delighted to know that in a time when his hardtack is not
sought for by sailors with such avidity as should be; a time
also when some shipmasters privily resent the borrowing
from them a tar or two for the sevice; His Majesty, I say,
will be delighted to learn that *one* shipmaster at least cheerfully surrenders to the King, the flower of his flock, a sailor
who with equal loyalty makes no dissent.—But where's

my beauty? Ah," looking through the cabin's open door "Here he comes; and, by Jove—lugging along his chest— Apollo with his portmanteau!—My man," stepping out to him, "you can't take that big box aboard a warship. The boxes there are mostly shot-boxes. Put your duds in a bag, lad. Boot and saddle for the cavalryman, bag and hammock for the man-of-war's man."

The transfer from chest to bag was made. And, after seeing his man into the cutter and then following him down, the lieutenant pushed off from the *Rights-of-Man*. That was the merchant ship's name; though by her master and crew abbreviated in sailor fashion into *The Rights*. The hard-headed Dundee owner was a staunch admirer of Thomas Paine whose book in rejoinder to Burke's arraignment of the French Revolution had then been published for some time and had gone everywhere. In christening his vessel after the title of Paine's volume the man of Dundee was something like his contemporary shipowner, Stephen Girard of Philadelphia, whose sympathies, alike with his native land and its liberal philosophers, he evinced by naming his ships after Voltaire, Diderot, and so forth.

But now, when the boat swept under the merchantman's stern, and officer and oarsmen were noting—some bitterly and others with a grin,—the name emblazoned there; just then it was that the new recruit jumped up from the bow where the coxswain had directed him to sit, and waving his hat to his silent shipmates sorrowfully looking over at him from the taffrail, bade the lads a genial good-bye. Then making a salutation as to the ship herself, "And good-bye to you too, old *Rights of Man!*"

"Down, Sir!" roared the lieutenant, instantly assuming all the rigor of his rank, though with difficulty repressing a smile.

To be sure, Billy's action was a terrible breach of naval decorum. But in that decorum he had never been instructed; in consideration of which the lieutenant would hardly have been so energetic in reproof but for the concluding farewell to the ship. This he rather took as meant to convey a covert sally on the new recruit's part, a sly slur at impressment in general, and that of himself in especial. And yet, more likely, if satire it was in effect, it was hardly so by intention, for Billy, though happily endowed with the gaiety of high health, youth and a free heart, was yet by no means of a satirical turn. The will to it and the sinister dexterity were alike wanting. To deal in double meaning and insinuations of any sort was quite foreign to his nature.

As to his enforced enlistment, that he seemed to take pretty much as he was wont to take any vicissitude of weather. Like the animals, though no philosopher, he was, without knowing it, practically a fatalist. And, it may be, that he rather liked this adventurous turn in his affairs, which promised an opening into novel scenes and martial excitements.

Aboard the *Indomitable* our merchant-sailor was forthwith rated as an able-seaman and assigned to the starboard watch of the foretop. He was soon at home in the service, not at all disliked for his unpretentious good looks and a sort of genial happy-go-lucky air. No merrier man in his mess: in marked contrast to certain other individuals included like himself among the impressed portion of the ship's company; for these when not actively employed were sometimes, and more particularly in the last dog-watch when the drawing near of twilight induced revery, apt to fall into a saddish mood which in some partook of sullenness. But they were not so young as our foretopman, and no few of them must have known a hearth of some sort, others may have had wives and children left, too probably, in uncertain circumstances, and hardly any but must have had acknowledged kith and kin, while for Billy, as will shortly be seen, his entire family was practically invested in himself.

2

THOUGH our new-made foretopman was well received in the top and on the gun-decks, hardly here was he that cynosure he had previously been among those minor ship's companies of the merchant marine, with which companies only had he hitherto consorted.

He was young; and despite his all but fully developed frame in aspect looked even younger than he really was, owing to a lingering adolescent expression in the as yet smooth face all but feminine in purity in natural complexion but where, thanks to his seagoing, the lily was quite suppressed and the rose had some ado visibly to flush through the tan.

To one essentially such a novice in the complexities of factious life, the abrupt transition from his former and simpler sphere to the ampler and more knowing world of a great warship; this might well have abashed him had there been any conceit or vanity in his composition. Among her miscellaneous multitude, the *Indomitable* mustered several individuals who however inferior in grade were of no common natural stamp, sailors more signally susceptive of that air which continuous martial discipline and repeated presence in battle can in some degree impart even to the average man. As the *handsome sailor* Billy Budd's position aboard the seventy-four was something analogous to that of a rustic beauty transplanted from the provinces and brought into competition with the high-born dames of the court. But this change of circumstances he scarce noted. As little did he observe that something about him provoked an ambiguous smile in one or two harder faces among the blue-jackets. Nor less unaware was he of the peculiar fa-

vorable effect his person and demeanor had upon the more
intelligent gentlemen of the quarter-deck. Nor could this
well have been otherwise. Cast in a mould peculiar to the
finest physical examples of those Englishmen in whom the
Saxon strain would seem not at all to partake of any Nor-
man or other admixture, he showed in face that humane
look of reposeful good nature which the Greek sculptor in
some instances gave to his heroic strong man, Hercules.
But this again was subtly modified by another and perva-
sive quality. The ear, small and shapely, the arch of the
foot, the curve in mouth and nostril, even the indurated
hand dyed to the orange-tawny of the toucan's bill, a hand
telling alike of the halyards and tar-bucket; but, above all,
something in the mobile expression, and every chance attitude and movement, something suggestive of a mother
eminently favored by Love and the Graces; all this strangely
indicated a lineage in direct contradiction to his lot.
The mysteriousness here, became less mysterious through a
matter-of-fact elicited when Billy at the capstan was being
formally mustered into the service. Asked by the officer, a
small brisk little gentleman as it chanced among other
questions, his place of birth, he replied, "Please, Sir, I
don't know."

"Don't know where you were born?—Who was your
father?"

"God knows, Sir."

Struck by the straightforward simplicity of these replies,
the officer next asked "Do you know anything about your
beginning?"

"No, Sir. But I have heard that I was found in a pretty
silk-lined basket hanging one morning from the knocker
of a good man's door in Bristol."

"*Found* say you? Well," throwing back his head and
looking up and down the new recruit; "Well it turns out to

have been a pretty good find. Hope they'll find some more like you, my man; the fleet sadly needs them."

Yes, Billy Budd was a foundling, a presumable bye-blow, and, evidently, no ignoble one. Noble descent was as evident in him as in a blood horse.

For the rest, with little or no sharpness of faculty or any trace of the wisdom of the serpent, nor yet quite a dove, he possessed that kind and degree of intelligence going along with the unconventional rectitude of a sound human creature, one to whom not yet has been proffered the questionable apple of knowledge. He was illiterate; he could not read, but he could sing, and like the illiterate nightingale was sometimes the composer of his own song.

Of self-consciousness he seemed to have little or none, or about as much as we may reasonably impute to a dog of St. Bernard's breed.

Habitually living with the elements and knowing little more of the land than as a beach, or, rather, that portion of the terraqueous globe providentially set apart for dance-houses doxies and tapsters, in short what sailors call a "fiddlers' green," his simple nature remained unsophisticated by those moral obliquities which are not in every case incompatible with that manufacturable thing known as respectability. But are sailors, frequenters of "fiddlers' greens," without vices? No; but less often than with landsmen do their vices, so called, partake of crookedness of heart, seeming less to proceed from viciousness than exuberance of vitality after long constraint; frank manifestations in accordance with natural law. By his original constitution aided by the coöperating influences of his lot, Billy in many respects, was little more than a sort of upright barbarian, much such perhaps as Adam presumably might have been ere the urbane Serpent wriggled himself into his company.

And here be it submitted that apparently going to corroborate the doctrine of man's fall, a doctrine now popularly ignored, it is observable that where certain virtues pristine and unadulterate peculiarly characterize anybody in the external uniform of civilization, they will upon scrutiny seem not to be derived from custom or convention but rather to be out of keeping with these, as if indeed exceptionally transmitted from a period prior to Cain's city and citified man. The character marked by such qualities has to an unvitiated taste an untampered-with flavor like that of berries while the man thoroughly civilized even in a fair specimen of the breed has to the same moral palate a questionable smack as of a compounded wine. To any stray inheritor of these primitive qualities found, like Caspar Hauser, wandering dazed in any Christian capital of our time the good-natured poet's famous invocation, near two thousand years ago, of the good rustic out of his latitude in the Rome of the Caesars, still appropriately holds:—

> "Honest and poor, faithful in word and thought,
> What has thee, Fabian, to the city brought."

Though our Handsome Sailor had as much of masculine beauty as one can expect anywhere to see; nevertheless, like the beautiful woman in one of Hawthorne's minor tales, there was just one thing amiss in him. No visible blemish, indeed, as with the lady; no, but an occasional liability to a vocal defect. Though in the hour of elemental uproar or peril, he was everything that a sailor should be, yet under sudden provocation of strong heart-feeling his voice otherwise singularly musical, as if expressive of the harmony within, was apt to develop an organic hesitancy, in fact more or less of a stutter or even worse. In this particular Billy was a striking instance that the arch interferer, the envious marplot of Eden still has more or less to do with every human consignment to this planet of earth. In every case, one way or another he is sure to slip in his little card, as much as to remind us—I too have a hand here.

The avowal of such an imperfection in the Handsome Sailor should be evidence not alone that he is not presented as a conventional hero, but also that the story in which he is the main figure is no romance.

3

At the time of Billy Budd's arbitrary enlistment into the *Indomitable* that ship was on her way to join the Mediterranean fleet. No long time elapsed before the junction was effected. As one of that fleet the seventy-four participated in its movements, though at times on account of her superior sailing qualities, in the absence of frigates, despatched on separate duty as a scout and at times on less temporary service. But with all this the story has little concernment, restricted as it is to the inner life of one particular ship and the career of an individual sailor.

It was the summer of 1797. In the April of that year had occurred the commotion at Spithead followed in May by a second and yet more serious outbreak in the fleet at the Nore. The latter is known, and without exaggeration in the epithet, as the Great Mutiny. It was indeed a demonstration more menacing to England than the contemporary manifestoes and conquering and proselyting armies of the French Directory.

To the British Empire the Nore Mutiny was what a strike in the fire-brigade would be to London threatened by general arson. In a crisis when the Kingdom might well have anticipated the famous signal that some years later published along the naval line of battle what it was that upon occasion England expected of Englishmen; *that* was the time when at the mast-heads of the three-deckers and seventy-fours moored in her own roadstead—a fleet, the right arm of a Power then all but the sole free conservative one of the Old World, the blue-jackets, to be numbered by thousands, ran up with huzzas the British colors with the union and cross wiped out; by that cancellation transmuting the flag of founded law and freedom defined, into the enemy's red meteor of unbridled and unbounded revolt. Reasonable discontent growing out of practical grievances in the fleet had been ignited into irrational combustion as by live cinders blown across the Channel from France in flames.

The event converted into irony for a time those spirited strains of Dibdin—as a song-writer no mean auxiliary to the English Government at the European conjuncture—strains celebrating, among other things, the patriotic devotion of the British tar:

> *"And as for my life, 'tis the King's!"*

Such an episode in the Island's grand naval story her naval historians naturally abridge; one of them (G. P. R. James) candidly acknowledging that fain would he pass it over did not "impartiality forbid fastidiousness." And yet his mention is less a narration than a reference, having to do hardly at all with details. Nor are these readily to be found in the libraries. Like some other events in every age befalling states everywhere including America the Great Mutiny was of such character that national pride along with views of policy would fain shade it off into the historical background. Such events cannot be ignored, but there is a considerate way of historically treating them. If a well-constituted individual refrains from blazoning aught amiss or calamitous in his family; a nation in the like circumstance may without reproach be equally discreet.

Though after parleyings between Government and the ring-leaders, and concessions by the former as to some glar-

ing abuses, the first uprising—that at Spithead—with difficulty was put down, or matters for a time pacified; yet at
the Nore the unforeseen renewal of insurrection on a yet
larger scale, and emphasized in the conferences that ensued
by demands deemed by the authorities not only inadmis-
sible but aggressively insolent, indicated—if the red flag did
not sufficiently do so, what was the spirit animating the
men. Final suppression, however, there was; but only
made possible perhaps by the unswerving loyalty of the
marine corps a voluntary resumption of loyalty among influential sections of the crews.

To some extent the Nore Mutiny may be regarded as
analogous to the distempering irruption of contagious fever
in a frame constitutionally sound, and which anon throws
it off.

At all events, of these thousands of mutineers were some
of the tars who not so very long afterwards—whether
wholly prompted thereto by patriotism, or pugnacious instinct, or by both,—helped to win a coronet for Nelson at
the Nile, and the naval crown of crowns for him at Trafalgar. To the mutineers those battles and especially Trafalgar were a plenary absolution; and a grand one; for all that
goes to make up scenic naval display and heroic magnificence in arms, those battles especially Trafalgar stand
unmatched in human annals.

4

Concerning "The greatest sailor since the
world began"—Tennyson?

IN THIS matter of writing, resolve as one may to keep to the
main road, some by-paths have an enticement not readily
to be withstood. I am going to err into such a by-path. If
the reader will keep me company I shall be glad. At the

least we can promise ourselves that pleasure which is wickedly said to be in sinning, for a literary sin the divergence will be.

Very likely it is no new remark that the inventions of our time have at last brought about a change in sea-warfare in degree corresponding to the revolution in all warfare effected by the original introduction from China into Europe of gunpowder. The first European fire-arm, a clumsy contrivance, was, as is well known, scouted by no few of the knights as a base implement good enough peradventure for weavers too craven to stand up crossing steel with steel in frank fight. But as ashore knightly valor though shorn of its blazonry did not cease with the knights, neither on the seas though nowadays in encounters there a certain kind of displayed gallantry be fallen out of date as hardly applicable under changed circumstances, did the nobler qualities of such naval magnates as Don John of Austria, Doria, Van Tromp, Jean Bart, the long line of British admirals and the American Decaturs of 1812 become obsolete with their wooden walls.

Nevertheless, to anybody who can hold the Present at its worth without being inappreciative of the Past, it may be forgiven, if to such an one the solitary old hulk at Portsmouth, Nelson's *Victory,* seems to float there, not alone as the decaying monument of a fame incorruptible, but also as a poetic reproach, softened by its picturesqueness, to the *Monitors* and yet mightier hulls of the European ironclads. And this not altogether because such craft are unsightly, unavoidably lacking the symmetry and grand lines of the old battleships, but equally for other reasons.

There are some, perhaps, who while not altogether inaccessible to that poetic reproach just alluded to, may yet on behalf of the new order, be disposed to parry it; and this to the extent of iconoclasm, if need be. For example, prompted by the sight of the star inserted in the *Victory's* quarter-deck designating the spot where the Great Sailor fell, these martial utilitarians may suggest considerations implying that Nelson's ornate publication of his person in battle was not only unnecessary, but not military, nay, savored of foolhardiness and vanity. They may add, too, that at Trafalgar it was in effect nothing less than a challenge to death; and death came; and that but for his bravado the victorious admiral might possibly have survived the battle, and so, instead of having his sagacious dying injunctions overruled by his immediate successor in command he himself when the contest was decided might have brought his shattered fleet to anchor, a proceeding which might have averted the deplorable loss of life by shipwreck in the elemental tempest that followed the martial one.

Well, should we set aside the more disputable point whether for various reasons it was possible to anchor the fleet, then plausibly enough the Benthamites of war may urge the above.

But the *might-have-been* is but boggy ground to build on. And certainly in foresight as to the larger issue of an encounter, and anxious preparations for it—buoying the deadly way and mapping it out, as at Copenhagen—few commanders have been so painstakingly circumspect as this same reckless declarer of his person in fight.

Personal prudence even when dictated by quite other than selfish considerations surely is no special virtue in a military man; while an excessive love of glory, impassioning a less burning impulse the honest sense of duty, is the first. If the name *Wellington* is not so much of a trumpet to the blood as the simpler name *Nelson*, the reason for this may perhaps be inferred from the above. Alfred in his funeral ode on the victor of Waterloo ventures not to call him the greatest soldier of all time, though in the same ode he invokes Nelson as "the greatest sailor since the world began."

At Trafalgar Nelson on the brink of opening the fight sat down and wrote his last brief will and testament. If under the presentiment of the most magnificent of all victories to be crowned by his own glorious death, a sort of priestly motive led him to dress his person in the jewelled vouchers of his own shining deeds; if thus to have adorned himself for the altar and the sacrifice were indeed vainglory, then affectation and fustian is each more heroic line in the great epics and dramas, since in such lines the poet but embodies in verse those exaltations of sentiment that a nature like Nelson, the opportunity being given, vitalizes into acts.

5

Yes, the outbreak at the Nore was put down. But not every grievance was redressed. If the contractors, for example, were no longer permitted to ply some practices peculiar to their tribe everywhere, such as providing shoddy cloth, rations not sound, or false in the measure; not the less impressment, for one thing, went on. By custom sanctioned for centuries, and judicially maintained by a Lord Chancellor as late as Mansfield, that mode of manning the fleet, a mode now fallen into a sort of abeyance but never formally renounced, it was not practicable to give up in those years. Its abrogation would have crippled the indispensable fleet, one wholly under canvas, no steam-power, its innumerable sails and thousands of cannon, everything in short, worked by muscle alone; a fleet the more insatiate in demand for men, because then multiplying its ships of all grades against contingencies present and to come of the convulsed Continent.

Discontent foreran the Two Mutinies, and more or less it lurkingly survived them. Hence it was not unreasonable to apprehend some return of trouble sporadic or general. One instance of such apprehensions: In the same year with this story, Nelson, then Vice-Admiral Sir Horatio, being with the fleet off the Spanish coast, was directed by the Admiral in command to shift his pennant from the *Captain* to the *Theseus;* and for this reason: that the latter ship having newly arrived on the station from home where it had taken part in the Great Mutiny, danger was apprehended from the temper of the men; and it was thought that an officer like Nelson was the one, not indeed to terrorize the crew into base subjection, but to win them, by force of his mere presence back to an allegiance if not as enthusiastic as his own, yet as true. So it was that for a time on more than one quarter-deck anxiety did exist. At sea precautionary vigilance was strained against relapse. At short notice an engagement might come on. When it did, the lieutenants assigned to batteries felt it incumbent on them, in some instances to stand with drawn swords behind the men working the guns.

6

BUT on board the seventy-four in which Billy now swung his hammock, very little in the manner of the men and nothing obvious in the demeanor of the officers would have suggested to an ordinary observer that the Great Mutiny was a recent event. In their general bearing and conduct the commissioned officers of a warship naturally take their tone from the commander, that is if he have that ascendancy of character that ought to be his.

Captain the Honorable Edward Fairfax Vere, to give his full title, was a bachelor of forty or thereabouts, a sailor of distinction even in a time prolific of renowned seamen. Though allied to the higher nobility his advancement had not been altogether owing to influences connected with that circumstance. He had seen much service, been in various engagements, always acquitting himself as an officer mindful of the welfare of his men, but never tolerating an infraction of discipline; thoroughly versed in the science of his profession, and intrepid to the verge of temerity, though never injudiciously so. For his gallantry in the West Indian waters as flag-lieutenant under Rodney in that Admiral's crowning victory over De Grasse, he was made a post-captain.

Ashore in the garb of a civilian scarce any one would have taken him for a sailor, more especially that he never garnished unprofessional talk with nautical terms, and grave in his bearing, evinced little appreciation of mere humor. It was not out of keeping with these traits that on a passage when nothing demanded his paramount action, he was the most undemonstrative of men. Any landsman observing this gentleman not conspicuous by his stature and wearing no pronounced insignia, emerging from his cabin to the open deck and noting the silent deference of the officers retiring to leeward, might have taken him for the King's guest, a civilian aboard the King's ship, some highly honorable discreet envoy on his way to an important post. But in fact this unobtrusiveness of demeanor may have proceeded from a certain unaffected modesty of manhood sometimes accompanying a resolute nature, a modesty evinced at all times not calling for pronounced action, and which shown in any rank of life suggests a virtue aristocratic in kind.

As with some others engaged in various departments of the world's more heroic activities, Captain Vere though practical enough upon occasion would at times betray a certain dreaminess of mood. Standing alone on the weather-side of the quarter-deck, one hand holding by the rigging he would absently gaze off at the blank sea. At the presentation to him then of some minor matter interrupting the current of his thoughts he would show more or less irascibility; but instantly he would control it.

In the navy he was popularly known by the appellation —Starry Vere. How such a designation happened to fall upon one who whatever his sturdy qualities was without any brilliant ones was in this wise: A favorite kinsman, Lord Denton, a free-hearted fellow, had been the first to meet and congratulate him upon his return to England from his West Indian cruise; and but the day previous turning over a copy of Andrew Marvell's poems had lighted, not for the first time however, upon the lines entitled *Appleton House*, the name of one of the seats of their common ancestor, a hero in the German wars of the seventeenth century, in which poem occur the lines,

> "This 'tis to have been from the first
> In a domestic heaven nursed,
> Under the discipline severe
> Of Fairfax and the starry Vere."

And so, upon embracing his cousin fresh from Rodney's victory wherein he had played so gallant a part, brimming over with just family pride in the sailor of their house, he exuberantly exclaimed, "Give ye joy, Ed; give ye joy, my starry Vere!" This got currency, and the novel prefix serving in familiar parlance readily to distinguish the *Indomitable's* Captain from another Vere his senior, a distant relative an officer of like rank in the navy, it remained permanently attached to the surname.

7

IN VIEW of the part that the Commander of the *Indomitable* plays in scenes shortly to follow, it may be well to fill out that sketch of him outlined in the previous chapter. Aside from his qualities as a sea-officer Captain Vere was an exceptional character. Unlike no few of England's renowned sailors, long and arduous service with signal devotion to it, had not resulted in absorbing and *salting* the entire man. He had a marked leaning toward everything intellectual. He loved books, never going to sea without a newly replenished library, compact but of the best. The isolated leisure, in some cases so wearisome, falling at intervals to commanders even during a war-cruise, never was tedious to Captain Vere. With nothing of that literary taste which less heeds the thing conveyed than the vehicle, his bias was toward those books to which every serious mind of superior order occupying any active post of authority in the world, naturally inclines; books treating of actual men and events no matter of what era—history, biography and unconventional writers, who, free from cant and convention, like Montaigne, honestly, and in the spirit of common sense philosophize upon realities.

In this love of reading he found confirmation of his own more reserved thoughts—confirmation which he had vainly sought in social converse, so that as touching most fundamental topics, there had got to be established in him some positive convictions which he forefelt would abide in him essentially unmodified so long as his intelligent part remained unimpaired. In view of the troubled period in which his lot was cast this was well for him. His settled convictions were as a dyke against those invading waters of novel opinion social political and otherwise, which carried away as in a torrent no few minds in those days, minds by nature not inferior to his own. While other members of that aristocracy to which by birth he belonged were incensed at the innovators mainly because their theories were inimical to the privileged classes, not alone Captain Vere disinterestedly opposed them because they seemed to him incapable of embodiment in lasting institutions, but at war with the peace of the world and the true welfare of mankind.

With minds less stored than his and less earnest, some

officers of his rank, with whom at times he would necessarily consort, found him lacking in the companionable quality, a dry and bookish gentleman as they deemed. Upon any chance withdrawal from their company one would be apt to say to another something like this: "Vere is a noble fellow, Starry Vere. 'Spite the gazettes, Sir Horatio" meaning him with the Lord title "is at bottom scarce a better seaman or fighter. But between you and me now don't you think there is a queer streak of the pedantic running through him? Yes, like the King's yarn in a coil of navy-rope?"

Some apparent ground there was for this sort of confidential criticism; since not only did the Captain's discourse never fall into the jocosely familiar, but in illustrating of any point touching the stirring personages and events of the time he would be as apt to cite some historic character or incident of antiquity as that he would cite from the moderns. He seemed unmindful of the circumstance that to his bluff company such remote allusions however pertinent they might really be were altogether alien to men whose reading was mainly confined to the journals. But considerateness in such matters is not easy to natures constituted like Captain Vere's. Their honesty prescribes to them directness, sometimes far-reaching like that of a migratory fowl that in its flight never heeds when it crosses a frontier.

8

THE lieutenants and other commissioned gentlemen forming Captain Vere's staff it is not necessary here to particularize nor needs it to make any mention of any of the warrant-officers. But among the petty officers was one who having much to do with the story, may as well be forthwith introduced. This portrait I essay, but shall never hit it. This was John Claggart, the Master-at-arms. But that sea-title may to landsmen seem somewhat equivocal. Originally doubtless that petty-officer's function was the instruction of the men in the use of arms, sword or cutlass. But very long ago, owing to the advance in gunnery making hand-to-hand encounters less frequent and giving to nitre and sulphur the pre-eminence over steel, that function ceased; the master-at-arms of a great warship becoming a sort of Chief of Police charged among other matters with the duty of preserving order on the populous lower gun-decks.

Claggart was a man of about five-and-thirty, somewhat spare and tall, yet of no ill figure upon the whole. His hand was too small and shapely to have been accustomed to hard toil. The face was a notable one; the features all except the chin cleanly cut as those on a Greek medallion; yet the chin, beardless as Tecumseh's, had something of strange protuberant heaviness in its make that recalled the prints of the Rev. Dr. Titus Oates, the historic deponent with the clerical drawl in the time of Charles II and the fraud of the alleged Popish Plot. It served Claggart in his office that his eye could cast a tutoring glance. His brow was of the sort phrenologically associated with more than average intellect; silken jet curls partly clustering over it, making a foil to the pallor below, a pallor tinged with a faint shade of amber akin to the hue of time-tinted marbles of old. This complexion, singularly contrasting with the red or deeply bronzed visages of the sailors, and in part the result of his official seclusion from the sunlight, though it was not exactly displeasing, nevertheless seemed to hint of something defective or abnormal in the constitution and blood. But his general aspect and manner were so suggestive of an education and career incongruous with his naval function that when not actively engaged in it he looked like a man of high quality, social and moral, who for reasons of his own was keeping incog. Nothing was known of his former life. It might be that he was an Englishman;

and yet there lurked a bit of accent in his speech suggesting
that possibly he was not such by birth, but through natural-
ization in early childhood. Among certain grizzled sea-gos-
sips of the gun-decks and forecastle went a rumor perdue
that the master-at-arms was a *chevalier* who had volunteered
into the King's navy by way of compounding for some
mysterious swindle whereof he had been arraigned at the
King's Bench. The fact that nobody could substantiate this
report was, of course, nothing against its secret currency.
Such a rumor once started on the gun-decks in reference
to almost anyone below the rank of a commissioned officer
would, during the period assigned to this narrative, have
seemed not altogether wanting in credibility to the tarry
old wiseacres of a man-of-war crew. And indeed a man of
Claggart's accomplishments, without prior nautical experience entering the navy at mature life, as he did, and necessarily allotted at the start to the lowest grade in it; a man
too who never made allusion to his previous life ashore;
these were circumstances which in the dearth of exact
knowledge as to his true antecedents opened to the invidious a vague field for unfavorable surmise.

But the sailors' dog-watch gossip concerning him derived
a vague plausibility from the fact that now for some period
the British Navy could so little afford to be squeamish in
the matter of keeping up the muster-rolls, that not only
were press-gangs notoriously abroad both afloat and ashore,
but there was little or no secret about another matter,
namely that the London police were at liberty to capture
any able-bodied suspect, any questionable fellow at large
and summarily ship him to the dock-yard or fleet. Furthermore, even among voluntary enlistments there were
instances where the motive thereto partook neither of patriotic impulse nor yet of a random desire to experience a
bit of sea-life and martial adventure. Insolvent debtors of
minor grade, together with the promiscuous lame ducks of

morality found in the navy a convenient and secure refuge. Secure, because once enlisted aboard a King's-Ship, they were as much in sanctuary, as the transgressor of the middle ages harboring himself under the shadow of the altar. Such sanctioned irregularities which for obvious reasons the Government would hardly think to parade at the time and which consequently, and as affecting the least influential class of mankind, have all but dropped into oblivion lend color to something for the truth whereof I do not vouch, and hence have some scruple in stating; something I remember having seen in print, though the book I cannot recall; but the same thing was personally communicated to me now more than forty years ago by an old pensioner in a cocked hat with whom I had a most interesting talk on the terrace at Greenwich, a Baltimore negro, a Trafalgar man. It was to this effect: In the case of a warship short of hands whose speedy sailing was imperative, the deficient quota in lack of any other way of making it good, would be eked out by drafts culled direct from the jails. For reasons previously suggested it would not perhaps be easy at the present day directly to prove or disprove the allegation. But allowed as a verity, how significant would it be of England's straits at the time confronted by those wars which like a flight of harpies rose shrieking from the din and dust of the fallen Bastille. That era appears measurably clear to us who look back at it, and but read of it. But to the grandfathers of us gray-beards, the more thoughtful of them, the genius of it presented an aspect like that of Camoëns' Spirit of the Cape, an eclipsing menace mysterious and prodigious. Not America was exempt from apprehension. At the height of Napoleon's unexampled conquests, there were Americans who had fought at Bunker Hill who looked forward to the possibility that the Atlantic might prove no barrier against the ultimate schemes of this French portentous upstart from the revolutionary chaos who seemed in act of fulfilling judgment prefigured in the Apocalypse.

But the less credence was to be given to the gun-deck talk touching Claggart, seeing that no man holding his office in a man-of-war can ever hope to be popular with the crew. Besides, in derogatory comments upon anyone against whom they have a grudge, or for any reason or no reason mislike, sailors are much like landsmen, they are apt to exaggerate or romance it.

About as much was really known to the *Indomitable's* tars of the master-at-arms' career before entering the service as an astronomer knows about a comet's travels prior to its first observable appearance in the sky. The verdict of the sea quidnunc's has been cited only by way of showing what sort of moral impression the man made upon rude uncultivated natures whose conceptions of human wickedness were necessarily of the narrowest, limited to ideas of vulgar rascality,—a thief among the swinging hammocks during a night-watch, or the man-brokers and land-sharks of the sea-ports.

It was no gossip, however, but fact, that though, as before hinted, Claggart upon his entrance into the navy was, as a novice, assigned to the least honorable section of a man-of-war's crew, embracing the drudgery, he did not long remain there.

The superior capacity he immediately evinced, his constitutional sobriety, ingratiating deference to superiors, together with a peculiar ferreting genius manifested on a singular occasion, all this capped by a certain austere patriotism abruptly advanced him to the position of master-at-arms.

Of this maritime Chief of Police the ship's corporals, so called, were the immediate subordinates, and compliant ones; and this, as is to be noted in some business departments ashore, almost to a degree inconsistent with entire moral volition. His place put various converging wires of

underground influence under the Chief's control, capable
when astutely worked through his understrappers of operating to the mysterious discomfort if nothing worse, of any
of the sea-commonalty.

9

LIFE in the foretop well agreed with Billy Budd. There,
when not actually engaged on the yards yet higher aloft,
the topmen, who as such had been picked out for youth
and activity, constituted an aerial club lounging at ease
against the smaller stunsails rolled up into cushions, spin-
ning yarns like the lazy gods, and frequently amused with
what was going on in the busy world of the decks below.
No wonder then that a young fellow of Billy's disposition
was well content in such society. Giving no cause of offense
to anybody, he was always alert at a call. So in the merchant service it had been with him. But now such a punc-
tiliousness in duty was shown that his topmates would
sometimes good-naturedly laugh at him for it. This heightened alacrity had its cause, namely, the impression made
upon him by the first formal gangway-punishment he had
ever witnessed, which befell the day following his impressment. It had been incurred by a little fellow, young, a
novice an after-guardsman absent from his assigned post
when the ship was being put about; a dereliction resulting
in a rather serious hitch to that maneuver, one demanding
instantaneous promptitude in letting go and making fast.
When Billy saw the culprit's naked back under the scourge
gridironed with red welts, and worse; when he marked
the dire expression on the liberated man's face as with his
woolen shirt flung over him by the executioner he rushed
forward from the spot to bury himself in the crowd, Billy
was horrified. He resolved that never through remissness
would he make himself liable to such a visitation or do or

omit aught that might merit even verbal reproof. What then was his surprise and concern when ultimately he found himself getting into petty trouble occasionally about such matters as the stowage of his bag or something amiss in his hammock, matters under the police oversight of the ship's corporals of the lower decks, and which brought down on him a vague threat from one of them.

So heedful in all things as he was, how could this be? He could not understand it, and it more than vexed him. When he spoke to his young topmates about it they were either lightly incredulous, or found something comical in his unconcealed anxiety. "Is it your bag, Billy?" said one "well, sew yourself up in it, bully boy, and then you'll be sure to know if anybody meddles with it."

Now there was a veteran aboard who because his years began to disqualify him for more active work had been recently assigned duty as mainmast-man in his watch, looking to the gear belayed at the rail roundabout that great spar near the deck. At off-times the foretopman had picked up some acquaintance with him, and now in his trouble it occurred to him that he might be the sort of person to go to for wise counsel. He was an old Dansker long anglicized in the service, of few words, many wrinkles and some honorable scars. His wizened face, time-tinted and weather-stained to the complexion of an antique parchment, was here and there peppered blue by the chance explosion of a gun-cartridge in action. He was an *Agamemnon*-man; some two years prior to the time of this story having served under Nelson, when but Sir Horatio, in that ship immortal in naval memory, and which dismantled and in part broken up to her bare ribs is seen a grand skeleton in Haydon's etching. As one of a boarding-party from the *Agamemnon* he had received a cut slantwise along one temple and cheek, leaving a long pale scar like a streak of dawn's light falling athwart the dark visage. It was on account of that scar and the affair in which it was known that he had received it, as well as from his blue-peppered complexion that the Dansker went among the *Indomitable's* crew by the name of "Board-her-in-the-smoke."

Now the first time that his small weazel-eyes happened to light on Billy Budd, a certain grim internal merriment set all his ancient wrinkles into antic play. Was it that his eccentric unsentimental old sapience primitive in its kind saw or thought it saw something which in contrast with the warship's environment looked oddly incongruous in the handsome sailor? But after slyly studying him at intervals, the old Merlin's equivocal merriment was modified; for now when the twain would meet, it would start in his face a quizzing sort of look, but it would be but momentary and sometimes replaced by an expression of speculative query as to what might eventually befall a nature like that, dropped into a world not without some man-traps and against whose subtleties simple courage lacking experience and address and without any touch of defensive ugliness, is of little avail; and where such innocence as man is capable of does yet in a moral emergency not always sharpen the faculties or enlighten the will.

However it was the Dansker in his ascetic way rather took to Billy. Nor was this only because of a certain philosophic interest in such a character. There was another cause. While the old man's eccentricities, sometimes bordering on the ursine, repelled the juniors, Billy, undeterred thereby, revering him as a salt hero would make advances, never passing the old Agamemnon-man without a salutation marked by that respect which is seldom lost on the aged however crabbed at times or whatever their station in life. There was a vein of dry humor, or what not, in the mast-man; and, whether in freak of patriarchal irony touching Billy's youth and athletic frame, or for some other and more recondite reason, from the first in addressing him he always substituted Baby for Billy. The Dansker in fact being the originator of the name by which the foretopman eventually became known aboard ship.

Well then, in his mysterious little difficulty going in quest of the wrinkled one, Billy found him off duty in a dog-watch ruminating by himself seated on a shot-box of the upper gun-deck now and then surveying with a somewhat cynical regard certain of the more swaggering promenaders there. Billy recounted his trouble, again wondering how it all happened. The salt seer attentively listened, accompanying the foretopman's recital with queer twitchings of his wrinkles and problematical little sparkles of his small ferret eyes. Making an end of his story, the foretopman asked, "And now, Dansker, do tell me what you think of it."

The old man, shoving up the front of his tarpaulin and deliberately rubbing the long slant scar at the point where it entered the thin hair, laconically said, "Baby Budd, *Jemmy Legs*" (meaning the master-at-arms) "is down on you."

"*Jemmy Legs!*" ejaculated Billy his welkin eyes expanding; "what for? Why he calls me *the sweet and pleasant young fellow,* they tell me."

"Does he so?" grinned the grizzled one; then said "Ay Baby Lad a sweet voice has *Jemmy Legs.*"

"No, not always. But to me he has. I seldom pass him but there comes a pleasant word."

"And that's because he's down upon you, Baby Budd."

Such reiteration along with the manner of it, incomprehensible to a novice, disturbed Billy almost as much as the mystery for which he had sought explanation. Something less unpleasingly oracular he tried to extract; but the old sea-Chiron thinking perhaps that for the nonce he had sufficiently instructed his young Achilles, pursed his lips, gathered his wrinkles together and would commit himself to nothing further.

Years, and those experiences which befall certain shrewder men subordinated life-long to the will of superiors, all this had developed in the Dansker the pithy guarded cynicism that was his leading characteristic.

10

THE next day an incident served to confirm Billy Budd in his incredulity as to the Dansker's strange summing up of the case submitted.

The ship at noon going large before the wind was rolling on her course, and he below at dinner and engaged in some sportful talk with the members of his mess, chanced in a sudden lurch to spill the entire contents of his soup-pan upon the new scrubbed deck. Claggart, the Master-at-arms, official rattan in hand, happened to be passing along the battery in a bay of which the mess was lodged, and the greasy liquid streamed just across his path. Stepping over it, he was proceeding on his way without comment, since the matter was nothing to take notice of under the circumstances, when he happened to observe who it was that had done the spilling. His countenance changed. Pausing, he was about to ejaculate something hasty at the sailor, but checked himself, and pointing down to the streaming soup, playfully tapped him from behind with his rattan, saying in a low musical voice peculiar to him at times "Handsomely done, my lad! And handsome is as handsome did it too!" And with that passed on. Not noted by Billy as not coming within his view was the involuntary smile, or rather grimace, that accompanied Claggart's equivocal words. Aridly it drew down the thin corners of his shapely mouth. But everybody taking his remark as meant for humorous, and at which therefore as coming from a superior they were bound to laugh "with counterfeited glee," acted accordingly; and Billy tickled, it may be, by the allusion to his being the handsome sailor, merrily joined in; then addressing his messmates exclaimed "There now, who says that *Jemmy Legs* is down on me!"

"And who said he was, Beauty?" demanded one Donald with some surprise. Whereat the foretopman looked a little foolish recalling that it was only one person, Board-her-in-the-smoke who had suggested what to him was the smoky idea that this master-at-arms was in any peculiar way hostile to him. Meantime that functionary resuming his path must have momentarily worn some expression less guarded than that of the bitter smile and, usurping the face from the heart, some distorting expression perhaps, for a drummer-boy, heedlessly frolicking along from the opposite direction, and chancing to come into light collision with his person was strangely disconcerted by his aspect. Nor was the impression lessened when the official, impulsively giving him a sharp cut with the rattan, vehemently exclaimed "Look where you go!"

11

WHAT was the matter with the master-at-arms? And, be the matter what it might, how could it have direct relation to Billy Budd with whom prior to the affair of the spilled soup he had never come into any special contact official or otherwise? What indeed could the trouble have to do with one so little inclined to give offense as the merchant-ship's *peacemaker*, even him who in Claggart's own phrase was "the sweet and pleasant young fellow"? Yes, why should *Jemmy Legs*, to borrow the Dansker's expression, be *down* on the Handsome Sailor?

But at heart and not for nothing, as the late chance

encounter may indicate to the discerning, down on him, secretly down on him, he assuredly was.

Now to invent something touching the more private career of Claggart, something involving Billy Budd, of which something the latter should be wholly ignorant, some romantic incident implying that Claggart's knowledge of the young blue-jacket began at some period anterior to catching sight of him on board the seventy-four—all this, not so difficult to do, might avail in a way more or less interesting to account for whatever enigma may appear to lurk in the case. But in fact there was nothing of the sort. And yet the cause, necessarily to be assumed as the sole one assignable, is in its very realism as much charged with that prime element of Radcliffian romance, *the mysterious,* as any that the ingenuity of the author of the *Mysteries of Udolpho* could devise. For what can more partake of the mysterious than an antipathy spontaneous and profound such as is evoked in certain exceptional mortals by the mere aspect of some other mortal, however harmless he may be? if not called forth by this very harmlessness itself.

Now there can exist no irritating juxtaposition of dissimilar personalities comparable to that which is possible aboard a great warship fully manned and at sea. There, every day among all ranks almost every man comes into more or less of contact with almost every other man. Wholly there to avoid even the sight of an aggravating object one must needs give it Jonah's toss or jump overboard himself. Imagine how all this might eventually operate on some peculiar human creature the direct reverse of a saint?

But for the adequate comprehending of Claggart by a normal nature these hints are insufficient. To pass from a normal nature to him one must cross "the deadly space between." And this is best done by indirection.

Long ago an honest scholar my senior, said to me in reference to one who like himself is now no more, a man so unimpeachably respectable that against him nothing was ever openly said though among the few something was whispered, "Yes, X—— is a nut not to be cracked by the tap of a lady's fan. You are aware that I am the adherent of no organized religion much less of any philosophy built into a system. Well, for all that, I think that to try and get into X——, enter his labyrinth and get out again, without a clue derived from some source other than what is known as *knowledge of the world*—that were hardly possible, at least for me."

"Why," said I, "X—— however singular a study to some, is yet human, and knowledge of the world assuredly implies the knowledge of human nature, and in most of its varieties."

"Yes, but a superficial knowledge of it, serving ordinary purposes. But for anything deeper, I am not certain whether to know the world and to know human nature be not two distinct branches of knowledge, which while they may coexist in the same heart, yet either may exist with little or nothing of the other. Nay, in an average man of the world, his constant rubbing with it blunts that fine spiritual insight indispensable to the understanding of the essential in certain exceptional characters, whether evil ones or good. In a matter of some importance I have seen a girl wind an old lawyer about her little finger. Nor was it the dotage of senile love. Nothing of the sort. But he knew law better than he knew the girl's heart. Coke and Blackstone hardly shed so much light into obscure spiritual places as the Hebrew prophets. And who were they? Mostly recluses."

At the time my inexperience was such that I did not quite see the drift of all this. It may be that I see it now. And, indeed, if that lexicon which is based on Holy Writ were any longer popular, one might with less difficulty define and denominate certain phenomenal men. As it is, one must turn to some authority not liable to the charge of being tinctured with the Biblical element.

In a list of definitions included in the authentic translation of Plato, a list attributed to him, occurs this: "Natural Depravity: a depravity according to nature." A definition which though savoring of Calvinism, by no means involves Calvin's dogma as to total mankind. Evidently its intent makes it applicable but to individuals. Not many are the examples of this depravity which the gallows and jail supply. At any rate for notable instances, since these have no vulgar alloy of the brute in them, but invariably are dominated by intellectuality, one must go elsewhere. Civilization, especially if of the austerer sort, is auspicious to it. It folds itself in the mantle of respectability. It has its certain negative virtues serving as silent auxiliaries. It never allows wine to get within its guard. It is not going too far to say that it is without vices or small sins. There is a phenomenal pride in it that excludes them from anything mercenary or avaricious. In short the depravity here meant partakes nothing of the sordid or sensual. It is serious, but free from acerbity. Though no flatterer of mankind it never speaks ill of it.

But the thing which in eminent instances signalizes so exceptional a nature is this: though the man's even temper and discreet bearing would seem to intimate a mind peculiarly subject to the law of reason, not the less in his heart he would seem to riot in complete exemption from that law having apparently little to do with reason further than to employ it as an ambidexter implement for effecting the irrational. That is to say: toward the accomplishment of an aim which in wantonness of malignity would seem to partake of the insane, he will direct a cool judgment sagacious and sound.

These men are true madmen, and of the most dangerous sort, for their lunacy is not continuous but occasional evoked by some special object; it is probably secretive which is as much to say it is self-contained, so that when moreover, most active it is to the average mind not distinguishable from sanity, and for the reason above suggested that whatever its aims may be, and the aim is never declared—the method and the outward proceeding is always perfectly rational.

Now something such an one was Claggart, in whom was the mania of an evil nature, not engendered by vicious training or corrupting books or licentious living, but born with him and innate, in short "a depravity according to nature."

12

Lawyers, Experts, Clergy
An Episode

By the way, can it be the phenomenon, disowned or at least concealed, that in some criminal cases puzzles the courts? For this cause have our juries at times not only to endure the prolonged contentions of lawyers with their fees, but also the yet more perplexing strife of the medical experts with theirs? But why leave it to them? Why not subpoena (?) as well the clerical proficients? Their vocation bringing them into peculiar contact with so many human beings, and sometimes in their least guarded hour, in interviews very much more confidential than those of physician and patient; this would seem to qualify them to know something about those intricacies involved in the question of moral responsibility; whether in a given case, say, the crime proceeded from mania in the brain or rabies of the heart. As to any differences among themselves these clerical proficients might develop on the stand, these could hardly be greater than the direct contradictions exchanged between the remunerated medical experts.

Dark sayings are these, some will say. But why? Is it because they somewhat savor of Holy Writ in its phrase "mysteries of iniquity"? If they do, such savor was far from being intended for little will it commend these pages to many a reader of today.

The point of the present story turning on the hidden nature of the master-at-arms has necessitated this chapter. With an added hint or two in connection with the incident at the mess, the resumed narrative must be left to vindicate as it may, its own credibility.

13

Pale ire, envy and despair

THAT Claggart's figure was not amiss, and his face, save the chin, well moulded, has already been said. Of these favorable points he seemed not insensible, for he was not only neat but careful in his dress. But the form of Billy Budd was heroic; and if his face was without the intellectual look of the pallid Claggart's, not the less was it lit, like his, from within, though from a different source. The bonfire in his heart made luminous the rose-tan in his cheek.

In view of the marked contrast between the persons of the twain, it is more than probable that when the master-at-arms in the scene last given applied to the sailor the proverb *Handsome is as handsome does*; he there let escape an ironic inkling, not caught by the young sailors who heard it, as to what it was that had first moved him against Billy, namely, his significant personal beauty.

Now envy and antipathy passions irreconcilable in reason, nevertheless in fact may spring conjoined like Chang and Eng in one birth. Is Envy then such a monster? Well, though many an arraigned mortal has in hopes of mitigated penalty pleaded guilty to horrible actions, did ever anybody seriously confess to envy? Something there is in it universally felt to be more shameful than even felonious crime. And not only does everybody disown it but the better sort are inclined to incredulity when it is in earnest imputed to an intelligent man. But since its lodgment is in the heart not the brain, no degree of intellect supplies a guarantee against it. But Claggart's was no vulgar form of the passion. Nor, as directed toward Billy Budd, did it partake of that streak of apprehensive jealousy that marred Saul's visage perturbedly brooding on the comely young David. Claggart's envy struck deeper. If askance he eyed the good looks, cheery health and frank enjoyment of young life in Billy Budd, it was because these went along with a nature that as Claggart magnetically felt, had in its simplicity never willed malice or experienced the reactionary bite of that serpent. To him, the spirit lodged within Billy, and looking out from his welkin eyes as from windows, that ineffability it was which made the dimple in his dyed cheek, suppled his joints, and dancing in his yellow curls made him preeminently the Handsome Sailor. One person excepted the master-at-arms was perhaps the only man in the ship intellectually capable of adequately appreciating the moral phenomenon presented in Billy Budd. And the insight but intensified his passion, which assuming various secret forms within him, at times assumed that of cynic disdain —disdain of innocence—To be nothing more than innocent! Yet in an aesthetic way he saw the charm of it, the courageous free-and-easy temper of it, and fain would have shared it, but he despaired of it.

With no power to annul the elemental evil in him, though readily enough he could hide it; apprehending the good, but powerless to be it; a nature like Claggart's surcharged with energy as such natures almost invariably are, what recourse is left to it but to recoil upon itself and like the scorpion for which the Creator alone is responsible, act out to the end the part allotted it.

14

PASSION, and passion in its profoundest, is not a thing demanding a palatial stage whereon to play its part. Down among the groundlings, among the beggars and rakers of the garbage, profound passion is enacted. And the circumstances that provoke it, however trivial or mean, are no measure of its power. In the present instance the stage is a scrubbed gun-deck, and one of the external provocations a man-of-war's man's spilled soup.

Now when the Master-at-arms noticed whence came that greasy fluid streaming before his feet, he must have taken it—to some extent wilfully,—perhaps not for the mere accident it assuredly was, but for the sly escape of a spontaneous feeling on Billy's part more or less answering to the antipathy on his own. In effect a foolish demonstration he must have thought, and very harmless, like the futile kick of a heifer, which yet were the heifer a shod stallion, would not be so harmless. Even so was it that into the gall of Claggart's envy he infused the vitriol of his contempt. But the incident confirmed to him certain tell-tale reports purveyed to his ear by *Squeak,* one of his more cunning corporals, a grizzled little man, so nicknamed by the sailors on account of his squeaky voice, and sharp visage ferreting about the dark corners of the lower decks after interlopers, satirically suggesting to them the idea of a rat in a cellar.

From his Chief's employing him as an implicit tool in laying little traps for the worriment of the Foretopman—for it was from the Master-at-arms that the petty persecutions heretofore adverted to had proceeded—the corporal having naturally enough concluded that his master could have no love for the sailor, made it his business, faithful understrapper that he was, to foment the ill blood by perverting to his Chief certain innocent frolics of the good natured Foretopman, besides inventing for his mouth sundry contumelious epithets he claimed to have overheard him let fall. The Master-at-arms never suspected the veracity of these reports, more especially as to the epithets, for he well knew how secretly unpopular may become a master-at-arms at least a master-at-arms of those days zealous in his function, and how the blue-jackets shoot at him in private their raillery and wit; the nickname by which he goes among them (*Jemmy Legs*) implying under the form of merriment their cherished disrespect and dislike.

But in view of the greediness of hate for patrolmen it hardly needed a purveyor to feed Claggart's passion. An uncommon prudence is habitual with the subtler depravity, for it has everything to hide. And in case of an injury but suspected its secretiveness voluntarily cuts it off from enlightenment or disillusion; and, not unreluctantly, action is taken upon surmise as upon certainty. And the retaliation is apt to be in monstrous disproportion to the supposed offense; for when in anybody was revenge in its exactions aught else but an inordinate usurer? But how with Claggart's conscience? For though consciences are unlike as foreheads, every intelligence, not excluding the Scriptural devils who "believe and tremble," has one. But Claggart's conscience being but the lawyer to his will, made ogres of trifles, probably arguing that the motive imputed to Billy in spilling the soup just when he did, together with the epithets alleged, these, if nothing more, made a strong case against him; nay, justified animosity into a sort of retributive righteousness. The Pharisee is the Guy Fawkes prowling in the hid chambers underlying the Claggarts. And they can really form no conception of an unreciprocated malice. Probably, the master-at-arms' clandestine persecutions of Billy were started to try the temper of the man; but it had not developed any quality in him that enmity could make official use of or even pervert into even plausible self-justification; so that the occurrence at the mess, petty if it were, was a welcome one to that peculiar conscience assigned to be the private mentor of Claggart; and for the rest, not improbably it put him upon new experiments.

15

NOT many days after the last incident narrated something befell Billy Budd that more gravelled him than aught that had previously occurred.

It was a warm night for the latitude; and the Foretopman, whose watch at the time was properly below, was dozing on the uppermost deck whither he had ascended from his hot hammock one of hundreds suspended so closely wedged together over a lower gun-deck that there was little or no swing to them. He lay as in the shadow of a hill-side stretched under the lee of the *booms,* a piled ridge of spare spars amidships between foremast and main mast and among which the ship's largest boat, the launch, was stowed. Alongside of three other slumberers from below, he lay near that end of the booms which approaches from the foremast; his station aloft on duty as a foretopman being just over the deck-station of the forecastlemen, entitling him according to usage to make himself more or less at home in that neighborhood.

Presently he was stirred into semi-consciousness by somebody, who must have previously sounded the sleep of the others, touching his shoulder, and then as the Foretopman raised his head, breathing into his ear in a quick whisper, "Slip into the lee forechains, Billy; there is something in the wind. Don't speak. Quick. I will meet you there;" and disappeared.

Now Billy like sundry other essentially goodnatured ones had some of the weaknesses inseparable from essential good-nature; and among these was a reluctance, almost an incapacity of plumply saying *no* to an abrupt proposition not obviously absurd, on the face of it, nor obviously unfriendly, nor iniquitous. And being of warm blood he had not the phlegm tacitly to negative any proposition by an unresponsive inaction. Like his sense of fear, his apprehension as to aught outside of the honest and natural was seldom very quick. Besides, upon the present occasion, the drowse from his sleep still hung upon him.

However it was, he mechanically rose, and sleepily wondering what could be in the wind, betook himself to the designated place, a narrow platform, one of six, outside of the high bulwarks and screened by the great dead-eyes and multiple columned lanyards of the shrouds and backstays; and, in a great warship of that time, of dimensions commensurate to the hull's magnitude; a tarry balcony in short overhanging the sea, and so secluded that one mariner of the *Indomitable,* a nonconformist old tar of a serious turn, made it even in daytime his private oratory.

In this retired nook the stranger soon joined Billy Budd. There was no moon as yet; a haze obscured the star-light. He could not distinctly see the stranger's face. Yet from something in the outline and carriage, Billy took him to be, and correctly, one of the afterguard.

"Hist! Billy," said the man; in the same quick cautionary whisper as before, "You were impressed, weren't you? Well, so was I;" and he paused as to mark the effect. But Billy not knowing exactly what to make of this said nothing. Then the other: "We are not the only impressed ones, Billy. There's a gang of us.—Couldn't you—help—at a pinch?"

"What do you mean?" demanded Billy here thoroughly shaking off his drowse.

"Hist, hist!" the hurried whisper now growing husky, "see here;" and the man held up two small objects faintly twinkling in the night light; "see, they are yours, Billy if you'll only—"

But Billy broke in, and in his resentful eagerness to deliver himself his vocal infirmity somewhat intruded; "D-D-Damme, I don't know what you are d-d-driving at, or what you mean, but you had better g-g-go where you belong!" For the moment the fellow, as confounded, did not stir; and Billy, springing to his feet, said "If you d-don't start I'll t-t-toss you back over the r-rail!" There was no mistaking this and the mysterious emissary decamped, disappearing in the direction of the mainmast in the shadow of the booms.

"Hallo, what's the matter?" here came growling from a forecastleman awakened from his deck-doze by Billy's raised voice. And as the foretopman reappeared and was recognized by him; "Ah, *Beauty*, is it you? Well, something must have been the matter for you st-st-stuttered."

"Oh," rejoined Billy, now mastering the impediment; "I found an afterguardsman in our part of the ship here and I bid him be off where he belongs."

"And is that all you did about it, foretopman?" gruffly demanded another, an irascible old fellow of brick-colored visage and hair, and who was known to his associate forecastlemen as *Red Pepper*; "Such sneaks I should like to marry to the gunner's daughter!" by that expression meaning that he would like to subject them to disciplinary castigation over a gun.

However, Billy's rendering of the matter satisfactorily accounted to these inquirers for the brief commotion, since of all the sections of a ship's company the forecastlemen, veterans for the most part and bigoted in their sea-prejudices, are the most jealous in resenting territorial encroachments, especially on the part of any of the afterguard, of whom they have but a sorry opinion, chiefly landsmen, never going aloft except to reef or furl the mainsail, and in no wise competent to handle a marlinspike or turn in a *dead-eye,* say.

16

THIS incident sorely puzzled Billy Budd. It was an entirely new experience; the first time in his life that he had ever been personally approached in underhand intriguing fashion. Prior to this encounter he had known nothing of the afterguardsman, the two men being stationed wide apart, one forward and aloft during his watch, the other on deck and aft.

What could it mean? And could they really be guineas, those two glittering objects the interloper had held up to his (Billy's) eyes? Where could the fellow get guineas? Why even buttons spare buttons are not so plentiful at sea. The more he turned the matter over, the more he was nonplussed, and made uneasy and discomforted. In his disgustful recoil from an overture which though he but ill comprehended he instinctively knew must involve evil of some sort, Billy Budd was like a young horse fresh from the pasture suddenly inhaling a vile whiff from some chemical factory and by repeated snortings tries to get it out of his nostrils and lungs. This frame of mind barred all desire of holding further parley with the fellow, even were it but for the purpose of gaining some enlightenment as to his design in approaching him. And yet he was not without natural curiosity to see how such a visitor in the dark would look in broad day.

He espied him the following afternoon in his first dogwatch below one of the smokers on that forward part of the upper gun-deck allotted to the pipe. He recognized him by his general cut and build, more than by his round freckled face and glassy eyes of pale blue, veiled with lashes all but white.

And yet Billy was a bit uncertain whether indeed it were he—yonder chap about his own age, chatting and laughing in free-hearted way, leaning against a gun; a genial young fellow enough to look at, and something of a rattle-brain, to all appearance. Rather chubby too for a sailor even an afterguardsman. In short the last man in the world, one would think, to be overburdened with thoughts, especially those perilous thoughts that must needs belong to a conspirator in any serious project, or even to the underling of such a conspirator.

Although Billy was not aware of it, the fellow, with a sidelong watchful glance had perceived Billy first, and then noting that Billy was looking at him, thereupon nodded a familiar sort of friendly recognition as to an old acquaintance, without interrupting the talk he was engaged in with the group of smokers. A day or two afterwards chancing in the evening promenade on a gun-deck, to pass Billy, he offered a flying word of good-fellowship as it were, which by its unexpectedness, and equivocalness under the circumstances so embarrassed Billy that he knew not how to respond to it, and let it go unnoticed.

Billy was now left more at a loss than before. The ineffectual speculations into which he was led were so disturbingly alien to him that he did his best to smother them. It never entered his mind that here was a matter which from its extreme questionableness, it was his duty as a loyal blue-jacket to report in the proper quarter. And, probably, had such a step been suggested to him, he would have been deterred from taking it by the thought, one of novice-magnanimity, that it would savor overmuch of the dirty work of a tell-tale. He kept the thing to himself. Yet upon one occasion, he could not forbear a little disburthening himself to the old Dansker, tempted thereto perhaps by the influence of a balmy night when the ship lay becalmed; the twain, silent for the most part, sitting together on deck, their heads propped against the bulwarks. But it was only a partial and anonymous account that Billy gave, the unfounded scruples above referred to preventing full disclosure to anybody. Upon hearing Billy's version, the sage Dansker seemed to divine more than he was told; and after a little meditation during which his wrinkles were pursed as into a point, quite effacing for the time that quizzing expression his face sometimes wore,—"Didn't I say so, Baby Budd?"

"Say what?" demanded Billy.

"Why, *Jemmy Legs* is *down* on you."

"And what" rejoined Billy in amazement, "has *Jemmy Legs* to do with that cracked afterguardsman?"

"Ho, it was an afterguardsman, then. A cat's-paw, a cat's-paw!" And with that exclamation, which, whether it had reference to a light puff of air just then coming over the calm sea, or subtler relation to the afterguardsman, there is no telling, the old Merlin gave a twisting wrench with his black teeth at his plug of tobacco, vouchsafing no reply to Billy's impetuous question, though now repeated, for it was his wont to relapse into grim silence when interrogated in skeptical sort as to any of his sententious oracles, not always very clear ones, rather partaking of that obscurity which invests most Delphic deliverances from any quarter. Long experience had very likely brought this old man to that bitter prudence which never interferes in aught and never gives advice.

17

Yes, despite the Dansker's pithy insistence as to the Master-at-arms being at the bottom of these strange experiences of Billy on board the *Indomitable,* the young sailor was ready to ascribe them to almost anybody but the man who, to use Billy's own expression, "always had a pleasant word for him." This is to be wondered at. Yet not so much to be wondered at. In certain matters, some sailors even in mature life remain unsophisticated enough. But a young seafarer of the disposition of our athletic Foretopman is much of a child-man. And yet a child's utter innocence is but its blank ignorance, and the innocence more or less wanes as intelligence waxes. But in Billy Budd intelligence such as it was, had advanced, while yet his simple-mindedness remained for the most part unaffected. Experience is a teacher indeed; yet did Billy's years make his experience small. Besides, he had none of that intuitive knowledge of the bad which in natures not good or incompletely so foreruns experience, and therefore may pertain, as in some instances it too clearly does pertain, even to youth.

And what could Billy know of man except of man as a mere sailor? And the old-fashioned sailor, the veritable man-before-the-mast, the sailor from boyhood up, he, though indeed of the same species as a landsman is in some respects singularly distinct from him. The sailor is frankness, the landsman is finesse. Life is not a game with the sailor, demanding the long head; no intricate game of chess where few moves are made in straightforwardness, and ends are attained by indirection; an oblique, tedious, barren game hardly worth that poor candle burnt out in playing it.

Yes, as a class, sailors are in character a juvenile race. Even their deviations are marked by juvenility. And this more especially holding true with the sailors of Billy's time. Then, too, certain things which apply to all sailors, do more pointedly operate here and there, upon the junior one. Every sailor, too is accustomed to obey orders without debating them; his life afloat is externally ruled for him; he

is not brought into that promiscuous commerce with mankind where unobstructed free agency on equal terms—
equal superficially, at least—soon teaches one that unless
upon occasion he exercises a distrust keen in proportion to
the fairness of the appearance, some foul turn may be
served him. A ruled undemonstrative distrustfulness is so
habitual, not with business-men so much, as with men
who know their kind in less shallow relations than business, namely certain men-of-the-world, that they come at
last to employ it all but unconsciously; and some of them
would very likely feel real surprise at being charged with
it as one of their general characteristics.

18

BUT after the little matter at the mess Billy Budd no more
found himself in strange trouble at times about his hammock or his clothes-bag or what not. While, as to that smile
that occasionally sunned him, and the pleasant passing
word, these were if not more frequent, yet if anything
more pronounced than before.

But for all that, there were certain other demonstrations
now. When Claggart's unobserved glance happened to
light on belted Billy rolling along the upper gun-deck in
the leisure of the second dog-watch exchanging passing
broadsides of fun with other young promenaders in the
crowd; that glance would follow the cheerful sea-Hype-
rion with a settled meditative and melancholy expression,
his eyes strangely suffused with incipient feverish tears
Then would Claggart look like the man of sorrows. Yes,
and sometimes the melancholy expression would have in
it a touch of soft yearning, as if Claggart could even have
loved Billy but for fate and ban. But this was an evanes-
cence, and quickly repented of, as it were, by an immiti-
gable look, pinching and shrivelling the visage into the

momentary semblance of a wrinkled walnut. But sometimes catching sight in advance of the foretopman coming in his direction, he would, upon their nearing, step aside a little to let him pass, dwelling upon Billy for the moment with the glittering dental satire of a Guise. But upon any abrupt unforeseen encounter a red light would flash forth from his eye like a spark from an anvil in a dusk smithy. That quick fierce light was a strange one, darted from orbs which in repose were of a color nearest approaching a deeper violet, the softest of shades.

Though some of these caprices of the pit could not but be observed by their object, yet were they beyond the construing of such a nature. And the *thews* of Billy were hardly compatible with that sort of sensitive spiritual organization which in some cases instinctively conveys to ignorant innocence an admonition of the proximity of the malign. He thought the Master-at-arms acted in a manner rather queer at times. That was all. But the occasional frank air and pleasant word went for what they purported to be, the young sailor never having heard as yet of the "too fair-spoken man."

Had the foretopman been conscious of having done or said anything to provoke the ill will of the official, it would have been different with him, and his sight might have been purged if not sharpened. As it was innocence was his blinder.

So was it with him in yet another matter. Two minor officers—the Armorer, and Captain of the Hold, with whom he had never exchanged a word, his position on the ship not bringing him into contact with them; these men now for the first began to cast upon Billy when they chanced to encounter him, that peculiar glance which evidences that the man from whom it comes has been some way tampered with and to the prejudice of him upon whom the glance lights. Never did it occur to Billy as a thing to be noted or a thing suspicious, though he well knew the fact, that the Armorer and Captain of the Hold, with the ship's yeoman, apothecary and others of that grade, were by naval usage, messmates of the master-at-arms men with ears convenient to his confidential tongue.

But the general popularity that our Handsome Sailor's manly forwardness upon occasion, and irresistible good nature indicating no mental superiority tending to excite an invidious feeling; this good will on the part of most of his shipmates made him the less to concern himself about such mute aspects toward him as those whereto allusion has just been made as far as he could not so fathom as to infer their whole import.

As to the afterguardsman, though Billy for reasons already given necessarily saw little of him, yet when the two did happen to meet, invariably came the fellow's offhand cheerful recognition, sometimes accompanied by a passing pleasant word or two. Whatever that equivocal young person's original design may really have been, or the design of which he might have been the deputy, certain it was from his manner upon these occasions, that he had wholly dropped it.

It was as if his precocity of crookedness (and every vulgar villain is precocious) had for once deceived him, and the man he had sought to entrap as a simpleton had, through his very simplicity ignorantly baffled him.

But shrewd ones may opine that it was hardly possible for Billy to refrain from going up to the afterguardsman and bluntly demanding to know his purpose in the initial interview, so abruptly closed in the fore-chains. Shrewd ones may also think it but natural in Billy to set about sounding some of the other impressed men of the ship in order to discover what basis, if any, there was for the emissary's obscure suggestions as to plotting disaffection aboard. Yes, the shrewd may so think. But something more, or rather, something else than mere shrewdness is perhaps needful for the due understanding of such a character as Billy Budd's.

As to Claggart, the monomania in the man—if that indeed it were—as involuntarily disclosed by starts in the manifestations detailed, yet in general covered over by his self-contained and rational demeanor; this, like a subterranean fire was eating its way deeper and deeper in him. Something decisive must come of it.

19

AFTER the mysterious interview in the fore-chains, the one so abruptly ended there by Billy, nothing especially german to the story occurred until the events now about to be narrated.

Elsewhere it has been said that in the lack of frigates (of course better sailers than line-of-battle ships) in the English squadron up the Straits at that period, the *Indomitable* was occasionally employed not only as an available substitute for a scout, but at times on detached service of more important kind. This was not alone because of her sailing qualities, not common in a ship of her rate, but quite as much, probably, that the character of her commander, it was thought, specially adapted him for any duty where under unforeseen difficulties a prompt initiative might have to be taken in some matter demanding knowledge and ability in addition to those qualities implied in good seamanship. It was on an expedition of the latter sort, a somewhat distant one, and when the *Indomitable* was almost at her furthest remove from the fleet that in the latter part of an afternoon-watch she unexpectedly came in sight of a ship of the enemy. It proved to be frigate. The latter, perceiving through the glass that the weight of men and metal would be heavily against her, invoking her light heels crowded sail to get away. After a chase urged almost against hope and lasting until about the middle of the first dog-watch, she signally succeeded in effecting her escape.

Not long after the pursuit had been given up, and ere the excitement incident thereto had altogether waned away, the master-at-arms ascending from his cavernous sphere made his appearance cap in hand by the mainmast respectfully awaiting the notice of Captain Vere then solitary walking the weather-side of the quarter-deck doubtless somewhat chafed at the failure of the pursuit. The spot where Claggart stood was the place allotted to men of lesser grades seeking some more particular interview either with the officer-of-the-deck or the Captain himself. But from the latter it was not often that a sailor or petty-officer of those days would seek a hearing; only some exceptional cause, would, according to established custom, have warranted that.

Presently, just as the Commander absorbed in his reflections was on the point of turning aft in his promenade, he became sensible of Claggart's presence, and saw the doffed cap held in deferential expectancy. Here be it said that Captain Vere's personal knowledge of this petty-officer had only begun at the time of the ship's last sailing from home, Claggart then for the first, in transfer from a ship detained for repairs, supplying on board the *Indomitable* the place of a previous master-at-arms disabled and ashore.

No sooner did the Commander observe who it was that now so deferentially stood awaiting his notice, than a peculiar expression came over him. It was not unlike that which uncontrollably will flit across the countenance of one at unawares encountering a person who though known to him indeed has hardly been long enough known for thorough knowledge, but something in whose aspect nevertheless now for the first provokes a vaguely repellent distaste. But coming to a stand and resuming much of his wonted official manner, save that a sort of impatience lurked in the intonation of the opening word, he said, "Well? what is it, master-at-arms?"

With the air of a subordinate grieved at the necessity of being a messenger of ill tidings, and while conscientiously determined to be frank, yet equally resolved upon shunning overstatement, Claggart at this invitation or rather summons to disburthen, spoke up. What he said, conveyed in the language of no uneducated man, was to the effect following if not altogether in these words, namely, that during the chase and preparations for the possible encounter he had seen enough to convince him that at least one sailor aboard was a dangerous character in a ship mustering some who not only had taken a guilty part in the late serious troubles, but others also who, like the man in question, had entered His Majesty's service under another form than enlistment.

At this point Captain Vere with some impatience, interrupted him:

"Be direct, man; say impressed men."

Claggart made a gesture of subservience, and proceeded.

Quite lately whereof he (Claggart) had begun to suspect that on the gun-decks some sort of movement prompted by the sailor in question was covertly going on, but he had not thought himself warranted in reporting the suspicion so long as it remained indistinct. But from what he had that afternoon observed in the man referred to, the suspicion of something clandestine going on had advanced to a point less removed from certainty. He deeply felt, he added, the serious responsibility assumed in making a report involving such possible consequences to the individual mainly concerned, besides tending to augment those natural anxieties which every naval commander must feel in view of extraordinary outbreaks so recent as those which, he sorrowfully said it, it needed not to name.

Now at the first broaching of the matter Captain Vere taken by surprise could not wholly dissemble his disquietude. But as Claggart went on, the former's aspect changed into restiveness under something in the witness's manner in giving his testimony. However, he refrained from interrupting him. And Claggart, continuing, concluded with this:

"God forbid, your honor, that the *Indomitable's* should be the experience of the—"

"Never mind that!" here peremptorily broke in the superior, his face altering with anger, instinctively divining the ship that the other was about to name, one in which the Nore Mutiny had assumed a singularly tragical character that for a time jeopardized the life of its commander. Under the circumstances he was indignant at the purposed allusion. When the commissioned officers themselves were on all occasions very heedful how they referred to the recent events, for a petty-officer unnecessarily to allude to them in the presence of his Captain, this struck him as a most immodest presumption. Besides, to his quick sense of self-respect, it even looked under the circumstances something like an attempt to alarm him. Nor at first was he without some surprise that one who so far as he had hitherto come under his notice had shown considerable tact in his function should in this particular evince such lack of it.

But these thoughts and kindred dubious ones flitting across his mind were suddenly replaced by an intuitional surmise which though as yet obscure in form served practically to affect his reception of the ill tidings. Certain it is, that long versed in everything pertaining to the complicated gun-deck life, which like every other form of life has its secret mines and dubious side the side popularly disclaimed, Captain Vere did not permit himself to be unduly disturbed by the general tenor of his subordinate's report. Furthermore, if in view of recent events prompt action should be taken at the first palpable sign of recurring insubordination, for all that, not judicious would it be, he thought, to keep the idea of lingering disaffection alive by undue forwardness in crediting an informer even if his own subordinate and charged among other things with police surveillance of the crew. This feeling would not perhaps have so prevailed with him were it not that upon a prior occasion the patriotic zeal officially evinced by Claggart had somewhat irritated him as appearing rather supersensible and strained. Furthermore something even in the official's self-possessed and somewhat ostentatious manner in making his specifications strangely reminded him of a bandsman, a perjurous witness in a capital case before a court-martial ashore of which when a lieutenant he Captain Vere had been a member.

Now the peremptory check given to Claggart in the matter of the arrested allusion was quickly followed up by this: "You say that there is at least one dangerous man aboard. Name him."

"William Budd. A foretopman, your honor—"

"William Budd" repeated Captain Vere with unfeigned astonishment; "and mean you the man that Lieutenant Ratcliffe took from the merchantman not very long ago—the young fellow who seems to be so popular with the men—Billy, the Handsome Sailor, as they call him?"

"The same, your honor; but for all his youth and good looks, a deep one. Not for nothing does he insinuate himself into the good will of his shipmates, since at the least all hands will at a pinch say a good word for him at all hazards. Did Lieutenant Ratcliffe happen to tell your honor of that adroit fling of Budd's jumping up in the cutter's bow under the merchantman's stern when he was being taken off? It is even masqued by that sort of good humored air that at heart he resents his impressment. You have but noted his fair cheek. A man-trap may be under his ruddy-tipped daisies."

Now the *Handsome Sailor* as a signal figure among the crew, had naturally enough attracted the Captain's attention from the first. Though in general not very demonstrative to his officers, he had congratulated Lieutenant Ratcliffe upon his good fortune in lighting on such a fine specimen of the genus homo, who in the nude might have posed for a statue of young Adam before the Fall.

As to Billy's adieu to the ship *Rights-of-Man*, which the boarding lieutenant had indeed reported to him, Captain Vere, but in a deferential way more as a good story than aught else, though mistakenly understanding it as a satiric sally, had but thought so much the better of the impressed man for it; as a military sailor, admiring the spirit that could take an arbitrary enlistment so merrily and sensibly. The foretopman's conduct, too, so far as it had fallen under the Captain's notice had confirmed the first happy augury, while the new recruit's qualities as a *sailor-man* seemed to be such that he had thought of recommending him to the executive officer for promotion to a place that would more frequently bring him under his own observation, namely, the captaincy of the mizzen-top, replacing there in the starboard watch a man not so young whom partly for that reason he deemed less fitted for the post. Be it parenthesized here that since the mizzen-top-men having not to handle such breadths of heavy canvas as the lower sails on the main-mast and fore-mast, a young man if of the right stuff not only seems best adapted to duty there, but in fact is generally selected for the captaincy of that top, and the company under him are light hands and often but striplings. In sum, Captain Vere had from the beginning deemed Billy Budd to be what in the naval parlance of the time was called a *"King's bargain,"* that is to say, for His Britannic Majesty's navy a capital investment at small outlay or none at all.

After a brief pause during which the reminiscences above mentioned passed vividly through his mind and he weighed the import of Claggart's last suggestion, conveyed in the phrase, "pitfall under the clover," and the more he weighed it the less reliance he felt in the informer's good faith. Suddenly he turned upon him and in a low voice: "Do you come to me, master-at-arms, with so foggy a tale? As to Budd, cite me an act or spoken word of his confirmatory of what you in general charge against him. Stay," drawing nearer to him "heed what you speak. Just now and in a case like this, there is a yard-arm-end for the false-witness."

"Ah, your honor!" sighed Claggart mildly shaking his shapely head as in sad deprecation of such unmerited severity of tone. Then, bridling—erecting himself as in virtuous self-assertion, he circumstantially alleged certain words and acts, which collectively, if credited, led to presumptions mortally inculpating Budd. And for some of these averments, he added, substantiating proof was not far.

With gray eyes impatient and distrustful essaying to fathom to the bottom Claggart's calm violet ones, Captain Vere again heard him out; then for the moment stood ruminating. The mood he evinced, Claggart—himself for the time liberated from the other's scrutiny—steadily regarded with a look difficult to render,—a look curious of the operation of his tactics, a look such as might have been that of the spokesman of the envious children of Jacob deceptively imposing upon the troubled patriarch the blood-dyed coat of young Joseph.

Though something exceptional in the moral quality of Captain Vere made him, in earnest encounter with a fellow-man, a veritable touch-stone of that man's essential nature, yet now as to Claggart and what was really going on in him his feeling partook less of intuitional conviction than of strong suspicion clogged by strange dubieties. The perplexity he evinced proceeded less from aught touching the man informed against—as Claggart doubtless opined—than from considerations how best to act in regard to the informer. At first indeed he was naturally for summoning that substantiation of his allegations which Claggart said was at hand. But such a proceeding would result in the matter at once getting abroad, which in the present stage of it, he thought, might undesirably affect the ship's company. If Claggart was a false witness,—that closed the affair. And therefore before trying the accusation, he would first practically test the accuser; and he thought this could be done in a quiet undemonstrative way.

The measure he determined upon involved a shifting of the scene, a transfer to a place less exposed to observation than the broad quarter-deck. For although the few gun-room officers there at the time had, in due observance of naval etiquette, withdrawn to leeward the moment Captain Vere had begun his promenade on the deck's weather-side; and though during the colloquy with Claggart they of course ventured not to diminish the distance; and though throughout the interview Captain Vere's voice was far from high, and Claggart's silvery and low; and the wind in the cordage and the wash of the sea helped the more to put them beyond ear-shot; nevertheless, the interview's continuance already had attracted observation from some topmen aloft and other sailors in the waist or further forward.

Having determined upon his measures, Captain Vere forthwith took action. Abruptly turning to Claggart he asked "Master-at-arms, is it now Budd's watch aloft?"

"No, your honor." Whereupon, "Mr. Wilkes!" summoning the nearest midshipman, "tell Albert to come to me." Albert was the Captain's hammock-boy, a sort of sea-valet in whose discretion and fidelity his master had much confidence. The lad appeared. "You know Budd the foretopman?"

"I do, Sir."

"Go find him. It is his watch off. Manage to tell him out of ear-shot that he is wanted aft. Contrive it that he speaks to nobody. Keep him in talk yourself. And not till you get well aft here, not till then let him know that the place where he is wanted is my cabin. You understand. Go.—Master-at-arms, show yourself on the decks below, and when you think it time for Albert to be coming with his man, stand by quietly to follow the sailor in."

20

Now when the foretopman found himself closeted there, as it were, in the cabin with the Captain and Claggart, he was surprised enough. But it was a surprise unaccompanied by apprehension or distrust. To an immature nature essentially honest and humane, forewarning intimations of subtler danger from one's kind come tardily if at all. The only thing that took shape in the young sailor's mind was this: Yes, the Captain, I have always thought, looks kindly upon me. Wonder if he's going to make me his coxswain. I should like that. And maybe now he is going to ask the master-at-arms about me.

"Shut the door there, sentry," said the commander; "stand without, and let nobody come in.—Now, master-at-arms, tell this man to his face what you told of him to me;" and stood prepared to scrutinize the mutually confronting visages.

With the measured step and calm collected air of an asylum-physician approaching in the public hall some patient beginning to show indications of a coming paroxysm,

Claggart deliberately advanced within short range of Billy, and mesmerically looking him in the eye, briefly recapitulated the accusation.

Not at first did Billy take it in. When he did the rose-tan of his cheek looked struck as by white leprosy. He stood like one impaled and gagged. Meanwhile the accuser's eyes removing not as yet from the blue dilated ones, underwent a phenomenal change, their wonted rich violet color blurring into a muddy purple. Those lights of human intelligence losing human expression, gelidly protruding like the alien eyes of certain uncatalogued creatures of the deep. The first mesmeric glance was one of serpent fascination; the last was as the hungry lurch of the torpedo-fish.

"Speak, man!" said Captain Vere to the transfixed one struck by his aspect even more than by Claggart's, "Speak! defend yourself." Which appeal caused but a strange dumb gesturing and gurgling in Billy; amazement at such an accusation so suddenly sprung on inexperienced nonage; this, and, it may be, horror of the accuser, serving to bring out his lurking defect and in this instance for the time intensifying it into a convulsed tongue-tie; while the intent head and entire form straining forward in an agony of ineffectual eagerness to obey the injunction to speak and defend himself, gave an expression to the face like that of a condemned Vestal priestess in the moment of being buried alive, and in the first struggle against suffocation.

Though at the time Captain Vere was quite ignorant of Billy's liability to vocal impediment, he now immediately divined it, since vividly Billy's aspect recalled to him that of a bright young schoolmate of his whom he had once seen struck by much the same startling impotence in the act of eagerly rising in the class to be foremost in response to a testing question put to it by the master. Going close up to the young sailor, and laying a soothing hand on his shoulder, he said: "There is no hurry, my boy. Take your time, take your time." Contrary to the effect intended, these words so fatherly in tone, doubtless touching Billy's heart to the quick, prompted yet more violent efforts at utterance—efforts soon ending for the time in confirming the paralysis, and bringing to his face an expression which was as a crucifixion to behold. The next instant, quick as the flame from a discharged cannon at night, his right arm shot out, and Claggart dropped to the deck. Whether intentionally or but owing to the young athlete's superior height, the blow had taken effect full upon the forehead, so shapely and intellectual-looking a feature in the master-at-arms; so that the body fell over lengthwise, like a heavy plank tilted from erectness. A gasp or two, and he lay motionless.

"Fated boy," breathed Captain Vere in tone so low as to be almost a whisper, "what have you done! But here, help me."

The twain raised the felled one from the loins up into a sitting position. The spare form flexibly acquiesced, but inertly. It was like handling a dead snake They lowered it back. Regaining erectness Captain Vere with one hand covering his face stood to all appearance as impassive as the object at his feet. Was he absorbed in taking in all the bearings of the event and what was best not only now at once to be done, but also in the sequel? Slowly he uncovered his face; and the effect was as if the moon emerging from eclipse should reappear with quite another aspect than that which had gone into hiding. The father in him, manifested towards Billy thus far in the scene, was replaced by the military disciplinarian. In his official tone he bade the foretopman retire to a state-room aft (pointing it out) and there remain till thence summoned. This order Billy in silence mechanically obeyed. Then going to the cabin-door where it opened on the quarter-deck, Captain

Vere said to the sentry without, "Tell somebody to send Albert here." When the lad appeared his master so contrived it that he should not catch sight of the prone one. "Albert," he said to him, "tell the Surgeon I wish to see him. You need not come back till called."

When the Surgeon entered—a self-poised character of that grave sense and experience that hardly anything could take him aback,—Captain Vere advanced to meet him, thus unconsciously intercepting his view of Claggart and interrupting the other's wonted ceremonious salutation, said, "Nay, tell me how it is with yonder man," directing his attention to the prostrate one.

The Surgeon looked, and for all his self-command, somewhat started at the abrupt revelation. On Claggart's always pallid complexion, thick black blood was now oozing from nostril and ear. To the gazer's professional eye it was unmistakably no living man that he saw.

"Is it so then?" said Captain Vere intently watching him. "I thought it. But verify it." Whereupon the customary tests confirmed the Surgeon's first glance, who now looking up in unfeigned concern, cast a look of intense inquisitiveness upon his superior. But Captain Vere, with one hand to his brow was standing motionless. Suddenly, catching the Surgeon's arm convulsively, he exclaimed pointing down to the body—"It is the divine judgment on Ananias! Look!"

Disturbed by the excited manner he had never before observed in the *Indomitable's* Captain, and as yet wholly ignorant of the affair, the prudent Surgeon nevertheless held his peace, only again looking an earnest interrogation as to what it was that had resulted in such a tragedy.

But Captain Vere was now again motionless standing absorbed in thought. But again starting, he vehemently exclaimed—"Struck dead by an angel of God. Yet the angel must hang!"

At these passionate interjections, mere incoherences to the listener as yet unapprised of the antecedent events, the Surgeon was profoundly discomposed. But now as recollecting himself, Captain Vere in less harsh tone briefly related the circumstances leading up to the event.

"But come; we must despatch" he added. "Help me to remove him (meaning the body) to yonder compartment," designating one opposite that where the foretopman remained immured. Anew disturbed by a request that as implying a desire for secrecy, seemed unaccountably strange to him, there was nothing for the subordinate to do but comply.

"Go now" said Captain Vere with something of his wonted manner, "Go now. I shall presently call a drumhead court. Tell the lieutenants what has happened, and tell Mr. Mordant," meaning the captain of marines, "and charge them to keep the matter to themselves."

21

FULL of disquietude and misgiving the Surgeon left the cabin. Was Captain Vere suddenly affected in his mind, or was it but a transient excitement, brought about by so strange and extraordinary happening? As to the drumhead court, it struck the Surgeon as impolitic, if nothing more. The thing to do, he thought, was to place Billy Budd in confinement, and in a way dictated by usage, and postpone further action in so extraordinary a case to such time as they should rejoin the squadron, and then refer it to the Admiral. He recalled the unwonted agitation of Captain Vere and his excited exclamations so at variance with his normal manner. Was he unhinged? But assuming that he is, it is not so susceptible of proof. What then could he do? No more trying situation is conceivable than that of an officer subordinate under a Captain whom he suspects to be, not mad indeed, but yet not quite unaffected in his intellect. To argue his order to him would be insolence. To resist him would be mutiny. In obedience to Captain Vere he communicated what had happened to the lieutenants and captain of marines; saying nothing as to the Captain's state. They fully shared his own surprise and concern. Like him they seemed to think that such a matter should be referred to the Admiral.

22

WHO in the rainbow can draw the line where the violet tint ends and the orange tint begins? Distinctly we see the difference of the colors, but where exactly does the one first blendingly enter into the other? So with sanity and insanity. In pronounced cases there is no question about them. But in some supposed cases, in various degrees supposedly less pronounced, to draw the exact line of demarkation few will undertake though for a fee some professional experts will. There is nothing namable but that some men will undertake to do it for pay.

Whether Captain Vere, as the Surgeon professionally and primarily surmised, was really the sudden victim of any degree of aberration, one must determine for himself by such light as this narrative may afford.

That the unhappy event which has been narrated could not have happened at a worse juncture was but too true. For it was close on the heel of the suppressed insurrections, an after-time very critical to naval authority, demanding from every English sea-commander two qualities not readily interfusable—prudence and rigor. Moreover there was something crucial in the case.

In the jugglery of circumstances preceding and attending the event on board the *Indomitable* and in the light of that martial code whereby it was formally to be judged, innocence and guilt personified in Claggart and Budd—in effect changed places.

In a legal view the apparent victim of the tragedy was he who had sought to victimize a man blameless; and the indisputable deed of the latter, navally regarded, consti- tuted the most heinous of military crimes. Yet more. The essential right and wrong involved in the matter, the clearer that might be, so much the worse for the respon- sibility of a loyal sea-commander inasmuch as he was not authorized to determine the matter on that primitive basis.

Small wonder then that the *Indomitable's* Captain though in general a man of rapid decision, felt that circum- spectness not less than promptitude was necessary. Until he could decide upon his course, and in each detail; and not only so, but until the concluding measure was upon the point of being enacted, he deemed it advisable, in view of all the circumstances to guard as much as possible against publicity. Here he may or may not have erred. Cer- tain it is however that subsequently in the confidential talk of more than one or two gun-rooms and cabins he was not a little criticized by some officers, a fact imputed by his friends, and vehemently by his cousin Jack Denton, to pro- fessional jealousy of *Starry Vere*. Some imaginative ground for invidious comment there was. The maintenance of se- crecy in the matter, the confining all knowledge of it for a time to the place where the homicide occurred, the quarter-deck cabin; in these particulars lurked some resem- blance to the policy adopted in those tragedies of the pal- ace which have occurred more than once in the capital founded by Peter the Barbarian.

The case indeed was such that fain would the *Indomi- table's* Captain have deferred taking any action whatever respecting it further than to keep the foretopman a close prisoner till the ship rejoined the squadron and then submitting the matter to the judgment of his Admiral.

But a true military officer is in one particular like a true monk. Not with more of self-abnegation will the latter keep his vows of monastic obedience than the former his vows of allegiance to martial duty.

Feeling that unless quick action were taken on it, the deed of the foretopman, so soon as it should be known on the gun-decks would tend to awaken any slumbering embers of the Nore among the crew, a sense of the urgency of the case overruled in Captain Vere every other consideration. But though a conscientious disciplinarian he was no lover of authority for mere authority's sake. Very far was he from embracing opportunities for monopolizing to himself the perils of moral responsibility none at least that could properly be referred to an official superior or shared with him by his official equals or even subordinates. So thinking he was glad it would not be at variance with usage to turn the matter over to a summary court of his own officers, reserving to himself as the one on whom the ultimate accountability would rest, the right of maintaining a supervision of it, or formally or informally interposing at need. Accordingly a drumhead court was summarily convened, he electing the individuals composing it, the First Lieutenant, the Captain of marines, and the Sailing Master.

In associating an officer of marines with the sea-lieutenants in a case having to do with a sailor the Commander perhaps deviated from general custom. He was prompted thereto by the circumstance that he took that soldier to be a judicious person, thoughtful, and not altogether incapable of grappling with a difficult case unprecedented in his prior experience. Yet even as to him he was not without some latent misgiving, for withal he was an extremely good-natured man, an enjoyer of his dinner, a sound sleeper, and inclined to obesity. A man who though he would always maintain his manhood in battle might not prove altogether reliable in a moral dilemma involving aught of the tragic. As to the First Lieutenant and the Sailing Master Captain Vere could not but be aware that though honest natures, of approved gallantry upon occasion their intelligence was mostly confined to the matter of active seamanship and the fighting demands of their profession. The court was held in the same cabin where the unfortunate affair had taken place. This cabin, the Commander's, embraced the entire area under the poop-deck. Aft, and on either side was a small state-room the one room temporarily a jail and the other a dead-house and a yet smaller compartment leaving a space between, expanding forward into a goodly oblong of length coinciding with the ship's beam. A sky-light of moderate dimension was overhead and at each end of the oblong space were two sashed port-hole windows easily convertible back into embrasures for short carronades.

All being quickly in readiness, Billy Budd was arraigned, Captain Vere necessarily appearing as the sole witness in the case, and as such temporarily sinking his rank, though singularly maintaining it in a matter apparently trivial, namely, that he testified from the ship's weather-side with that object having caused the court to sit on the lee-side. Concisely he narrated all that had led up to the catastrophe, omitting nothing in Claggart's accusation and deposing as to the manner in which the prisoner had received it. At this testimony the three officers glanced with no little surprise at Billy Budd, the last man they would have suspected either of the mutinous design alleged by Claggart or the undeniable deed he himself had done. The First Lieutenant, taking judicial primacy and turning toward the prisoner, said, "Captain Vere has spoken. Is it or is it not as Captain Vere says?" In response came syllables not so much impeded in the utterance as might have been anticipated. They were these: "Captain Vere tells the truth. It is just as Captain Vere says, but it is not as the Master-at-Arms said. I have eaten the King's bread and I am true to the King."

"I believe you, my man," said the witness his voice indicating a suppressed emotion not otherwise betrayed.

"God will bless you for that, Your Honor!" not without stammering said Billy, and all but broke down. But immediately was recalled to self-control by another question, to which with the same emotional difficulty of utterance he said "No, there was no malice between us. I never bore malice against the Master-at-arms. I am sorry that he is dead. I did not mean to kill him. Could I have used my tongue I would not have struck him. But he foully lied to my face and in presence of my Captain, and I had to say something, and I could only say it with a blow, God help me!"

In the impulsive above-board manner of the frank one the court saw confirmed all that was implied in words that just previously had perplexed them coming as they did from the testifier to the tragedy and promptly following Billy's impassioned disclaimer of mutinous intent—Captain Vere's words, "I believe you, my man."

Next it was asked of him whether he knew of or suspected aught savoring of incipient trouble (meaning mutiny, though the explicit term was avoided) going on in any section of the ship's company.

The reply lingered. This was naturally imputed by the court to the same vocal embarrassment which had retarded or obstructed previous answers. But in main it was otherwise here; the question immediately recalling to Billy's mind the interview with the afterguardsman in the forechains. But an innate repugnance to playing a part at all

approaching that of an informer against one's own shipmates—the same erring sense of uninstructed honor which
had stood in the way of his reporting the matter at the time
though as a loyal man-of-war-man it was incumbent on
him and failure so to do if charged against him and proven,
would have subjected him to the heaviest of penalties;
this, with the blind feeling now his, that nothing really
was being hatched, prevailed with him. When the answer
came it was a negative.

"One question more," said the officer of marines now
first speaking and with a troubled earnestness, "You tell
us that what the Master-at-arms said against you was a lie.
Now why should he have so lied, so maliciously lied, since
you declare there was no malice between you?"

At that question unintentionally touching on a spiritual
sphere wholly obscure to Billy's thoughts, he was nonplussed, evincing a confusion indeed that some observers,
such as can readily be imagined, would have construed
into involuntary evidence of hidden guilt. Nevertheless
he strove some way to answer, but all at once relinquished
the vain endeavor, at the same time turning an appealing
glance towards Captain Vere as deeming him his best
helper and friend. Captain Vere who had been seated for
a time, rose to his feet, addressing the interrogator. "The
question you put to him comes naturally enough. But how
can he rightly answer it? or anybody else? unless indeed it
be he who lies within there" designating the compartment
where lay the corpse. "But the prone one there will not
rise to our summons. In effect though, as it seems to me,
the point you make is hardly material. Quite aside from
any conceivable motive actuating the Master-at-arms, and
irrespective of the provocation to the blow, a martial court
must needs in the present case confine its attention to the
blow's consequence, which consequence justly is to be
deemed not otherwise than as the striker's deed."

This utterance the full significance of which it was not at all likely that Billy took in, nevertheless caused him to turn a wistful interrogative look toward the speaker. a look in its dumb expressiveness not unlike that which a dog of generous breed might turn upon his master seeking in his face some elucidation of a previous gesture ambiguous to the canine intelligence. Nor was the same utterance without marked effect upon the three officers, more especially the soldier. Couched in it seemed to them a meaning unanticipated, involving a prejudgment on the speaker's part. It served to augment a mental disturbance previously evident enough.

The soldier once more spoke; in a tone of suggestive dubiety addressing at once his associates and Captain Vere: "Nobody is present—none of the ship's company, I mean, who might shed lateral light, if any is to be had, upon what remains mysterious in this matter."

"That is thoughtfully put" said Captain Vere; "I see your drift. Ay, there is a mystery; but to use a Scriptural phrase, it is 'a mystery of iniquity,' a matter for psychologic theologians to discuss. But what has a military court to do with it? Not to add that for us any possible investigation of it is cut off by the lasting tongue-tie of—him—in yonder," again designating the mortuary state-room. "The prisoner's deed,—with that alone we have to do."

To this, and particularly the closing reiteration, the marine soldier knowing not how aptly to reply, sadly abstained from saying aught. The First Lieutenant who at the outset had not unnaturally assumed primacy in the court, now overrulingly instructed by a glance from Captain Vere, a glance more effective than words, resumed that primacy. Turning to the prisoner, "Budd," he said, and scarce in equable tones, "Budd, if you have aught further to say for yourself, say it now."

Upon this the young sailor turned another quick glance

toward Captain Vere; then, as taking a hint from that aspect, a hint confirming his own instinct that silence was now best, replied to the Lieutenant, "I have said all, Sir."

The marine—the same who had been the sentinel without the cabin-door at the time that the foretopman followed by the master-at-arms, entered it—he, standing by the sailor throughout these judicial proceedings, was now directed to take him back to the after compartment originally assigned to the prisoner and his custodian. As the twain disappeared from view, the three officers as partially liberated from some inward constraint associated with Billy's mere presence, simultaneously stirred in their seats. They exchanged looks of troubled indecision, yet feeling that decide they must and without long delay. For Captain Vere was for the time standing unconsciously with his back toward them, apparently in one of his absent fits, gazing out from a sashed port-hole to windward upon the monotonous blank of the twilight sea. But the court's silence continuing, broken only at moments by brief consultations in low earnest tones, this seemed to assure him and encourage him. Turning, he to-and-fro paced the cabin athwart; in the returning ascent to windward, climbing the slant deck in the ship's lee roll; without knowing it symbolizing thus in his action a mind resolute to surmount difficulties even if against primitive instincts strong as the wind and the sea. Presently he came to a stand before the three. After scanning their faces he stood less as mustering his thoughts for expression, than as one inly deliberating how best to put them to well-meaning men not intellectually mature, men with whom it was necessary to demonstrate certain principles that were axioms to himself. Similar impatience as to talking is perhaps one reason that deters some minds from addressing any popular assemblies.

When speak he did, something both in the substance of what he said and his manner of saying it, showed the influence of unshared studies modifying and tempering the practical training of an active career. This, along with his phraseology now and then was suggestive of the grounds whereon rested that imputation of a certain pedantry socially alleged against him by certain naval men of wholly practical cast, captains who nevertheless would frankly concede that His Majesty's navy mustered no more efficient officer of their grade than 'Starry Vere.'

What he said was to this effect: "Hitherto I have been but the witness, little more; and I should hardly think now to take another tone, that of your coadjutor, for the time, did I not perceive in you—at the crisis too—a troubled hesitancy, proceeding, I doubt not from the clash of military duty with moral scruple—scruple vitalized by compassion. For the compassion how can I otherwise than share it. But, mindful of paramount obligations I strive against scruples that may tend to enervate decision. Not, gentlemen, that I hide from myself that the case is an exceptional one. Speculatively regarded, it well might be referred to a jury of casuists. But for us here acting not as casuists or moralists, it is a case practical, and under martial law practically to be dealt with.

"But your scruples: do they move as in a dusk? Challenge them. Make them advance and declare themselves. Come now: do they import something like this: If, mindless of palliating circumstances we are bound to regard the death of the Master-at-arms as the prisoner's deed, then does that deed constitute a capital crime whereof the penalty is a mortal one. But in natural justice is nothing but the prisoner's overt act to be considered? How can we adjudge to summary and shameful death a fellow-creature innocent before God, and whom we feel to be so?—Does that state it aright? You sign sad assent. Well, I too feel that, the full force of that. It is Nature. But do these buttons that we wear attest that our allegiance is to Nature?

No, to the King. Though the ocean, which is inviolate Nature primeval, though this be the element where we move and have our being as sailors, yet as the King's officers lies our duty in a sphere correspondingly natural? So little is that true, that in receiving our commissions we in the most important regards ceased to be natural free-agents. When war is declared, are we the commissioned fighters previously consulted? We fight at command. If our judgments approve the war, that is but coincidence. So in other particulars. So now. For suppose condemnation to follow these present proceedings. Would it be so much we ourselves that would condemn as it would be martial law operating through us? For that law and the rigor of it, we are not responsible. Our vowed responsibility is in this: That however pitilessly that law may operate, we nevertheless adhere to it and administer it.

"But the exceptional in the matter moves the hearts within you. Even so too is mine moved. But let not warm hearts betray heads that should be cool. Ashore in a criminal case will an upright judge allow himself off the bench to be waylaid by some tender kinswoman of the accused seeking to touch him with her tearful plea? Well the heart sometimes the feminine in man, here is as that piteous woman. And hard though it be, she must here be ruled out."

He paused, earnestly studying them for a moment; then resumed.

"But something in your aspect seems to urge that it is not solely the heart that moves in you, but also the conscience, the private conscience. But tell me whether or not, occupying the position we do, private conscience should not yield to that imperial one formulated in the code under which alone we officially proceed?"

Here the three men moved in their seats, less convinced

than agitated by the course of an argument troubling but the more the spontaneous conflict within.

Perceiving which, the speaker paused for a moment; then abruptly changing his tone, went on.

"To steady us a bit, let us recur to the facts.—In war-time at sea a man-of-war's-man strikes his superior in grade, and the blow kills. Apart from its effect the blow itself is, according to the Articles of War, a capital crime. Furthermore—"

"Ay, Sir," emotionally broke in the officer of marines, "in one sense it was. But surely Budd purposed neither mutiny nor homicide."

"Surely not, my good man. And before a court less arbitrary and more merciful than a martial one that plea would largely extenuate. At the Last Assizes it shall acquit. But how here? We proceed under the law of the Mutiny Act. In feature no child can resemble his father more than that Act resembles in spirit the thing from which it derives— War. In His Majesty's service—in this ship indeed—there are Englishmen forced to fight for the King against their will. Against their conscience, for aught we know. Though as their fellow-creatures some of us may appreciate their position, yet as Navy Officers, what reck we of it? Still less recks the enemy. Our impressed men he would fain cut down in the same swath with our volunteers. As regards the enemy's naval conscripts, some of whom may even share our own abhorrence of the regicidal French Directory, it is the same on our side. War looks but to the frontage, the appearance. And the Mutiny Act, War's child, takes after the father. Budd's intent or non-intent is nothing to the purpose.

"But while, put to it by those anxieties in you which I can not but respect, I only repeat myself—while thus strangely we prolong proceedings that should be summary

—the enemy may be sighted and an engagement result. We must do; and one of two things must we do—condemn or let go."

"Can we not convict and yet mitigate the penalty?" asked the junior Lieutenant here speaking, and falteringly, for the first.

"Lieutenant, were that clearly lawful for us under the circumstances consider the consequence of such clemency. The people" (meaning the ship's company) "have native sense; most of them are familiar with our naval usage and tradition; and how would they take it? Even could you explain to them—which our official position forbids—they, long moulded by arbitrary discipline have not that kind of intelligent responsiveness that might qualify them to comprehend and discriminate. No, to the people the foretopman's deed however it be worded in the announcement will be plain homicide committed in a flagrant act of mutiny. What penalty for that should follow, they know. But it does not follow. *Why?* They will ruminate. You know what sailors are. Will they not revert to the recent outbreak at the Nore? Ay. They know the well-founded alarm—the panic it struck throughout England. Your clement sentence they would account pusillanimous. They would think that we flinch, that we are afraid of them—afraid of practicing a lawful rigor singularly demanded at this juncture lest it should provoke new troubles. What shame to us such a conjecture on their part, and how deadly to discipline. You see then, whither prompted by duty and the law I steadfastly drive. But I beseech you, my friends, do not take me amiss. I feel as you do for this unfortunate boy. But did he know our hearts, I take him to be of that generous nature that he would feel even for us on whom in this military necessity so heavy a compulsion is laid."

With that, crossing the deck he resumed his place by the sashed port-hole, tacitly leaving the three to come to a decision. On the cabin's opposite side the troubled court sat silent. Loyal lieges, plain and practical, though at bottom they dissented from some points Captain Vere had put to them, they were without the faculty, hardly had the inclination to gainsay one whom they felt to be an earnest man, one too not less their superior in mind than in naval rank. But it is not improbable that even such of his words as were not without influence over them, less came home to them than his closing appeal to their instinct as sea-officers in the forethought he threw out as to the practical consequences to discipline, considering the unconfirmed tone of the fleet at the time, should a man-of-war's-man's violent killing at sea of a superior in grade be allowed to pass for aught else than a capital crime demanding prompt infliction of the penalty.

Not unlikely they were brought to something more or less akin to that harassed frame of mind which in the year 1842 actuated the commander of the U.S. brig-of-war *Somers* to resolve, under the so-called Articles of War, Articles modelled upon the English Mutiny Act, to resolve upon the execution at sea of a midshipman and two petty-officers as mutineers designing the seizure of the brig. Which resolution was carried out though in a time of peace and within not many days sail of home. An act vindicated by a naval court of inquiry subsequently convened ashore. History, and here cited without comment. True, the circumstances on board the *Somers* were different from those on board the *Indomitable*. But the urgency felt, well-warranted or otherwise, was much the same.

Says a writer whom few know, "Forty years after a battle it is easy for a non-combatant to reason about how it ought to have been fought. It is another thing personally and under fire to direct the fighting while involved in the obscuring smoke of it. Much so with respect to other emergencies involving considerations both practical and moral, and when it is imperative promptly to act. The greater the fog the more it imperils the steamer, and speed is put on though at the hazard of running somebody down. Little ween the snug card-players in the cabin of the responsibilities of the sleepless man on the bridge."

In brief, Billy Budd was formally convicted and sentenced to be hung at the yard-arm in the early morning-watch, it being now night. Otherwise, as is customary in such cases, the sentence would forthwith have been carried out. In war-time on the field or in the fleet, a mortal punishment decreed by a drumhead court—on the field sometimes decreed by but a nod from the General—follows without delay on the heel of conviction without appeal.

23

IT WAS Captain Vere himself who of his own motion communicated the finding of the court to the prisoner; for that purpose going to the compartment where he was in custody and bidding the marine there to withdraw for the time.

Beyond the communication of the sentence what took place at this interview was never known. But in view of the character of the twain briefly closeted in that state-room, each radically sharing in the rarer qualities of our nature—so rare indeed as to be all but incredible to average minds however much cultivated—some conjectures may be ventured.

It would have been in consonance with the spirit of Captain Vere should he on this occasion have concealed nothing from the condemned one—should he indeed have frankly disclosed to him the part he himself had played in bringing about the decision, at the same time revealing his actuating motives. On Billy's side it is not improbable that such a confession would have been received in much the same spirit that prompted it. Not without a sort of joy indeed he might have appreciated the brave opinion of him implied in his Captain making such a confidant of him. Nor, as to the sentence itself could he have been insensible that it was imparted to him as to one not afraid to die. Even more may have been. Captain Vere in the end may have developed the passion sometimes latent under an exterior stoical or indifferent. He was old enough to have been Billy's father. The austere devotee of military duty letting himself melt back into what remains primeval in our formalized humanity may in the end have caught Billy to his heart even as Abraham may have caught young Isaac on the brink of resolutely offering him up in obedience to the exacting behest. But there is no telling the sacrament, seldom if in any case revealed to the gadding world wherever under circumstances at all akin to those here attempted to be set forth two of great Nature's nobler order embrace. There is privacy at the time, inviolable to the survivor, and holy oblivion the sequel to each diviner magnanimity, providentially covers all at last.

The first to encounter Captain Vere in act of leaving the compartment was the senior Lieutenant. The face he beheld, for the moment one expressive of the agony of the strong, was to that officer, though a man of fifty, a startling revelation. That the condemned one suffered less than he who mainly had effected the condemnation was apparently indicated by the former's exclamation in the scene soon perforce to be touched upon.

24

Of a series of incidents within a brief term rapidly following each other, the adequate narration may take up a term less brief, especially if explanation or comment here and there seem requisite to the better understanding of such incidents. Between the entrance into the cabin of him who never left it alive, and him who when he did leave it left it as one condemned to die; between this and the closeted interview just given less than an hour and a half had elapsed. It was an interval long enough however to awaken speculations among no few of the ship's company as to what it was that could be detaining in the cabin the master-at-arms and the sailor; for a rumor that both of them had been seen to enter it and neither of them had been seen to emerge, this rumor had got abroad upon the gun-decks and in the tops; the people of a great war-ship being in one respect like villagers, taking microscopic note of every outward movement or non-movement going on. When therefore in weather not at all tempestuous all hands were called in the second dog-watch, a summons under such circumstances not usual in those hours, the crew were not wholly unprepared for some announcement extraordinary, one having connection too with the continued absence of the two men from their wonted haunts.

There was a moderate sea at the time; and the moon, newly risen and near to being at its full, silvered the white spar-deck wherever not blotted by the clear-cut shadows horizontally thrown of fixtures and moving men. On either side the quarter-deck the marine guard under arms was drawn up; and Captain Vere standing in his place surrounded by all the ward-room officers, addressed his men. In so doing his manner showed neither more nor less than that properly pertaining to his supreme position aboard his own ship. In clear terms and concise he told them what had taken place in the cabin; that the master-at-arms was dead; that he who had killed him had been already tried by a summary court and condemned to death; and that the execution would take place in the early morning watch. The word *mutiny* was not named in what he said. He refrained too from making the occasion an opportunity for any preachment as to the maintenance of discipline, thinking perhaps that under existing circumstances in the navy the consequence of violating discipline should be made to speak for itself.

Their Captain's announcement was listened to by the throng of standing sailors in a dumbness like that of a seated congregation of believers in hell listening to the clergyman's announcement of his Calvinistic text.

At the close, however, a confused murmur went up. It began to wax. All but instantly, then, at a sign, it was pierced and suppressed by shrill whistles of the Boatswain and his mates piping down one watch.

To be prepared for burial Claggart's body was delivered to certain petty-officers of his mess. And here, not to clog the sequel with lateral matters, it may be added that at a suitable hour, the Master-at-arms was committed to the sea with every funeral honor properly belonging to his naval grade.

In this proceeding as in every public one growing out of the tragedy strict adherence to usage was observed. Nor in any point could it have been at all deviated from either with respect to Claggart or Billy Budd without begetting undesirable speculations in the ship's company, sailors, and more particularly men-of-war's men, being of all men the greatest sticklers for usage.

For similar cause all communication between Captain Vere and the condemned one ended with the closeted interview already given, the latter being now surrendered to the ordinary routine preliminary to the end. This transfer under guard from the Captain's quarters was effected without unusual precautions—at least no visible ones.

If possible not to let the men so much as surmise that their officers anticipate aught amiss from them is the tacit rule in a military ship. And the more that some sort of trouble should really be apprehended the more do the officers keep that apprehension to themselves; though not the less unostentatious vigilance may be augmented.

In the present instance the sentry placed over the prisoner had strict orders to let no one have communication with him but the Chaplain. And certain unobtrusive measures were taken absolutely to insure this point.

25

IN A seventy-four of the old order the deck known as the upper gun-deck was the one covered over by the spar-deck which last though not without its armament was for the most part exposed to the weather. In general it was at all hours free from hammocks; those of the crew swinging on the lower gun-deck, and berth-deck, the latter being not only a dormitory but also the place for the stowing of the sailors' bags, and on both sides lined with the large chests or movable pantries of the many messes of the men.

On the starboard side of the *Indomitable's* upper gun-deck, behold Billy Budd under sentry lying prone in irons in one of the bays formed by the regular spacing of the guns comprising the batteries on either side. All these pieces were of the heavier caliber of that period. Mounted on lumbering wooden carriages they were hampered with cumbersome harness of breeching and strong side-tackles for running them out. Guns and carriages, together with the long rammers and shorter lintstocks lodged in loops overhead—all these, as customary, were painted black; and the heavy hempen breechings tarred to the same tint, wore the like livery of the undertakers. In contrast with the funereal tone of these surroundings the prone sailor's exterior apparel, white *jumper* and white duck trousers, each more or less soiled, dimly glimmered in the obscure light of the bay like a patch of discolored snow in early April lingering at some upland cave's black mouth. In effect he is already in his shroud or the garments that shall serve him in lieu of one. Over him but scarce illuminating him, two battle-lanterns swing from two massive beams of the deck above. Fed with the oil supplied by the war-contractors (whose gains, honest or otherwise, are in every land an anticipated portion of the harvest of death) with flickering splashes of dirty yellow light they pollute the pale moonshine all but ineffectually struggling in obstructed flecks through the open ports from which the tompioned cannon protrude. Other lanterns at intervals serve but to bring out somewhat the obscurer bays which like small confessionals or side-chapels in a cathedral branch from the long dim-vistaed broad aisle between the two batteries of that covered tier.

Such was the deck where now lay the Handsome Sailor. Through the rose-tan of his complexion, no pallor could have shown. It would have taken days of sequestration from the winds and the sun to have brought about the ef-facement of that. But the skeleton in the cheek-bone at the point of its angle was just beginning delicately to be defined under the warm-tinted skin. In fervid hearts self-contained some brief experiences devour our human tissue as secret fire in a ship's hold consumes cotton in the bale.

But now lying between the two guns, as nipped in the vice of fate, Billy's agony, mainly proceeding from a generous young heart's virgin experience of the diabolical incarnate and effective in some men—the tension of that agony was over now. It survived not the something healing in the closeted interview with Captain Vere. Without movement, he lay as in a trance. That adolescent expression previously noted as his, taking on something akin to the look of a slumbering child in the cradle when the warm hearth-glow of the still chamber at night plays on the dimples that at whiles mysteriously form in the cheek, silently coming and going there. For now and then in the gyved one's trance a serene happy light born of some wandering reminiscence or dream would diffuse itself over his face, and then wane away only anew to return.

The Chaplain coming to see him and finding him thus, and perceiving no sign that he was conscious of his presence, attentively regarded him for a space, then slipping aside, withdrew for the time, peradventure feeling that even he the minister of Christ though receiving his stipend from Mars had no consolation to proffer which could result in a peace transcending that which he beheld. But in the small hours he came again. And the prisoner now awake to his surroundings noticed his approach and civilly, all but cheerfully, welcomed him. But it was to little purpose that in the interview following the good man sought to bring Billy Budd to some Godly understanding that he must die, and at dawn. True, Billy himself freely referred to his death as a thing close at hand; but it was something in the way that children will refer to death in general, who yet among their other sports will play a funeral with hearse and mourners.

Not that like children Billy was incapable of conceiving what death really is. No, but he was wholly without irrational fear of it, a fear more prevalent in highly civilized communities than those so-called barbarous ones which in all respects stand nearer to unadulterate Nature. And, as elsewhere said, a barbarian Billy radically was; as much so, for all the costume, as his countrymen the British captives, living trophies, made to march in the Roman triumph of Germanicus. Quite as much so as those later barbarians, young men probably, and picked specimens among the earlier British converts to Christianity, at least nominally such and taken to Rome (as today converts from lesser isles of the sea may be taken to London) of whom the Pope of that time, admiring the strangeness of their personal beauty so unlike the Italian stamp, their clear ruddy complexion and curled flaxen locks, exclaimed, "Angles" (meaning *English* the modern derivative) "Angles do you call them? And is it because they look so like angels?" Had it been later in time one would think that the Pope had in mind Fra Angelico's seraphs some of whom, plucking apples in gardens of the Hesperides have the faint rosebud complexion of the more beautiful English girls.

If in vain the good Chaplain sought to impress the young barbarian with ideas of death akin to those conveyed in the skull, dial and cross-bones on old tombstones; equally futile to all appearance were his efforts to bring home to him the thought of salvation and a Saviour. Billy listened, but less out of awe or reverence perhaps than from a certain natural politeness; doubtless at bottom regarding all that in much the same way that most mariners of his class take any discourse abstract or out of the common tone of the work-a-day world. And this sailor way of taking clerical discourse is not wholly unlike the way in which the pioneer of Christianity full of transcendent miracles was received long ago on tropic isles by any superior *savage* so called—a Tahitian say of Captain Cook's time or shortly after that time. Out of natural courtesy he received but did not appropriate. It was like a gift placed in the palm of an outstretched hand upon which the fingers do not close.

But the *Indomitable's* Chaplain was a discreet man possessing the good sense of a good heart. So he insisted not in his vocation here. At the instance of Captain Vere, a lieutenant had apprised him of pretty much everything as to Billy; and since he felt that innocence was even a better thing than religion wherewith to go to Judgement, he reluctantly withdrew; but in his emotion not without first performing an act strange enough in an Englishman, and under the circumstances yet more so in any regular priest. Stooping over, he kissed on the fair cheek his fellow-man, a felon in martial law, one who though on the confines of death he felt he could never convert to a dogma; nor for all that did he fear for his future.

Marvel not that having been made acquainted with the young sailor's essential innocence (an irruption of heretic thought hard to suppress) the worthy man lifted not a finger to avert the doom of such a martyr to martial discipline. So to do would not only have been as idle as invoking the desert, but would also have been an audacious transgression of the bounds of his function, one as exactly prescribed to him by military law as that of the boatswain or any other naval officer. Bluntly put, a chaplain is the minister of the Prince of Peace serving in the host of the God of War—Mars. As such, he is as incongruous as that musket of Blücher etc. at Christmas. Why then is he there? Because he indirectly subserves the purpose attested by the cannon; because too he lends the sanction of the religion of the meek to that which practically is the abrogation of everything but brute Force.

26

THE night so luminous on the spar-deck but otherwise on the cavernous ones below, levels so like the tiered galleries in a coal-mine—the luminous night passed away. But, like the prophet in the chariot disappearing in heaven and dropping his mantle to Elisha, the withdrawing night transferred its pale robe to the breaking day. A meek shy light appeared in the East, where stretched a diaphanous fleece of white furrowed vapor. That light slowly waxed. Suddenly *eight bells* was struck aft, responded to by one louder metallic stroke from forward. It was four o'clock in the morning. Instantly the silver whistles were heard summoning all hands to witness punishment. Up through the great hatchways rimmed with racks of heavy shot, the watch below came pouring overspreading with the watch already on deck the space between the mainmast and foremast including that occupied by the capacious *launch* and the black booms tiered on either side of it, boat and booms making a summit of observation for the powder-boys and younger tars. A different group comprising one watch of topmen leaned over the rail of that sea-balcony, no small one in a seventy-four, looking down on the crowd below. Man or boy none spake but in whisper, and few spake at all. Captain Vere—as before, the central figure among the assembled commissioned officers—stood nigh the break of the poop-deck facing forward. Just below him on the quarter-deck the marines in full equipment were drawn up much as at the scene of the promulgated sentence.

At sea in the old time, the execution by halter of a military sailor was generally from the fore-yard. In the present instance for special reasons the main-yard was assigned. Under an arm of that weather or lee(?) yard the prisoner was presently brought up, the Chaplain attending him. It was noted at the time and remarked upon afterwards, that in this final scene the good man evinced little or nothing of the perfunctory. Brief speech indeed he had with the condemned one, but the genuine Gospel was less on his tongue than in his aspect and manner towards him. The final preparations personal to the latter being speedily brought to an end by two boatswain's-mates, the consummation impended. Billy stood facing aft. At the penultimate moment, his words, his only ones, words wholly unobstructed in the utterance were these—"God bless Captain Vere!" Syllables so unanticipated coming from one with the ignominious hemp about his neck—a conventional felon's benediction directed aft towards the quarters of honor; syllables too delivered in the clear melody of a singing-bird on the point of launching from the twig, had a phenomenal effect, not unenhanced by the rare personal beauty of the young sailor spiritualized now through late experiences so poignantly profound.

Without volition as it were, as if indeed the ship's populace were but the vehicles of some vocal current electric, with one voice from alow and aloft, came a resonant sympathetic echo—"God bless Captain Vere!" And yet at that instant Billy alone must have been in their hearts, even as he was in their eyes.

At the pronounced words and the spontaneous echo that voluminously rebounded them, Captain Vere, either through stoic self-control or a sort of momentary paralysis induced by emotional shock, stood erectly rigid as a musket in the ship-armorer's rack.

The hull deliberately recovering from the periodic roll to leeward was just regaining an even keel, when the last signal a preconcerted dumb one was given. At the same moment it chanced that the vapory fleece hanging low in the East, was shot through with a soft glory as of the fleece of the Lamb of God seen in mystical vision and simultaneously therewith, watched by the wedged mass of upturned faces, Billy ascended; and, ascending, took the full rose of the dawn.

In the pinioned figure, arrived at the yard-end, to the wonder of all no motion was apparent save that created by the ship's motion, in moderate weather so majestic in a great ship ponderously cannoned.

End of Chapter

27

A Digression

WHEN some days afterwards in reference to the singularity just mentioned, the Purser a rather ruddy rotund person more accurate as an accountant than profound as a philosopher said at mess to the Surgeon, "What testimony to the force lodged in will-power" the latter--saturnine spare and tall, one in whom a discreet causticity went along with a manner less genial than polite, replied, "Your pardon, Mr. Purser. In a hanging scientifically conducted—and under special orders I myself directed how Budd's was to be effected—any movement following the completed suspension and originating in the body suspended, such movement indicates mechanical spasm in the muscular system. Hence the absence of that is no more attributable to will-power as you call it than to horse-power—begging your pardon."

"But this muscular spasm you speak of, is not that in a degree more or less invariable in these cases?"

"Assuredly so, Mr. Purser."

"How then, my good Sir, do you account for its absence in this instance?"

"Mr. Purser, it is clear that your sense of the singularity in this matter equals not mine. You account for it by what you call will-power a term not yet included in the lexicon of science. For me I do not, with my present knowledge pretend to account for it at all. Even should one assume the hypothesis that at the first touch of the halyards the action of Budd's heart, intensified by extraordinary emotion at its climax, abruptly stopped—much like a watch when in carelessly winding it up you strain at the finish, thus snapping the chain—even under that hypothesis how account for the phenomenon that followed?"

"You admit then that the absence of spasmodic movement was phenomenal."

"It was phenomenal, Mr. Purser, in the sense that it was an appearance the cause of which is not immediately to be assigned."

"But tell me, my dear Sir," pertinaciously continued

the other, "was the man's death effected by the halter, or was it a species of euthanasia?"

"*Euthanasia*, Mr. Purser, is something like your *will-power*; I doubt its authenticity as a scientific term—begging your pardon again. It is at once imaginative and metaphysical,—in short, Greek. But" abruptly changing his tone, "there is a case in the sick-bay that I do not care to leave to my assistants. Beg your pardon, but excuse me." And rising from the mess he formally withdrew.

28

THE silence at the moment of execution and for a moment or two continuing thereafter, a silence but emphasized by the regular wash of the sea against the hull or the flutter of a sail caused by the helmsman's eyes being tempted astray, this emphasized silence was gradually disturbed by a sound not easily to be verbally rendered. Whoever has heard the freshet-wave of a torrent suddenly swelled by pouring showers in tropical mountains, showers not shared by the plain; whoever has heard the first muffled murmur of its sloping advance through precipitous woods, may form some conception of the sound now heard. The seeming remoteness of its source was because of its murmurous indistinctness since it came from close by, even from the men massed on the ship's open deck. Being inarticulate, it was dubious in significance further than it seemed to indicate some capricious revulsion of thought or feeling such as mobs ashore are liable to, in the present instance possibly implying a sullen revocation on the men's part of their involuntary echoing of Billy's benediction. But ere the murmur had time to wax into clamor it was met by a strategic command, the more telling that it came with abrupt unexpectedness.

"Pipe down the starboard watch Boatswain, and see that they go."

Shrill as the shriek of the sea-hawk the whistles of the Boatswain and his Mates pierced that ominous low sound, dissipating it; and yielding to the mechanism of discipline the throng was thinned by one half. For the remainder most of them were set to temporary employments connected with trimming the yards and so forth, business readily to be got up to serve occasion by any officer-of-the-deck.

Now each proceeding that follows a mortal sentence pronounced at sea by a drum-head court is characterized by promptitude not perceptibly merging into hurry, though bordering that. The hammock, the one which had been Billy's bed when alive, having already been ballasted with shot and otherwise prepared to serve for his canvas coffin, the last office of the sea-undertakers, the Sail-Maker's Mates, were now speedily completed. When everything was in readiness a second call for all hands made necessary by the strategic movement before mentioned was sounded and now to witness burial.

The details of this closing formality it needs not to give. But when the tilted plank let slide its freight into the sea, a second strange human murmur was heard, blended now with another inarticulate sound proceeding from certain larger sea-fowl whose attention having been attracted by the peculiar commotion in the water resulting from the heavy sloped dive of the shotted hammock into the sea flew screaming to the spot. So near the hull did they come, that the stridor or bony creak of their gaunt double-jointed pinions was audible. As the ship under light airs passed on, leaving the burial spot astern, they still kept circling it low down with the moving shadow of their outstretched wings and the croaked requiem of their cries.

Upon sailors as superstitious as those of the age preceding ours, men-of-war's men too who had just beheld the prodigy of repose in the form suspended in air and now foundering in the deeps; to such mariners the action of the sea-fowl though dictated by mere animal greed for prey, was big with no prosaic significance. An uncertain movement began among them, in which some encroachment was made. It was tolerated but for a moment. For suddenly the drum beat to quarters, which familiar sound happening at least twice every day, had upon the present occasion some signal peremptoriness in it. True martial discipline long continued superinduces in average man a sort of impulse of docility whose operation at the official sound of command much resembles in its promptitude the effect of an instinct.

The drum-beat dissolved the multitude, distributing most of them along the batteries of the two covered gun-decks. There, as wont, the guns' crews stood by their respective cannon erect and silent. In due course the First Officer, sword under arm and standing in his place on the quarter-deck formally received the successive reports of the sworded Lieutenants commanding the sections of batteries below; the last of which reports being made the summed report he delivered with the customary salute to the Commander. All this occupied time, which, in the present case, was the object of beating to quarters at an hour prior to the customary one. That such variance from usage was authorized by an officer like Captain Vere, a martinet as some deemed him, was evidence of the necessity for unusual action implied in what he deemed to be temporarily the mood of his men. "With mankind" he would say "forms, measured forms are everything; and that is the import couched in the story of Orpheus with his lyre spell-binding the wild denizens of the wood." And this he once applied to the disruption of forms going on across the Channel and the consequences thereof.

At this unwonted muster at quarters, all proceeded as at

the regular hour. The band on the quarter-deck played a sacred air. After which the Chaplain went through with the customary morning service. That done, the drum beat the retreat, and toned by music and religious rites subserving the discipline and purpose of war, the men in their wonted orderly manner dispersed to the places allotted them when not at the guns.

And now it was full day. The fleece of low-hanging vapor had vanished, licked up by the sun that late had so glorified it. And the circumambient air in the clearness of its serenity was like smooth white marble in the polished block not yet removed from the marble-dealer's yard.

29

THE symmetry of form attainable in pure fiction can not so readily be achieved in a narration essentially having less to do with fable than with fact. Truth uncompromisingly told will always have its ragged edges; hence the conclusion of such a narration is apt to be less finished than an architectural finial.

How it fared with the Handsome Sailor during the year of the great mutiny has been faithfully given. But though properly the story ends with his life something in way of sequel will not be amiss. Three brief chapters will suffice.

In the general re-christening under the Directory of the craft originally forming the navy of the French Monarchy, the *St. Louis* line-of-battle ship was named the *Athéiste.* Such a name, like some other substituted ones in the Revolutionary fleet while proclaiming the infidel audacity of the ruling power was yet, though not so intended to be, the aptest name, if one consider it, ever given to a warship; far more so indeed than the *Devastation,* the *Erebus* (the *Hell*) and similar names bestowed upon fighting-ships.

On the return-passage to the English fleet from the detached cruise during which occurred the events already recorded, the *Indomitable* fell in with the *Athéiste*. An engagement ensued; during which Captain Vere in the act of putting his ship alongside the enemy with a view of throwing his boarders across her bulwarks, was hit by a musket-ball from a port-hole of the enemy's main cabin. More than disabled he dropped to the deck and was carried below to the same cock-pit where some of his men already lay. The senior Lieutenant took command. Under him the enemy was finally captured and though much crippled was by rare good fortune successfully taken into Gibraltar, an English port not very distant from the scene of the fight. There, Captain Vere with the rest of the wounded was put ashore. He lingered for some days, but the end came. Unhappily he was cut off too early for the Nile and Trafalgar. The spirit that spite its philosophic austerity may yet have indulged in the most secret of all passions, ambition, never attained to the fullness of fame.

Not long before death while lying under the influence of that magical drug which soothing the physical frame mysteriously operates on the subtler element in man, he was heard to murmur words inexplicable to his attendant —"Billy Budd, Billy Budd." That these were not the accents of remorse, would seem clear from what the attendant said to the *Indomitable's* senior officer of marines who as the most reluctant to condemn of the members of the drumhead court, too well knew though here he kept the knowledge to himself, who Billy Budd was.

30

SOME few weeks after the execution, among other matters under the head of *News from the Mediterranean*, there appeared in a naval chronicle of the time, an authorized weekly publication, an account of the affair. It was doubtless for the most part written in good faith, though the medium, partly rumor, through which the facts must have reached the writer, served to deflect and in part falsify them. The account was as follows:—

"On the tenth of the last month a deplorable occurrence took place on board *H.M.S. Indomitable.* John Claggart, the ship's master-at-arms, discovering that some sort of plot was incipient among an inferior section of the ship's company, and that the ring-leader was one William Budd; he, Claggart in the act of arraigning the man before the Captain was vindictively stabbed to the heart by the suddenly drawn sheath-knife of Budd.

"The deed and the implement employed, sufficiently suggest that though mustered into the service under an English name, the assassin was no Englishman, but one of those aliens adopting English cognomens whom the present extraordinary necessities of the Service have caused to be admitted into it in considerable numbers.

"The enormity of the crime and the extreme depravity of the criminal, appear the greater in view of the character of the victim, a middle-aged man respectable and discreet, belonging to that minor official grade, the petty-officers, upon whom, as none know better than the commissioned gentlemen, the efficiency of His Majesty's navy so largely depends. His function was a responsible one; at once onerous and thankless and his fidelity in it the greater because of his strong patriotic impulse. In this instance as in so many other instances in these days, the character of this unfortunate man signally refutes, if refutation were needed, that peevish saying attributed to the late Dr. Johnson, that patriotism is the last refuge of a scoundrel.

"The criminal paid the penalty of his crime. The promptitude of the punishment has proved salutary. Nothing amiss is now apprehended aboard *H.M.S. Indomitable.*"

The above appearing in a publication now long ago superannuated and forgotten is all that hitherto has stood in human record to attest what manner of men respectively were John Claggart and Billy Budd.

31

EVERYTHING is for a term remarkable in navies. Any tangible object associated with some striking incident of the service is converted into a monument. The spar from which the Foretopman was suspended, was for some few years kept trace of by the blue-jackets. Then knowledge followed it from ship to dock-yard and again from dock-yard to ship, still pursuing it even when at last reduced to a mere dock-yard boom. To them a chip of it was as a piece of the Cross. Ignorant though they were of the secret facts of the tragedy, and not thinking but that the penalty was somehow unavoidably inflicted from the naval point of view, for all that they instinctively felt that Billy was a sort of man as incapable of mutiny as of wilful murder. They recalled the fresh young image of the Handsome Sailor, that face never deformed by a sneer or subtler vile freak of the heart within. This impression of him was doubtless deepened by the fact that he was gone, and in a measure mysteriously gone. On the gun-decks of the *Indomitable* the general estimate of his nature and its unconscious simplicity eventually found rude utterance from another foretopman, one of his own watch, gifted as some sailors are with an artless poetic temperament. The tarry hands made some lines which after circulating among the shipboard crew for a while, finally got rudely printed at Portsmouth as a ballad. The title given to it was the sailor's.

BILLY IN THE DARBIES

GOOD of the Chaplain to enter Lone Bay
And down on his marrow-bones here and pray

For the likes just o' me, Billy Budd.—But look:
Through the port comes the moon-shine astray!
It tips the guard's cutlass and silvers this nook;
But 'twill die in the dawning of Billy's last day.
A jewel-block they'll make of me tomorrow,
Pendant pearl from the yard-arm-end
Like the ear-drop I gave to Bristol Molly—
O, 'tis me, not the sentence they'll suspend.
Ay, Ay, all is up; and I must up too
Early in the morning, aloft from alow.
On an empty stomach, now, never it would do.
They'll give me a nibble—bit o' biscuit ere I go.
Sure, a messmate will reach me the last parting cup;
But, turning heads away from the hoist and the belay,
Heaven knows who will have the running of me up!
No pipe to those halyards—but aren't it all sham?
A blur's in my eyes; it is dreaming that I am.
A hatchet to my painter? all adrift to go?
The drum roll to grog, and Billy never know?
But Donald he has promised to stand by the plank;
So I'll shake a friendly hand ere I sink.
But—no! It is dead then I'll be, come to think.—
I remember Taff the Welshman when he sank.
And his cheek it was like the budding pink.
But me they'll lash me in hammock, drop me deep.
Fathoms down, fathoms down, how I'll dream fast asleep.
I feel it stealing now. Sentry, are you there?
Just ease these darbies at the wrist,
And roll me over fair.
I am sleepy, and the oozy weeds about me twist.

END OF BOOK

April 19th, 1891